OUT
OF LEFT FIELD

Andrews McMeel Publishing
a division of Andrews McMeel Universal
1130 Walnut Street, Kansas City, Missouri 64106

www.andrewsmcmeel.com

24 25 26 27 28 TEN 10 9 8 7 6 5 4 3 2 1

ISBN Paperback: 978-1-5248-8482-6
ISBN Hardback: 978-1-5248-8484-0

Library of Congress Control Number: 2023944333

Editor: Patty Rice
Designer: Brittany Lee
Production Editor: Brianna Westervelt
Production Manager: Julie Skalla
Color Flatting: Lynn Stoecklein

For Buba, who always
knew this would happen.
—J.N.

OUT OF

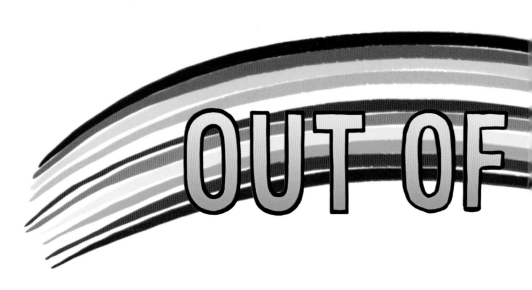

LEFT FIELD

Written and Illustrated by
JONAH NEWMAN

With Color by
DONNA OATNEY

Andrews McMeel
PUBLISHING®

CHAPTER 1

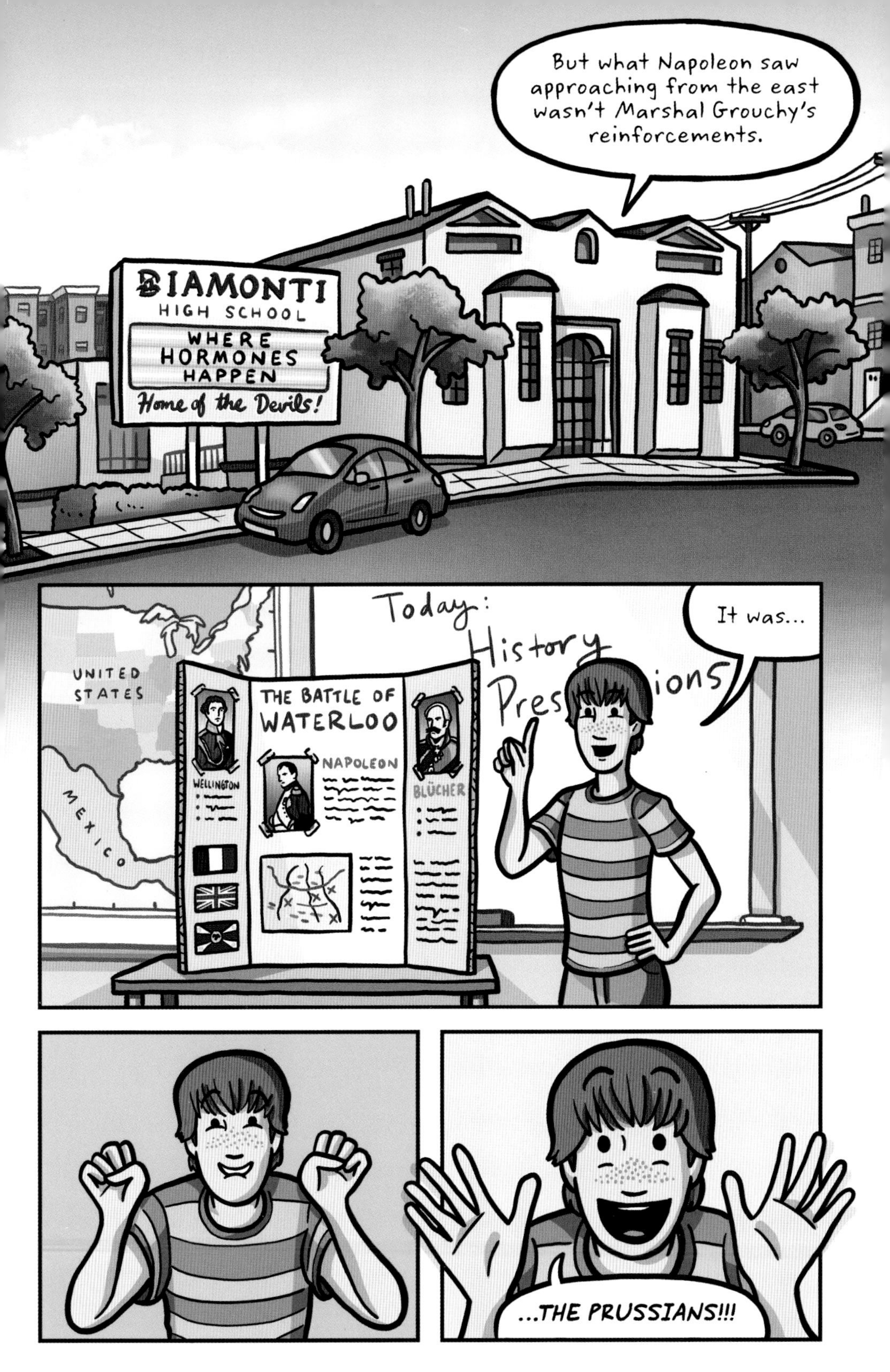
But what Napoleon saw approaching from the east wasn't Marshal Grouchy's reinforcements.
DIAMONTI HIGH SCHOOL
WHERE HORMONES HAPPEN
Home of the Devils!
UNITED STATES
MEXICO
Today:
History
Pres ions
THE BATTLE OF WATERLOO
WELLINGTON
NAPOLEON
BLÜCHER
It was...
...THE PRUSSIANS!!!

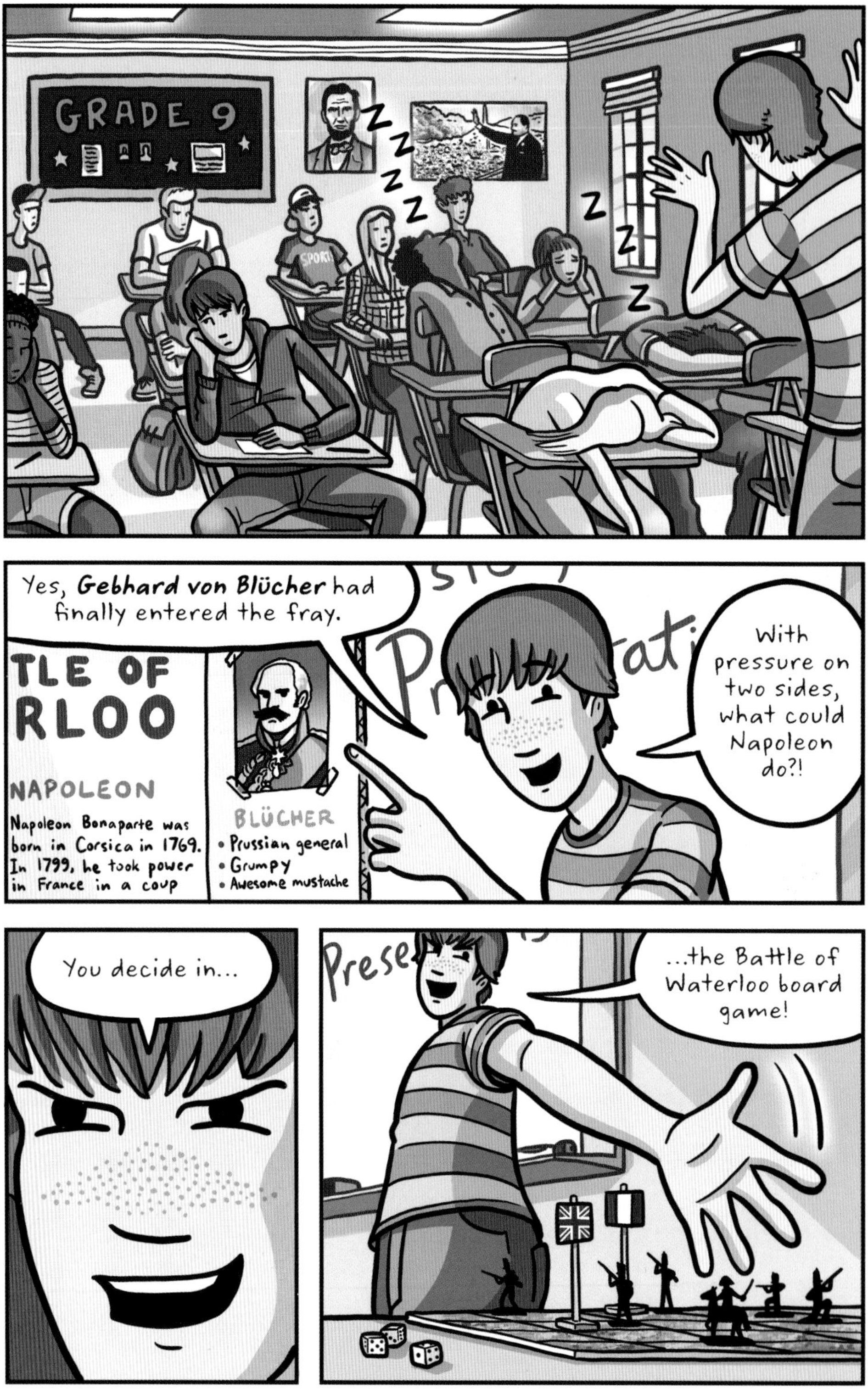
GRADE 9
Z Z Z Z
Z Z Z
Yes, **Gebhard von Blücher** had finally entered the fray.
TLE OF
RLOO
NAPOLEON
Napoleon Bonaparte was born in Corsica in 1769. In 1799, he took power in France in a coup
BLÜCHER
• Prussian general
• Grumpy
• Awesome mustache
With pressure on two sides, what could Napoleon do?!
You decide in...
...the Battle of Waterloo board game!

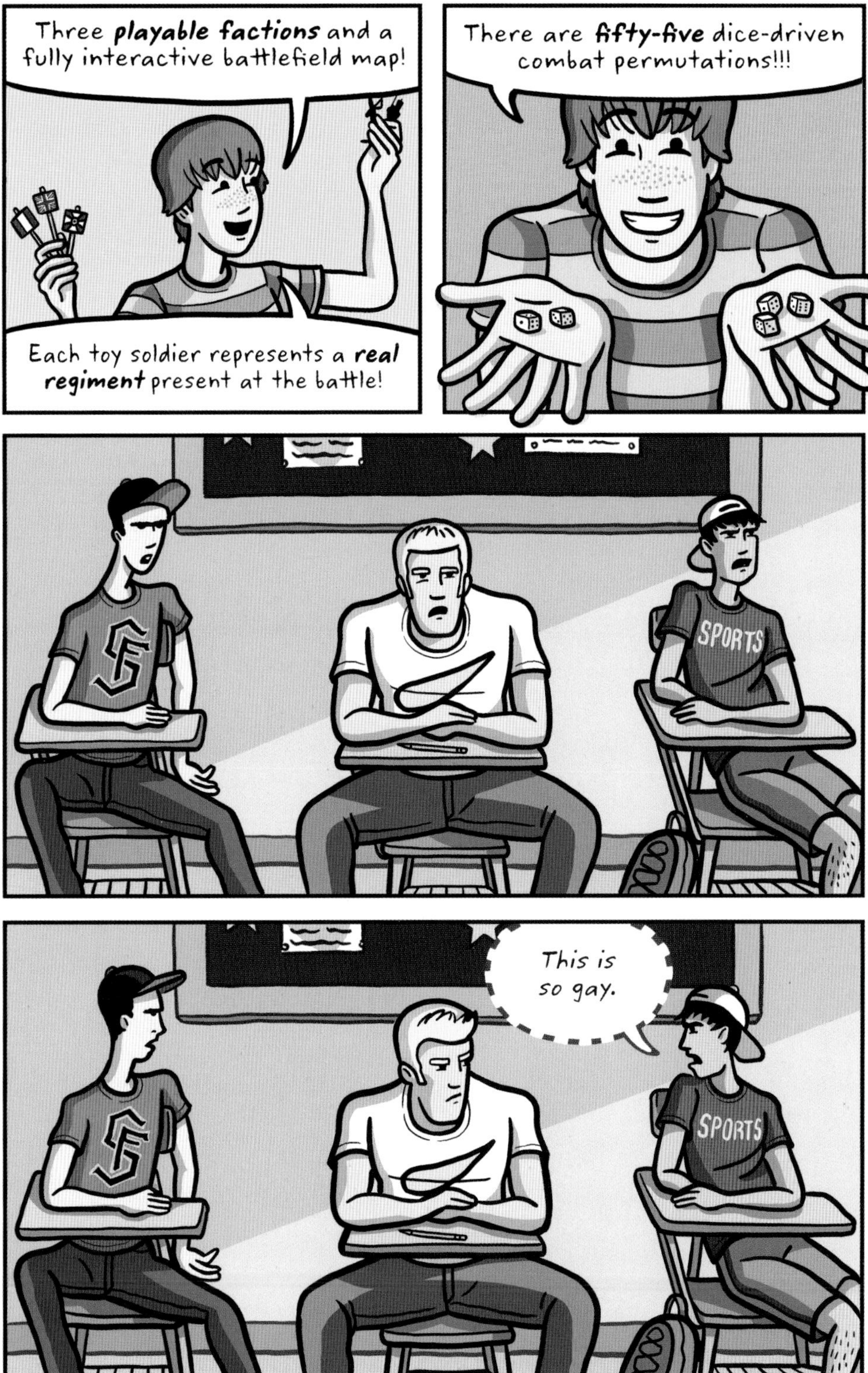
Three **playable factions** and a fully interactive battlefield map!
Each toy soldier represents a **real regiment** present at the battle!
There are **fifty-five** dice-driven combat permutations!!!
SPORTS
SPORTS
This is so gay.

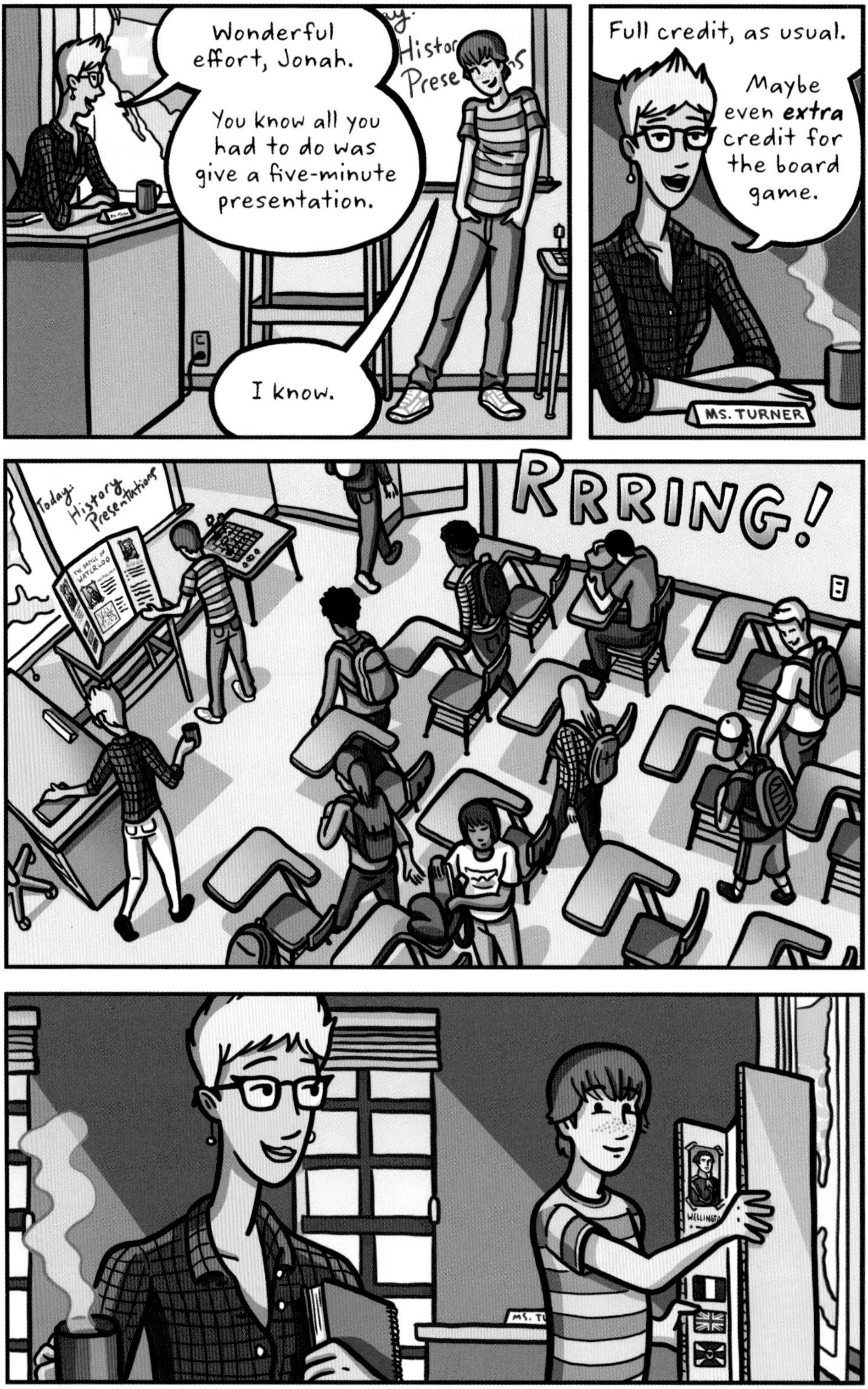
Wonderful effort, Jonah.
You know all you had to do was give a five-minute presentation.
I know.
Full credit, as usual.
Maybe even **extra** credit for the board game.
MS. TURNER
Today: History Presentations
THE BATTLE OF WATERLOO
RRRING!

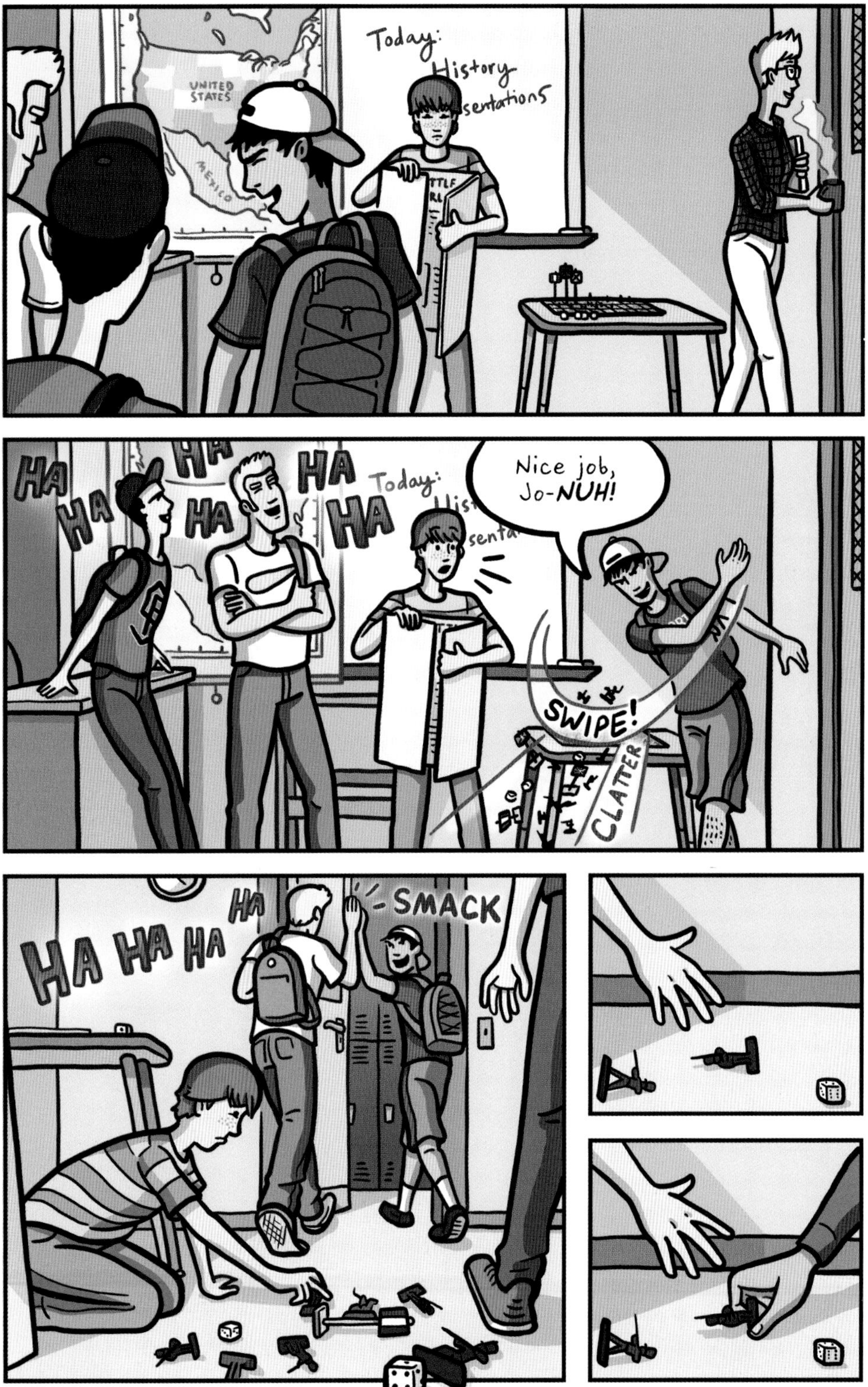
UNITED STATES
MEXICO
Today:
History
sentations
HA
HA
HA
HA
HA
HA
Nice job, Jo-NUH!
SWIPE!
CLATTER
HA HA HA HA
HA
SMACK

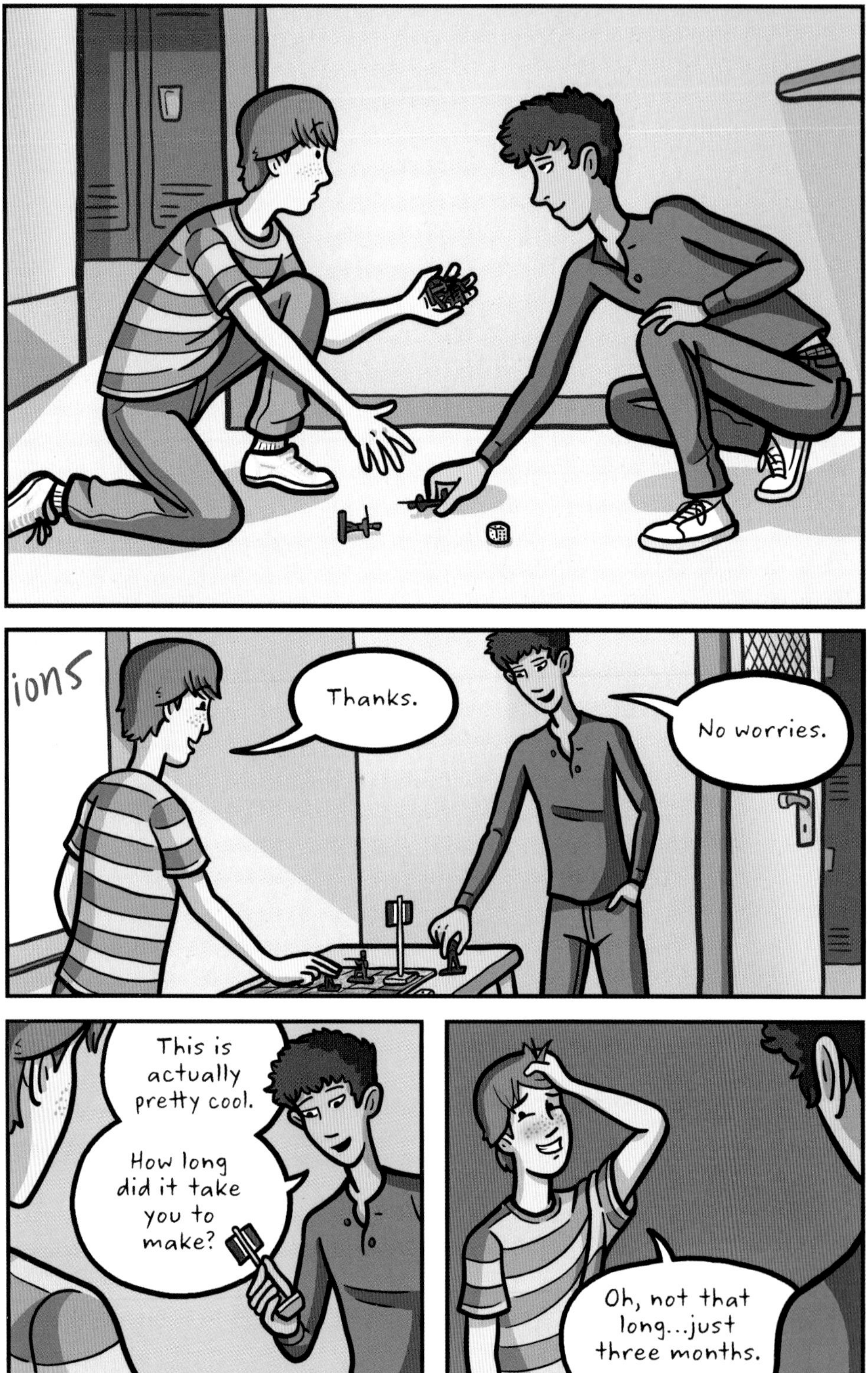
ions
Thanks.
No worries.
This is actually pretty cool.
How long did it take you to make?
Oh, not that long...just three months.

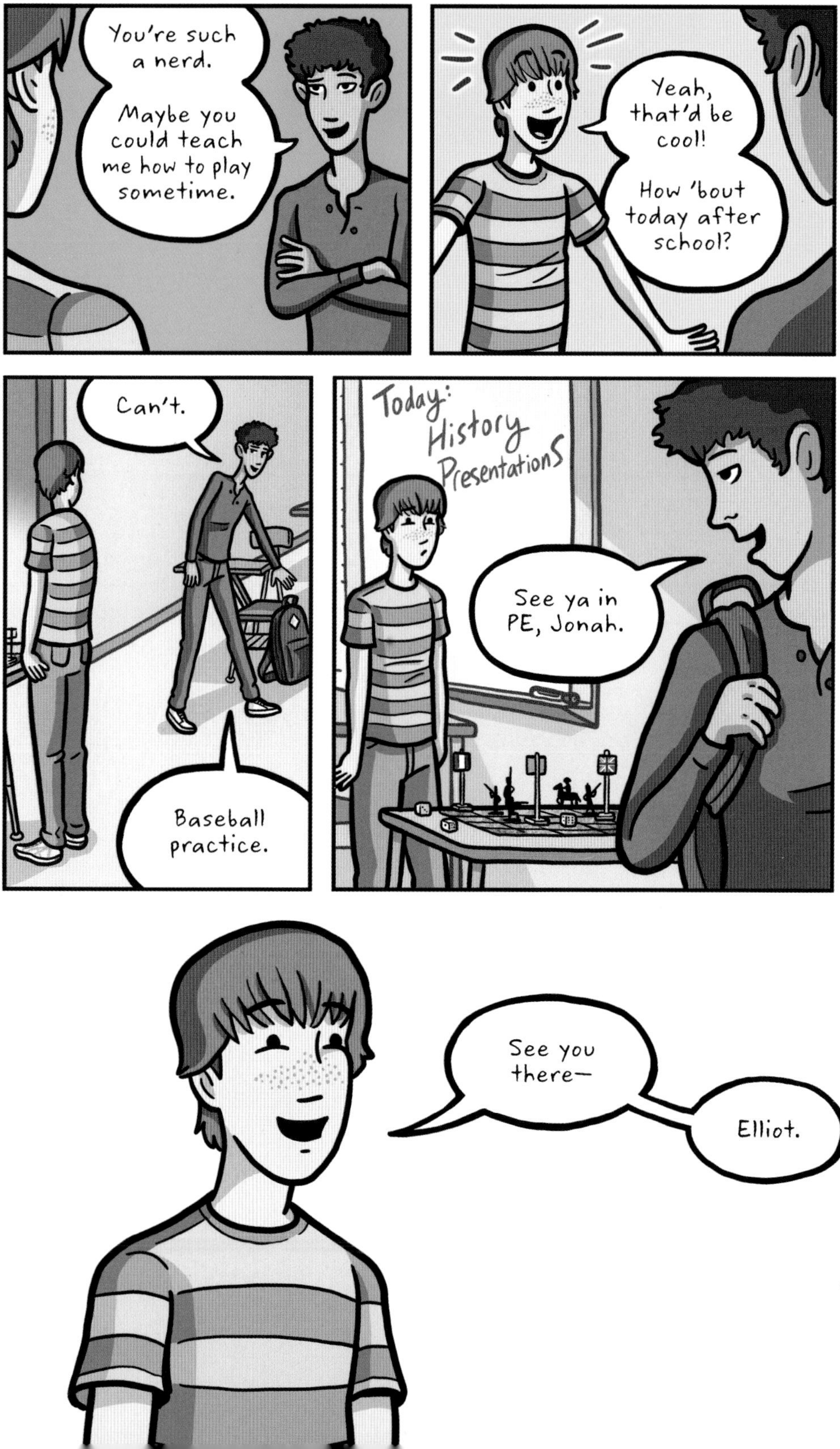
You're such a nerd.
Maybe you could teach me how to play sometime.
Yeah, that'd be cool!
How 'bout today after school?
Can't.
Baseball practice.
Today: History PresentationS
See ya in PE, Jonah.
See you there—
Elliot.

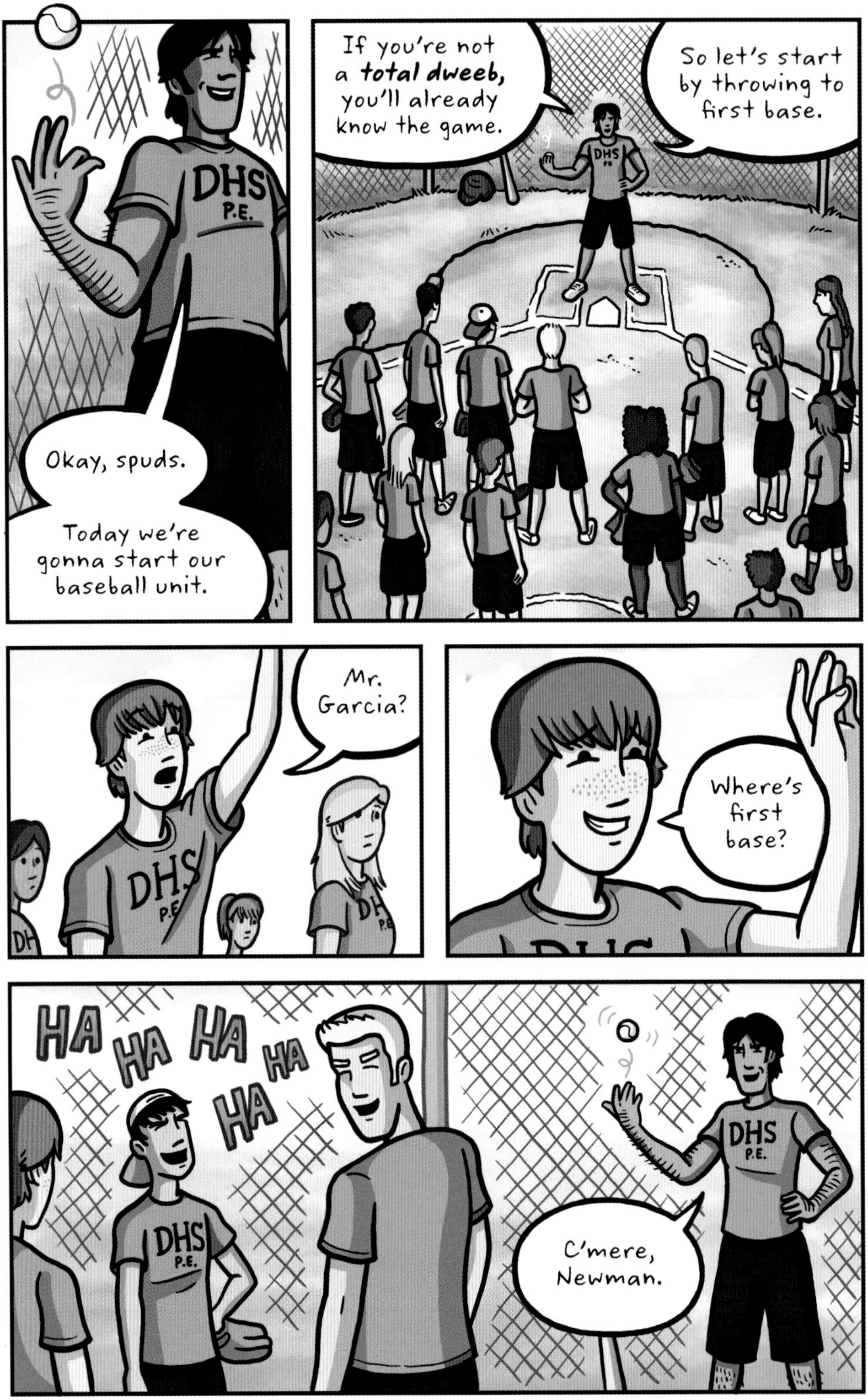
Okay, spuds.
Today we're gonna start our baseball unit.
If you're not a **total dweeb,** you'll already know the game.
So let's start by throwing to first base.
Mr. Garcia?
Where's first base?
HA HA HA HA HA
C'mere, Newman.

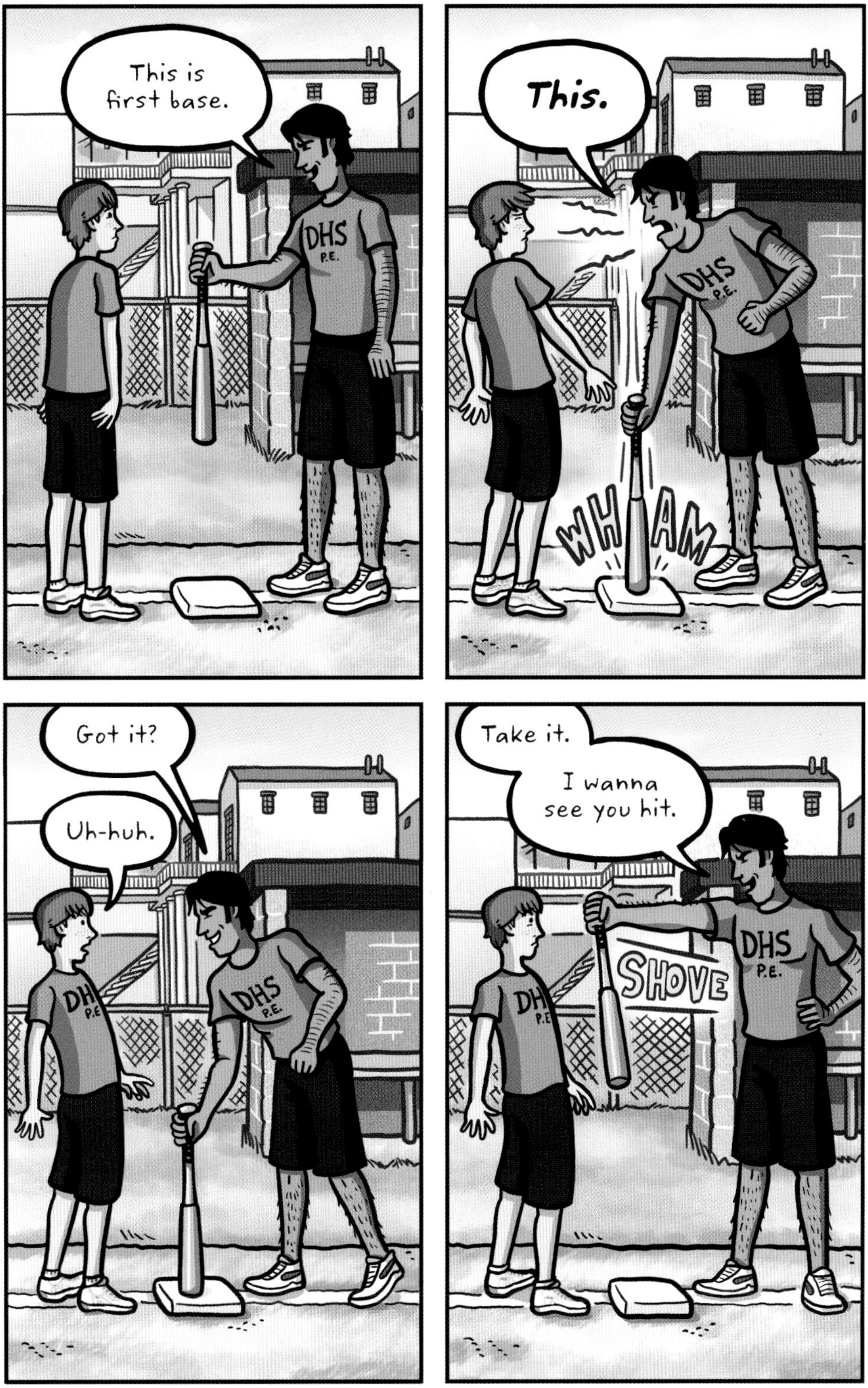
This is first base.
This.
WHAM
Got it?
Uh-huh.
Take it.
I wanna see you hit.
SHOVE

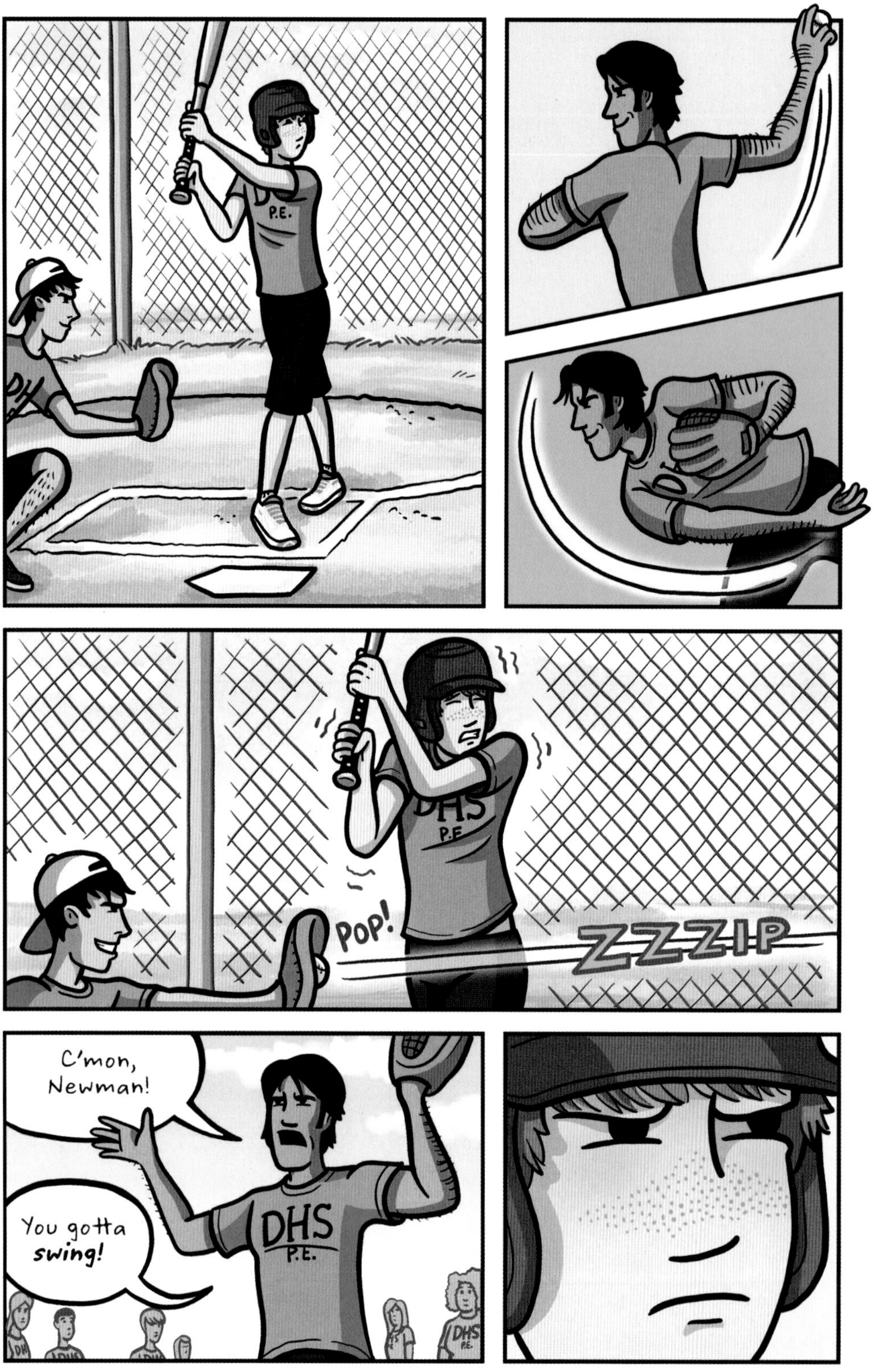
P.E.
DHS
P.E.
POP!
ZZZIP
C'mon, Newman!
You gotta swing!
DHS
P.E.
DHS
P.E.

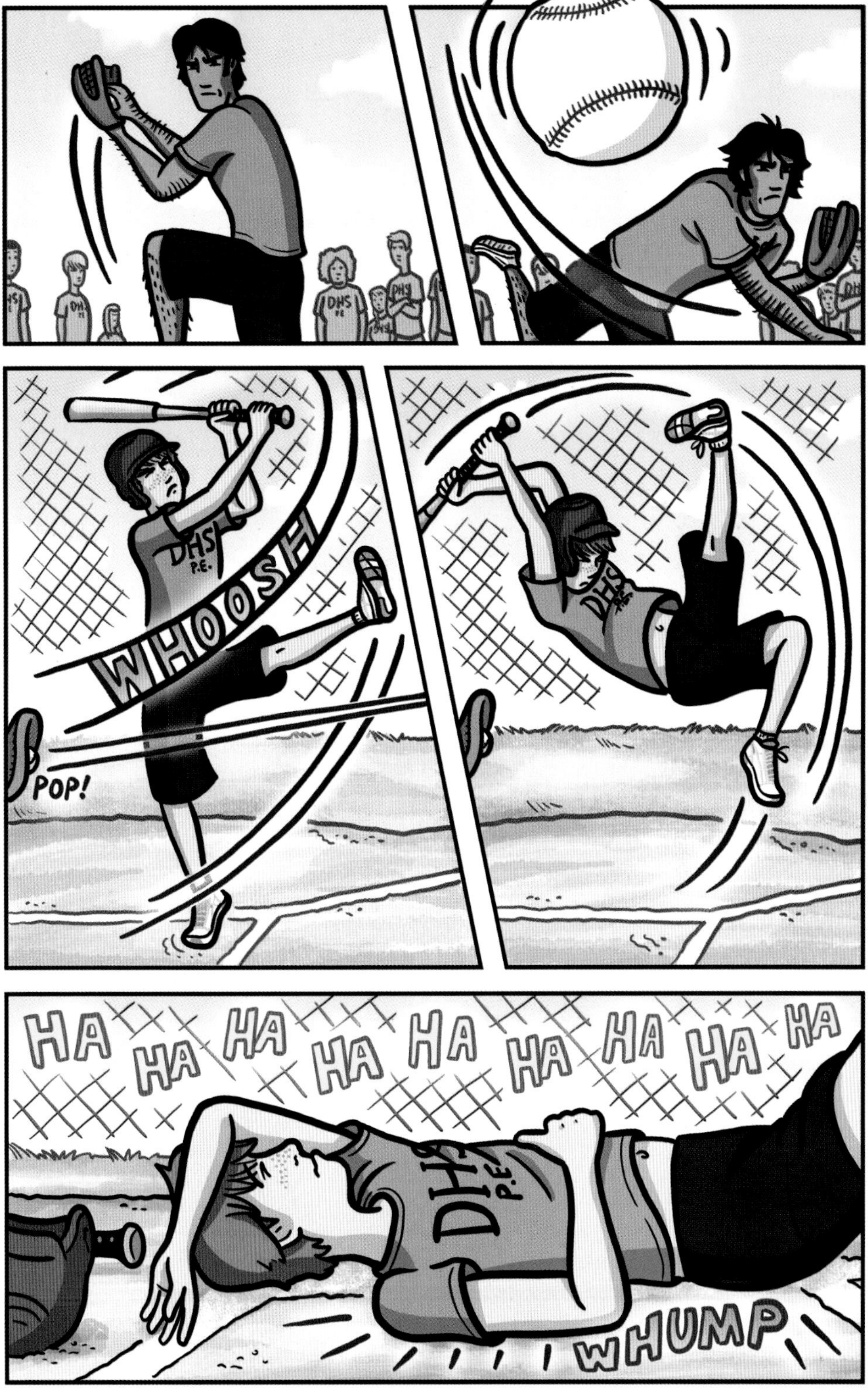
DHS
DHS P.E.
WHOOSH
DHS P.E.
POP!
DHS
HA HA HA HA HA HA HA HA HA
DHS P.E.
WHUMP

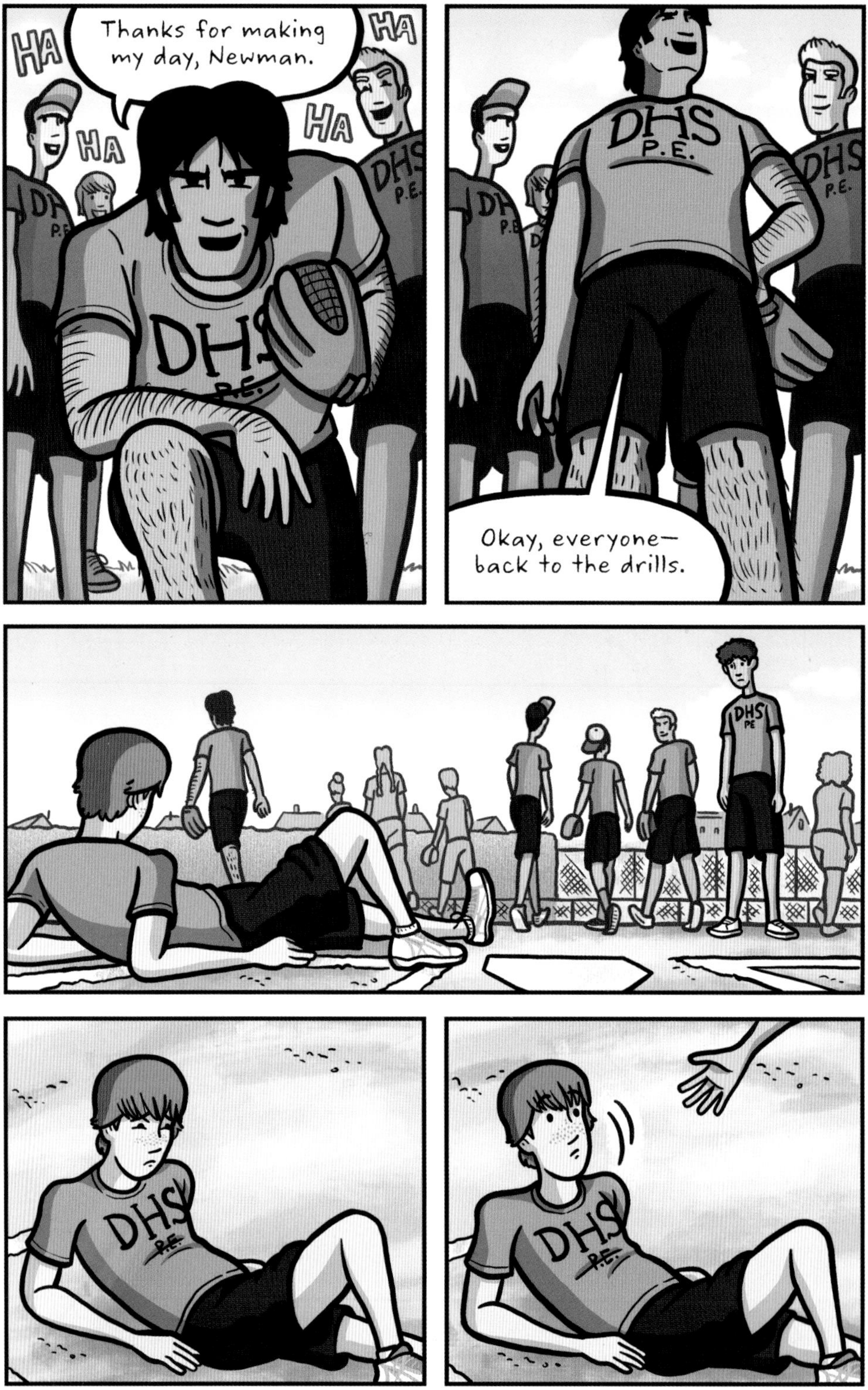
HA
Thanks for making my day, Newman.
HA
HA
HA
HA
Okay, everyone— back to the drills.

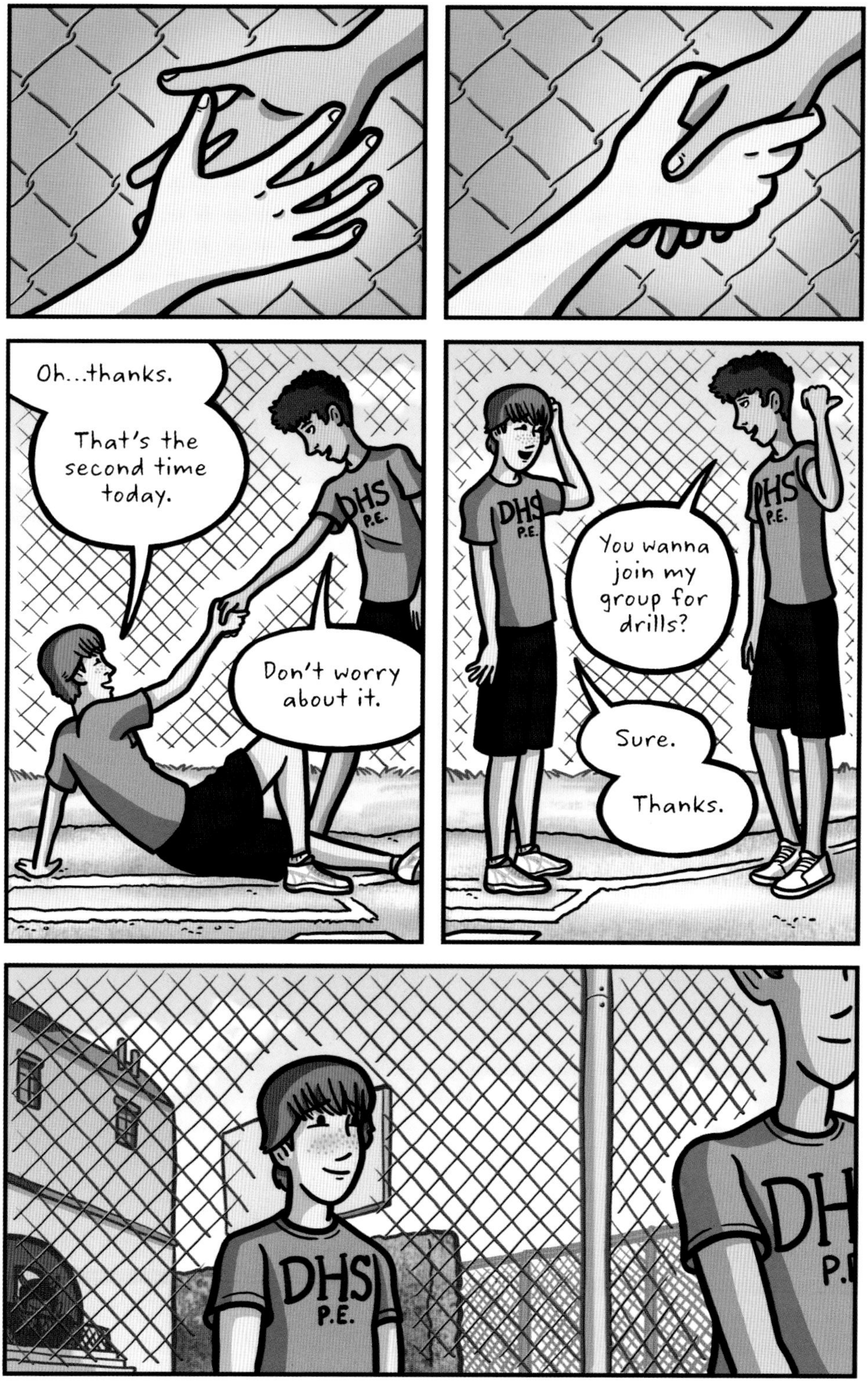
Oh...thanks.
That's the second time today.
Don't worry about it.
You wanna join my group for drills?
Sure.
Thanks.

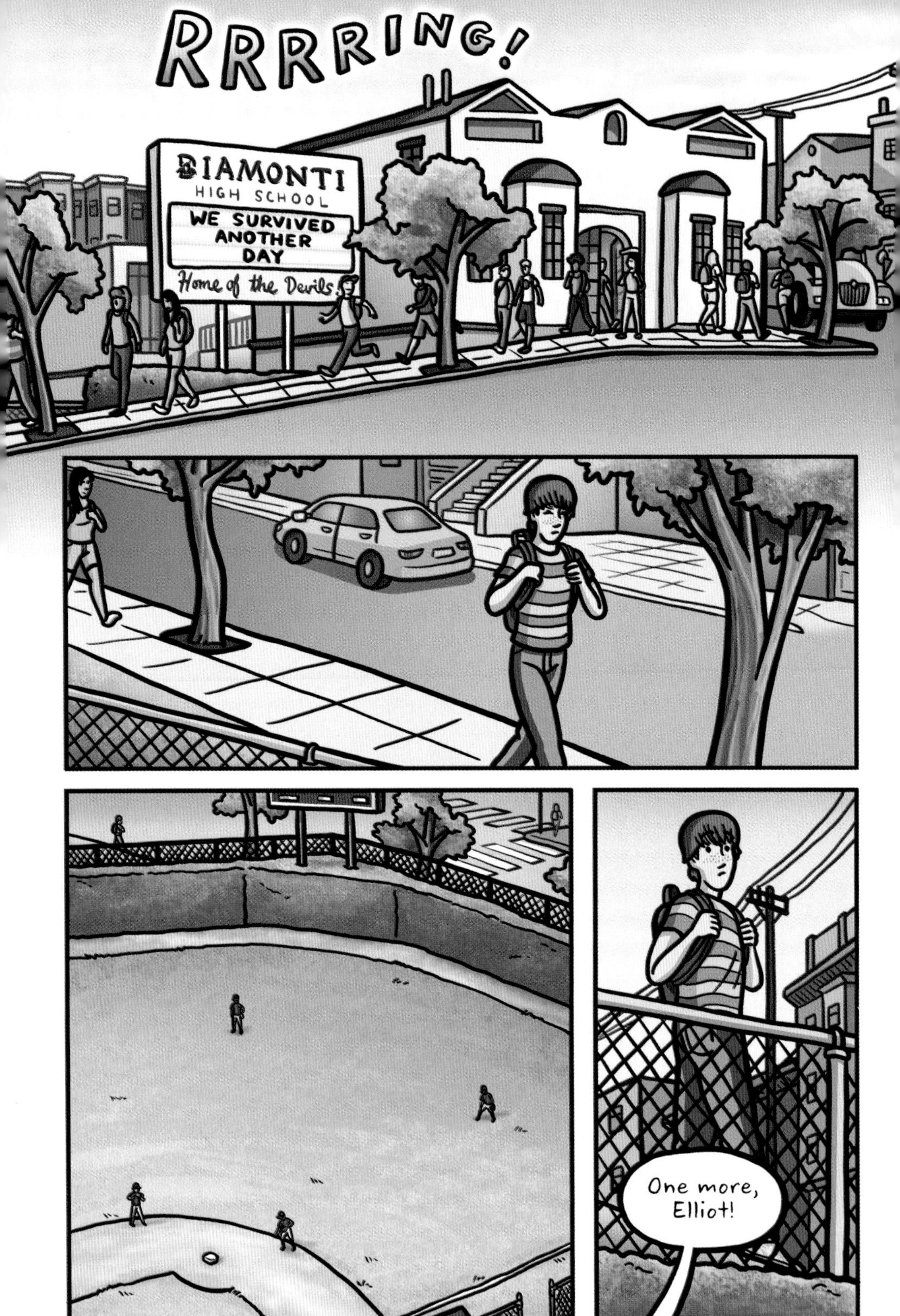
RRRRING!
DIAMONTI
HIGH SCHOOL
WE SURVIVED ANOTHER DAY
Home of the Devils!
One more, Elliot!

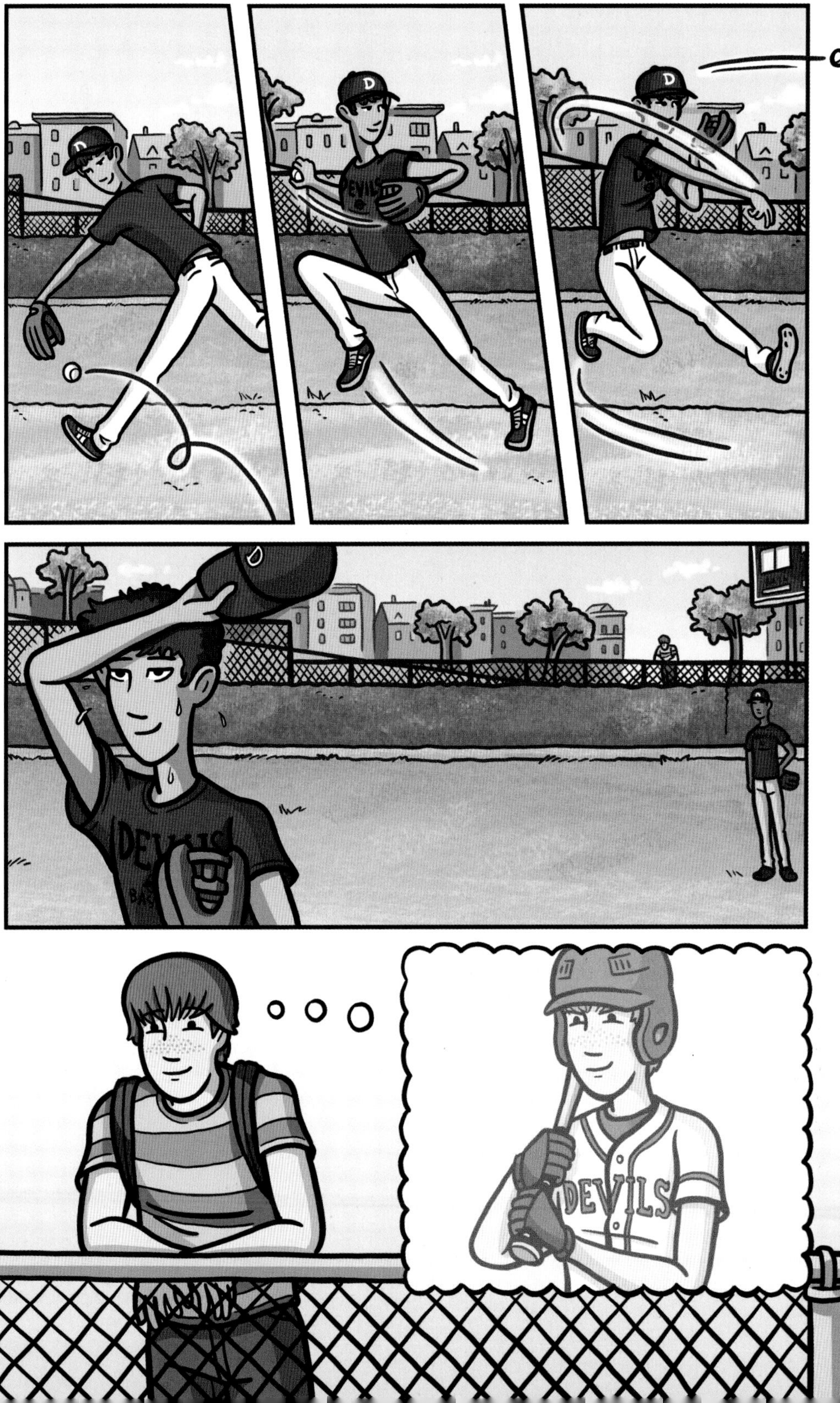
DEVILS
DEVILS
DEVILS

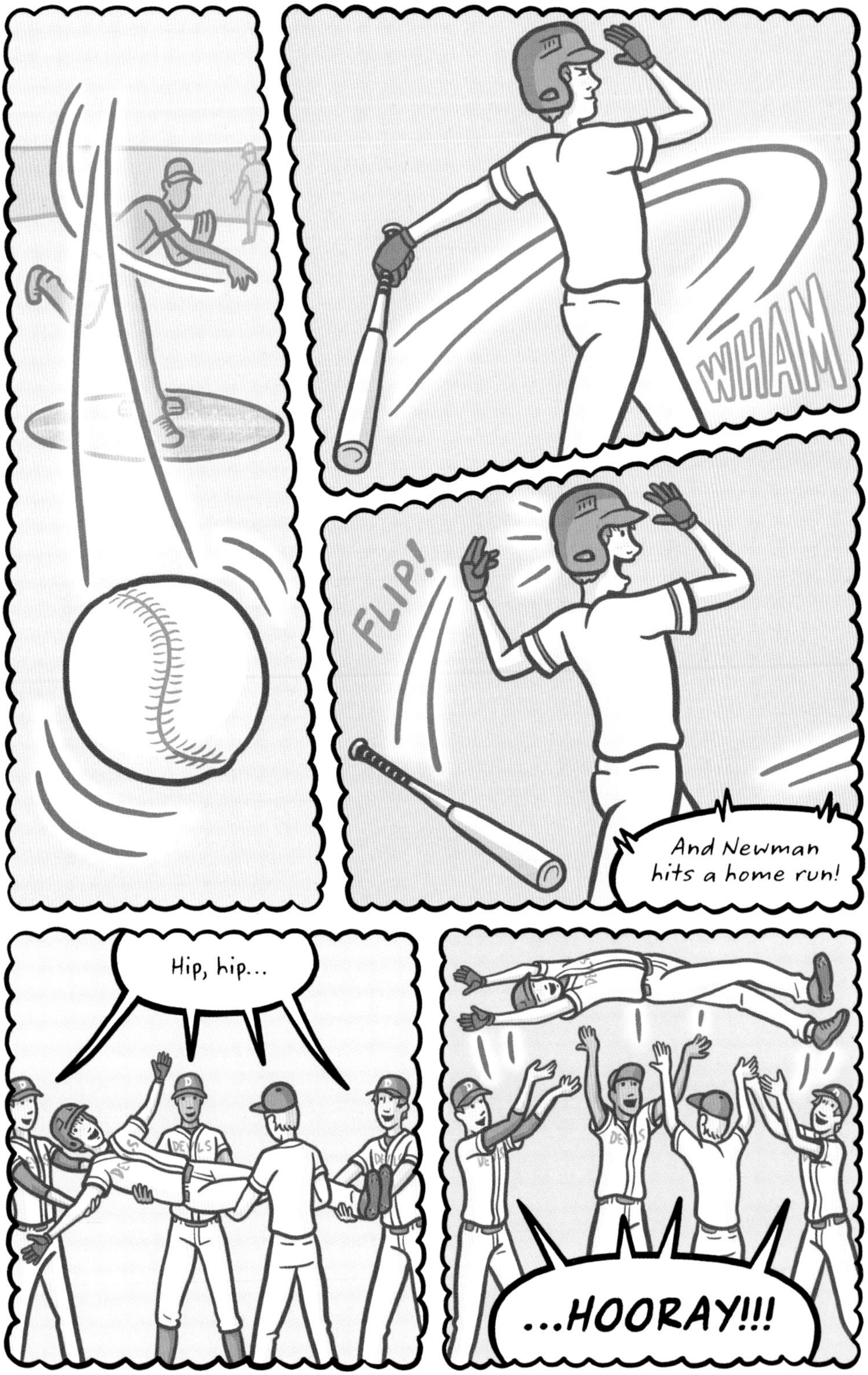
WHAM
FLIP!
And Newman hits a home run!
Hip, hip...
...HOORAY!!!

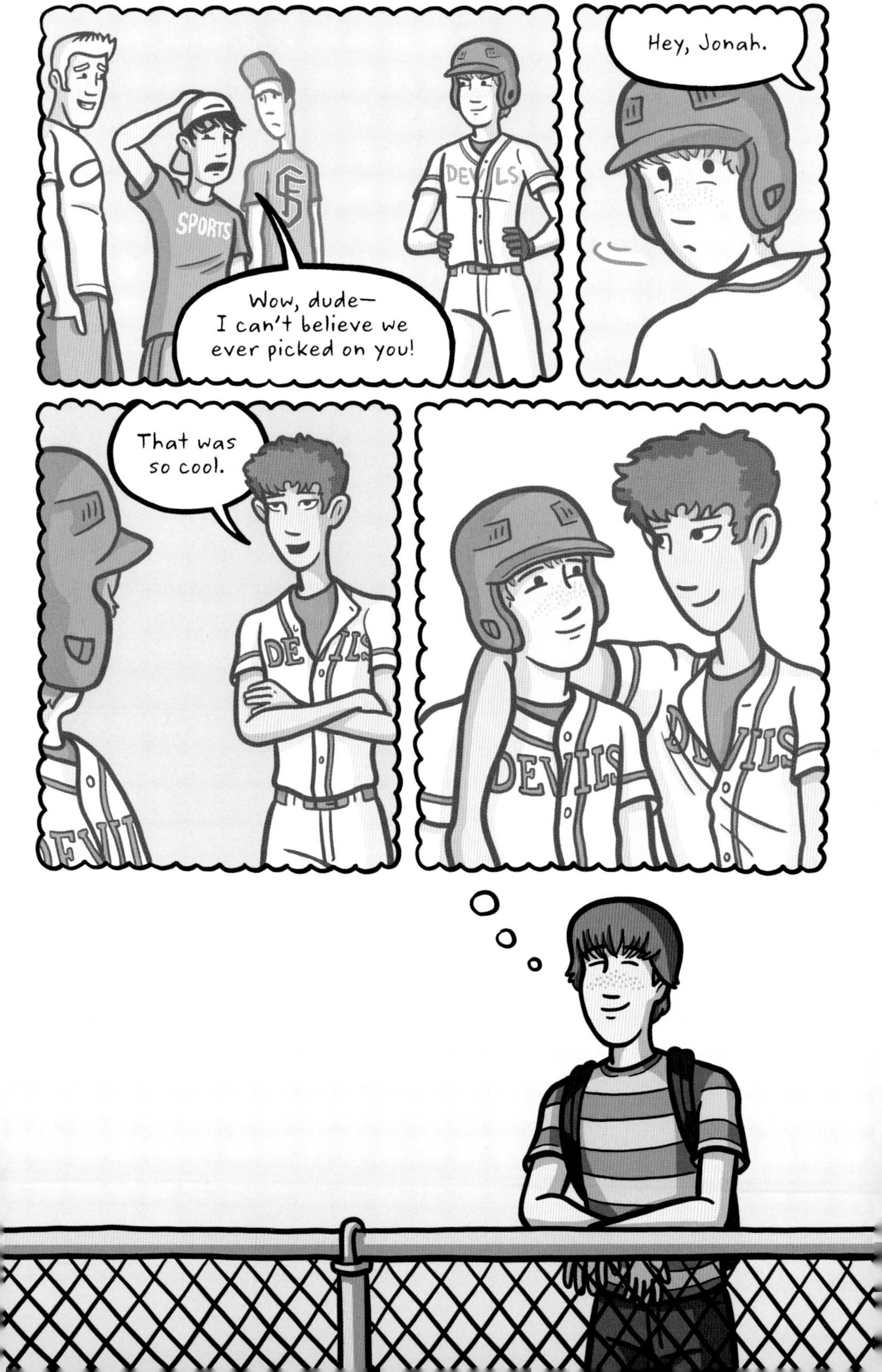
Wow, dude—
I can't believe we ever picked on you!
Hey, Jonah.
That was so cool.

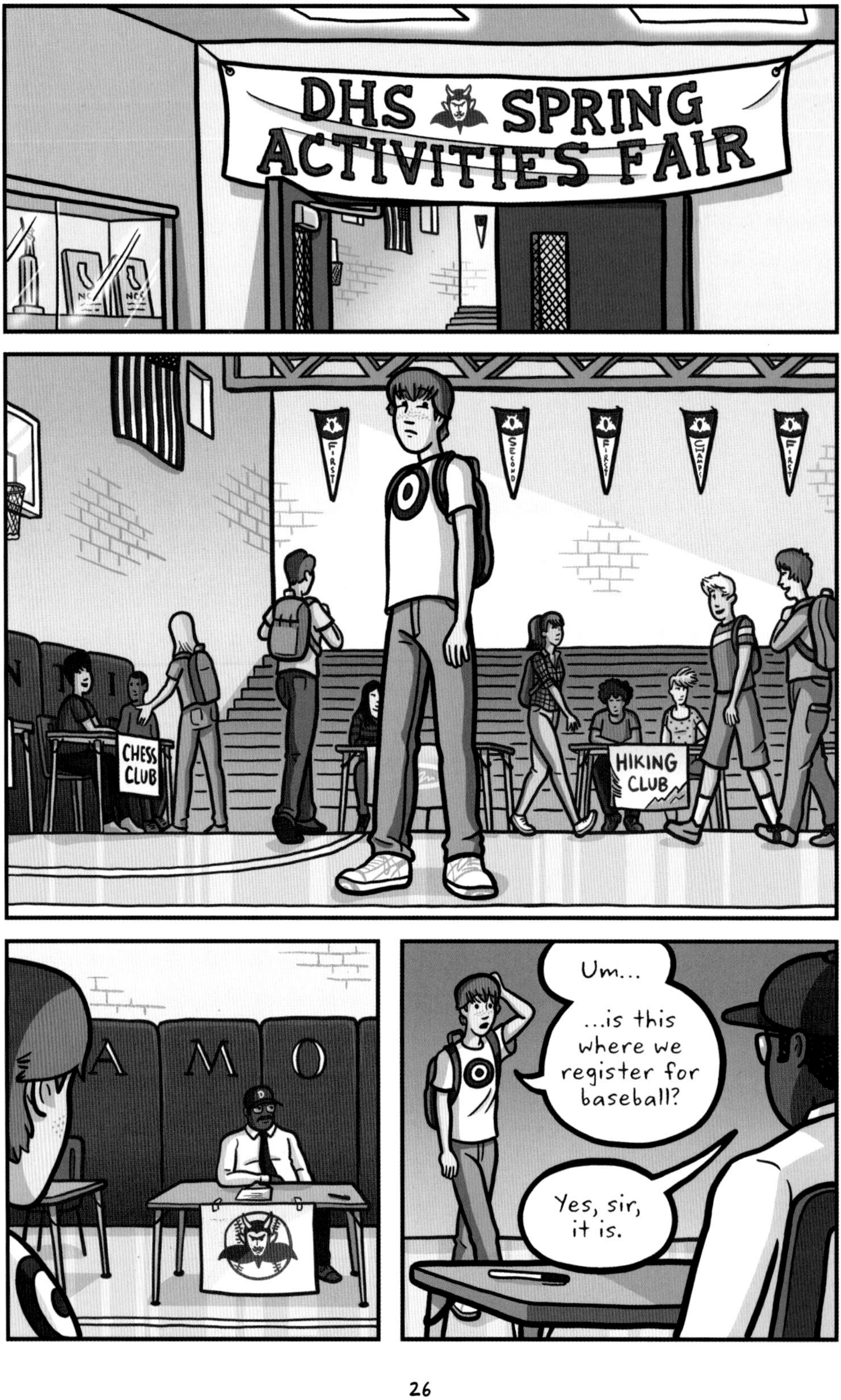
DHS SPRING ACTIVITIES FAIR
CHESS CLUB
HIKING CLUB
A M O
Um...
...is this where we register for baseball?
Yes, sir, it is.

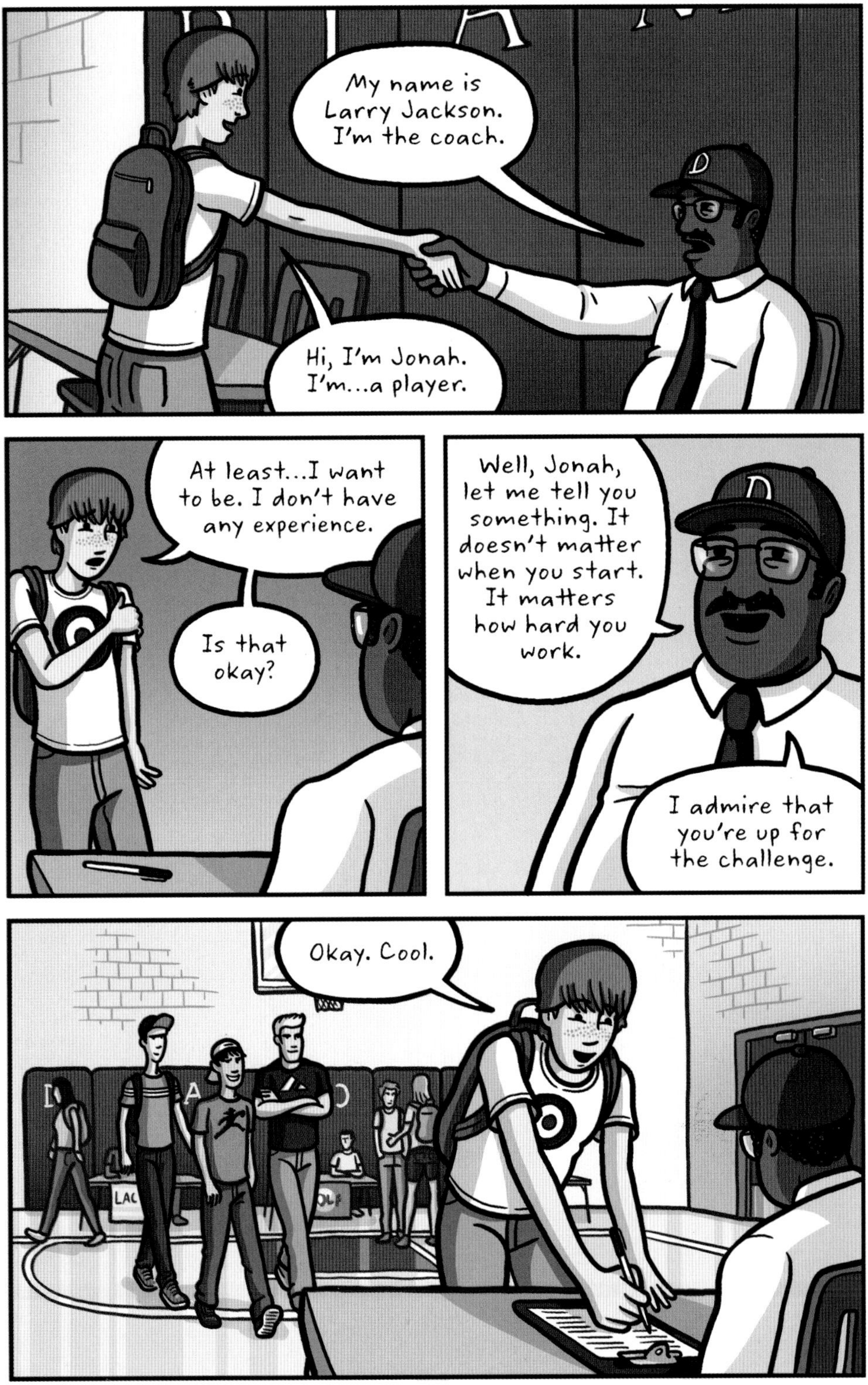
My name is Larry Jackson. I'm the coach.
Hi, I'm Jonah. I'm...a player.
At least...I want to be. I don't have any experience.
Is that okay?
Well, Jonah, let me tell you something. It doesn't matter when you start. It matters how hard you work.
I admire that you're up for the challenge.
Okay. Cool.

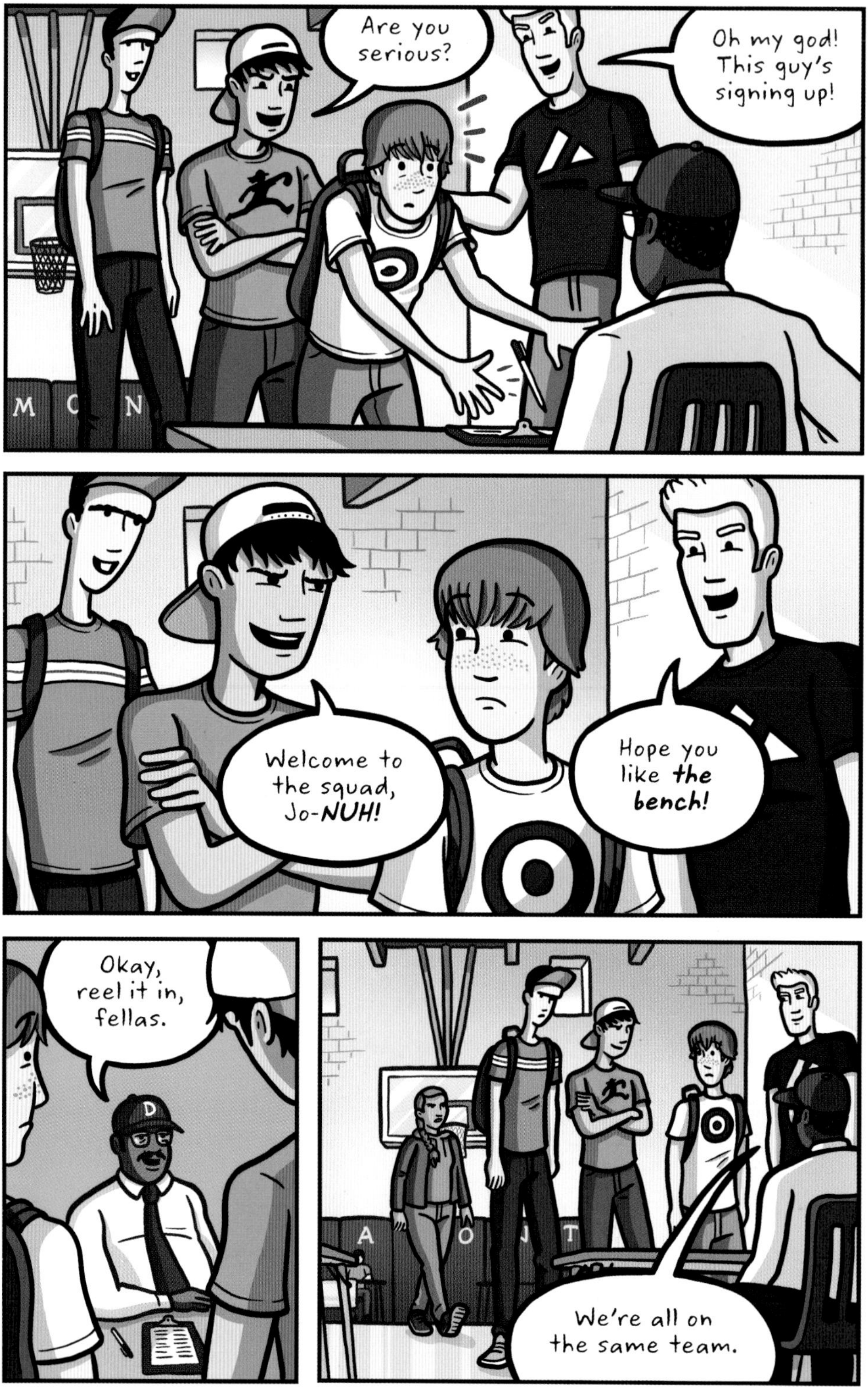
Are you serious?
Oh my god! This guy's signing up!
M O N
Welcome to the squad, Jo-**NUH!**
Hope you like **the bench!**
Okay, reel it in, fellas.
D
A O J T
We're all on the same team.

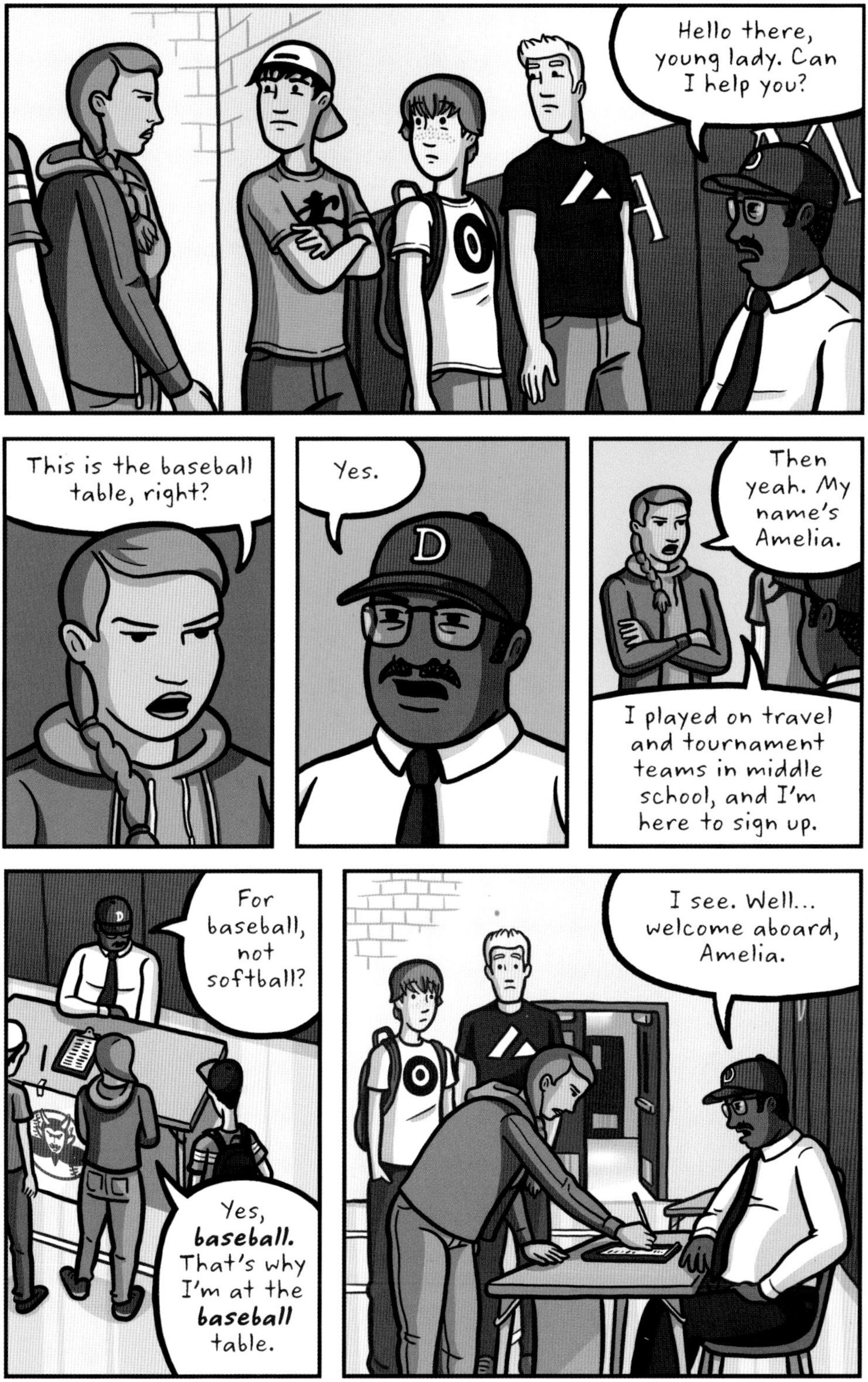

Hello there, young lady. Can I help you?
This is the baseball table, right?
Yes.
Then yeah. My name's Amelia.
I played on travel and tournament teams in middle school, and I'm here to sign up.
For baseball, not softball?
Yes, **baseball.** That's why I'm at the **baseball** table.
I see. Well... welcome aboard, Amelia.

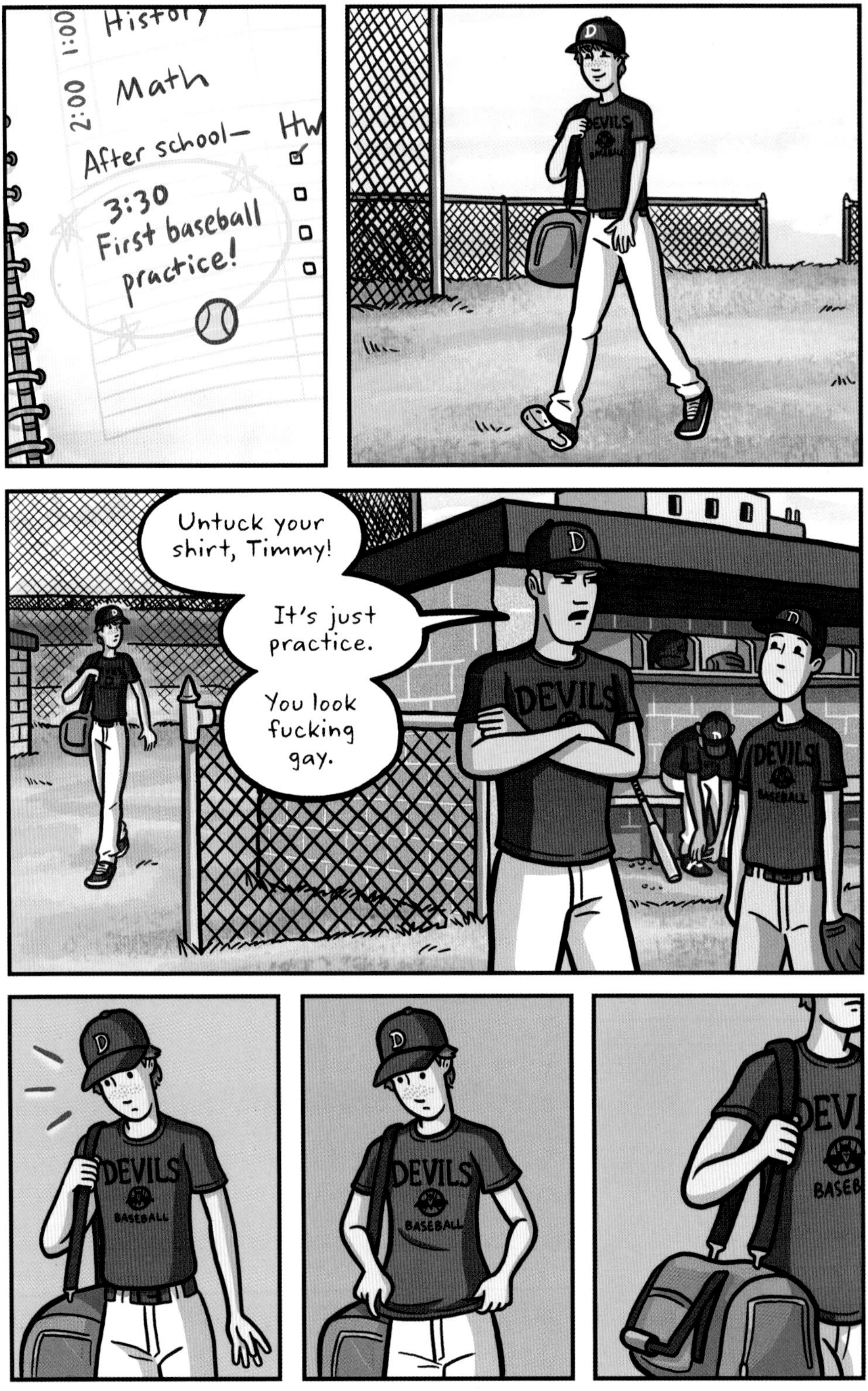
1:00 History
2:00 Math
After school—
3:30
First baseball
practice!
HW
DEVILS
BASEBALL
Untuck your shirt, Timmy!
It's just practice.
You look fucking gay.
DEVILS
BASEBALL
DEVILS
BASEBALL
DEVILS
BASEBALL

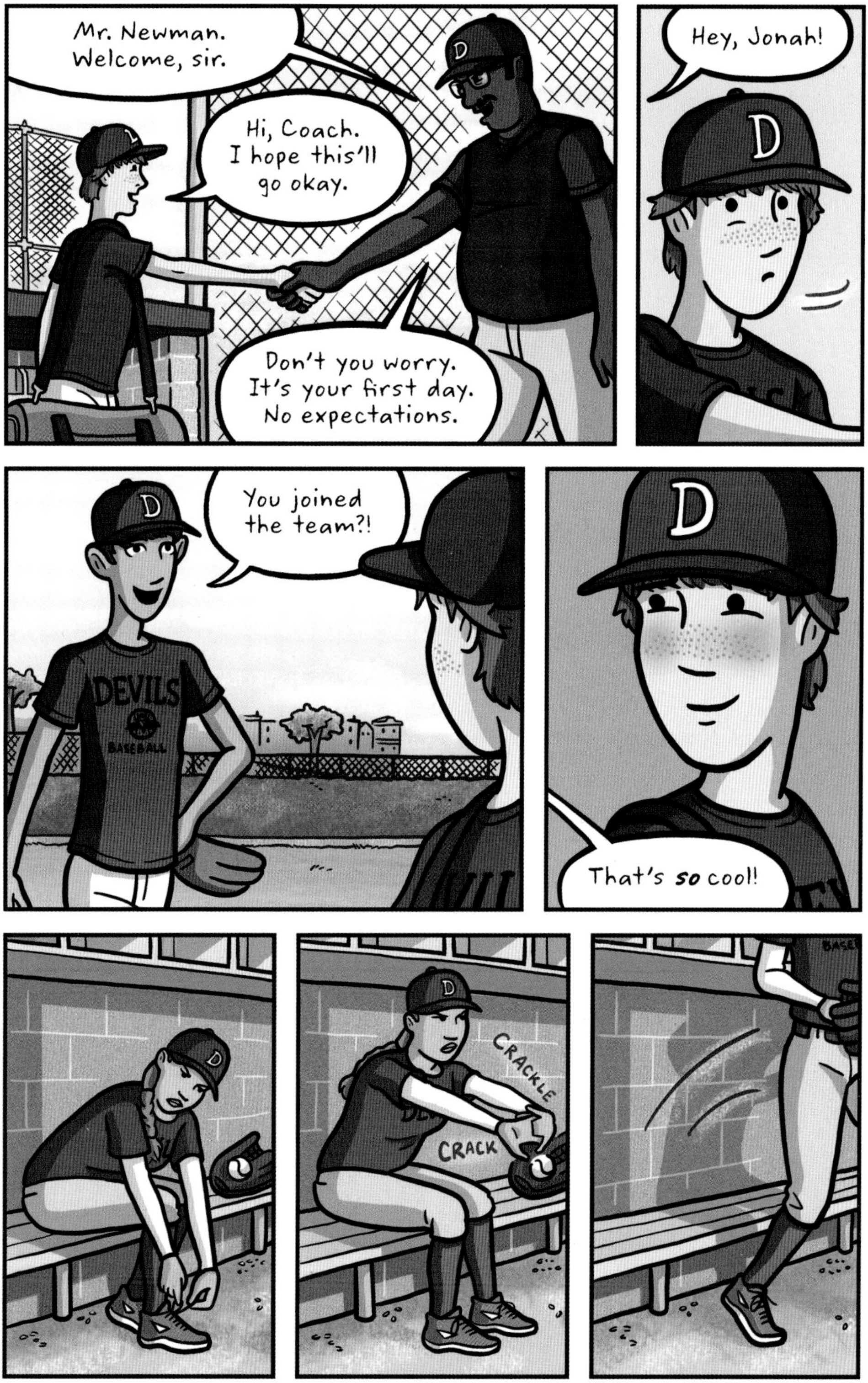
Mr. Newman. Welcome, sir.
Hi, Coach. I hope this'll go okay.
Don't you worry. It's your first day. No expectations.
Hey, Jonah!
You joined the team?!
DEVILS
BASEBALL
That's **so** cool!
CRACKLE
CRACK

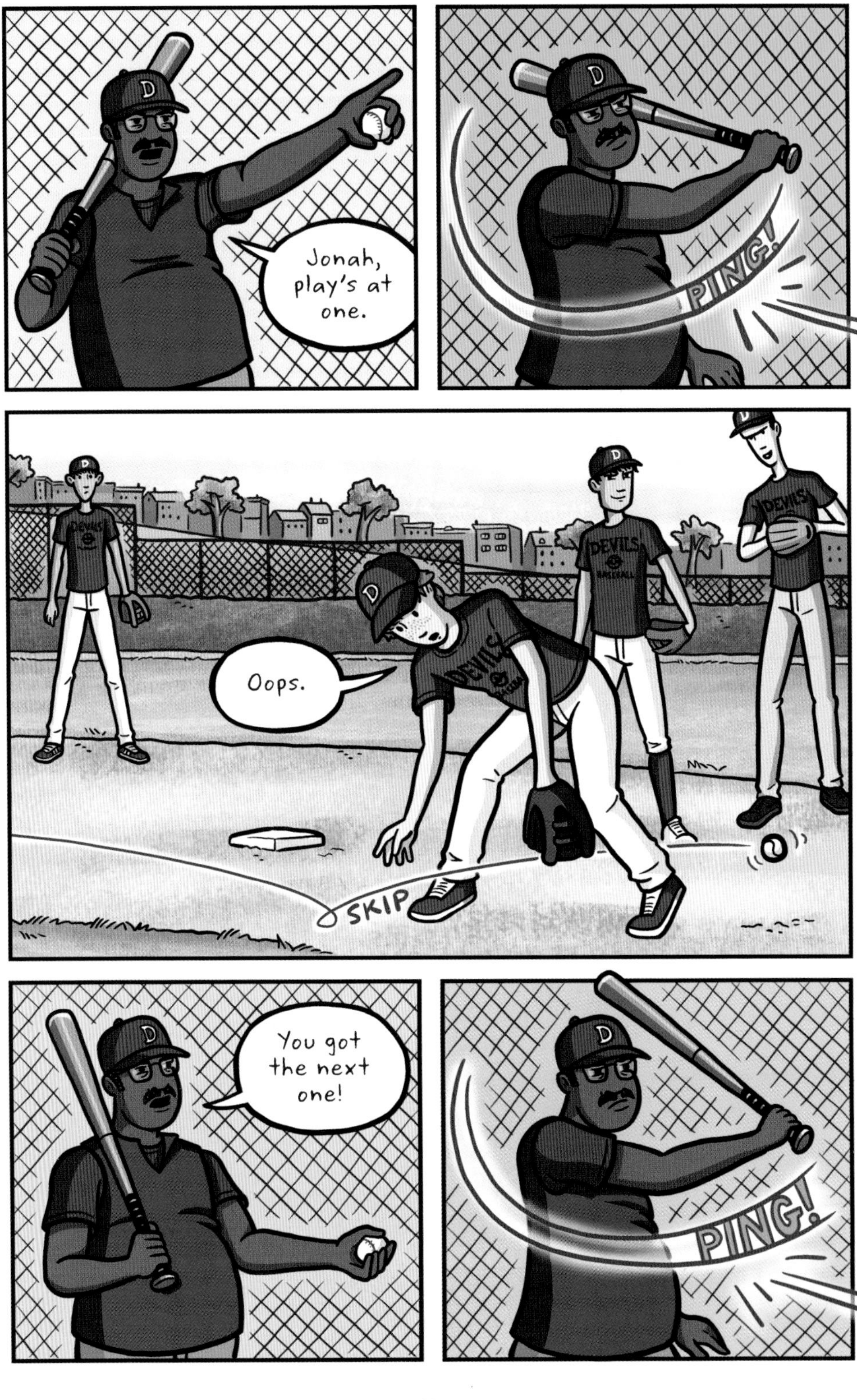
Jonah, play's at one.
PING!
Oops.
SKIP
You got the next one!
PING!

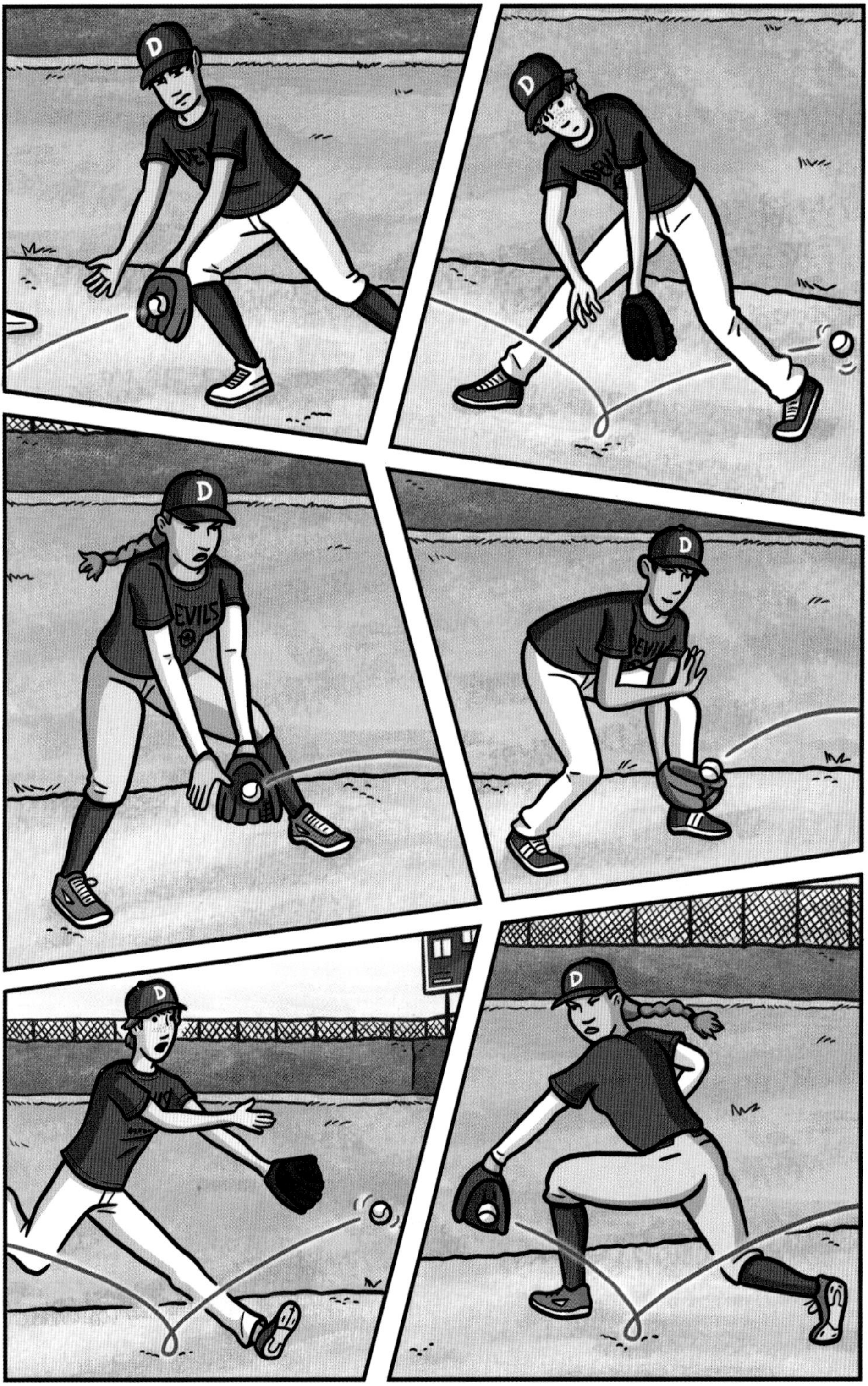
DEVILS

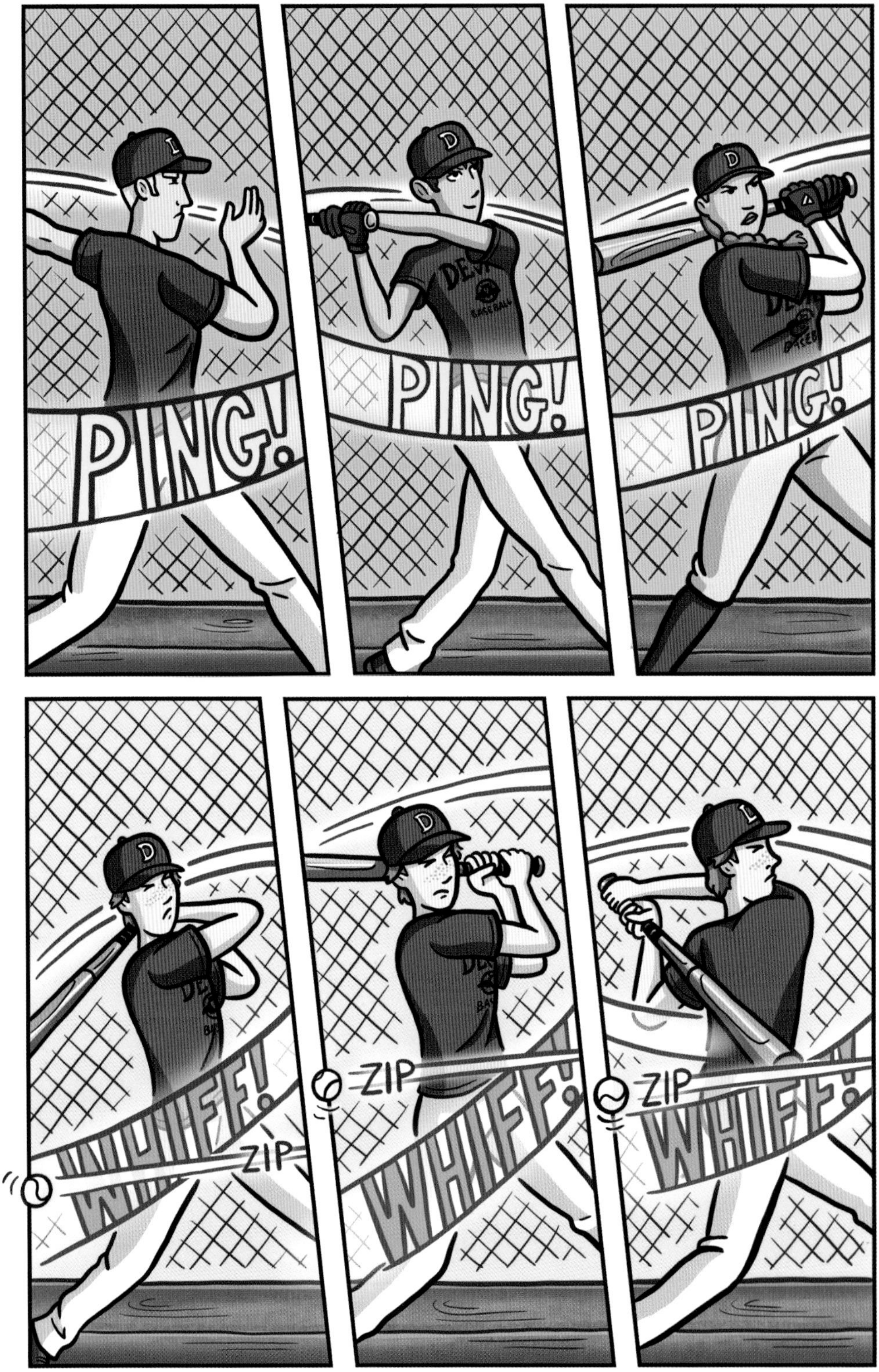
PING!
PING!
PING!
WHIFF!
ZIP
ZIP
WHIFF!
ZIP
WHIFF!

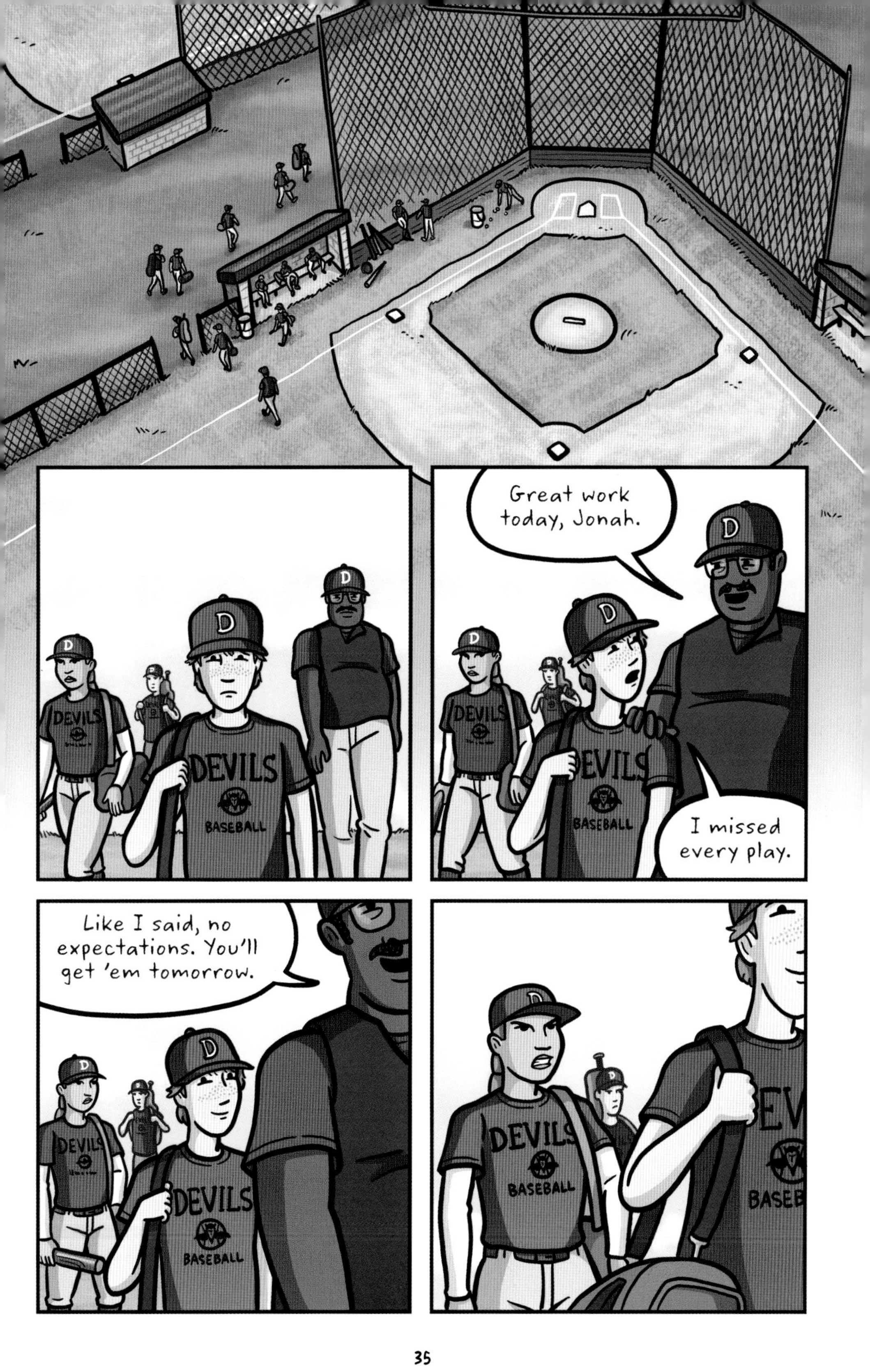
Great work today, Jonah.
I missed every play.
Like I said, no expectations. You'll get 'em tomorrow.

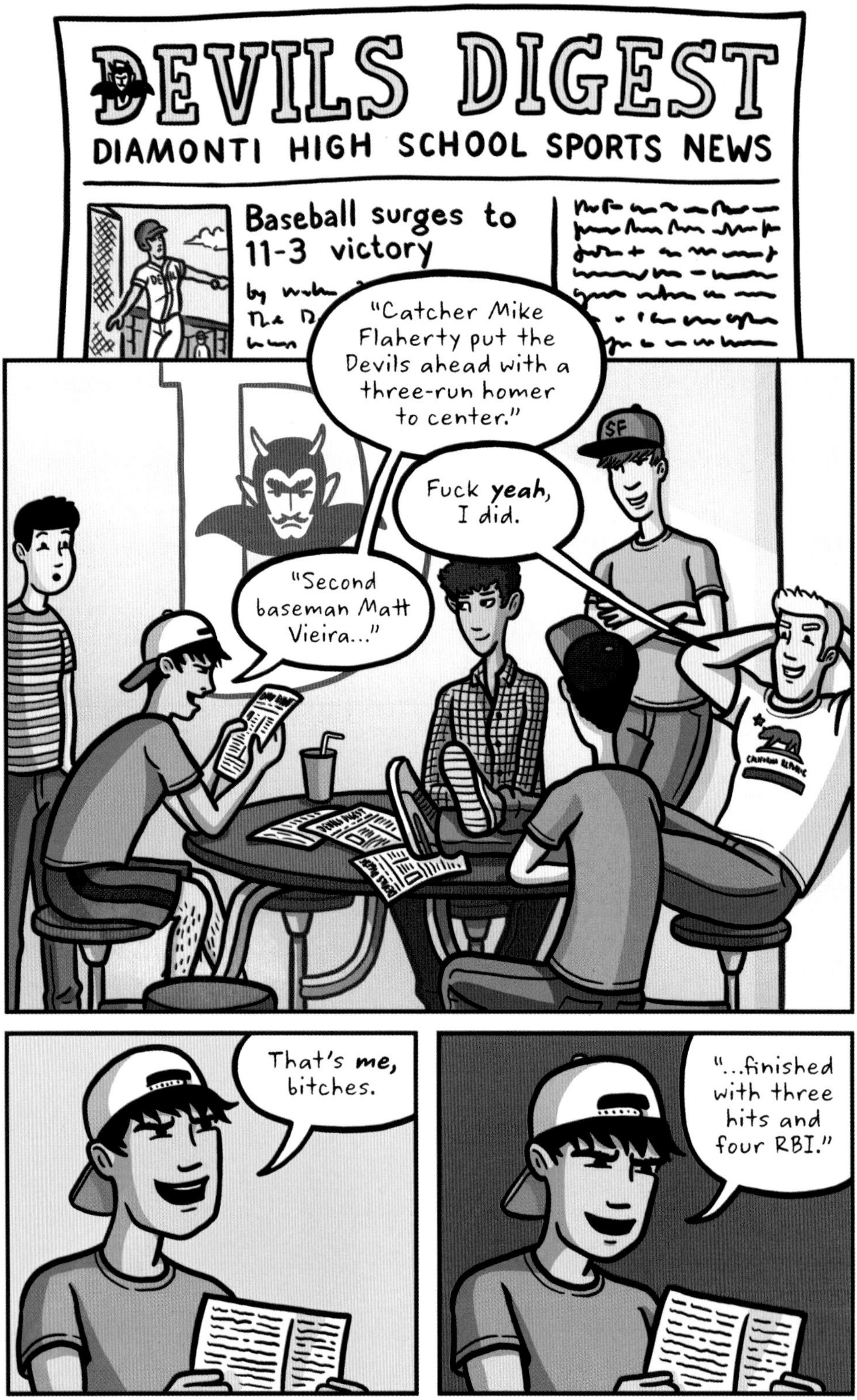
DEVILS DIGEST
DIAMONTI HIGH SCHOOL SPORTS NEWS
Baseball surges to 11-3 victory
"Catcher Mike Flaherty put the Devils ahead with a three-run homer to center."
Fuck **yeah**, I did.
"Second baseman Matt Vieira..."
That's **me**, bitches.
"...finished with three hits and four RBI."

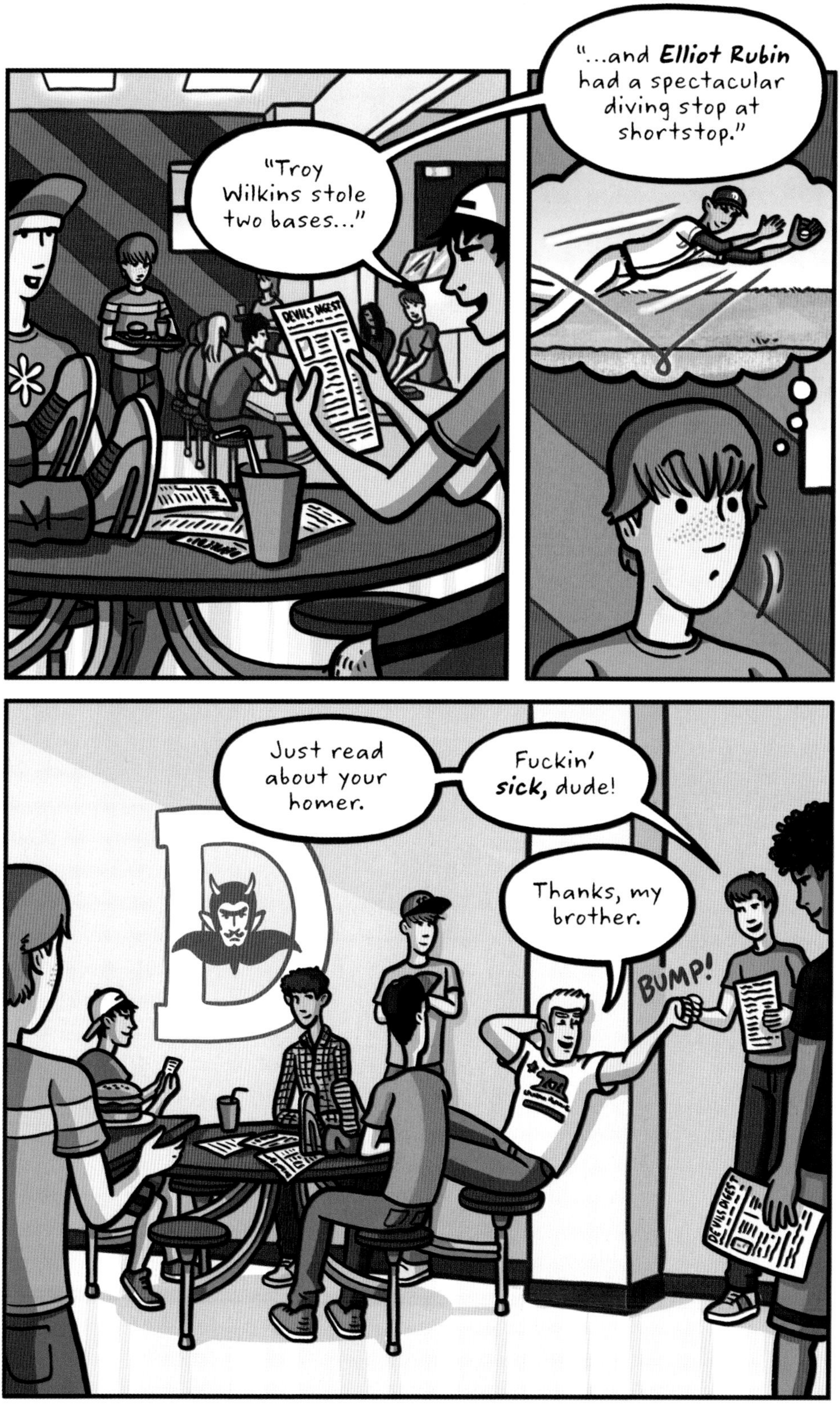
"Troy Wilkins stole two bases..."
"...and **Elliot Rubin** had a spectacular diving stop at shortstop."
DEVILS DIGEST
Just read about your homer.
Fuckin' **sick,** dude!
Thanks, my brother.
BUMP!
DEVILS DIGEST

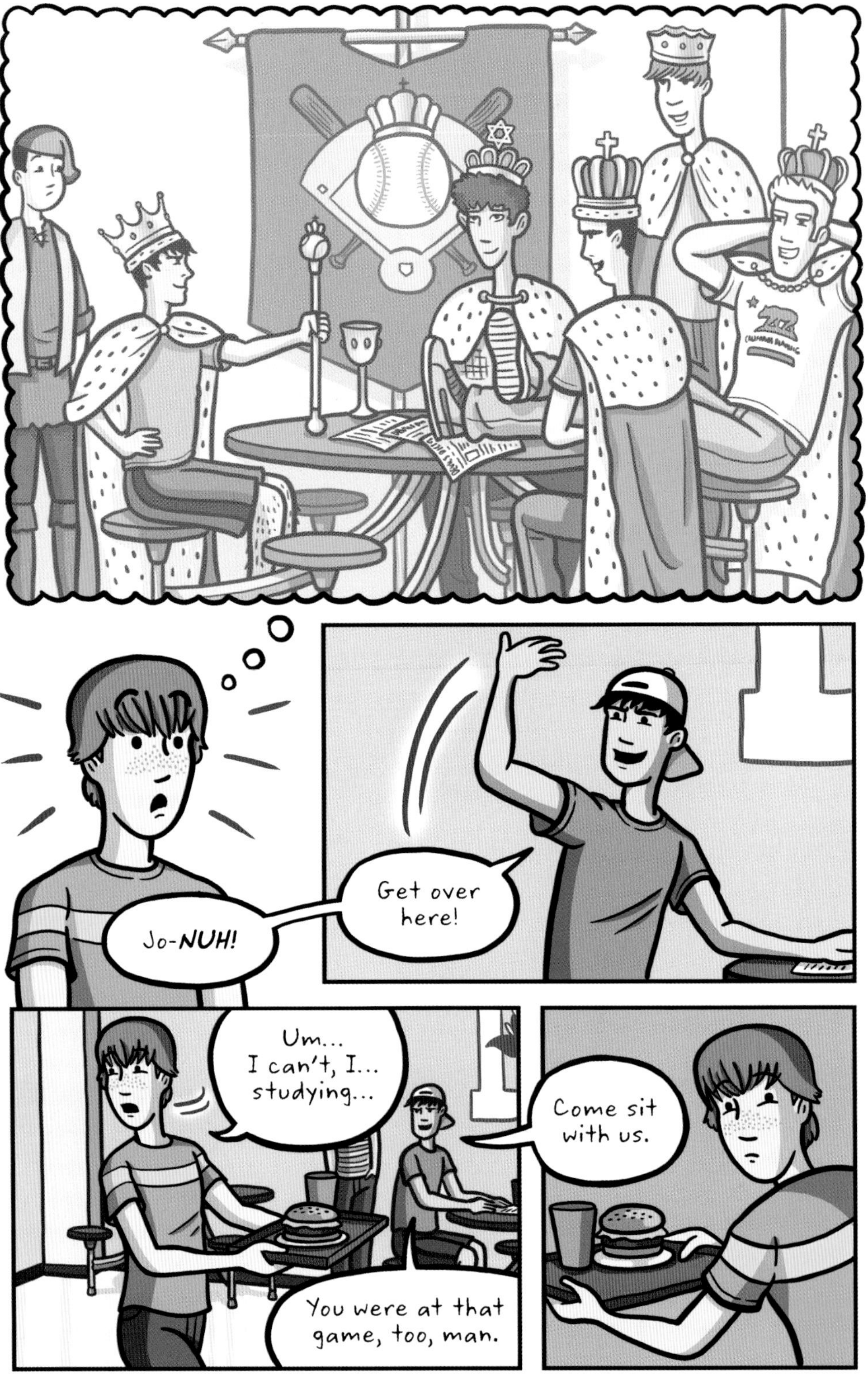
Jo-**NUH!**
Get over here!
Um... I can't, I... studying...
Come sit with us.
You were at that game, too, man.

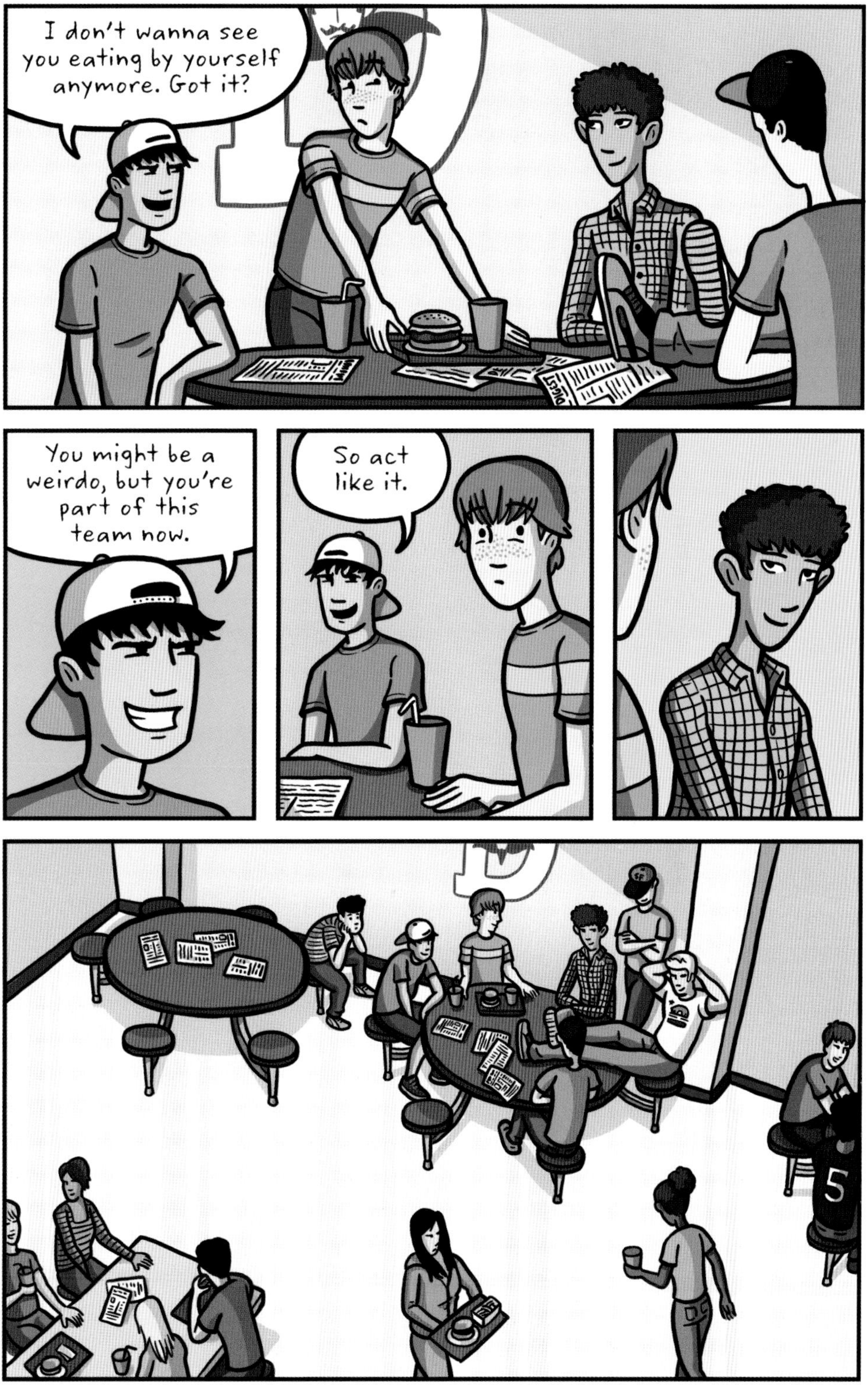
I don't wanna see you eating by yourself anymore. Got it?
DIGEST
You might be a weirdo, but you're part of this team now.
So act like it.
5

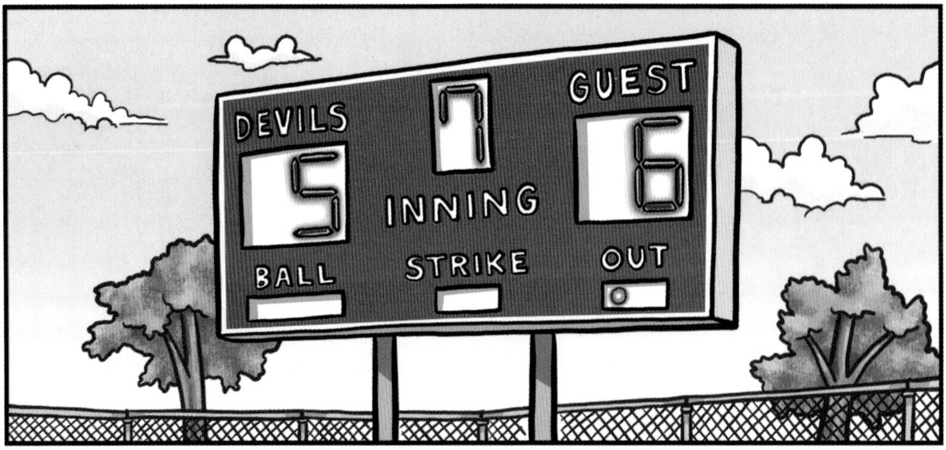
DEVILS
7
GUEST
5
INNING
6
BALL
STRIKE
OUT

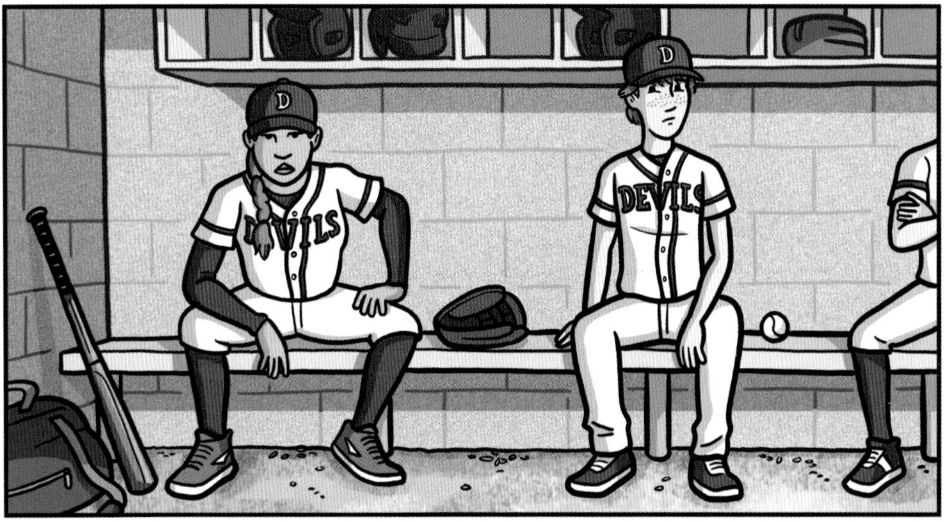
DEVILS
DEVILS

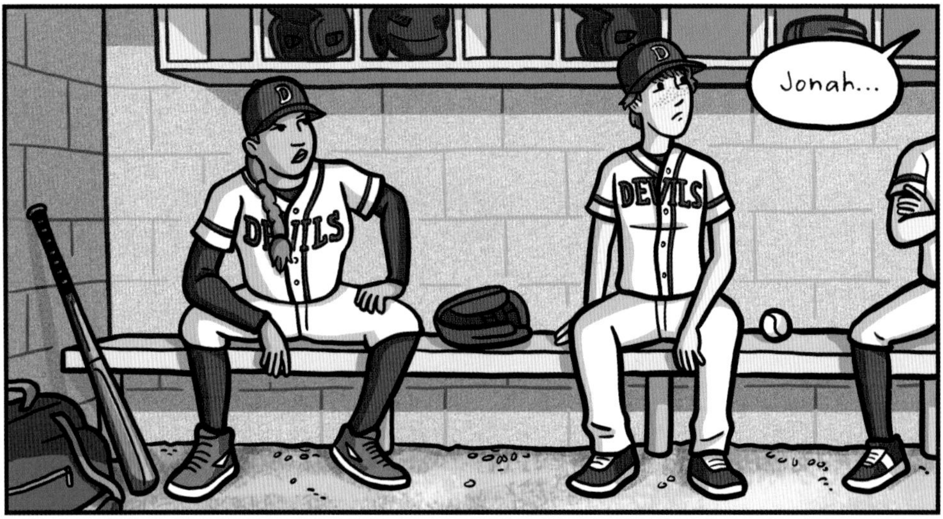
Jonah...
DEVILS
DEVILS

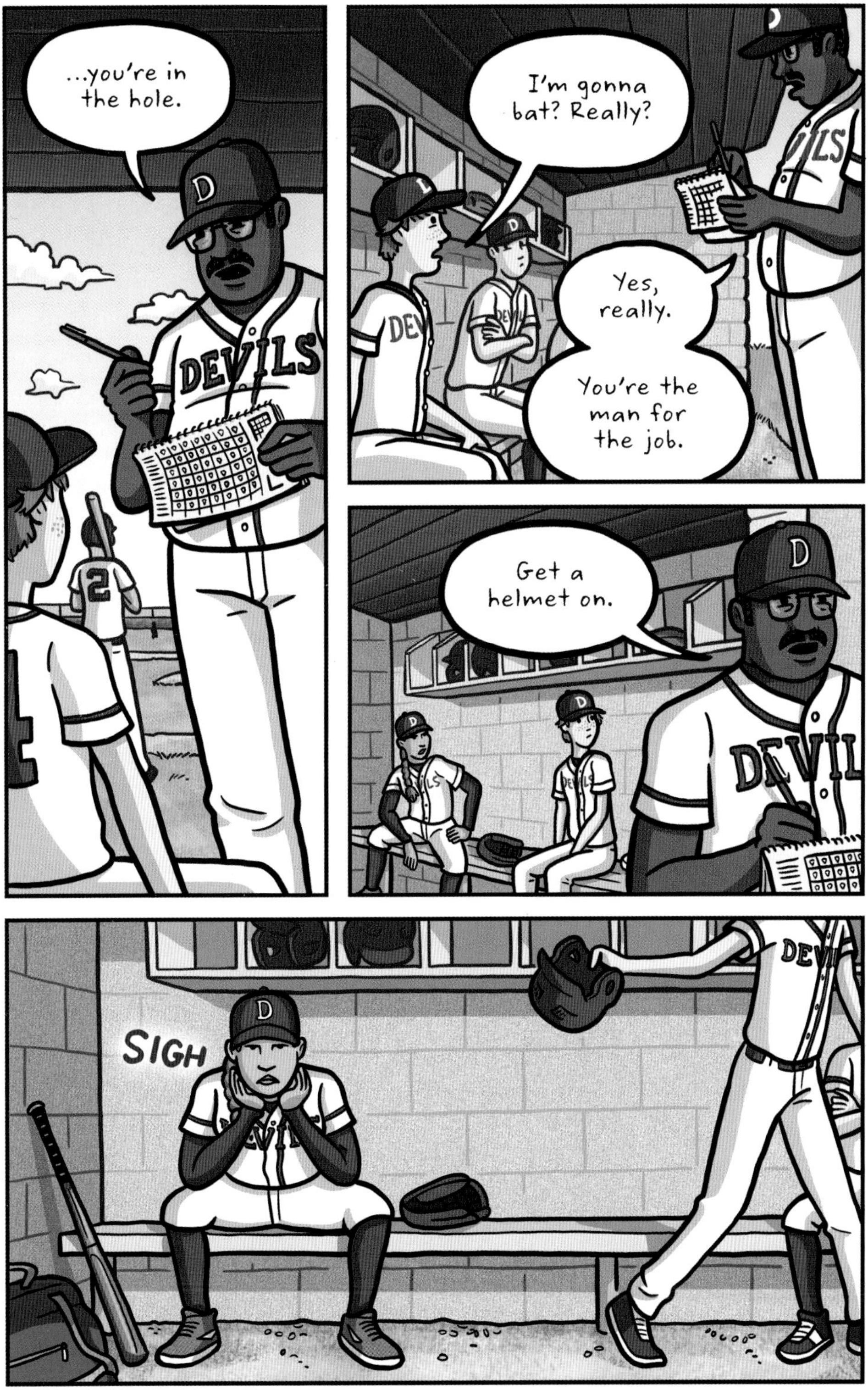

...you're in the hole.
I'm gonna bat? Really?
Yes, really.
You're the man for the job.
Get a helmet on.
SIGH

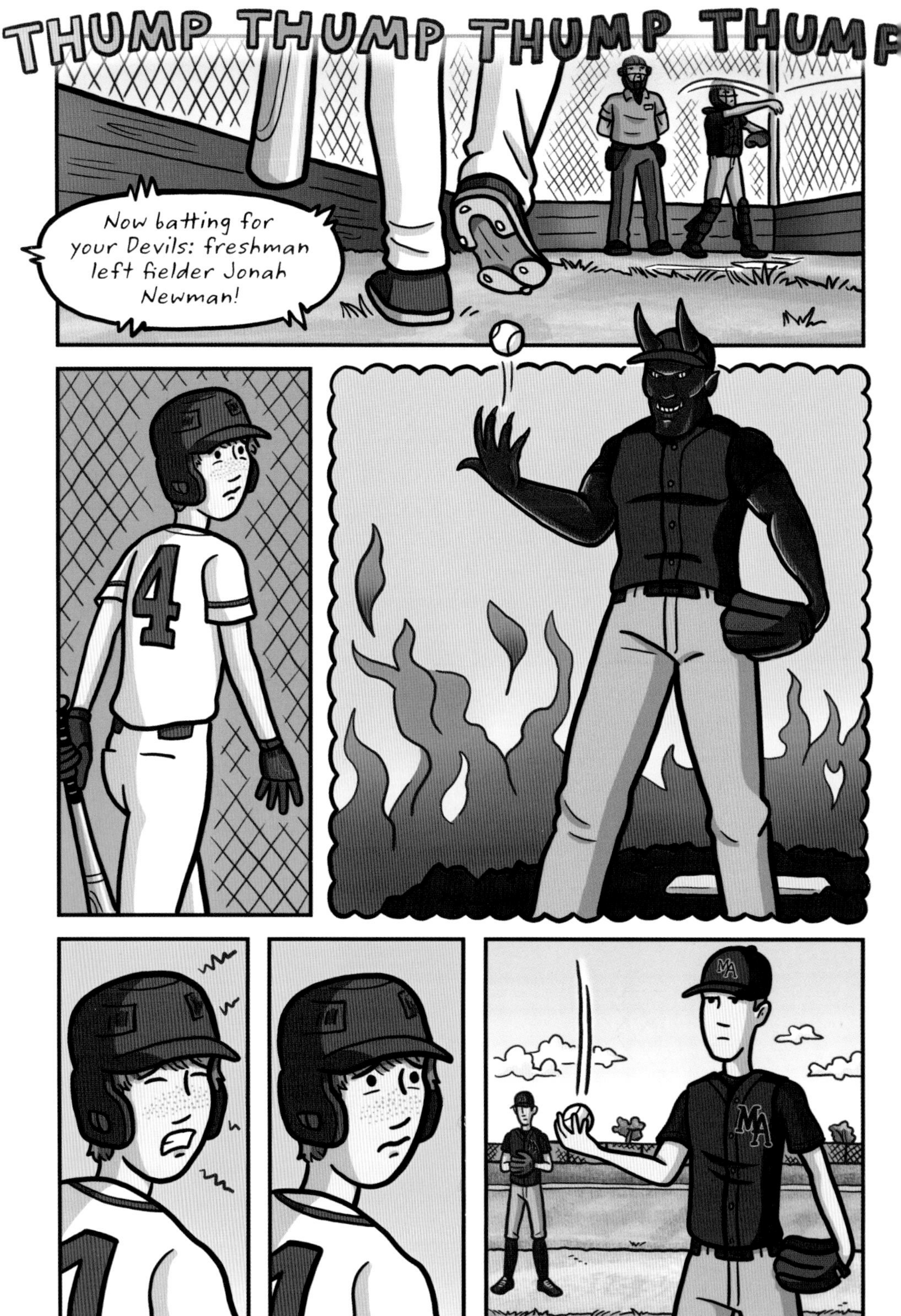
THUMP THUMP THUMP THUMP
Now batting for your Devils: freshman left fielder Jonah Newman!
MA
MA

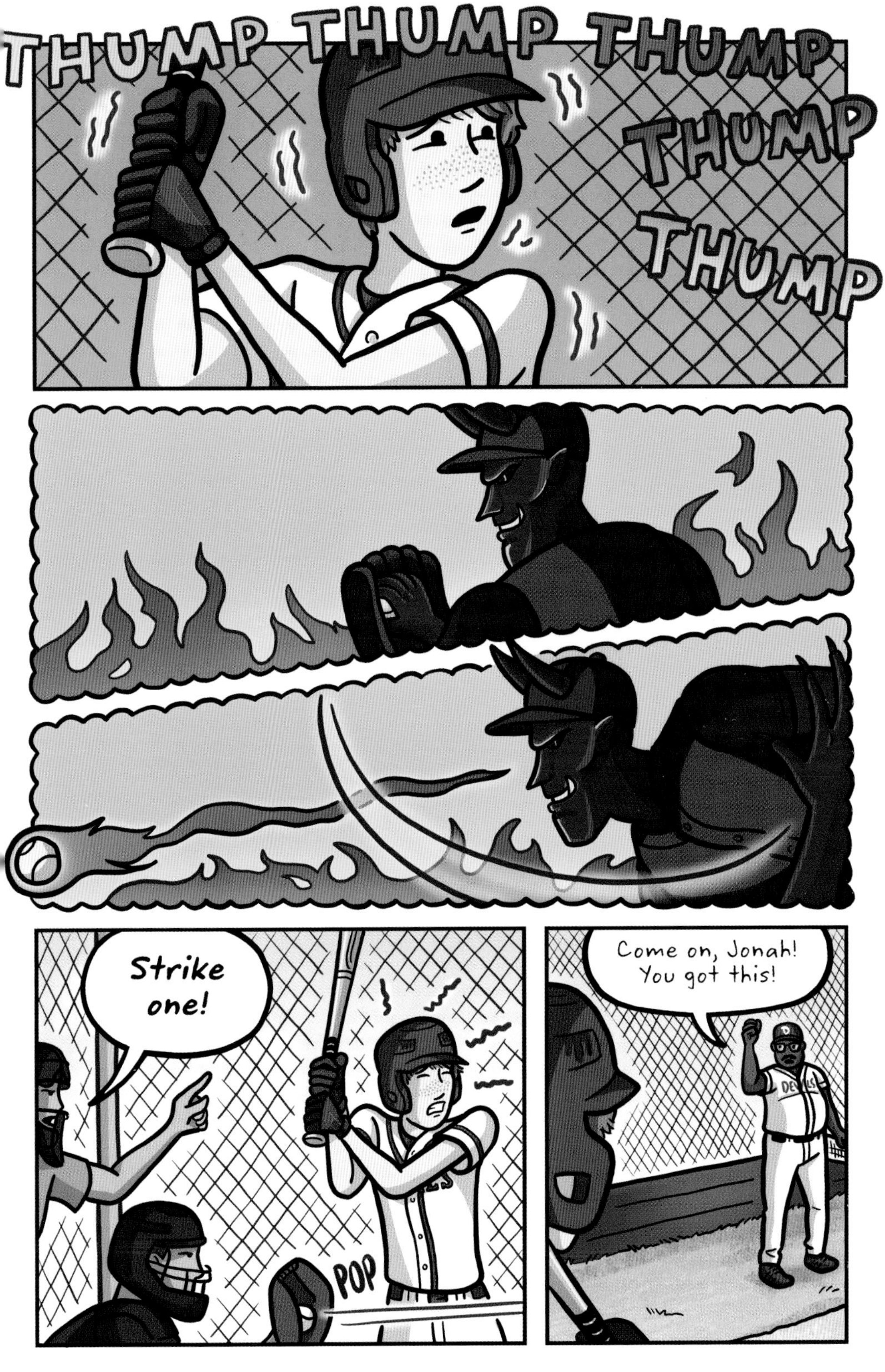
THUMP THUMP THUMP
THUMP
THUMP
Strike one!
POP
Come on, Jonah! You got this!

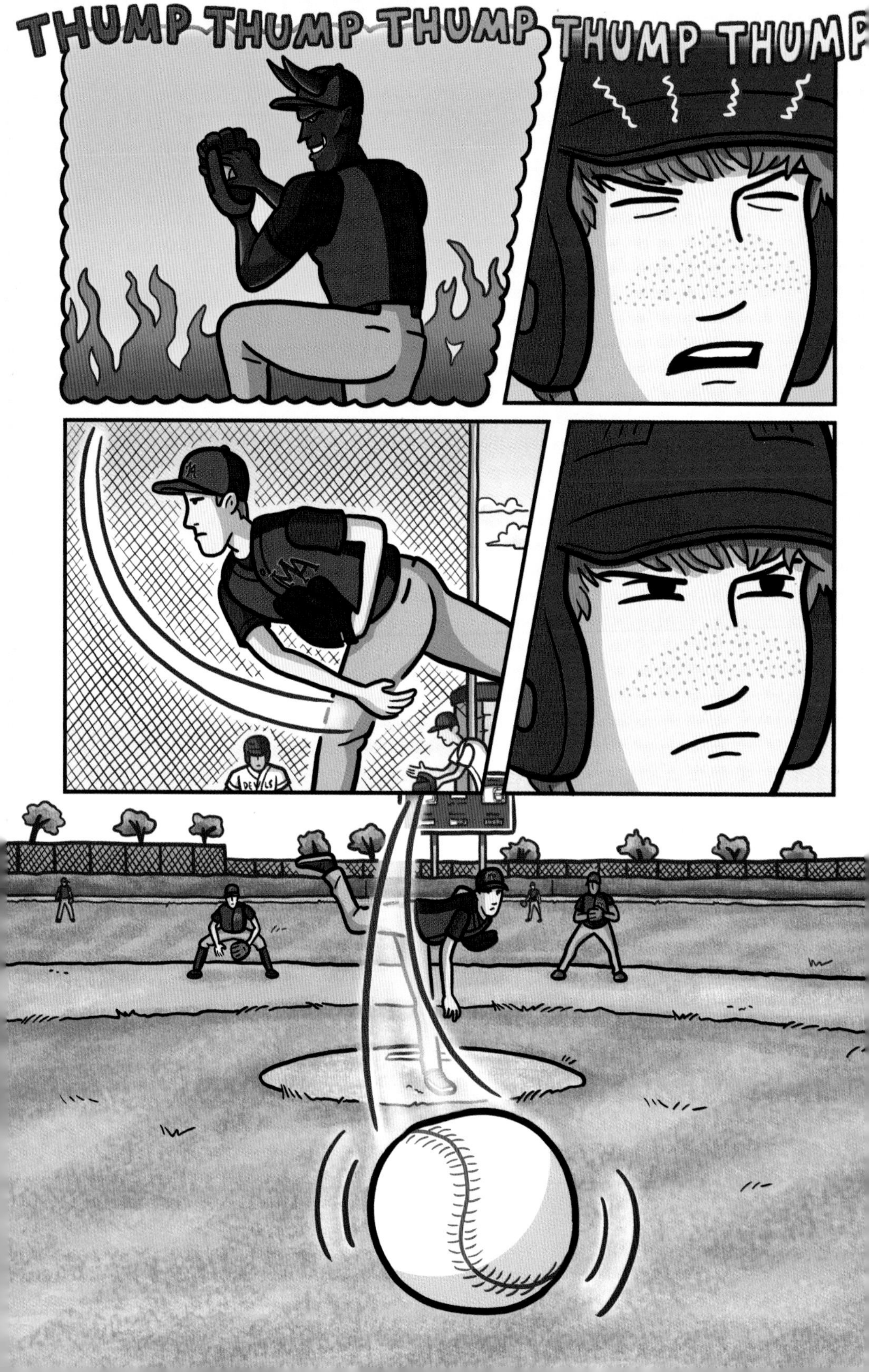
THUMP THUMP THUMP
THUMP THUMP
DEVILS

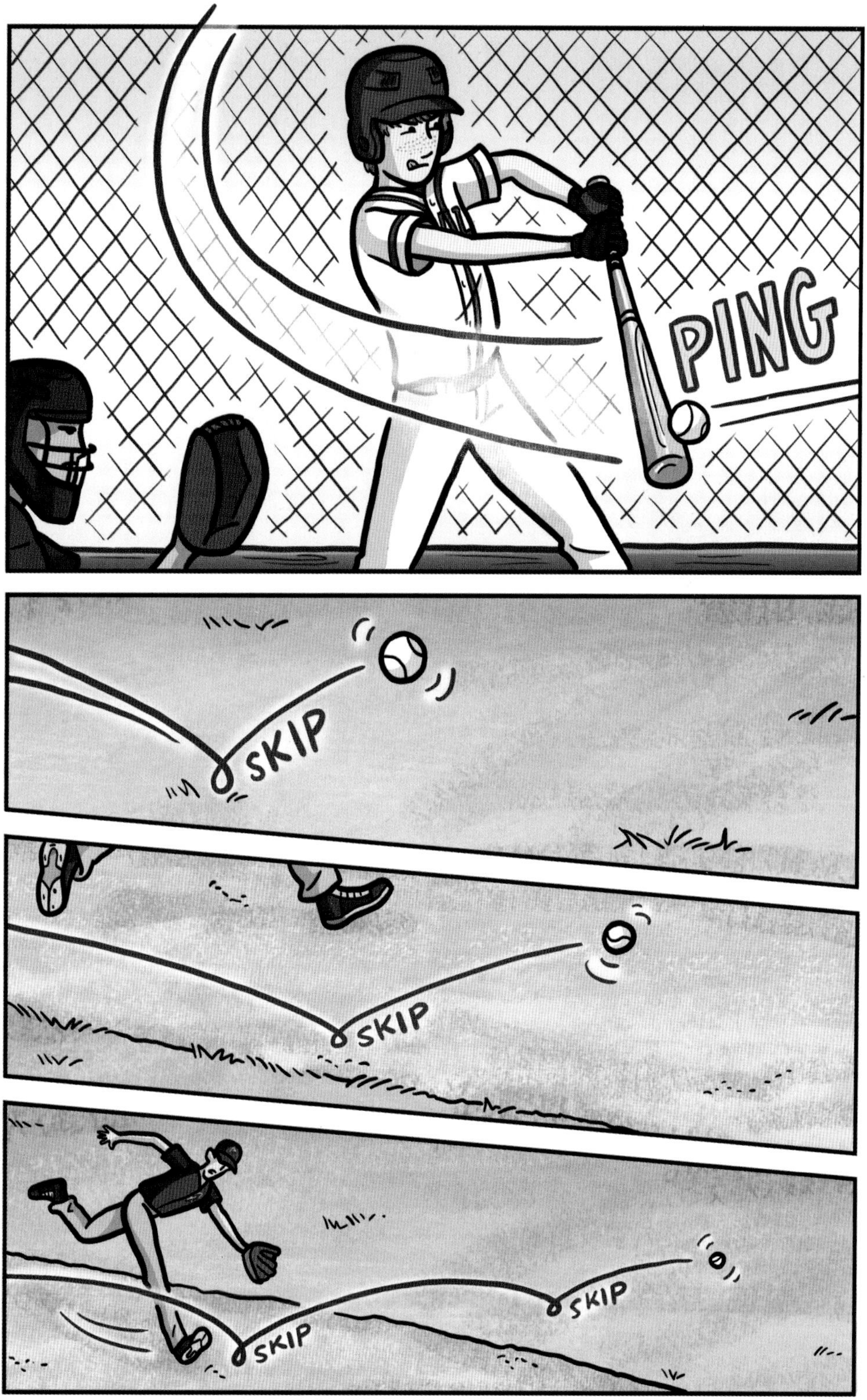
PING
SKIP
SKIP
SKIP
SKIP

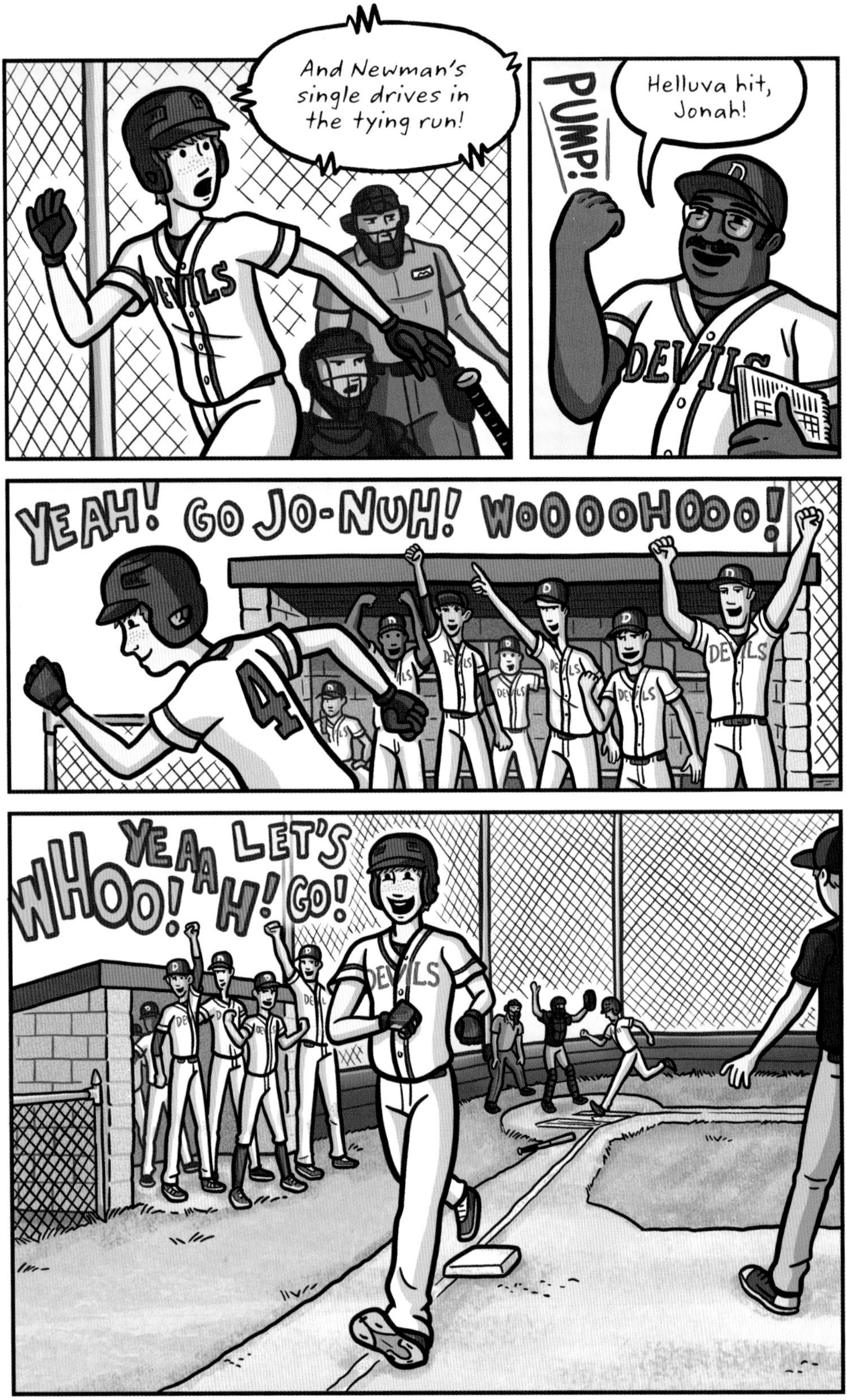
And Newman's single drives in the tying run!
PUMP!
Helluva hit, Jonah!
YEAH! GO JO-NUH! WOOOOOHOOO!
WHOO! YEAAAH! LET'S GO!

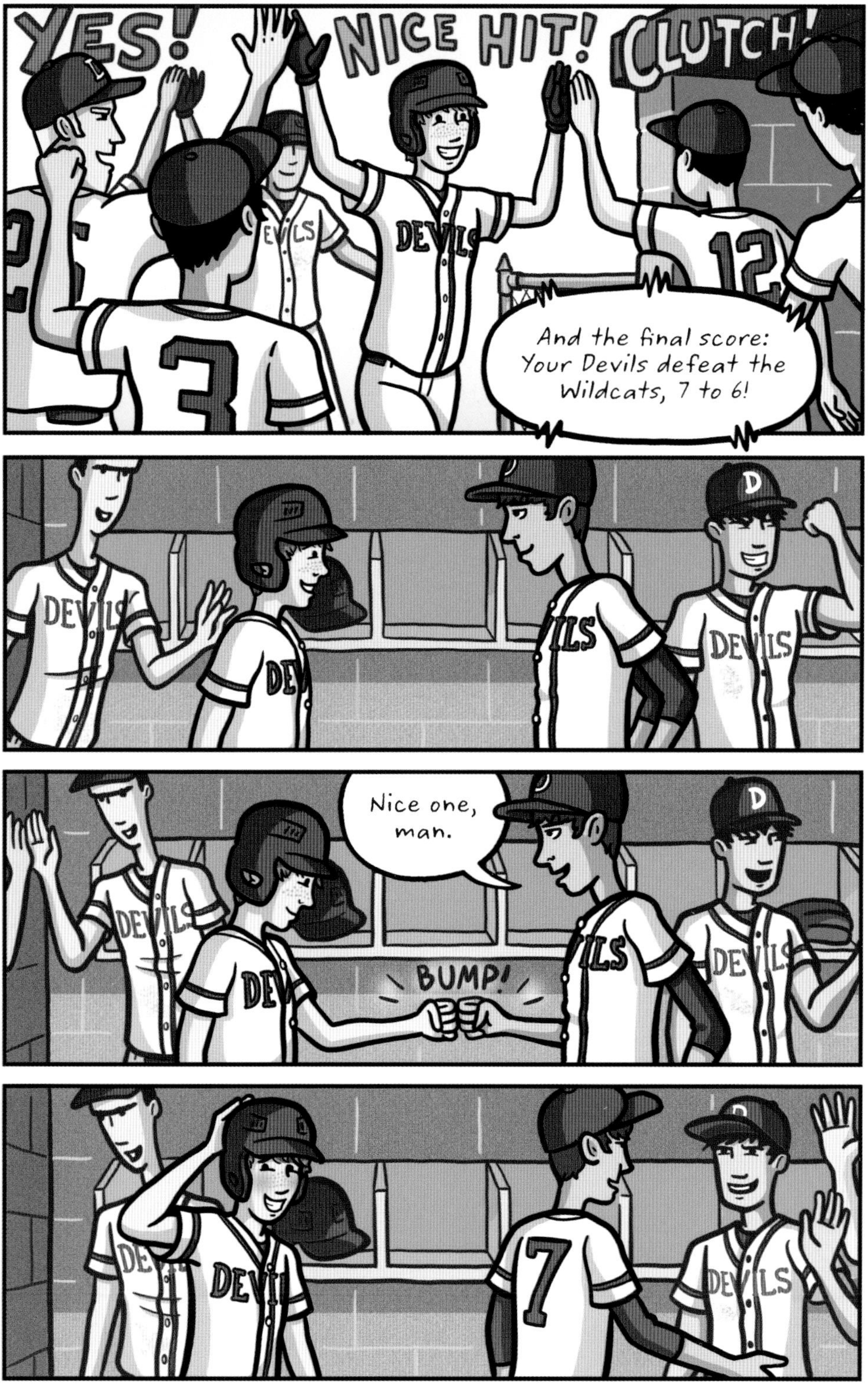
YES!
NICE HIT!
CLUTCH!
And the final score: Your Devils defeat the Wildcats, 7 to 6!
Nice one, man.
BUMP!

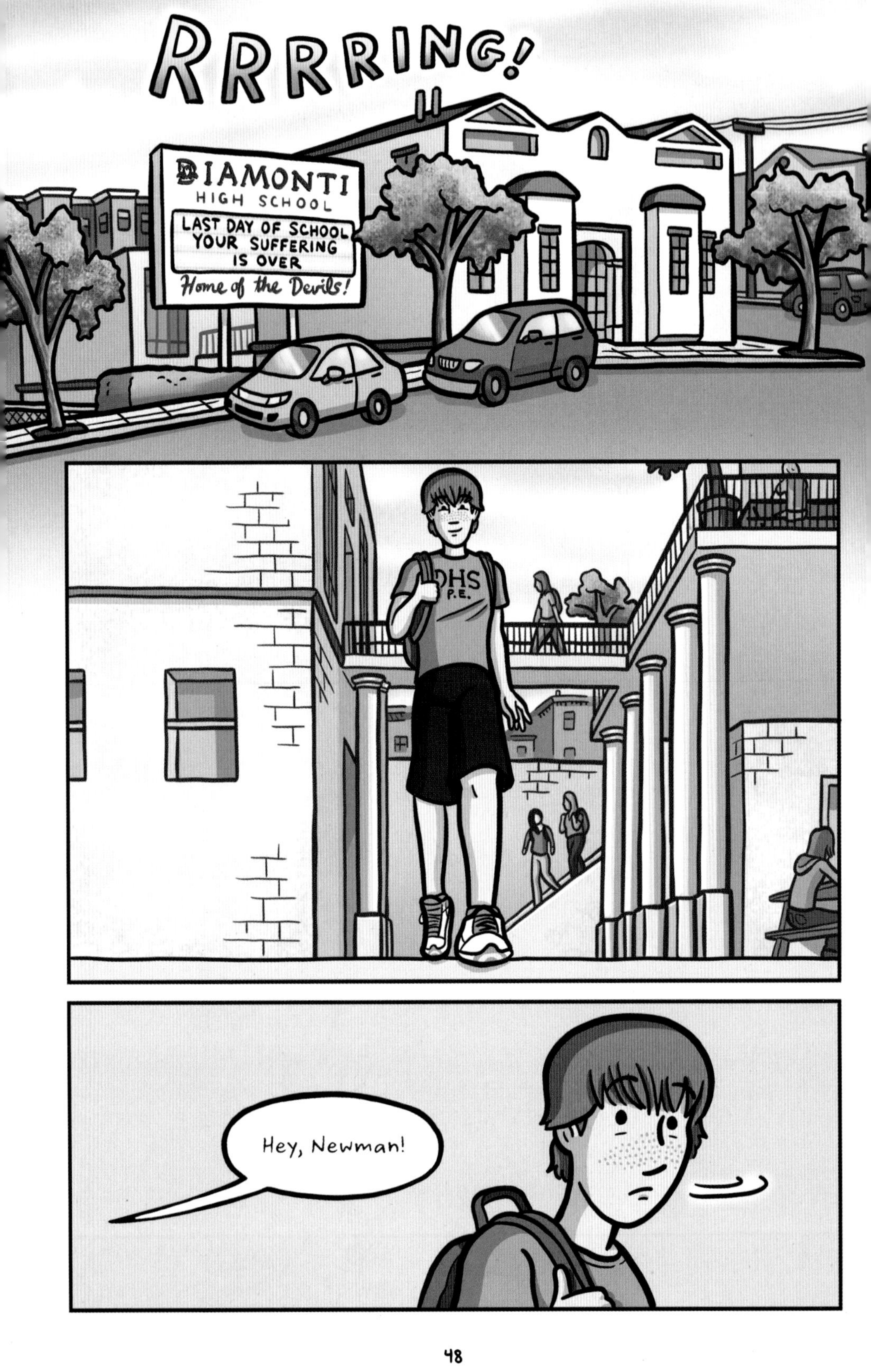
RRRRING!
DIAMONTI HIGH SCHOOL
LAST DAY OF SCHOOL YOUR SUFFERING IS OVER
Home of the Devils!
DHS P.E.
Hey, Newman!

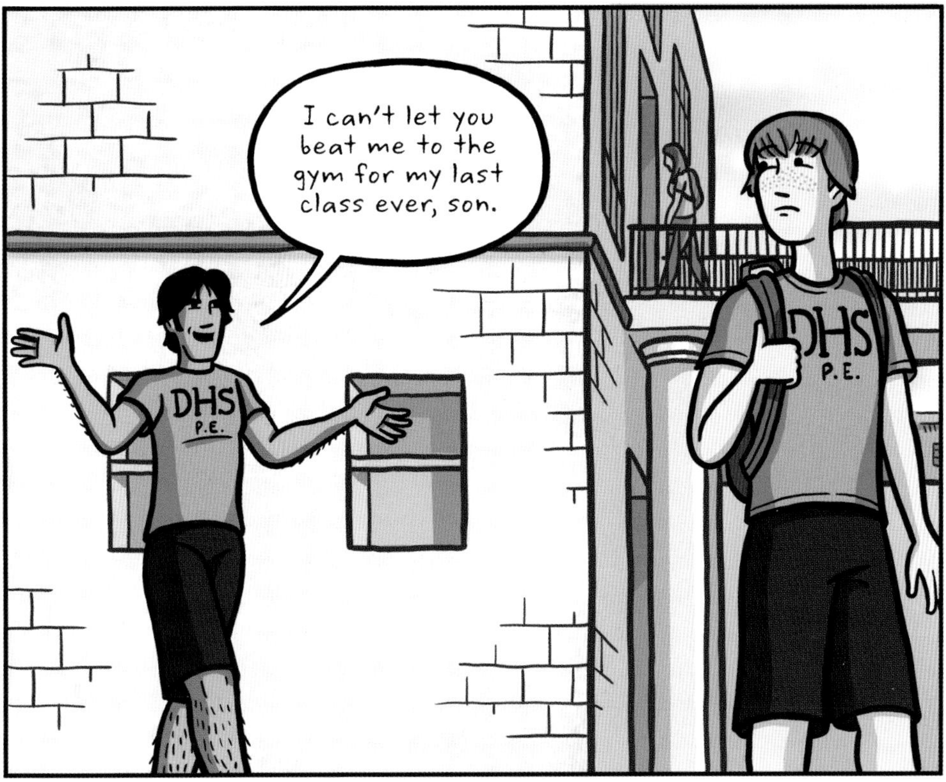
I can't let you beat me to the gym for my last class ever, son.
DHS P.E.
DHS P.E.

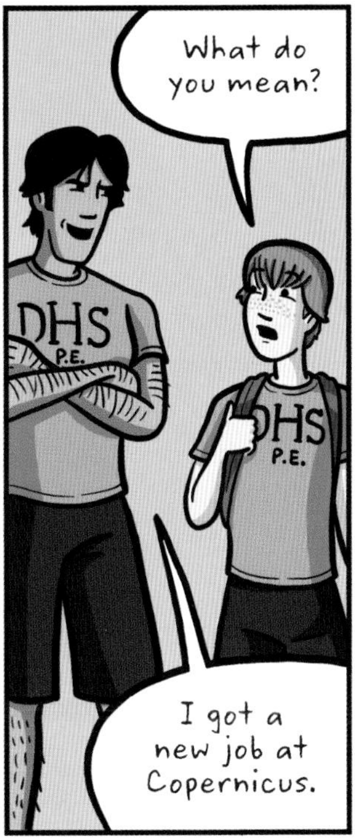
What do you mean?
I got a new job at Copernicus.
DHS P.E.
DHS P.E.

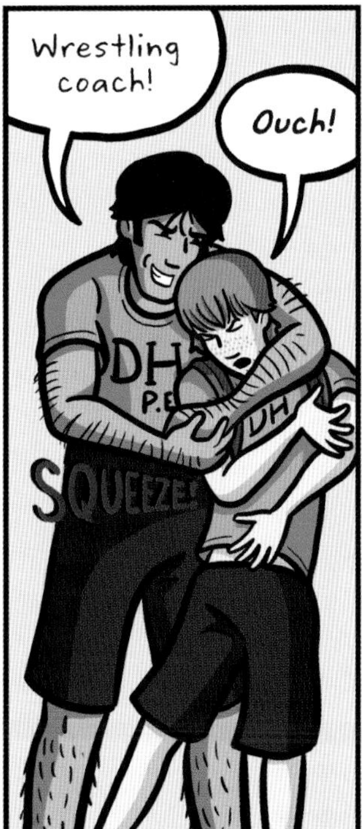
Wrestling coach!
Ouch!
SQUEEZE!

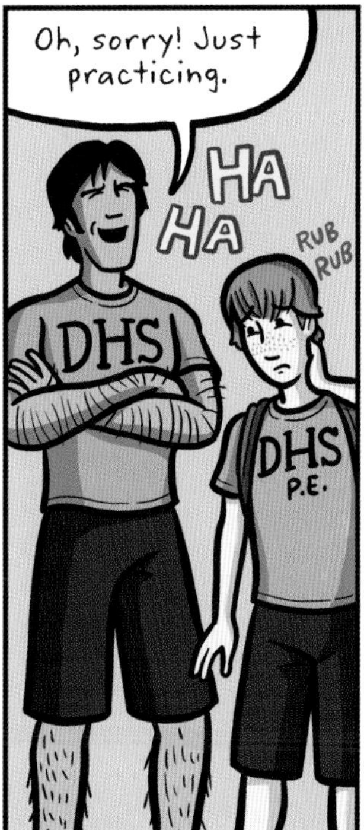
Oh, sorry! Just practicing.
HA HA
RUB RUB
DHS
DHS P.E.

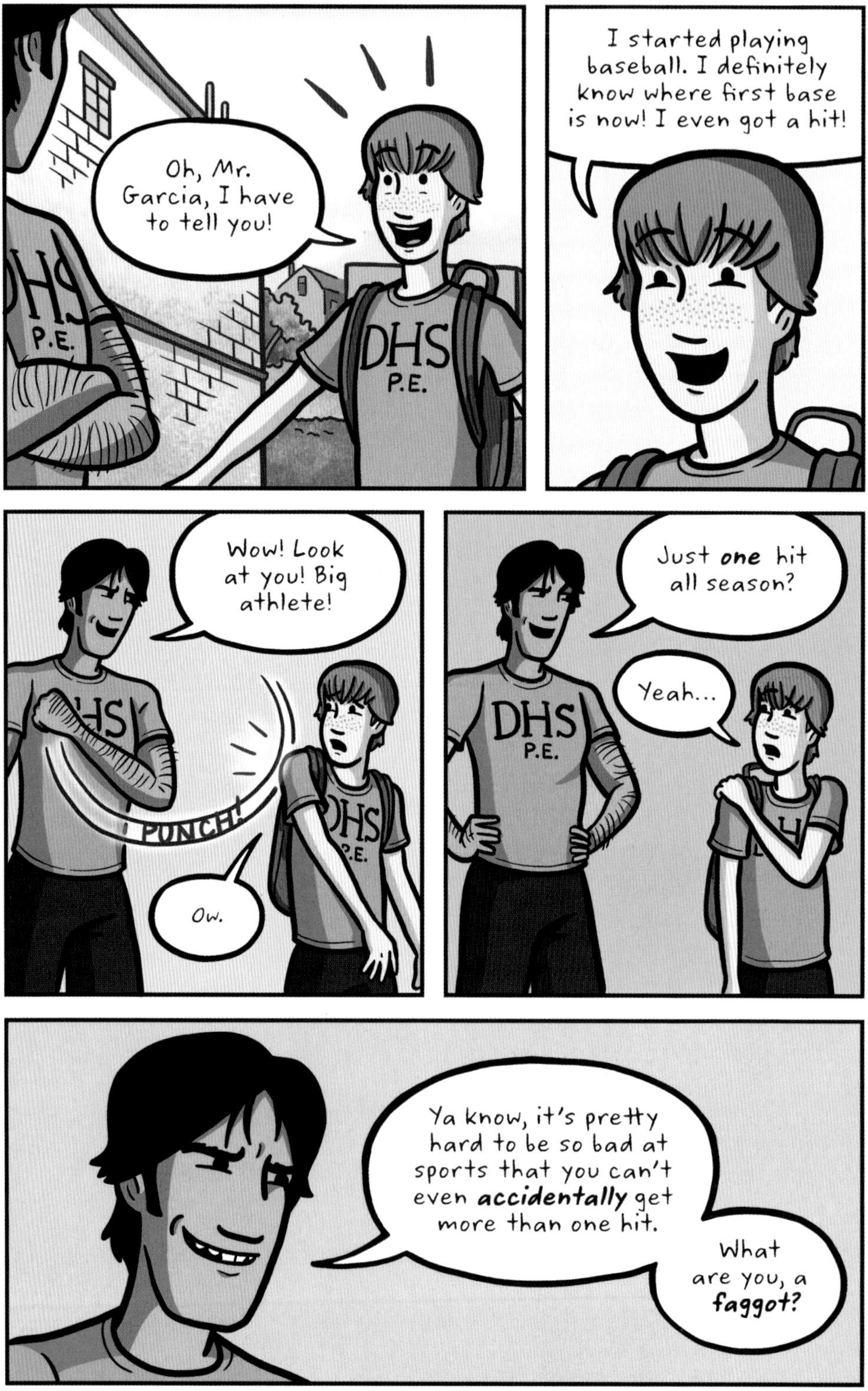
Oh, Mr. Garcia, I have to tell you!
I started playing baseball. I definitely know where first base is now! I even got a hit!
Wow! Look at you! Big athlete!
PUNCH!
Ow.
Just **one** hit all season?
Yeah...
Ya know, it's pretty hard to be so bad at sports that you can't even **accidentally** get more than one hit.
What are you, a **faggot?**

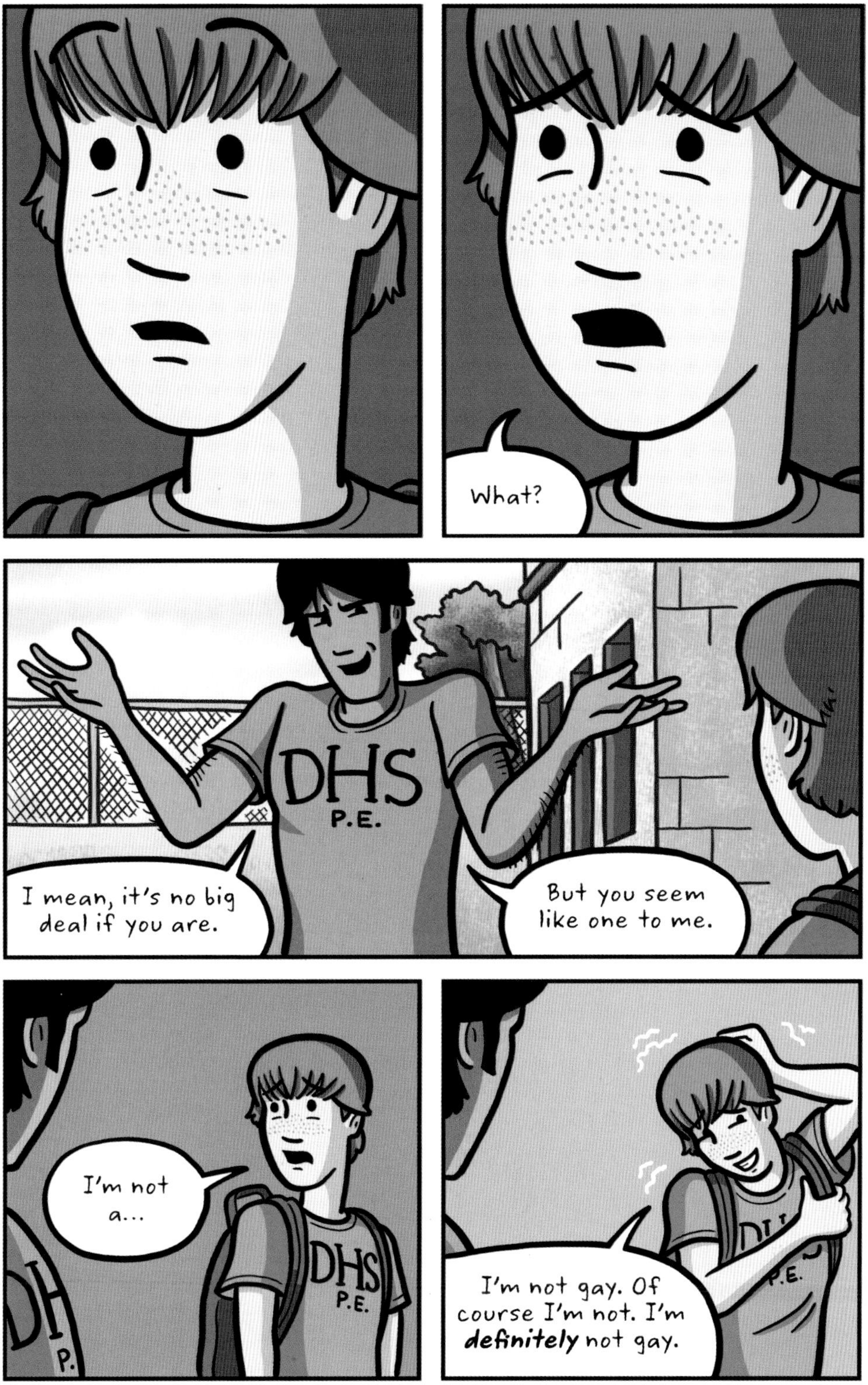
What?
I mean, it's no big deal if you are.
But you seem like one to me.
I'm not a...
I'm not gay. Of course I'm not. I'm *definitely* not gay.

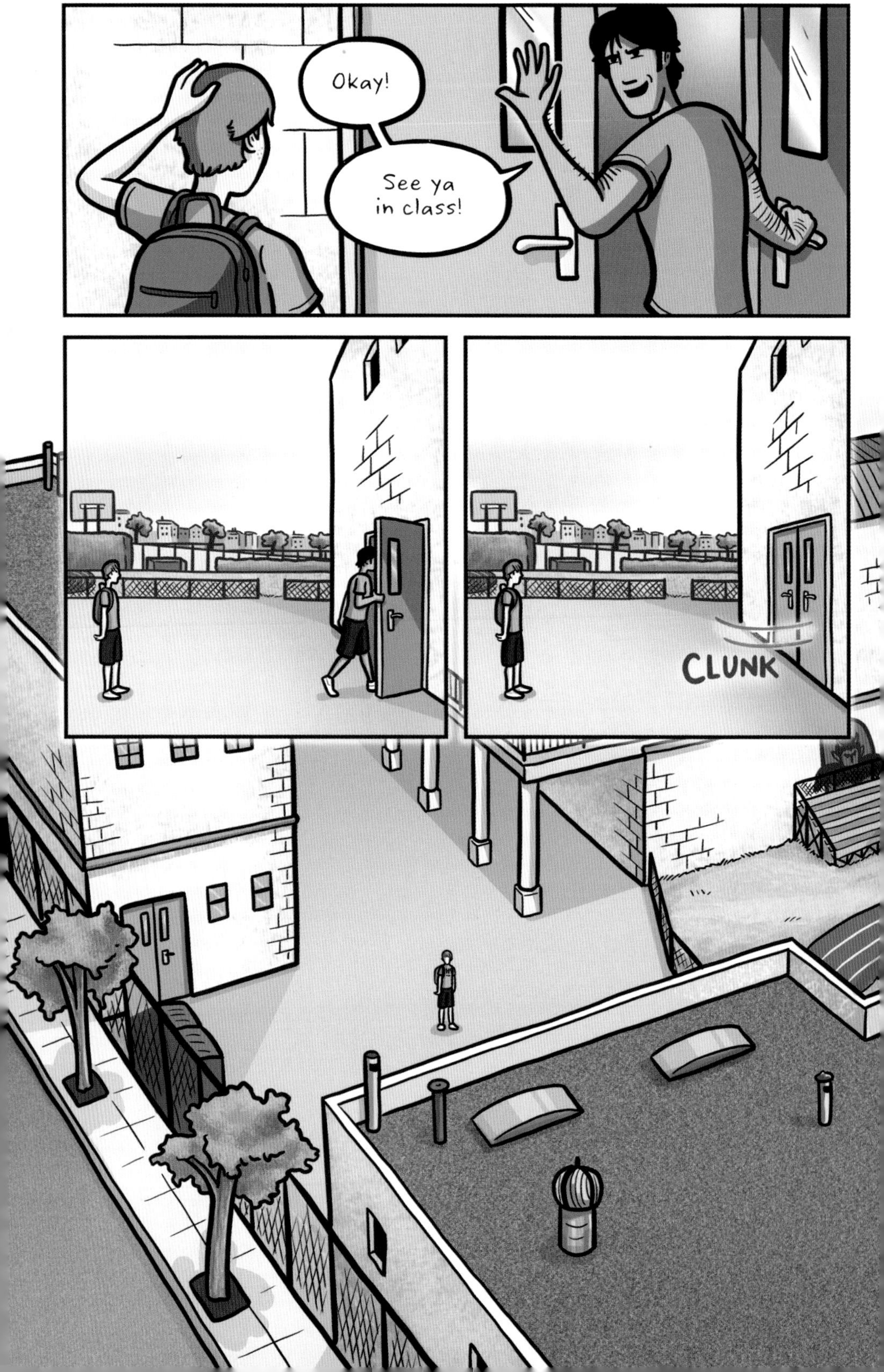
Okay!
See ya in class!
CLUNK

CHAPTER 2

NOW SHOWING SUMMER

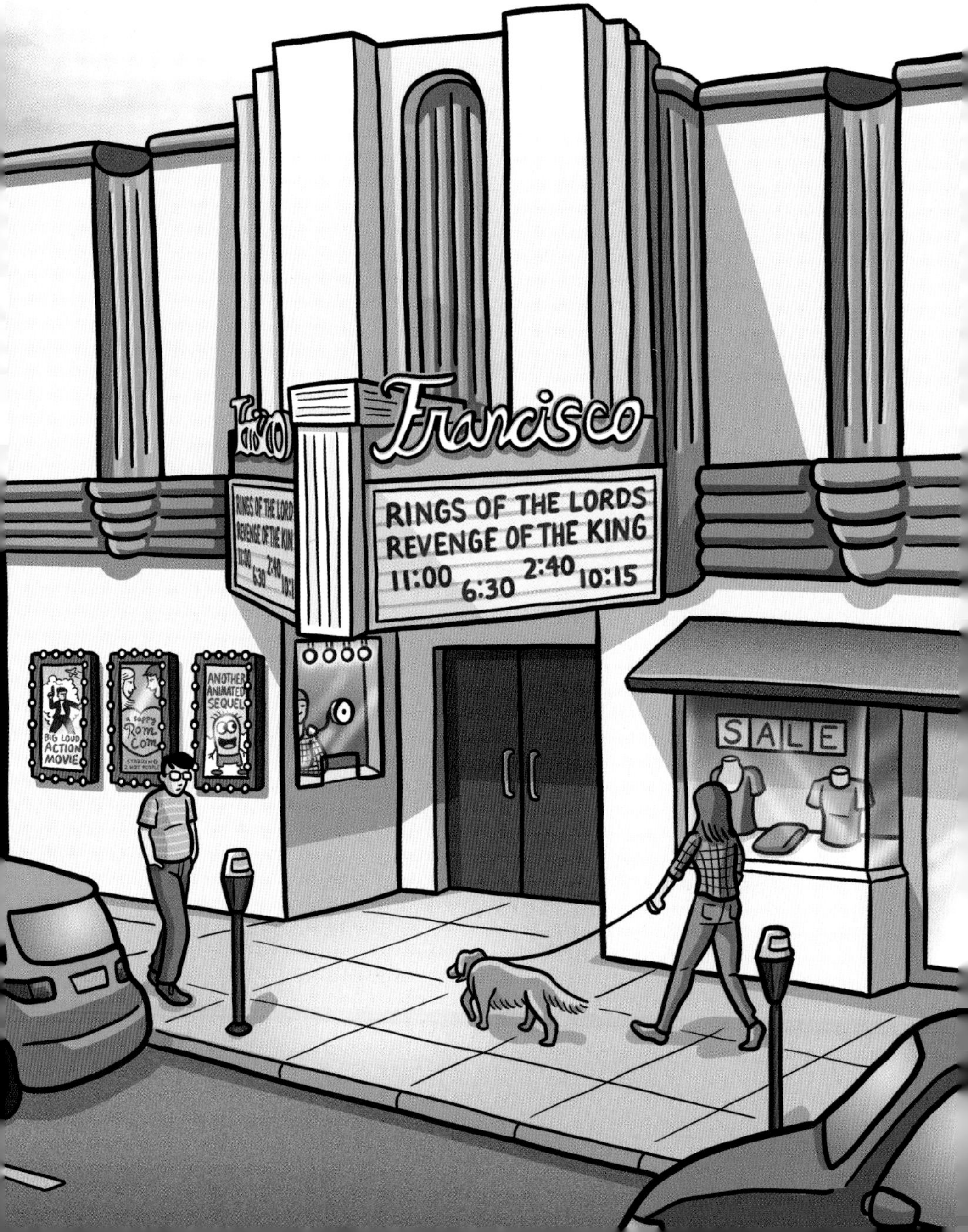
Francisco
RINGS OF THE LORDS
REVENGE OF THE KING
11:00 6:30 2:40 10:15
BIG LOUD ACTION MOVIE
a sappy Rom Com
STARRING 2 HOT PEOPLE
ANOTHER ANIMATED SEQUEL
SALE

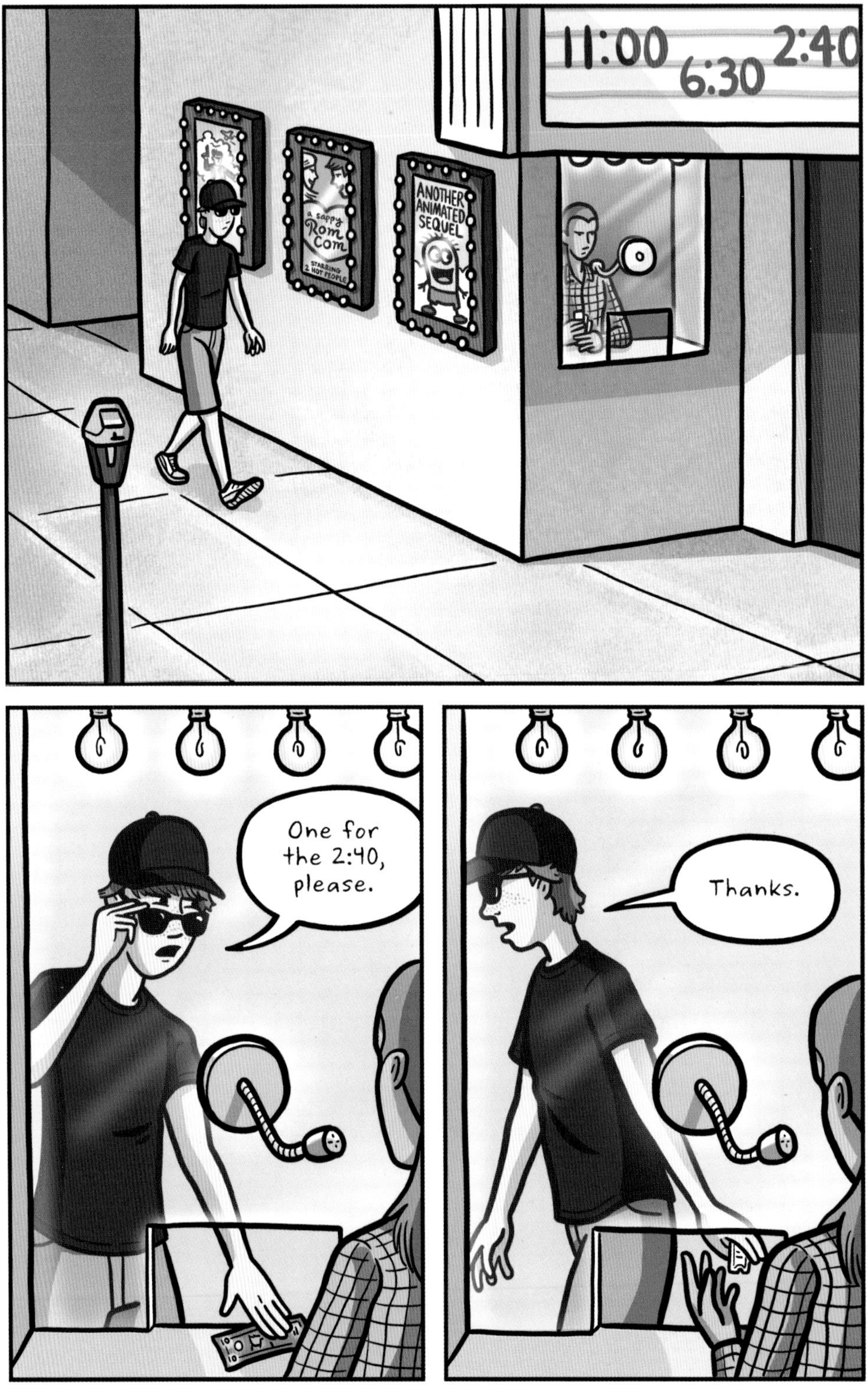
11:00 6:30 2:40
a sappy Rom Com
STARRING 2 HOT PEOPLE
ANOTHER ANIMATED SEQUEL
One for the 2:40, please.
Thanks.

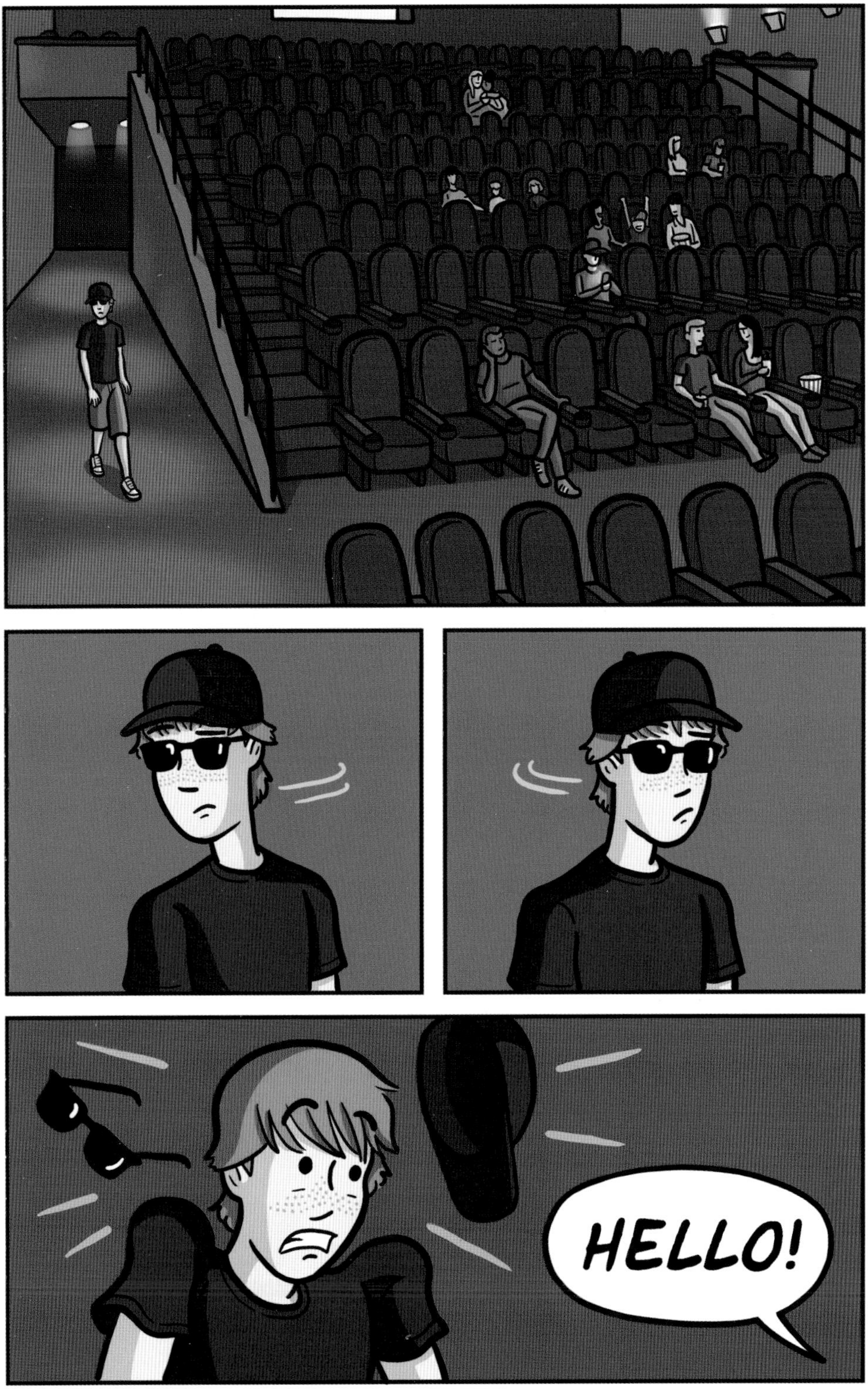
HELLO!

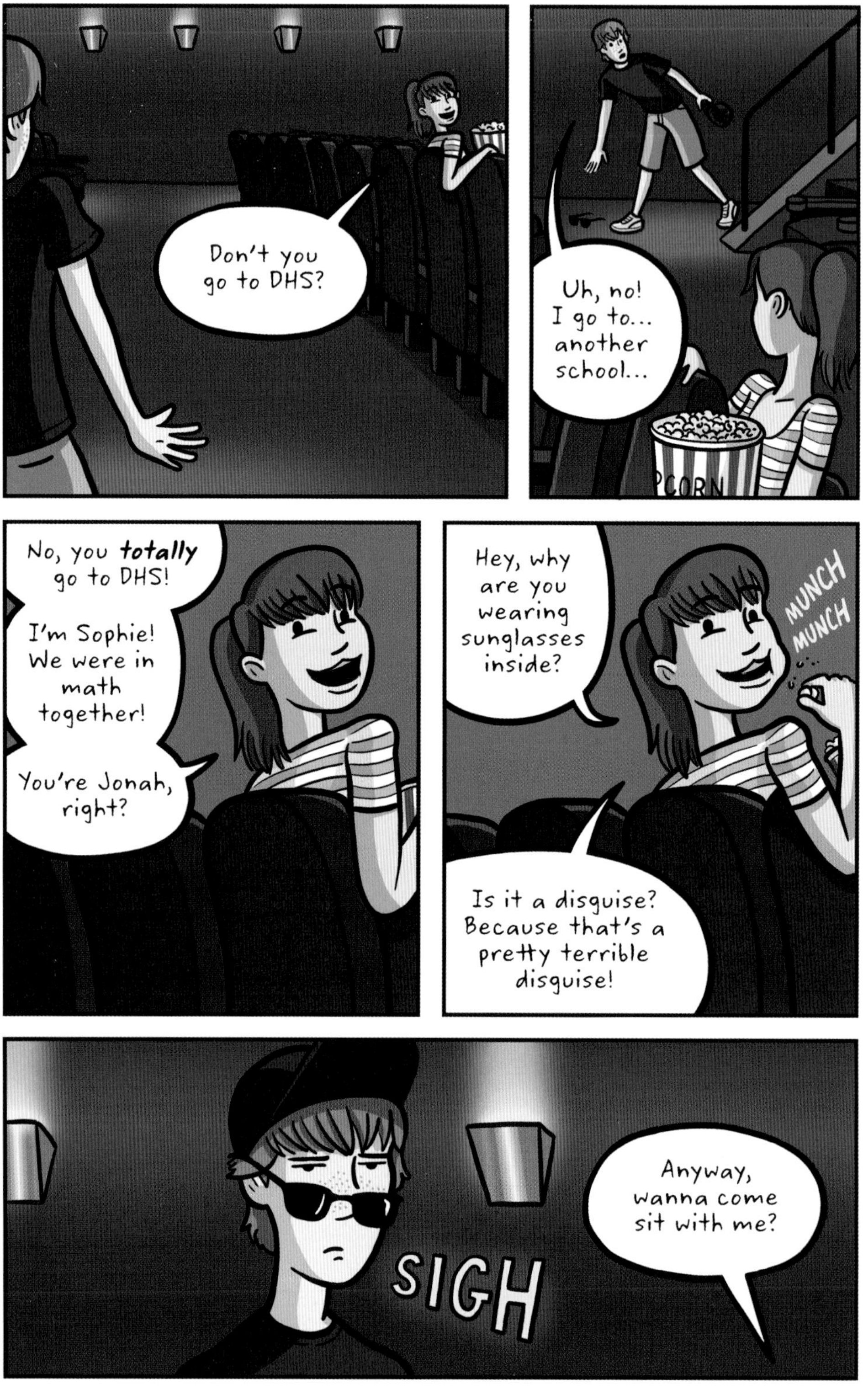
Don't you go to DHS?
Uh, no! I go to... another school...
POPCORN
No, you **totally** go to DHS!
I'm Sophie! We were in math together!
You're Jonah, right?
Hey, why are you wearing sunglasses inside?
MUNCH MUNCH
Is it a disguise? Because that's a pretty terrible disguise!
SIGH
Anyway, wanna come sit with me?

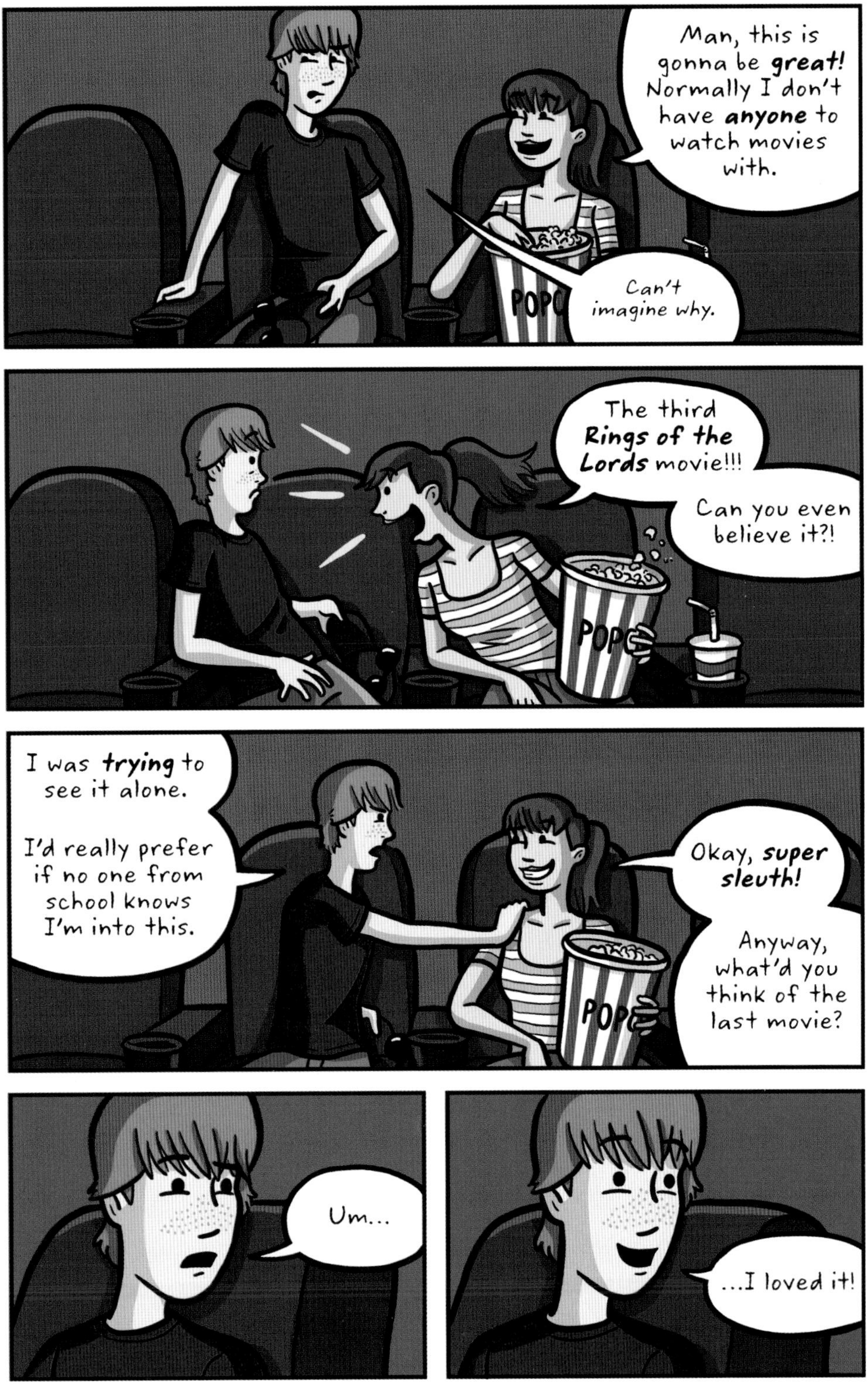
Man, this is gonna be **great!** Normally I don't have **anyone** to watch movies with.
Can't imagine why.
The third **Rings of the Lords** movie!!!
Can you even believe it?!
I was **trying** to see it alone.
I'd really prefer if no one from school knows I'm into this.
Okay, **super sleuth!**
Anyway, what'd you think of the last movie?
Um...
...I loved it!

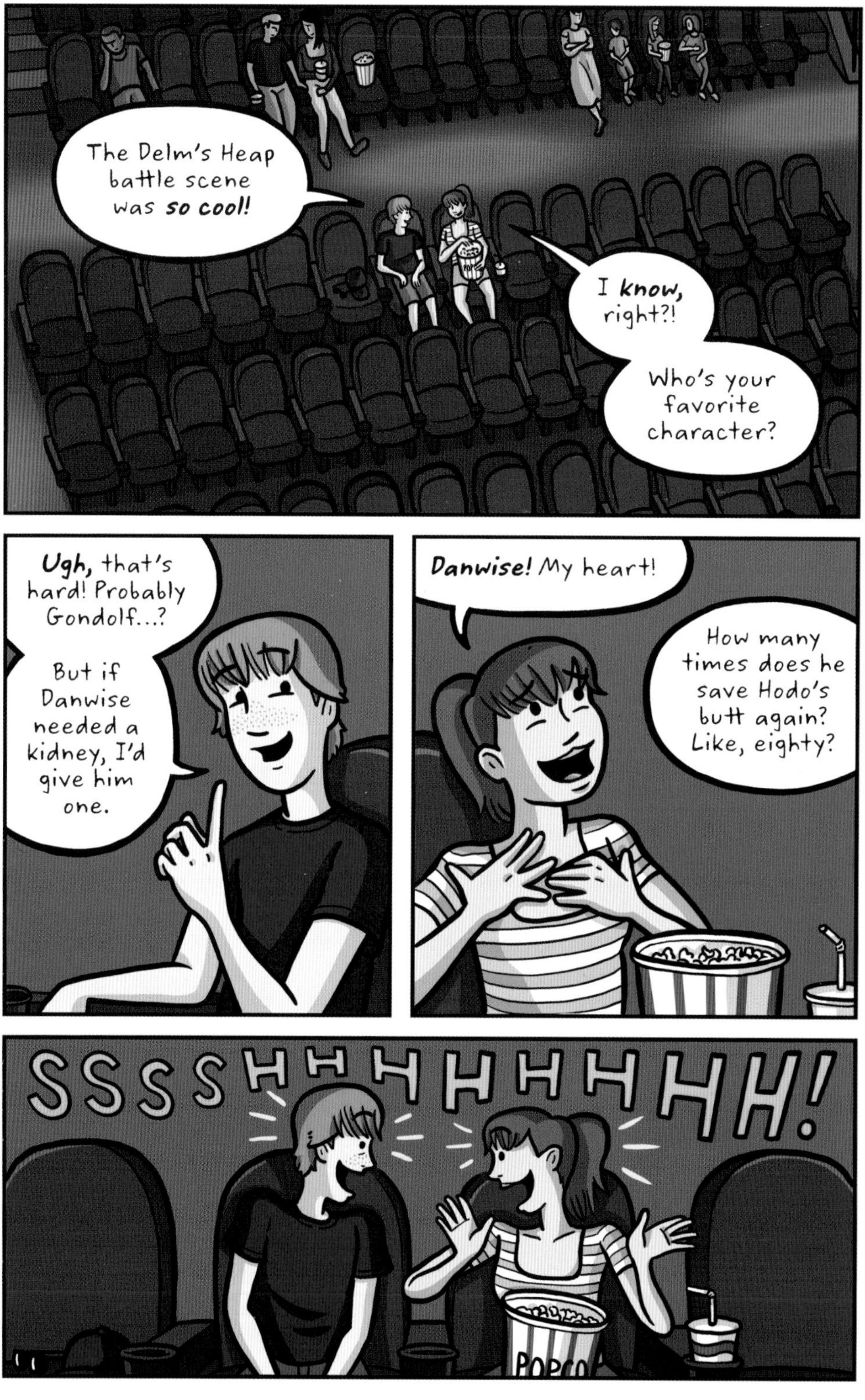
The Delm's Heap battle scene was **so cool!**
I **know,** right?!
Who's your favorite character?
Ugh, that's hard! Probably Gondolf...?
But if Danwise needed a kidney, I'd give him one.
Danwise! My heart!
How many times does he save Hodo's butt again? Like, eighty?
SSSSHHHHHHHHH!
POPCO

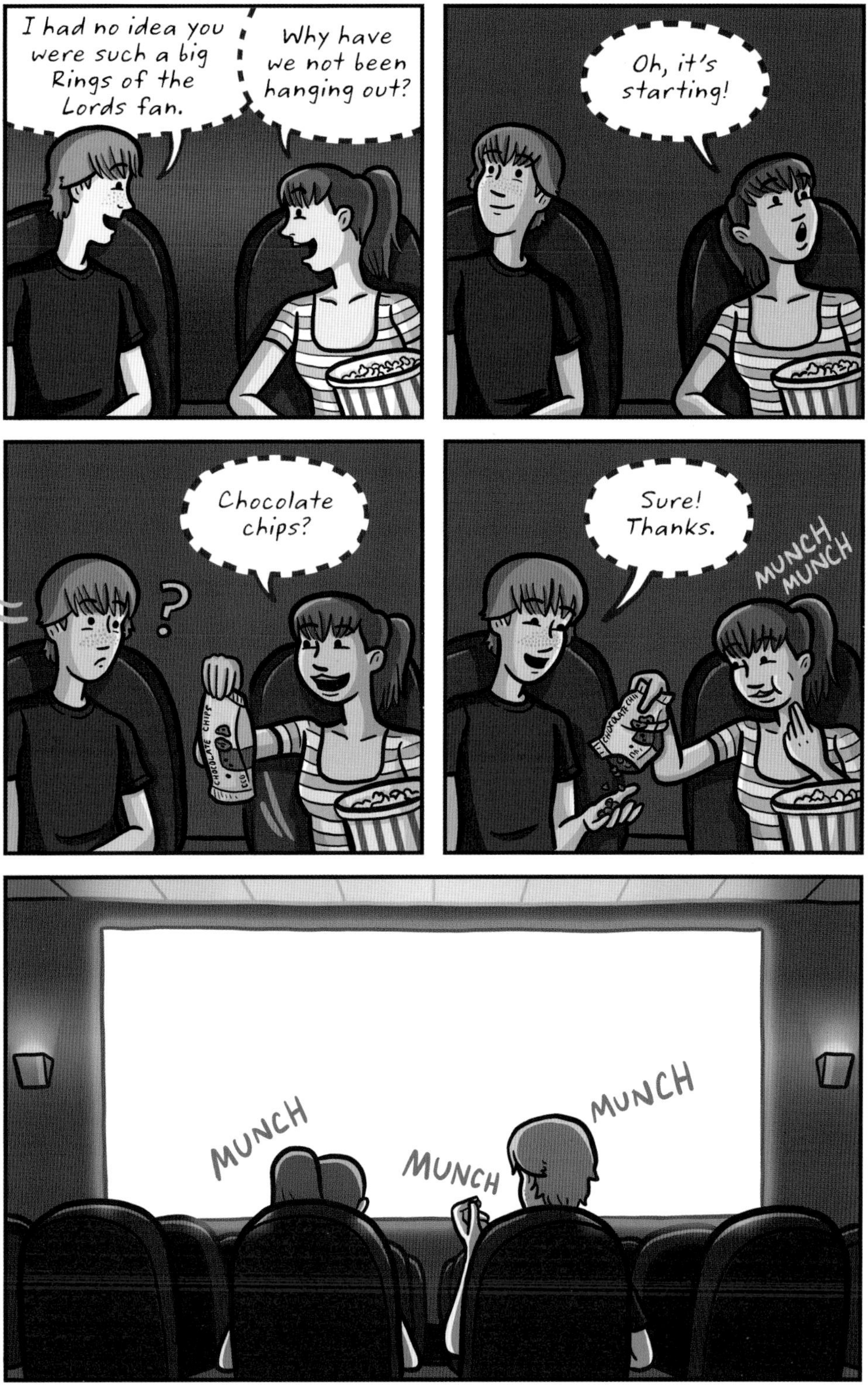
I had no idea you were such a big Rings of the Lords fan.
Why have we not been hanging out?
Oh, it's starting!
Chocolate chips?
?
CHOCOLATE CHIPS
Sure! Thanks.
MUNCH MUNCH
MUNCH
MUNCH
MUNCH

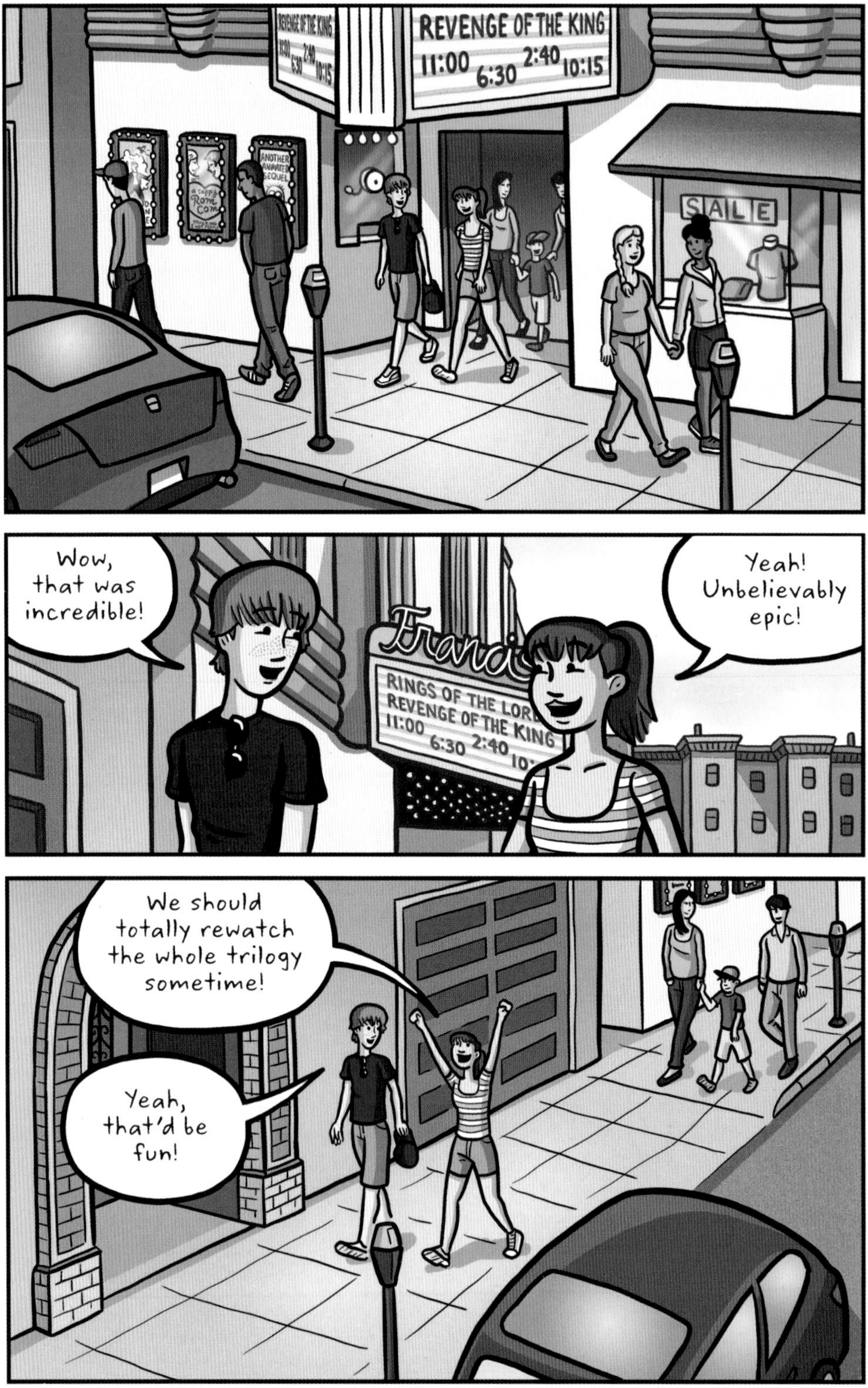
REVENGE OF THE KING
11:00 6:30 2:40 10:15
ANOTHER ANIMATED SEQUEL
SALE
Wow, that was incredible!
Yeah! Unbelievably epic!
We should totally rewatch the whole trilogy sometime!
Yeah, that'd be fun!

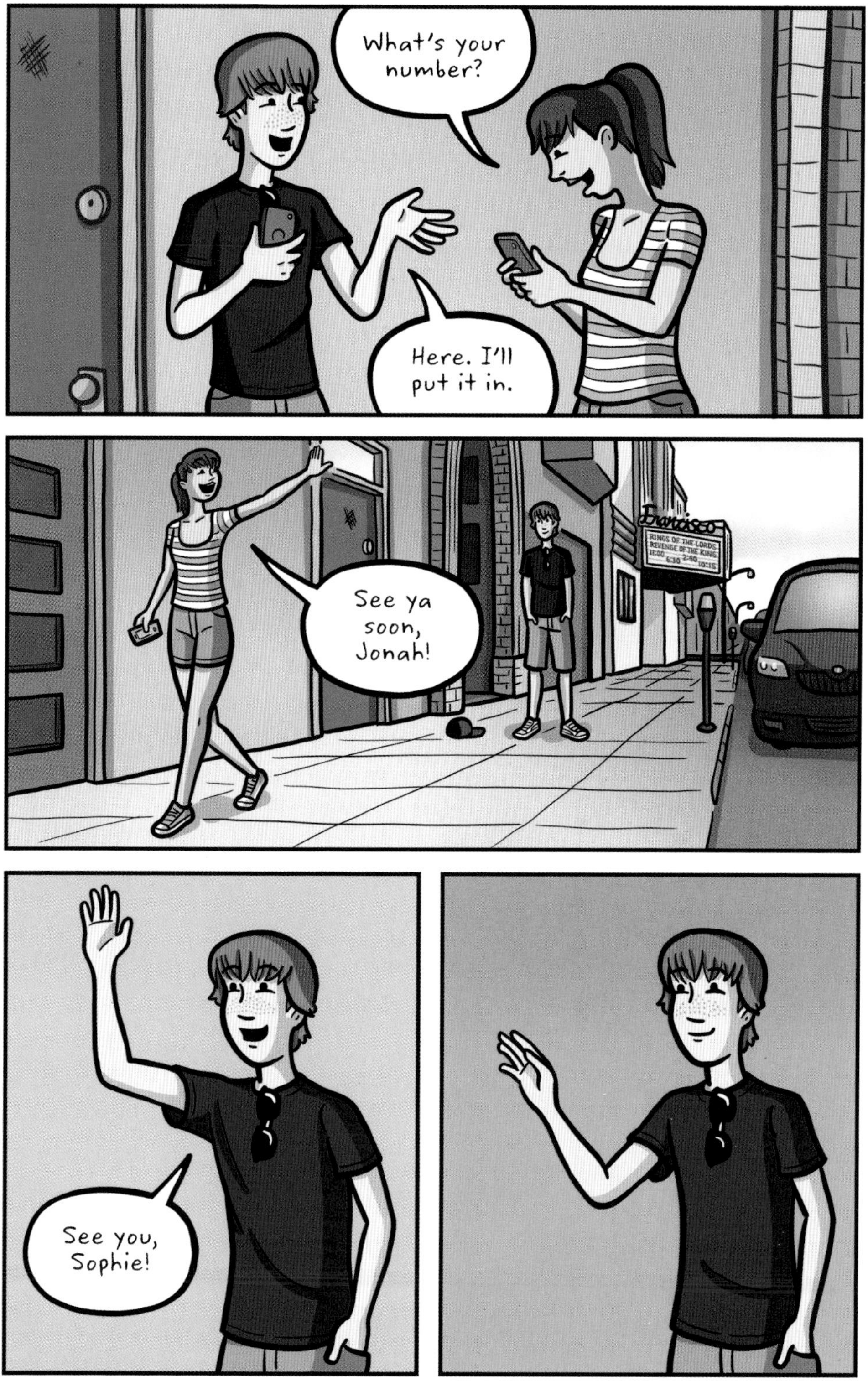
What's your number?
Here. I'll put it in.
Francisco
RINGS OF THE LORDS
REVENGE OF THE KING
11:00 2:40 6:30 10:15
See ya soon, Jonah!
See you, Sophie!

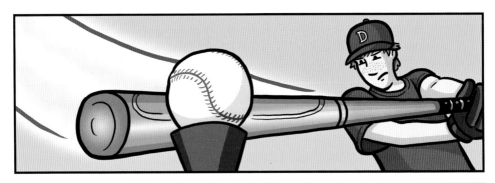

Good. Throw those hips.

Thanks for all your help this summer, Coach.

I can really feel myself getting better.

It's my pleasure, Jonah. Don't take this the wrong way, but you need more help than the other players.

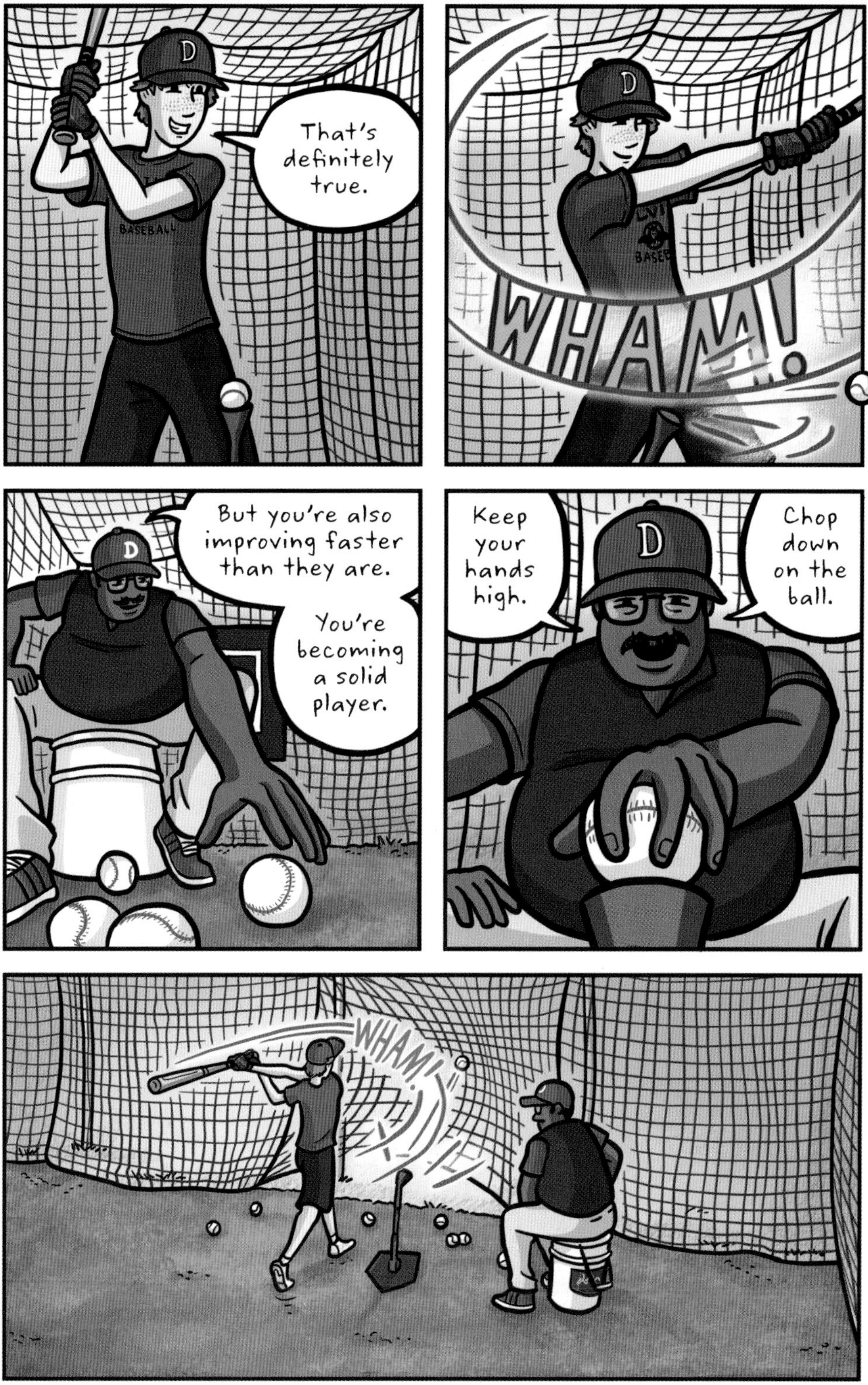
That's definitely true.
BASEBALL
WHAM!
But you're also improving faster than they are.
You're becoming a solid player.
Keep your hands high.
Chop down on the ball.
D
WHAM!

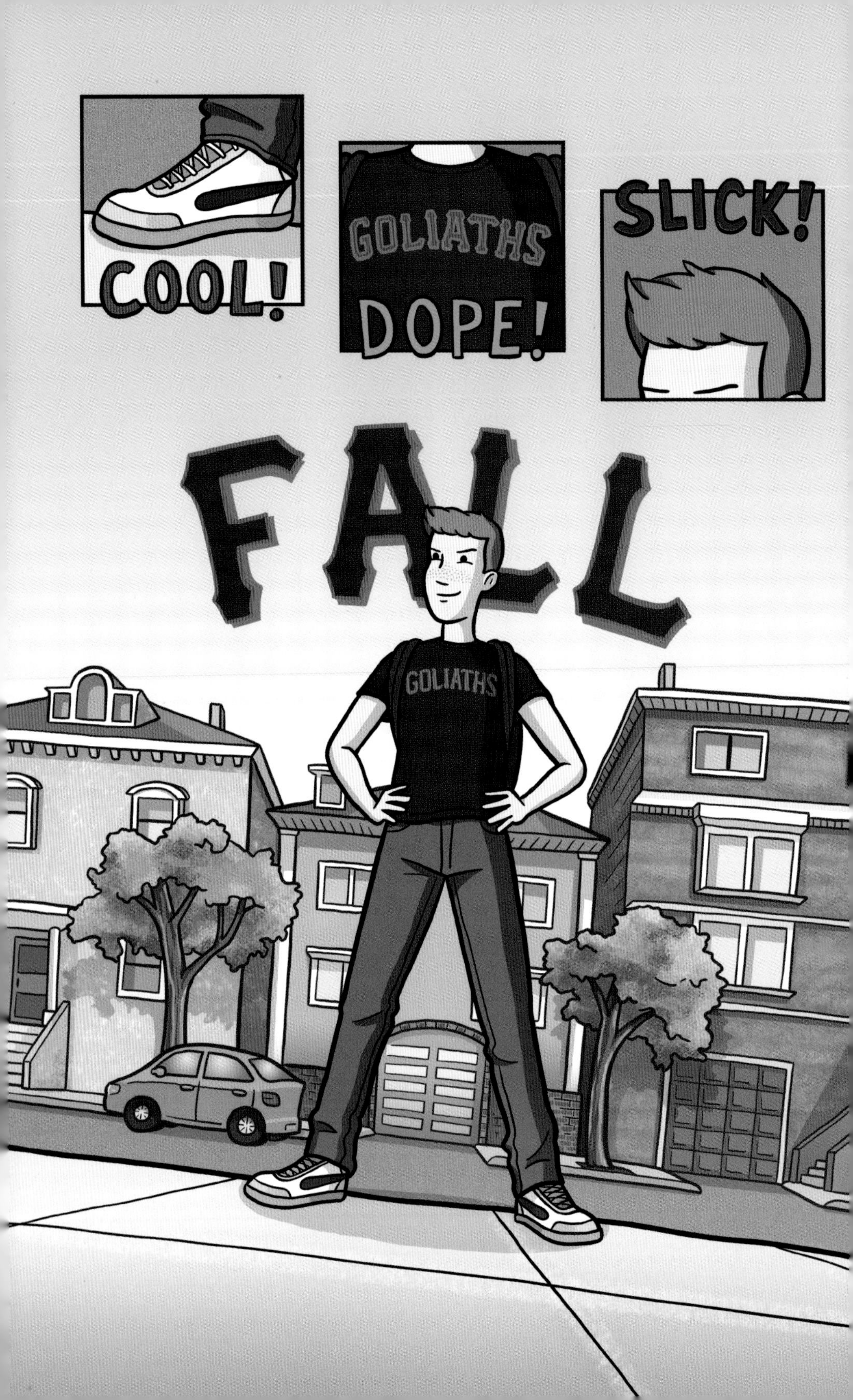
COOL!
GOLIATHS
DOPE!
SLICK!
FALL
GOLIATHS

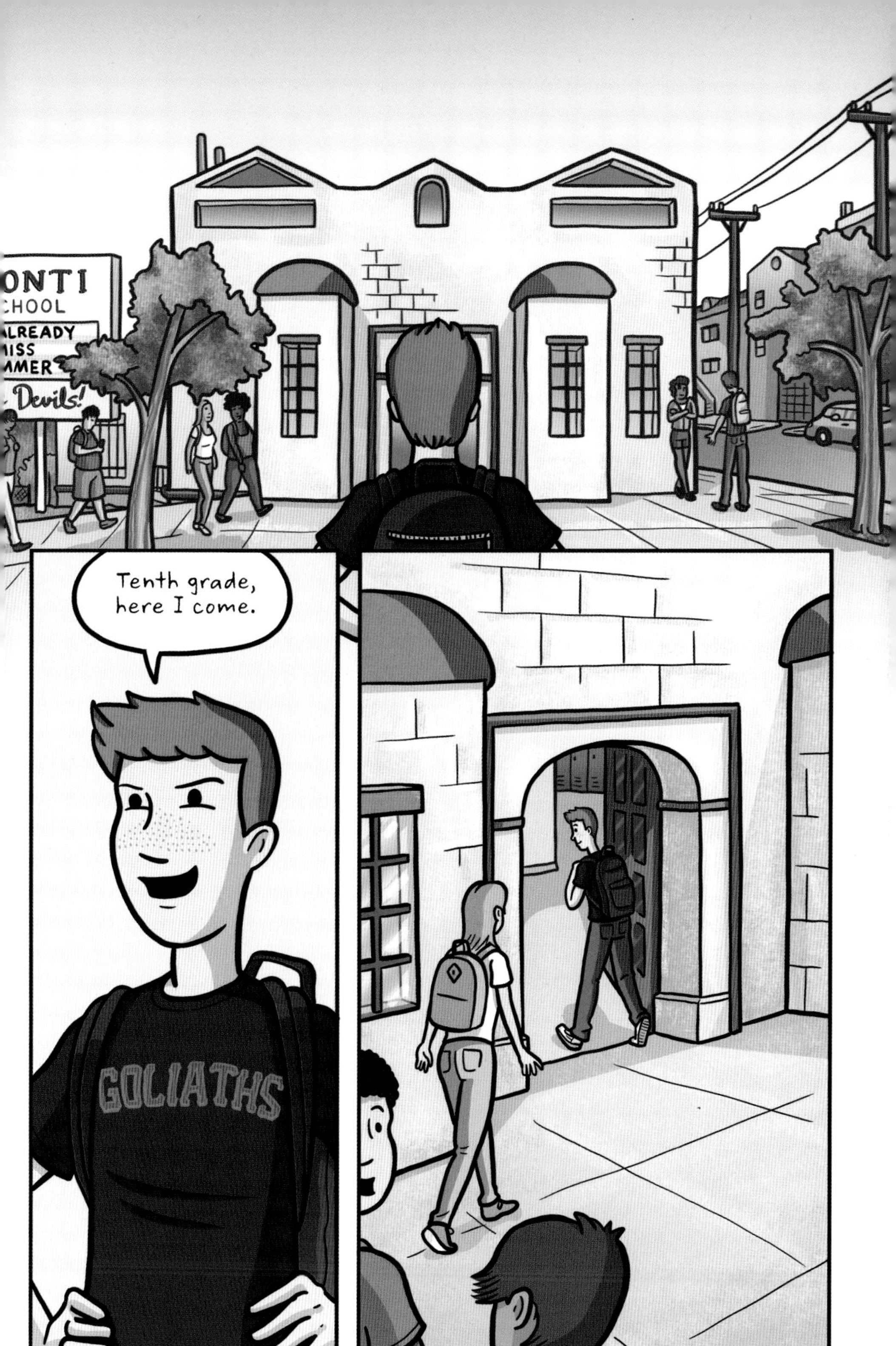

ONTI
CHOOL
LREADY
ISS
MMER
Devils!
Tenth grade, here I come.
GOLIATHS

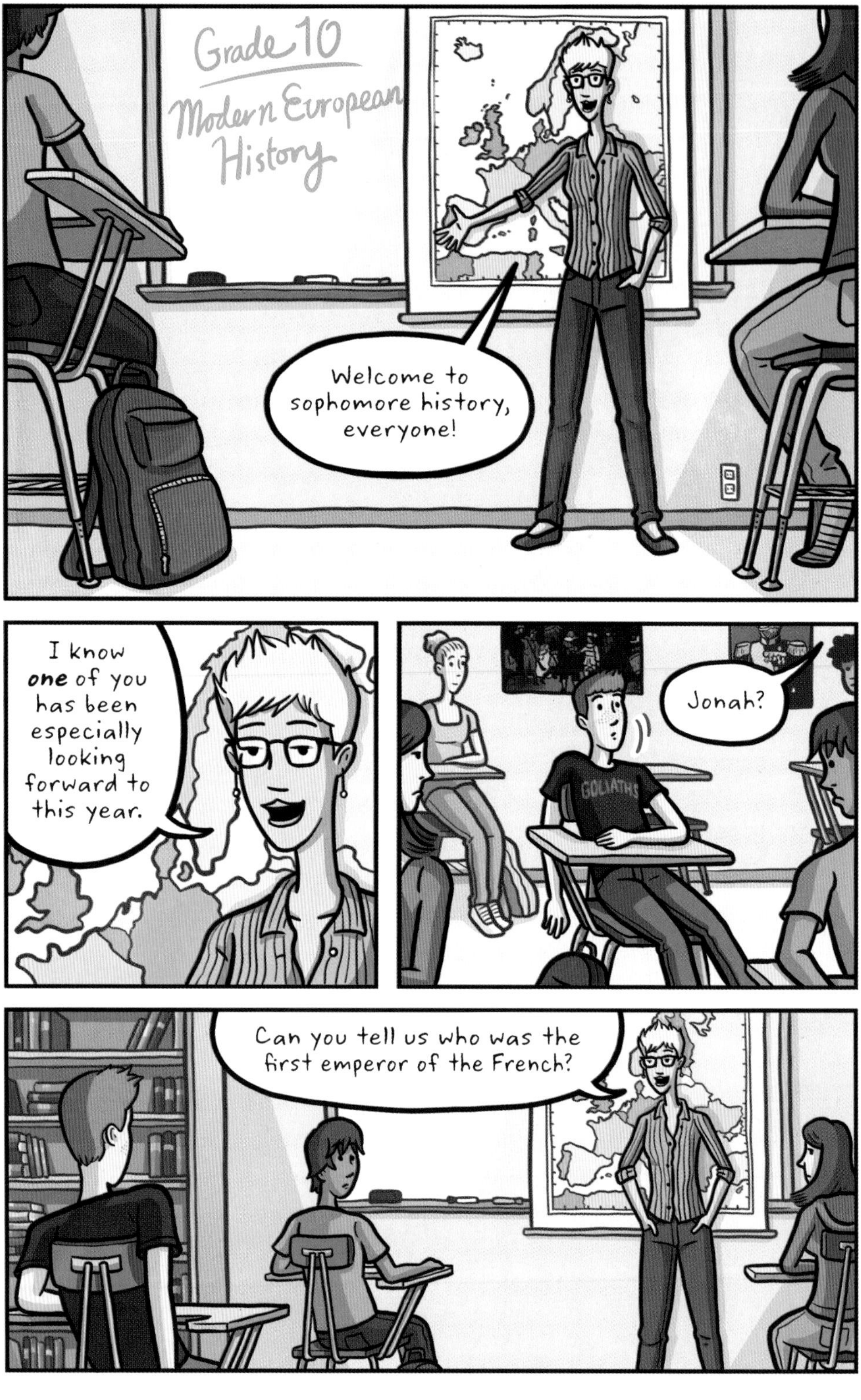
Grade 10
Modern European History
Welcome to sophomore history, everyone!
I know **one** of you has been especially looking forward to this year.
GOLIATHS
Jonah?
Can you tell us who was the first emperor of the French?

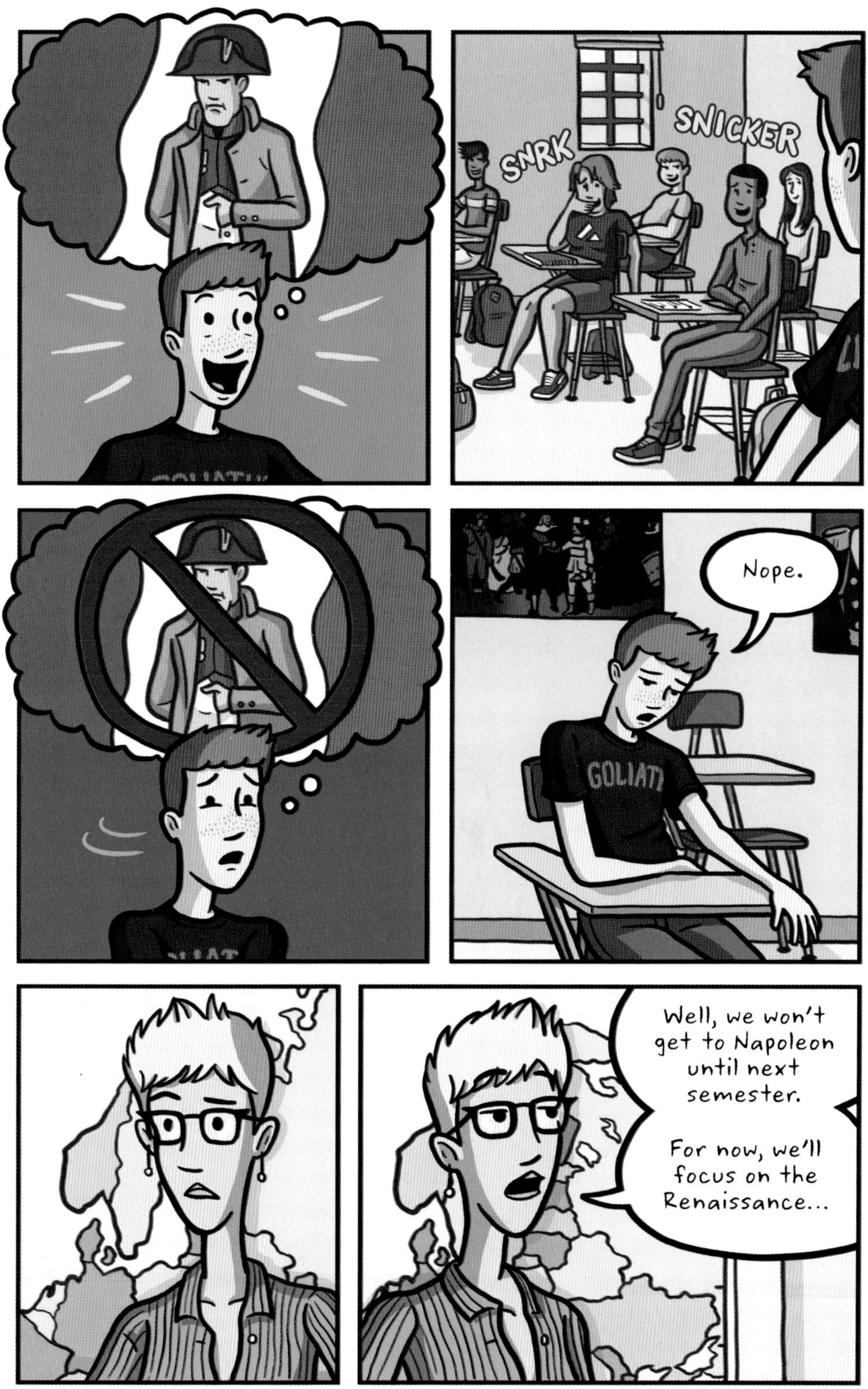
SNRK
SNICKER
Nope.
GOLIATH
Well, we won't get to Napoleon until next semester.
For now, we'll focus on the Renaissance...

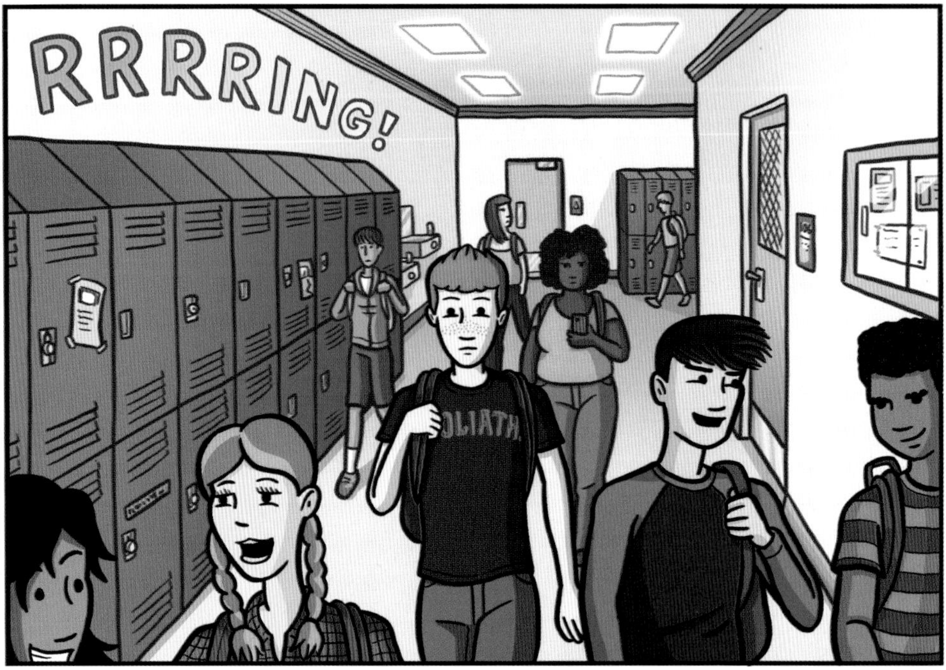
RRRRING!
OLIATH

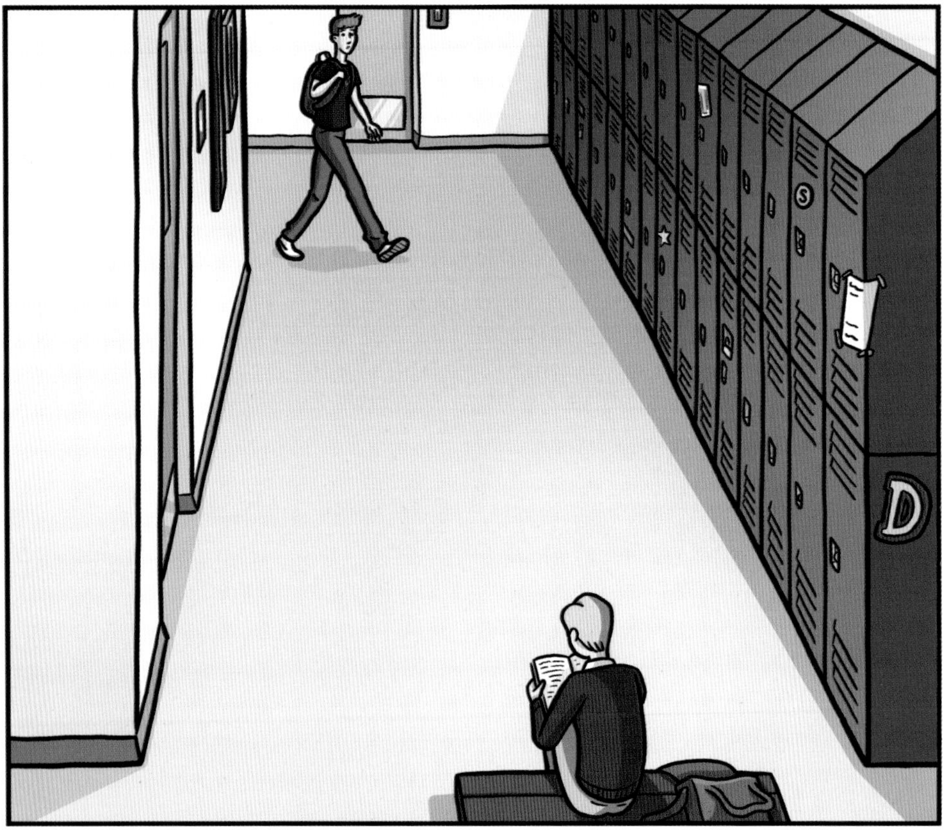
D

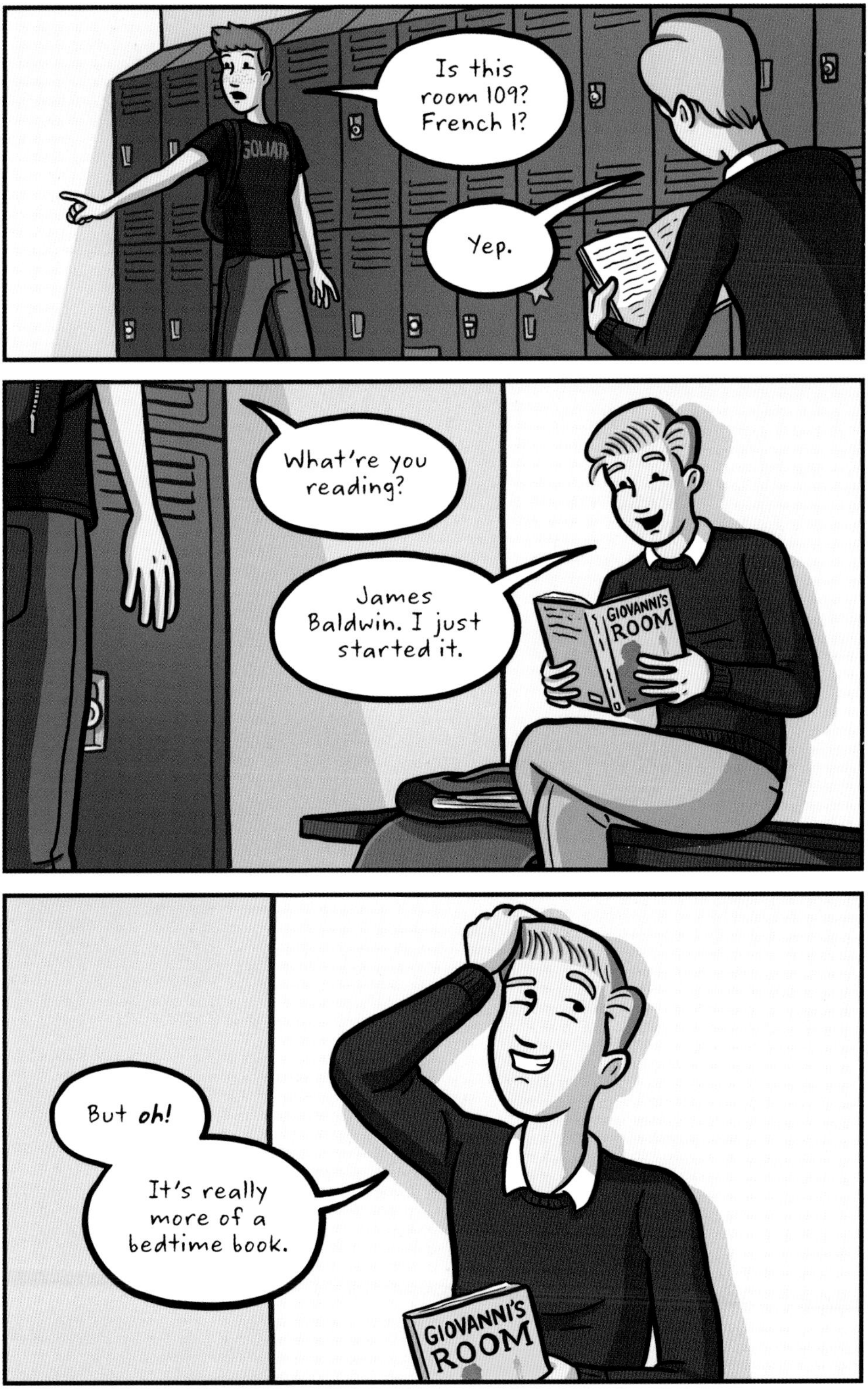

Is this room 109? French 1?
Yep.
What're you reading?
James Baldwin. I just started it.
GIOVANNI'S ROOM
But *oh!*
It's really more of a bedtime book.
GIOVANNI'S ROOM

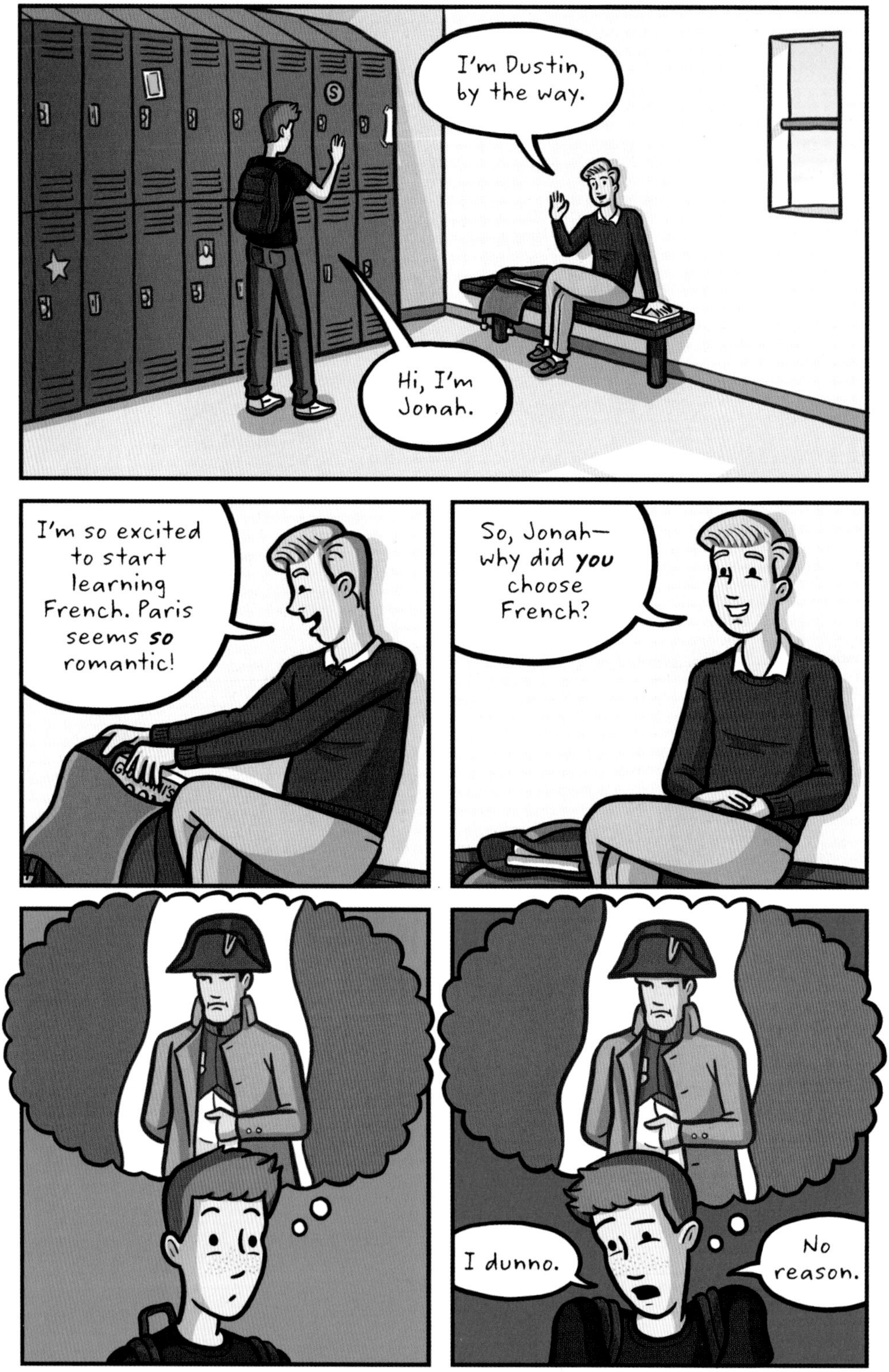
I'm Dustin, by the way.
Hi, I'm Jonah.
I'm so excited to start learning French. Paris seems *so* romantic!
So, Jonah— why did *you* choose French?
I dunno.
No reason.

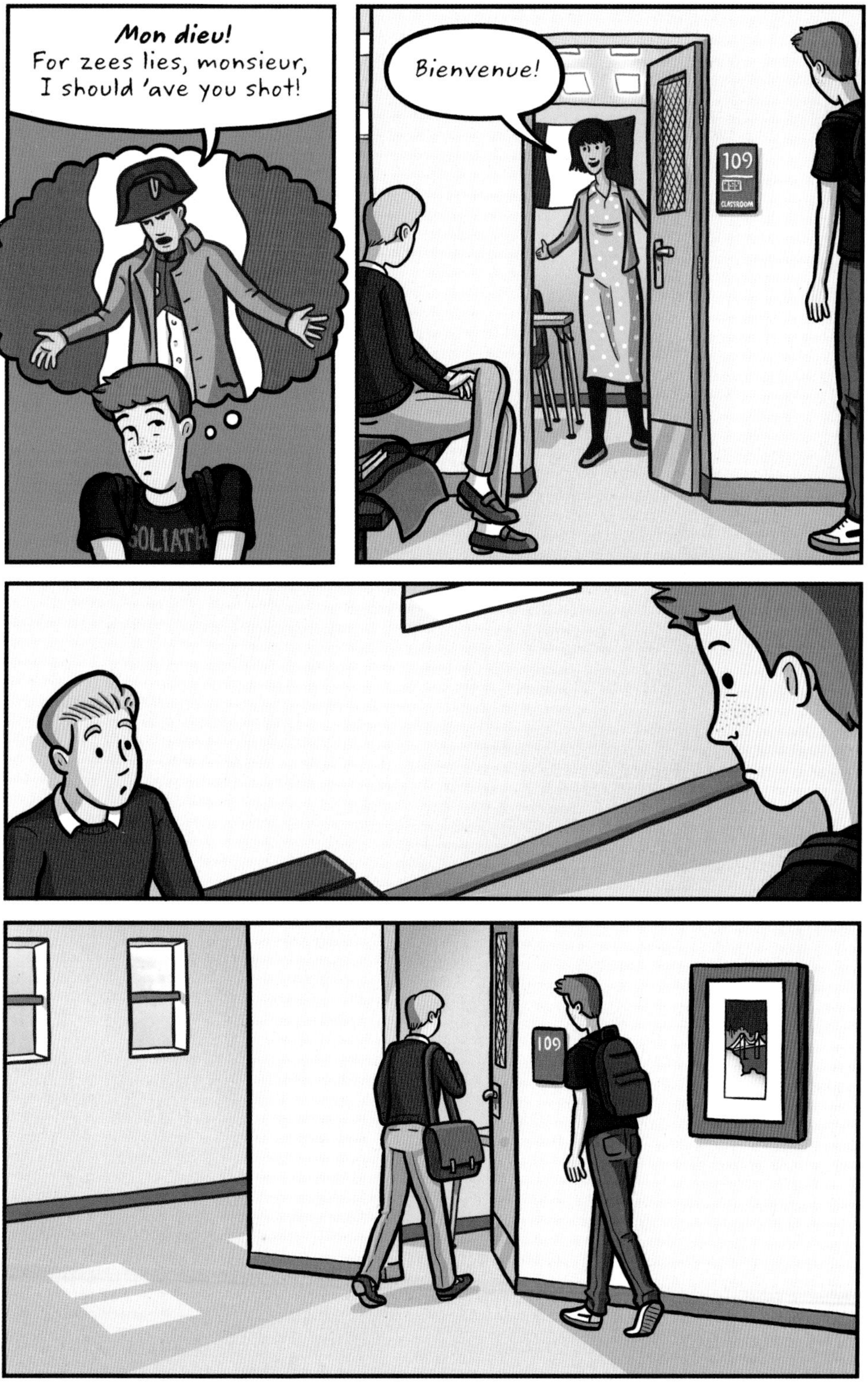

Mon dieu!
For zees lies, monsieur,
I should 'ave you shot!
GOLIATH
Bienvenue!
109
CLASSROOM
109

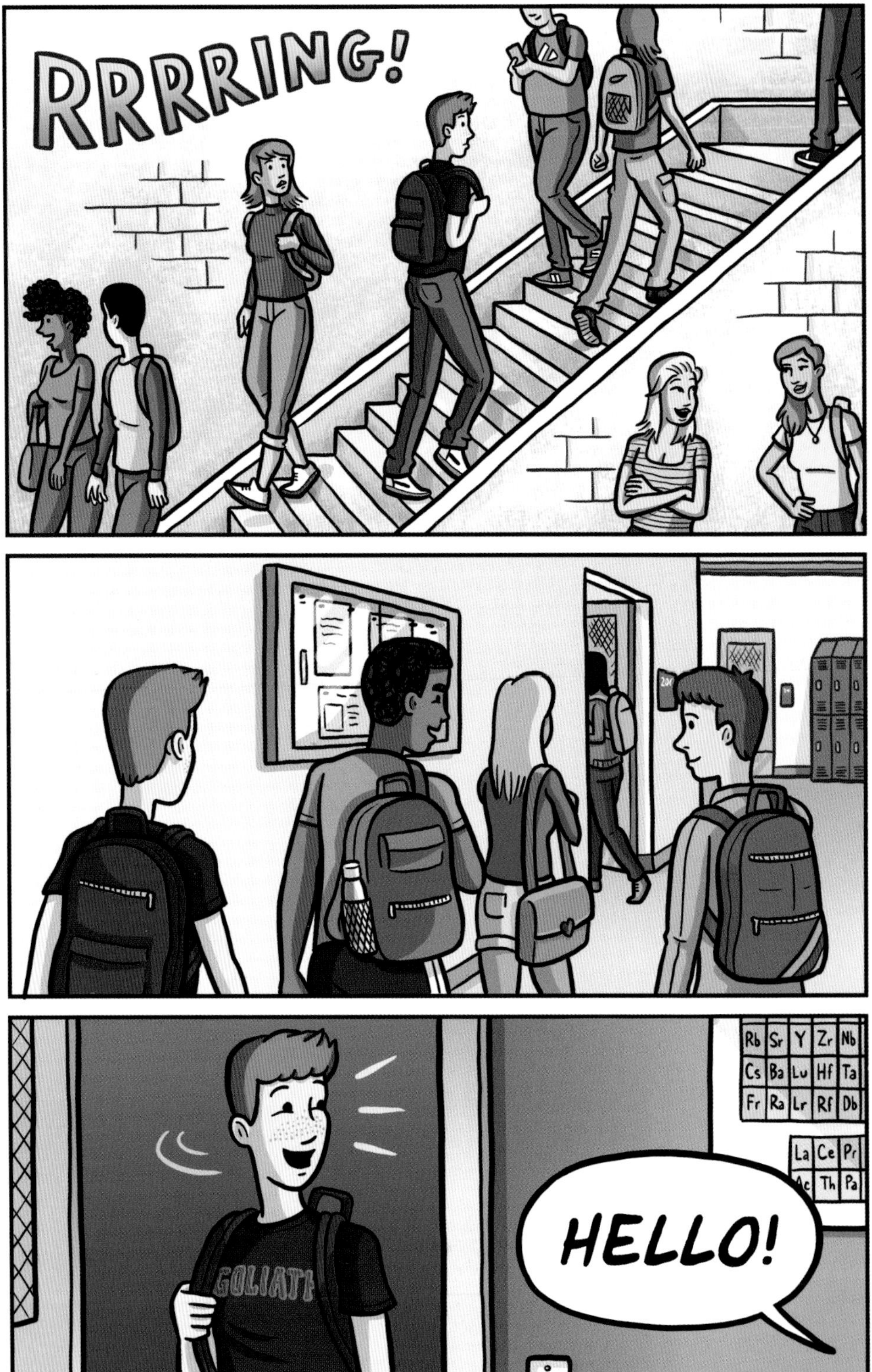
RRRRING!
GOLIATH
Rb Sr Y Zr Nb
Cs Ba Lu Hf Ta
Fr Ra Lr Rf Db
La Ce Pr
Ac Th Pa
HELLO!

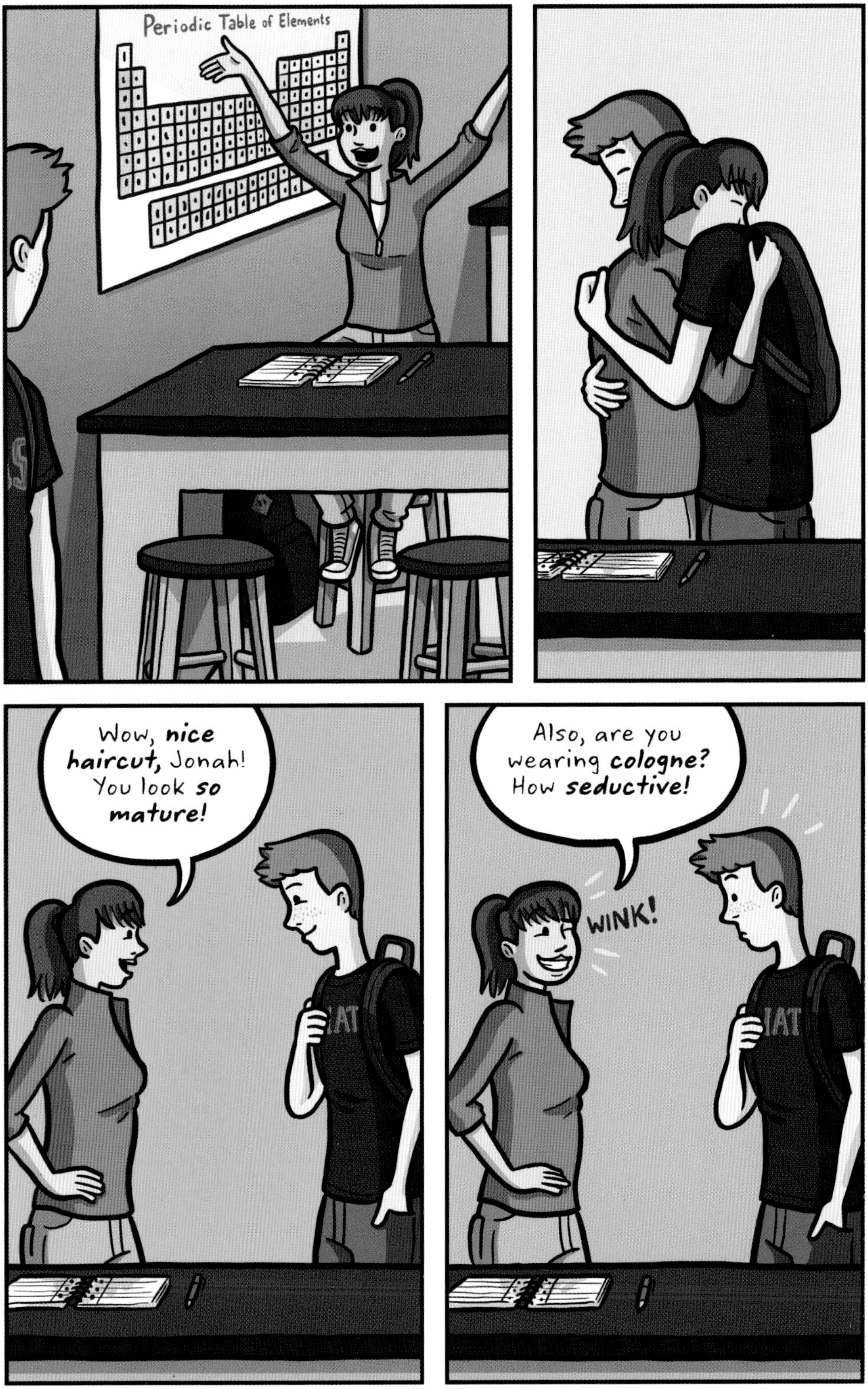
Periodic Table of Elements
Wow, **nice haircut,** Jonah! You look **so mature!**
Also, are you wearing **cologne?** How **seductive!**
WINK!

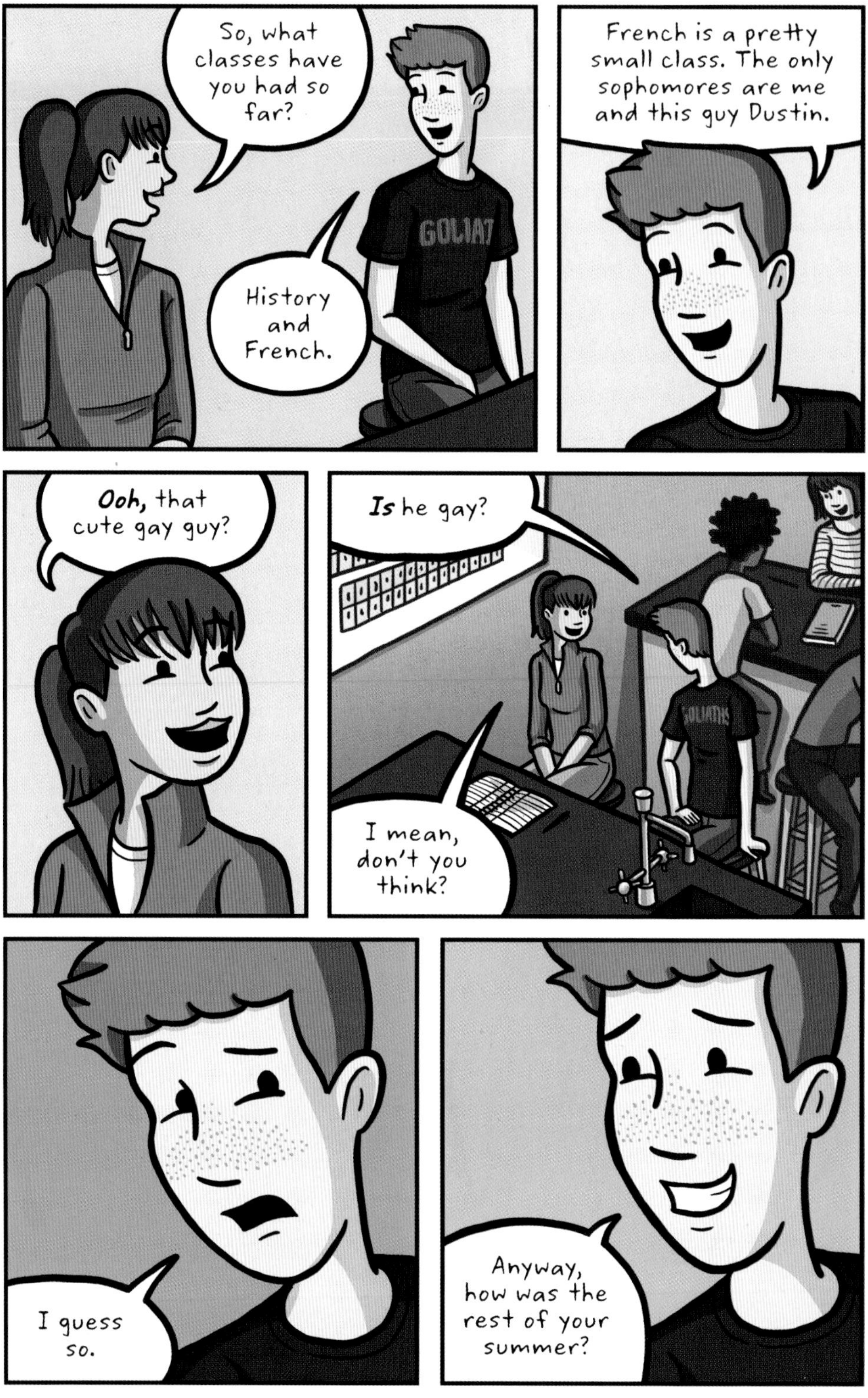
So, what classes have you had so far?
History and French.
French is a pretty small class. The only sophomores are me and this guy Dustin.
Ooh, that cute gay guy?
Is he gay?
I mean, don't you think?
I guess so.
Anyway, how was the rest of your summer?

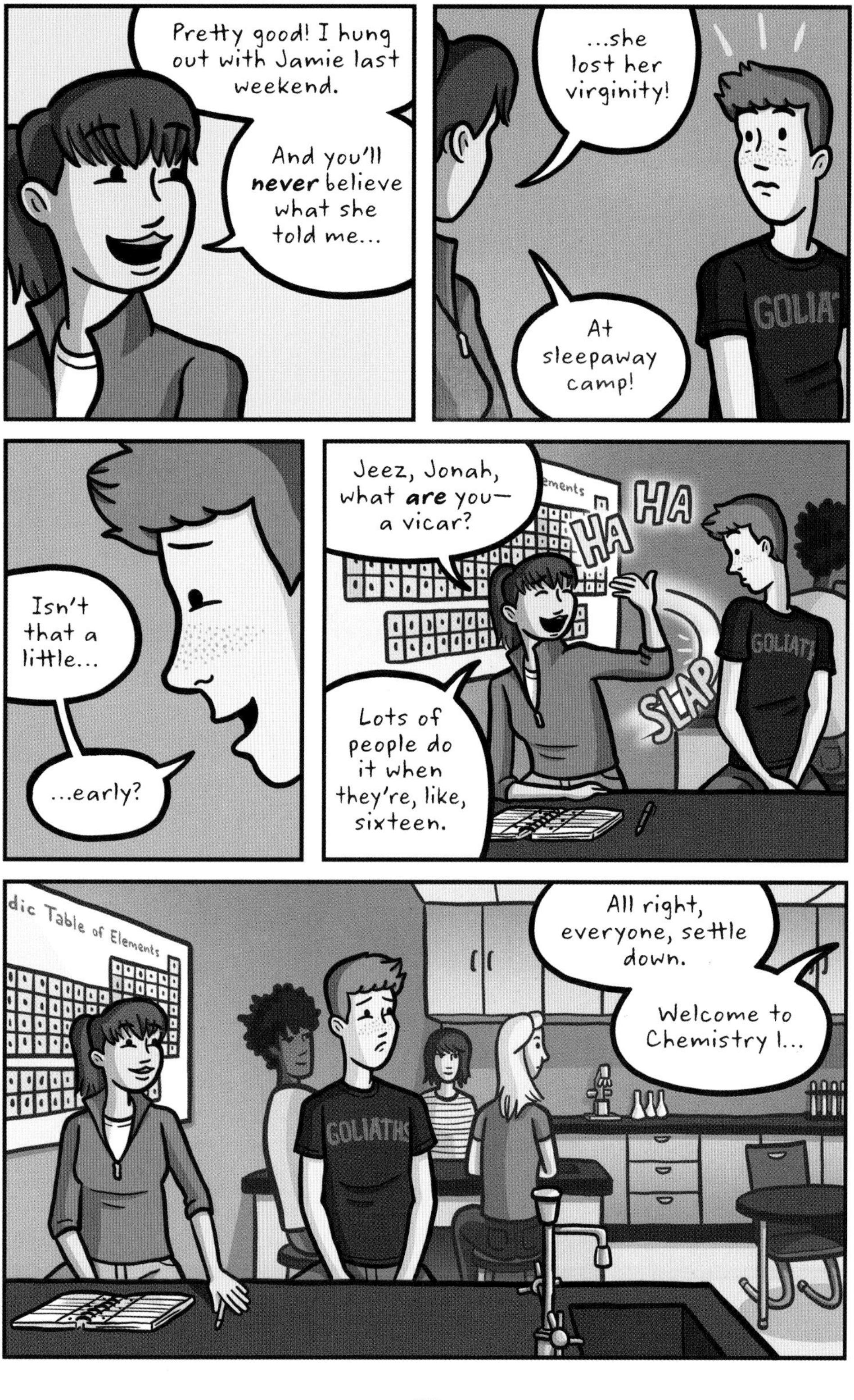
Pretty good! I hung out with Jamie last weekend.
And you'll **never** believe what she told me...
...she lost her virginity!
At sleepaway camp!
GOLIAT
Isn't that a little...
...early?
Jeez, Jonah, what **are** you—a vicar?
ements
HA
HA
SLAP
GOLIATH
Lots of people do it when they're, like, sixteen.
dic Table of Elements
GOLIATHS
All right, everyone, settle down.
Welcome to Chemistry I...

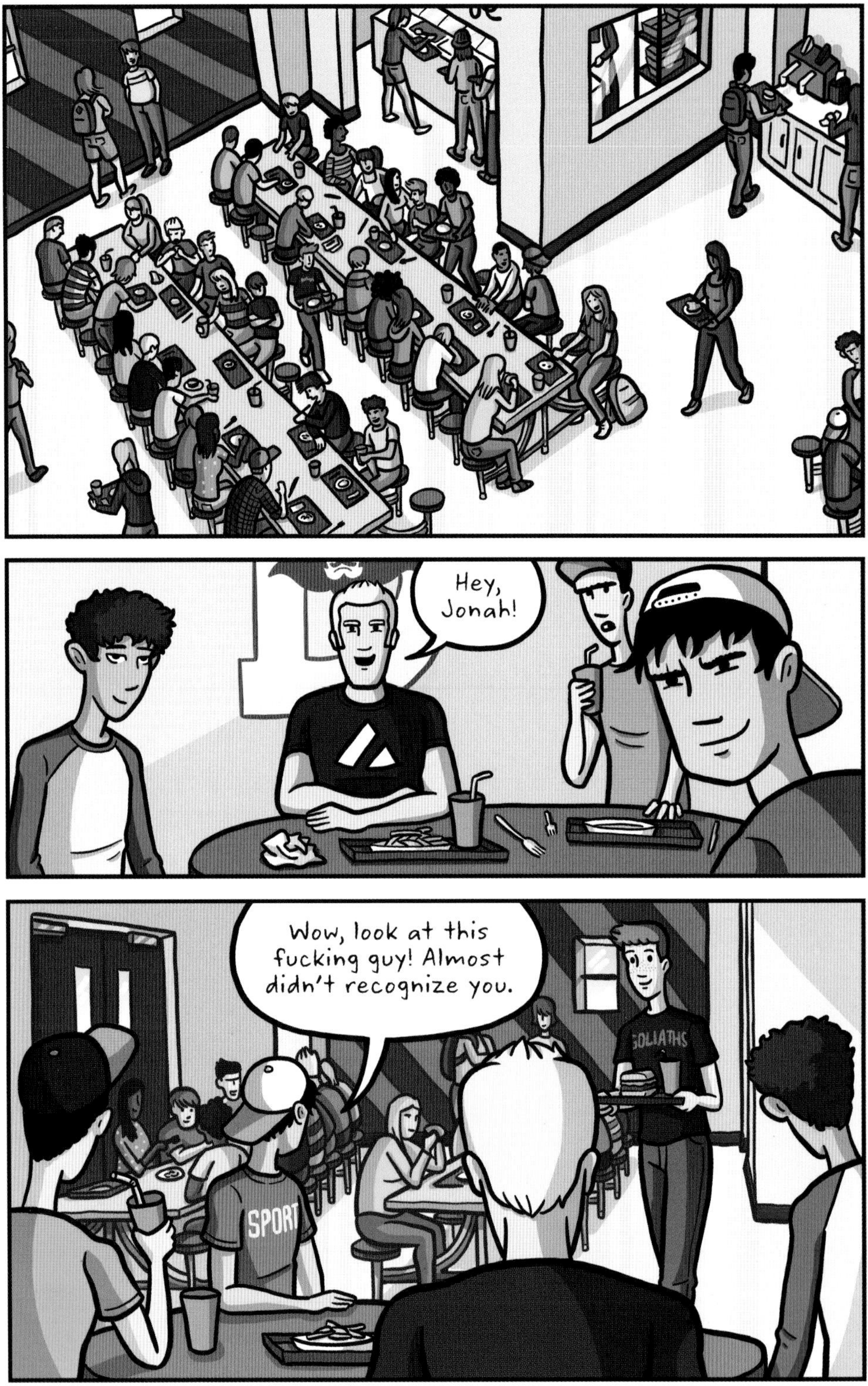
Hey, Jonah!
Wow, look at this fucking guy! Almost didn't recognize you.
GOLIATHS
SPORT

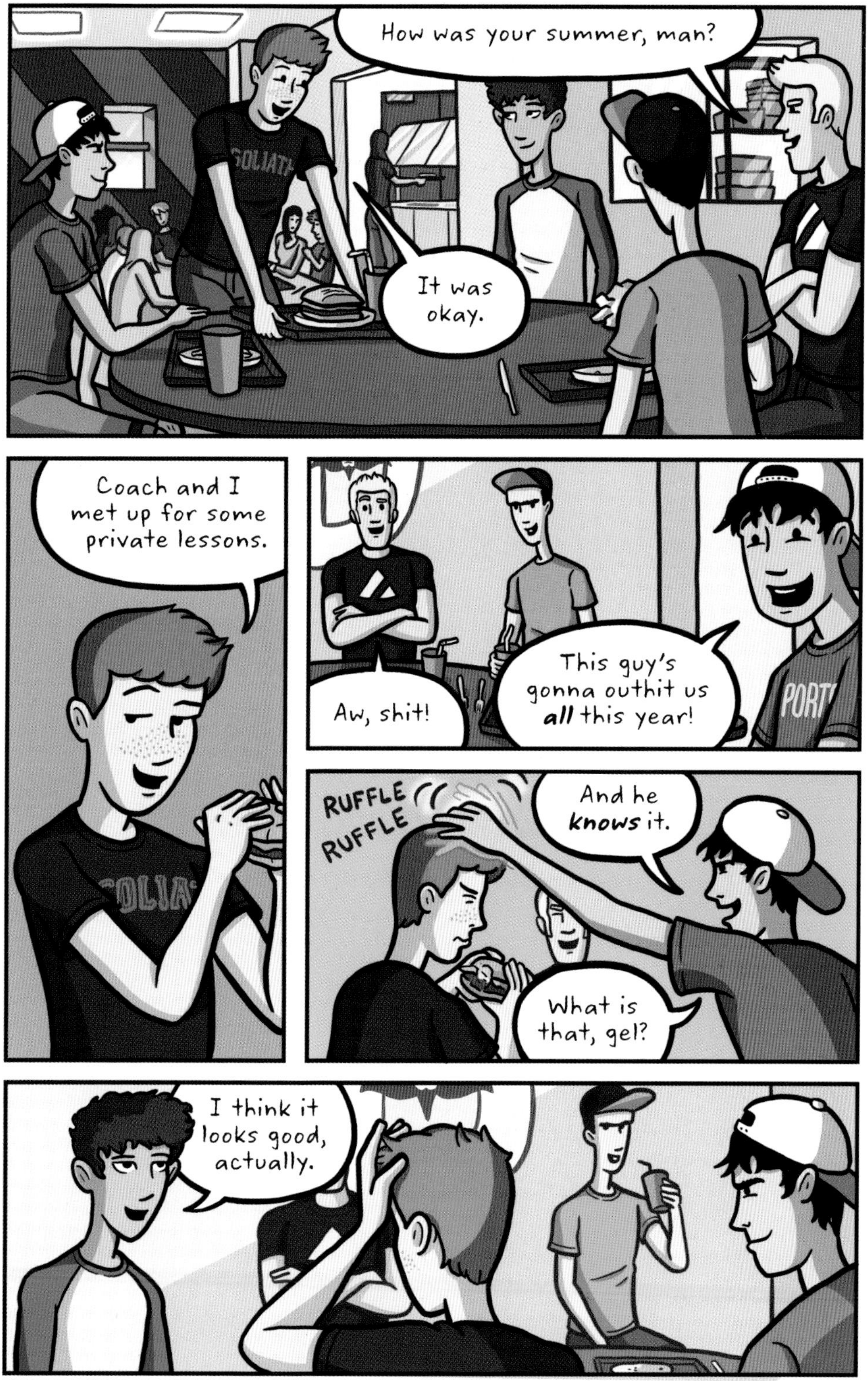

How was your summer, man?
It was okay.
Coach and I met up for some private lessons.
Aw, shit!
This guy's gonna outhit us **all** this year!
RUFFLE RUFFLE
And he **knows** it.
What is that, gel?
I think it looks good, actually.

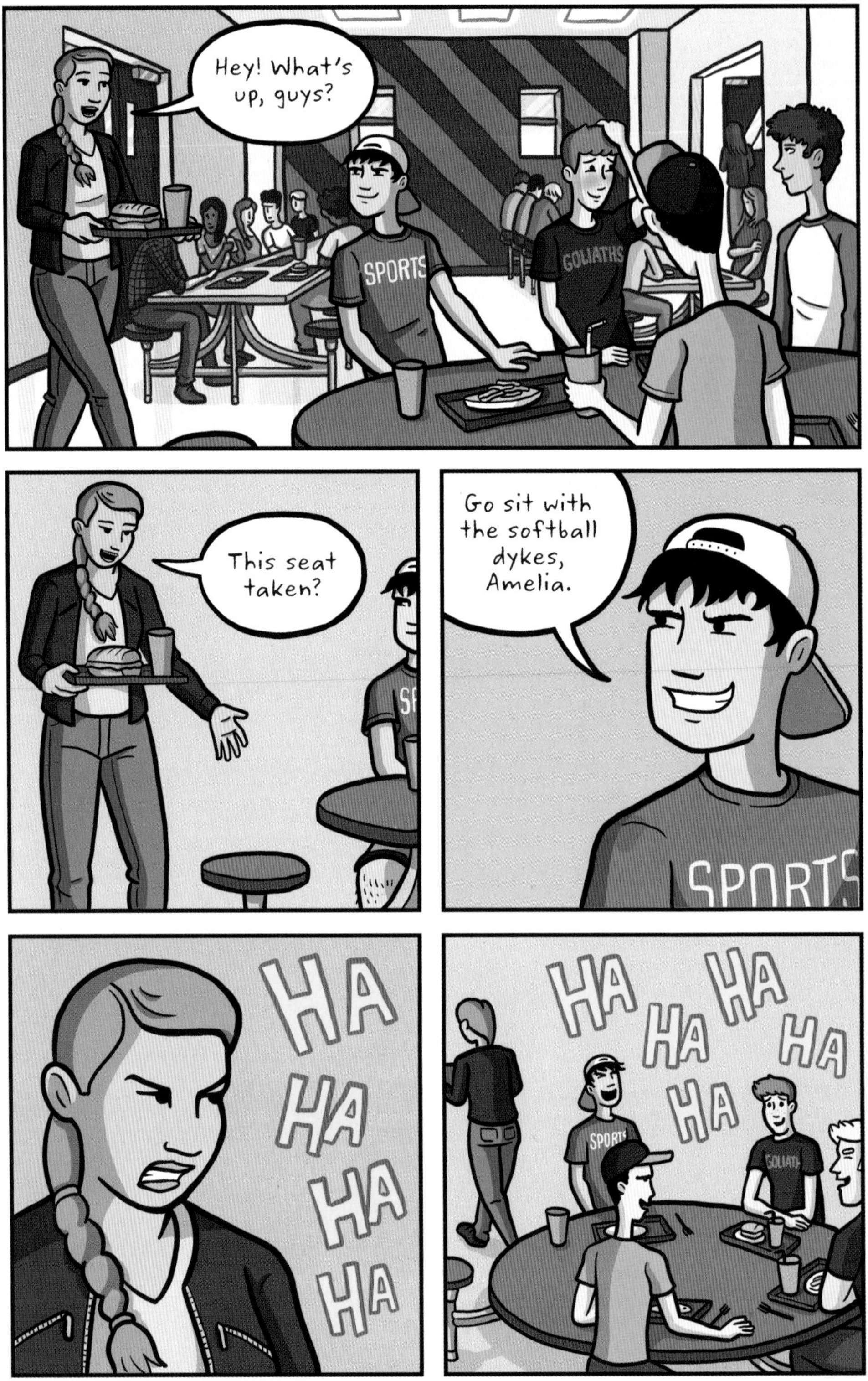
Hey! What's up, guys?
SPORTS
GOLIATHS
This seat taken?
Go sit with the softball dykes, Amelia.
SPORTS
HA HA HA HA
HA HA HA HA HA HA
SPORTS
GOLIATH

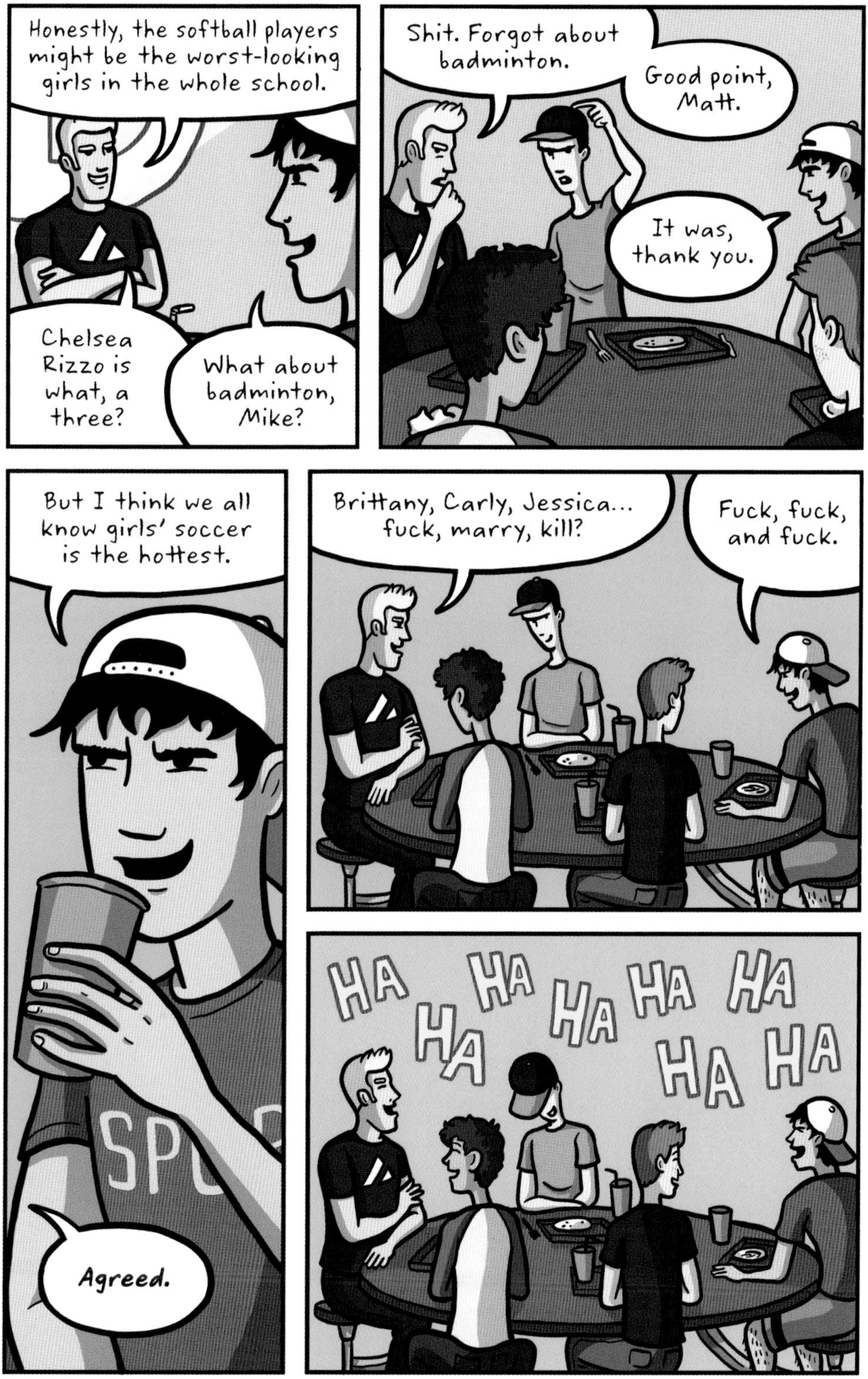
Honestly, the softball players might be the worst-looking girls in the whole school.
Chelsea Rizzo is what, a three?
What about badminton, Mike?
Shit. Forgot about badminton.
Good point, Matt.
It was, thank you.
But I think we all know girls' soccer is the hottest.
Agreed.
Brittany, Carly, Jessica... fuck, marry, kill?
Fuck, fuck, and fuck.
HA HA HA HA HA HA HA HA HA

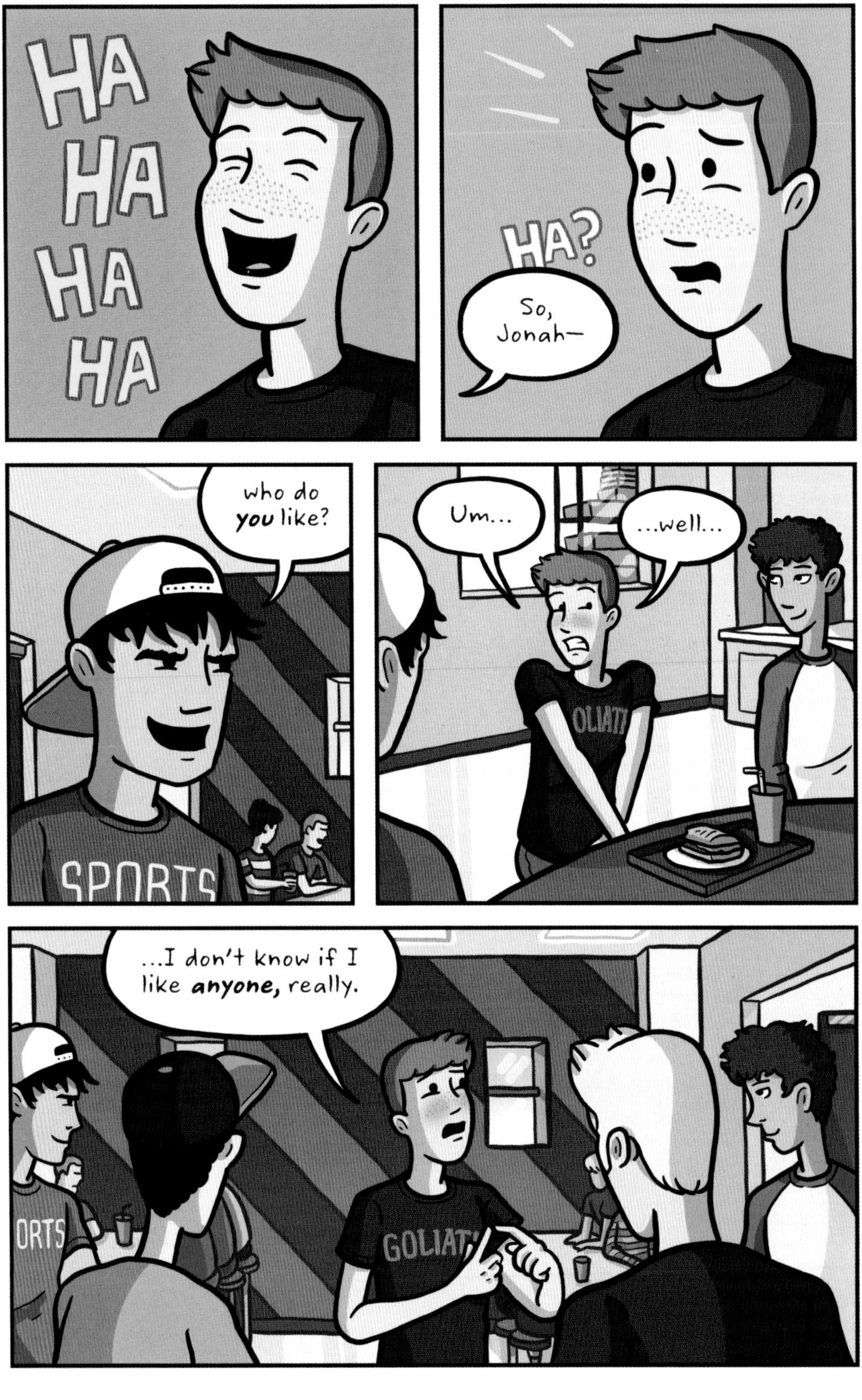
HA HA HA HA
HA?
So, Jonah—
who do *you* like?
Um...
...well...
...I don't know if I like **anyone,** really.
GOLIATH
SPORTS

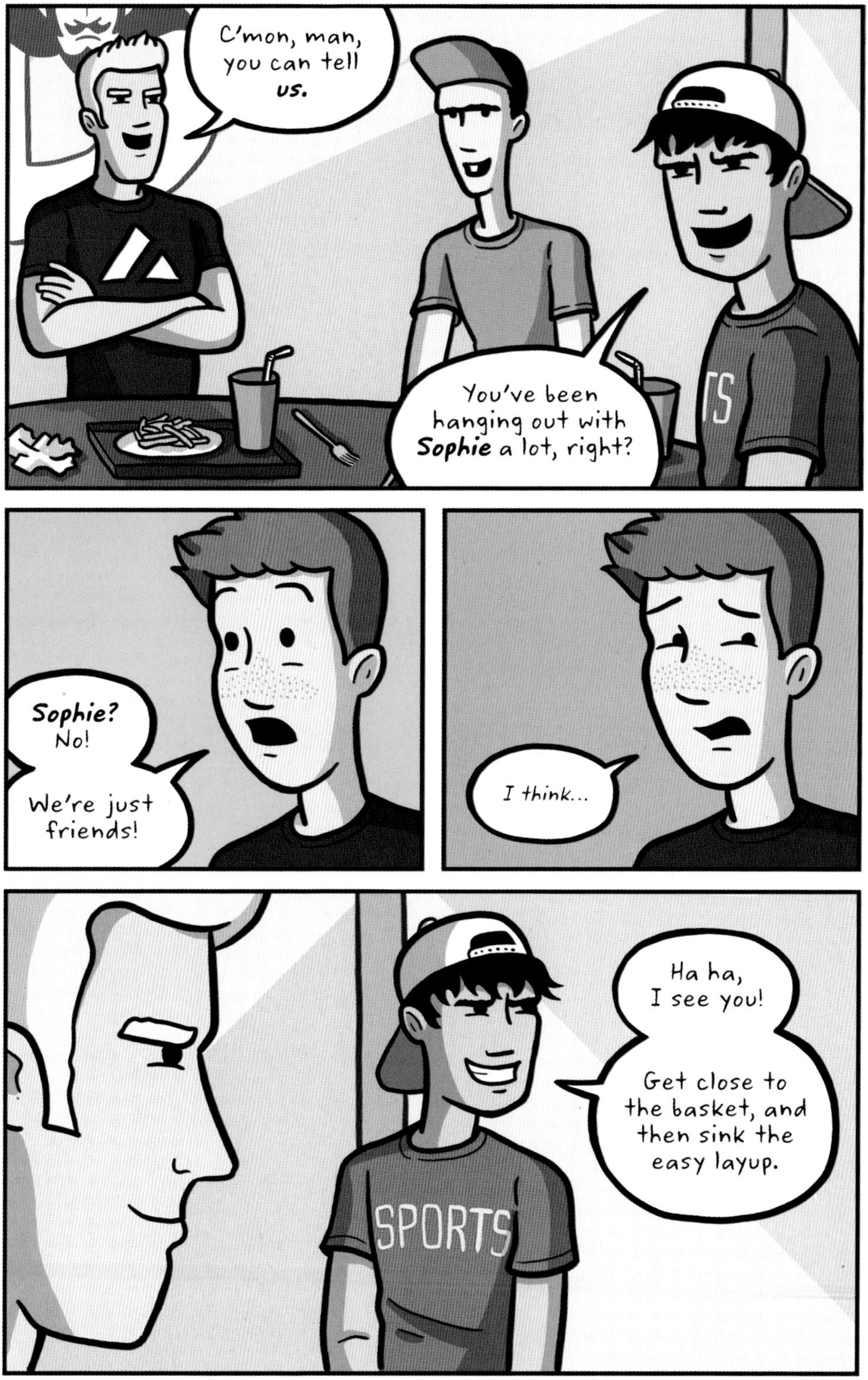
C'mon, man, you can tell **us.**
You've been hanging out with **Sophie** a lot, right?
Sophie? No!
We're just friends!
I think...
Ha ha, I see you!
Get close to the basket, and then sink the easy layup.
SPORTS

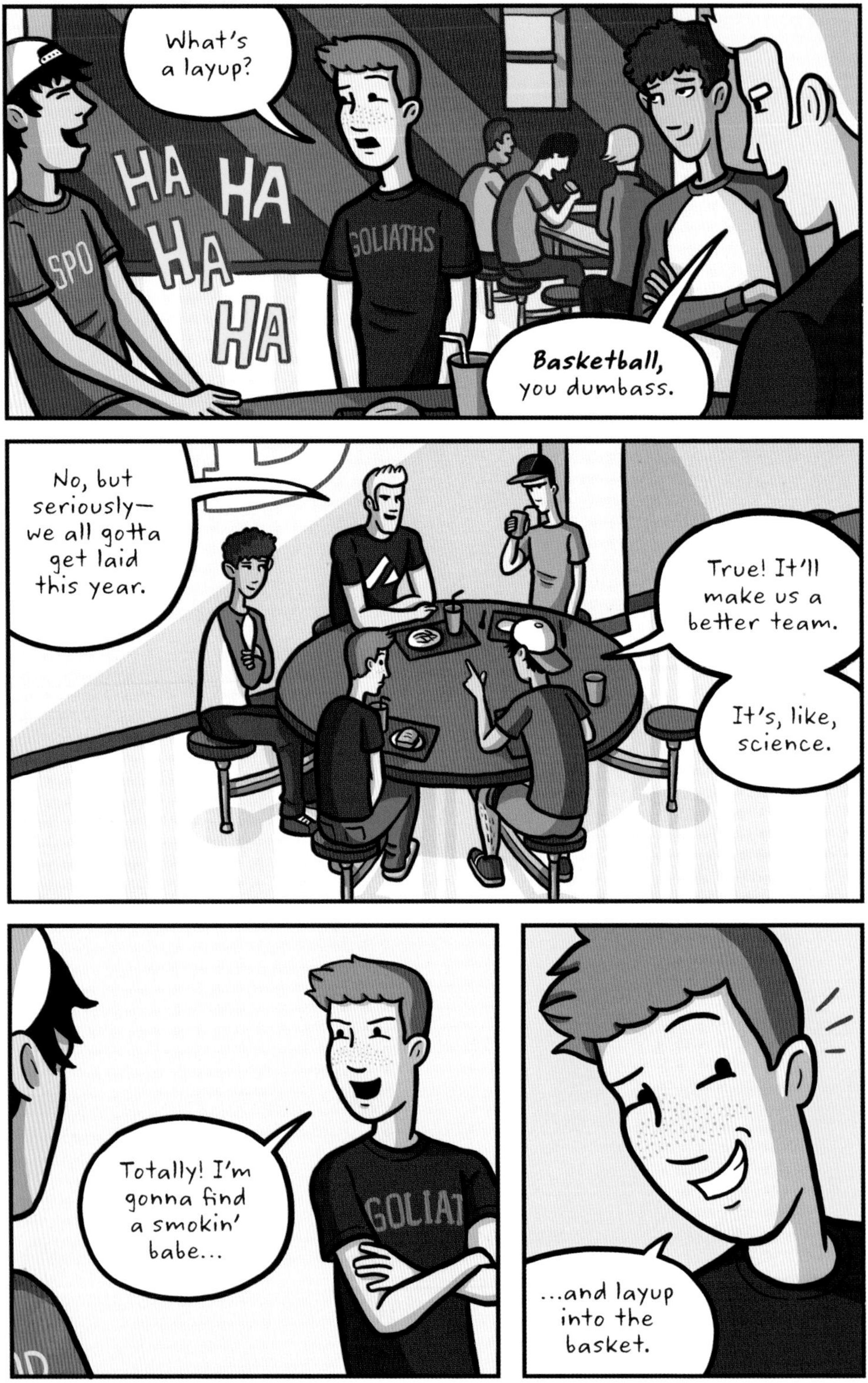
What's a layup?
HA HA HA HA
GOLIATHS
Basketball, you dumbass.
No, but seriously— we all gotta get laid this year.
True! It'll make us a better team.
It's, like, science.
Totally! I'm gonna find a smokin' babe...
...and layup into the basket.

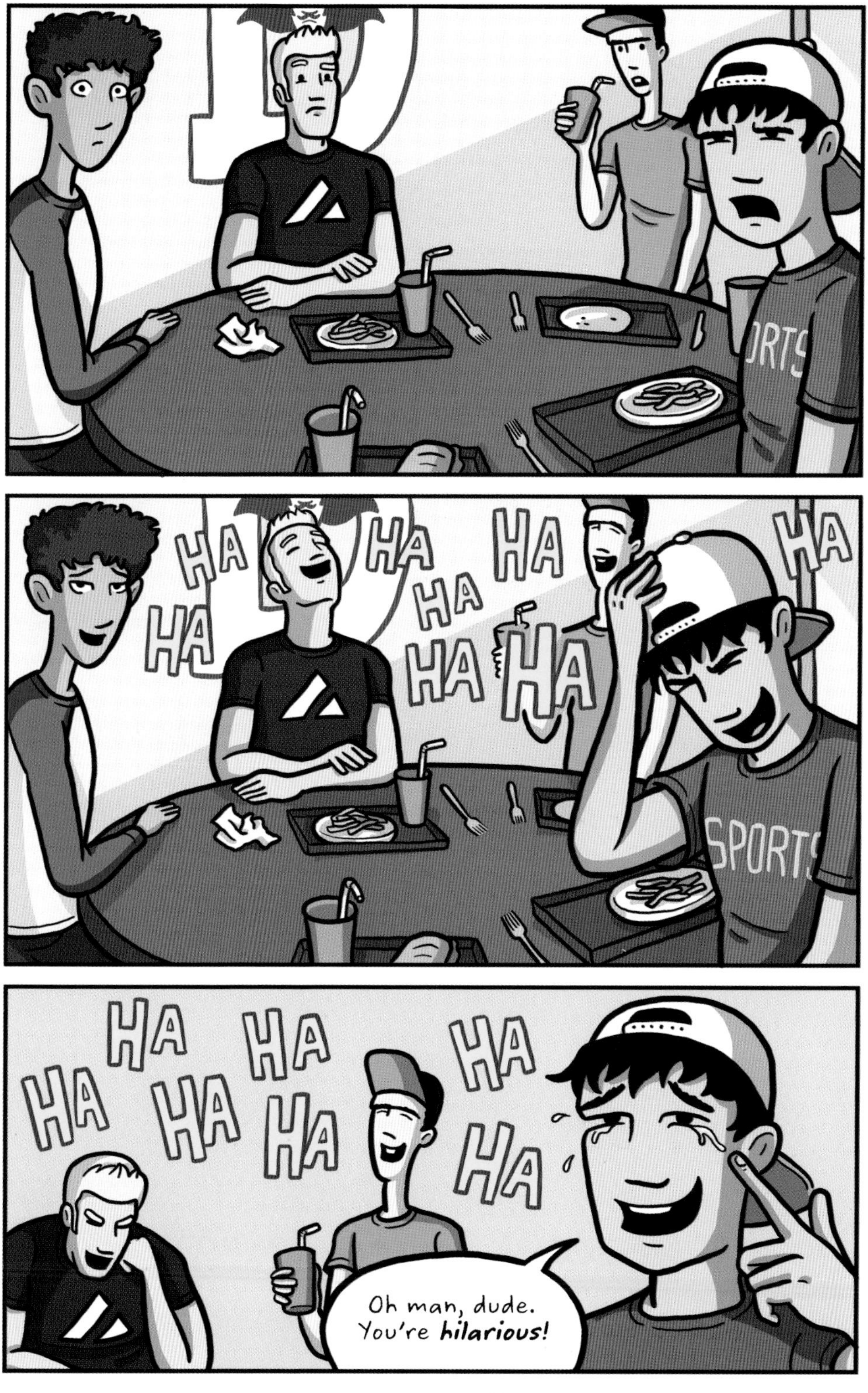
HA HA HA HA HA HA HA HA
SPORTS
HA HA HA HA HA HA HA
Oh man, dude. You're **hilarious**!

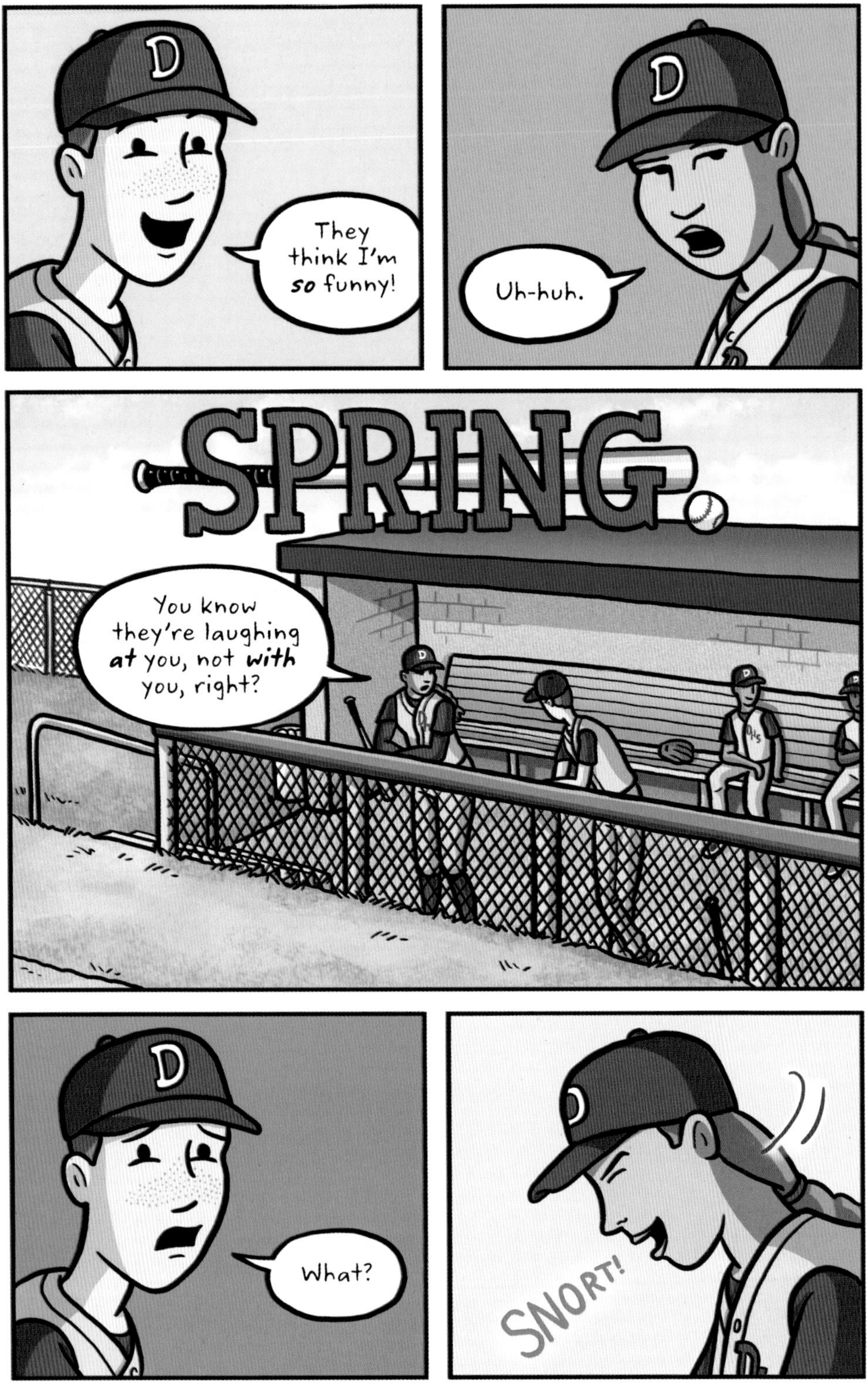
They think I'm so funny!
Uh-huh.
SPRING
You know they're laughing at you, not with you, right?
What?
SNORT!

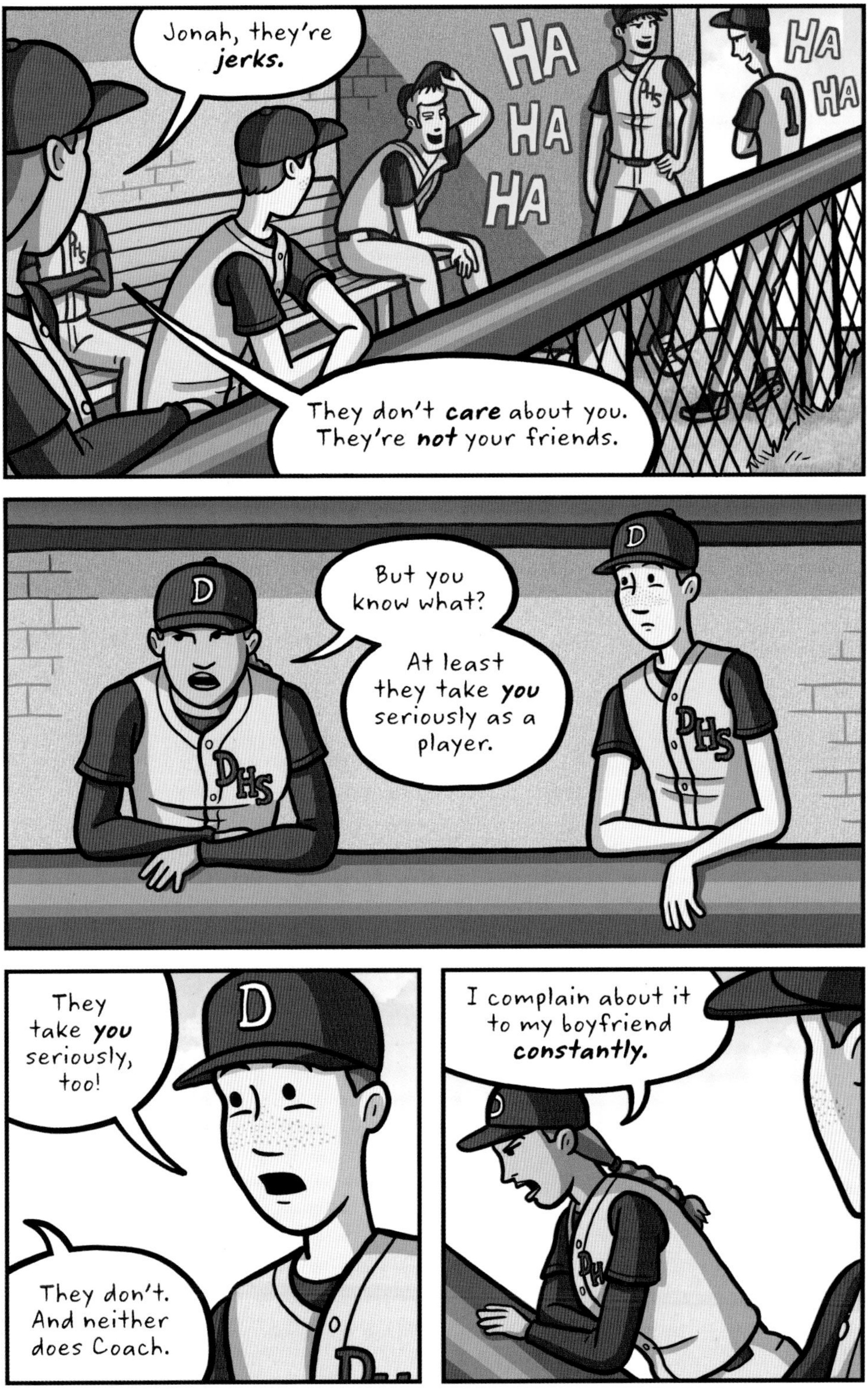
Jonah, they're **jerks.**
HA HA HA
HA HA
They don't **care** about you. They're **not** your friends.
But you know what?
At least they take **you** seriously as a player.
They take **you** seriously, too!
They don't. And neither does Coach.
I complain about it to my boyfriend **constantly.**

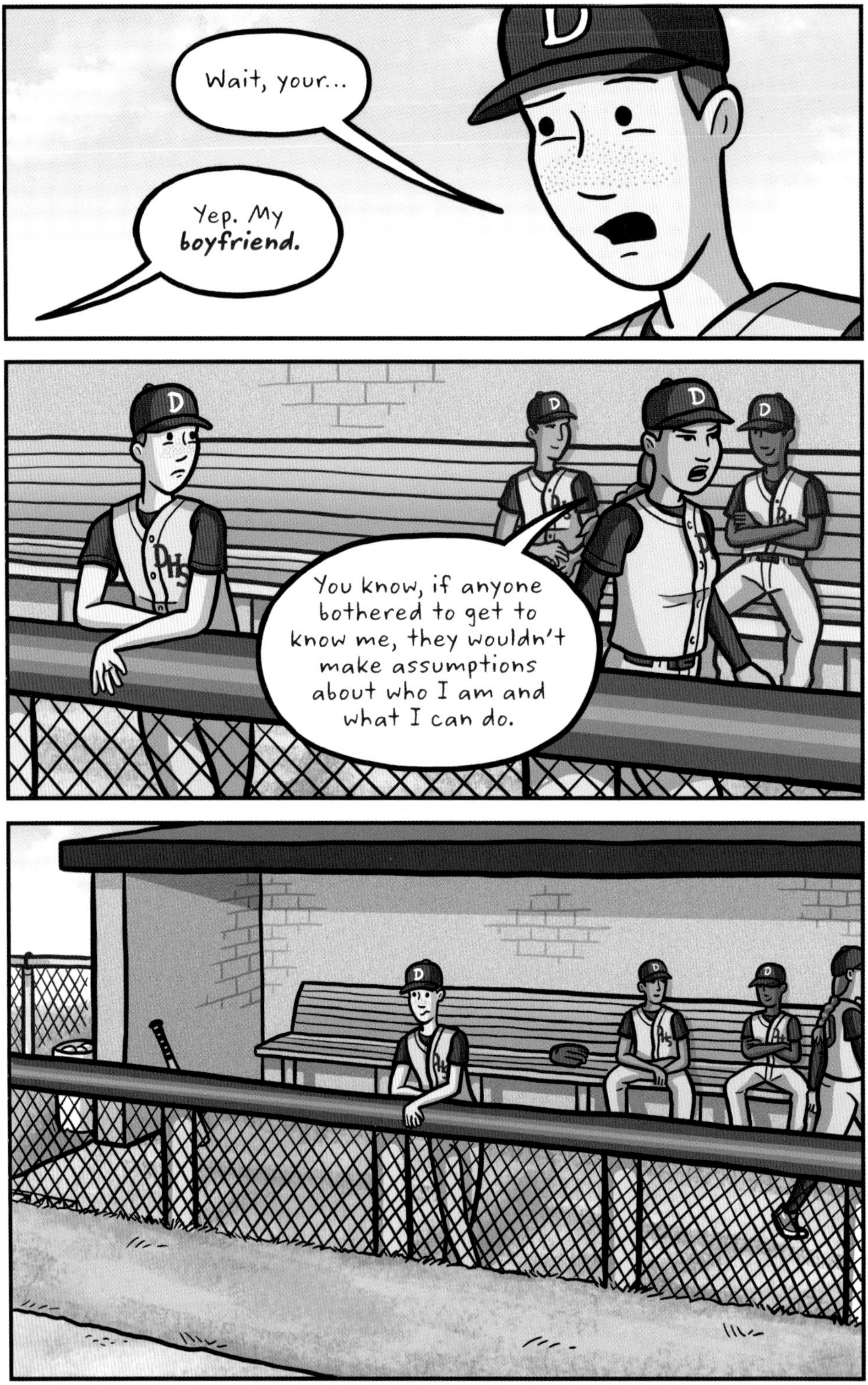
Wait, your...
Yep. My **boyfriend.**
You know, if anyone bothered to get to know me, they wouldn't make assumptions about who I am and what I can do.

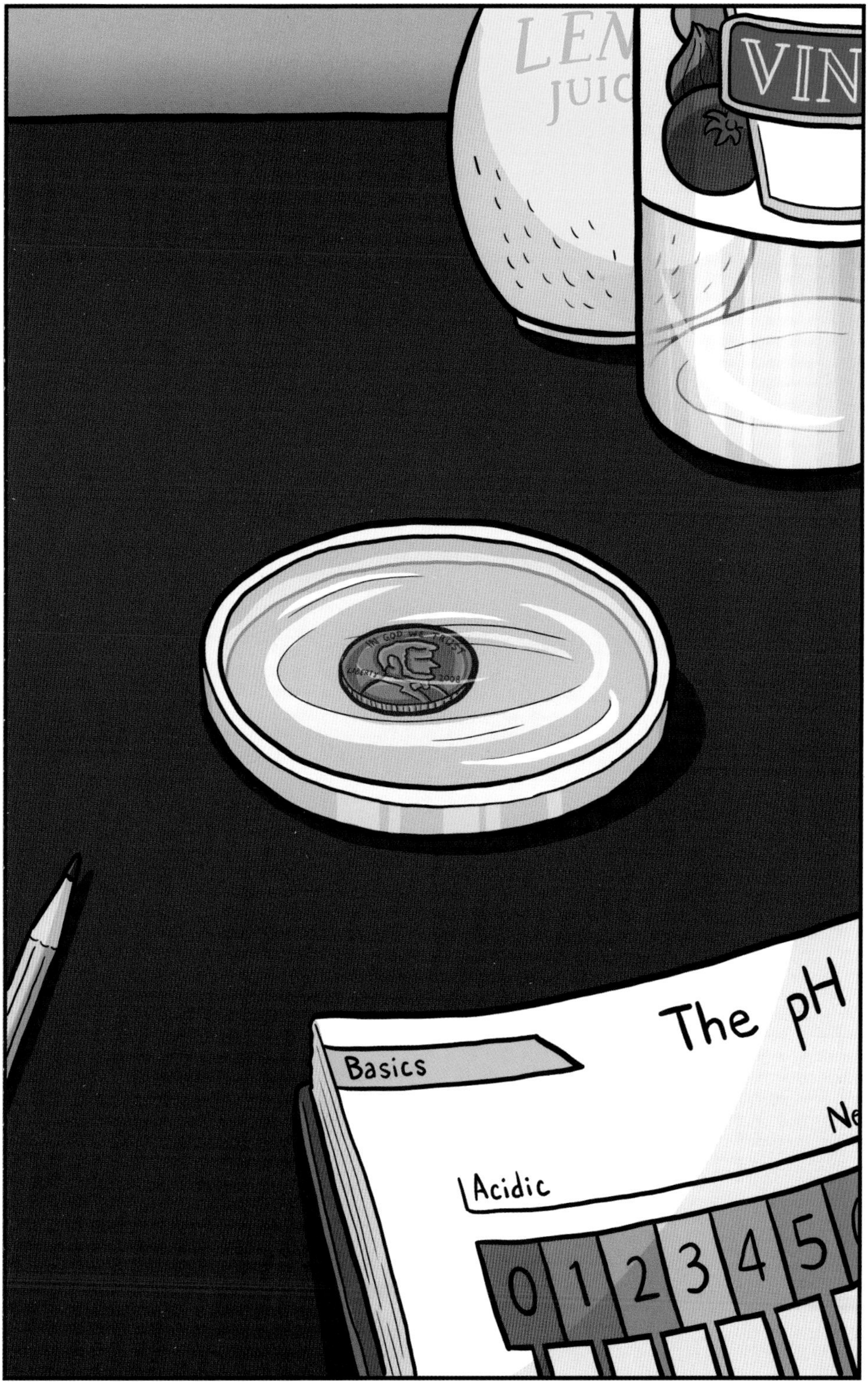
LEM
JUIC
VIN
The pH
Basics
Ne
Acidic
0 1 2 3 4 5

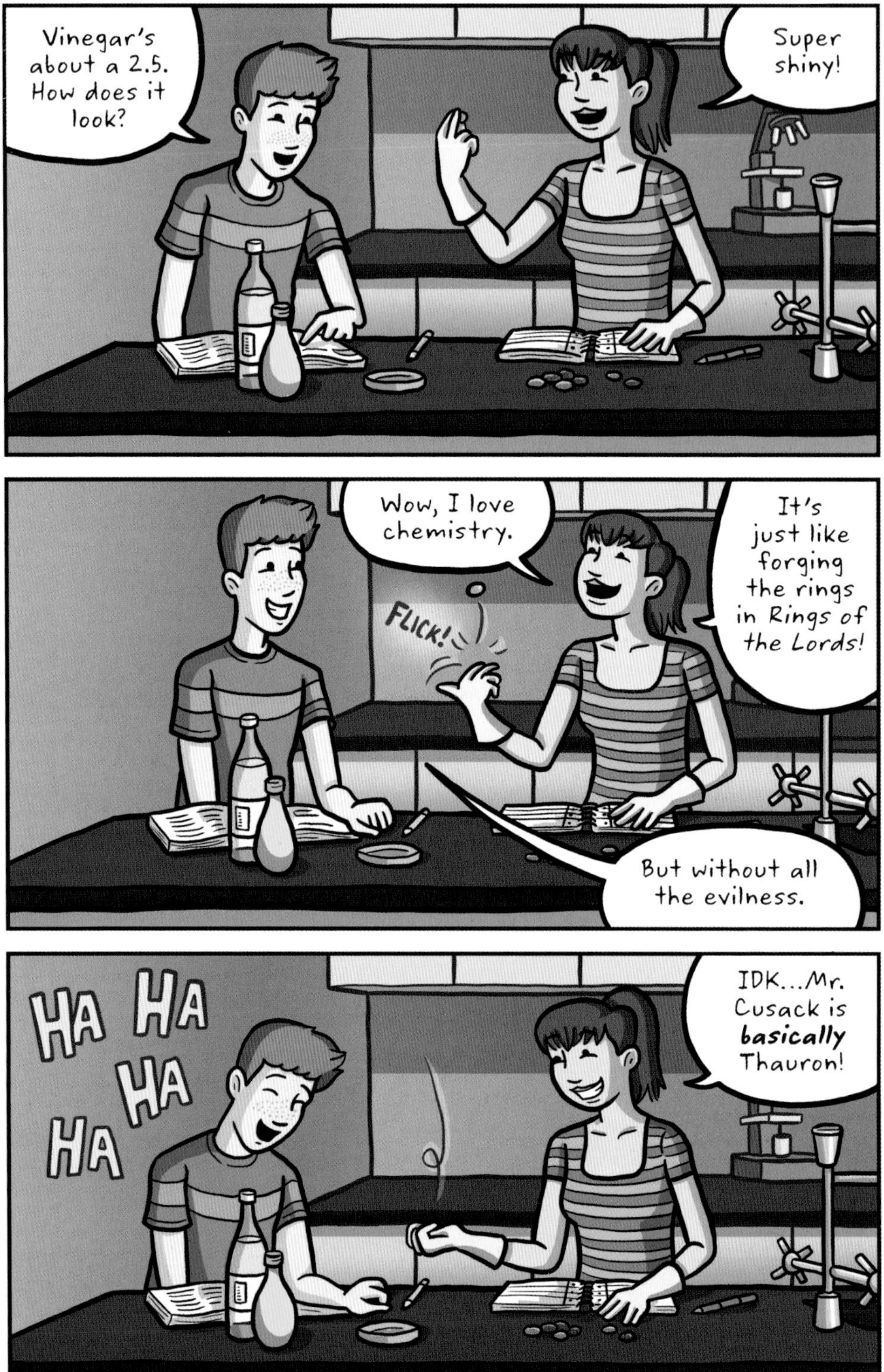
Vinegar's about a 2.5. How does it look?
Super shiny!
Wow, I love chemistry.
It's just like forging the rings in Rings of the Lords!
FLICK!
But without all the evilness.
HA HA HA HA
IDK...Mr. Cusack is **basically** Thauron!

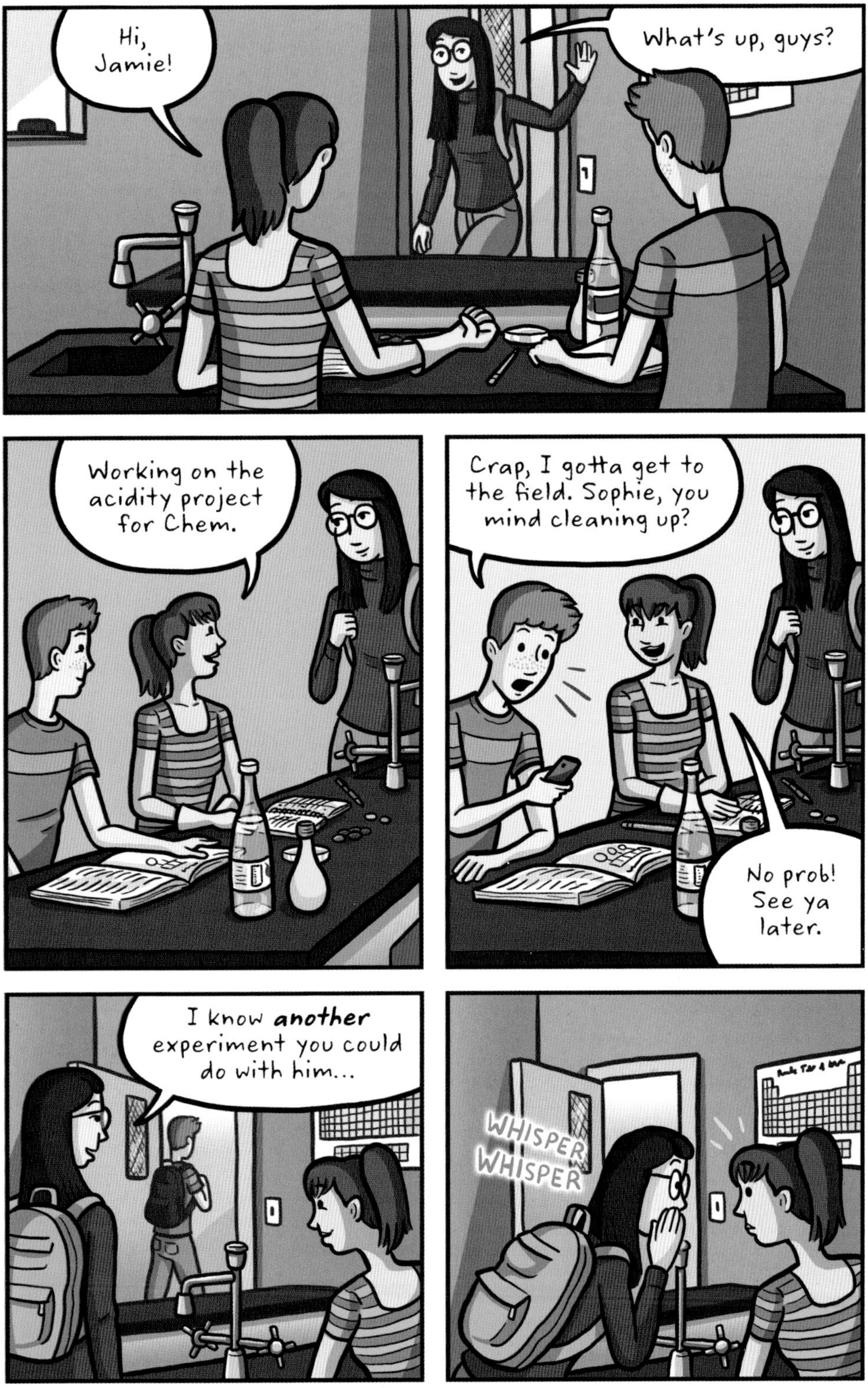
Hi, Jamie!
What's up, guys?
Working on the acidity project for Chem.
Crap, I gotta get to the field. Sophie, you mind cleaning up?
No prob! See ya later.
I know **another** experiment you could do with him...
WHISPER WHISPER

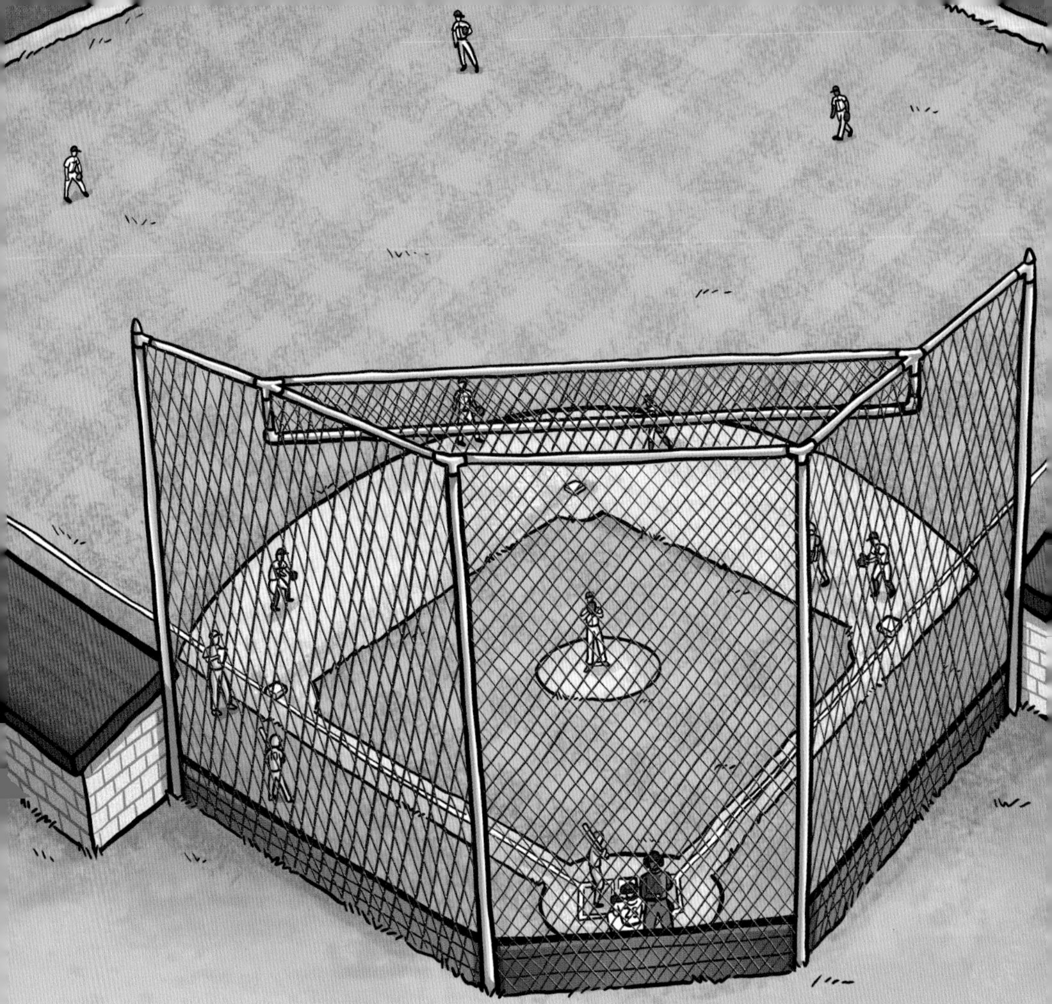

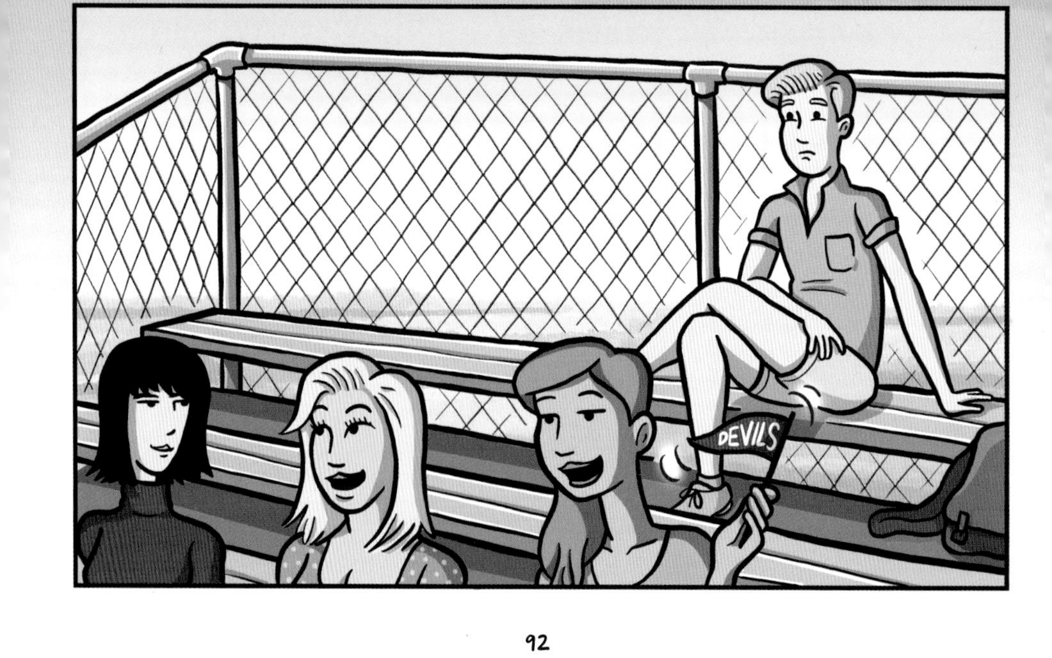
DEVILS

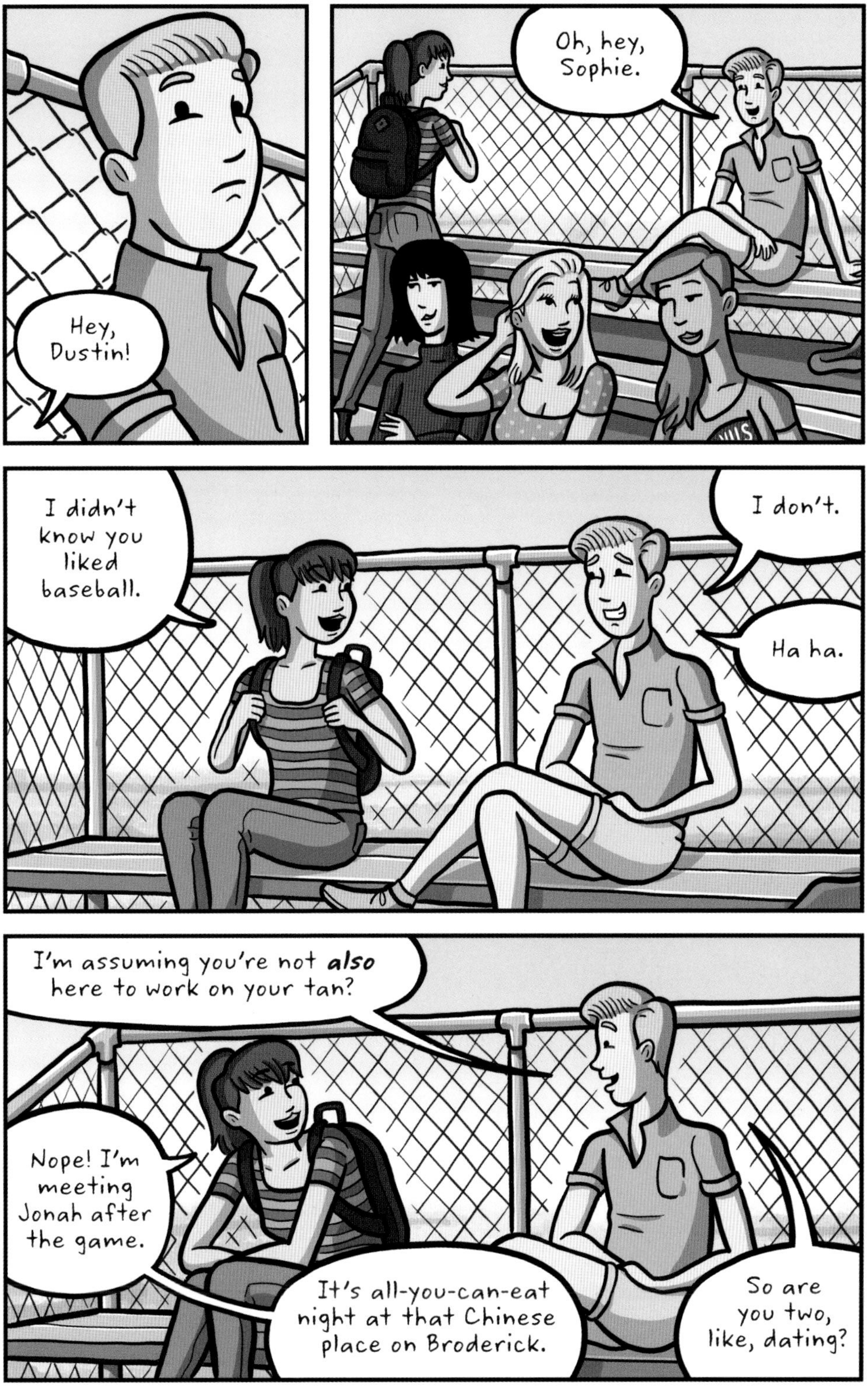
Hey, Dustin!
Oh, hey, Sophie.
I didn't know you liked baseball.
I don't.
Ha ha.
I'm assuming you're not ***also*** here to work on your tan?
Nope! I'm meeting Jonah after the game.
It's all-you-can-eat night at that Chinese place on Broderick.
So are you two, like, dating?

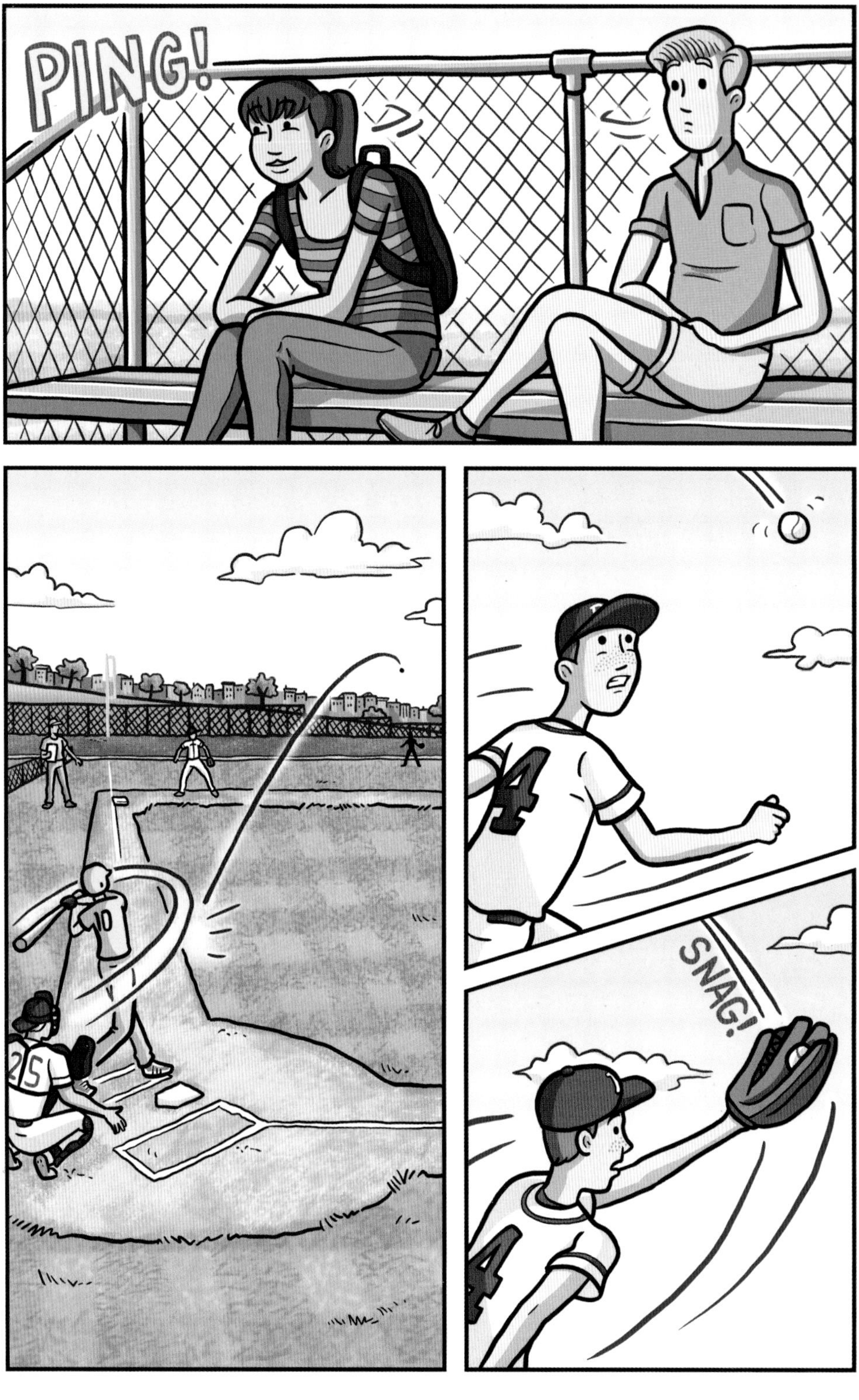
PING!
SNAG!

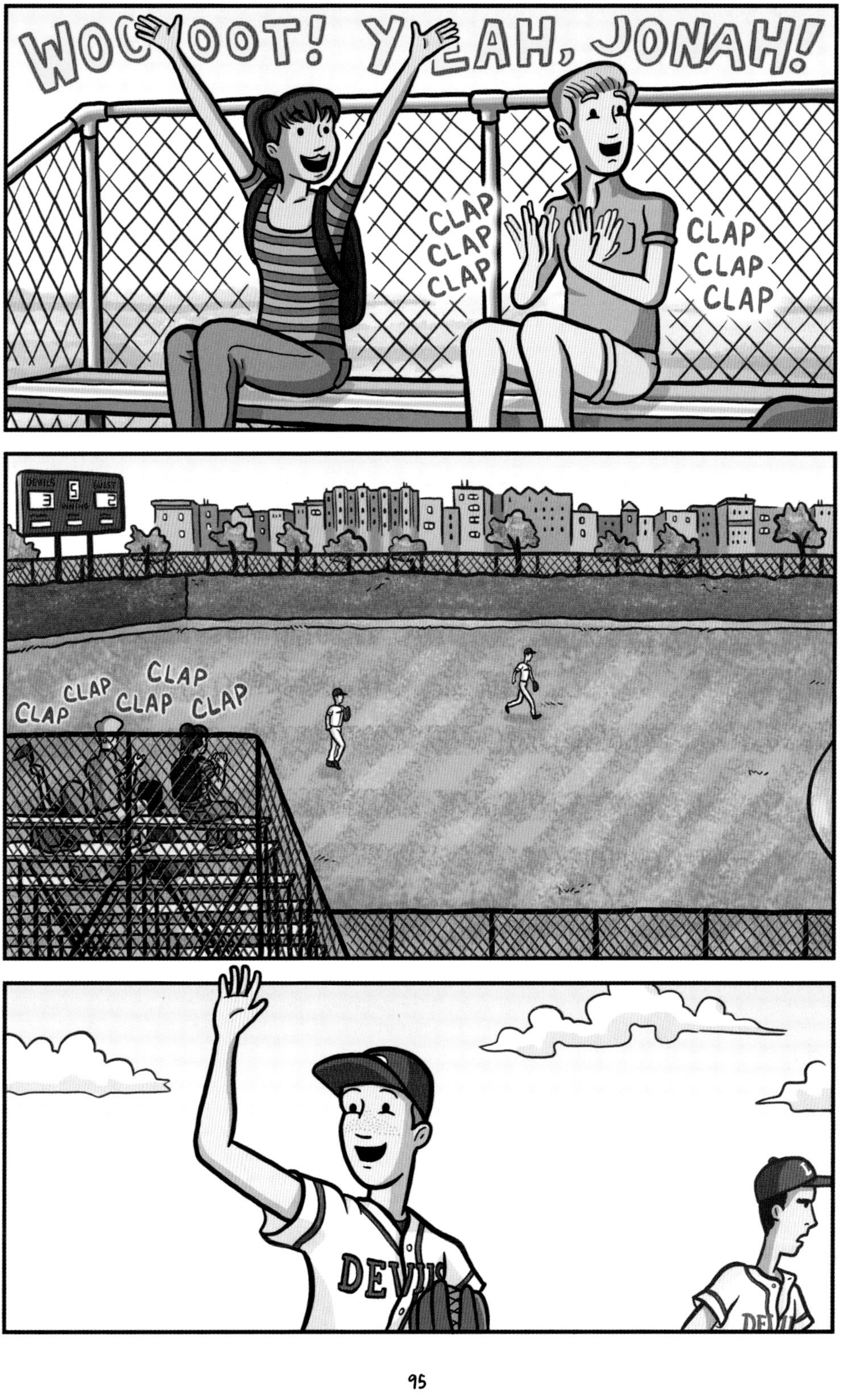
WOOHOOT! YEAH, JONAH!
CLAP CLAP CLAP
CLAP CLAP CLAP
DEVILS 3 5 GUEST 2
INNING
CLAP CLAP CLAP CLAP CLAP
DEVILS

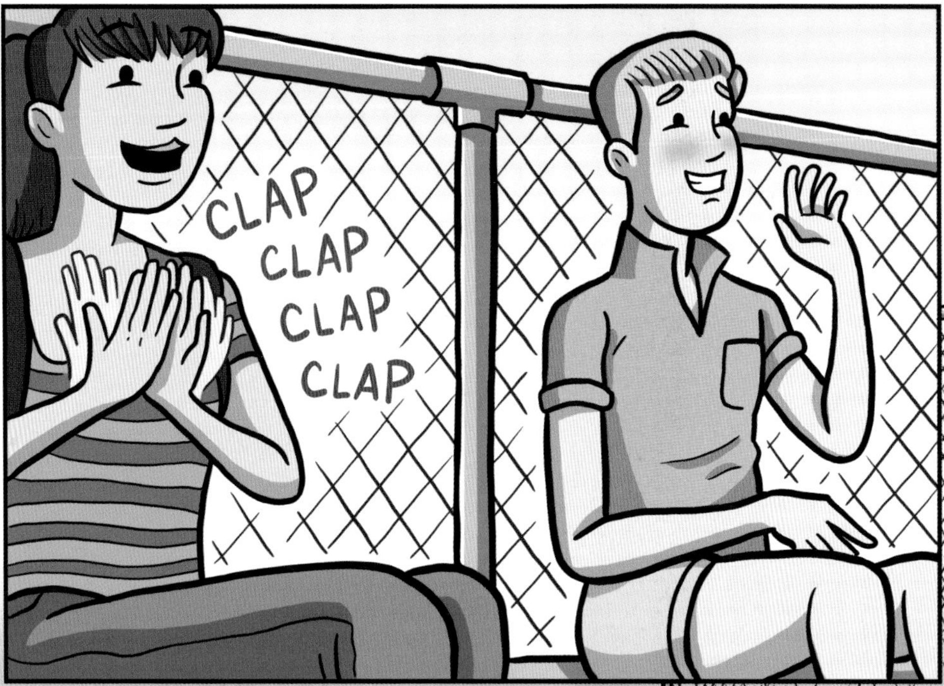
CLAP
CLAP
CLAP
CLAP

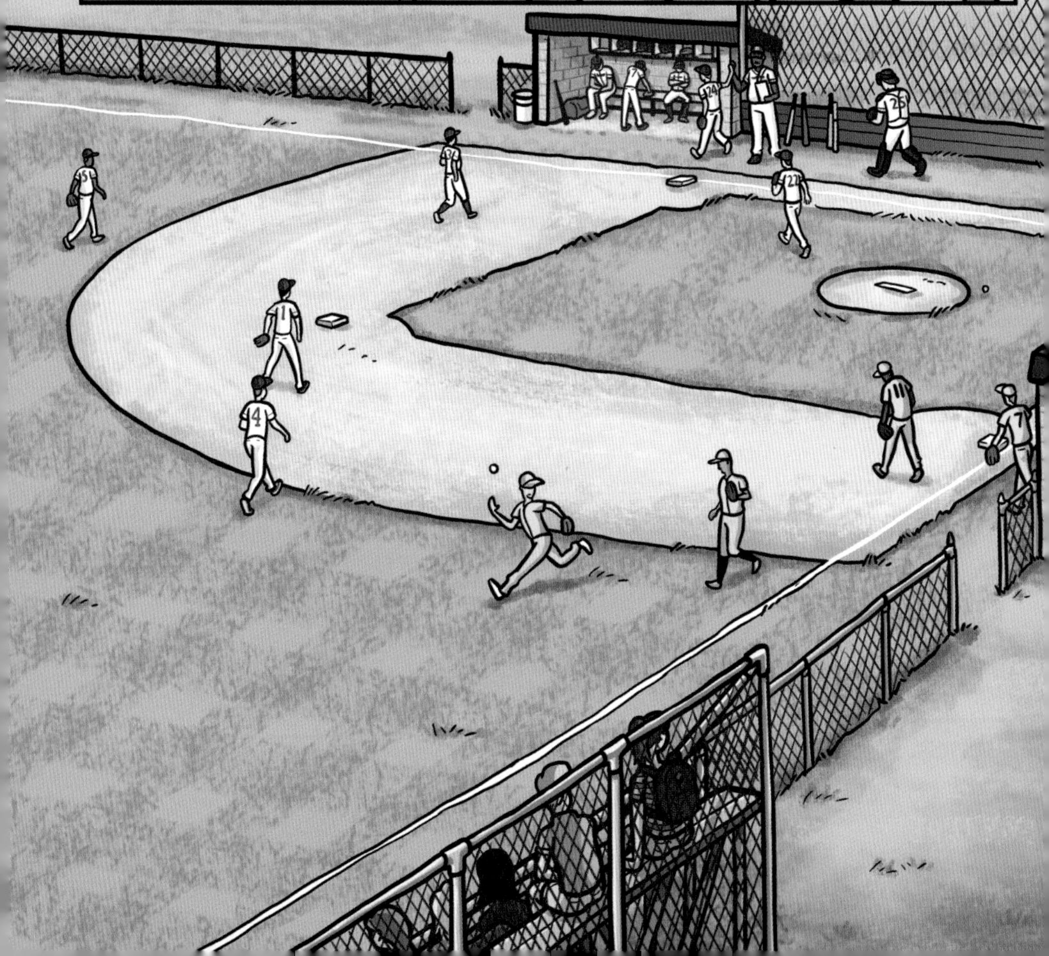

CHAPTER 3

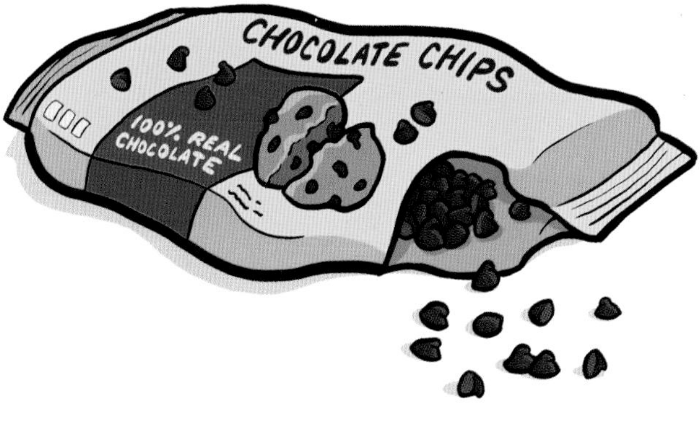

CHOCOLATE CHIPS
100% REAL CHOCOLATE

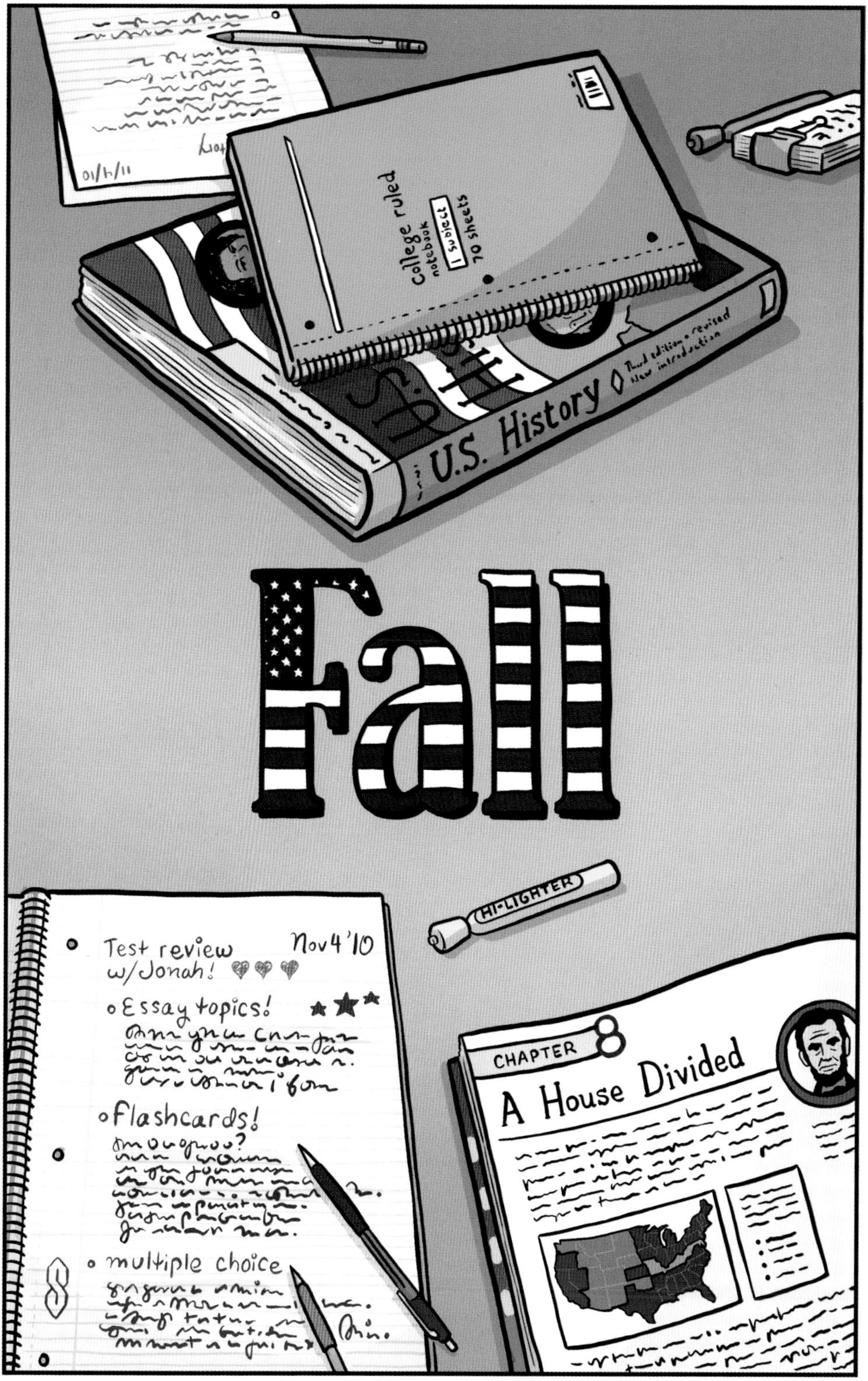
College ruled
notebook
1 subject
70 sheets
U.S. History
Fall
HI-LIGHTER
Test review
w/Jonah!
Nov 4 '10
Essay topics!
Flashcards!
multiple choice
CHAPTER 8
A House Divided

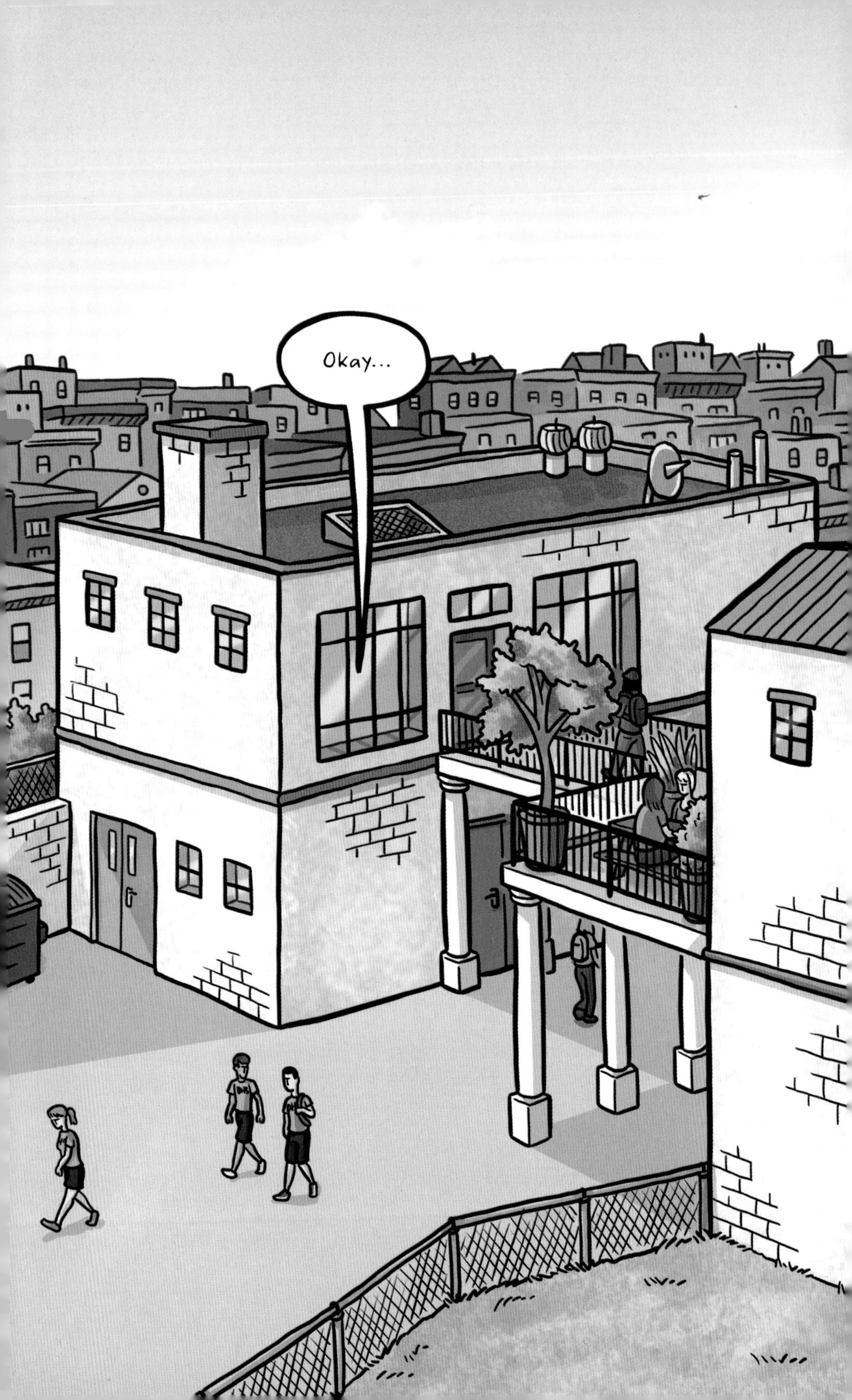
Okay...

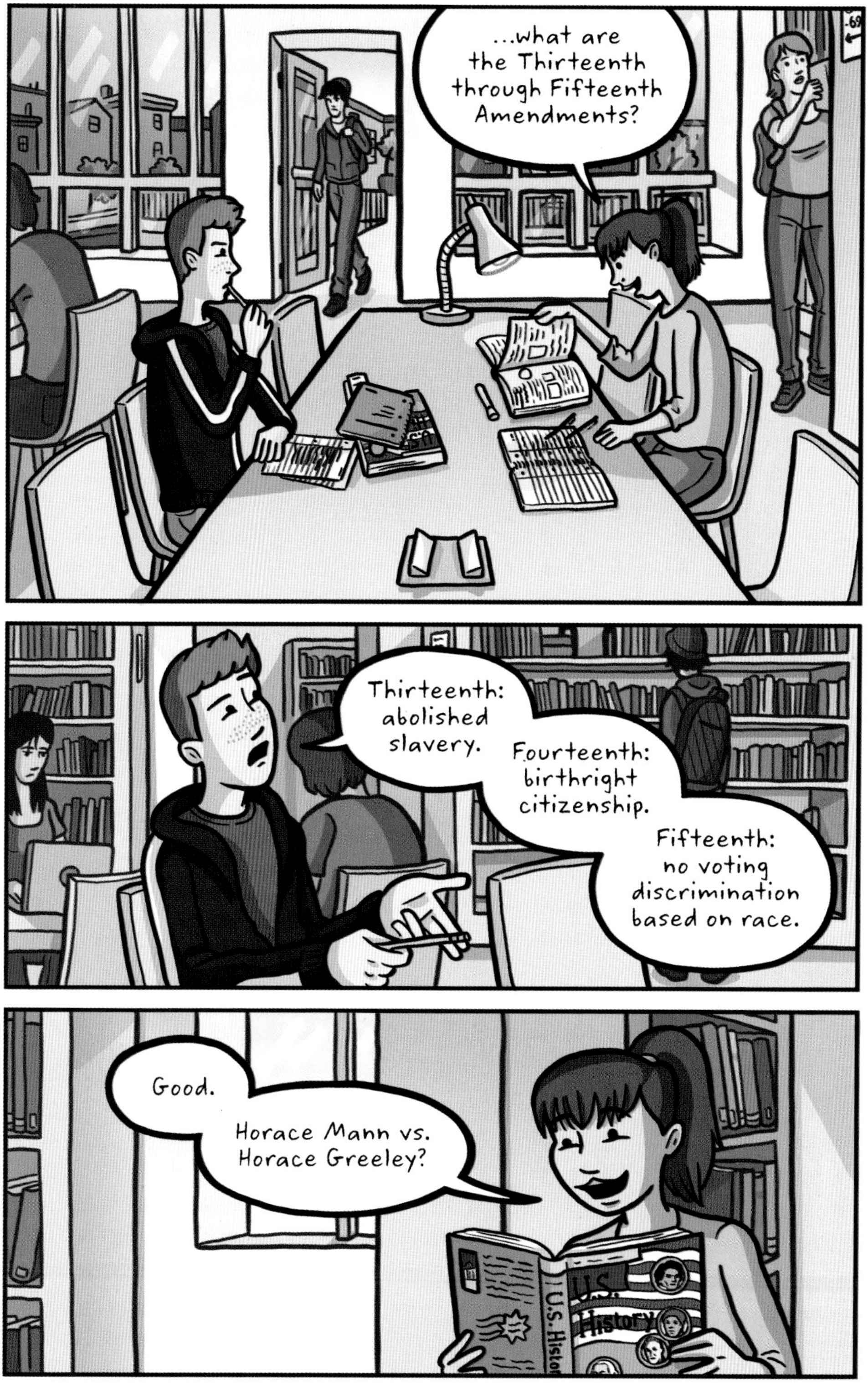
...what are the Thirteenth through Fifteenth Amendments?
Thirteenth: abolished slavery.
Fourteenth: birthright citizenship.
Fifteenth: no voting discrimination based on race.
Good.
Horace Mann vs. Horace Greeley?
U.S. History

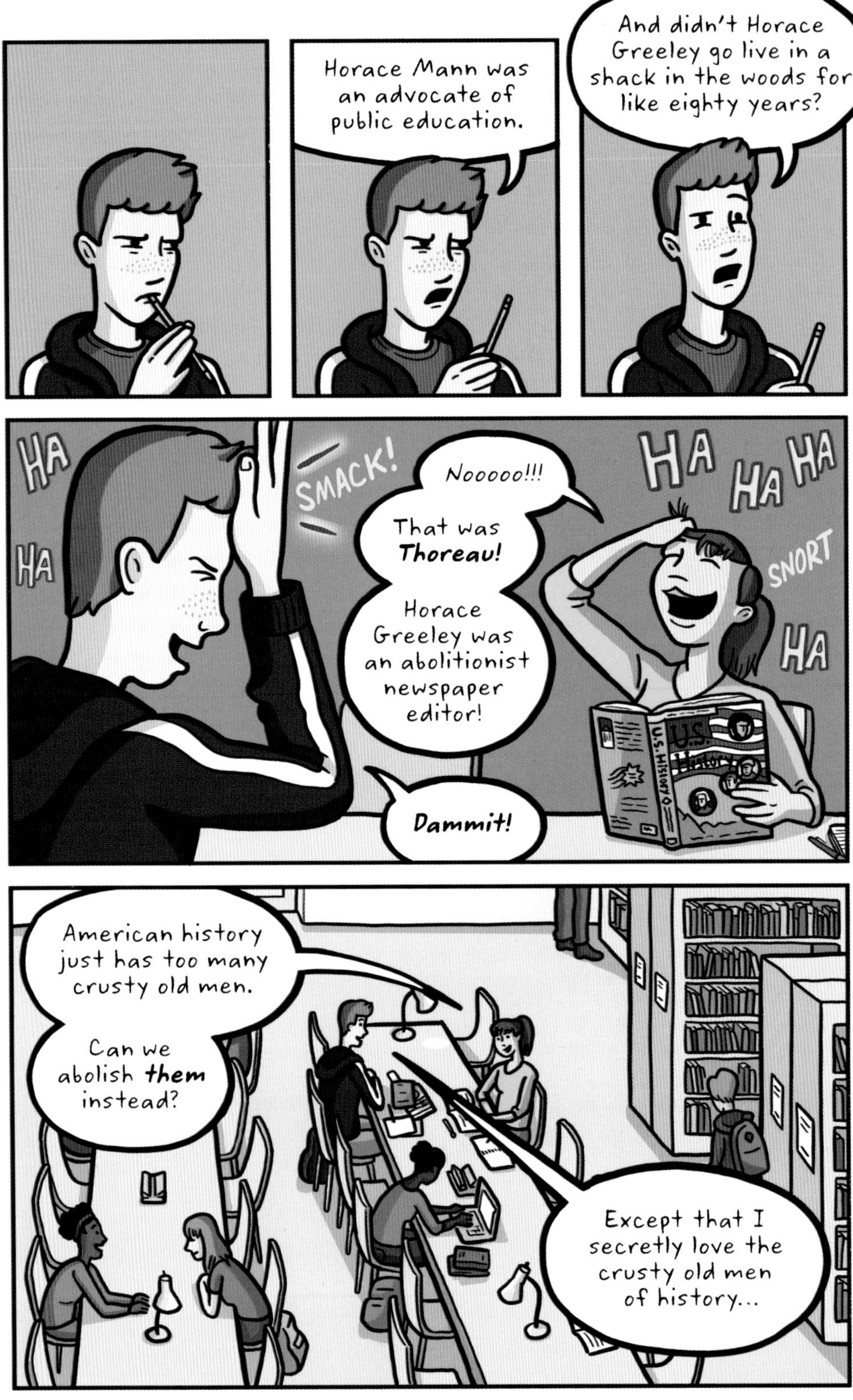

Horace Mann was an advocate of public education.
And didn't Horace Greeley go live in a shack in the woods for like eighty years?
HA
HA
SMACK!
Nooooo!!!
That was **Thoreau!**
Horace Greeley was an abolitionist newspaper editor!
Dammit!
HA
HA
HA
HA
SNORT
HA
U.S. History
American history just has too many crusty old men.
Can we abolish **them** instead?
Except that I secretly love the crusty old men of history...

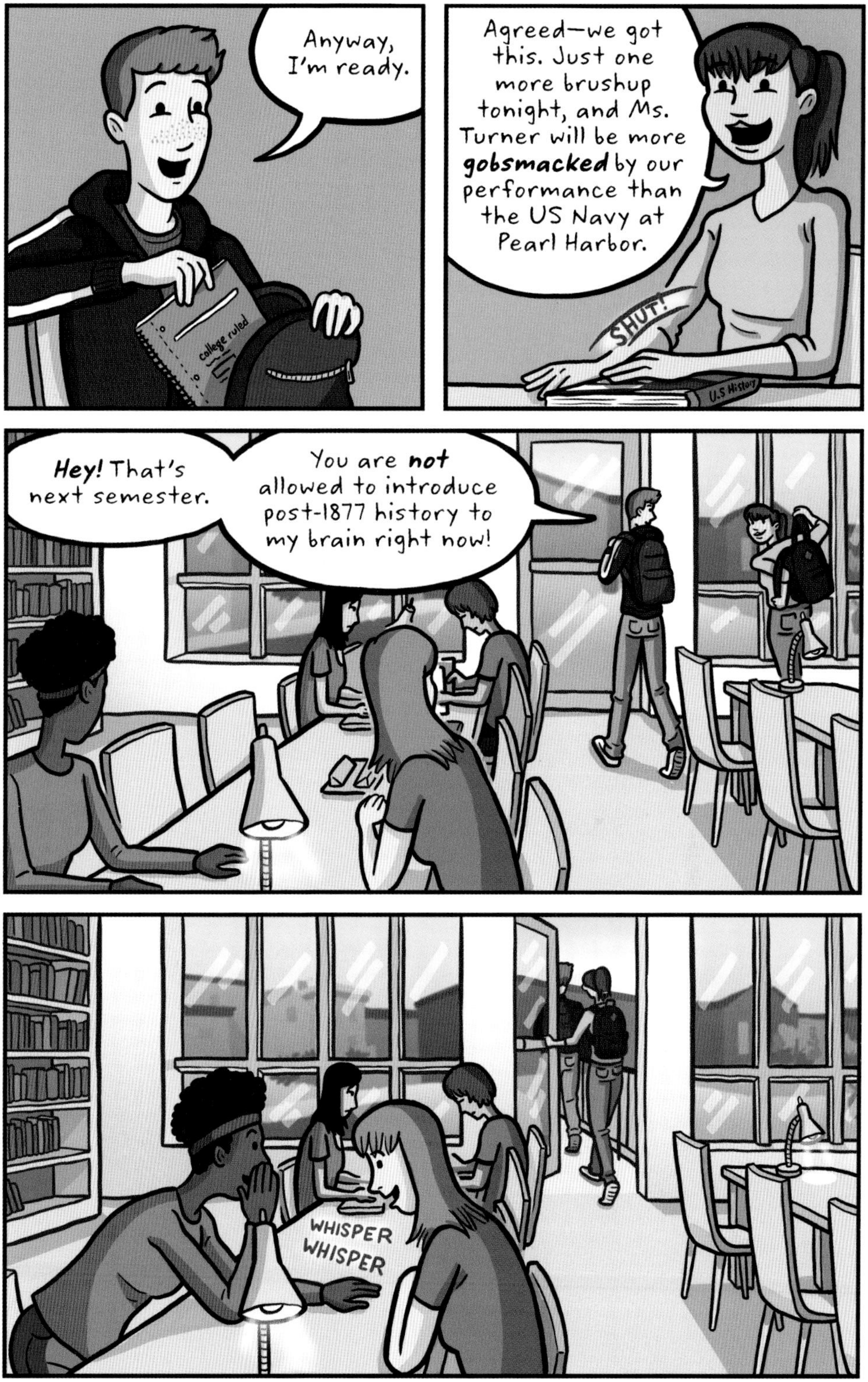
Anyway, I'm ready.
college ruled
Agreed—we got this. Just one more brushup tonight, and Ms. Turner will be more **gobsmacked** by our performance than the US Navy at Pearl Harbor.
SHUT!
U.S History
Hey! That's next semester.
You are **not** allowed to introduce post-1877 history to my brain right now!
WHISPER WHISPER

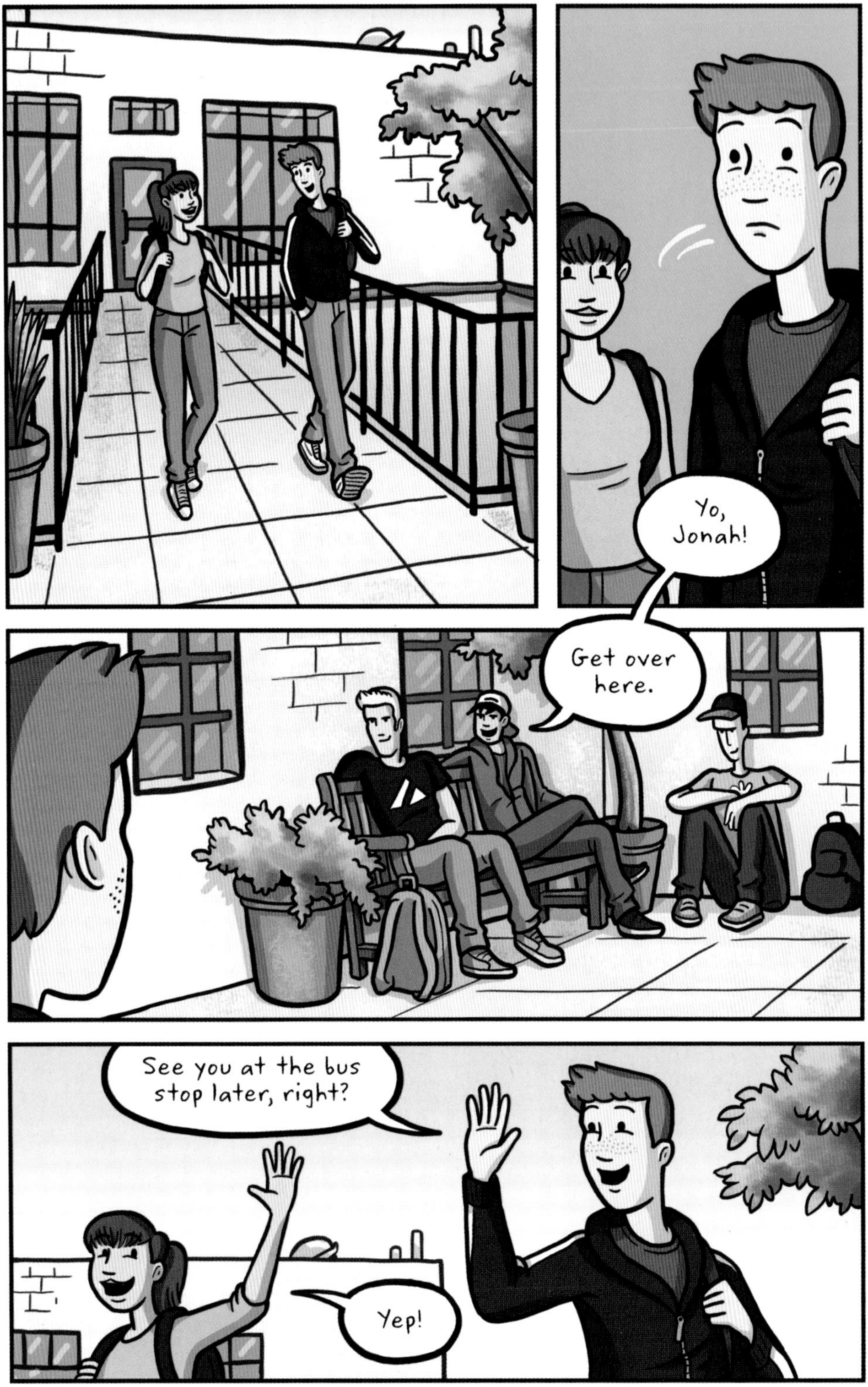
Yo, Jonah!
Get over here.
See you at the bus stop later, right?
Yep!

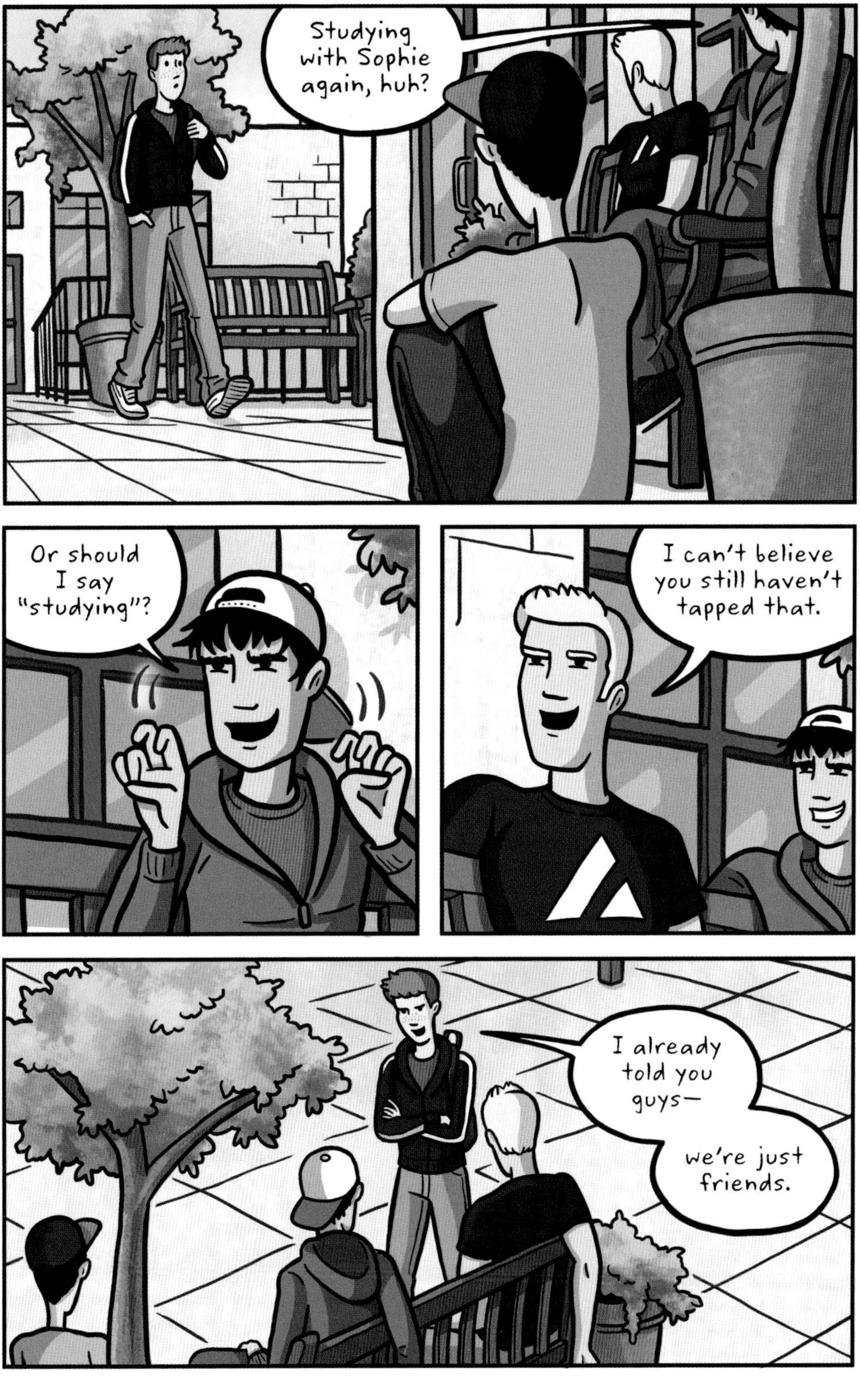
Studying with Sophie again, huh?
Or should I say "studying"?
I can't believe you still haven't tapped that.
I already told you guys—
we're just friends.

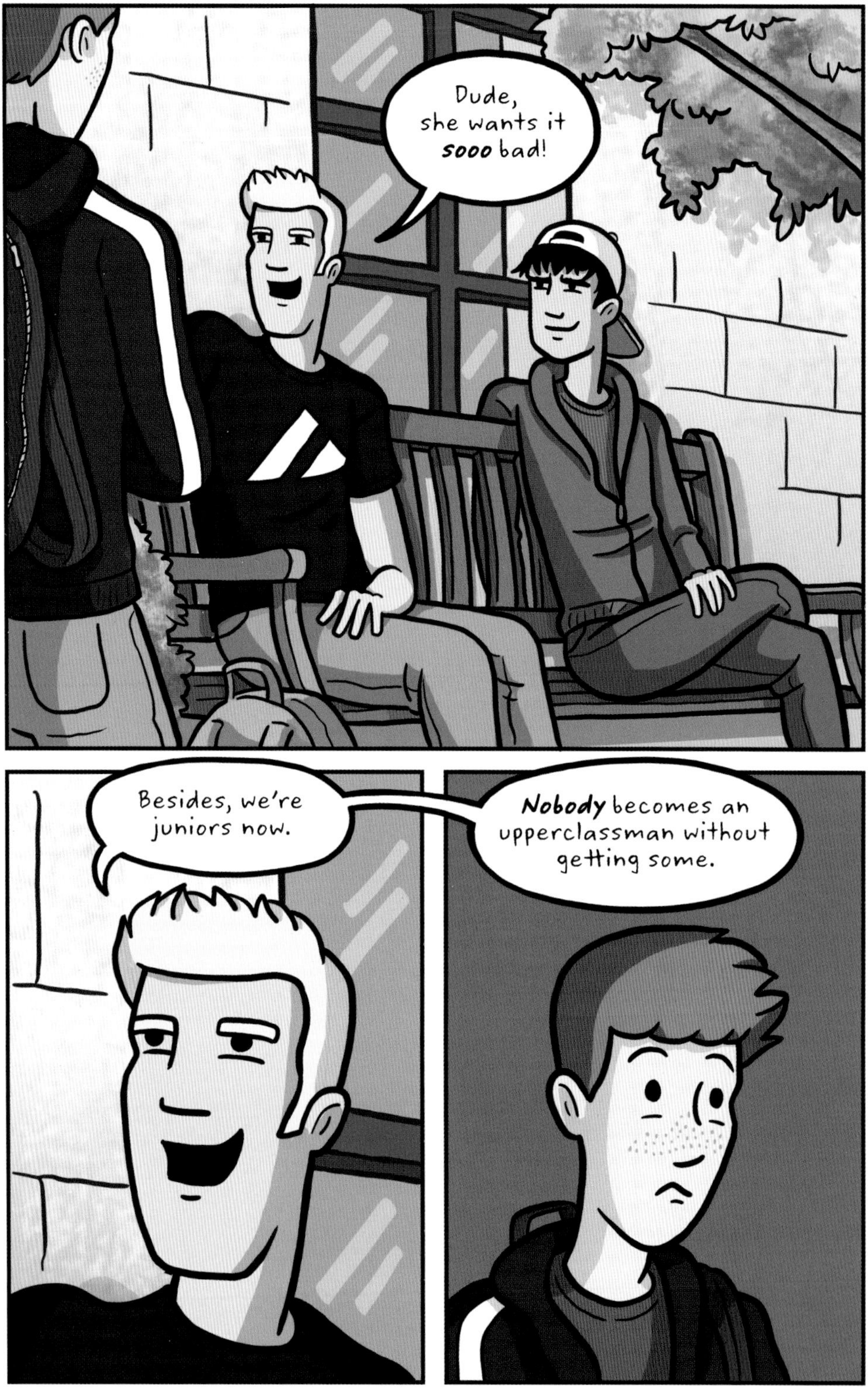
Dude, she wants it sooo bad!
Besides, we're juniors now.
Nobody becomes an upperclassman without getting some.

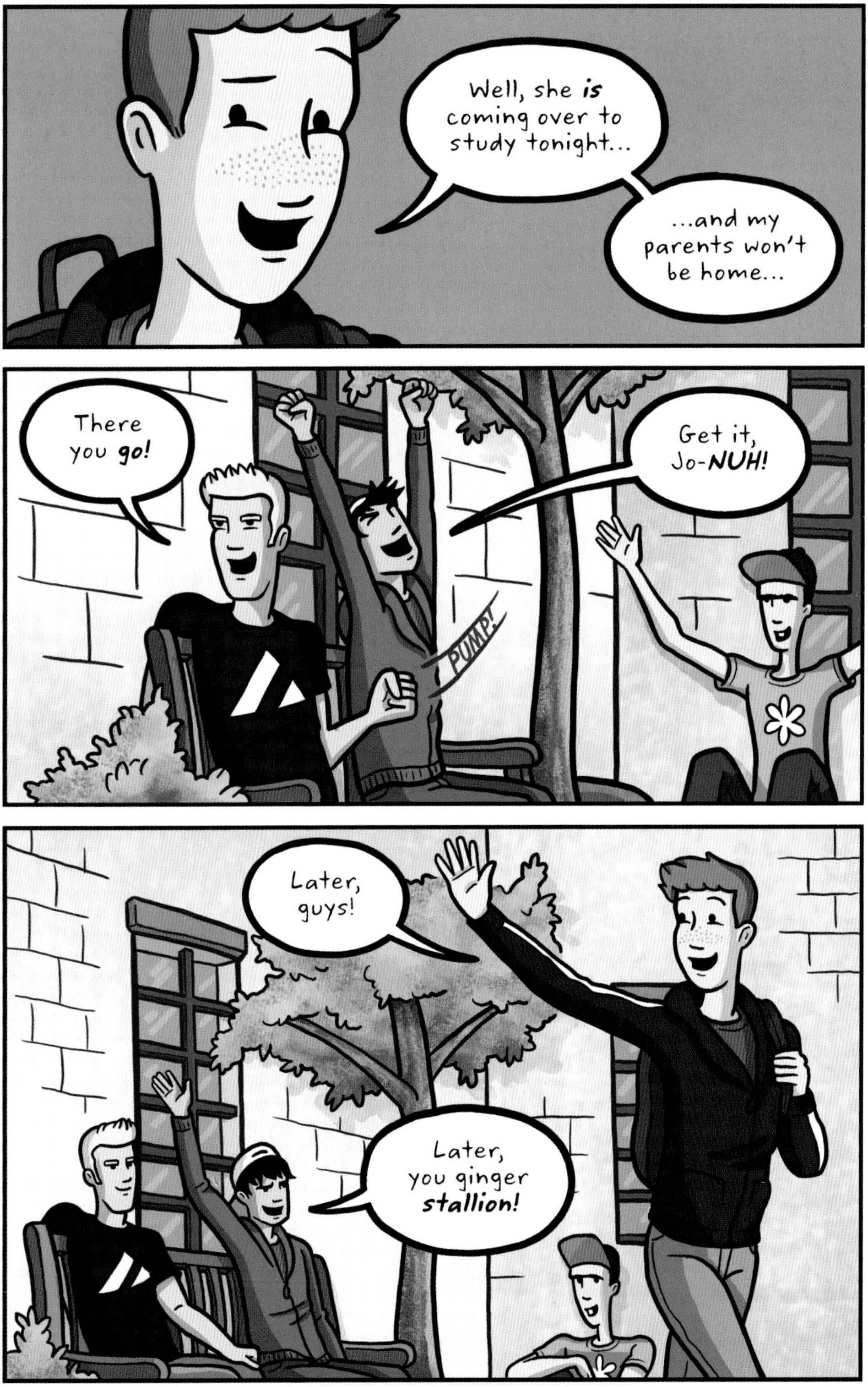
Well, she *is* coming over to study tonight...
...and my parents won't be home...
There you **go**!
Get it, Jo-**NUH**!
PUMP!
Later, guys!
Later, you ginger **stallion**!

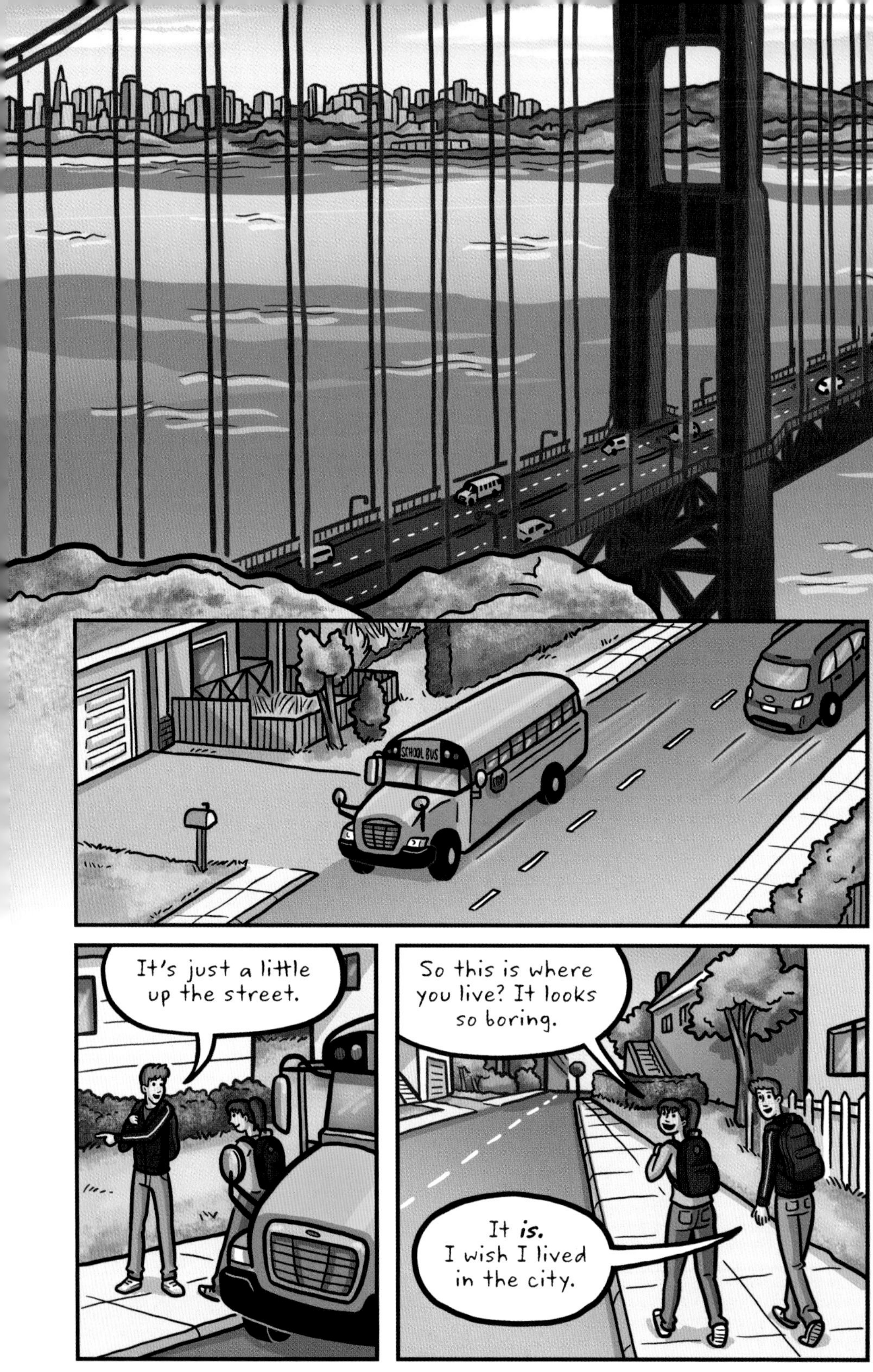
SCHOOL BUS
STOP
It's just a little up the street.
So this is where you live? It looks so boring.
It *is.* I wish I lived in the city.

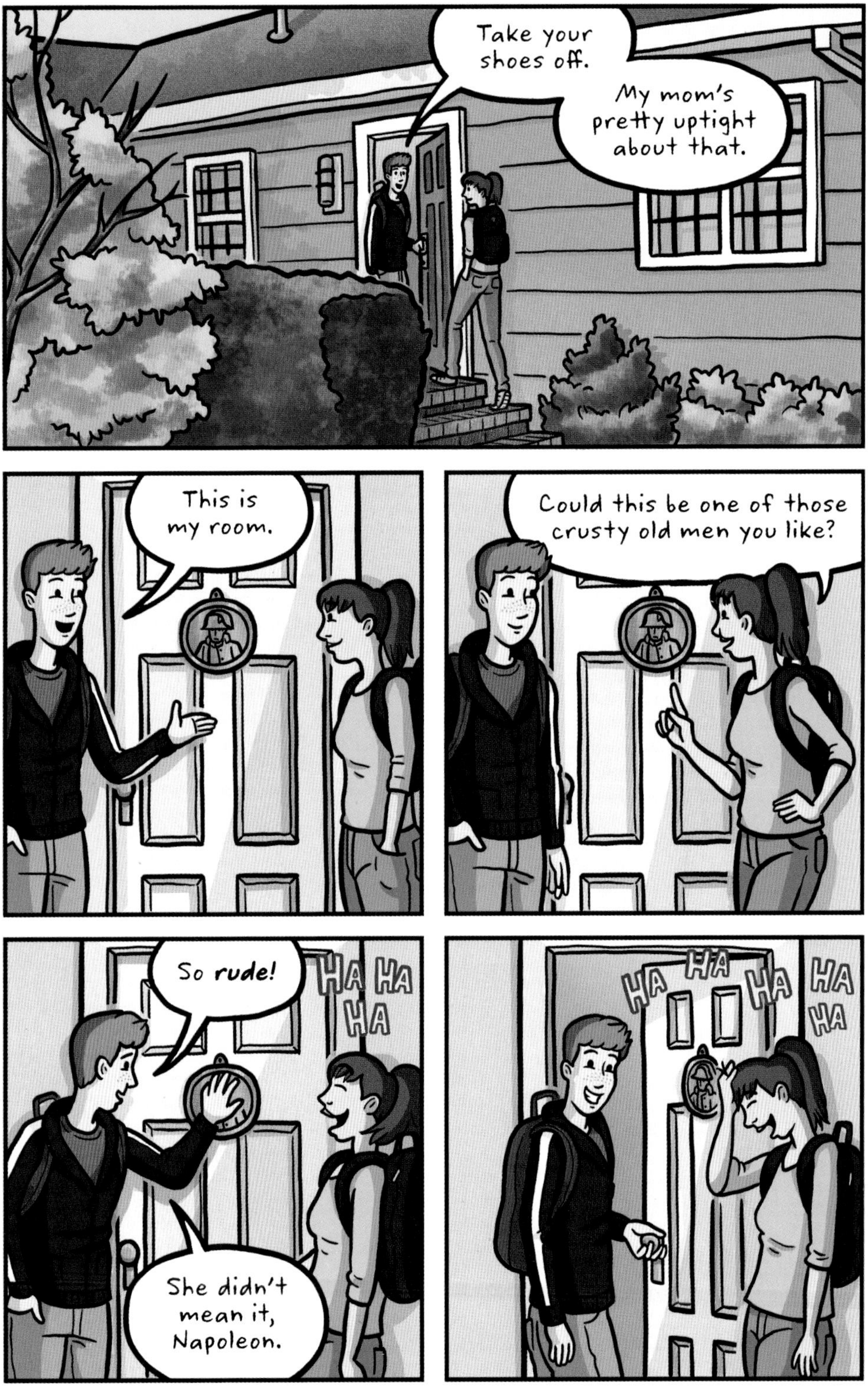
Take your shoes off.
My mom's pretty uptight about that.
This is my room.
Could this be one of those crusty old men you like?
So **rude**!
HA HA HA
She didn't mean it, Napoleon.
HA HA HA HA HA

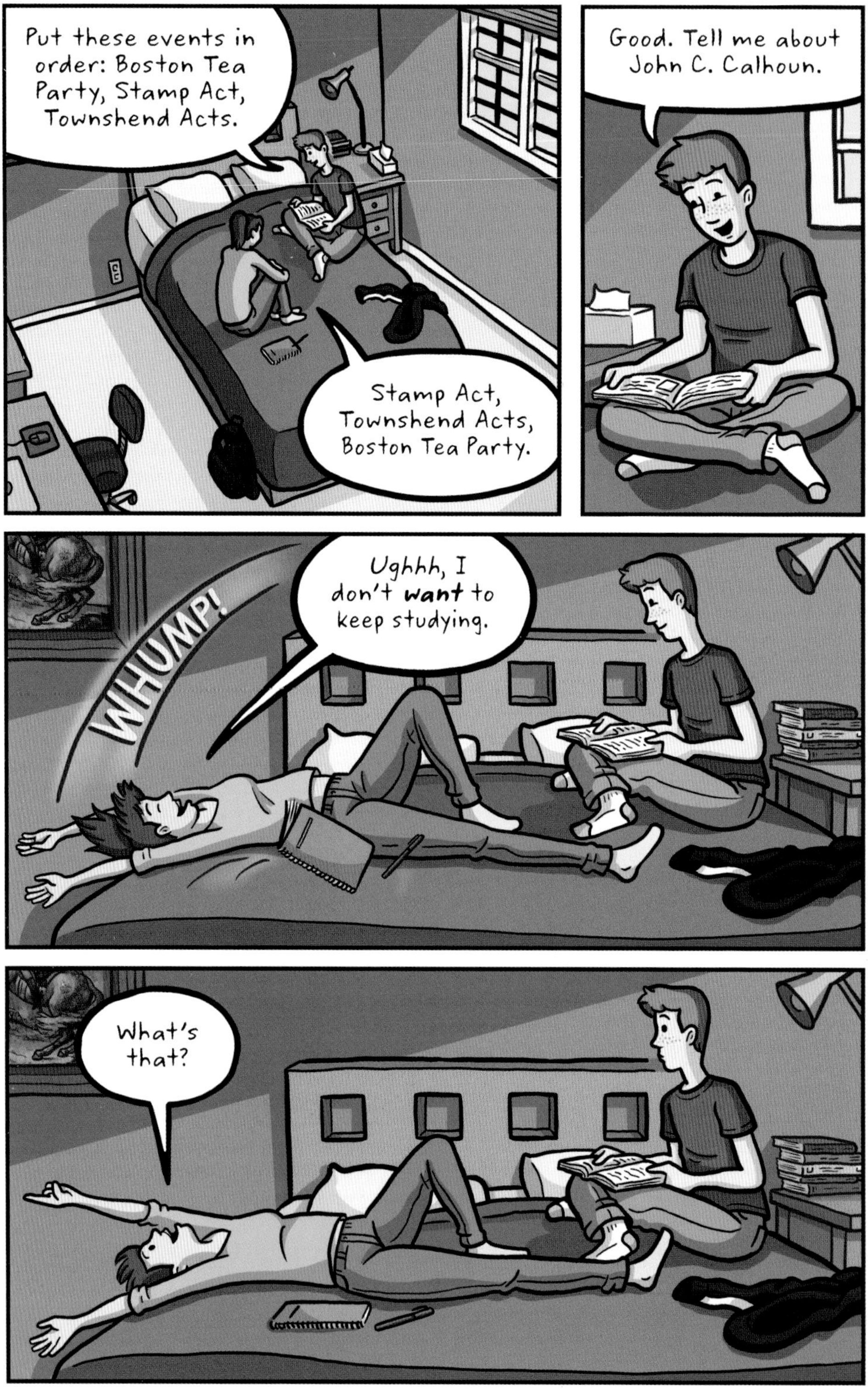

Put these events in order: Boston Tea Party, Stamp Act, Townshend Acts.
Stamp Act, Townshend Acts, Boston Tea Party.
Good. Tell me about John C. Calhoun.
WHUMP!
Ughhh, I don't **want** to keep studying.
What's that?

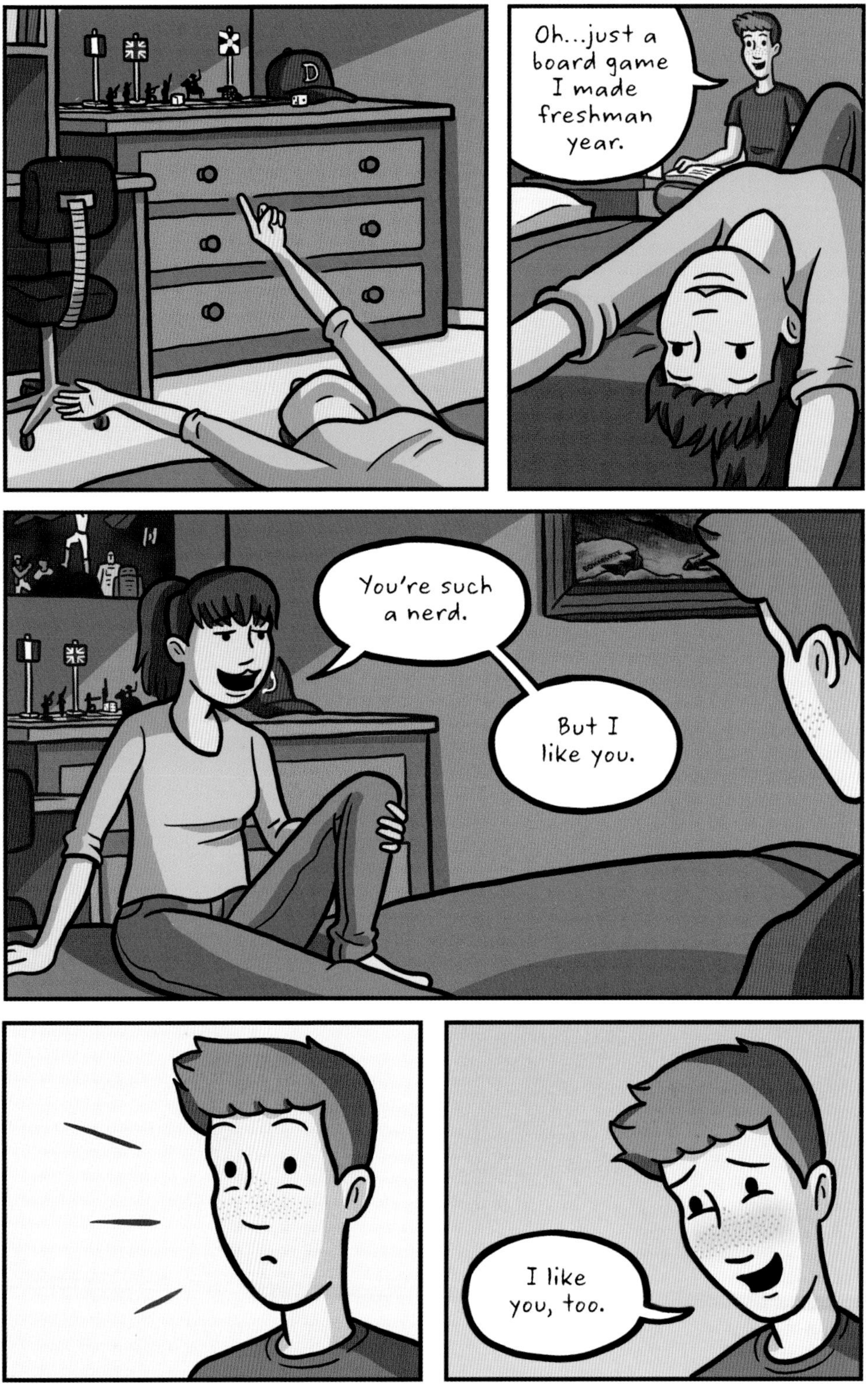
Oh...just a board game I made freshman year.
You're such a nerd.
But I like you.
I like you, too.

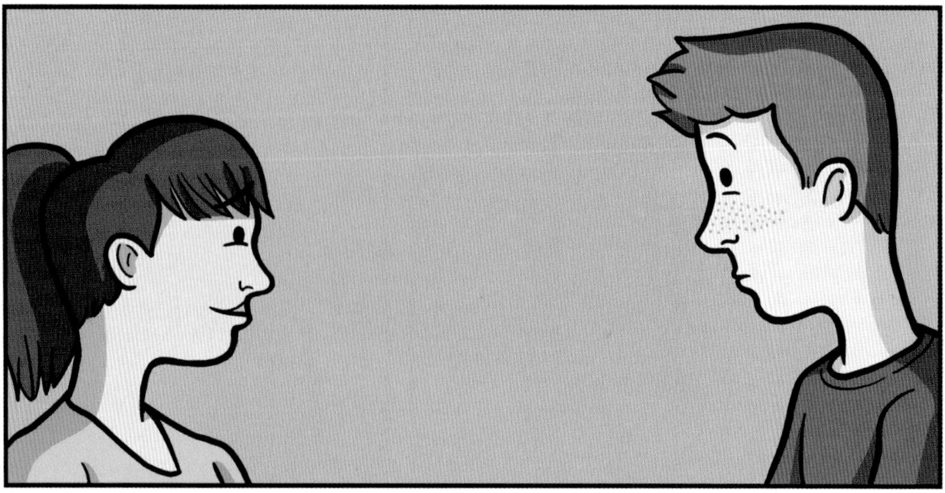

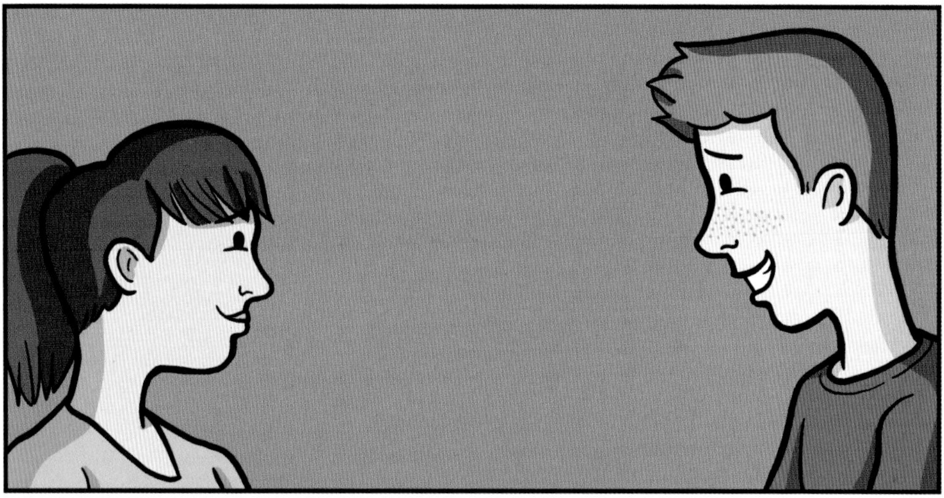

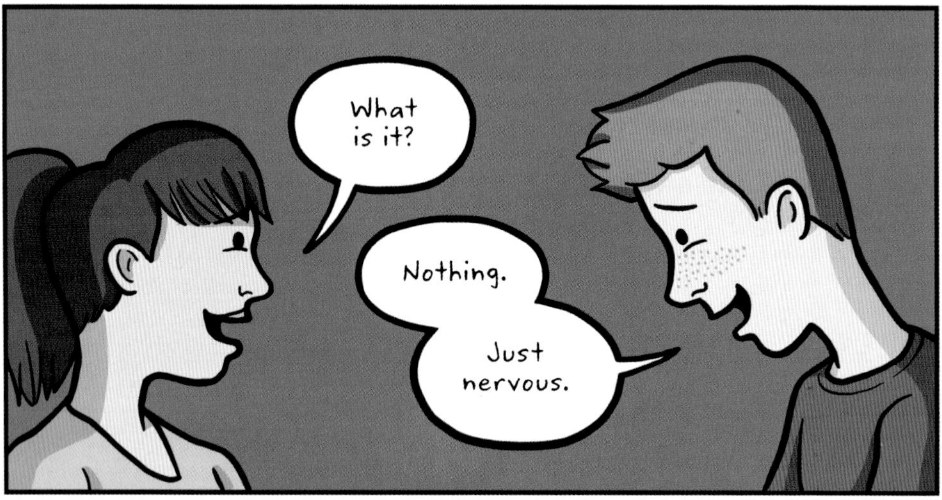
What is it?
Nothing.
Just nervous.

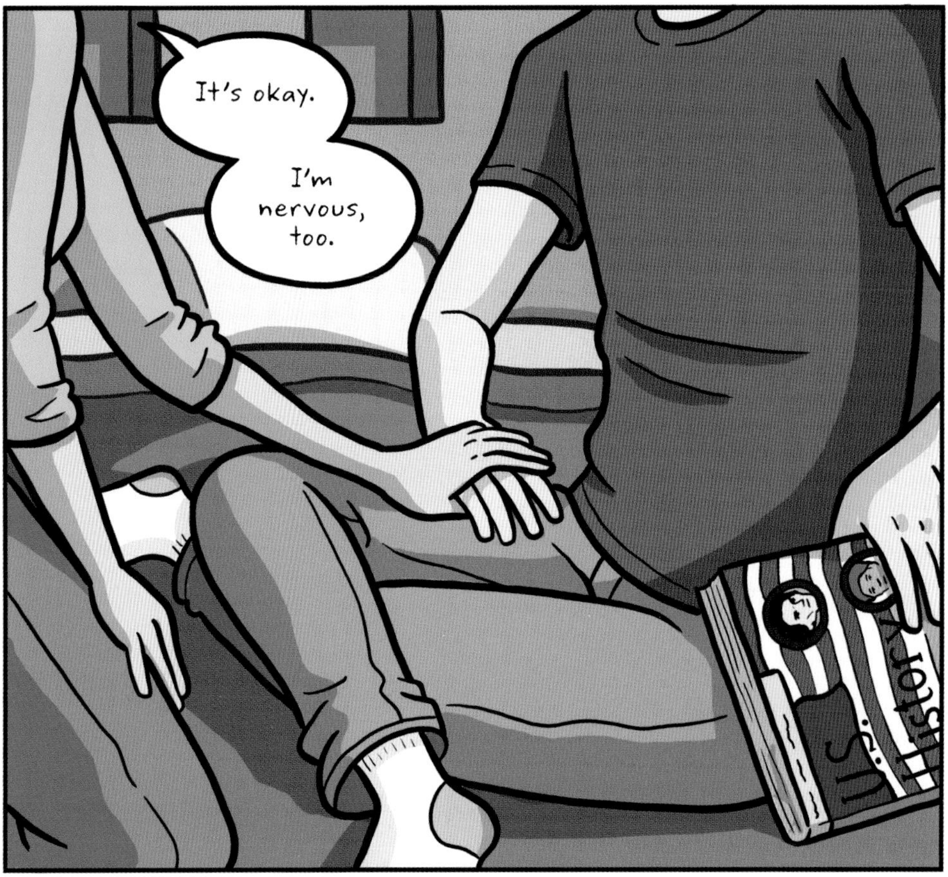
It's okay.
I'm nervous, too.

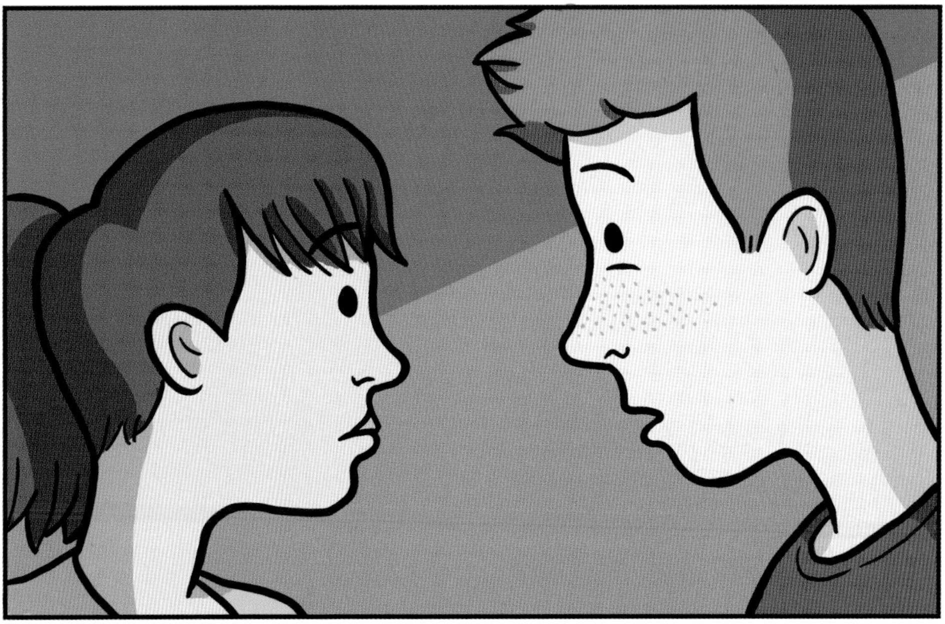

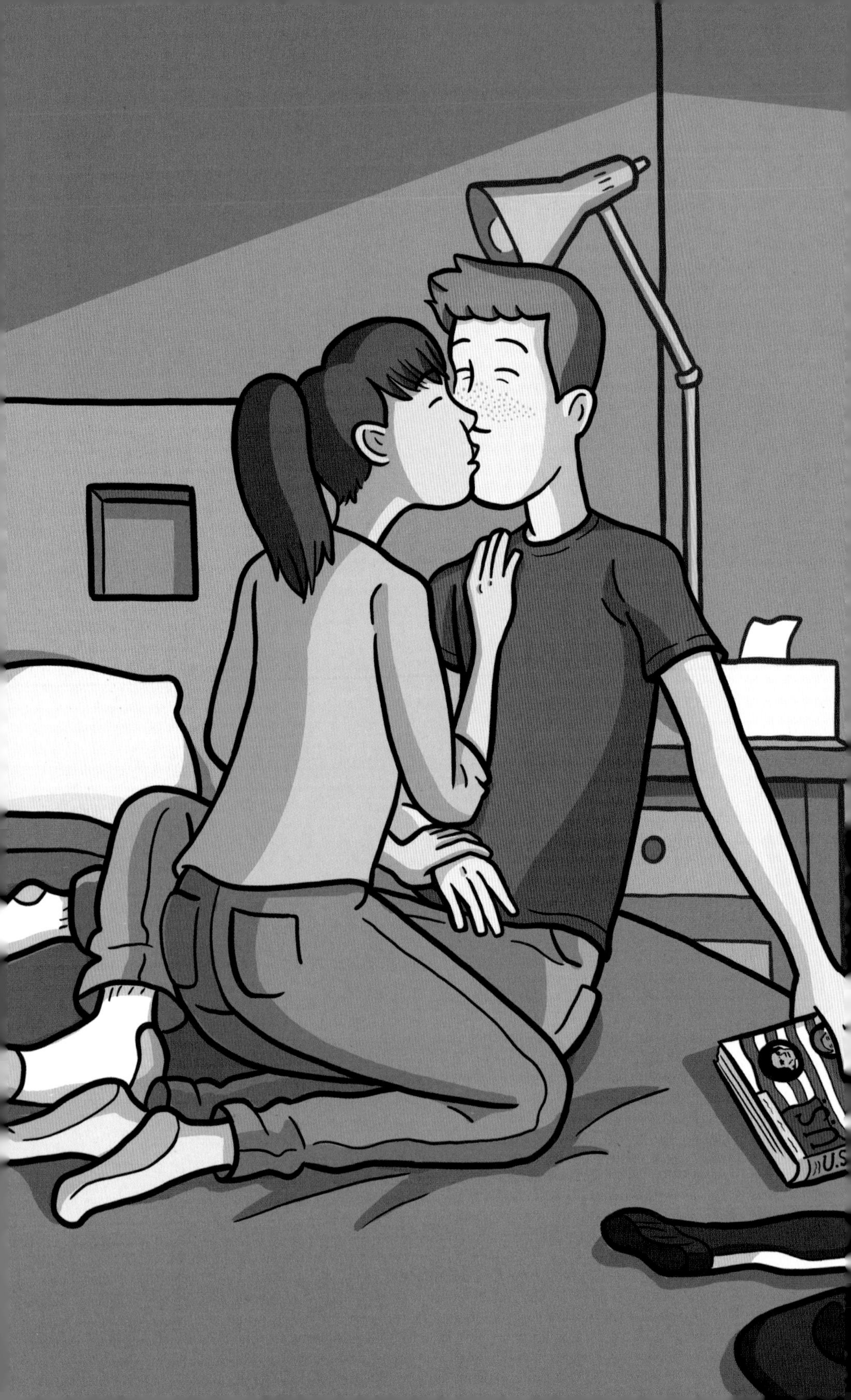

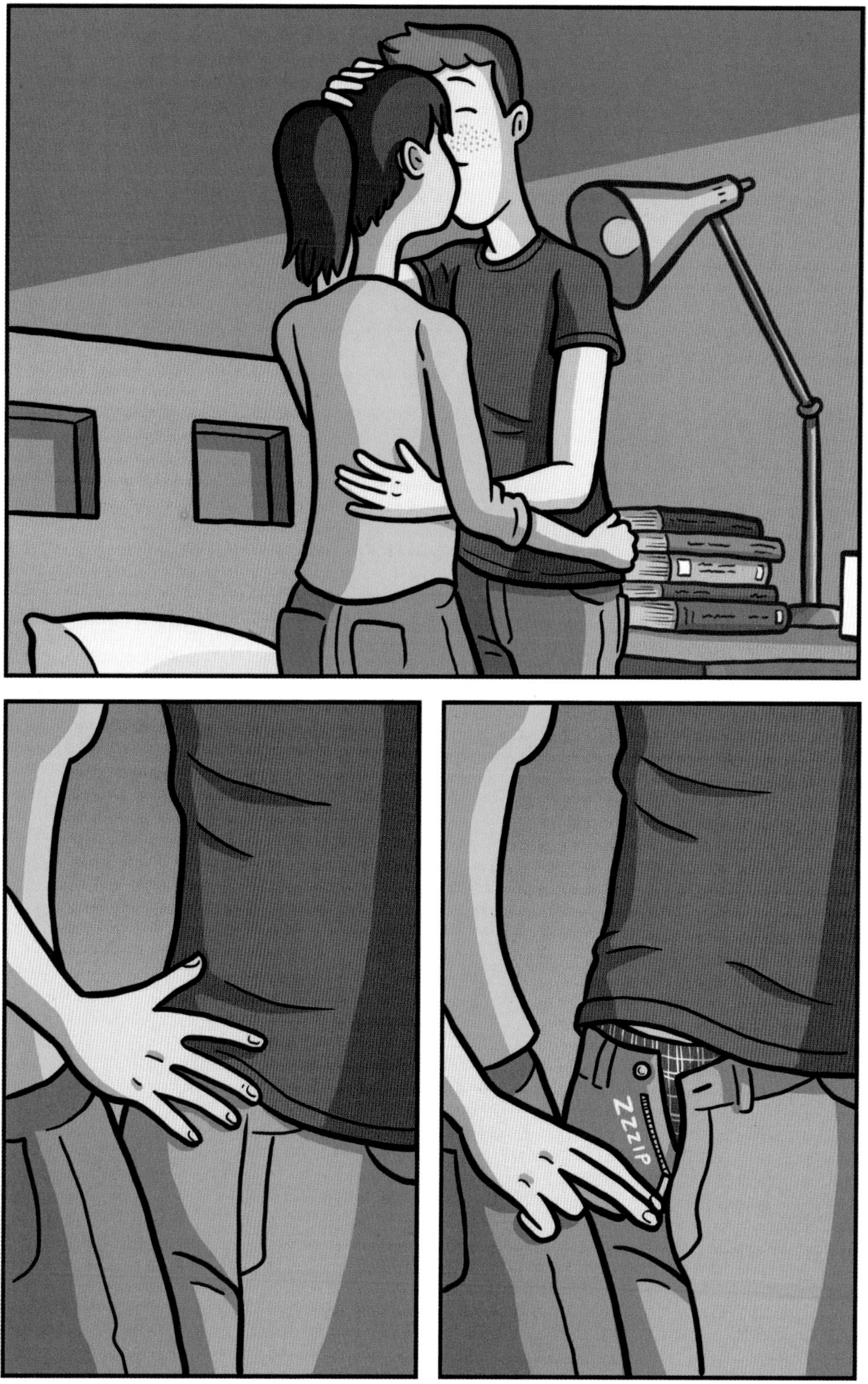
ZZZIP

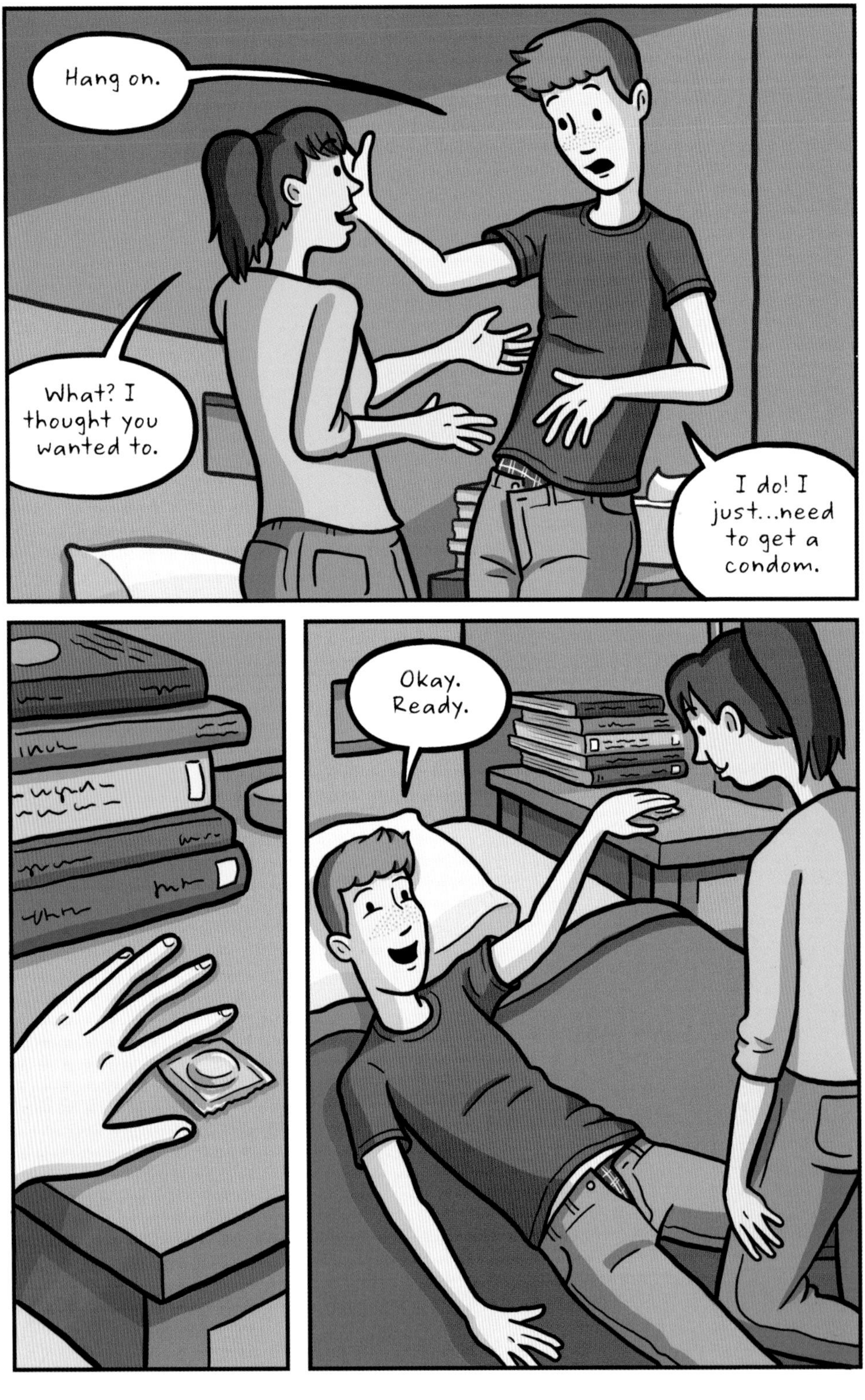
Hang on.
What? I thought you wanted to.
I do! I just...need to get a condom.
Okay. Ready.

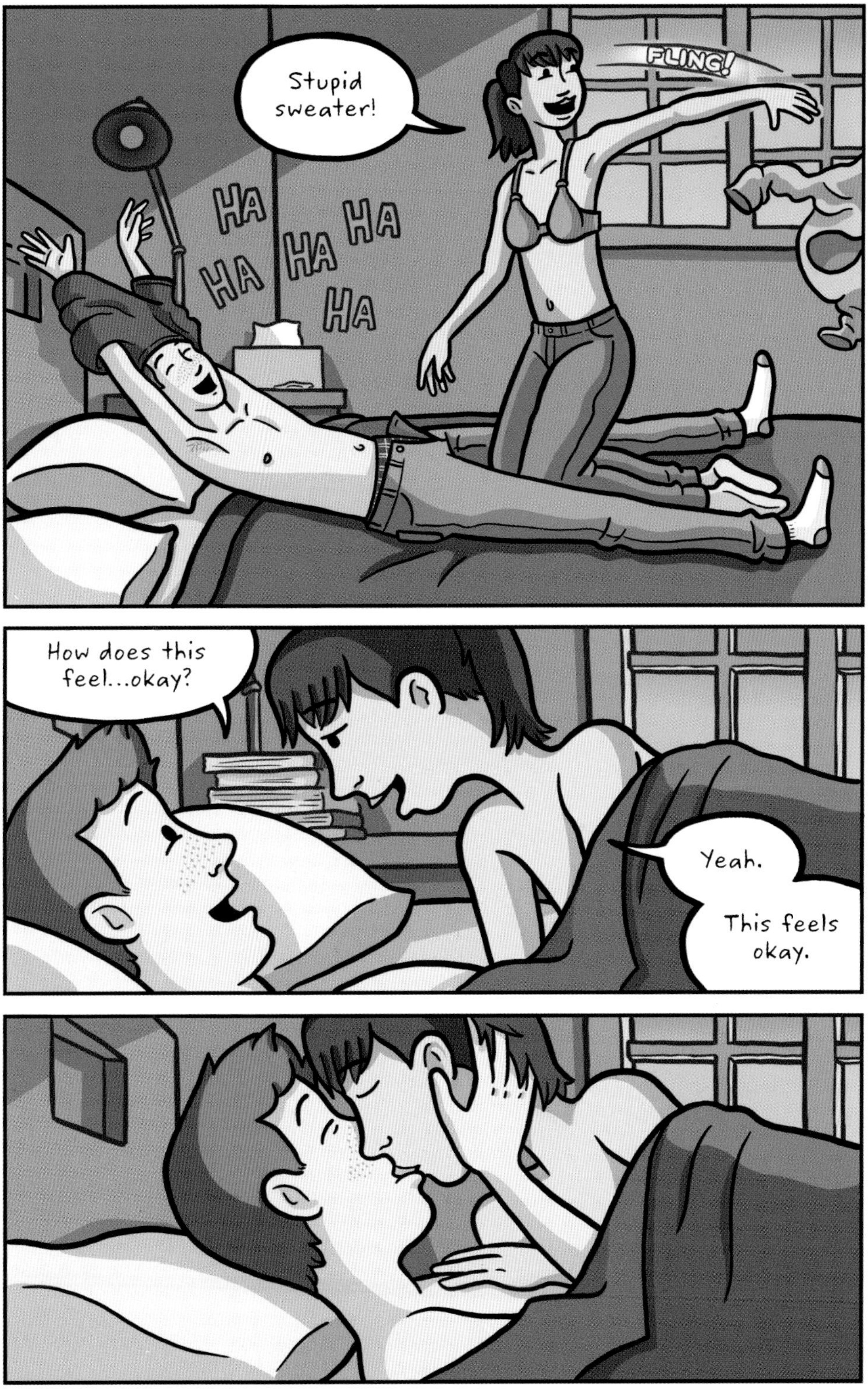
Stupid sweater!
FLING!
HA HA HA HA HA HA
How does this feel...okay?
Yeah.
This feels okay.

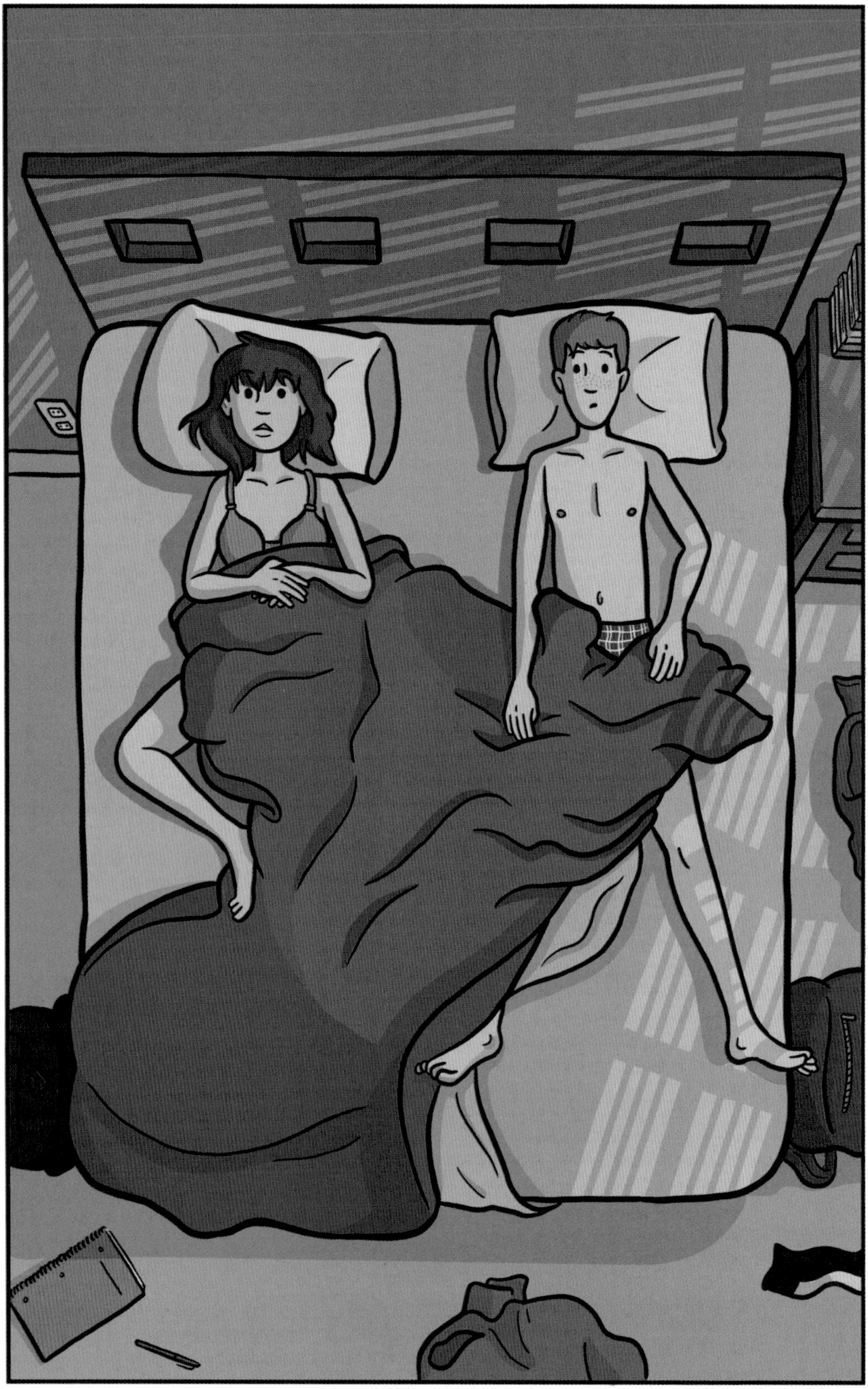

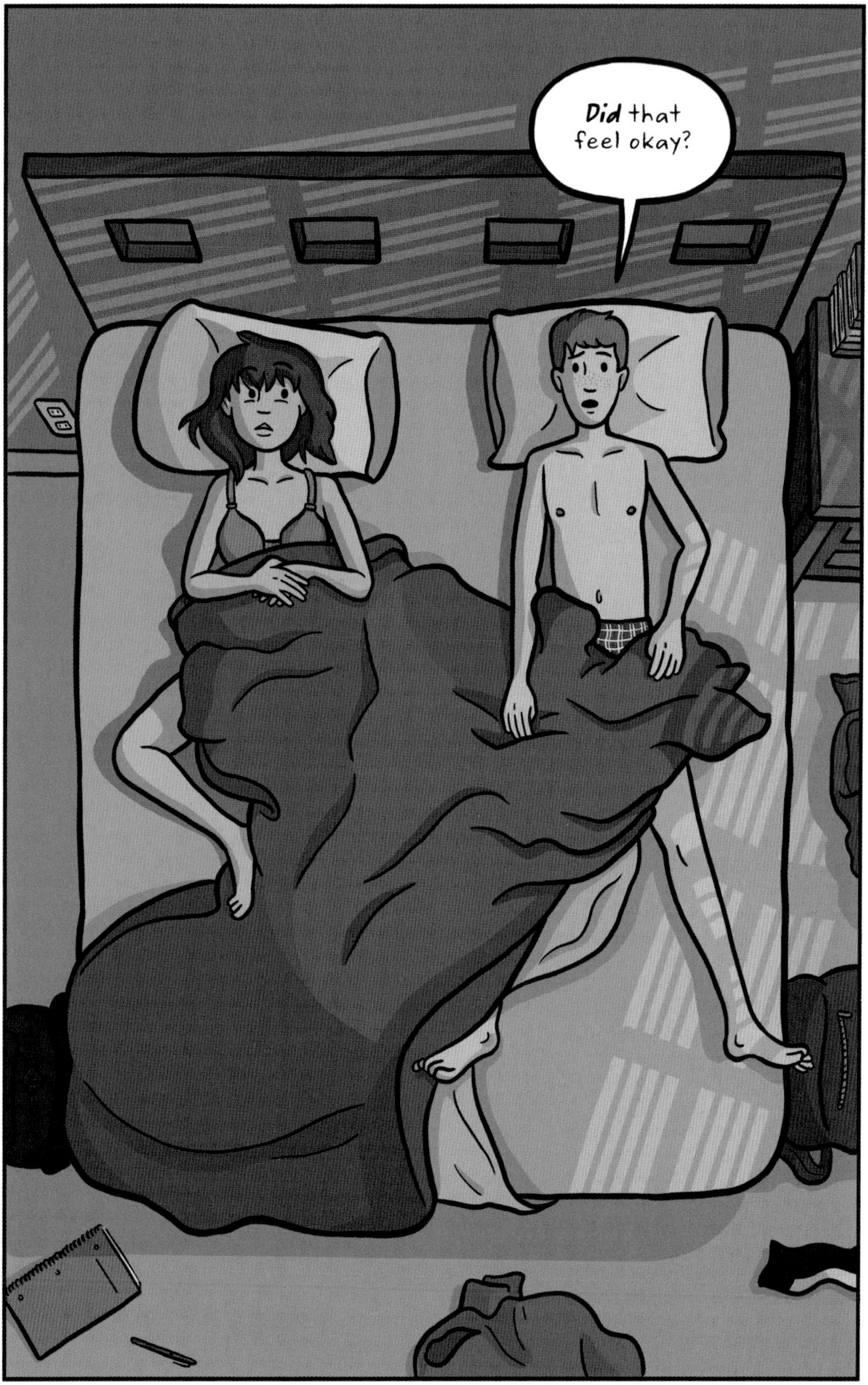
Did that feel okay?

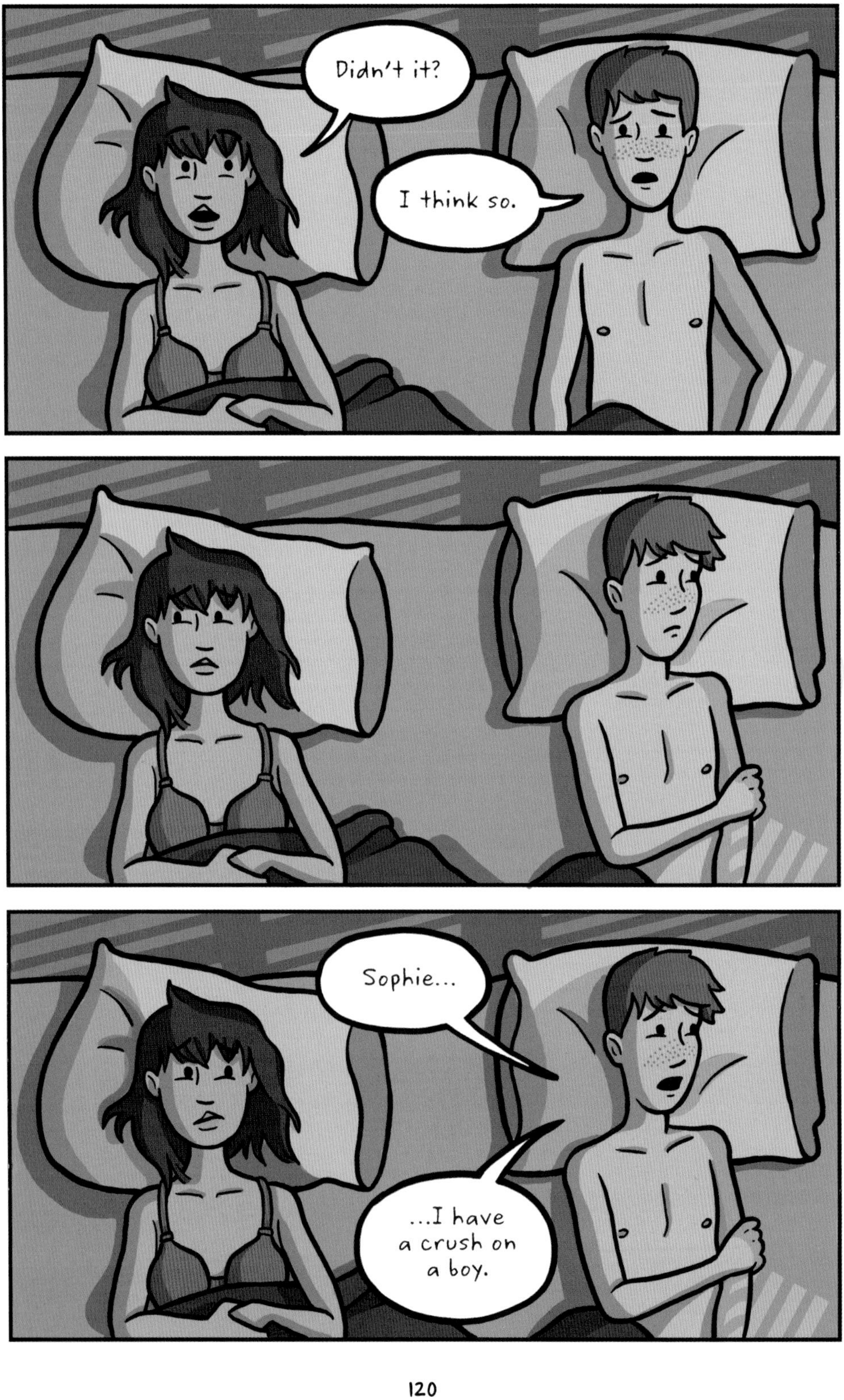
Didn't it?
I think so.
Sophie...
...I have a crush on a boy.

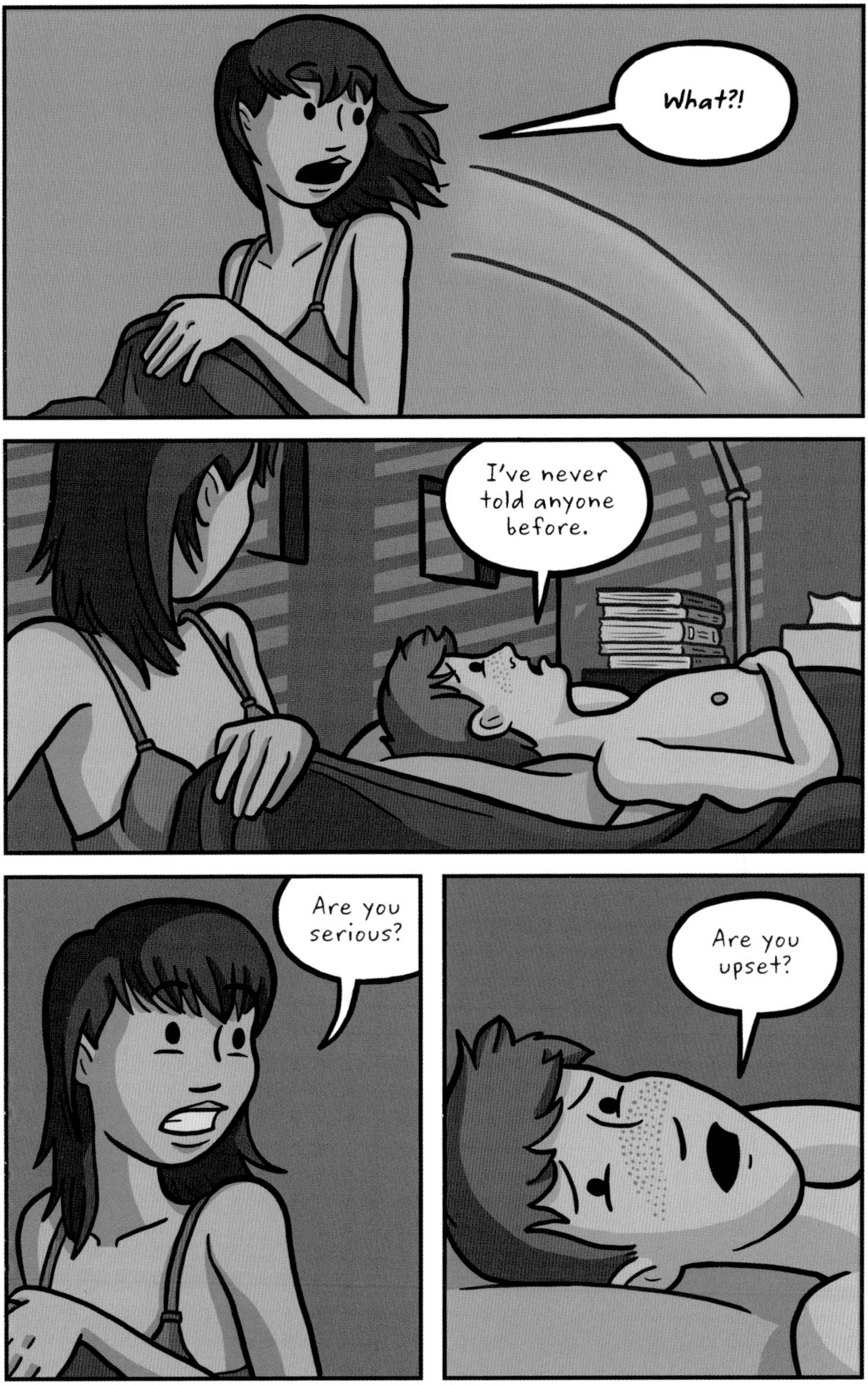
What?!
I've never told anyone before.
Are you serious?
Are you upset?

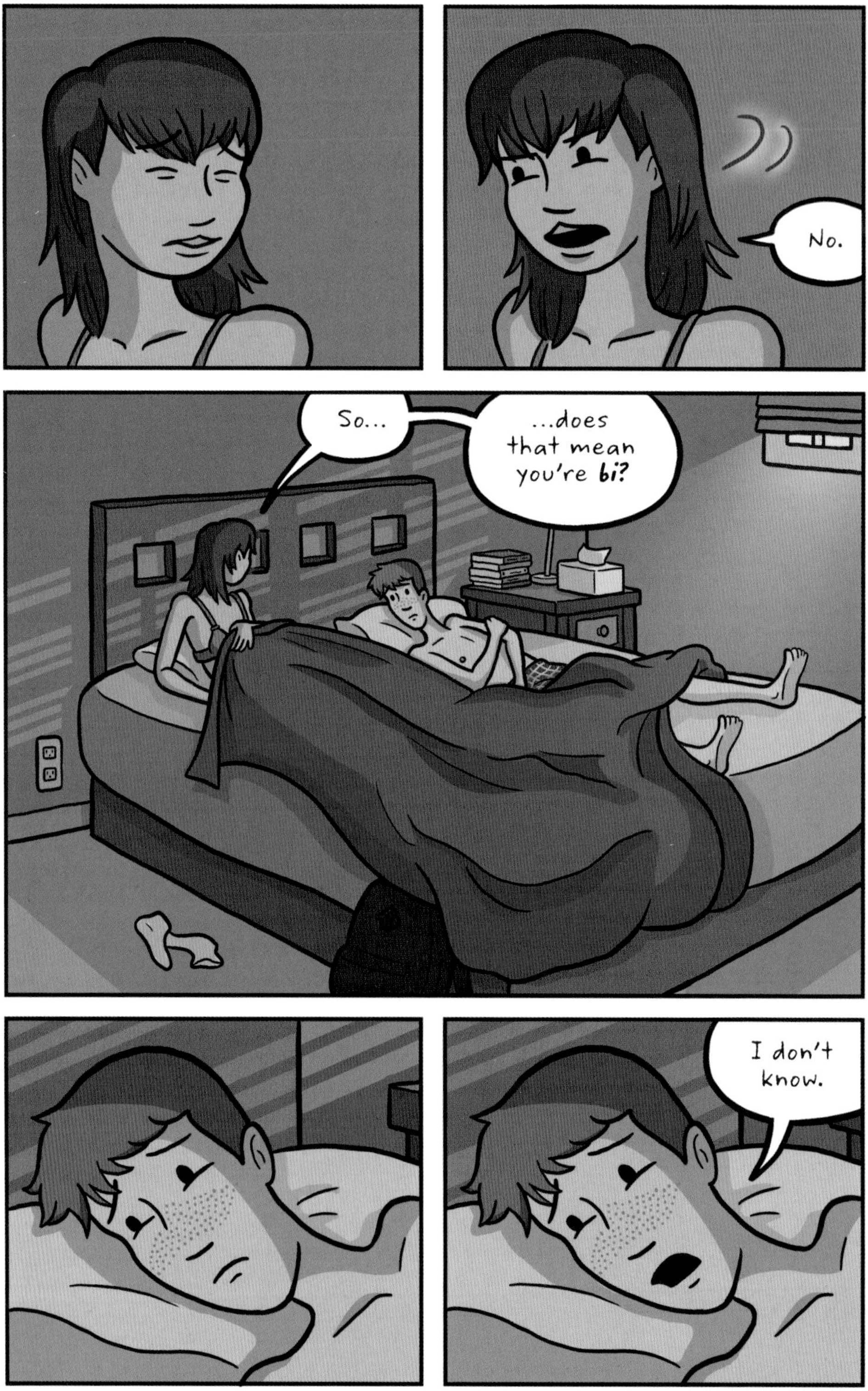
No.
So...
...does that mean you're **bi?**
I don't know.

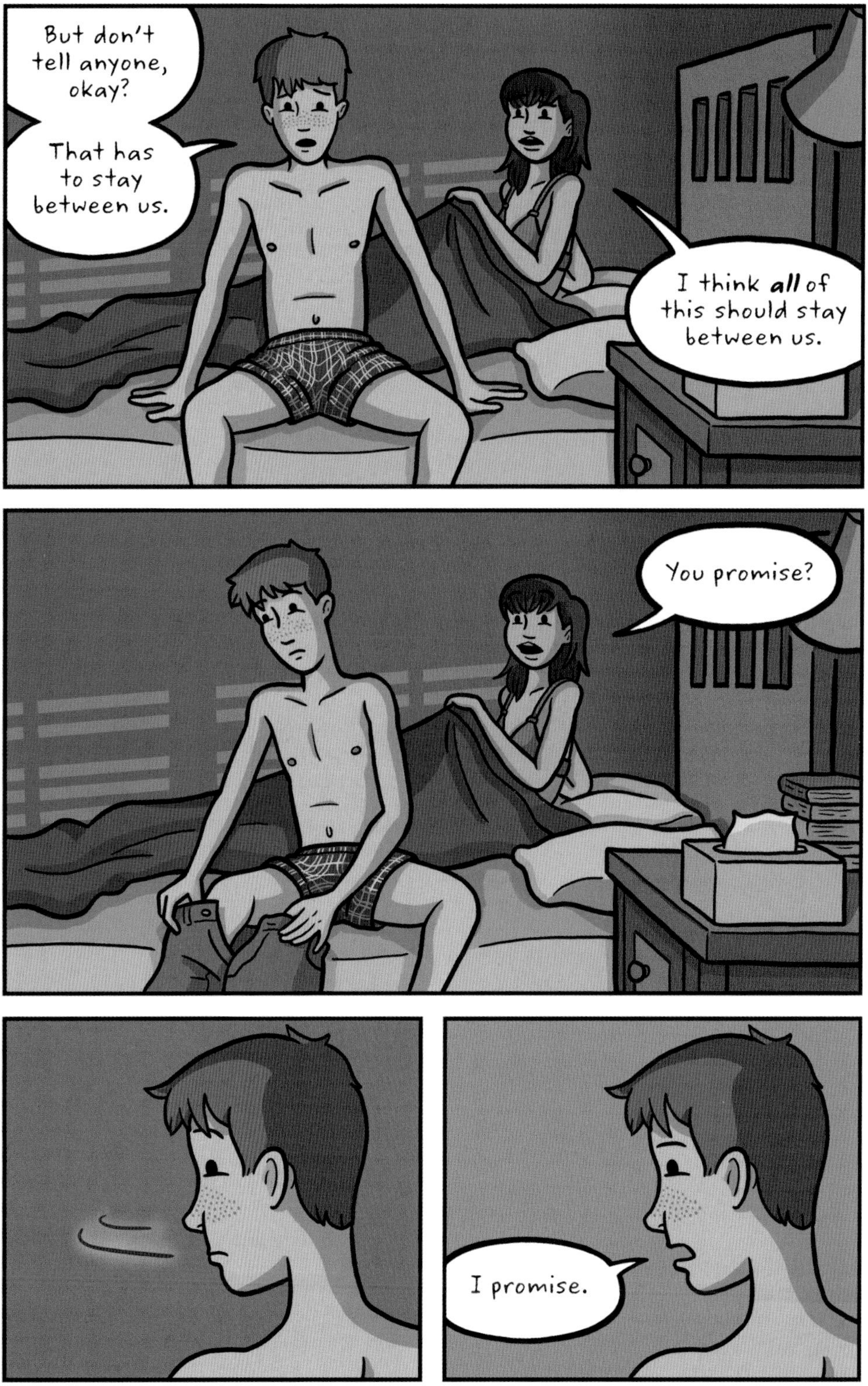
But don't tell anyone, okay?
That has to stay between us.
I think **all** of this should stay between us.
You promise?
I promise.

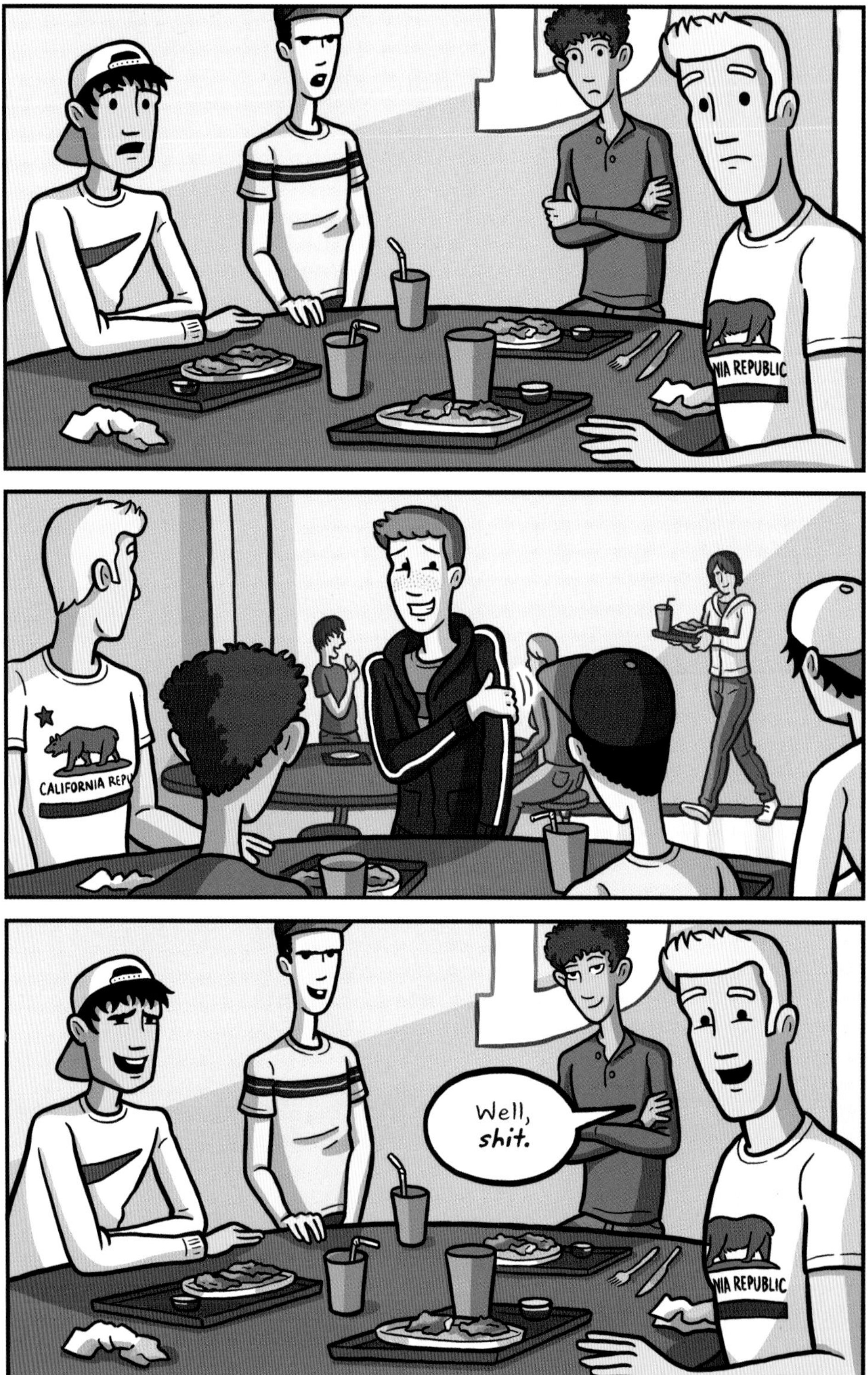

NIA REPUBLIC
CALIFORNIA REPU
Well, **shit.**
NIA REPUBLIC

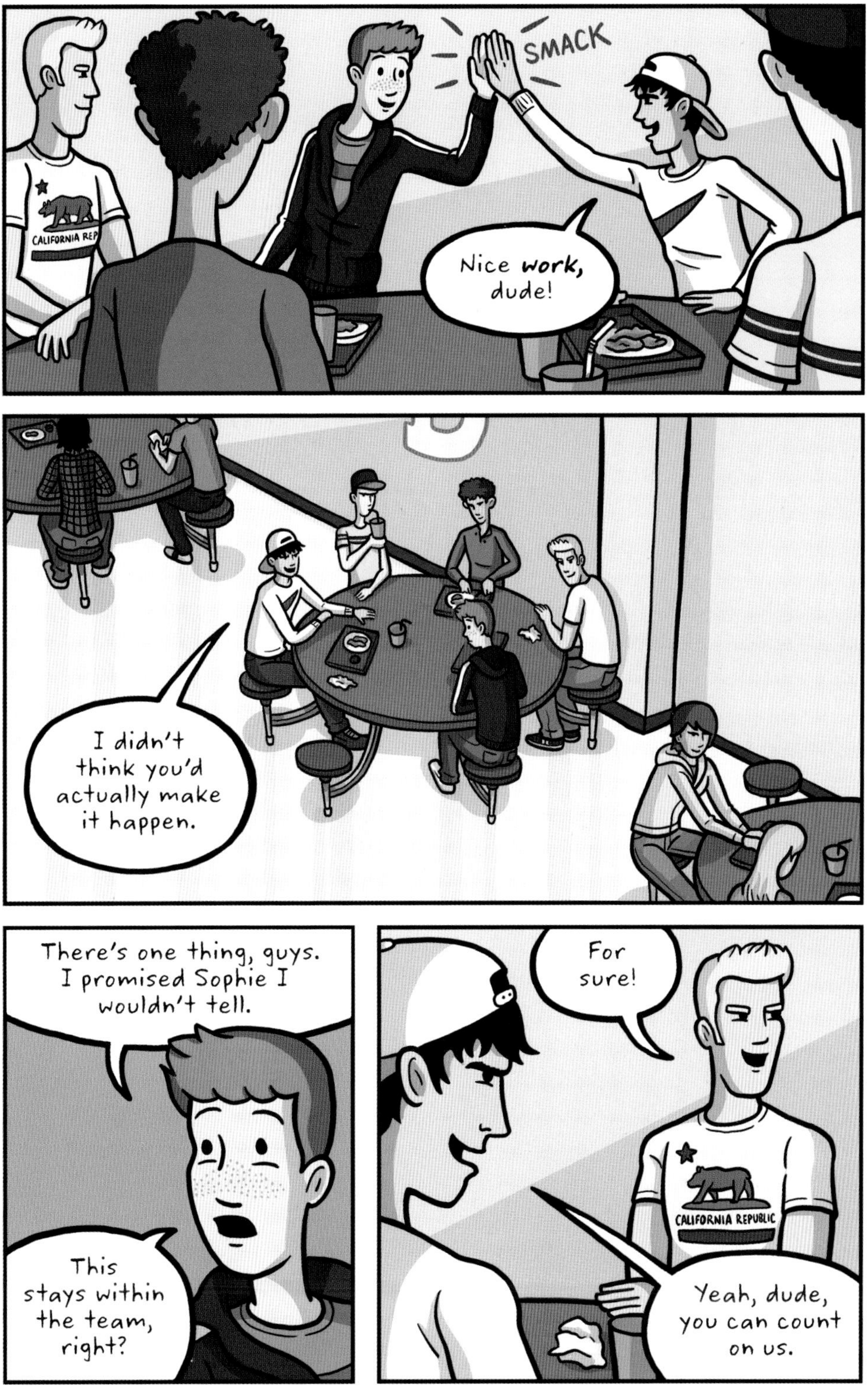
SMACK
Nice work, dude!
CALIFORNIA REP
I didn't think you'd actually make it happen.
There's one thing, guys. I promised Sophie I wouldn't tell.
This stays within the team, right?
For sure!
CALIFORNIA REPUBLIC
Yeah, dude, you can count on us.

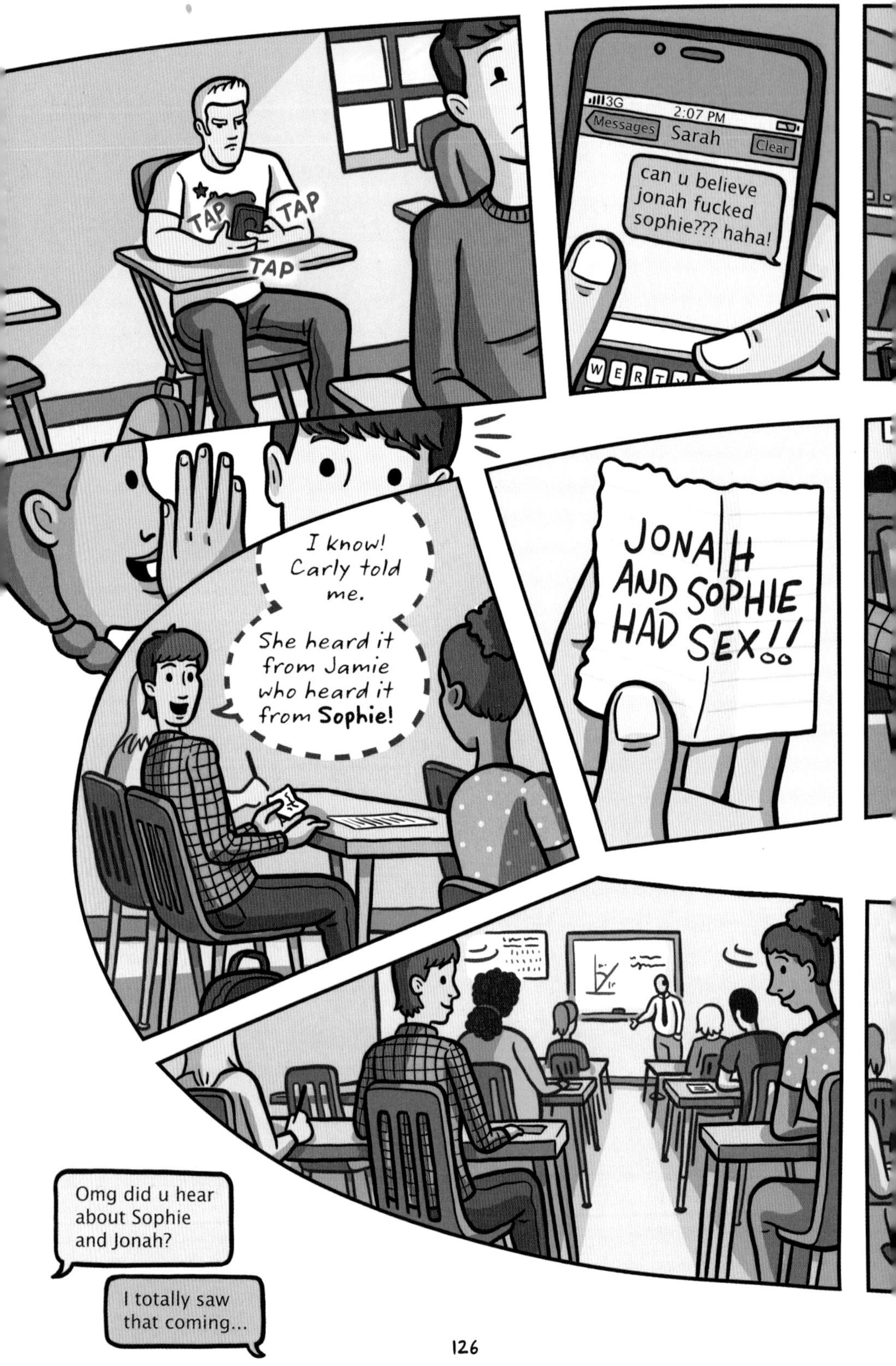
TAP
TAP
TAP
2:07 PM
Messages
Sarah
Clear
can u believe jonah fucked sophie??? haha!
I know! Carly told me.
She heard it from Jamie who heard it from **Sophie**!
JONAH AND SOPHIE HAD SEX!!
Omg did u hear about Sophie and Jonah?
I totally saw that coming...

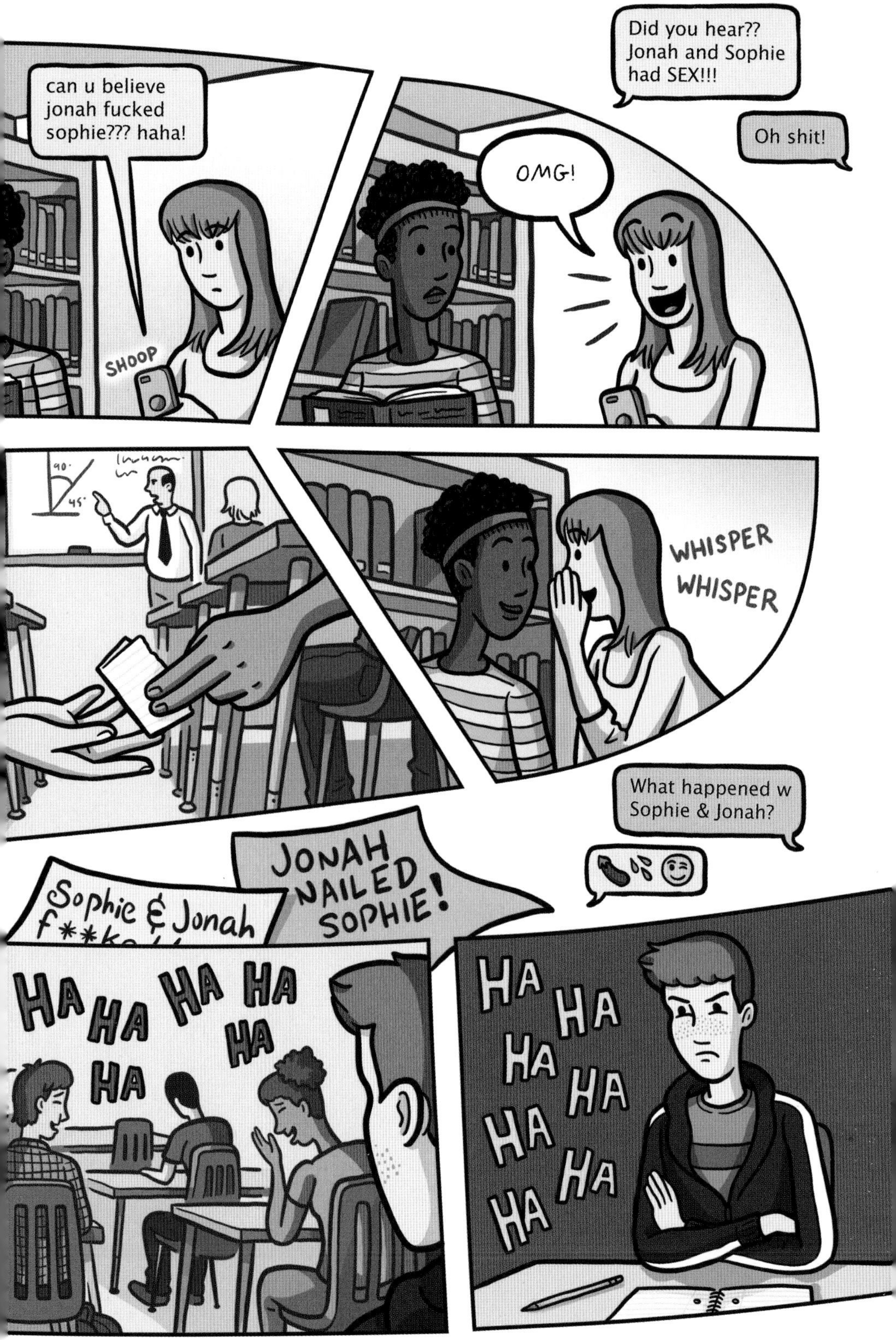
can u believe jonah fucked sophie??? haha!
SHOOP
Did you hear?? Jonah and Sophie had SEX!!!
Oh shit!
OMG!
WHISPER
WHISPER
What happened w Sophie & Jonah?
JONAH NAILED SOPHIE!
Sophie & Jonah
HA HA HA HA HA HA HA
HA HA HA HA HA HA HA HA

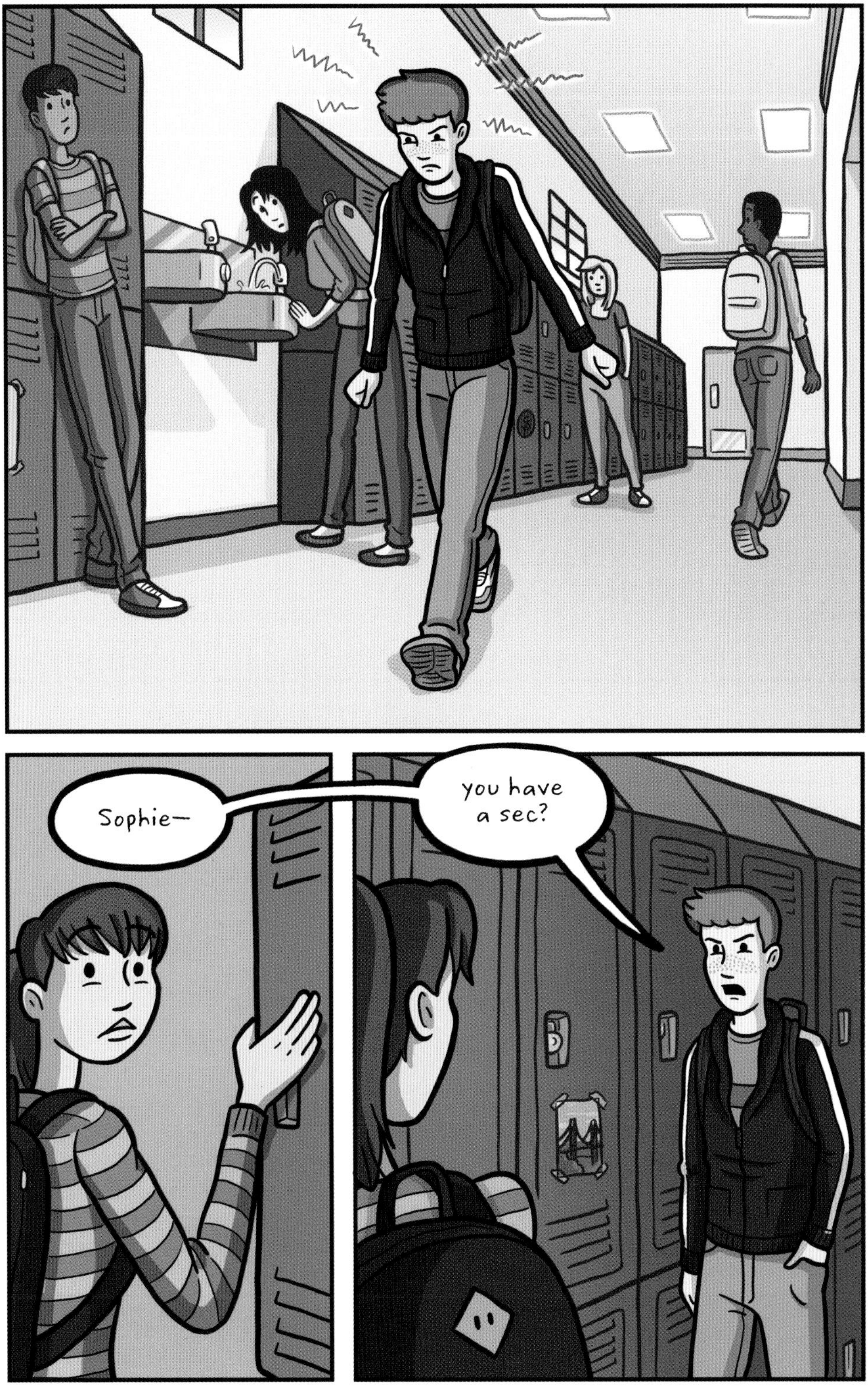
Sophie—
you have a sec?

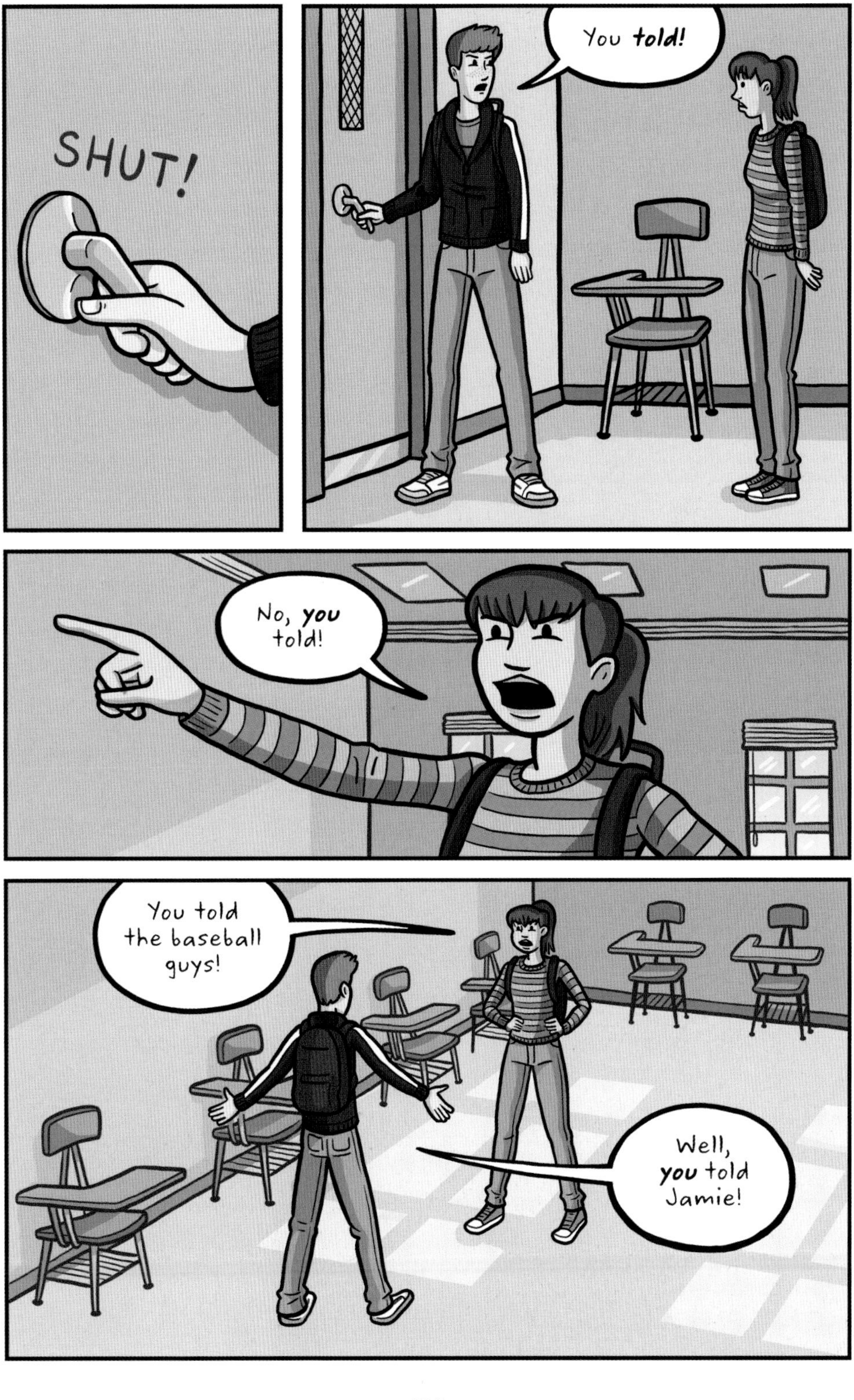
SHUT!
You **told!**
No, ***you*** told!
You told the baseball guys!
Well, ***you*** told Jamie!

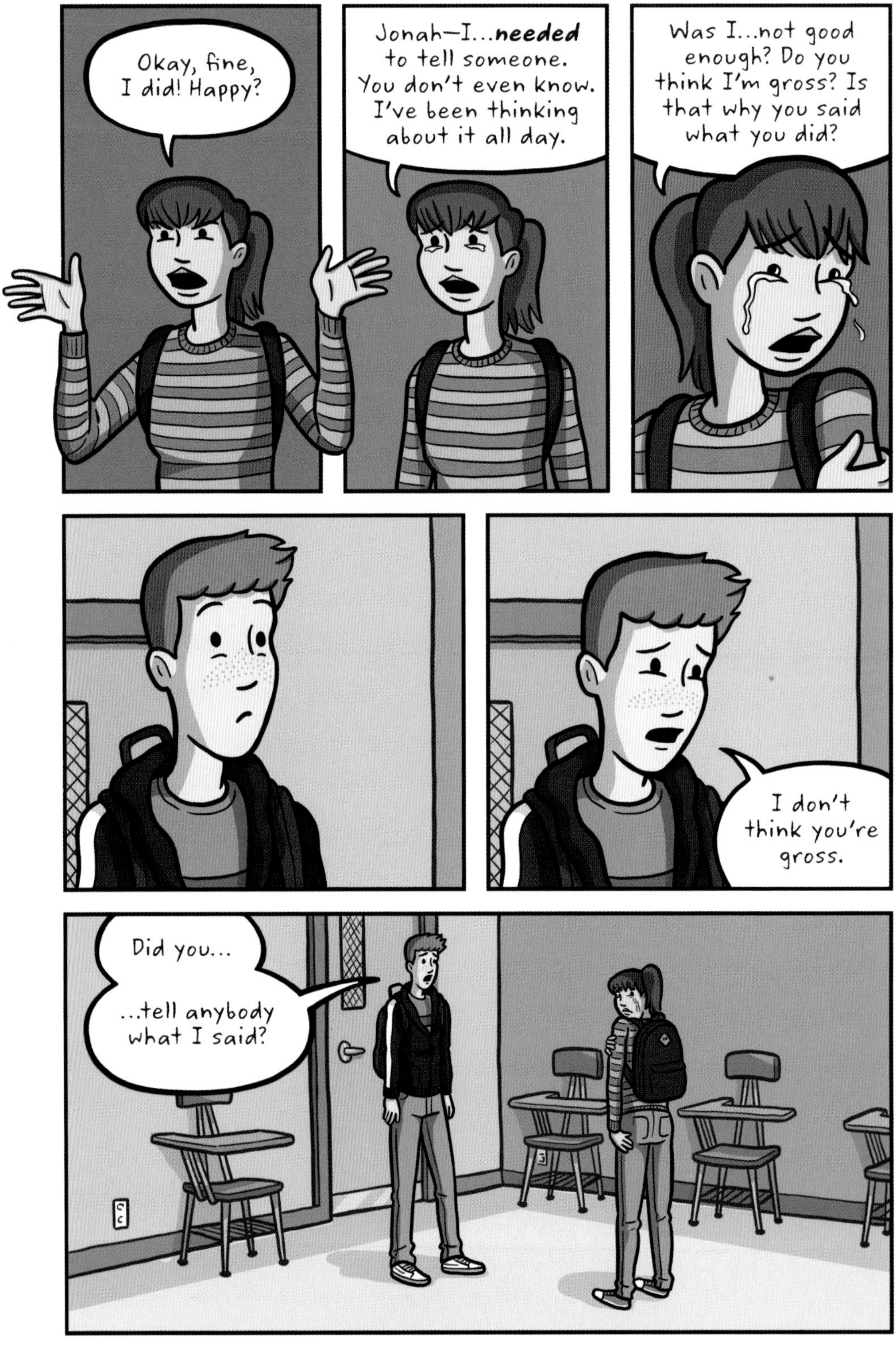

Okay, fine, I did! Happy?
Jonah—I...**needed** to tell someone. You don't even know. I've been thinking about it all day.
Was I...not good enough? Do you think I'm gross? Is that why you said what you did?
I don't think you're gross.
Did you...
...tell anybody what I said?

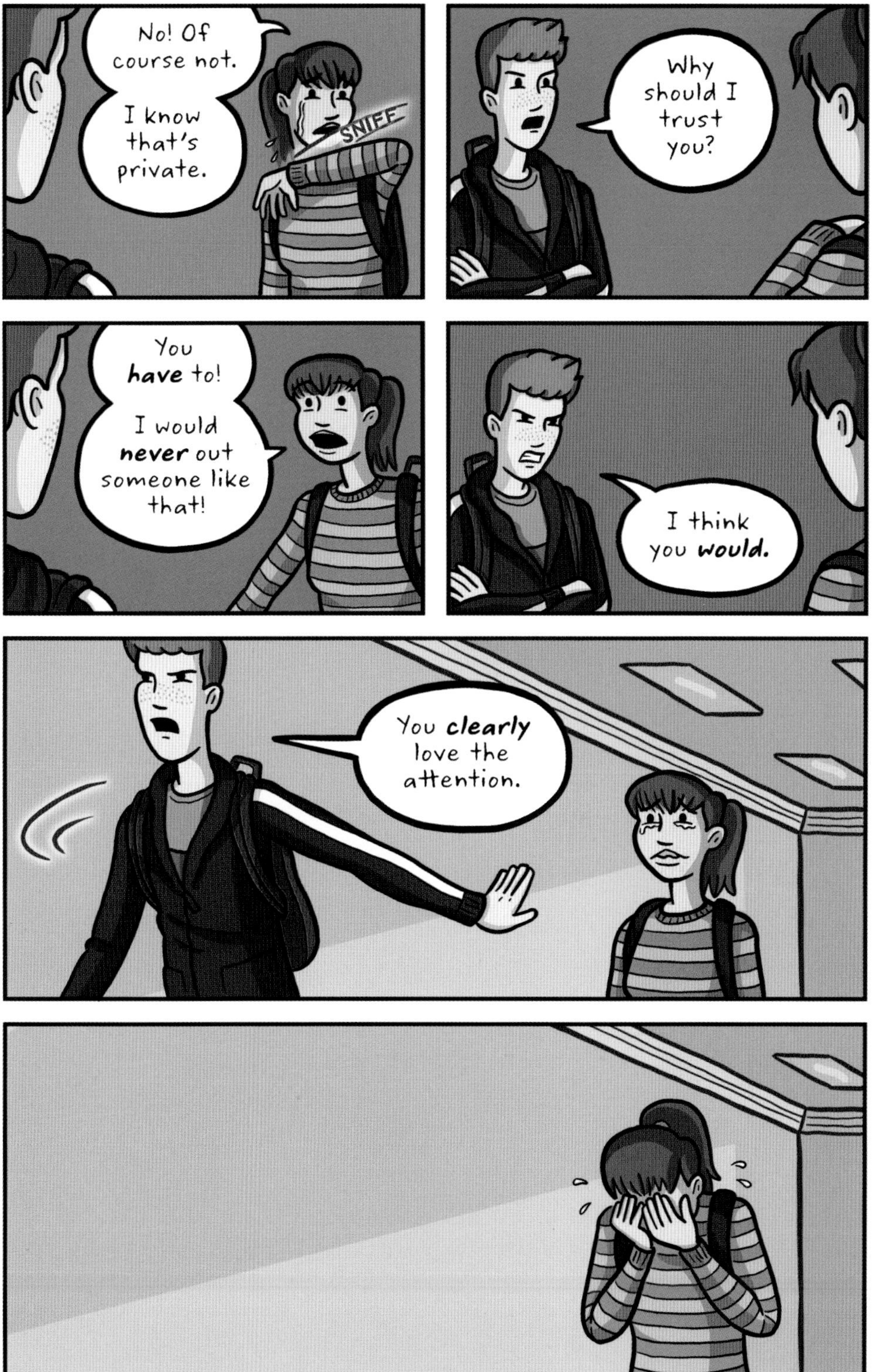
No! Of course not.
I know that's private.
SNIFF
Why should I trust you?
You **have** to!
I would **never** out someone like that!
I think you **would.**
You **clearly** love the attention.

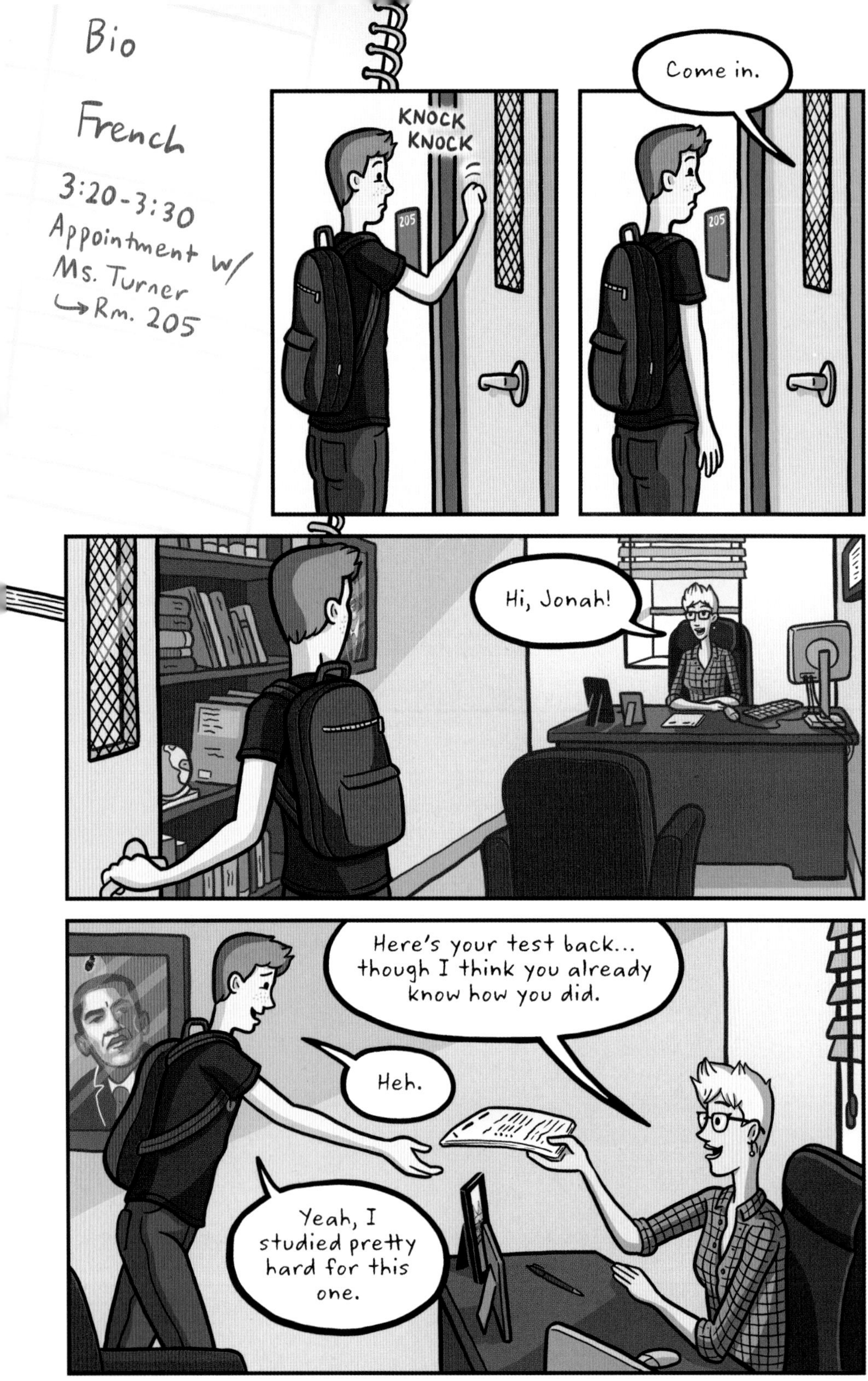
Bio
French
3:20-3:30
Appointment w/
Ms. Turner
→ Rm. 205
KNOCK
KNOCK
205
Come in.
205
Hi, Jonah!
Here's your test back... though I think you already know how you did.
Heh.
Yeah, I studied pretty hard for this one.

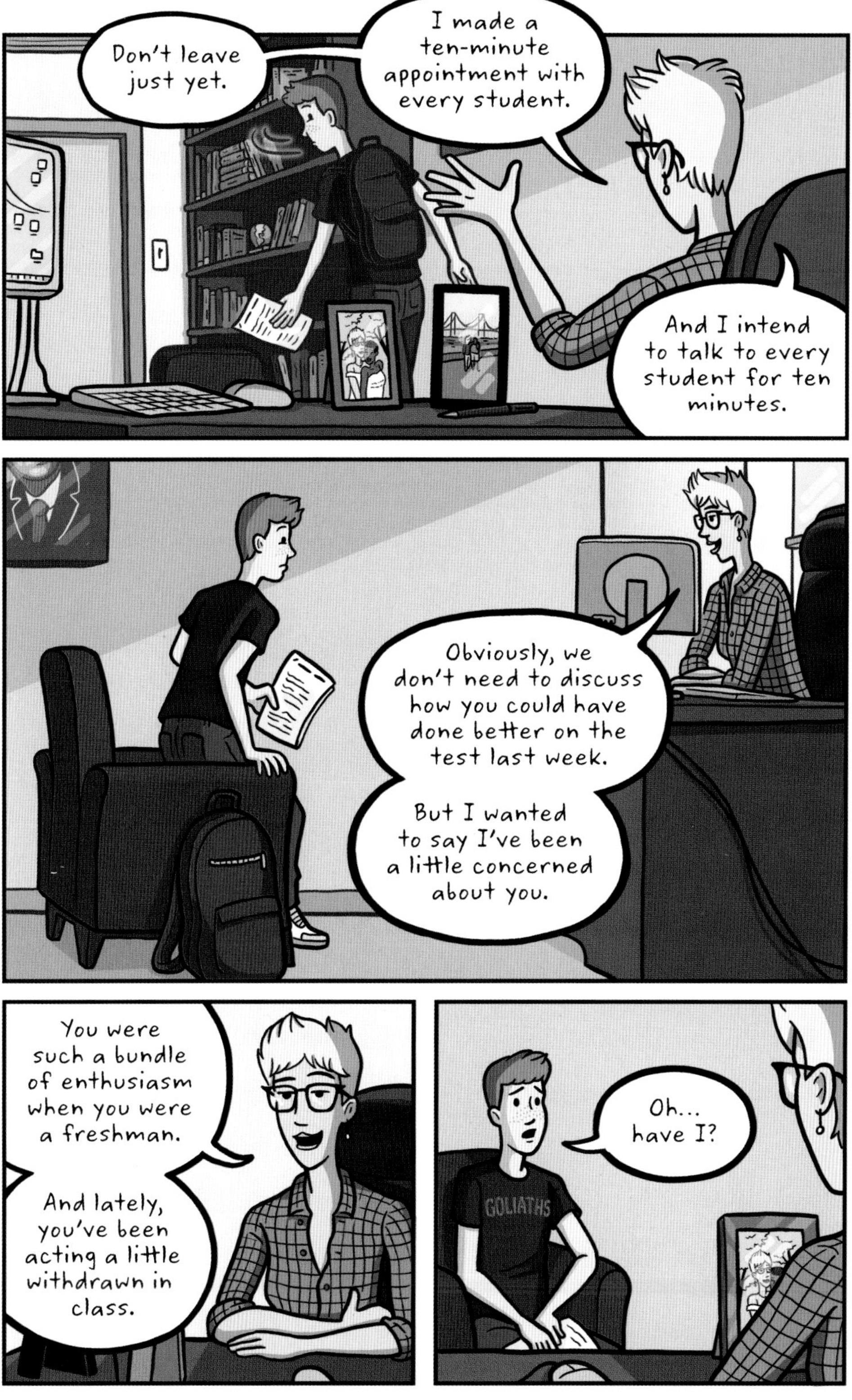
Don't leave just yet.
I made a ten-minute appointment with every student.
And I intend to talk to every student for ten minutes.
Obviously, we don't need to discuss how you could have done better on the test last week.
But I wanted to say I've been a little concerned about you.
You were such a bundle of enthusiasm when you were a freshman.
And lately, you've been acting a little withdrawn in class.
GOLIATHS
Oh... have I?

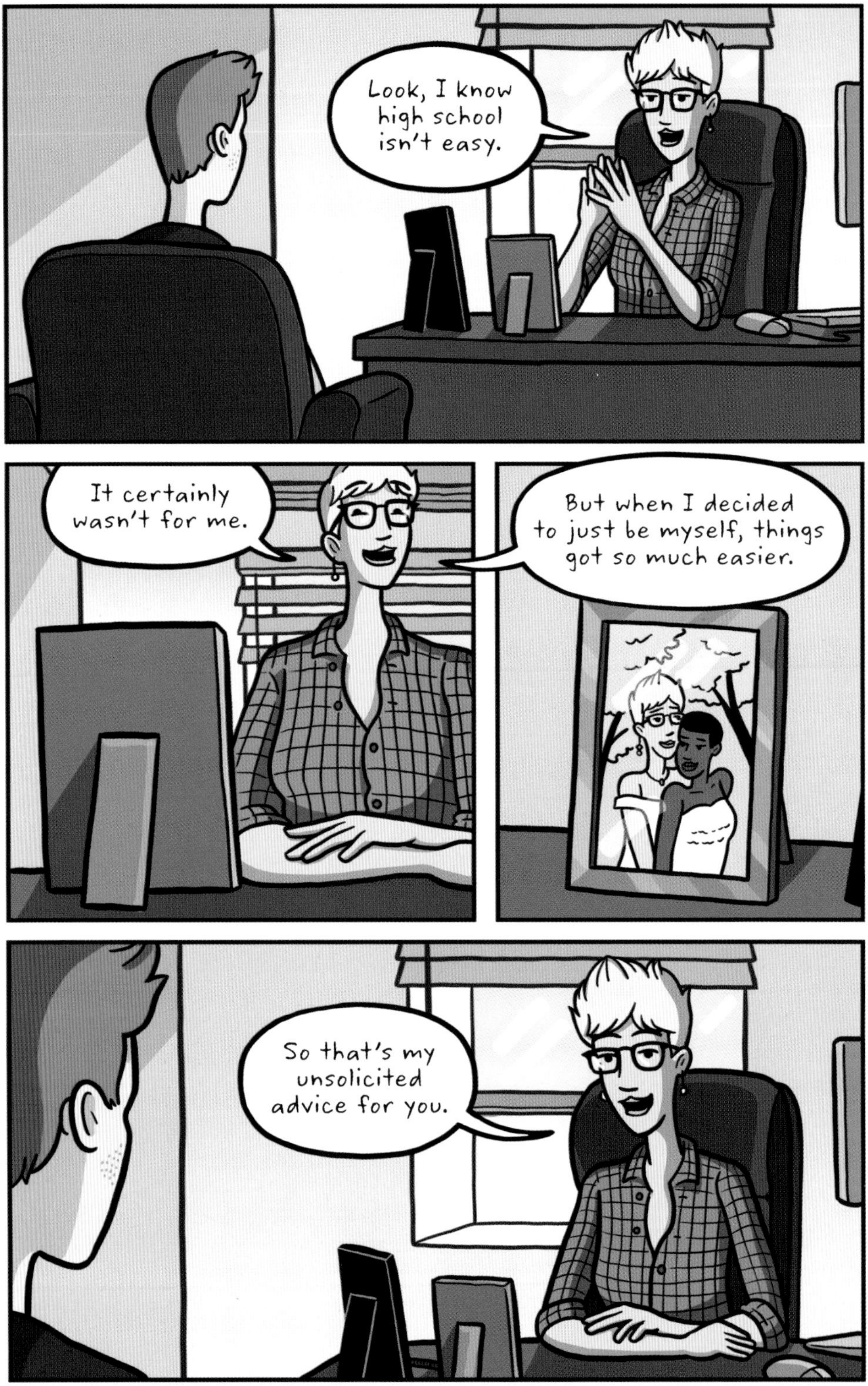
Look, I know high school isn't easy.
It certainly wasn't for me.
But when I decided to just be myself, things got so much easier.
So that's my unsolicited advice for you.

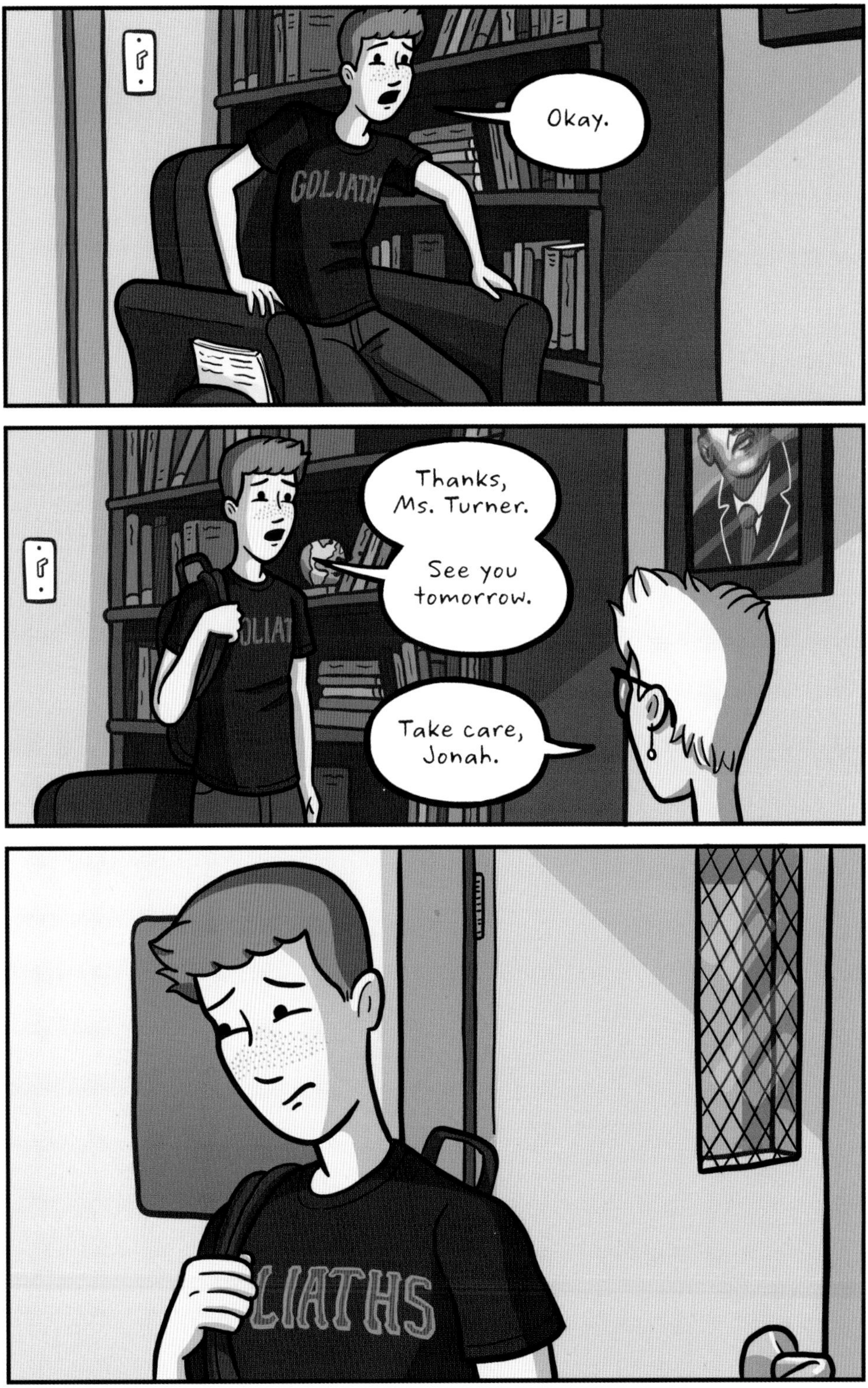
GOLIATH
Okay.
Thanks, Ms. Turner.
See you tomorrow.
Take care, Jonah.

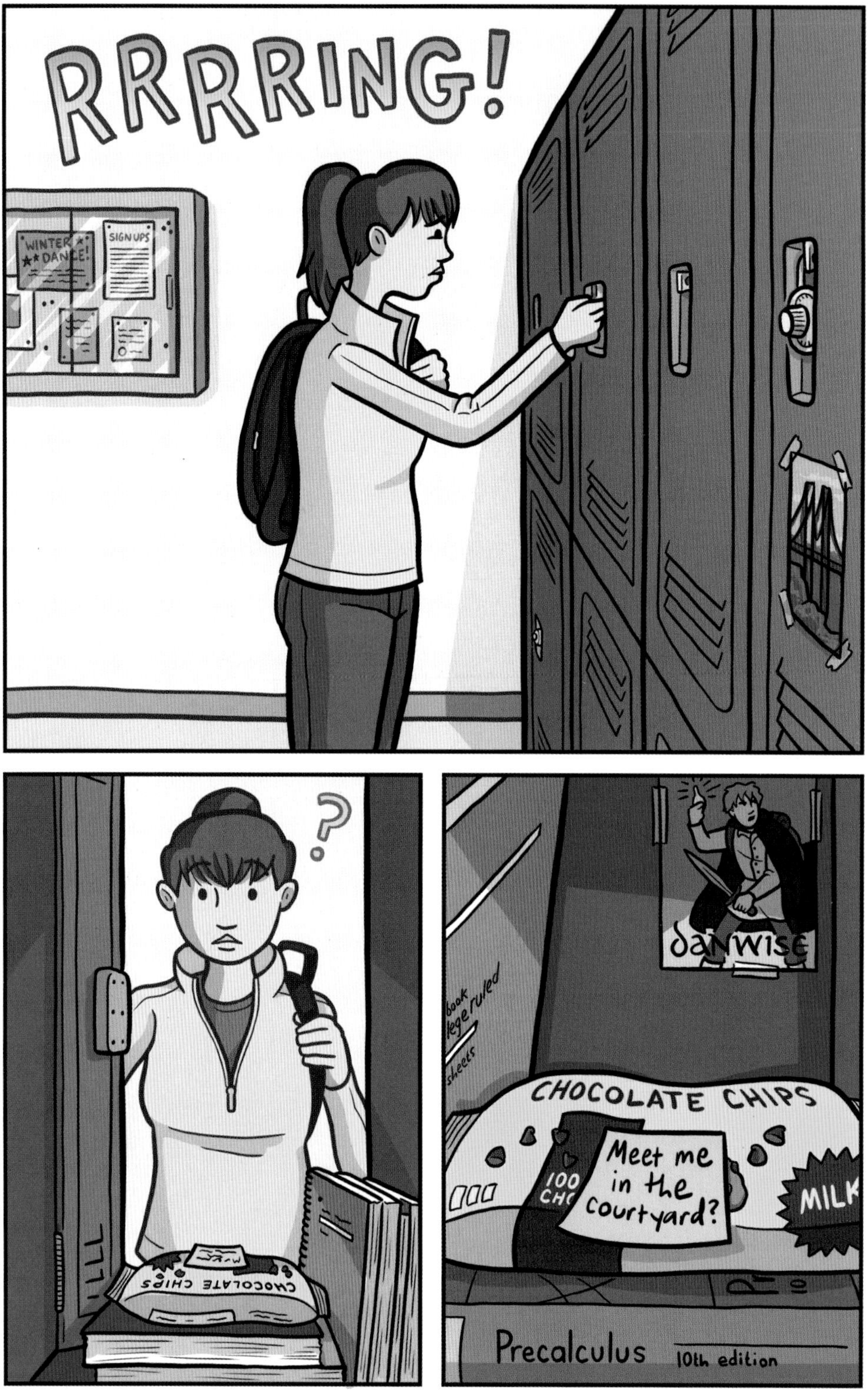
RRRRING!
WINTER DANCE!
SIGN UPS
?
CHOCOLATE CHIPS
danwise
CHOCOLATE CHIPS
Meet me in the courtyard?
MILK
Precalculus
10th edition

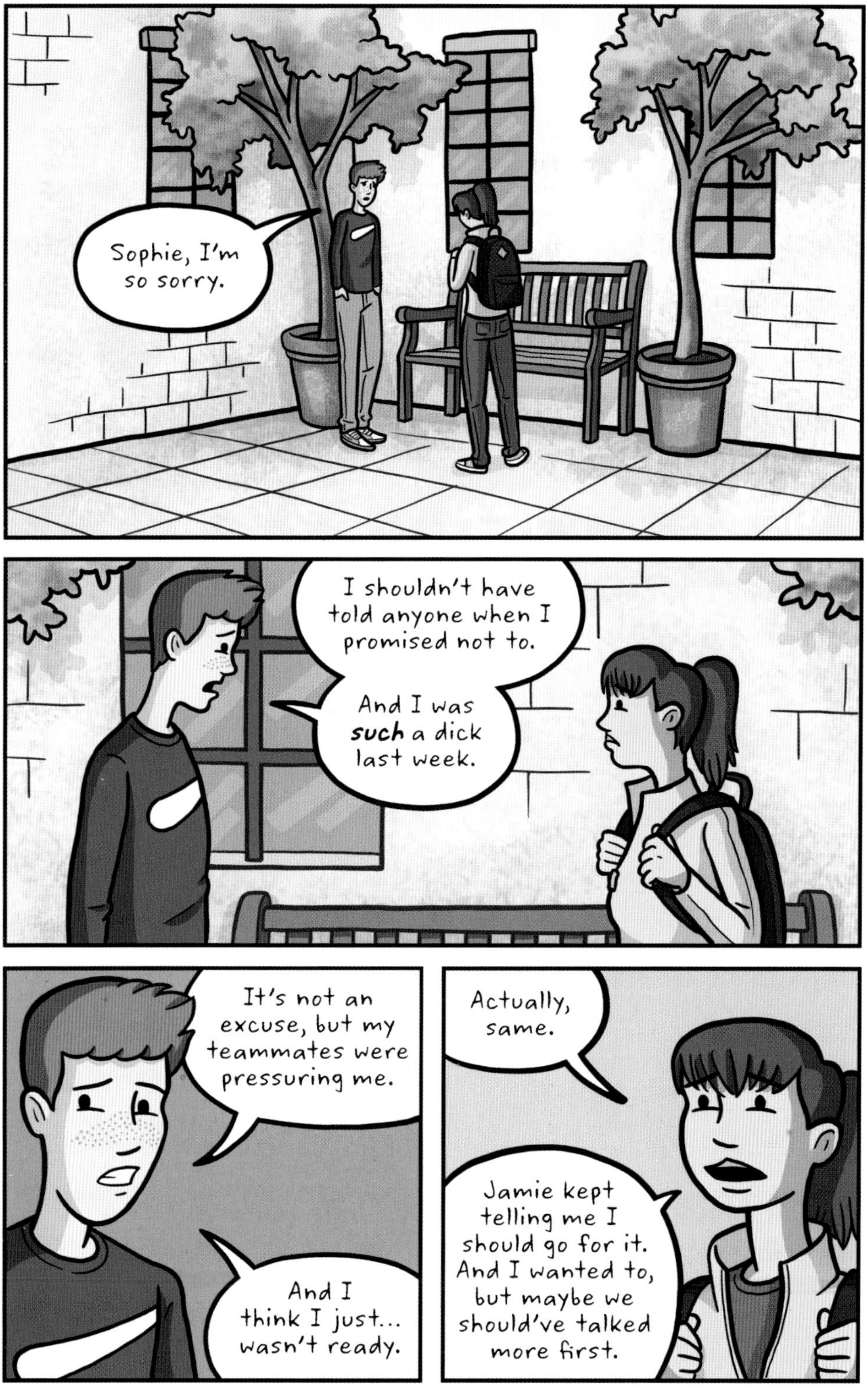
Sophie, I'm so sorry.
I shouldn't have told anyone when I promised not to.
And I was **such** a dick last week.
It's not an excuse, but my teammates were pressuring me.
And I think I just... wasn't ready.
Actually, same.
Jamie kept telling me I should go for it. And I wanted to, but maybe we should've talked more first.

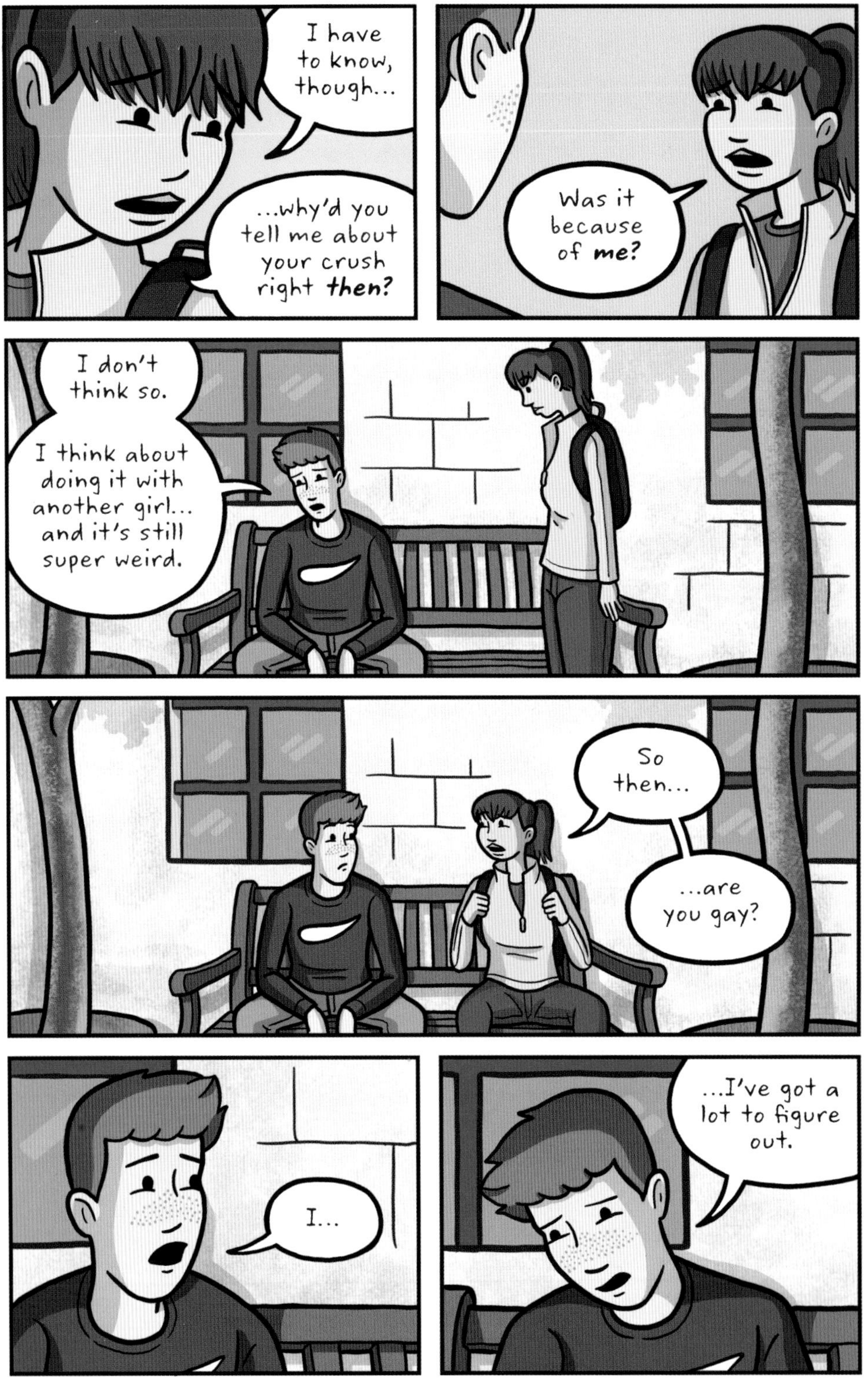
I have to know, though...
...why'd you tell me about your crush right **then?**
Was it because of **me?**
I don't think so.
I think about doing it with another girl... and it's still super weird.
So then...
...are you gay?
I...
...I've got a lot to figure out.

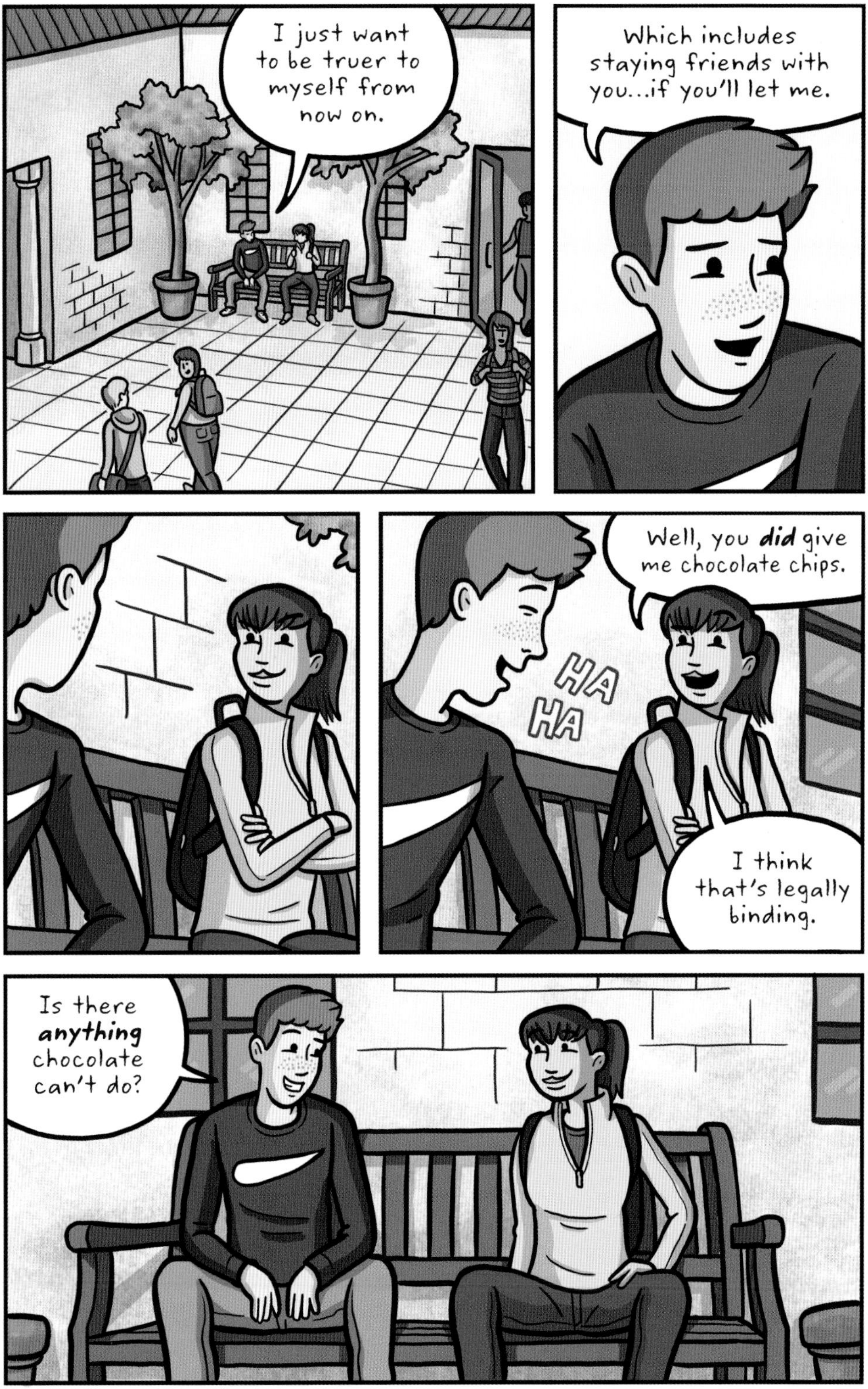
I just want to be truer to myself from now on.
Which includes staying friends with you...if you'll let me.
Well, you **did** give me chocolate chips.
HA HA
I think that's legally binding.
Is there **anything** chocolate can't do?

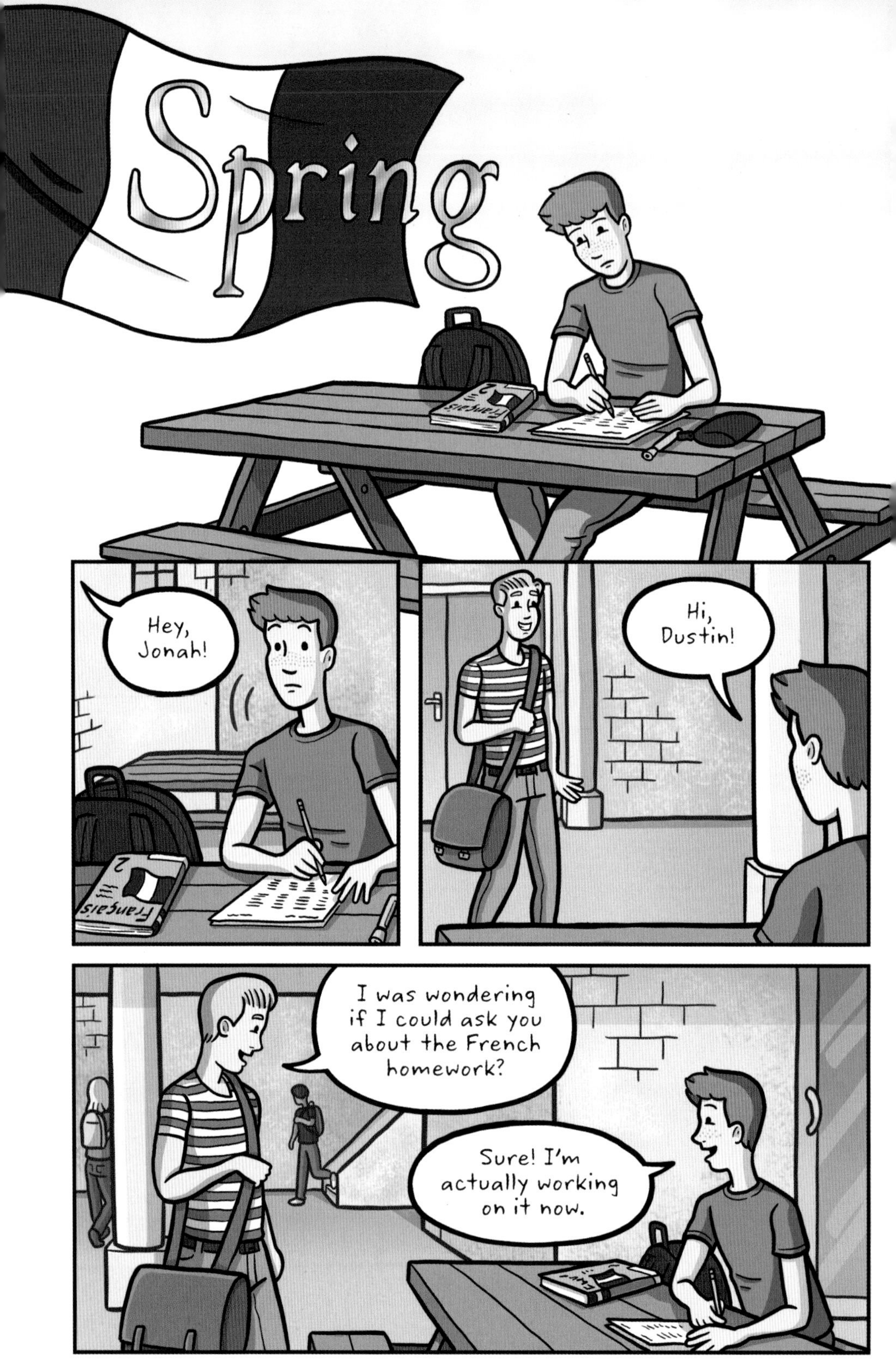
Spring
Français 2
Hey, Jonah!
Hi, Dustin!
I was wondering if I could ask you about the French homework?
Sure! I'm actually working on it now.

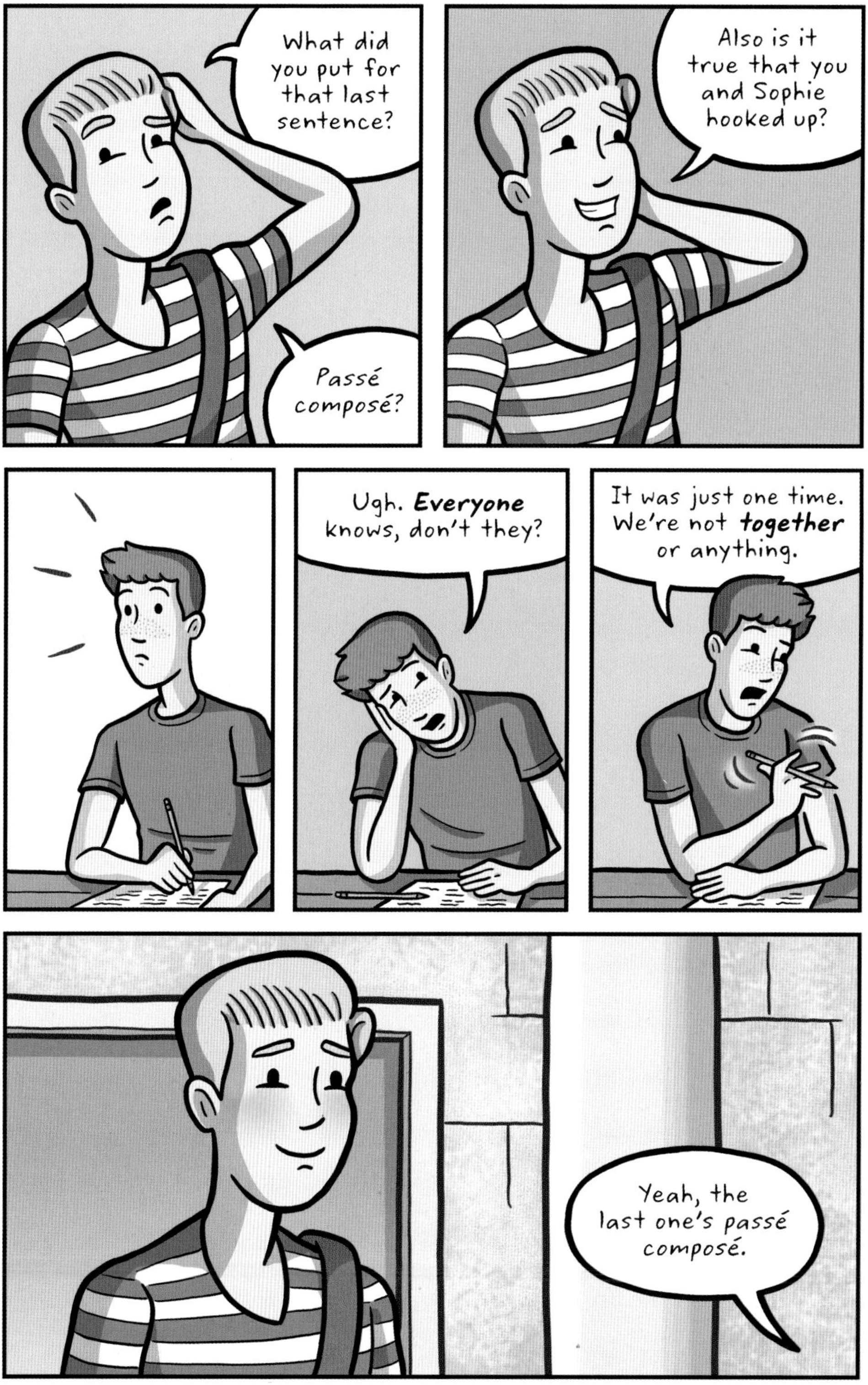
What did you put for that last sentence?
Passé composé?
Also is it true that you and Sophie hooked up?
Ugh. **Everyone** knows, don't they?
It was just one time. We're not **together** or anything.
Yeah, the last one's passé composé.

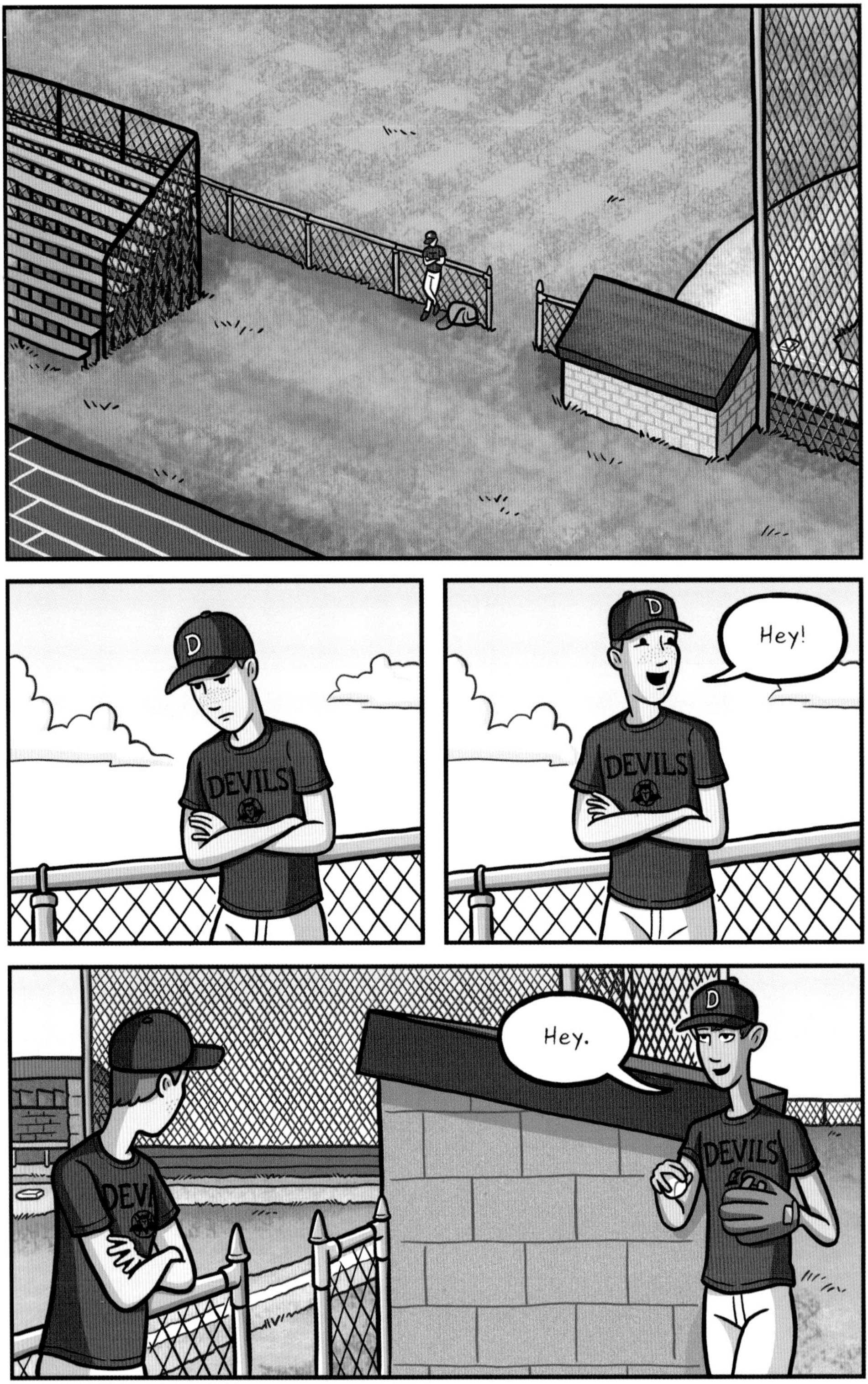
Hey!
Hey.

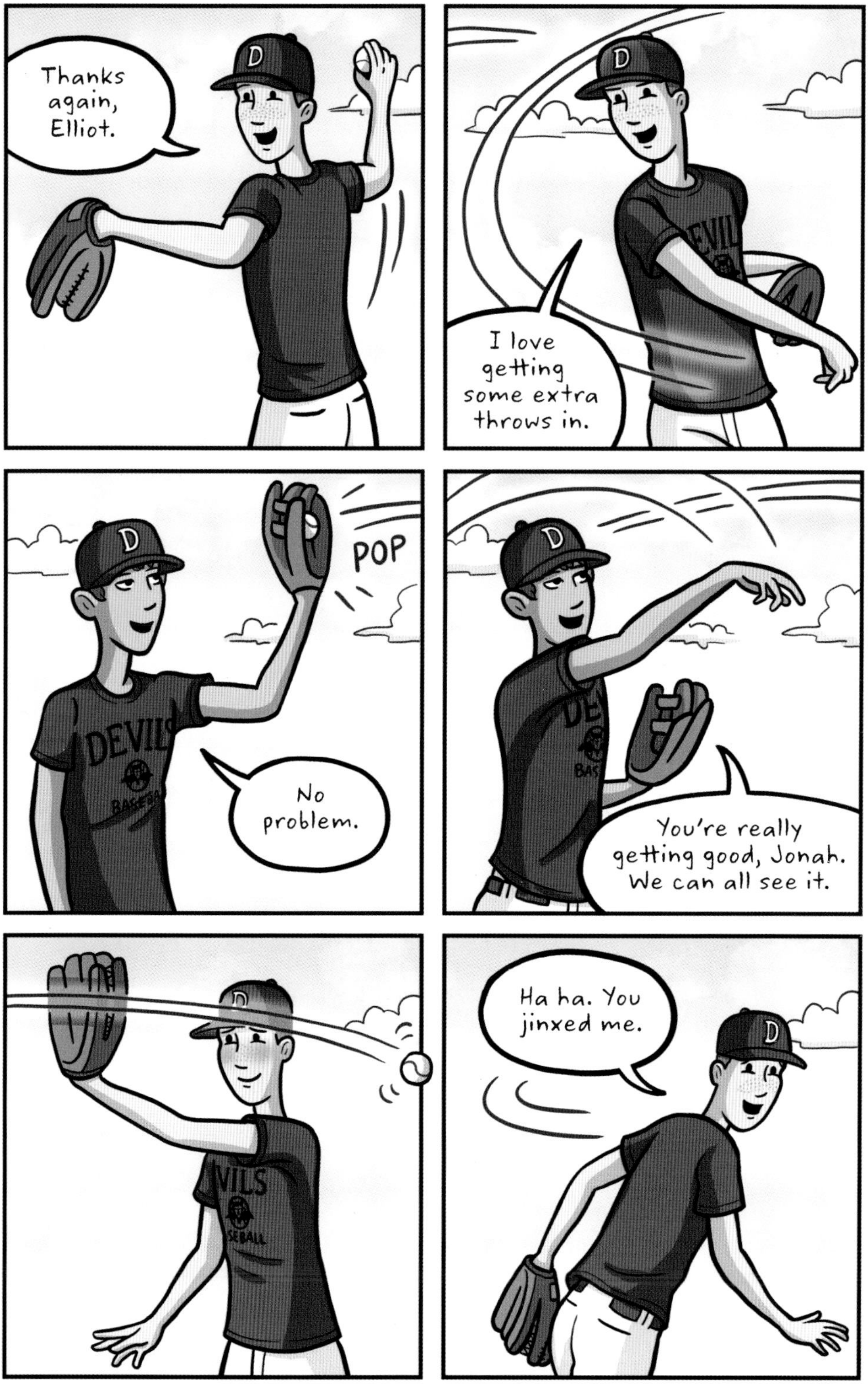
Thanks again, Elliot.
I love getting some extra throws in.
POP
No problem.
You're really getting good, Jonah. We can all see it.
Ha ha. You jinxed me.

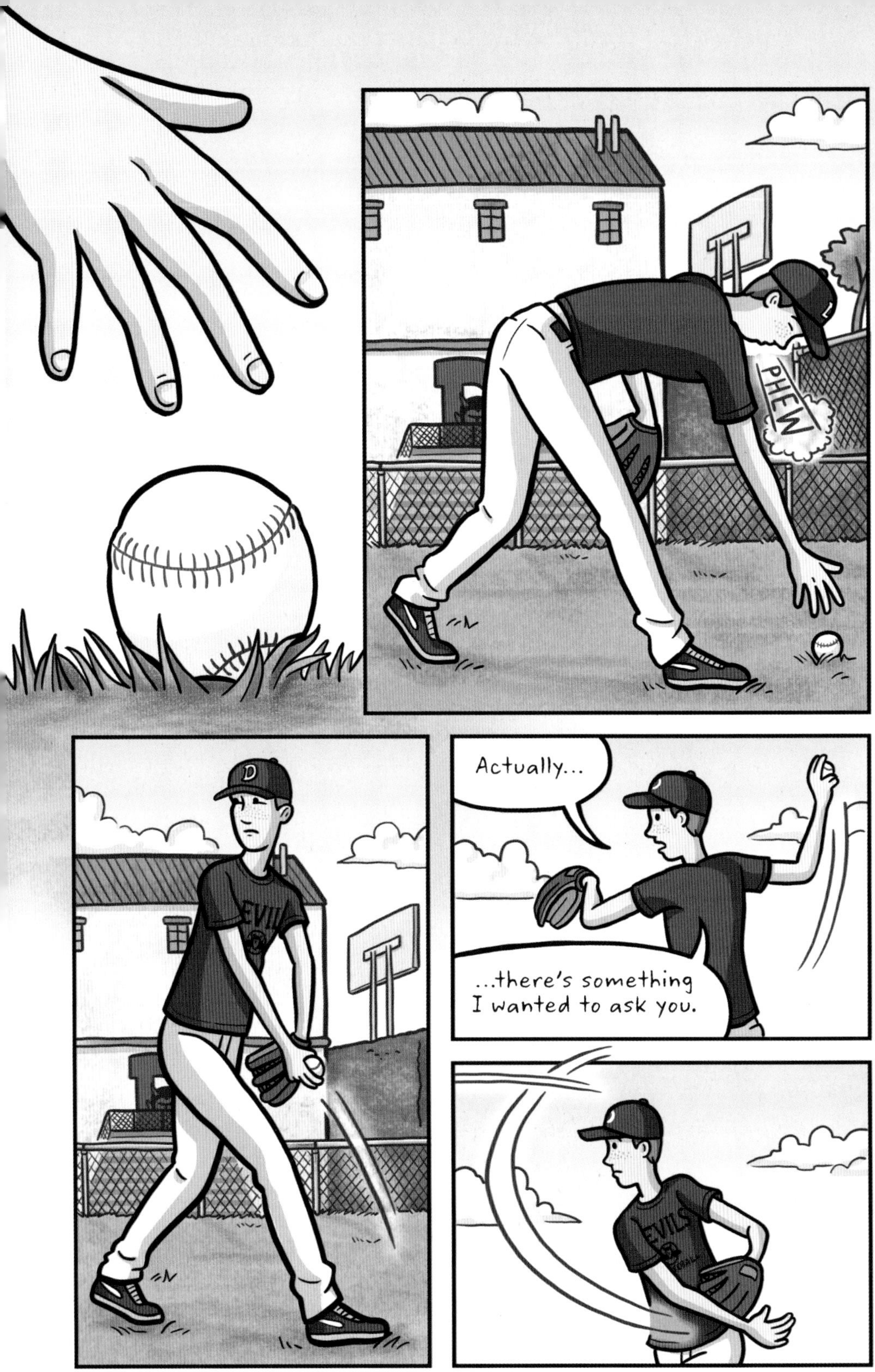
PHEW
Actually...
...there's something I wanted to ask you.

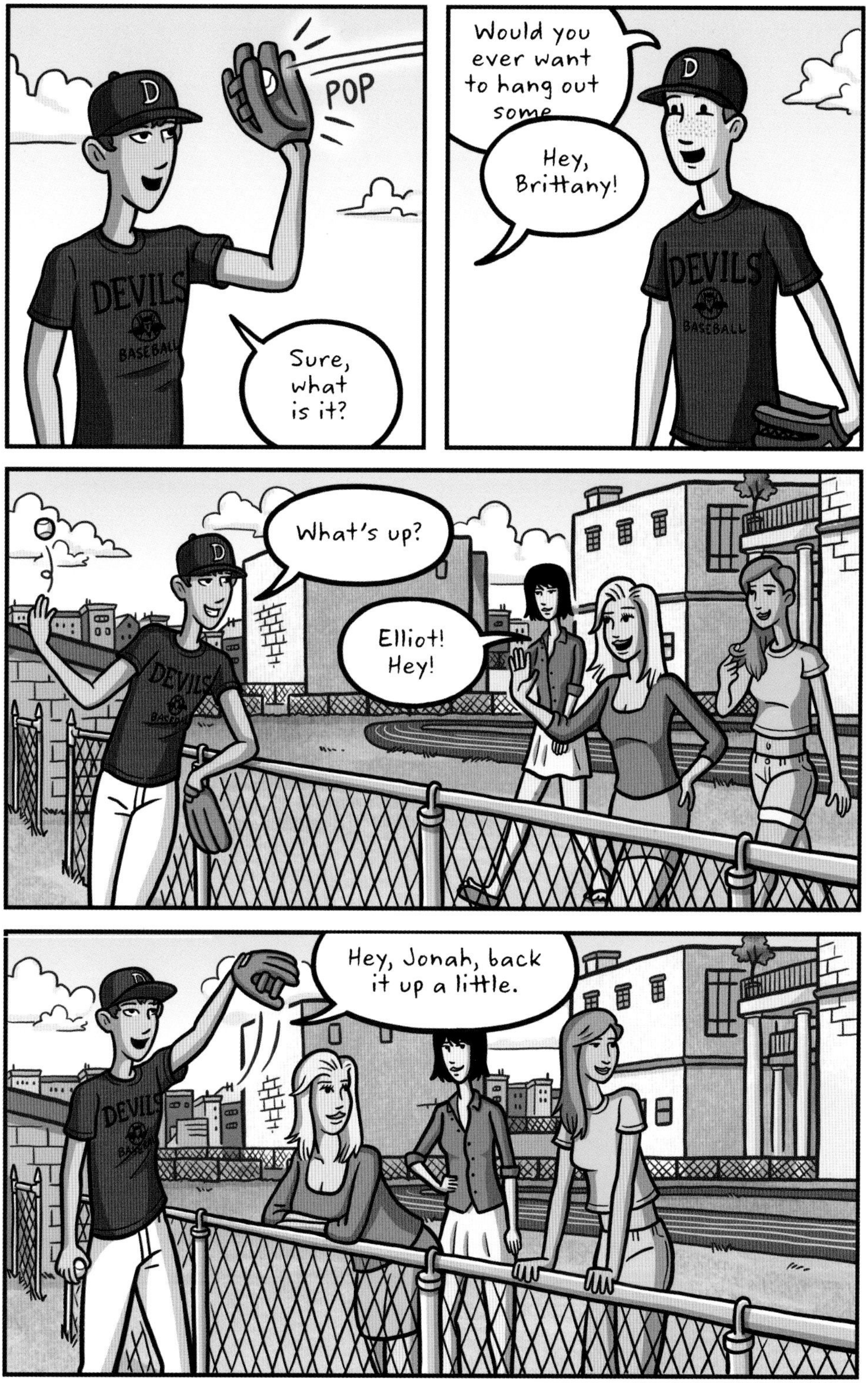
POP
Sure, what is it?
Would you ever want to hang out some
Hey, Brittany!
DEVILS BASEBALL
What's up?
Elliot! Hey!
Hey, Jonah, back it up a little.

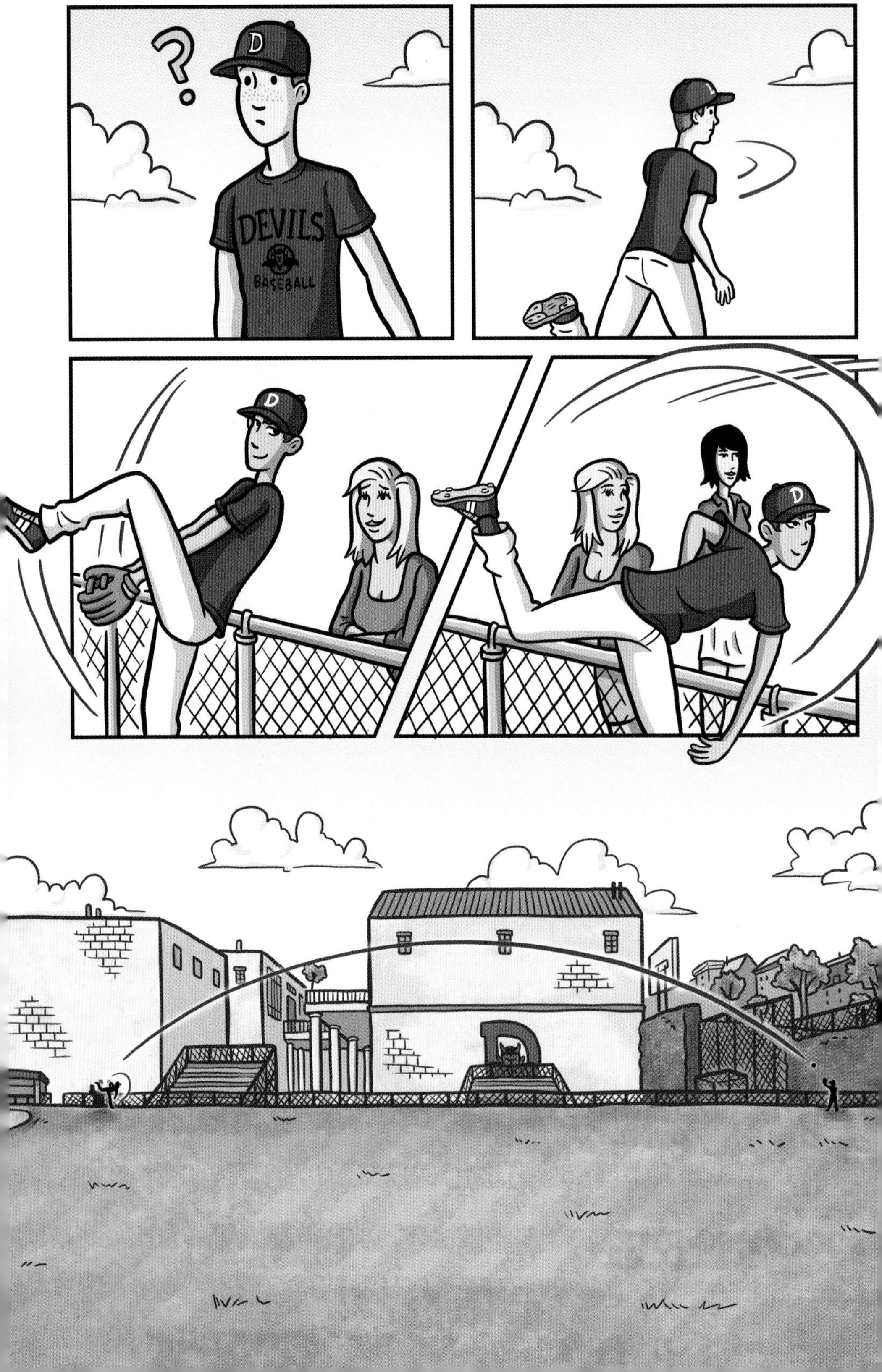
?
DEVILS
BASEBALL

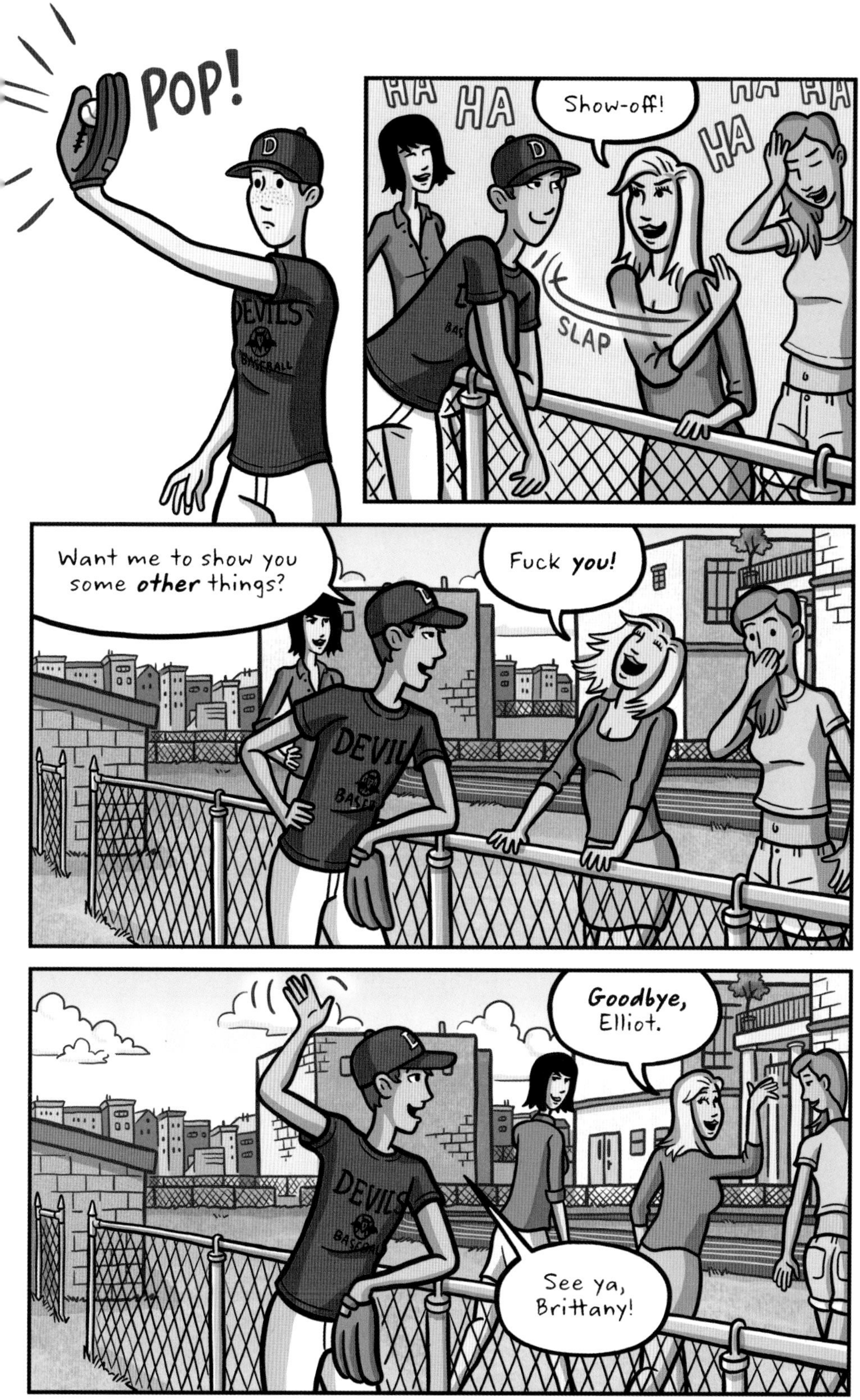
POP!
HA HA
Show-off!
HA HA HA
SLAP
Want me to show you some **other** things?
Fuck **you!**
Goodbye, Elliot.
See ya, Brittany!

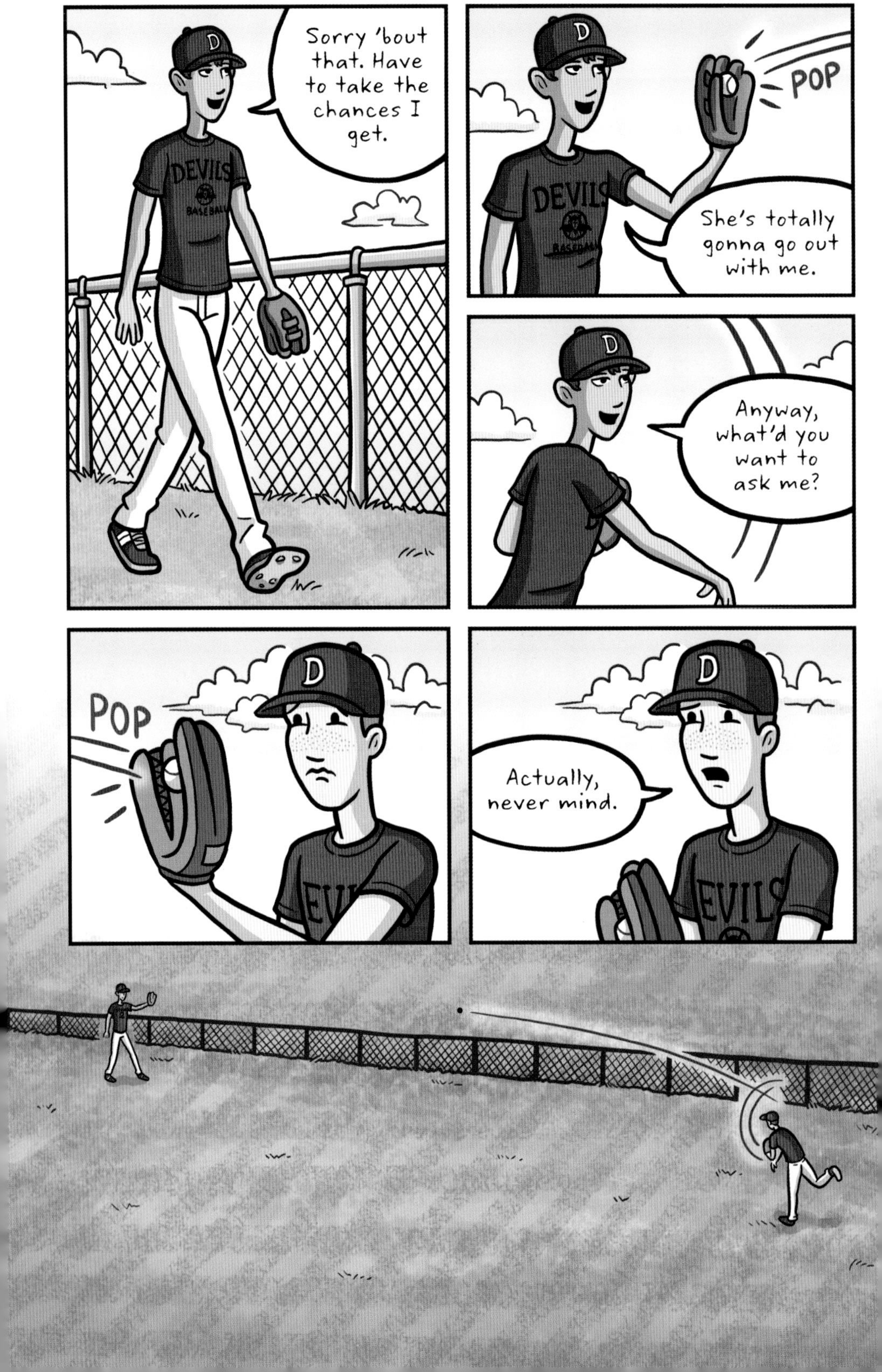
Sorry 'bout that. Have to take the chances I get.
POP
She's totally gonna go out with me.
Anyway, what'd you want to ask me?
POP
Actually, never mind.

CHAPTER 4

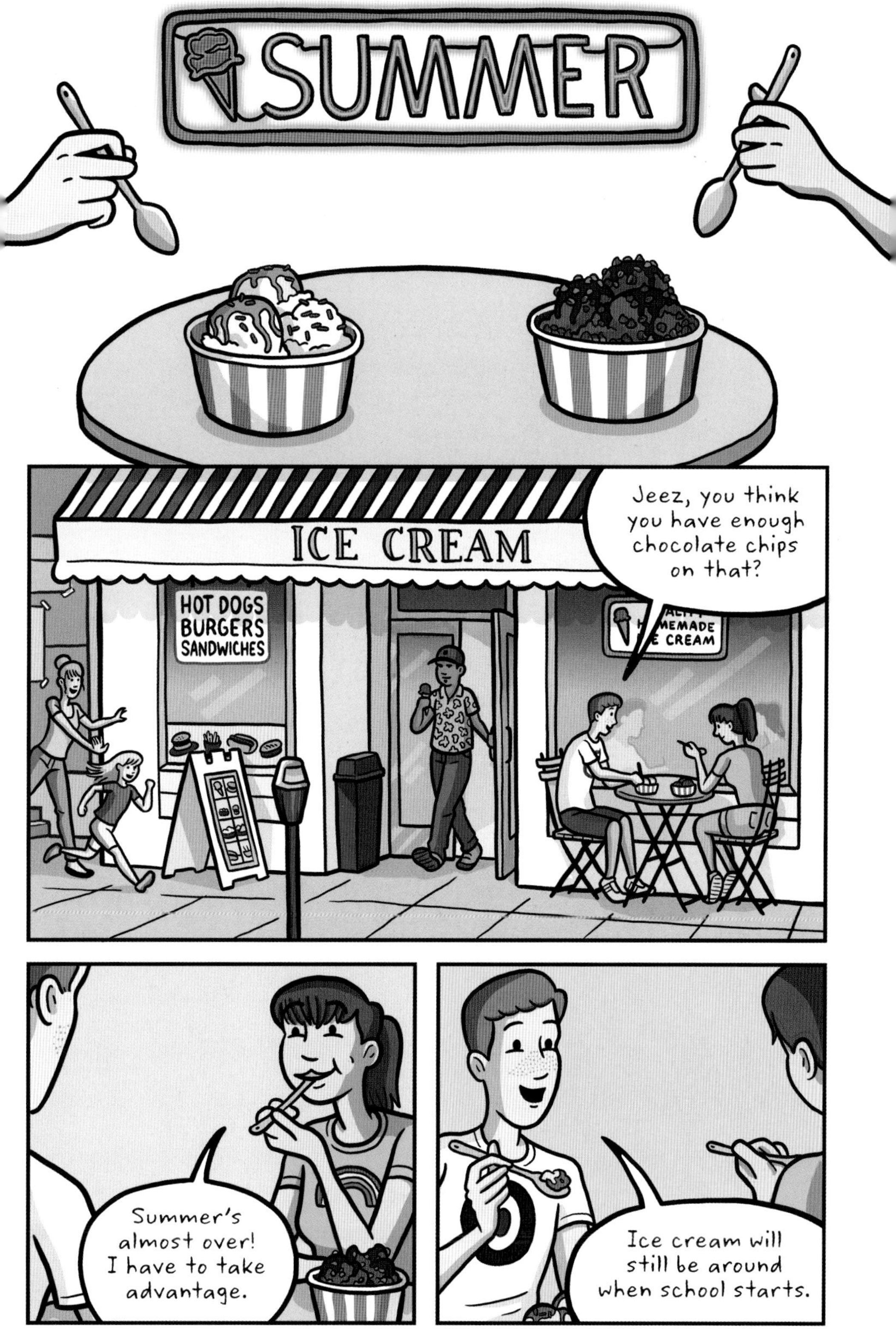
SUMMER
ICE CREAM
HOT DOGS
BURGERS
SANDWICHES
Jeez, you think you have enough chocolate chips on that?
Summer's almost over! I have to take advantage.
Ice cream will still be around when school starts.

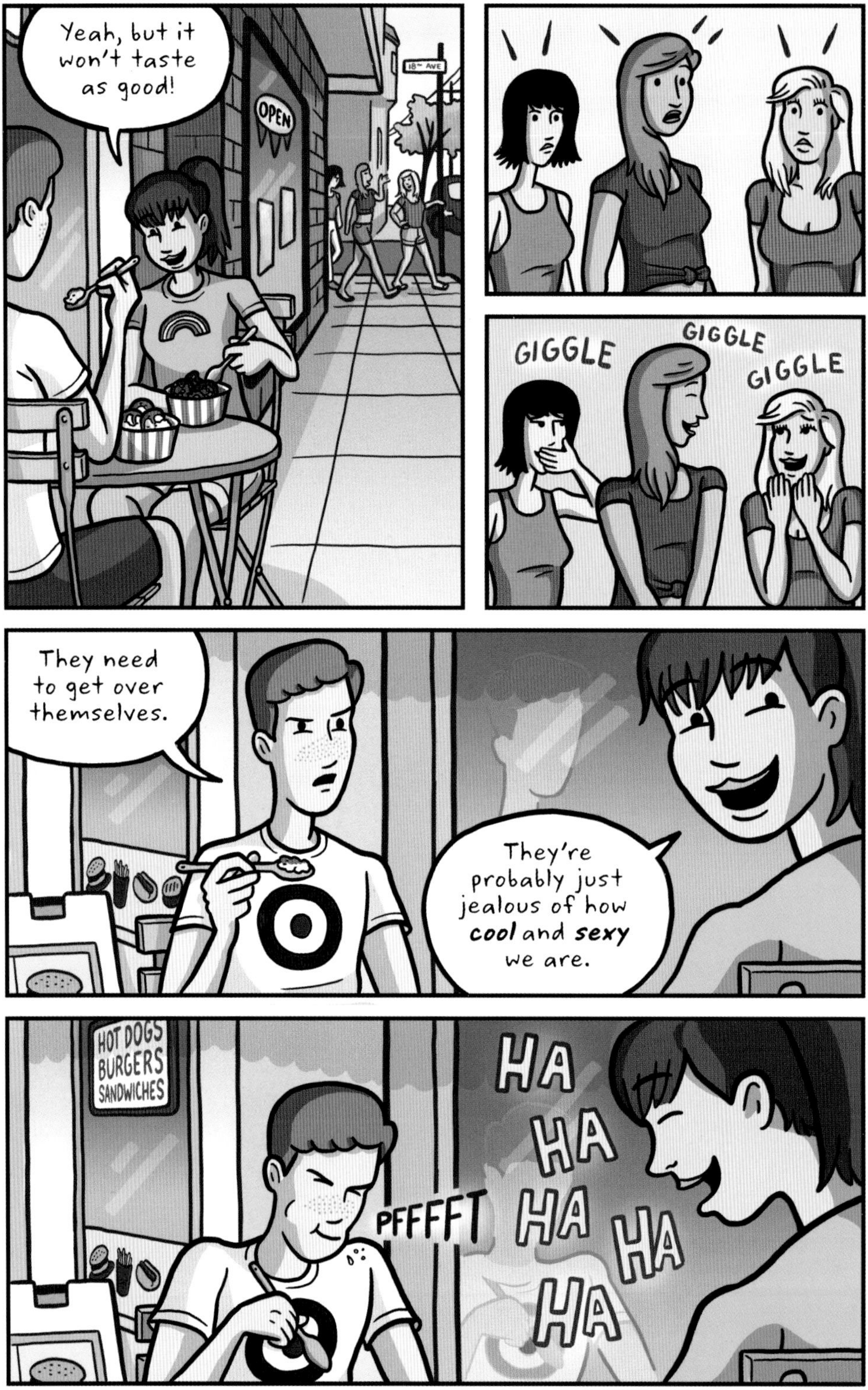
Yeah, but it won't taste as good!
18TH AVE
OPEN
GIGGLE
GIGGLE
GIGGLE
They need to get over themselves.
They're probably just jealous of how **cool** and **sexy** we are.
HOT DOGS
BURGERS
SANDWICHES
PFFFFT
HA
HA
HA
HA
HA

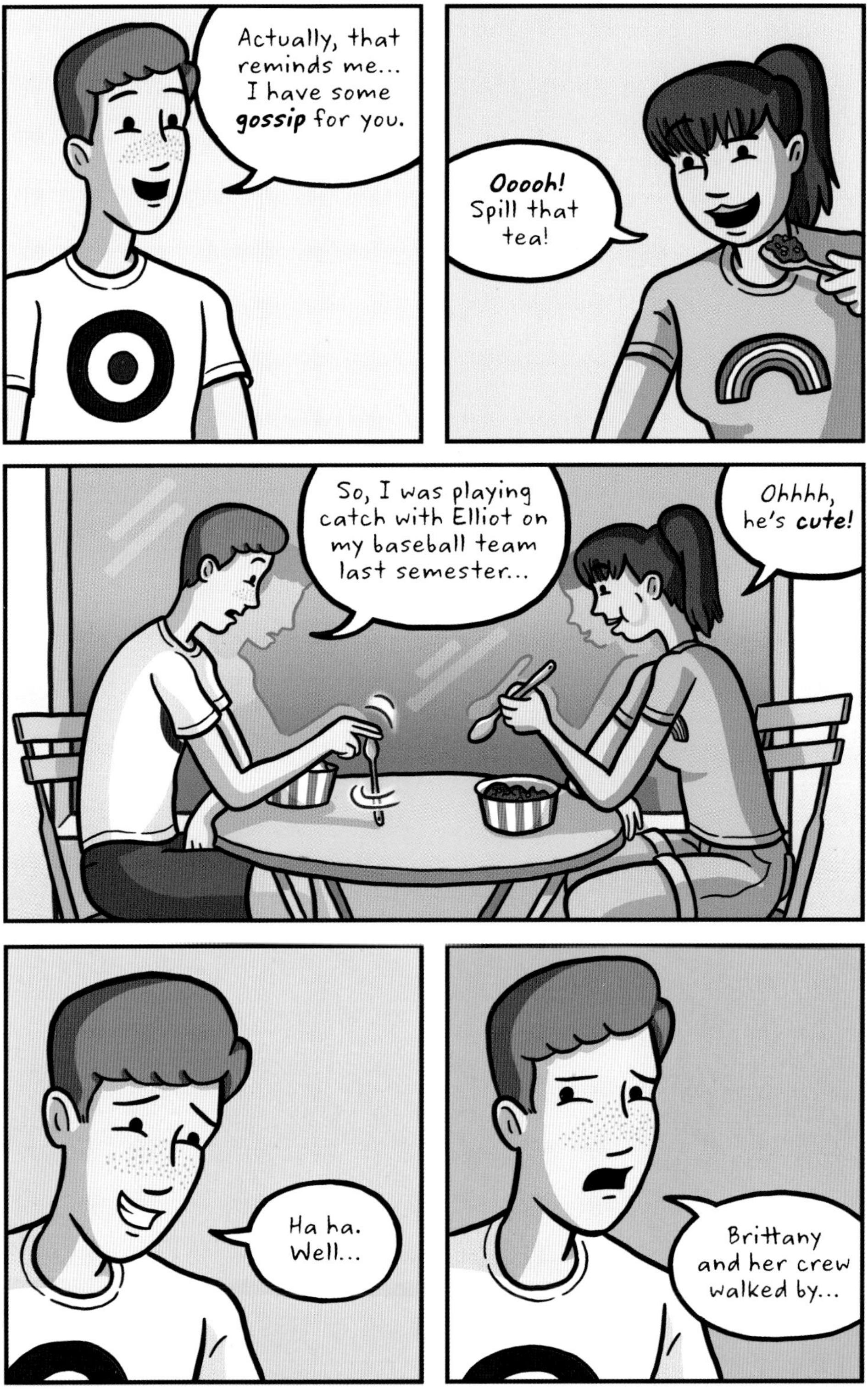
Actually, that reminds me... I have some **gossip** for you.
Ooooh! Spill that tea!
So, I was playing catch with Elliot on my baseball team last semester...
Ohhhh, he's **cute!**
Ha ha. Well...
Brittany and her crew walked by...

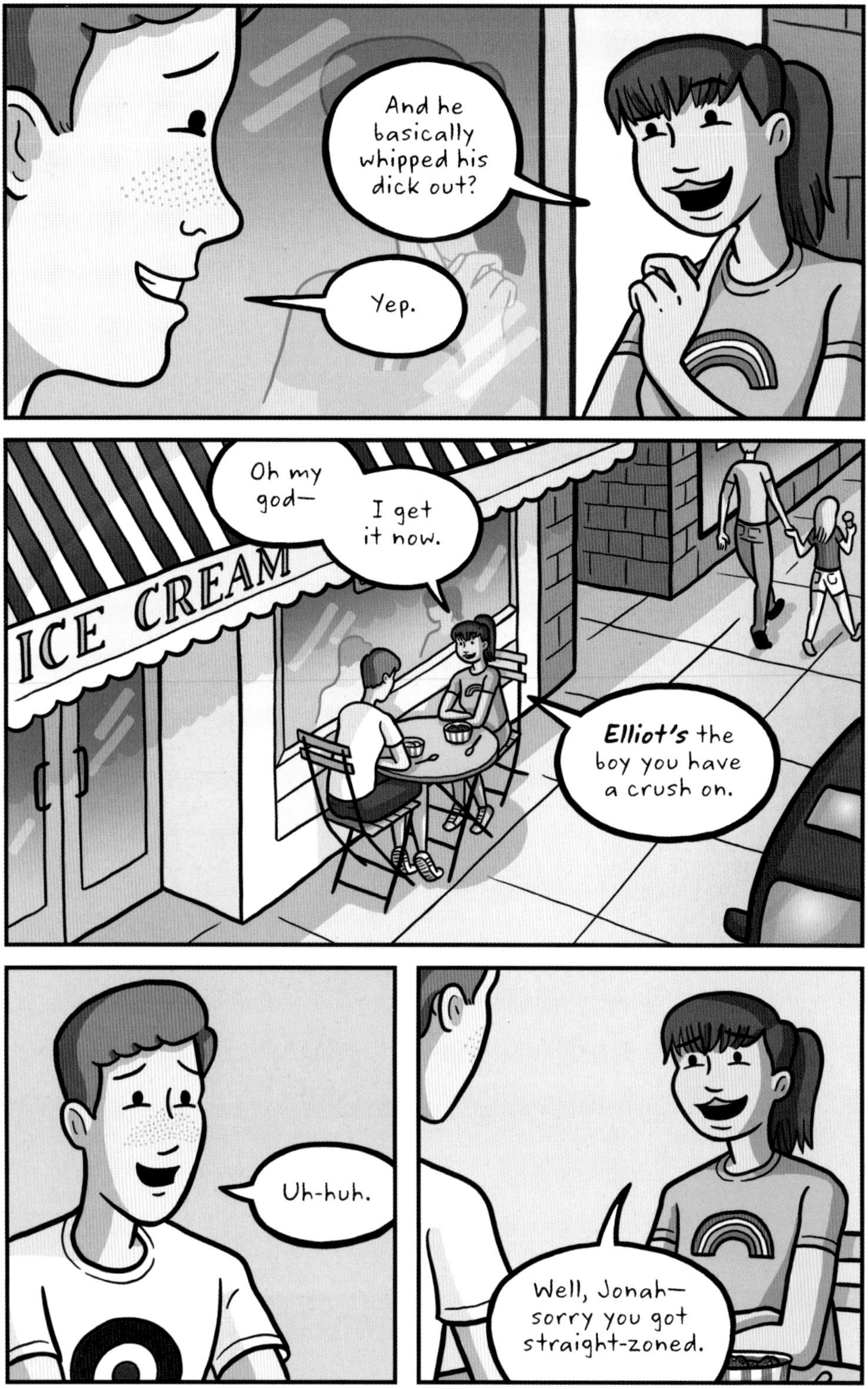
And he basically whipped his dick out?
Yep.
Oh my god—
I get it now.
Elliot's the boy you have a crush on.
Uh-huh.
Well, Jonah— sorry you got straight-zoned.

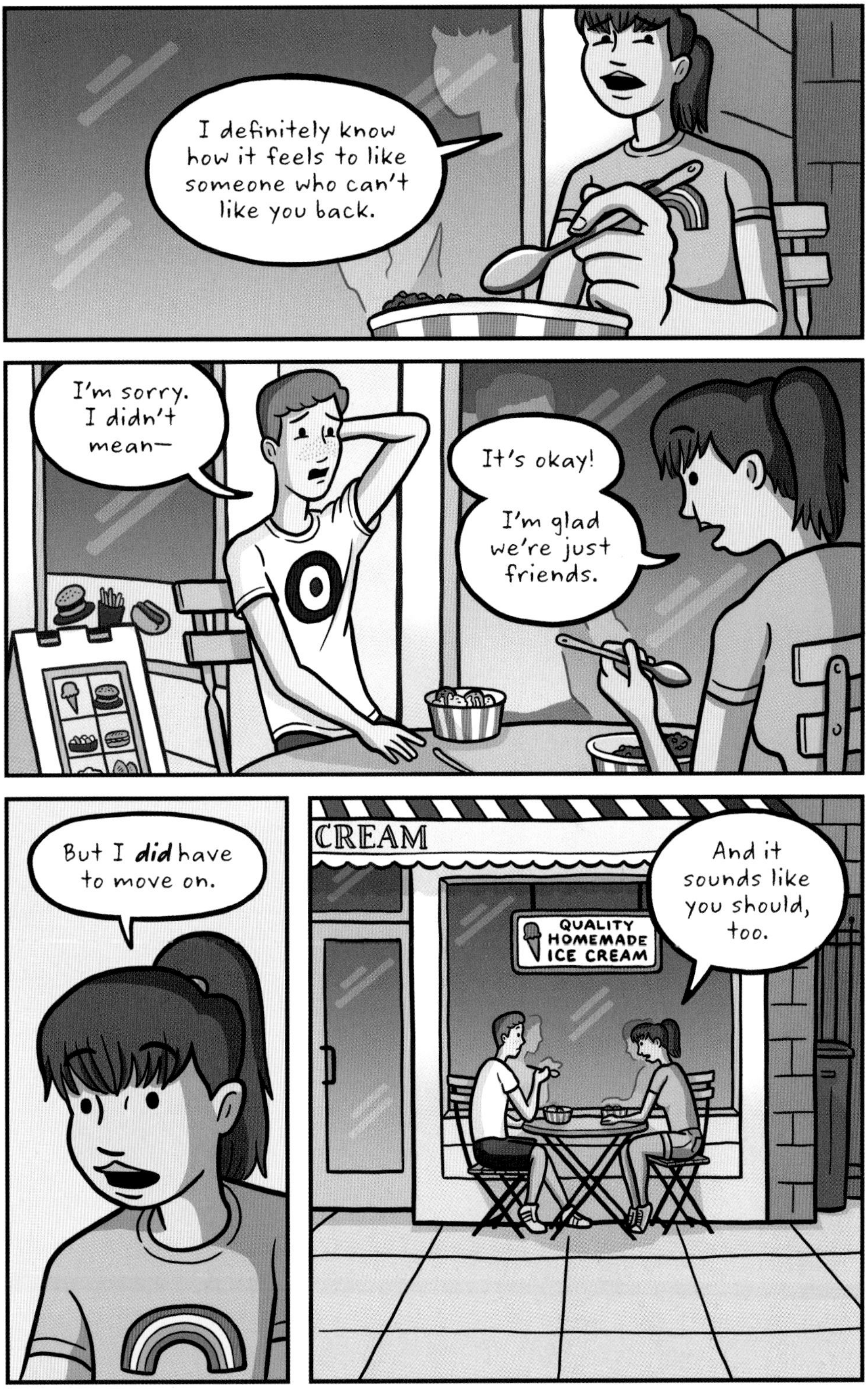
I definitely know how it feels to like someone who can't like you back.
I'm sorry. I didn't mean—
It's okay!
I'm glad we're just friends.
But I **did** have to move on.
CREAM
QUALITY HOMEMADE ICE CREAM
And it sounds like you should, too.

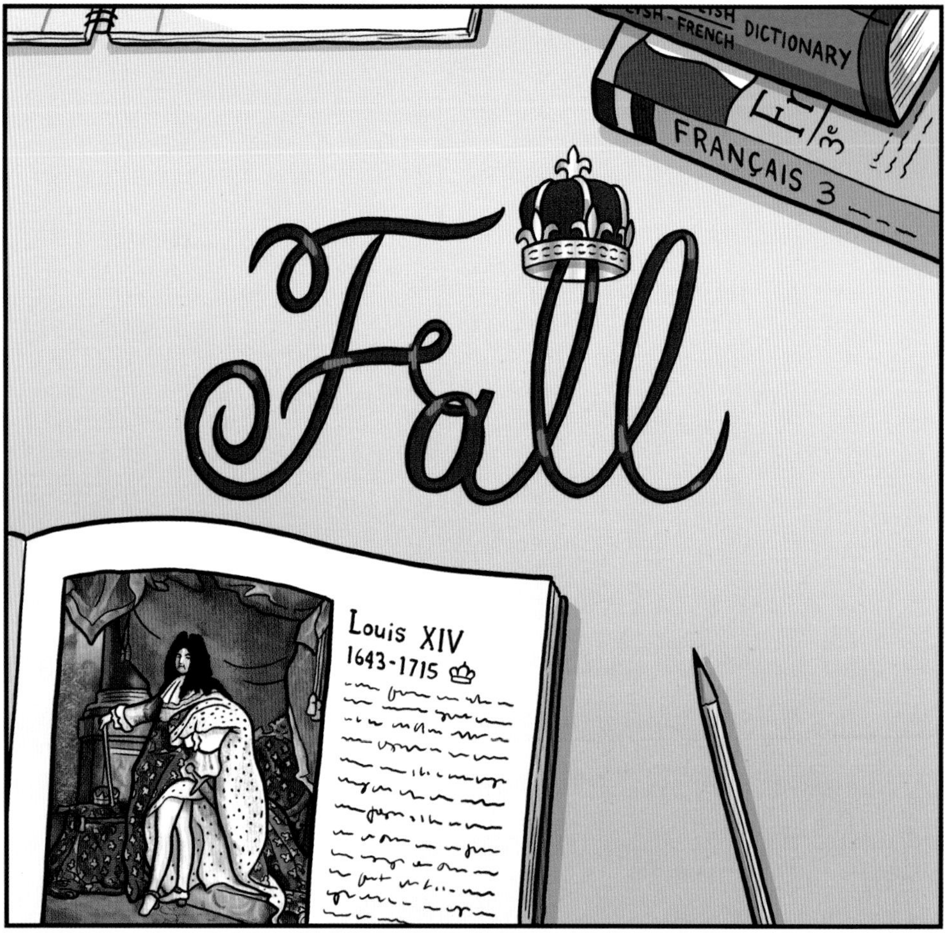

ENGLISH - FRENCH DICTIONARY
Fr 3e
FRANÇAIS 3
Fall
Louis XIV
1643-1715

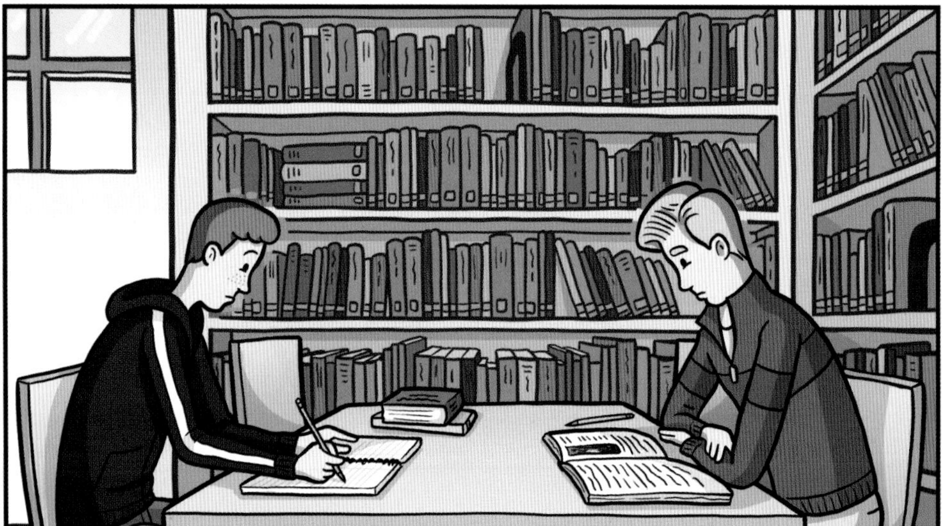

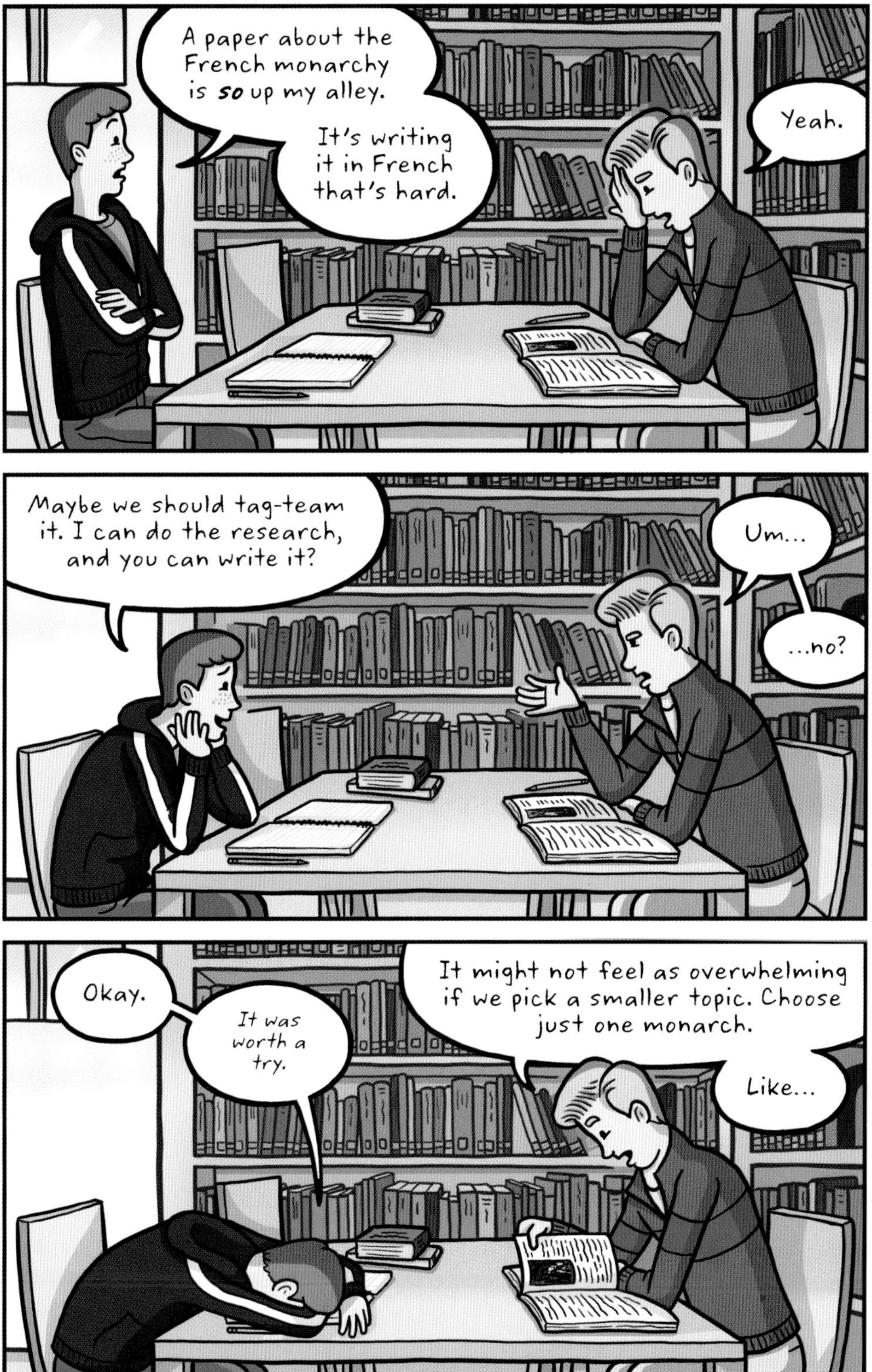
A paper about the French monarchy is **so** up my alley.
It's writing it in French that's hard.
Yeah.
Maybe we should tag-team it. I can do the research, and you can write it?
Um...
...no?
Okay.
It was worth a try.
It might not feel as overwhelming if we pick a smaller topic. Choose just one monarch.
Like...

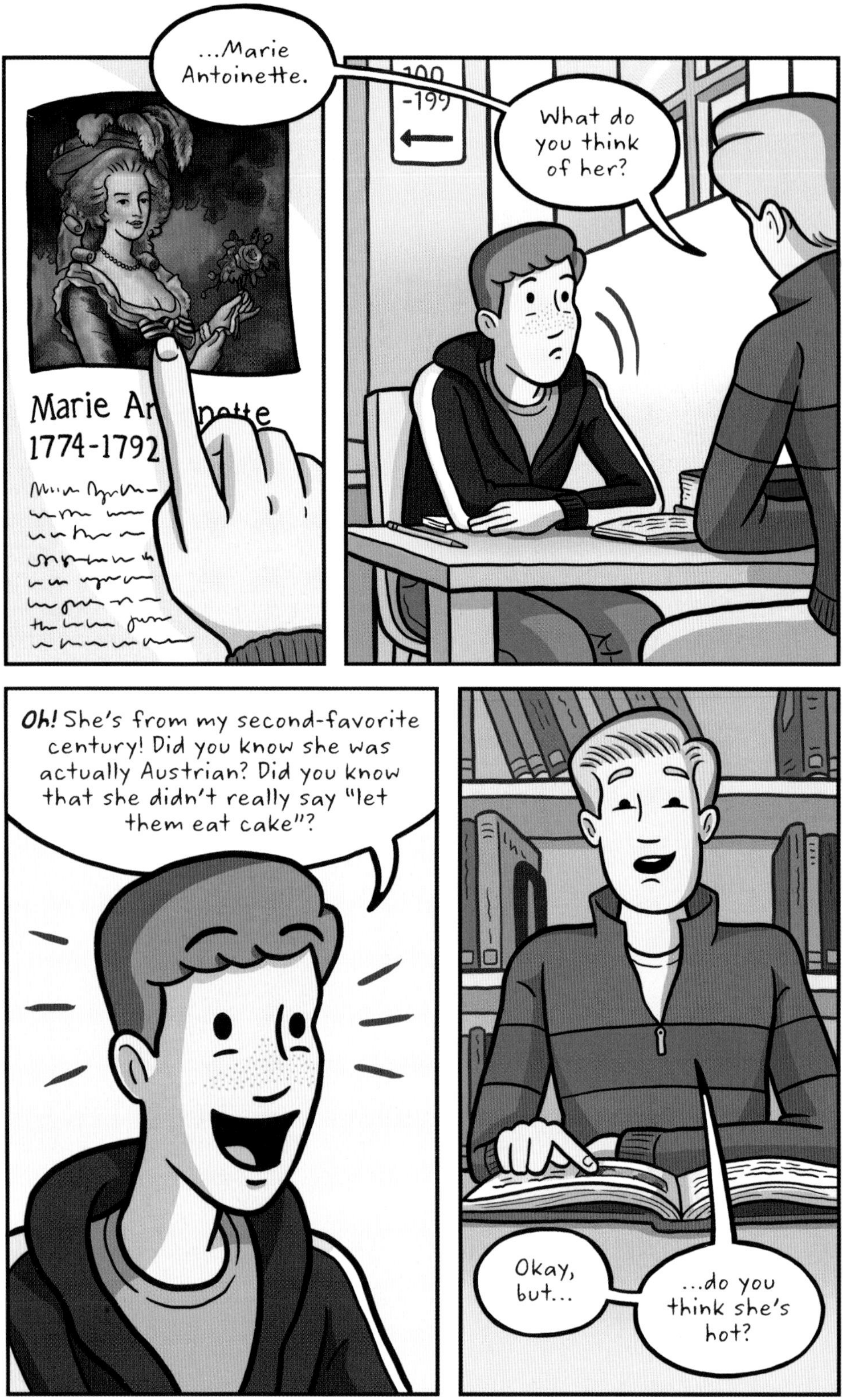
...Marie Antoinette.
100 -199
What do you think of her?
Oh! She's from my second-favorite century! Did you know she was actually Austrian? Did you know that she didn't really say "let them eat cake"?
Okay, but...
...do you think she's hot?

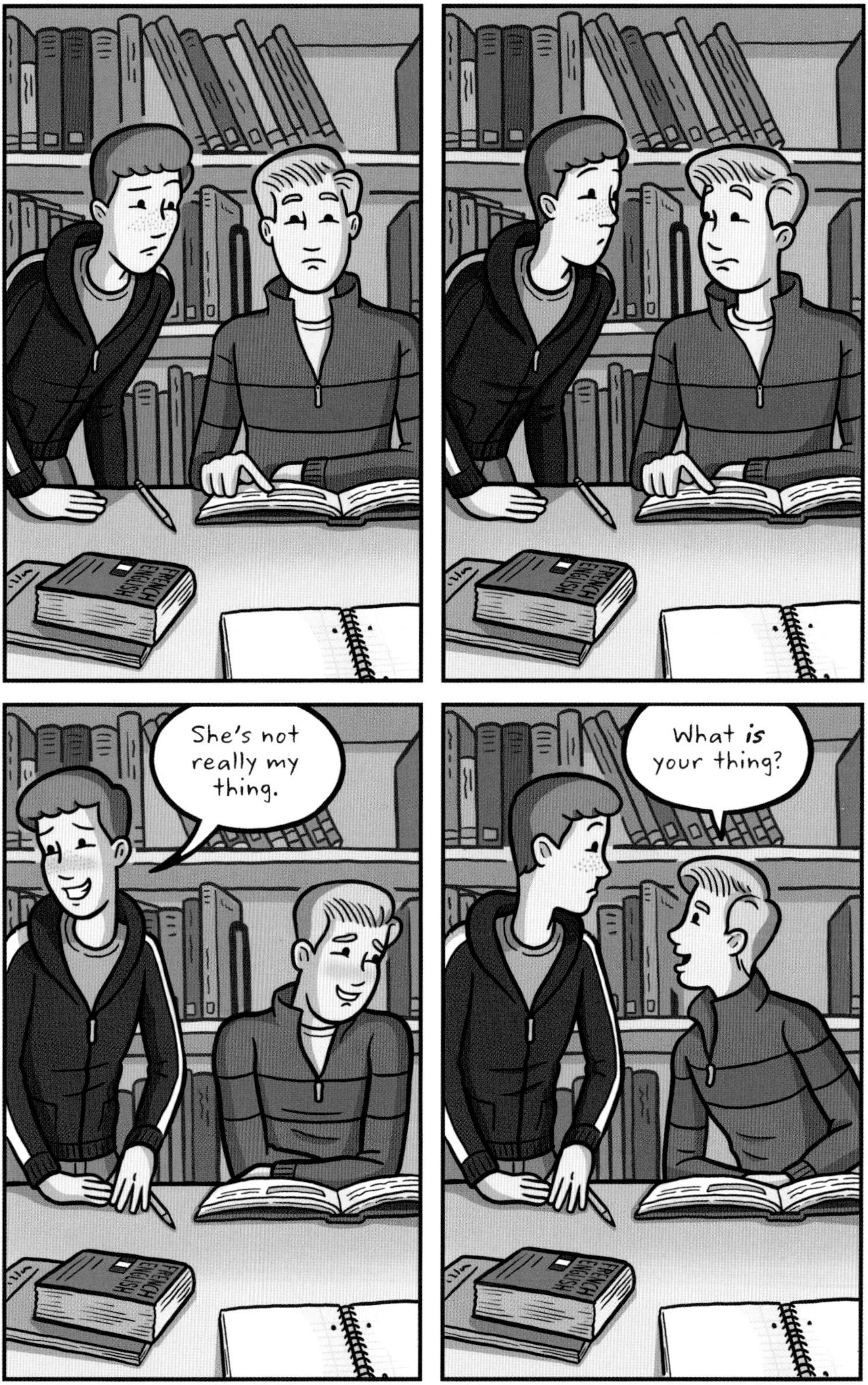
FRENCH ENGLISH
FRENCH ENGLISH
She's not really my thing.
FRENCH ENGLISH
What *is* your thing?
FRENCH ENGLISH

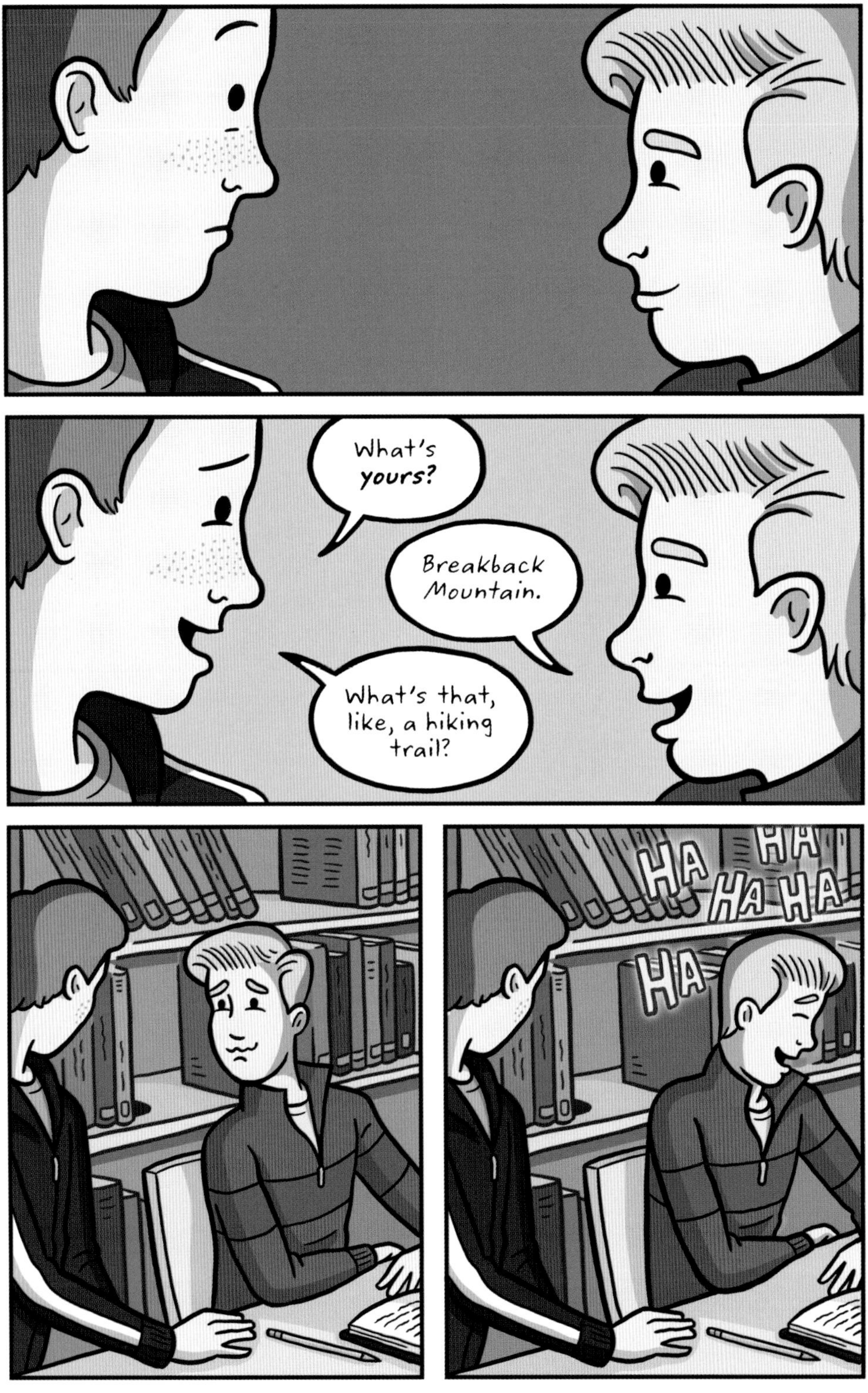
What's *yours?*
Breakback Mountain.
What's that, like, a hiking trail?
HA HA HA HA HA
HA

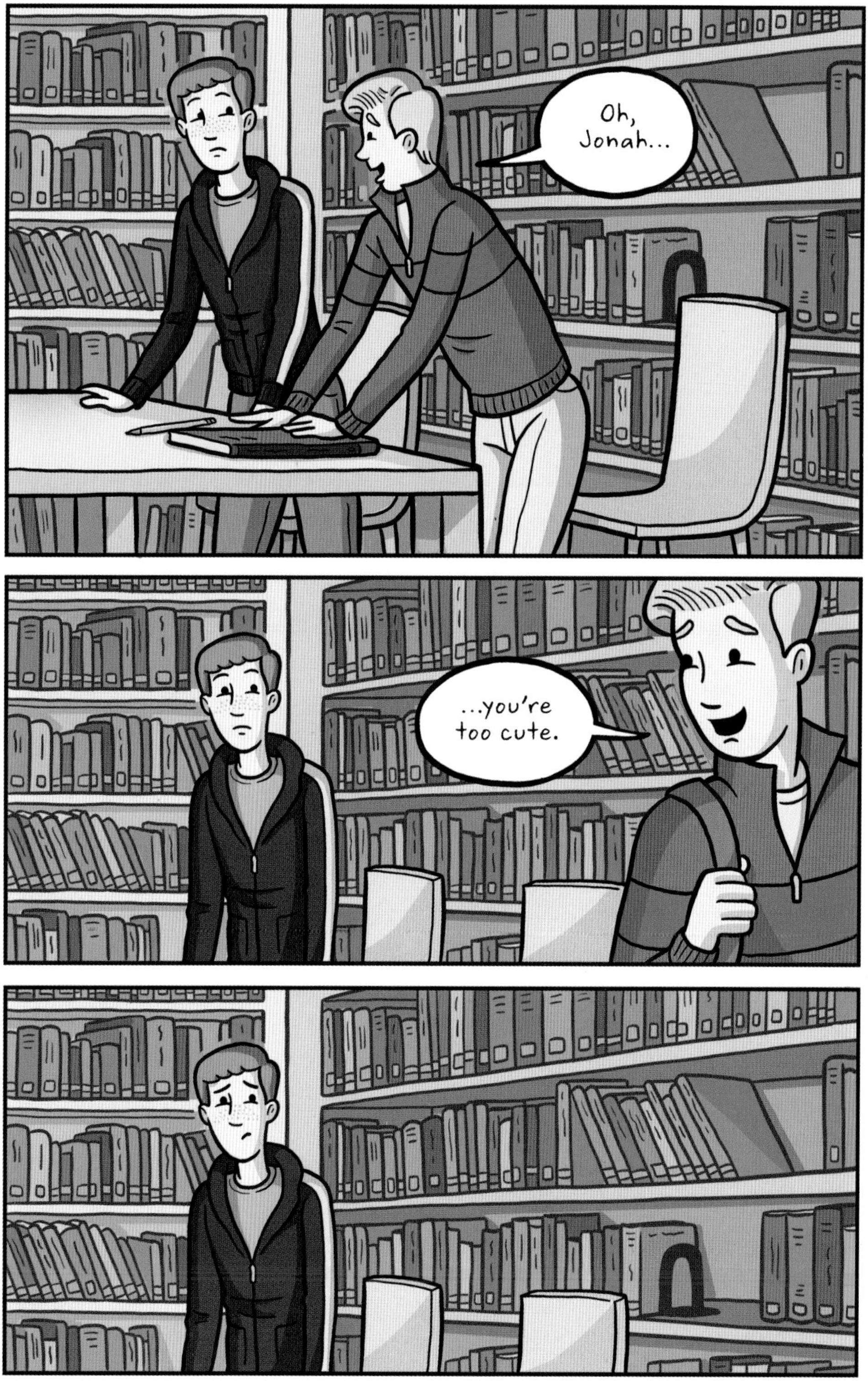
Oh, Jonah...
...you're too cute.

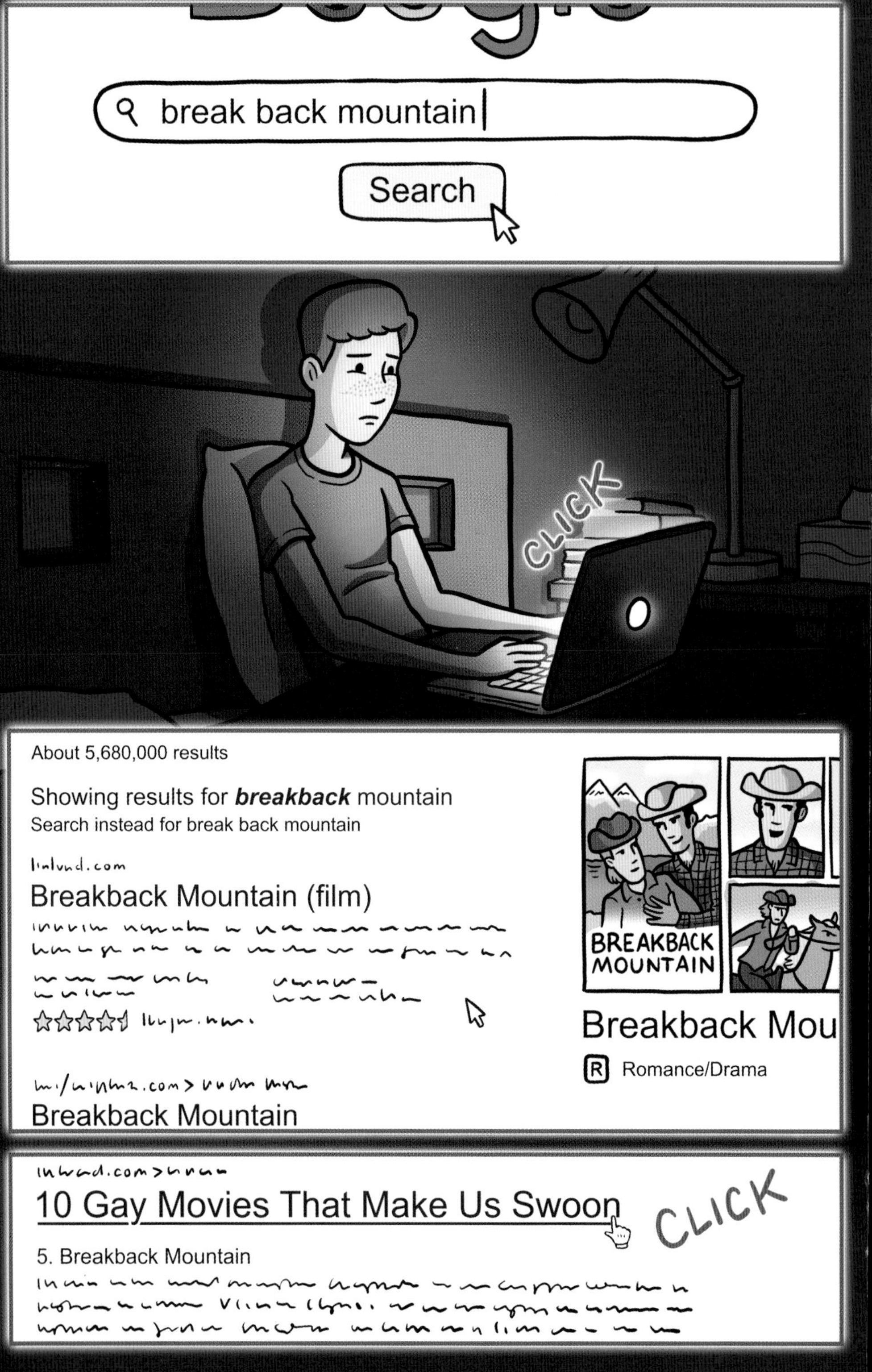

break back mountain
Search
CLICK
About 5,680,000 results
Showing results for ***breakback*** mountain
Search instead for break back mountain
Breakback Mountain (film)
Breakback Mountain
BREAKBACK MOUNTAIN
Breakback Mou
R Romance/Drama
10 Gay Movies That Make Us Swoon
CLICK
5. Breakback Mountain

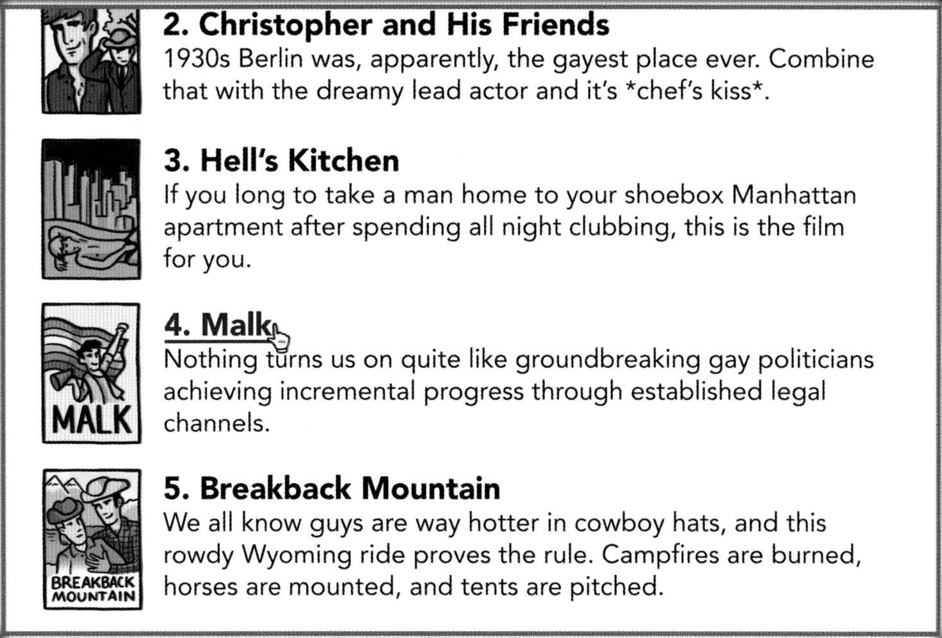
2. Christopher and His Friends
1930s Berlin was, apparently, the gayest place ever. Combine that with the dreamy lead actor and it's *chef's kiss*.
3. Hell's Kitchen
If you long to take a man home to your shoebox Manhattan apartment after spending all night clubbing, this is the film for you.
MALK
4. Malk
Nothing turns us on quite like groundbreaking gay politicians achieving incremental progress through established legal channels.
BREAKBACK MOUNTAIN
5. Breakback Mountain
We all know guys are way hotter in cowboy hats, and this rowdy Wyoming ride proves the rule. Campfires are burned, horses are mounted, and tents are pitched.

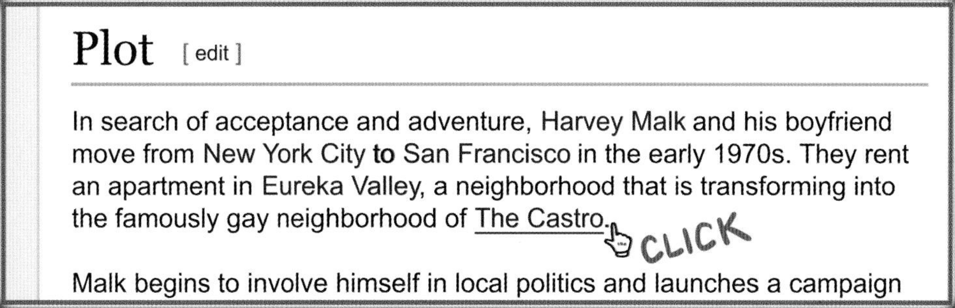
Plot [edit]
In search of acceptance and adventure, Harvey Malk and his boyfriend move from New York City to San Francisco in the early 1970s. They rent an apartment in Eureka Valley, a neighborhood that is transforming into the famously gay neighborhood of The Castro.
CLICK
Malk begins to involve himself in local politics and launches a campaign

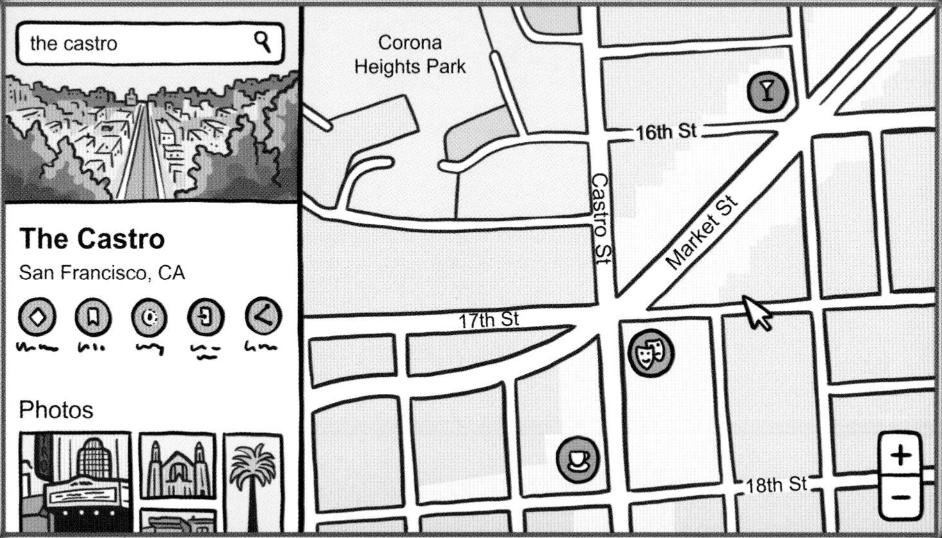
the castro
The Castro
San Francisco, CA
Photos
Corona Heights Park
16th St
Castro St
Market St
17th St
18th St

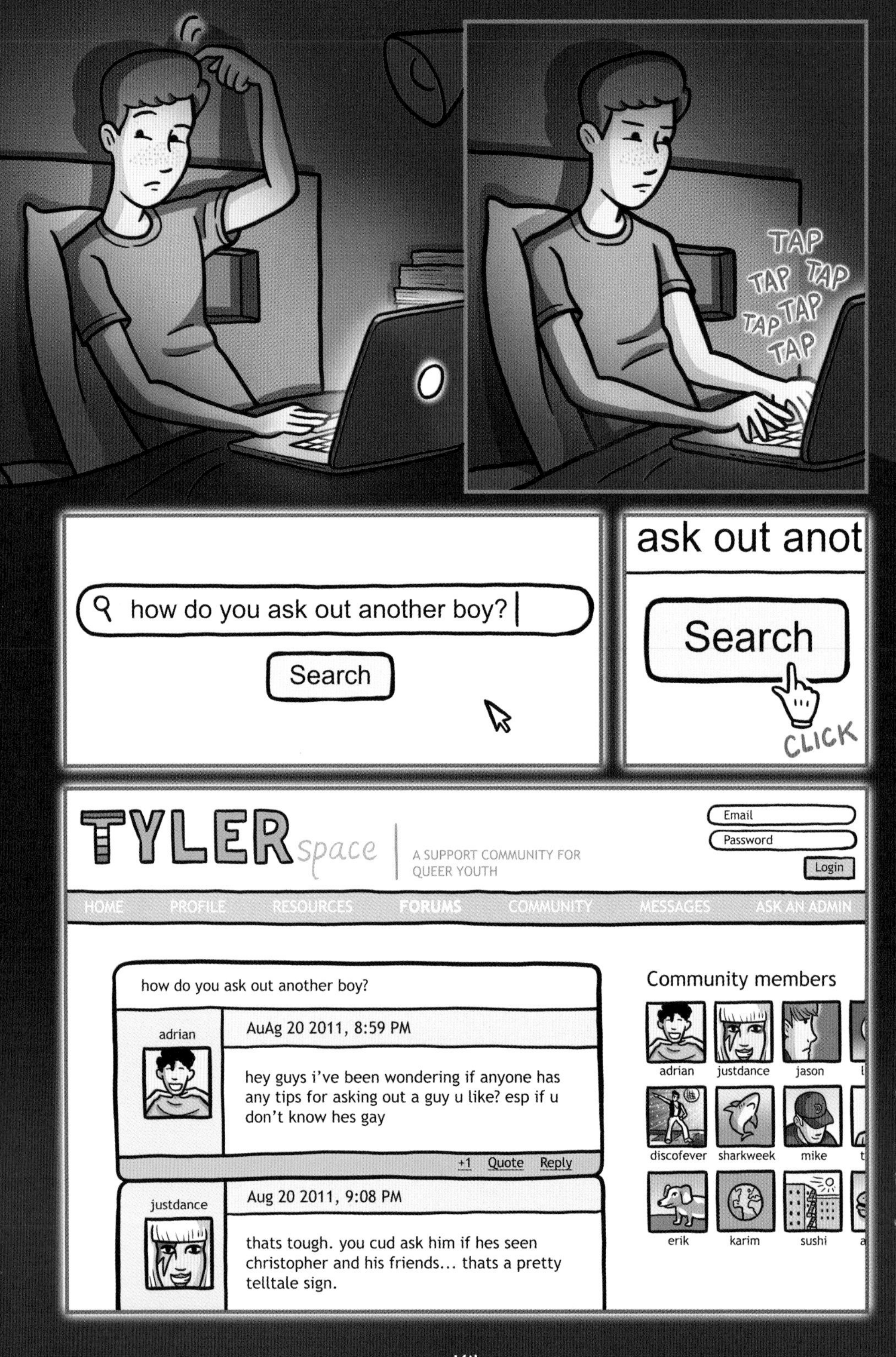

TAP TAP TAP TAP TAP TAP
how do you ask out another boy?
Search
ask out anot
Search
CLICK
TYLERspace
A SUPPORT COMMUNITY FOR QUEER YOUTH
Email
Password
Login
HOME PROFILE RESOURCES FORUMS COMMUNITY MESSAGES ASK AN ADMIN
how do you ask out another boy?
adrian
AuAg 20 2011, 8:59 PM
hey guys i've been wondering if anyone has any tips for asking out a guy u like? esp if u don't know hes gay
+1 Quote Reply
justdance
Aug 20 2011, 9:08 PM
thats tough. you cud ask him if hes seen christopher and his friends... thats a pretty telltale sign.
Community members
adrian justdance jason
discofever sharkweek mike
erik karim sushi

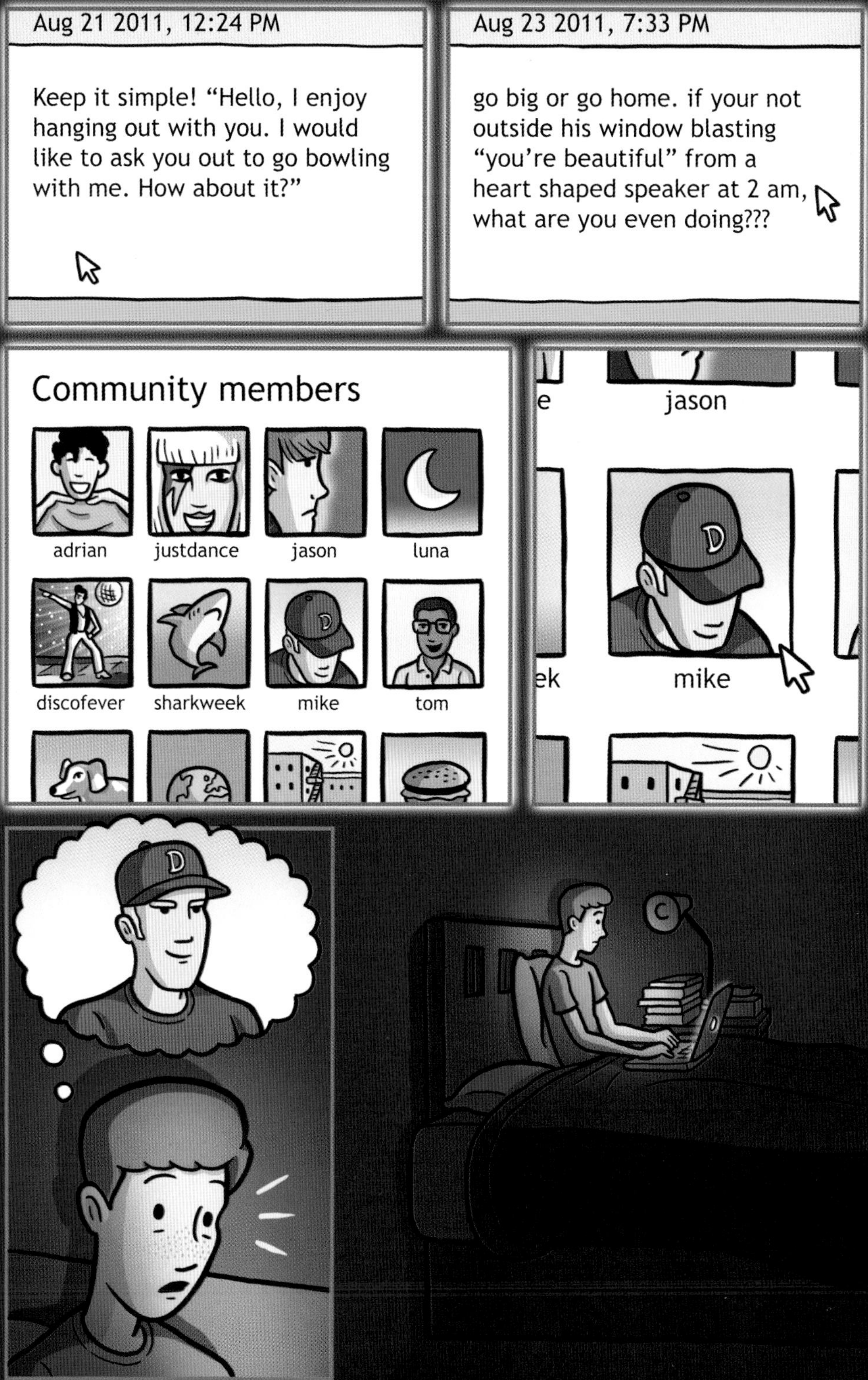

Aug 21 2011, 12:24 PM
Keep it simple! "Hello, I enjoy hanging out with you. I would like to ask you out to go bowling with me. How about it?"
Aug 23 2011, 7:33 PM
go big or go home. if your not outside his window blasting "you're beautiful" from a heart shaped speaker at 2 am, what are you even doing???
Community members
adrian
justdance
jason
luna
discofever
sharkweek
mike
tom
jason
mike

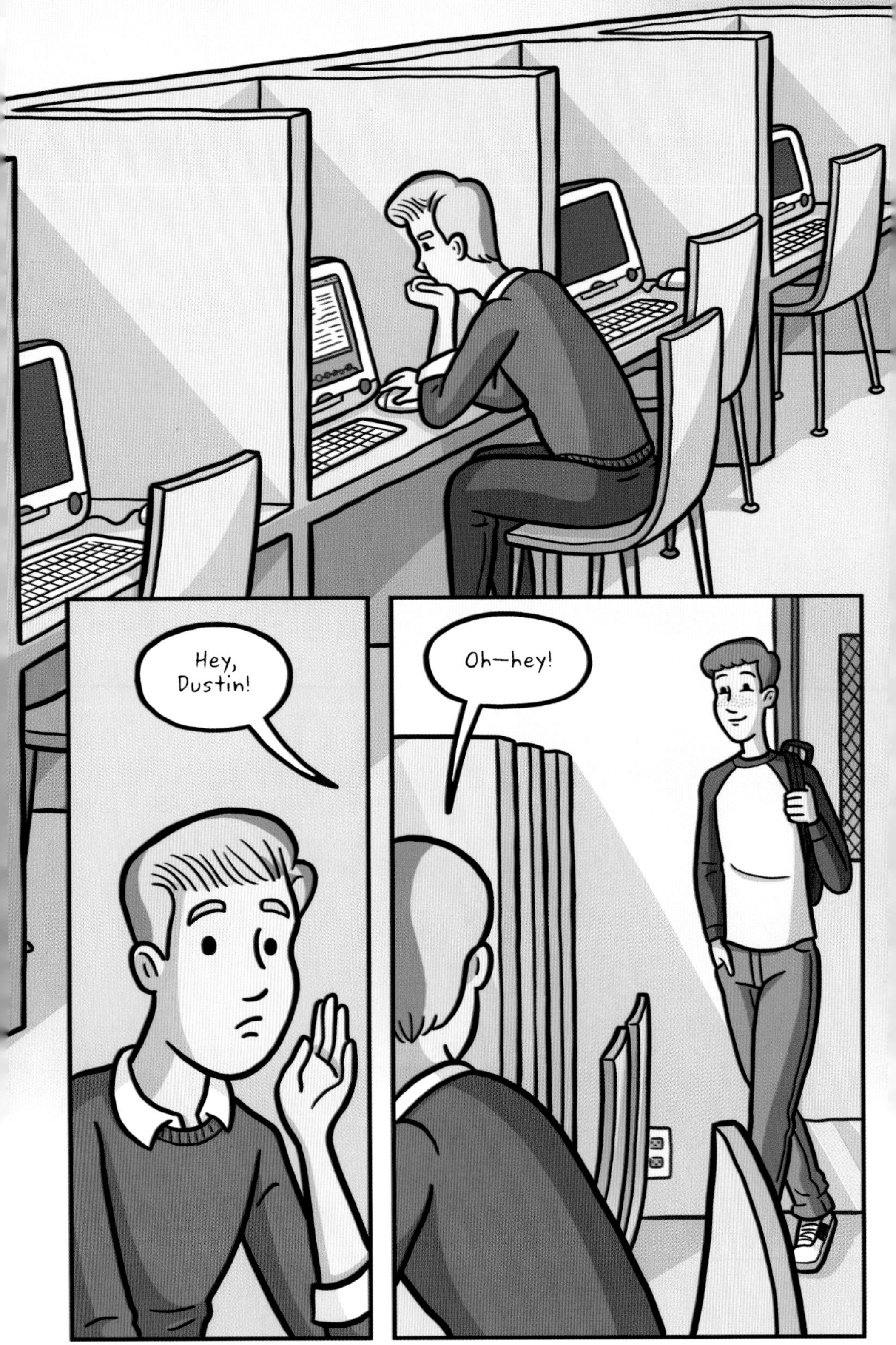
Hey, Dustin!
Oh—hey!

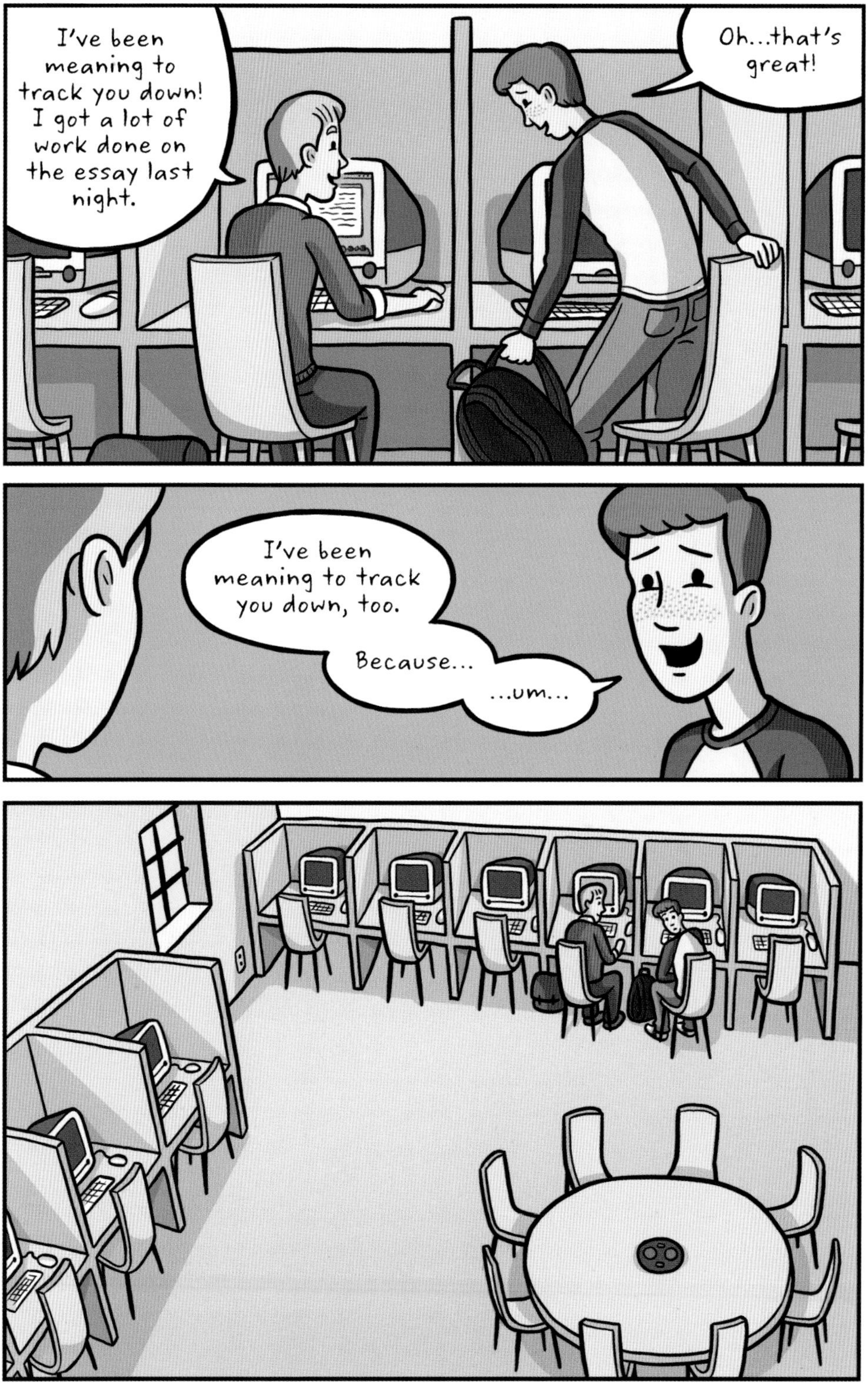
I've been meaning to track you down! I got a lot of work done on the essay last night.
Oh...that's great!
I've been meaning to track you down, too.
Because...
...um...

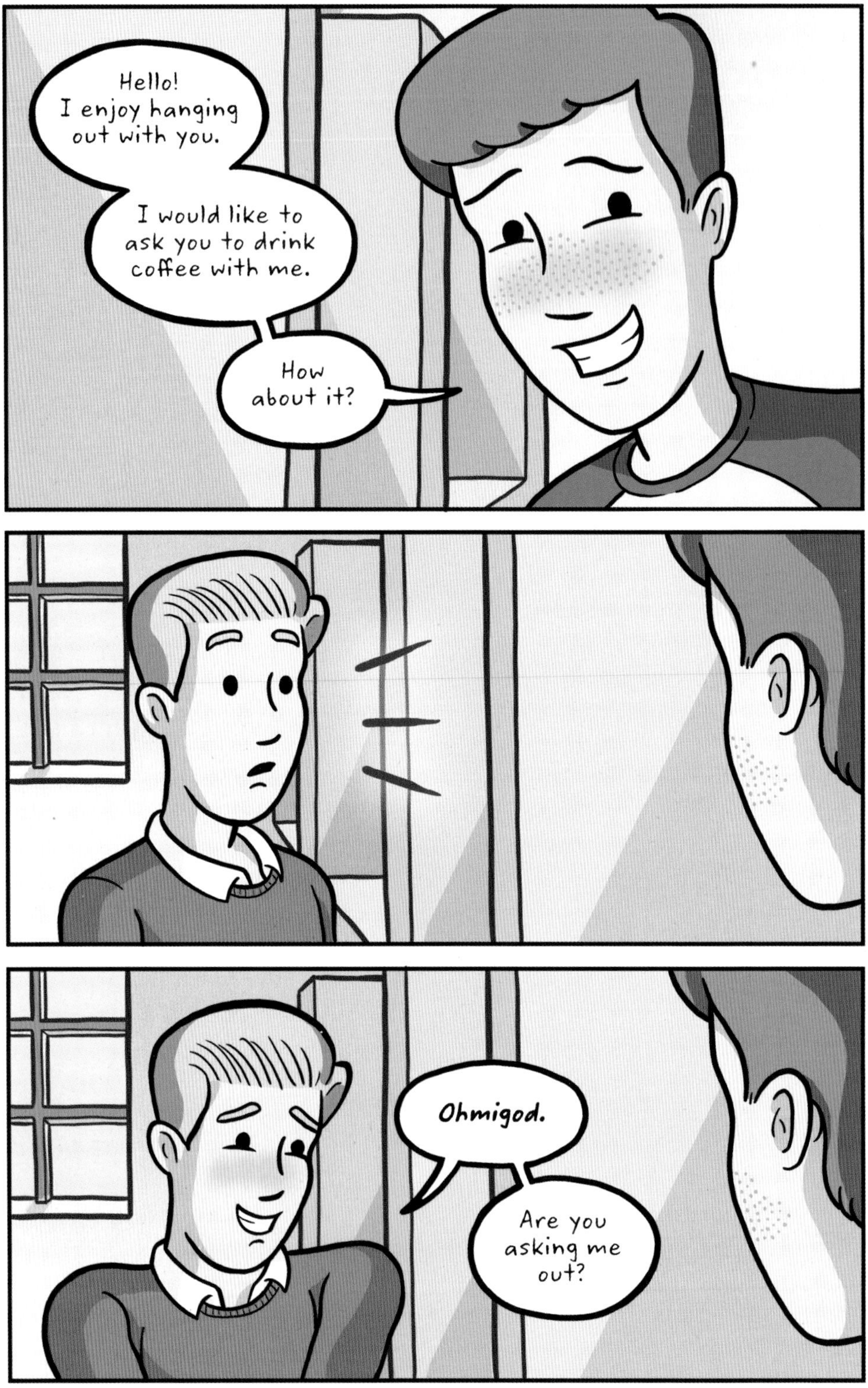
Hello!
I enjoy hanging out with you.
I would like to ask you to drink coffee with me.
How about it?
Ohmigod.
Are you asking me out?

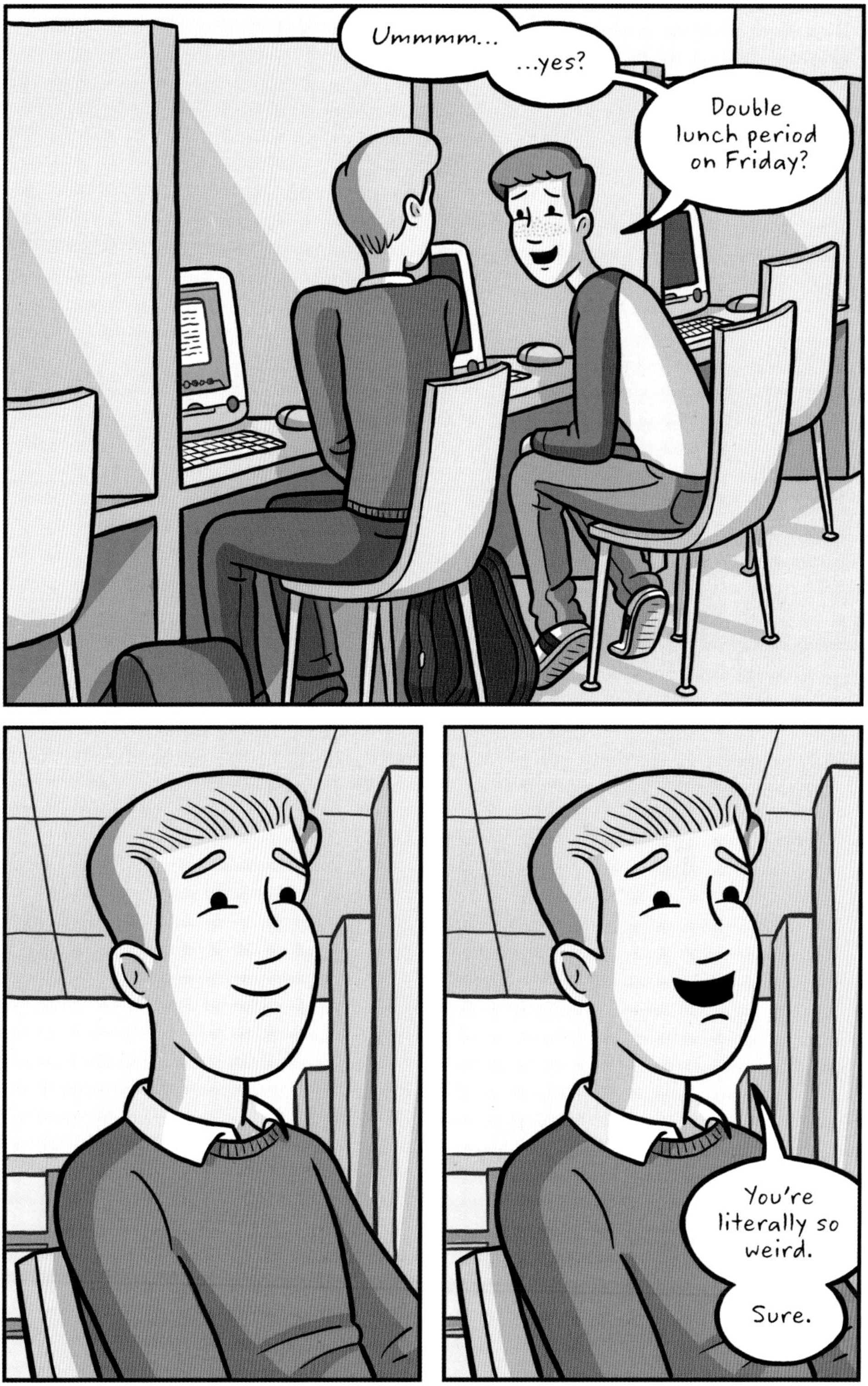
Ummmm...
...yes?
Double lunch period on Friday?
You're literally so weird.
Sure.

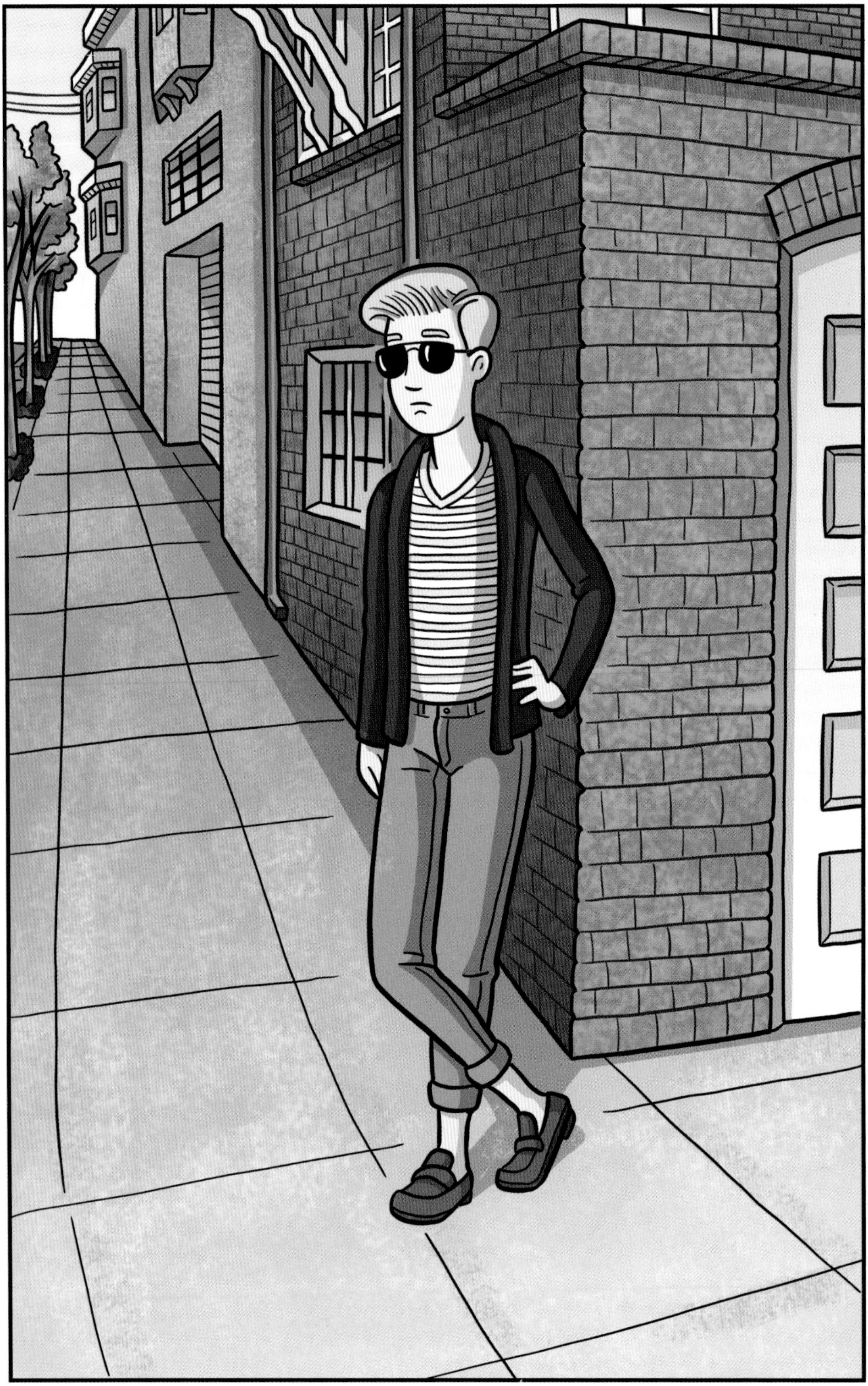

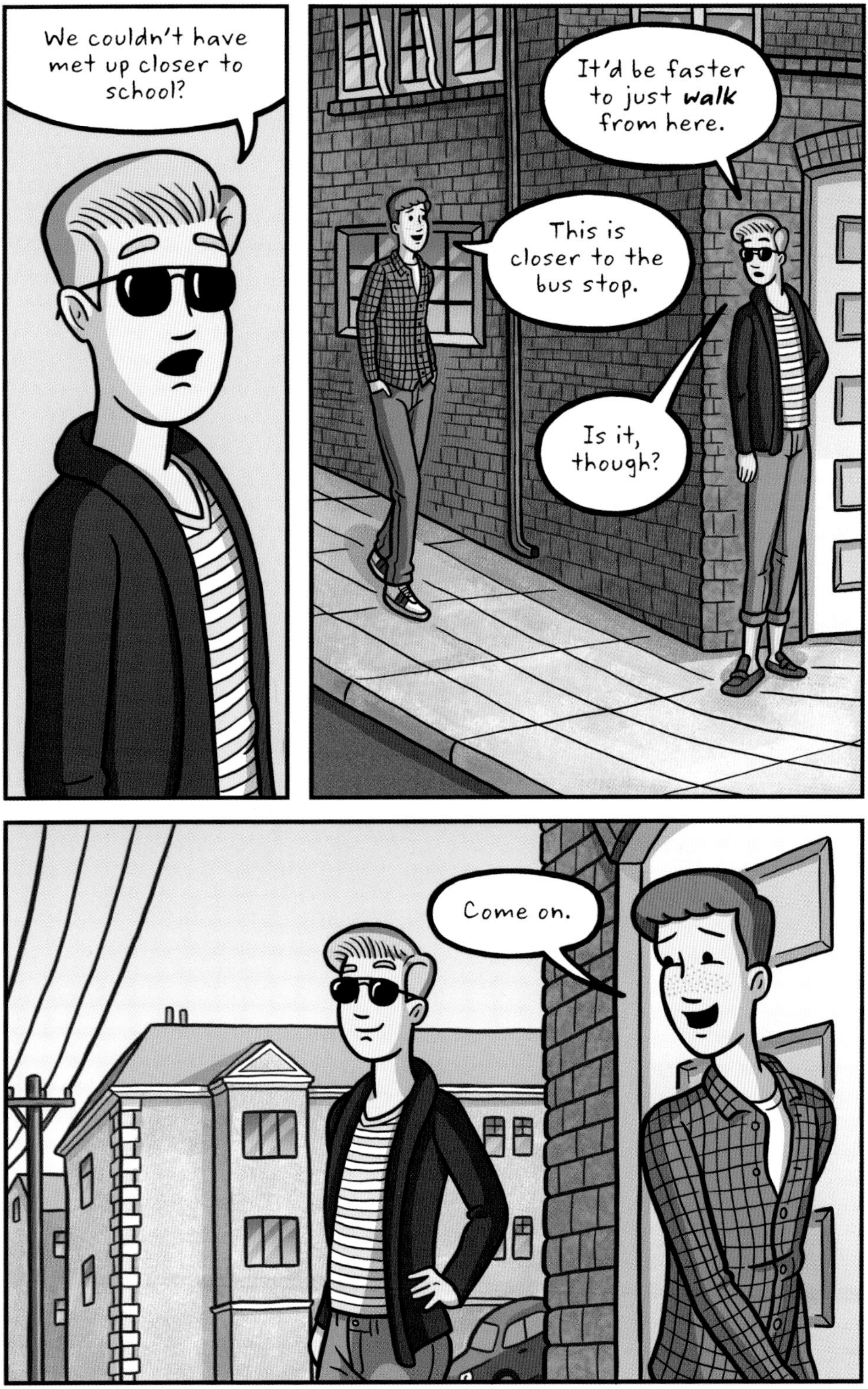
We couldn't have met up closer to school?
It'd be faster to just **walk** from here.
This is closer to the bus stop.
Is it, though?
Come on.

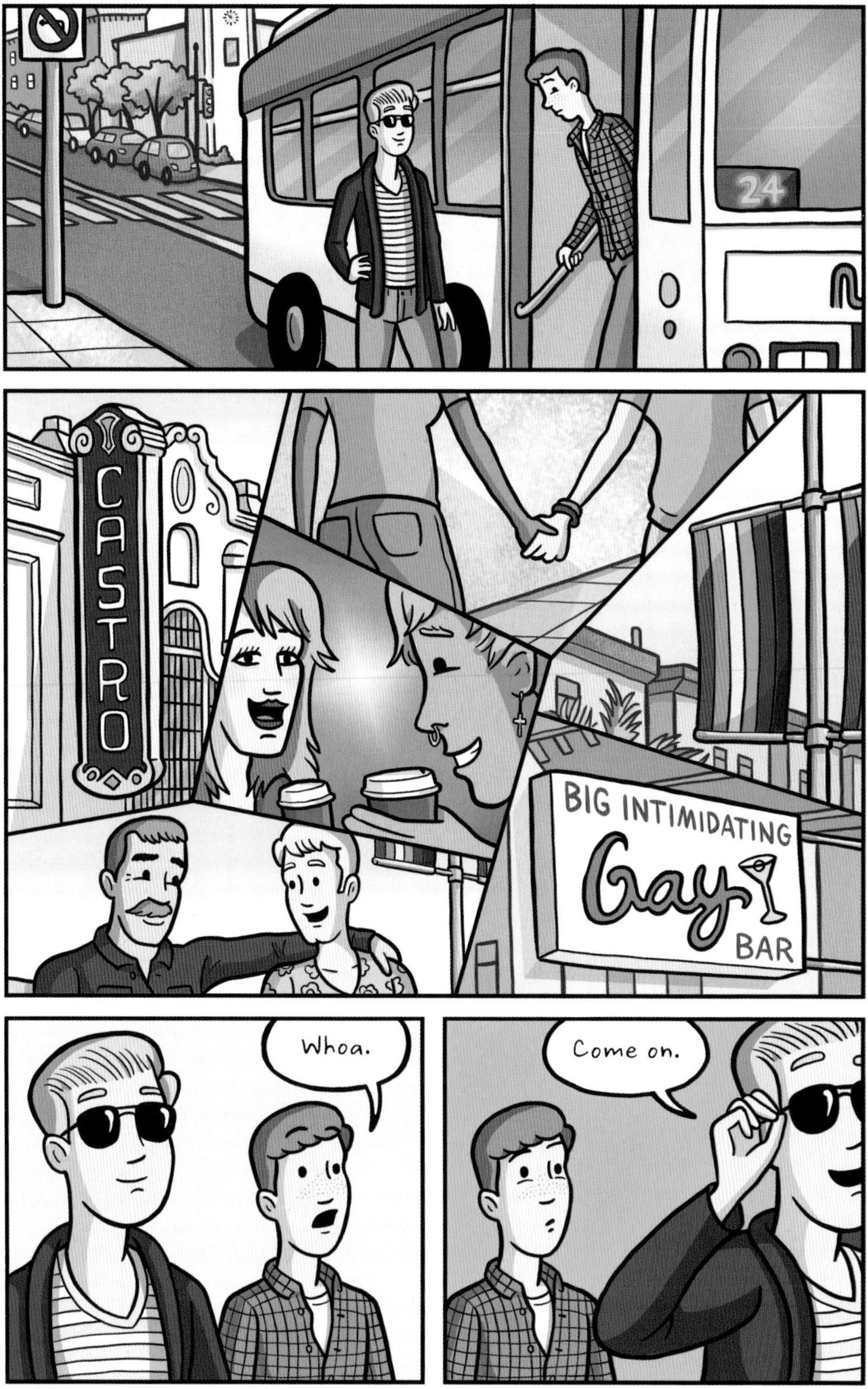
24
CASTRO
BIG INTIMIDATING
Gay
BAR
Whoa.
Come on.

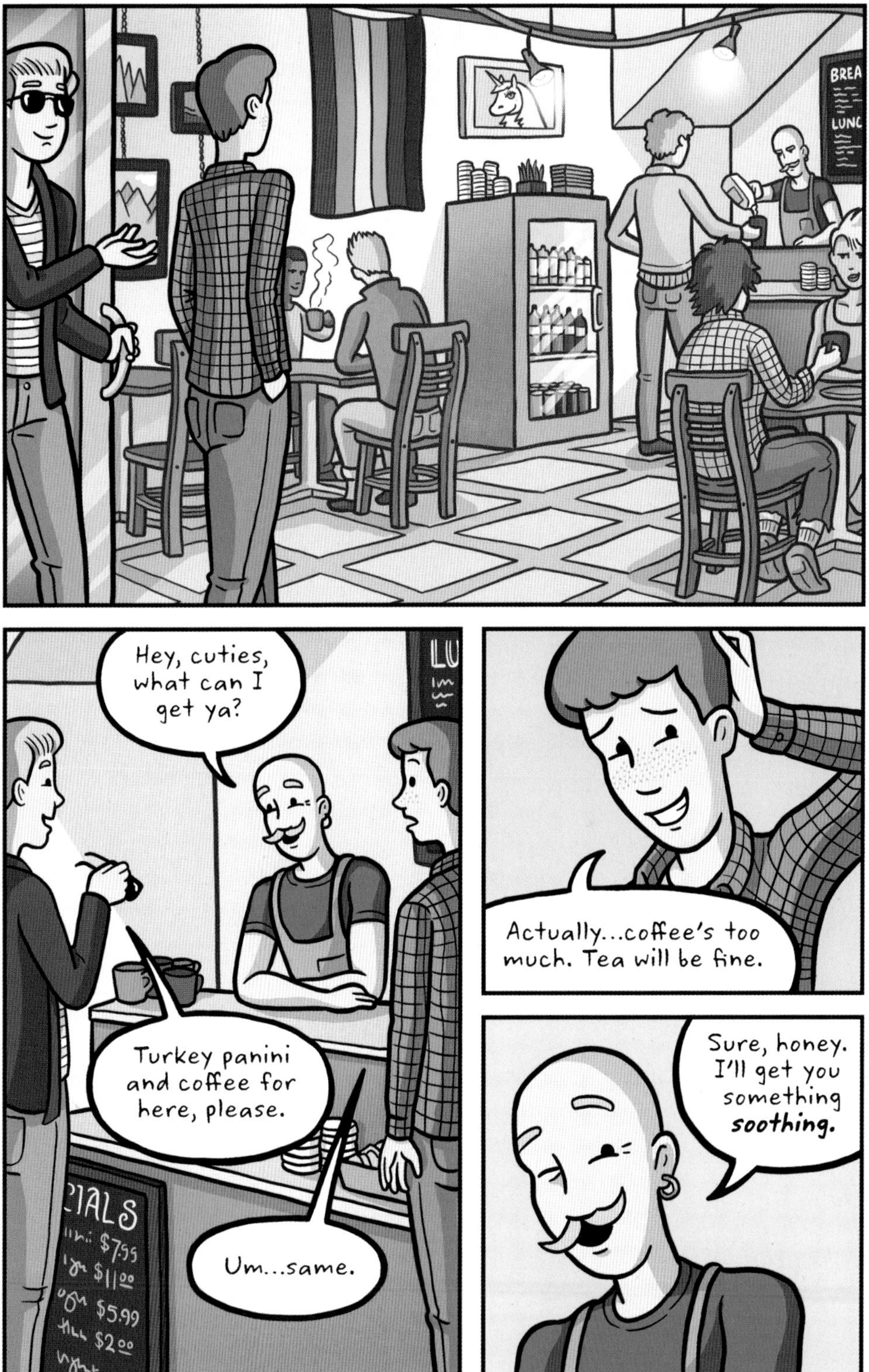
Hey, cuties, what can I get ya?
Turkey panini and coffee for here, please.
Um...same.
Actually...coffee's too much. Tea will be fine.
Sure, honey. I'll get you something **soothing.**

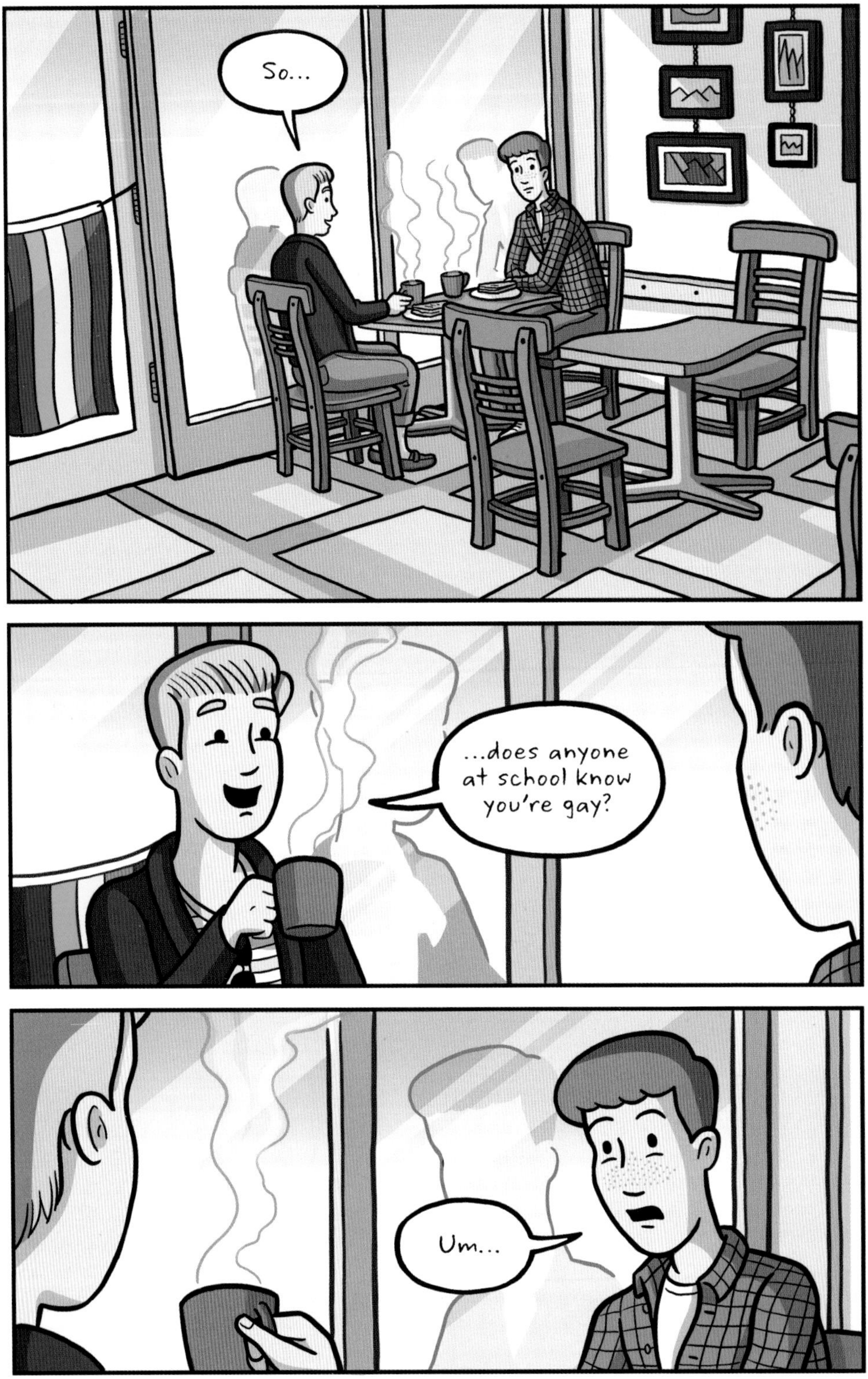
So...
...does anyone at school know you're gay?
Um...

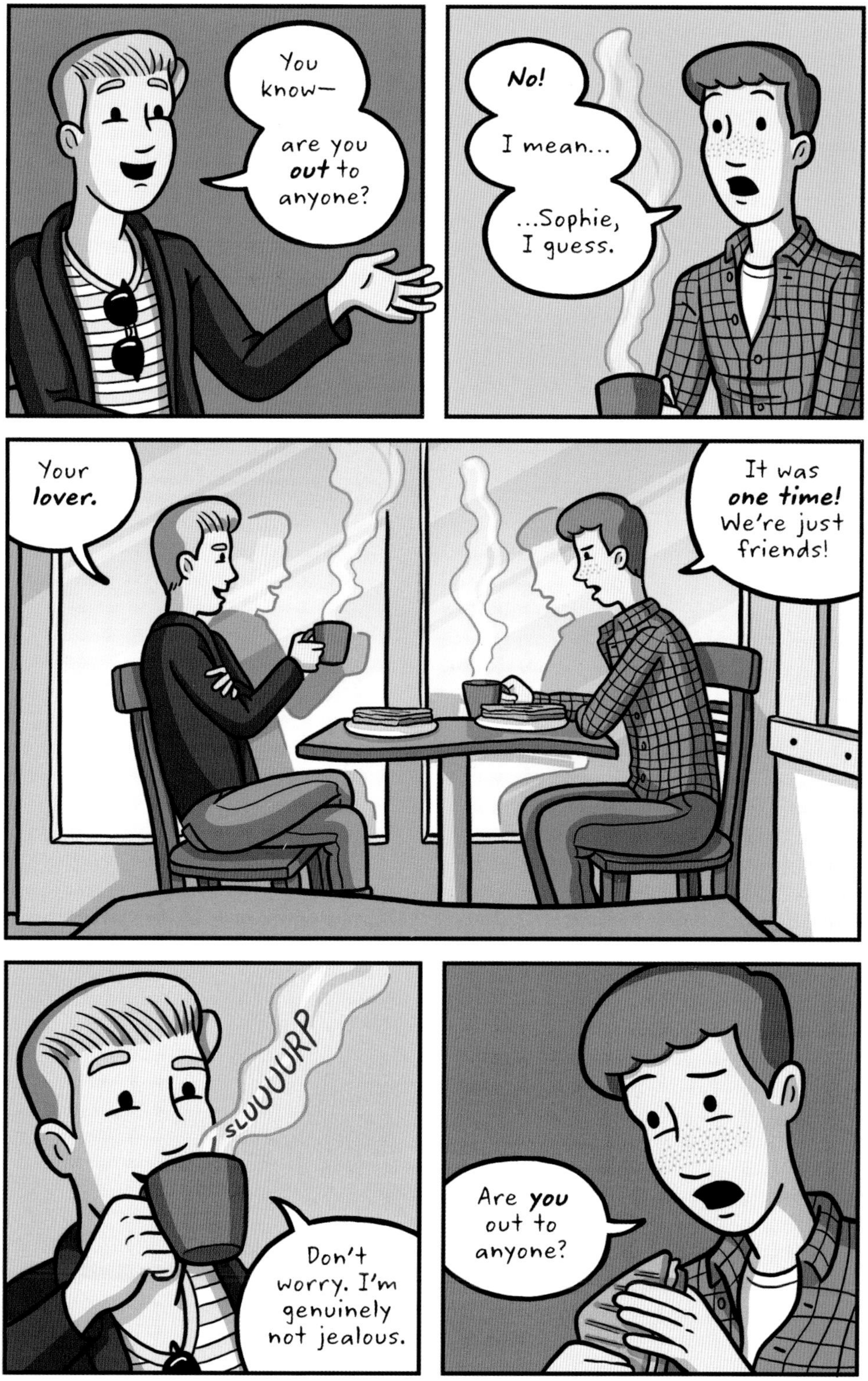
You know—
are you **out** to anyone?
No!
I mean...
...Sophie, I guess.
Your **lover.**
It was **one time!** We're just friends!
SLUUUURP
Don't worry. I'm genuinely not jealous.
Are **you** out to anyone?

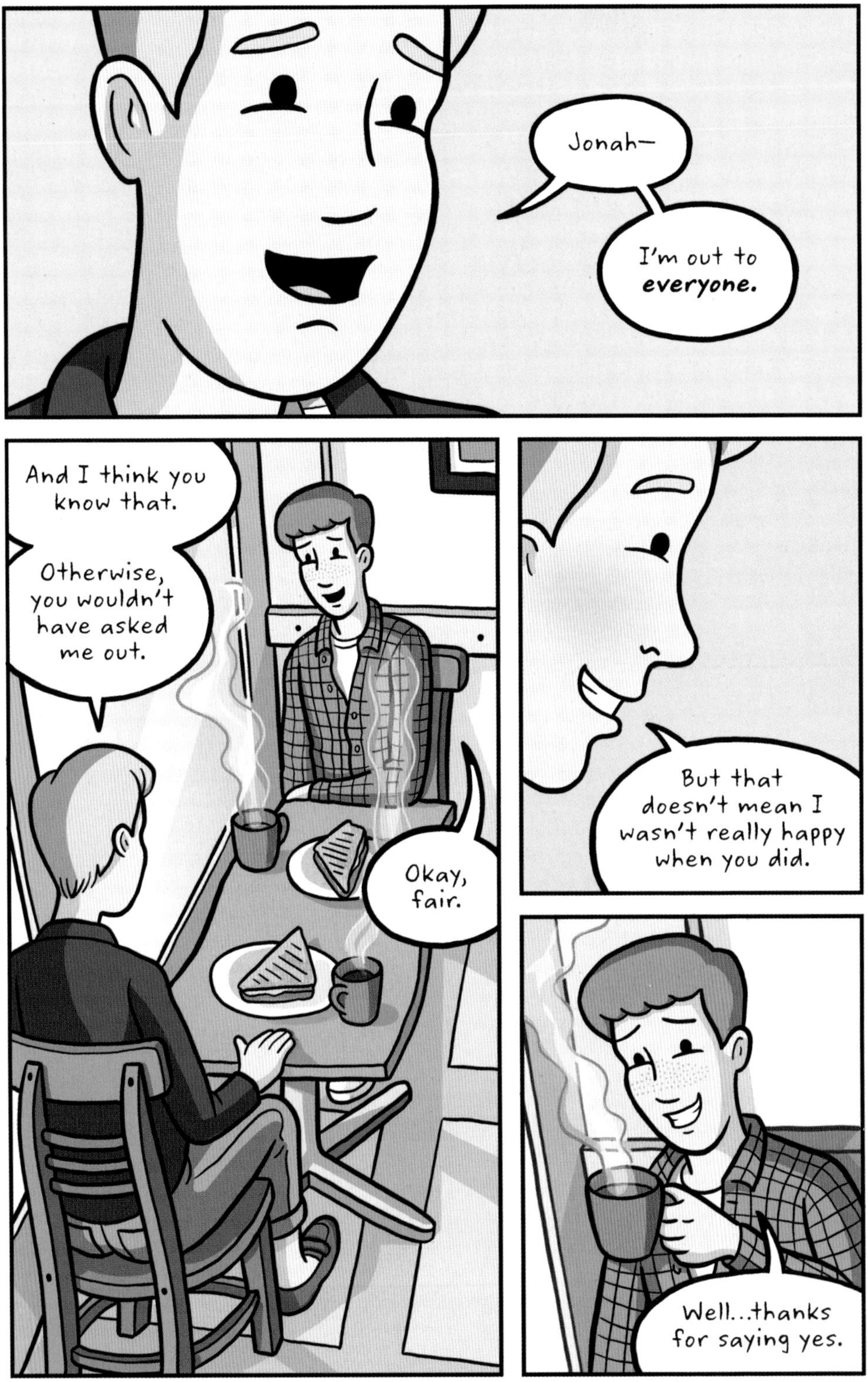
Jonah—
I'm out to **everyone.**
And I think you know that.
Otherwise, you wouldn't have asked me out.
Okay, fair.
But that doesn't mean I wasn't really happy when you did.
Well...thanks for saying yes.

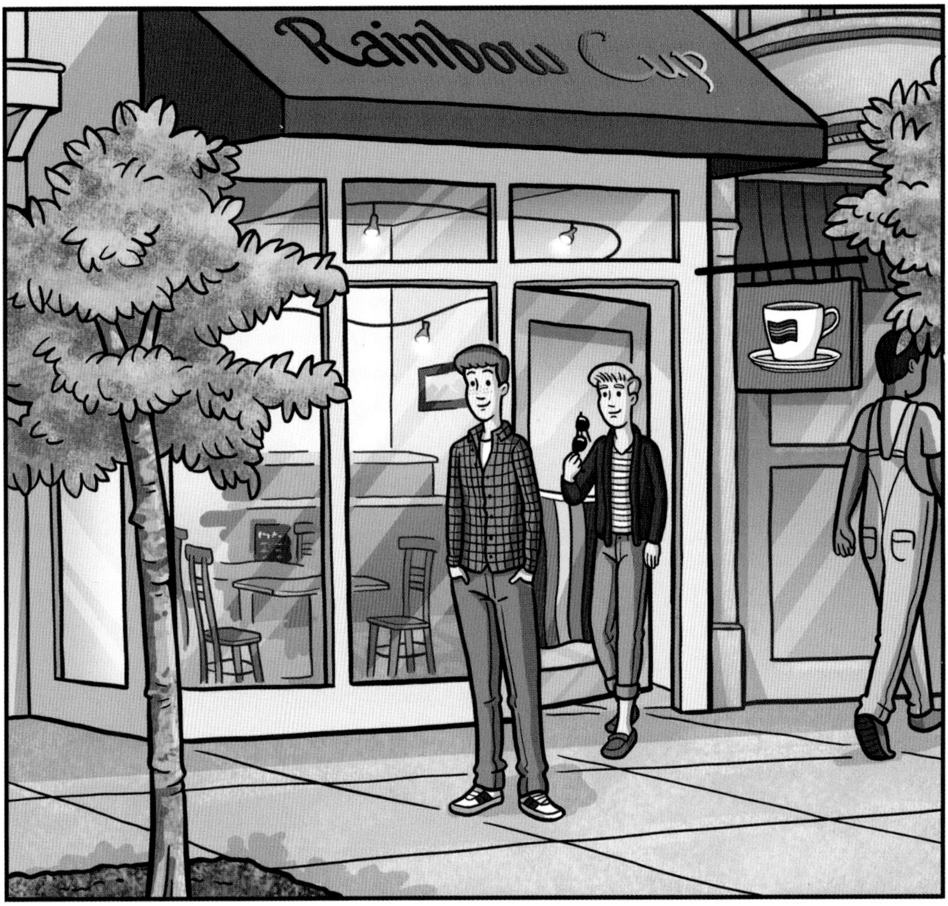
Rainbow Cup

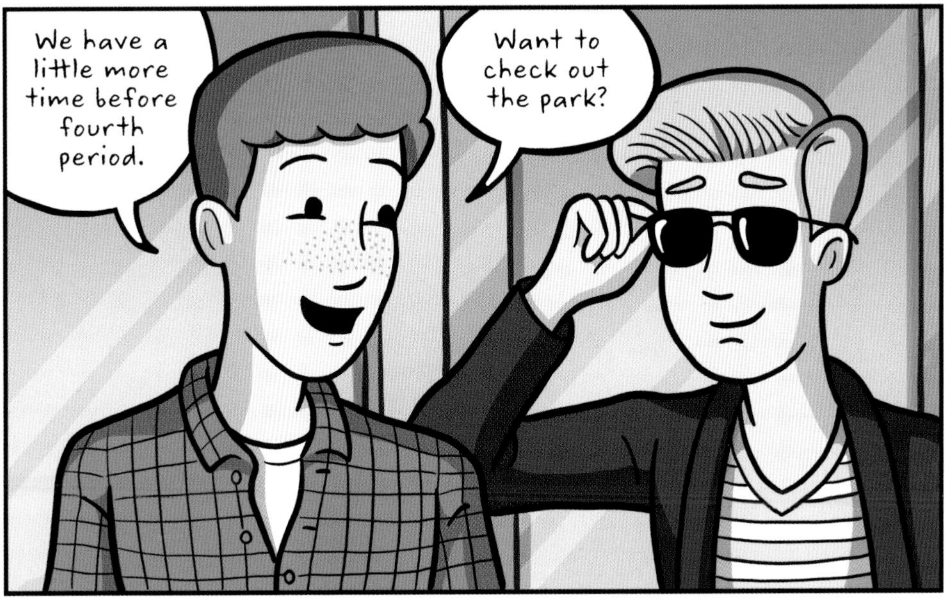
We have a little more time before fourth period.
Want to check out the park?

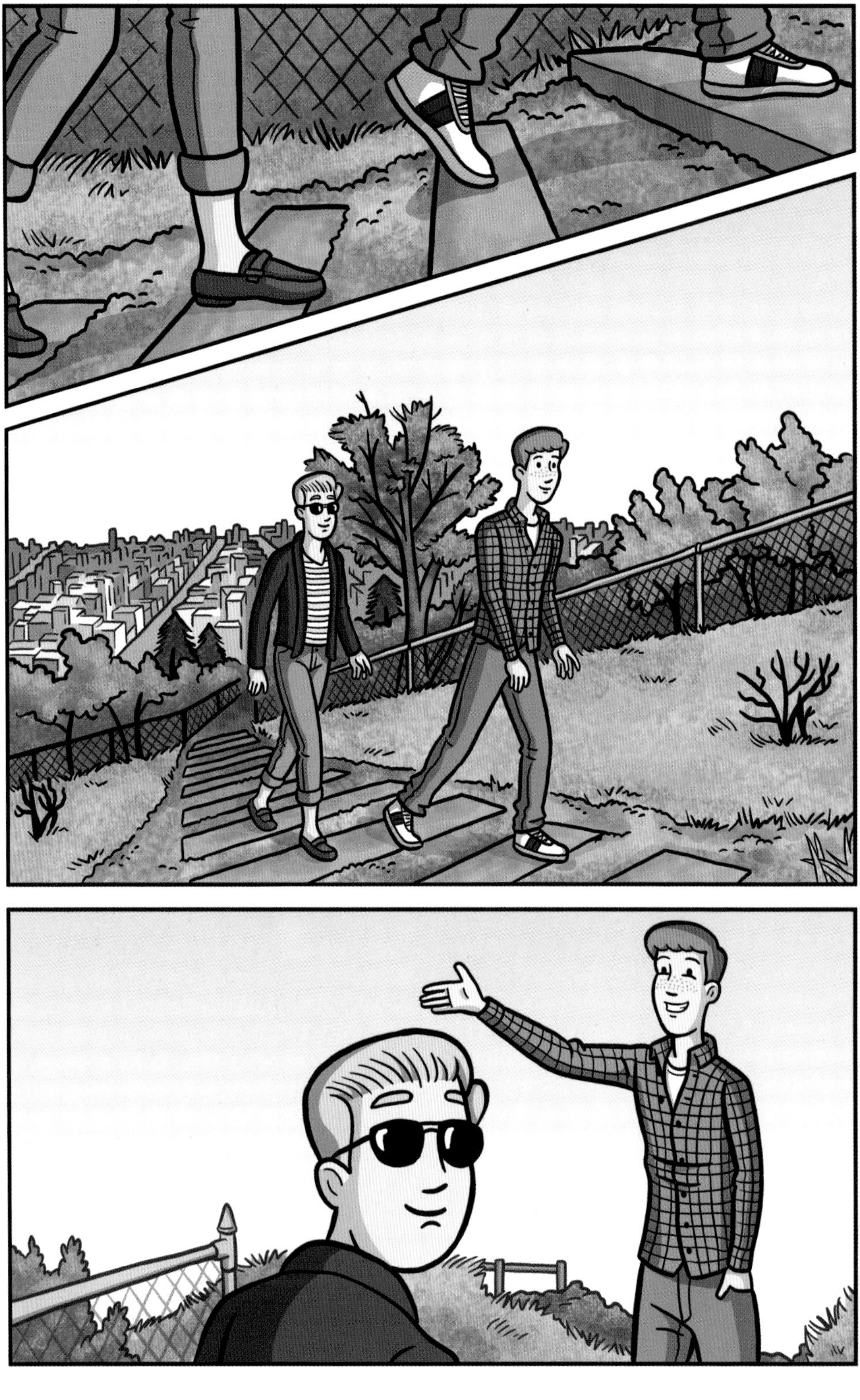

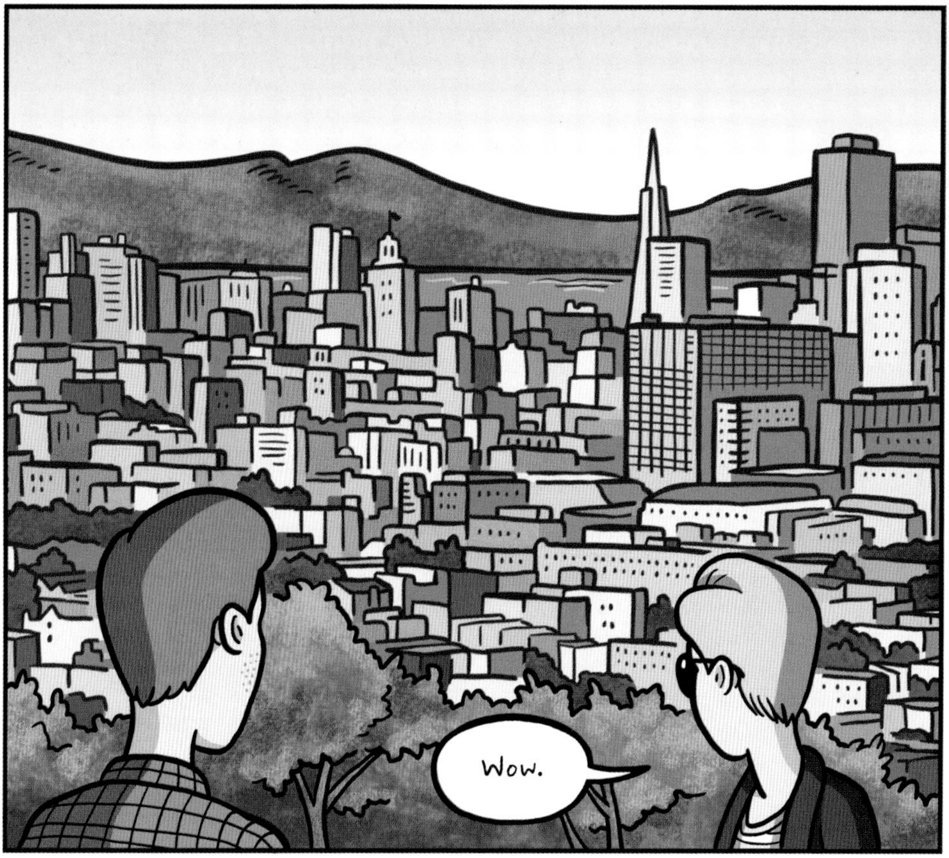
Wow.

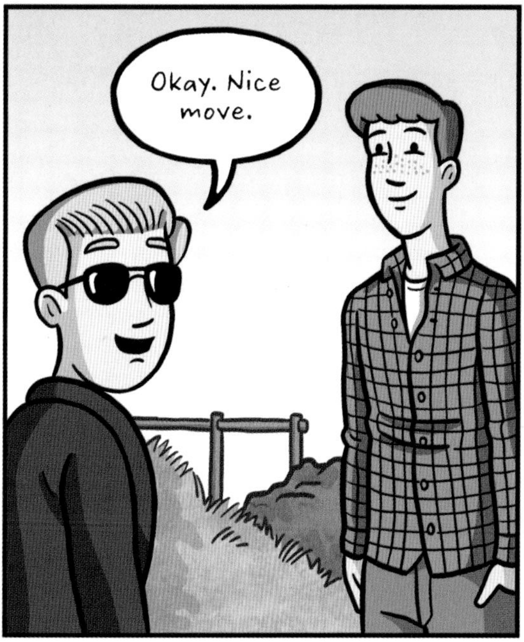
Okay. Nice move.

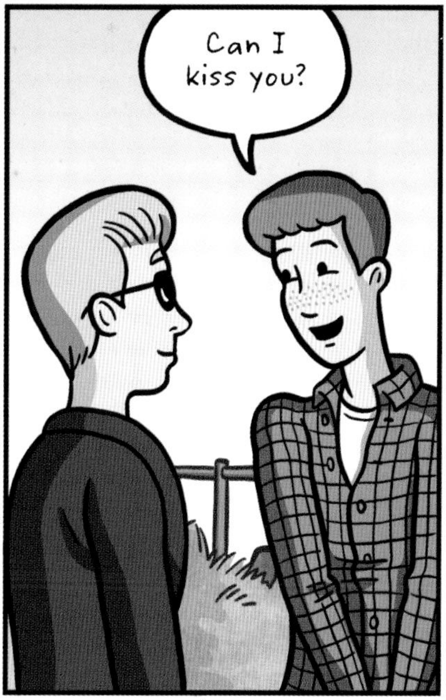
Can I kiss you?

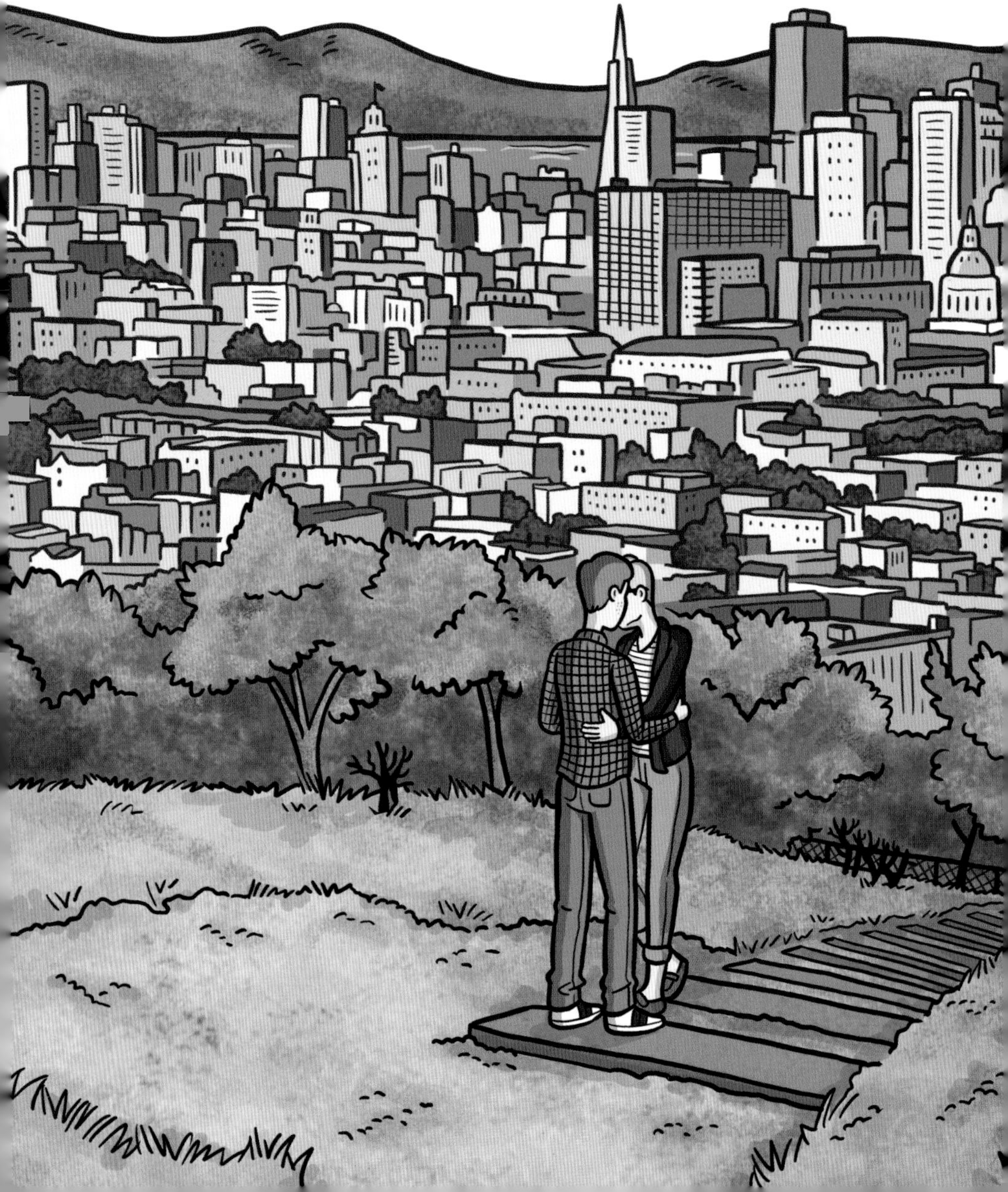

CHAPTER 5

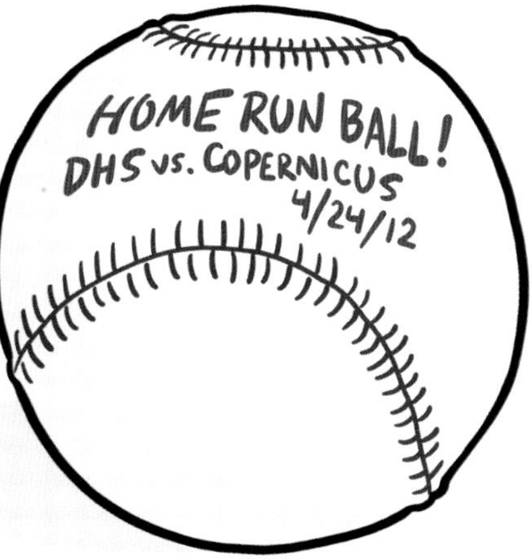
HOME RUN BALL!
DHS vs. COPERNICUS
4/24/12

SPRING

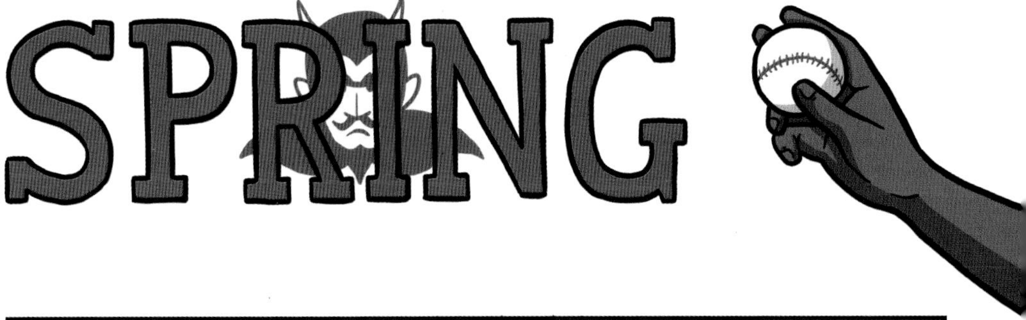

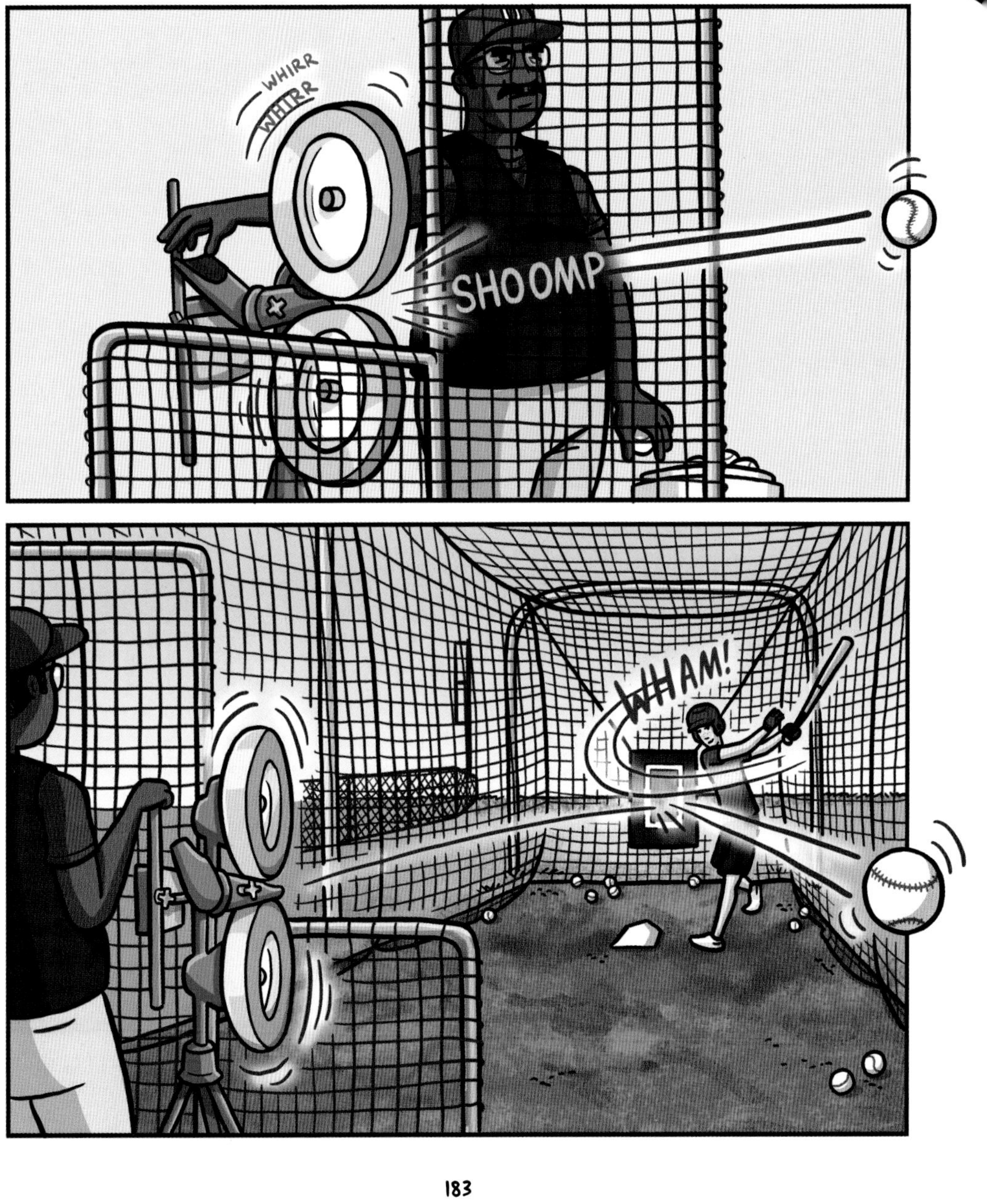
WHIRR
WHIRR
SHOOMP
WHAM!

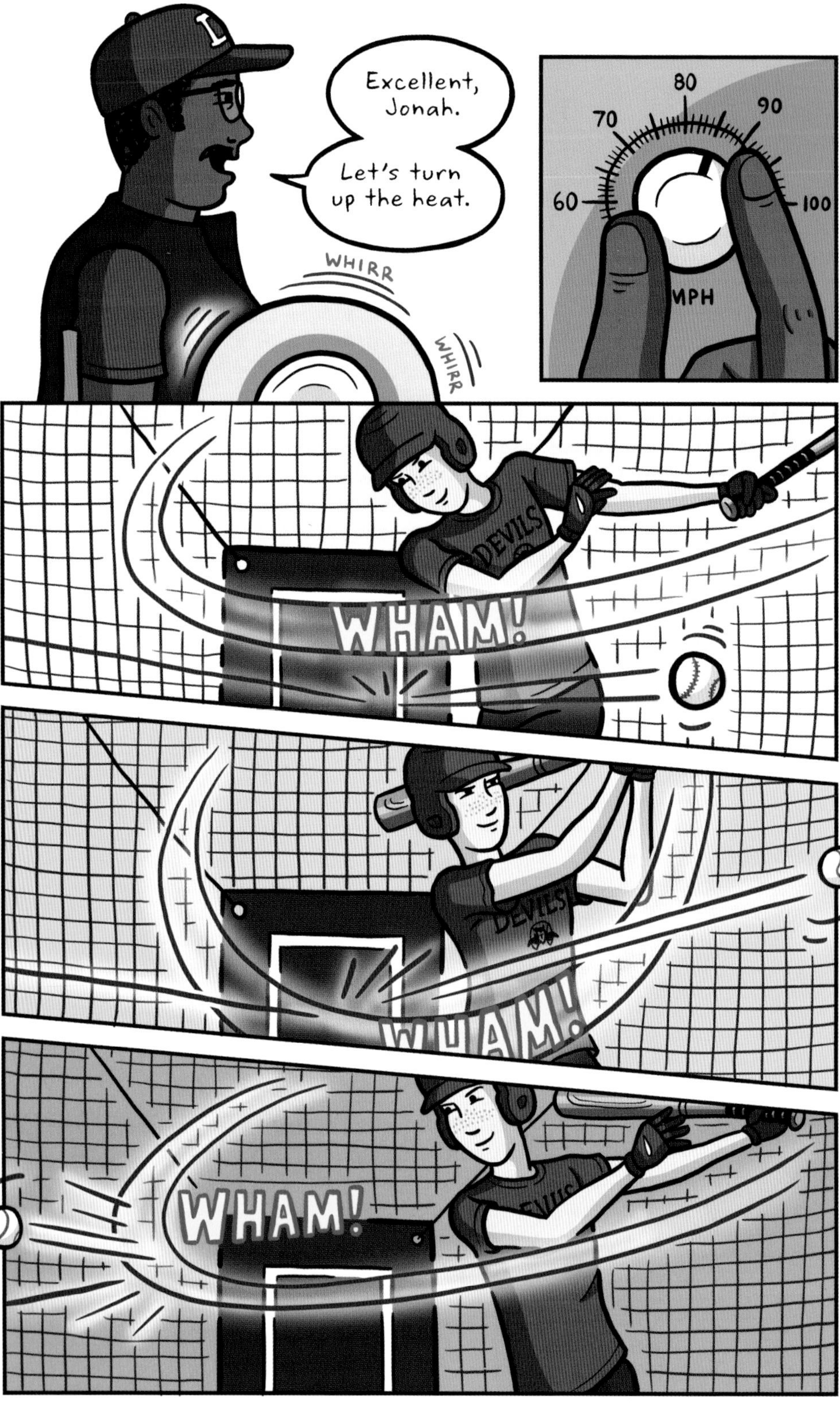
Excellent, Jonah.
Let's turn up the heat.
WHIRR
WHIRR
80
70
90
60
100
MPH
DEVILS
WHAM!
DEVILS
WHAM!
WHAM!

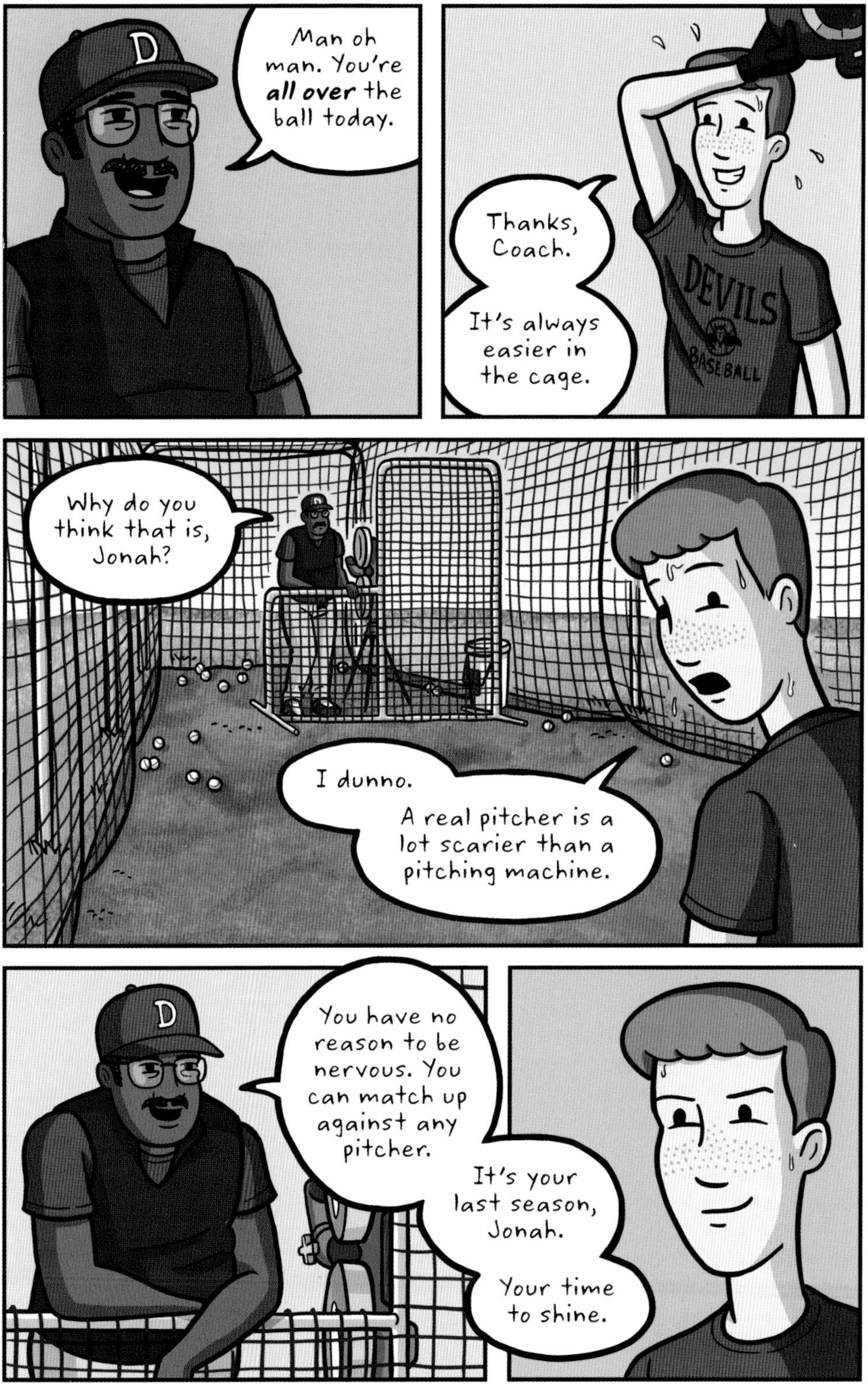
Man oh man. You're **all over** the ball today.
Thanks, Coach.
It's always easier in the cage.
DEVILS BASEBALL
Why do you think that is, Jonah?
I dunno.
A real pitcher is a lot scarier than a pitching machine.
You have no reason to be nervous. You can match up against any pitcher.
It's your last season, Jonah.
Your time to shine.

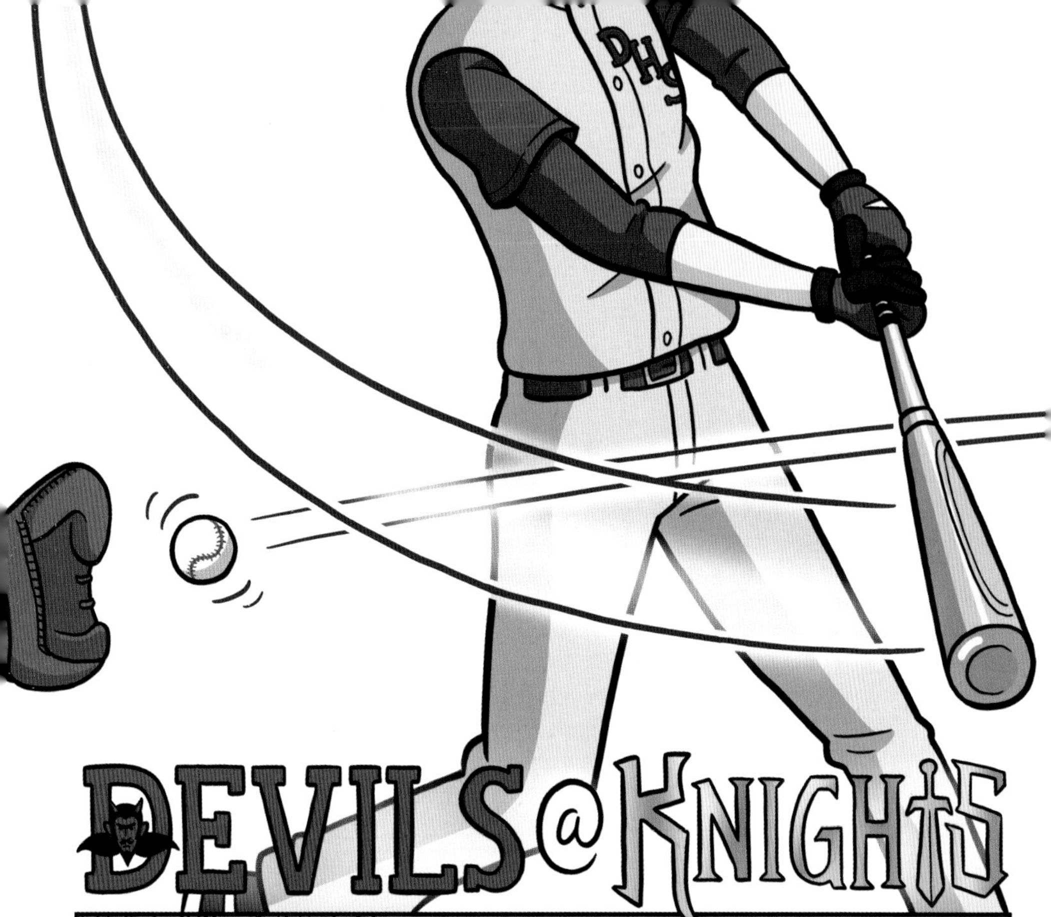
DEVILS @ KNIGHTS

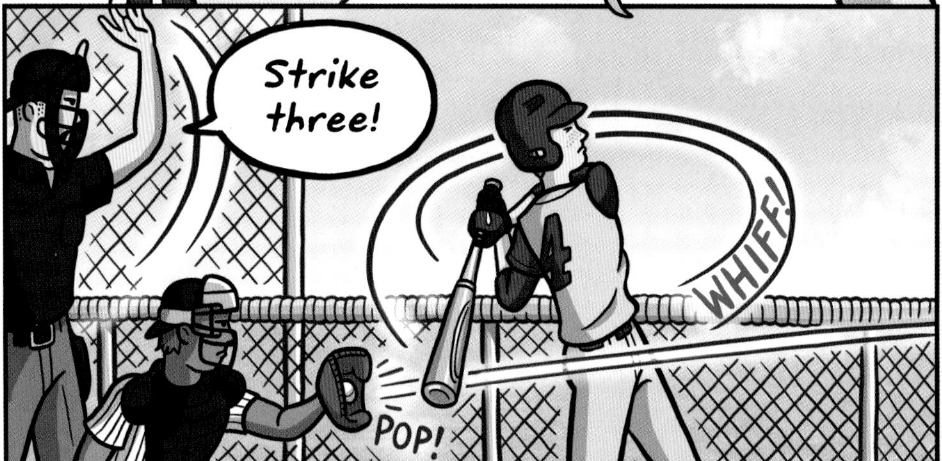
Strike three!
WHIFF!
POP!

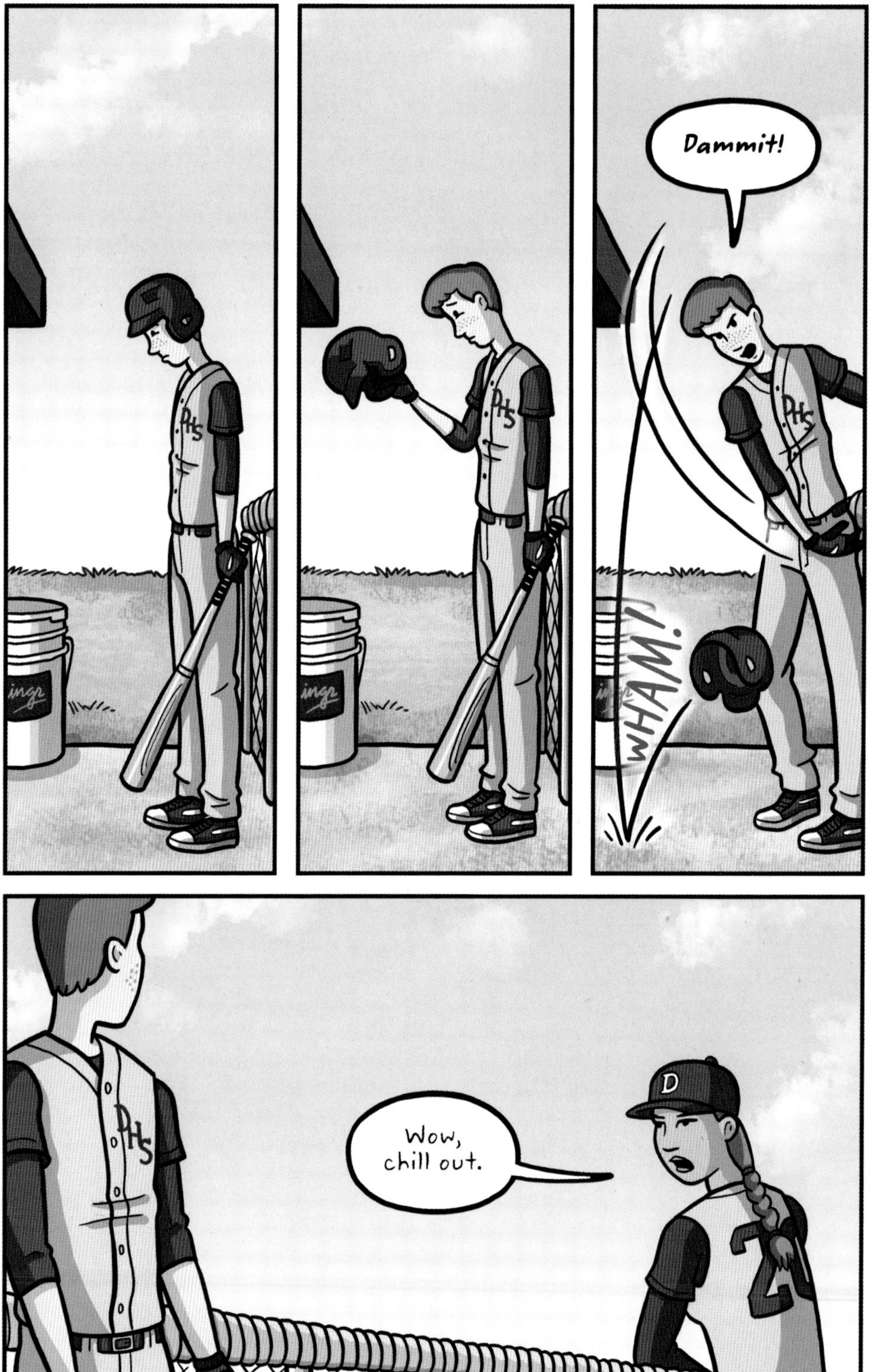
Dammit!
WHAM!
Wow, chill out.

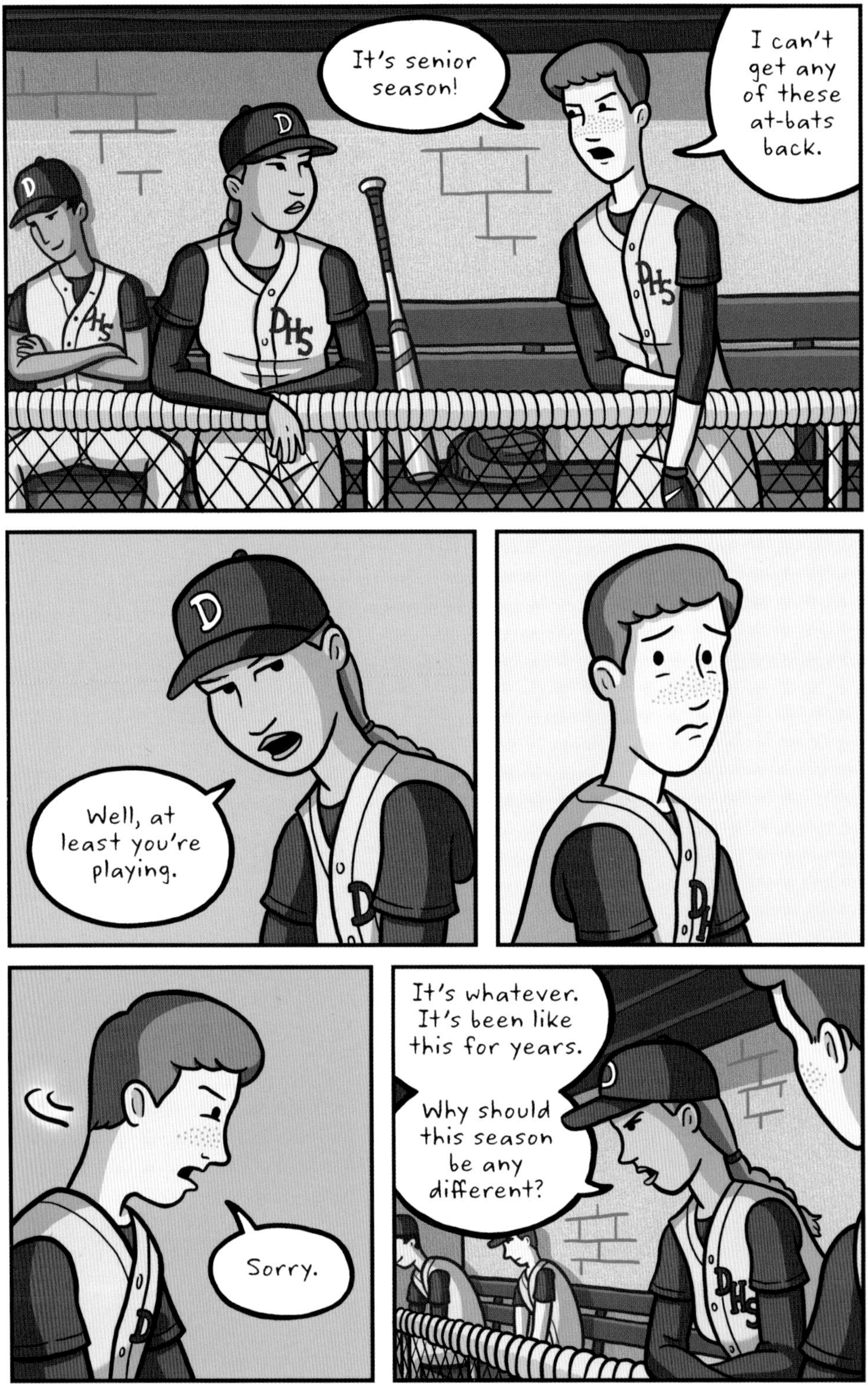
It's senior season!
I can't get any of these at-bats back.
Well, at least you're playing.
Sorry.
It's whatever. It's been like this for years.
Why should this season be any different?

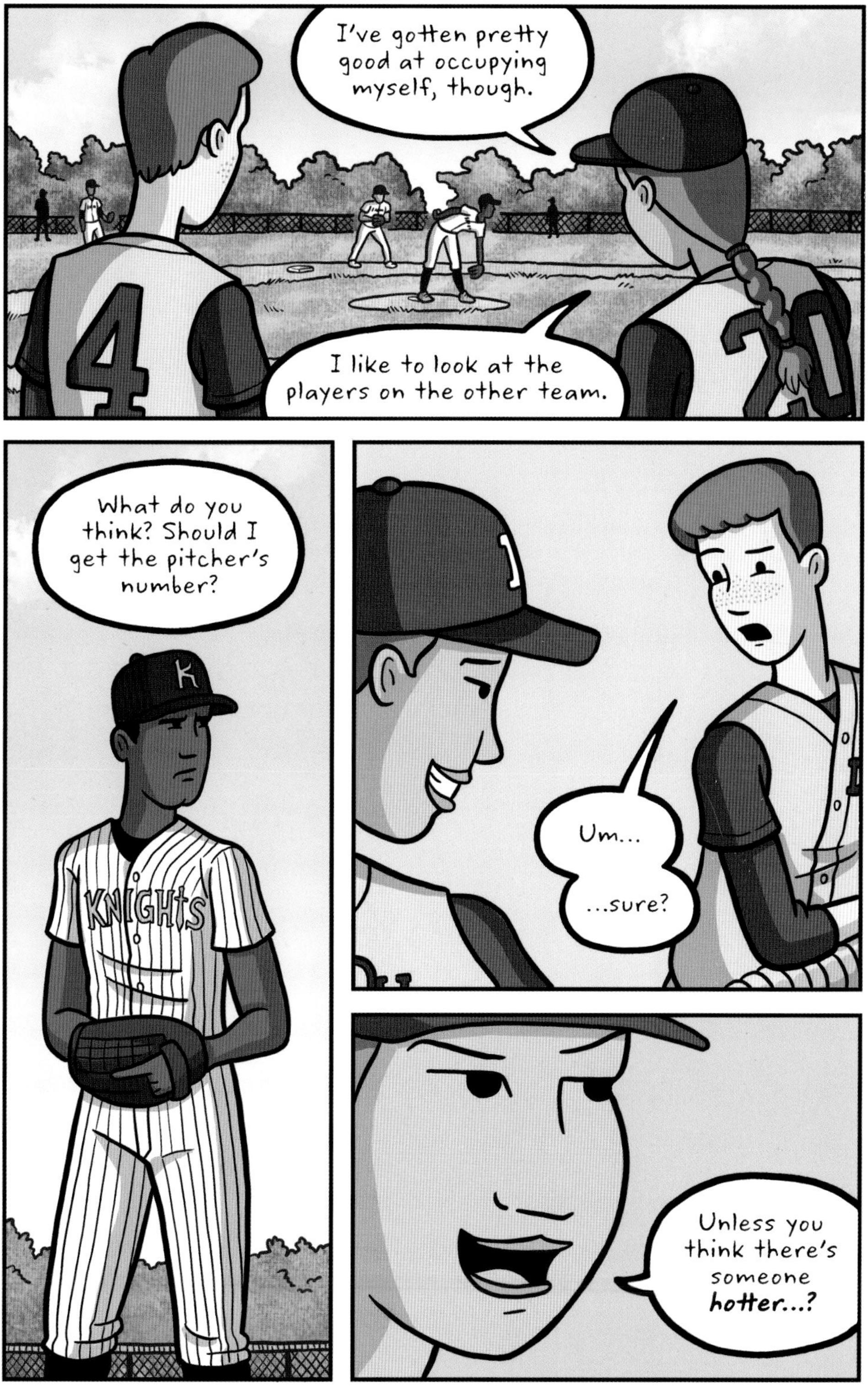
I've gotten pretty good at occupying myself, though.
I like to look at the players on the other team.
What do you think? Should I get the pitcher's number?
KNIGHTS
Um...
...sure?
Unless you think there's someone **hotter...?**

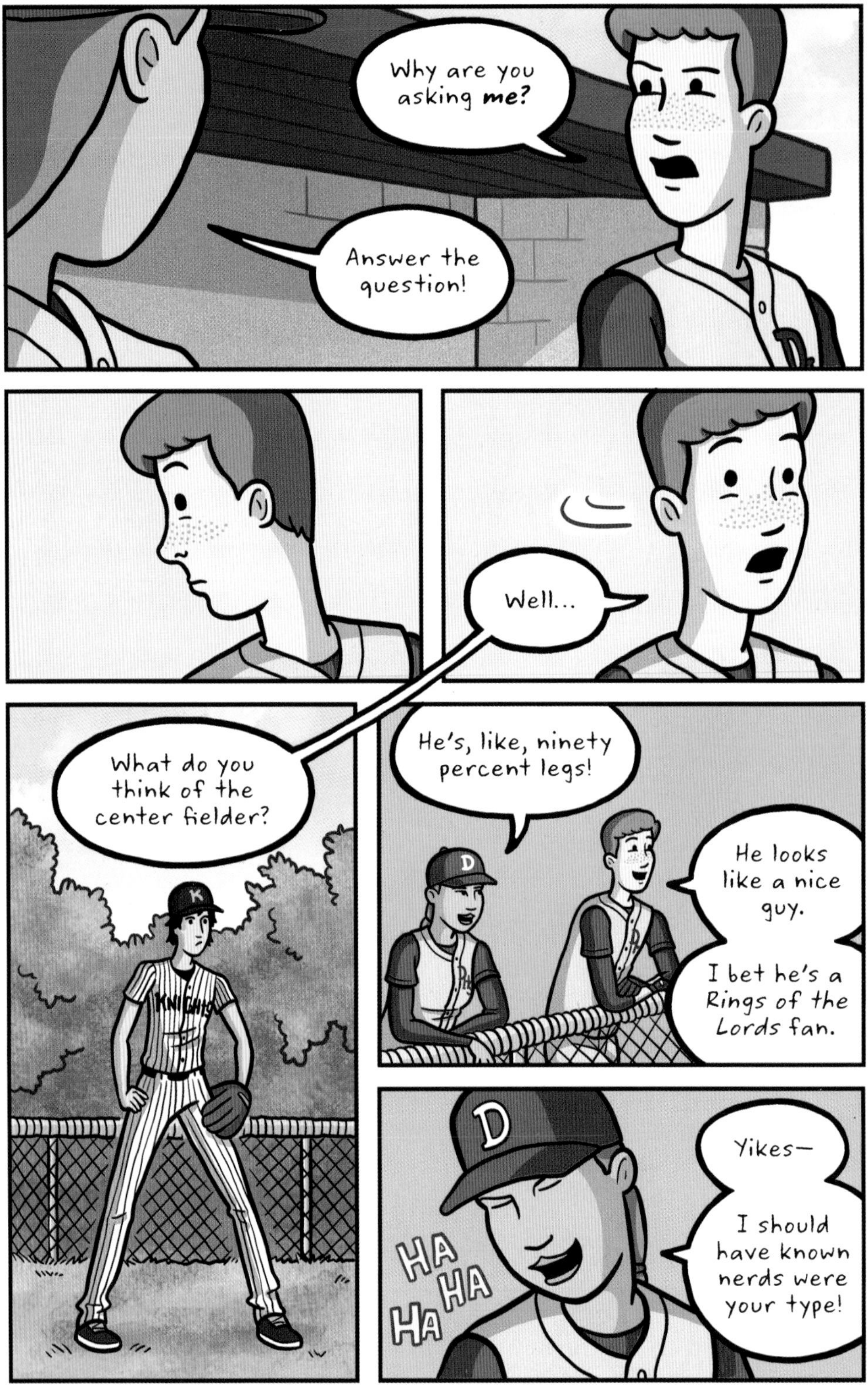
Why are you asking **me?**
Answer the question!
Well...
What do you think of the center fielder?
He's, like, ninety percent legs!
He looks like a nice guy.
I bet he's a Rings of the Lords fan.
Yikes—
I should have known nerds were your type!
HA HA HA

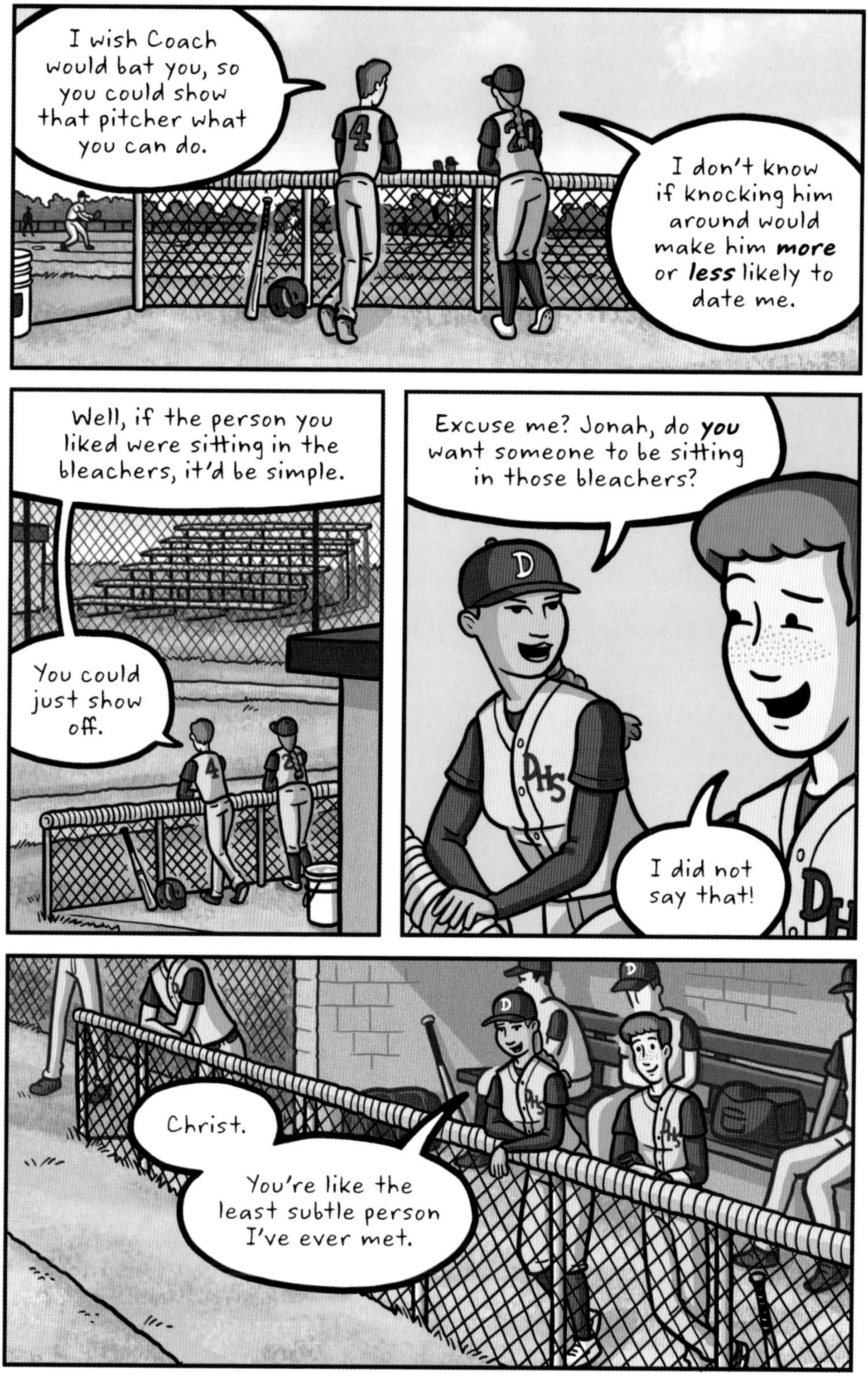
I wish Coach would bat you, so you could show that pitcher what you can do.
I don't know if knocking him around would make him **more** or **less** likely to date me.
Well, if the person you liked were sitting in the bleachers, it'd be simple.
You could just show off.
Excuse me? Jonah, do **you** want someone to be sitting in those bleachers?
I did not say that!
Christ.
You're like the least subtle person I've ever met.

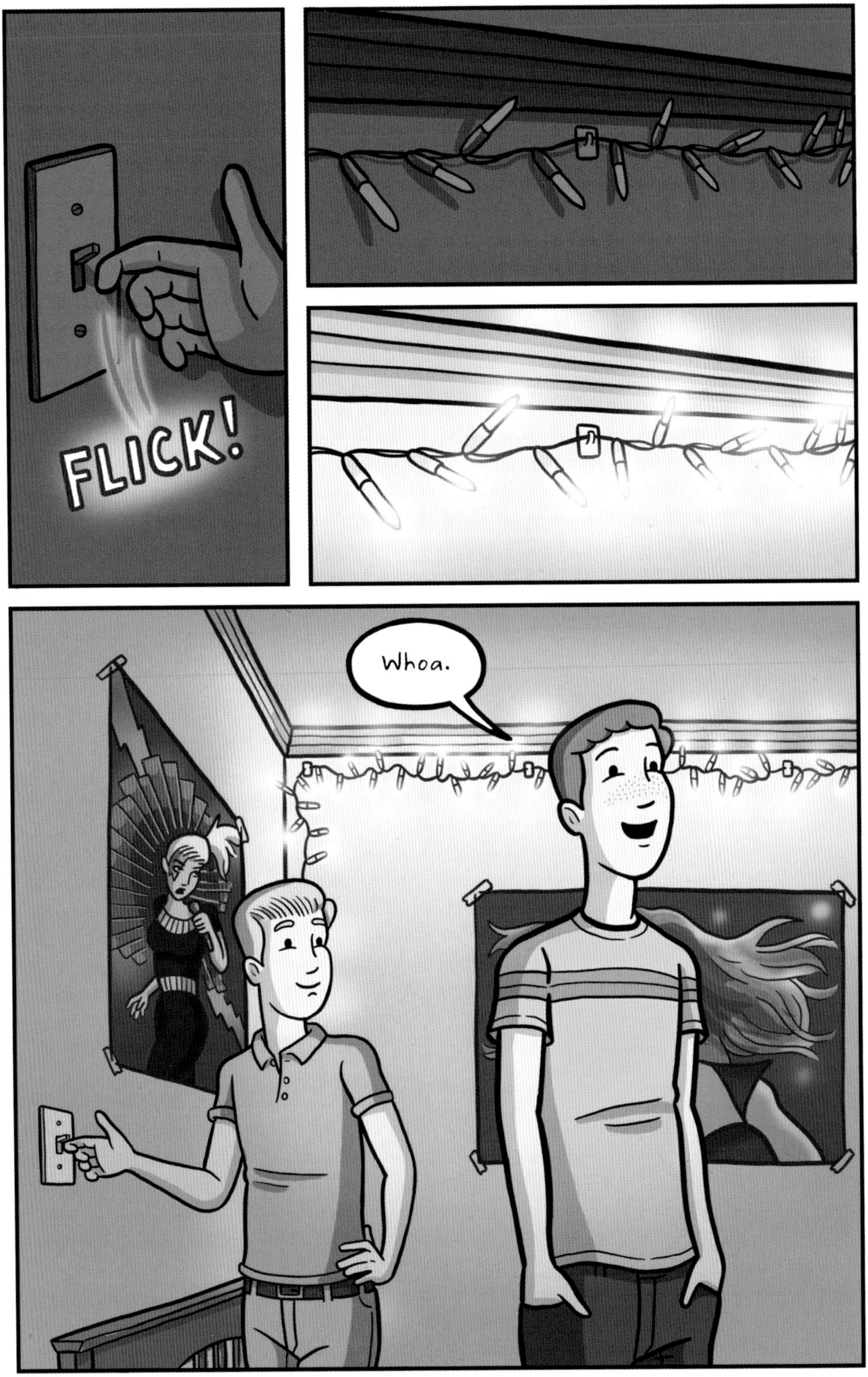
FLICK!
Whoa.

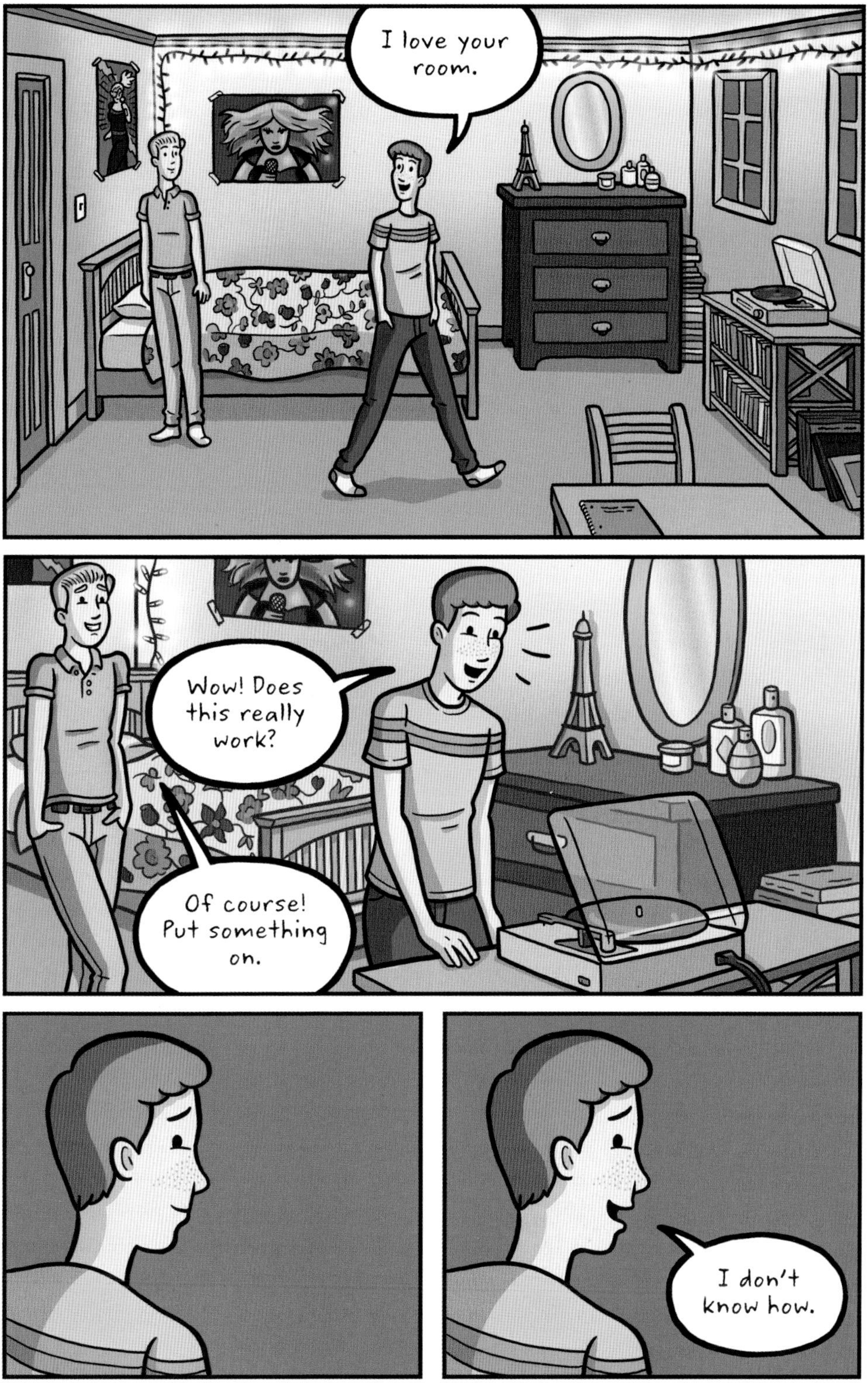
I love your room.
Wow! Does this really work?
Of course! Put something on.
I don't know how.

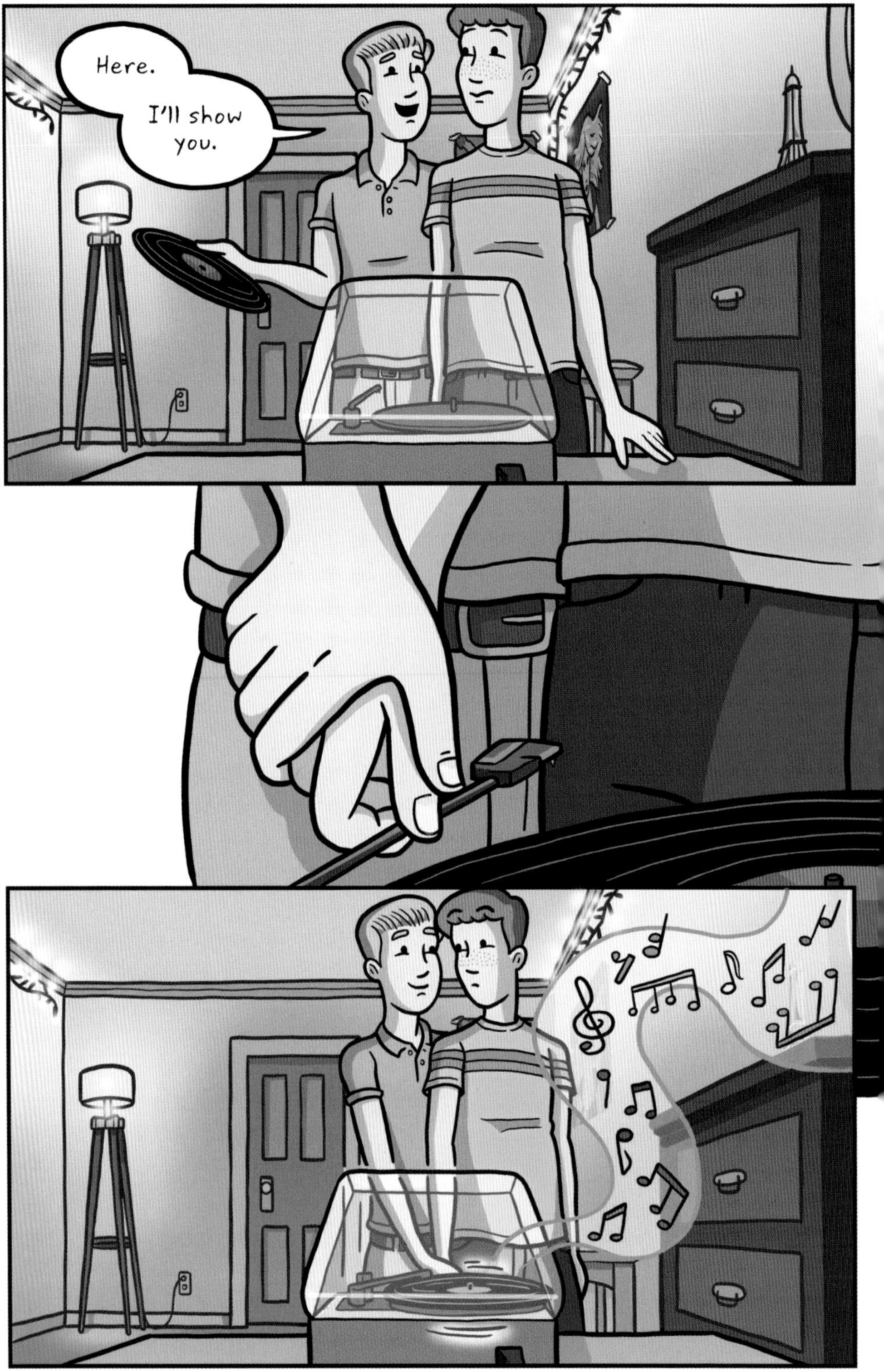
Here.
I'll show you.

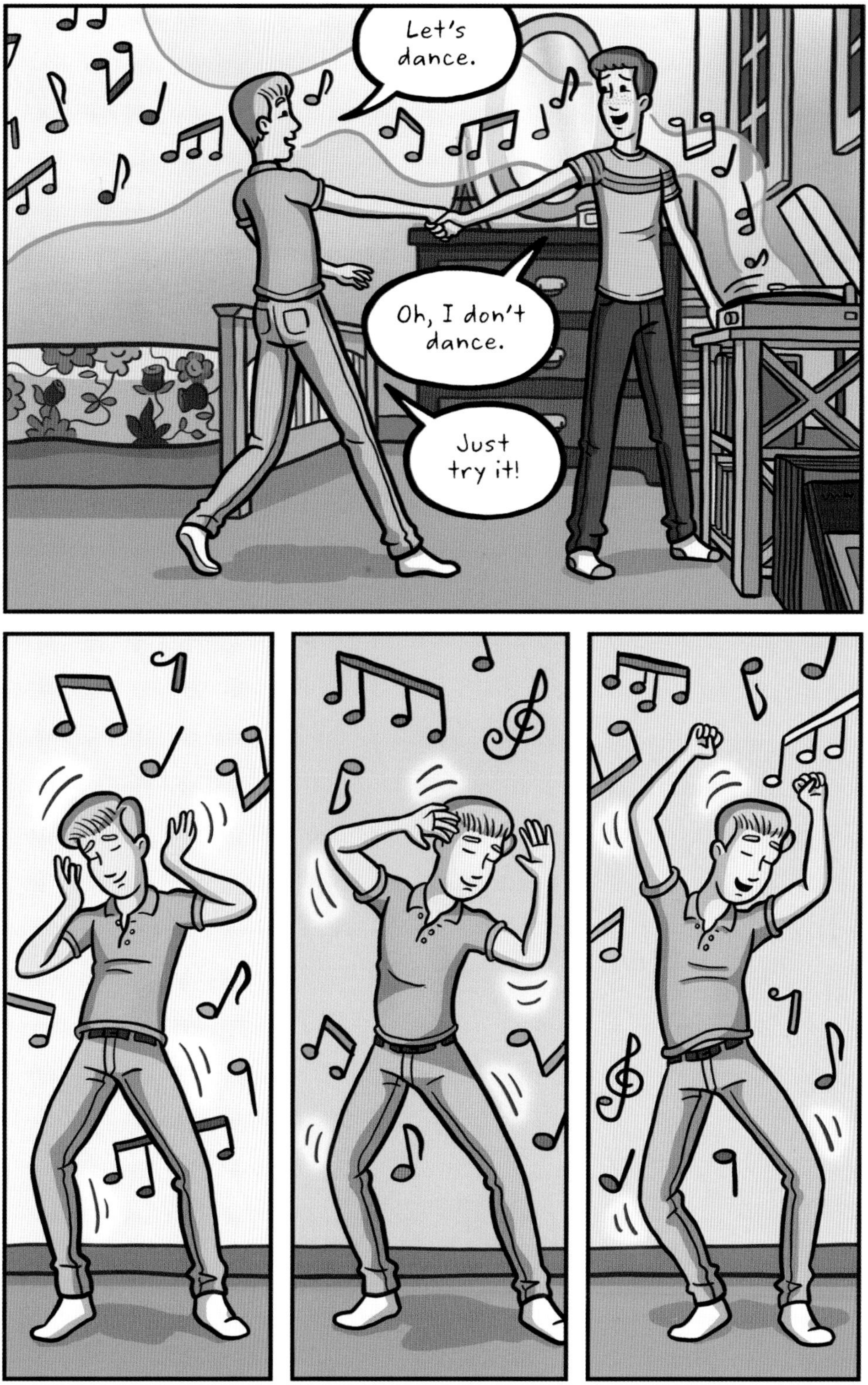
Let's dance.
Oh, I don't dance.
Just try it!

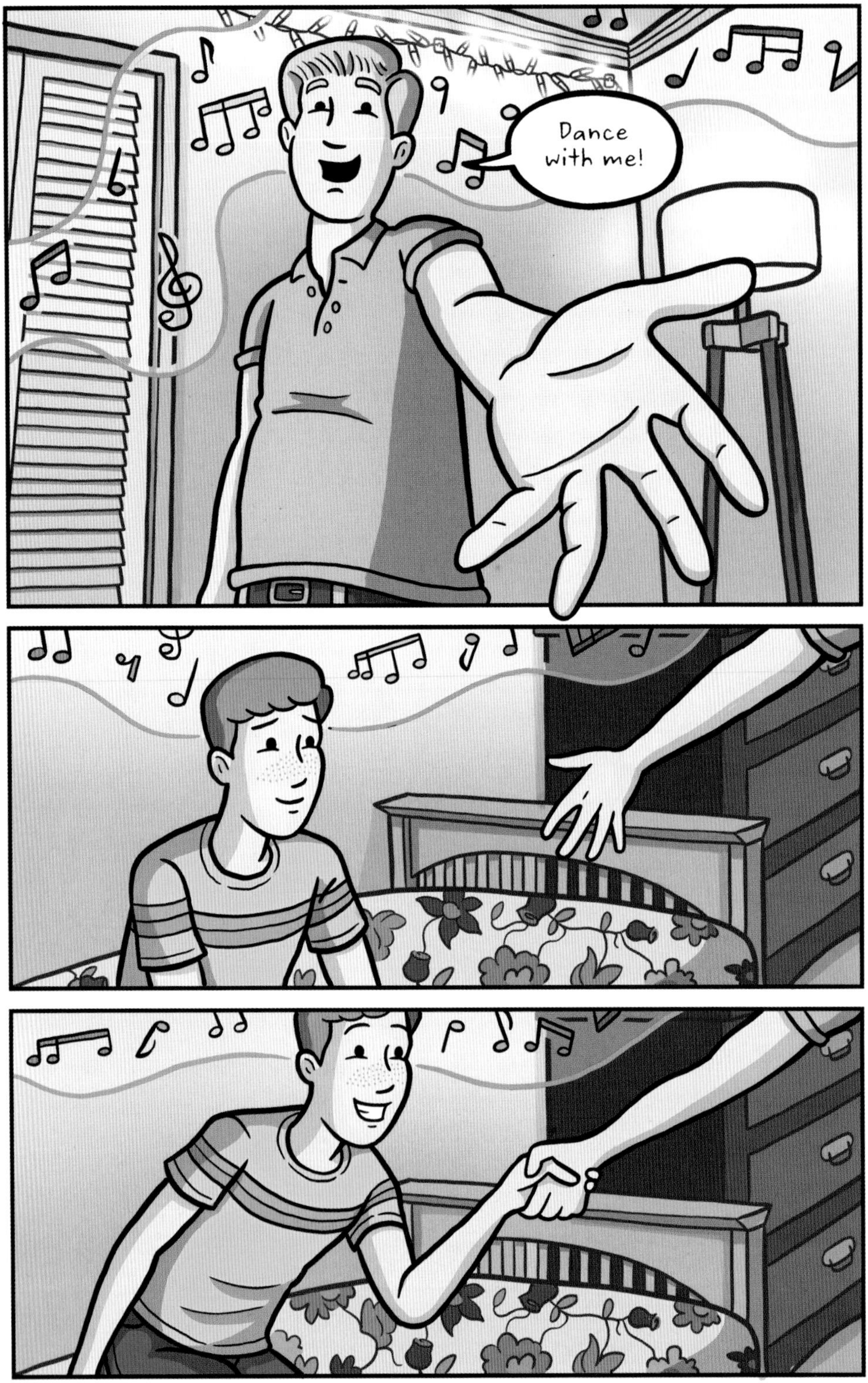
Dance with me!

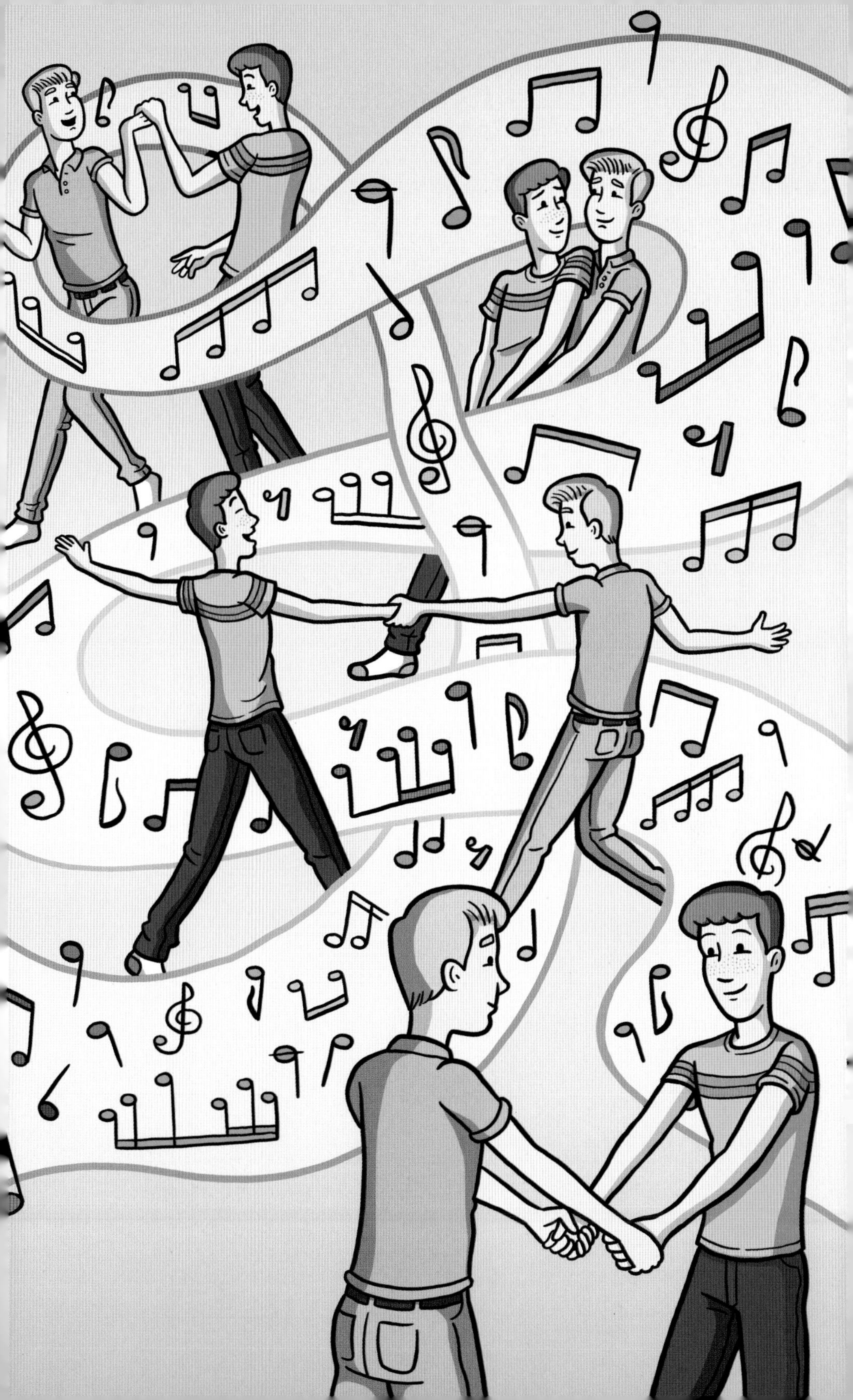

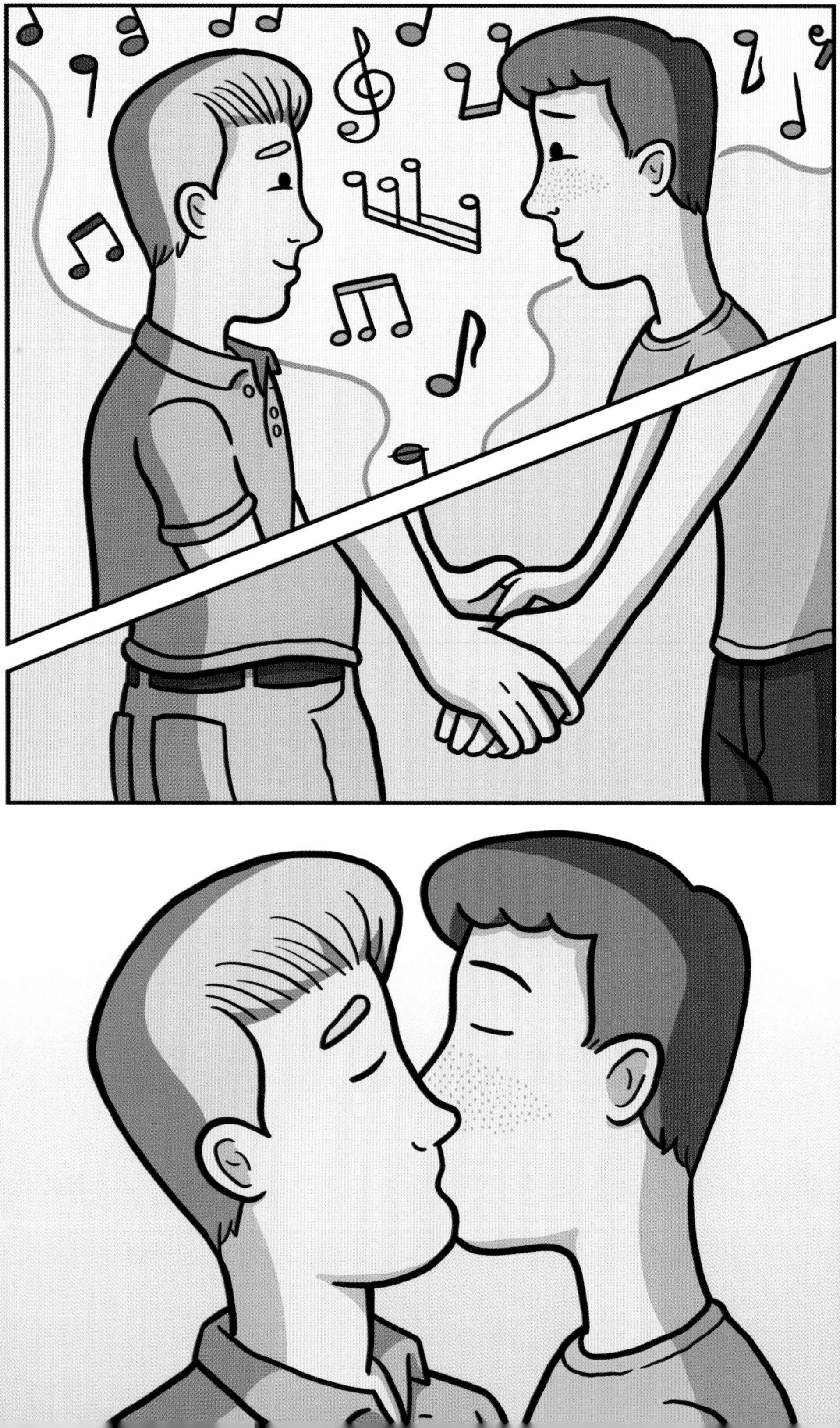

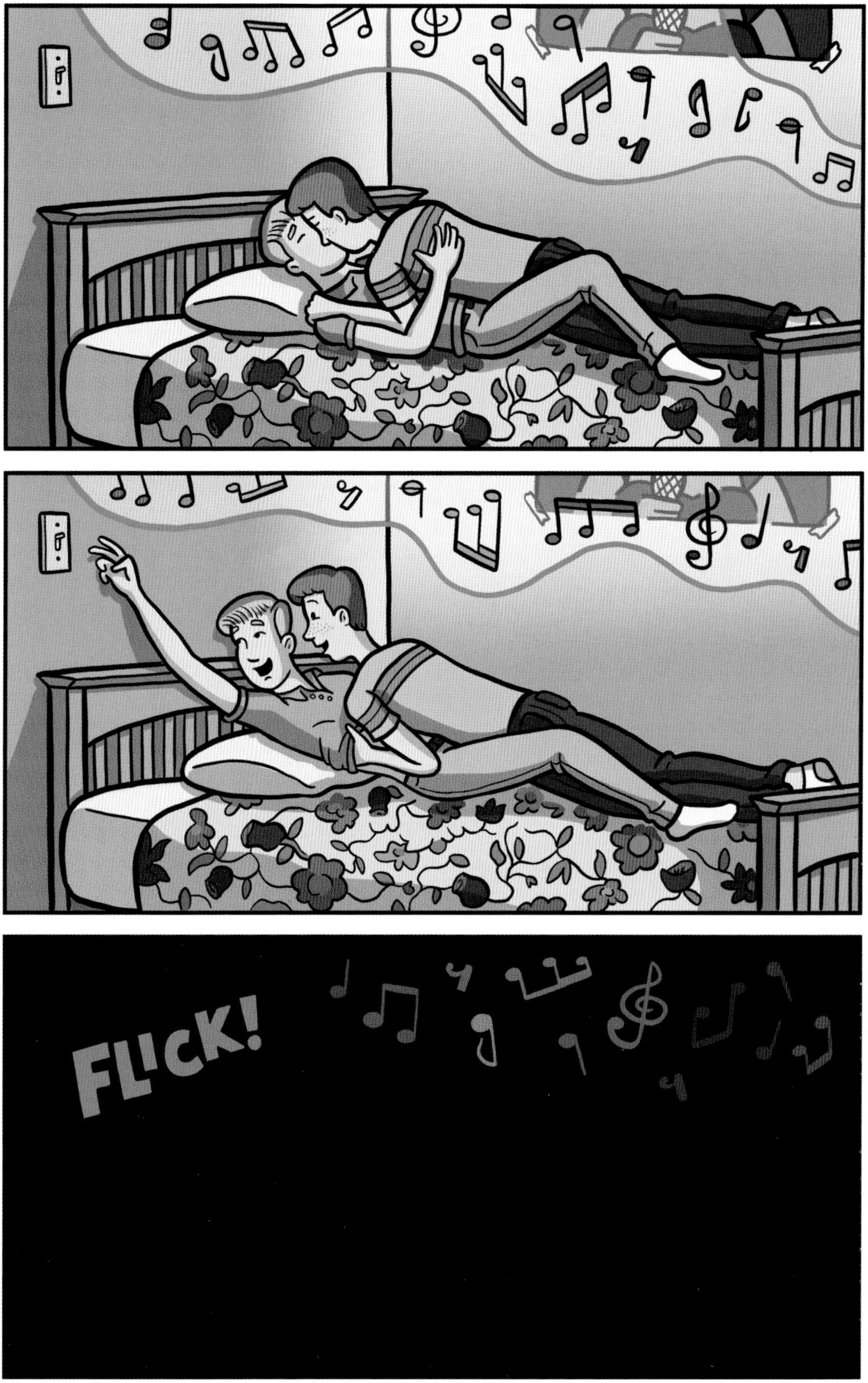
FLICK!

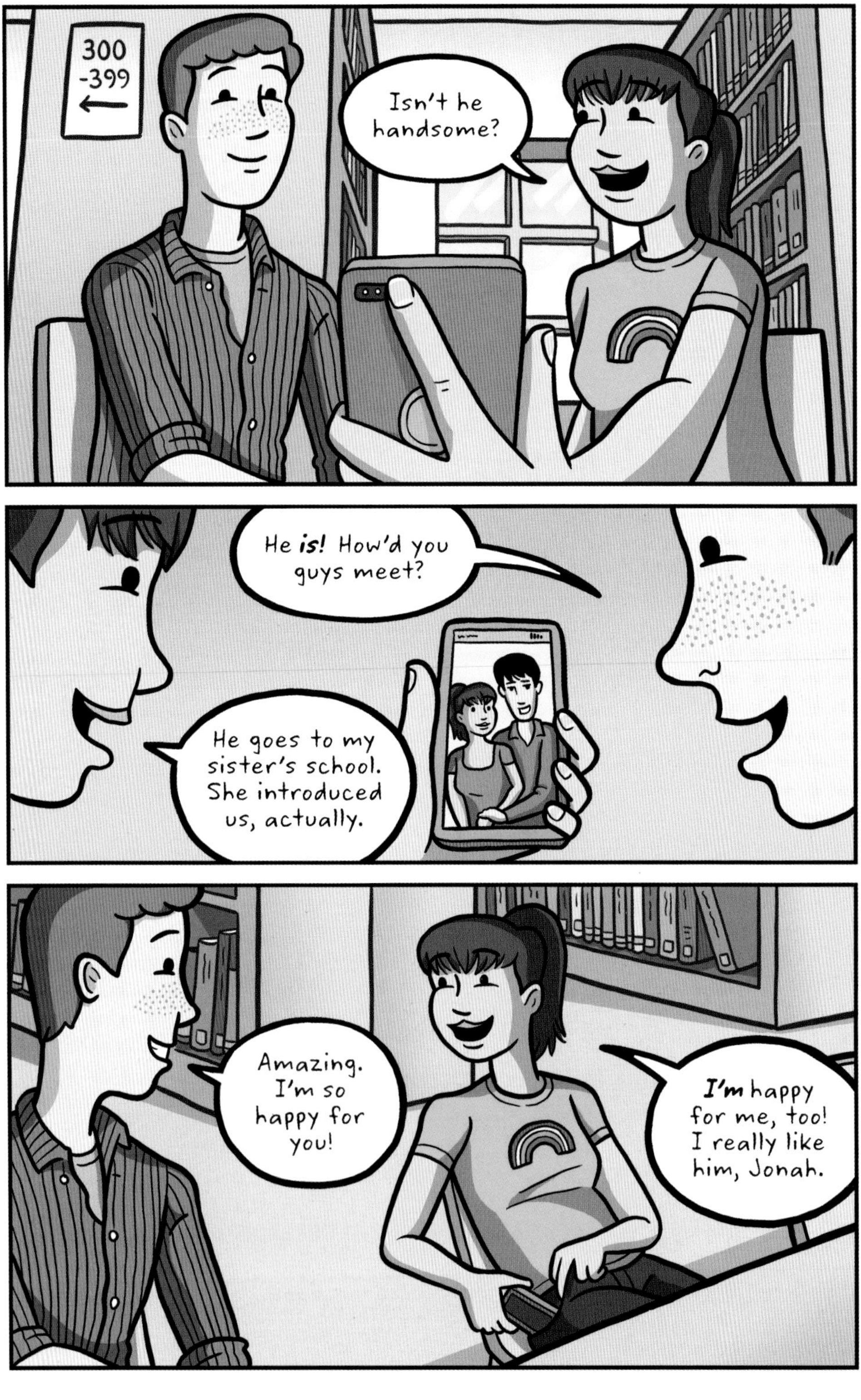
300
-399
Isn't he handsome?
He *is!* How'd you guys meet?
He goes to my sister's school. She introduced us, actually.
Amazing. I'm so happy for you!
I'm happy for me, too! I really like him, Jonah.

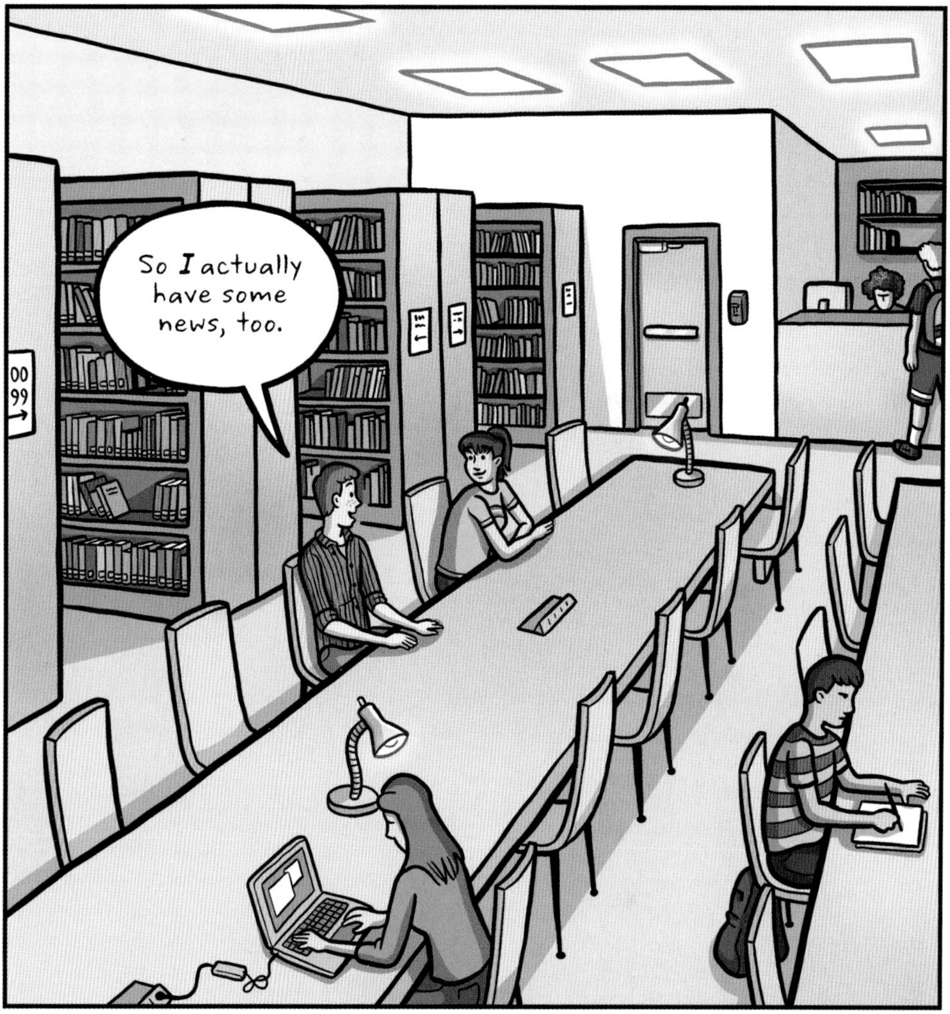
So I actually have some news, too.

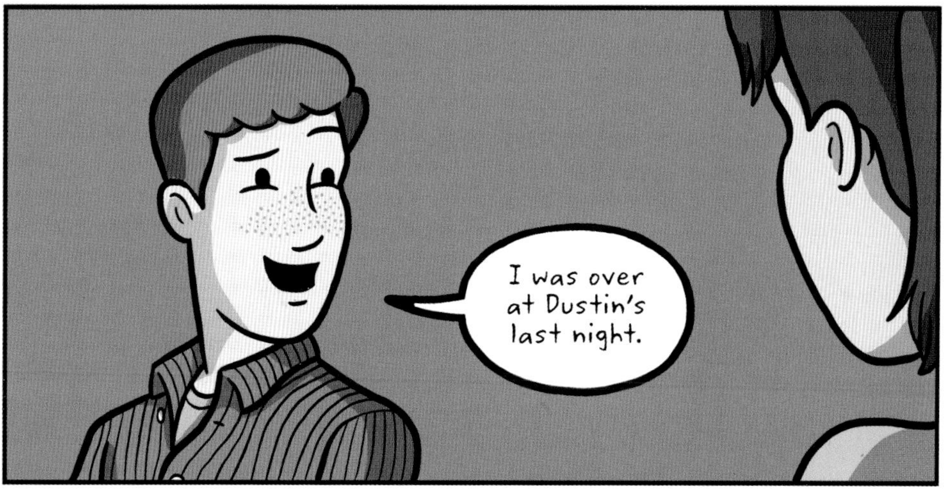
I was over at Dustin's last night.

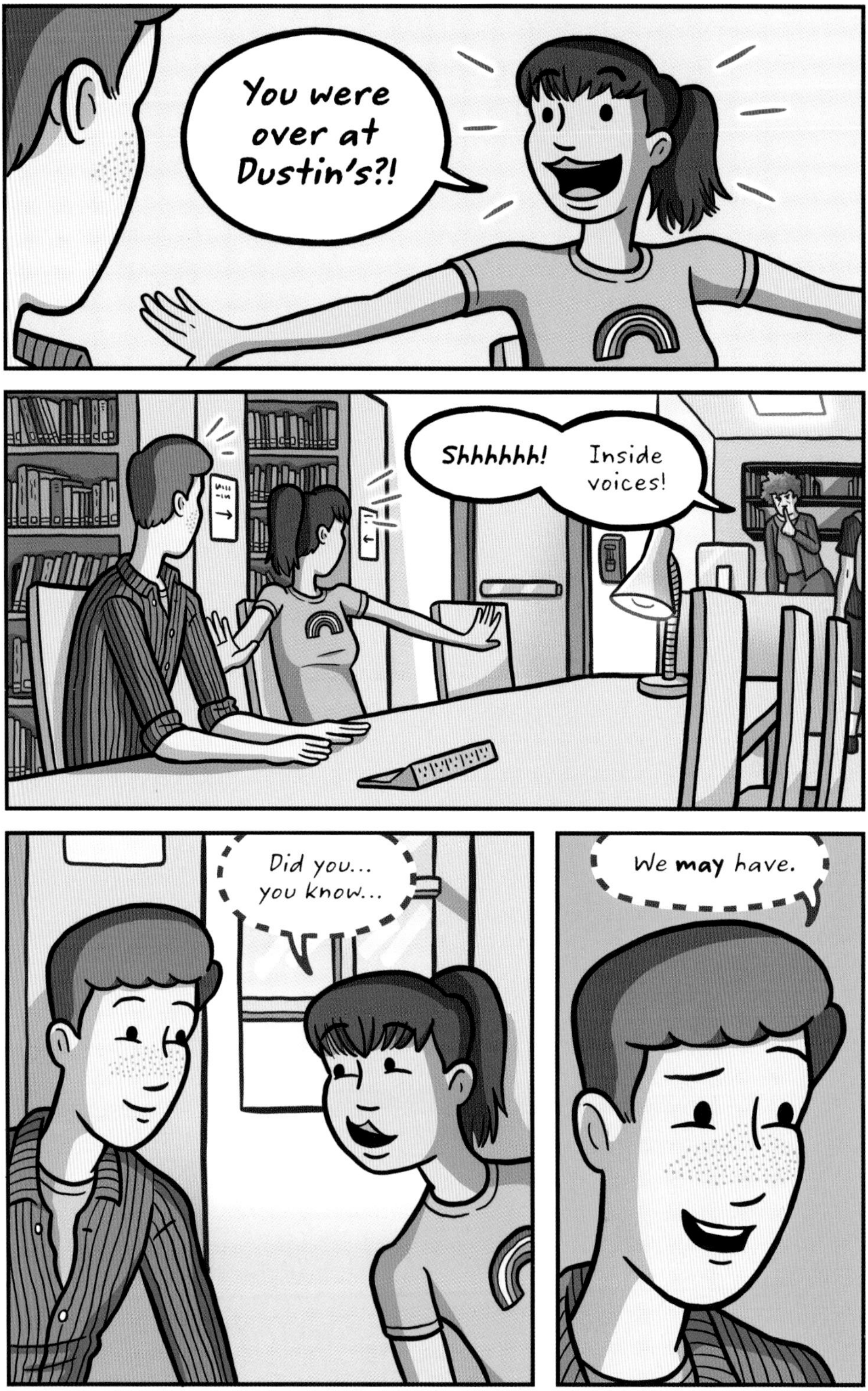
You were over at Dustin's?!
Shhhhhh! Inside voices!
Did you... you know...
We **may** have.

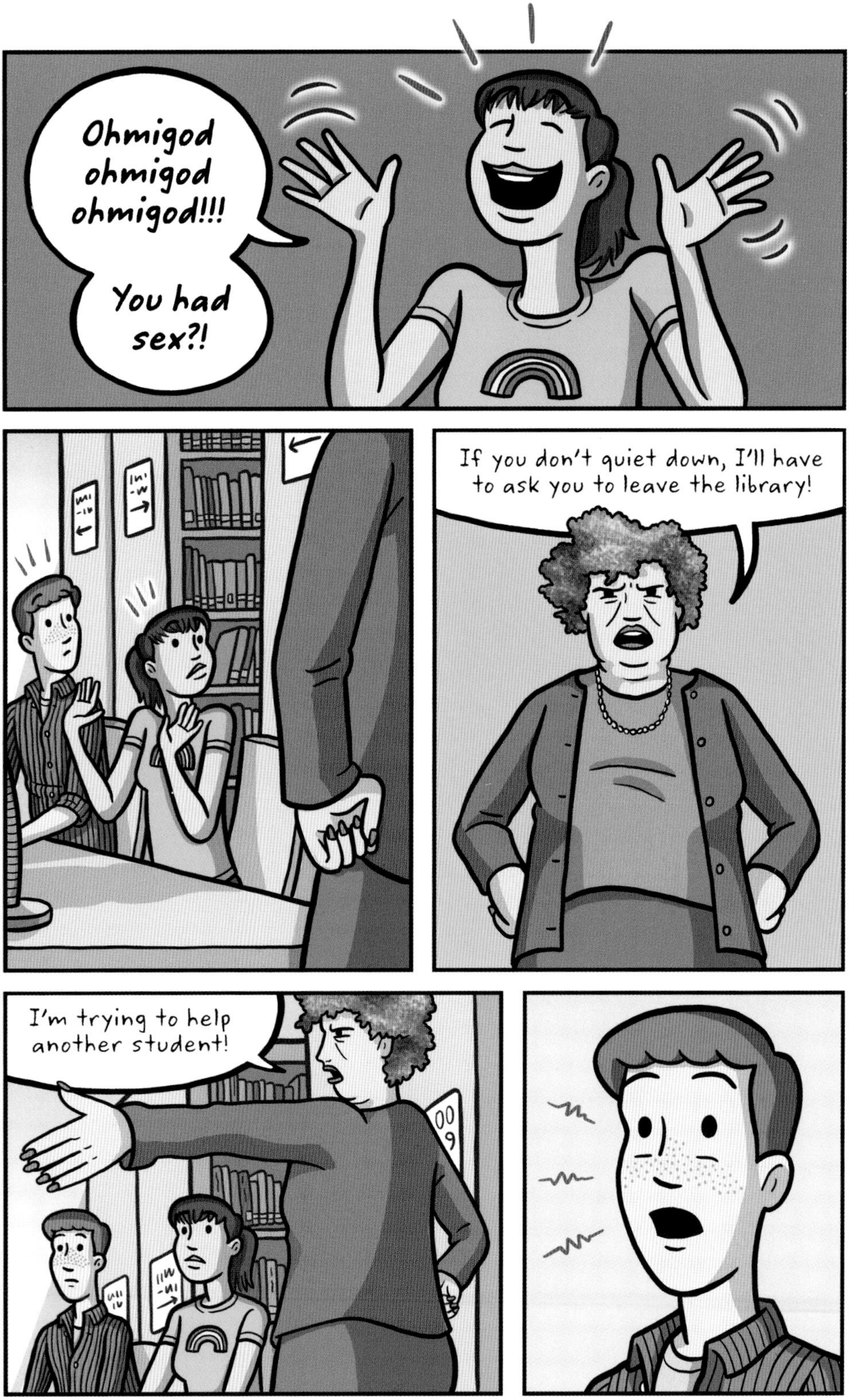
Ohmigod ohmigod ohmigod!!!
You had sex?!
If you don't quiet down, I'll have to ask you to leave the library!
I'm trying to help another student!

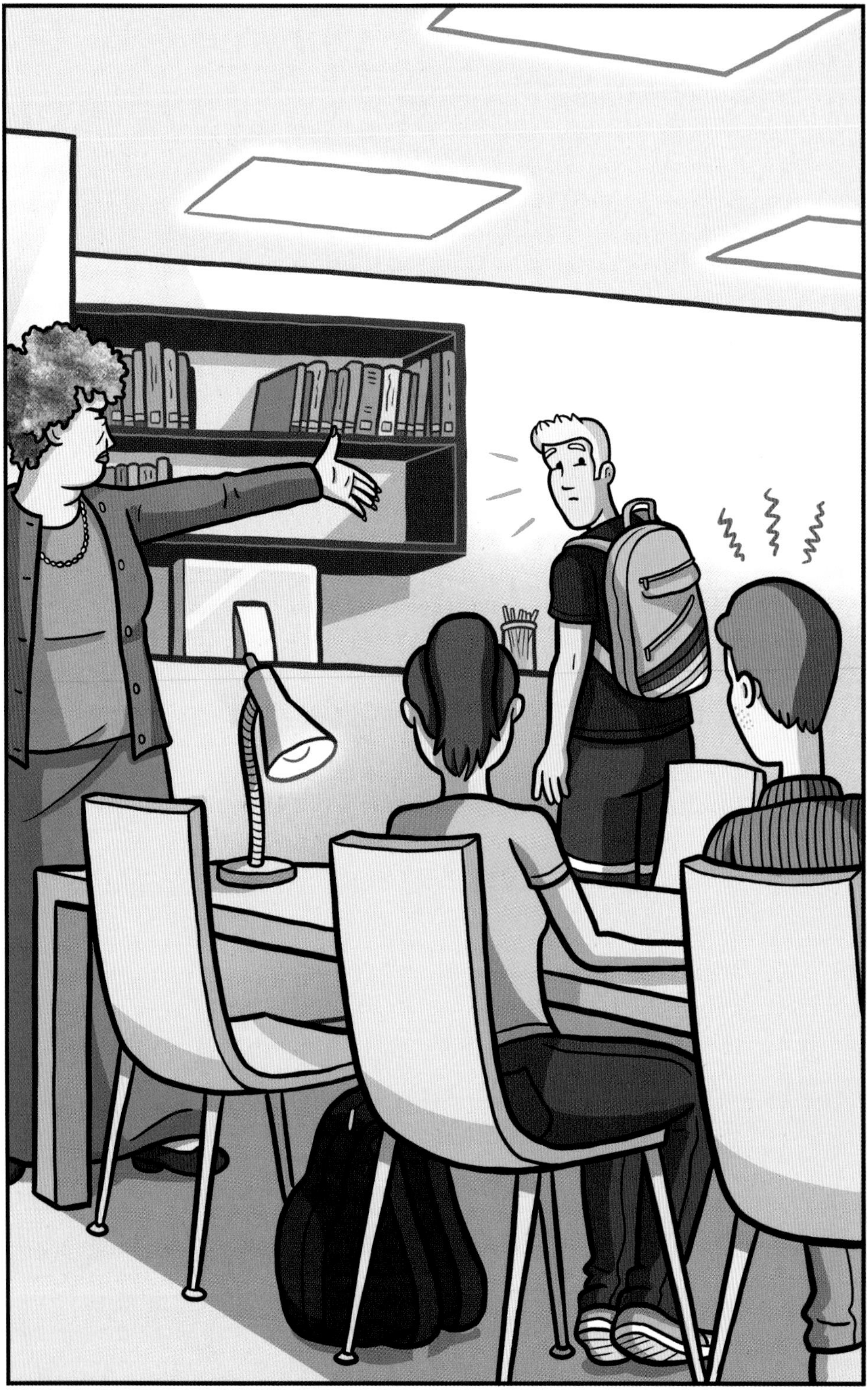

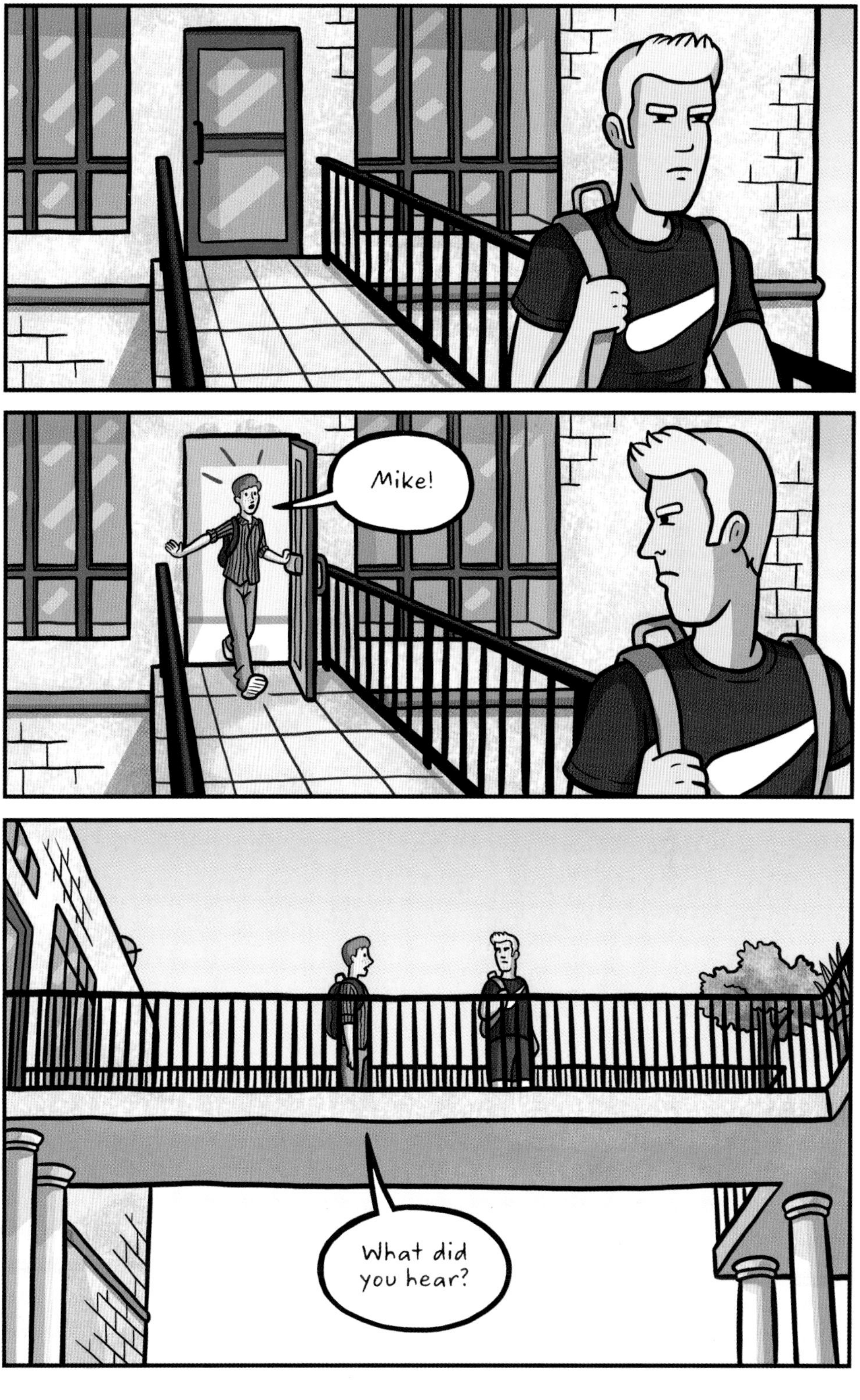
Mike!
What did you hear?

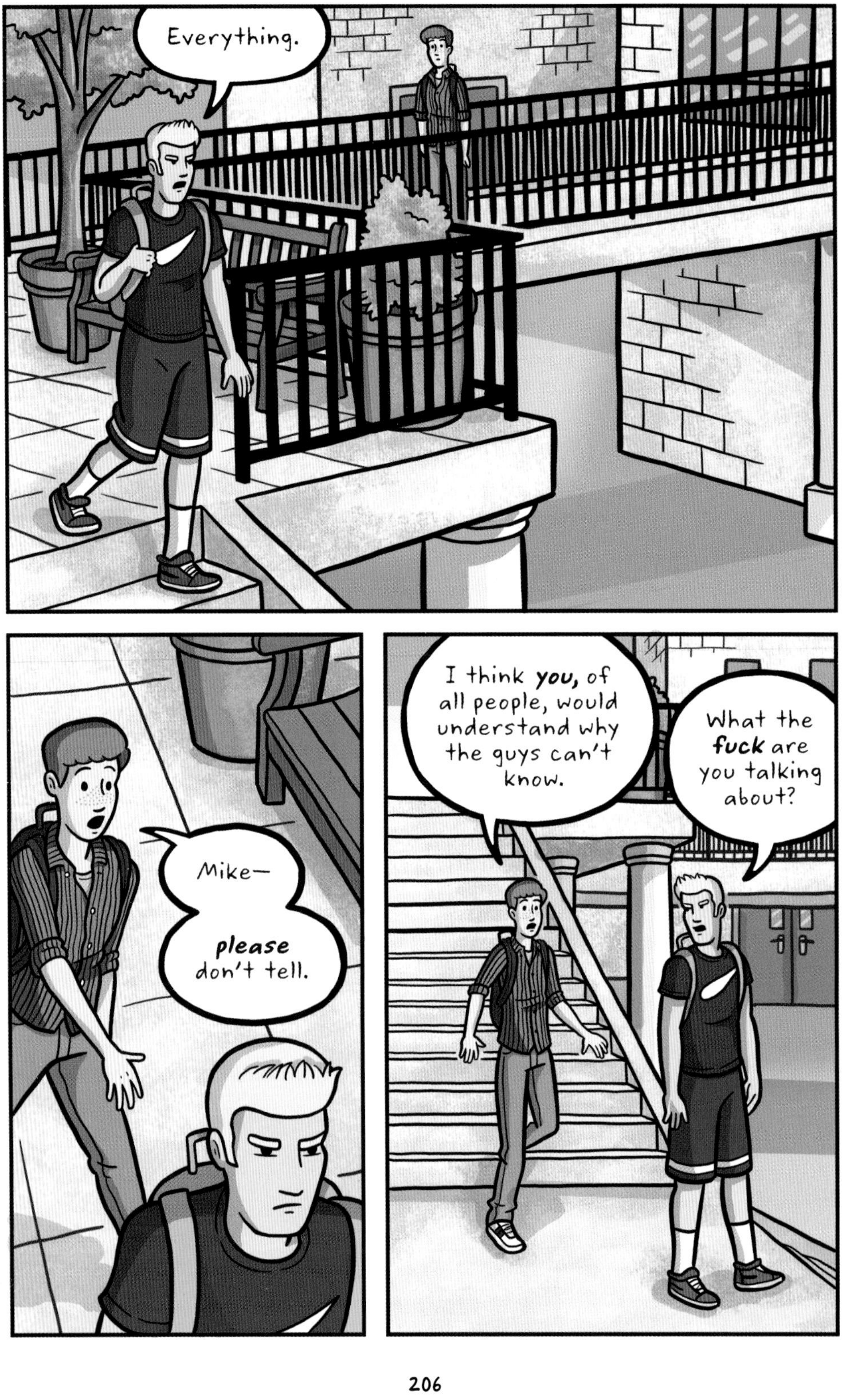
Everything.
Mike—
please don't tell.
I think **you,** of all people, would understand why the guys can't know.
What the **fuck** are you talking about?

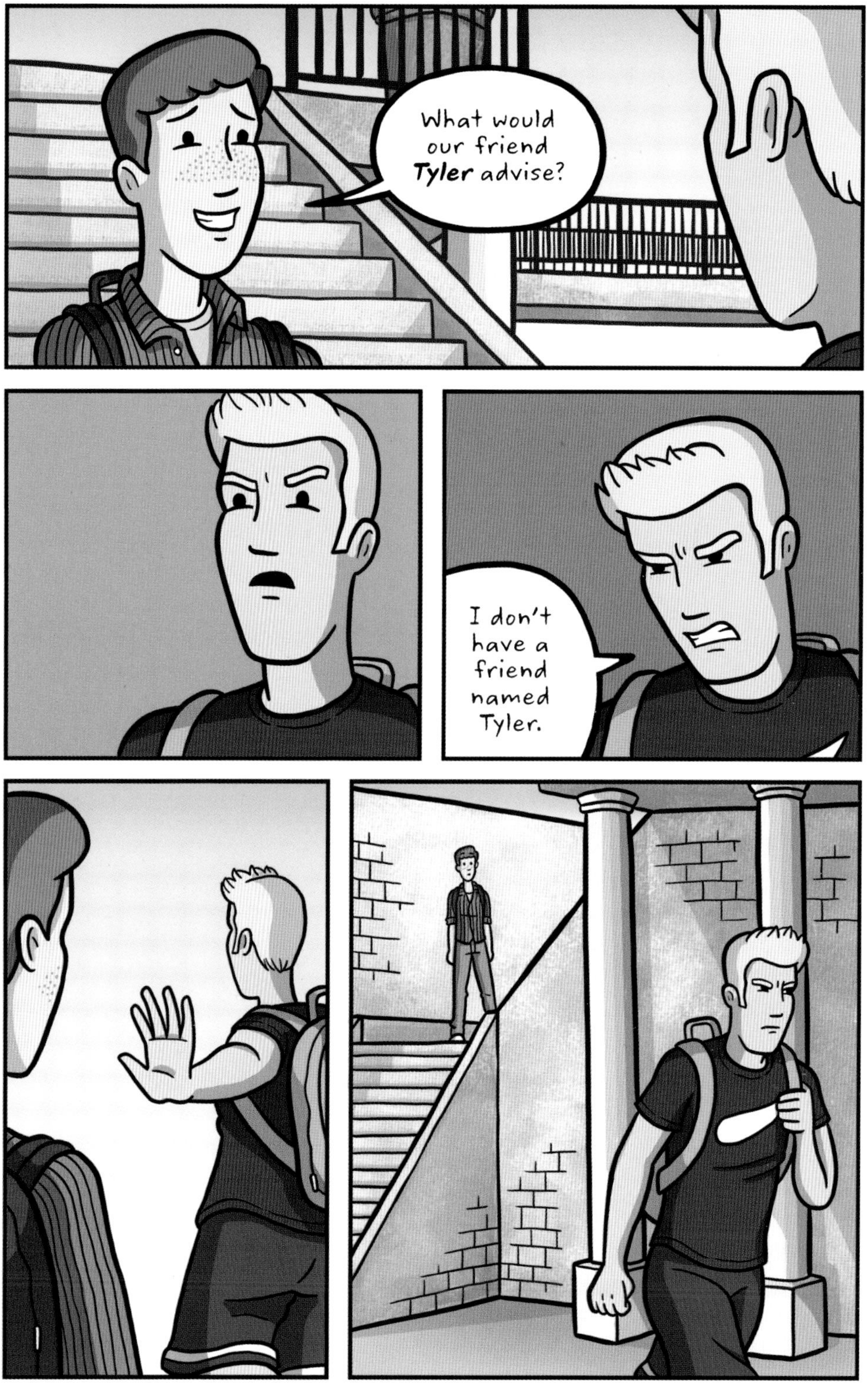
What would our friend **Tyler** advise?
I don't have a friend named Tyler.

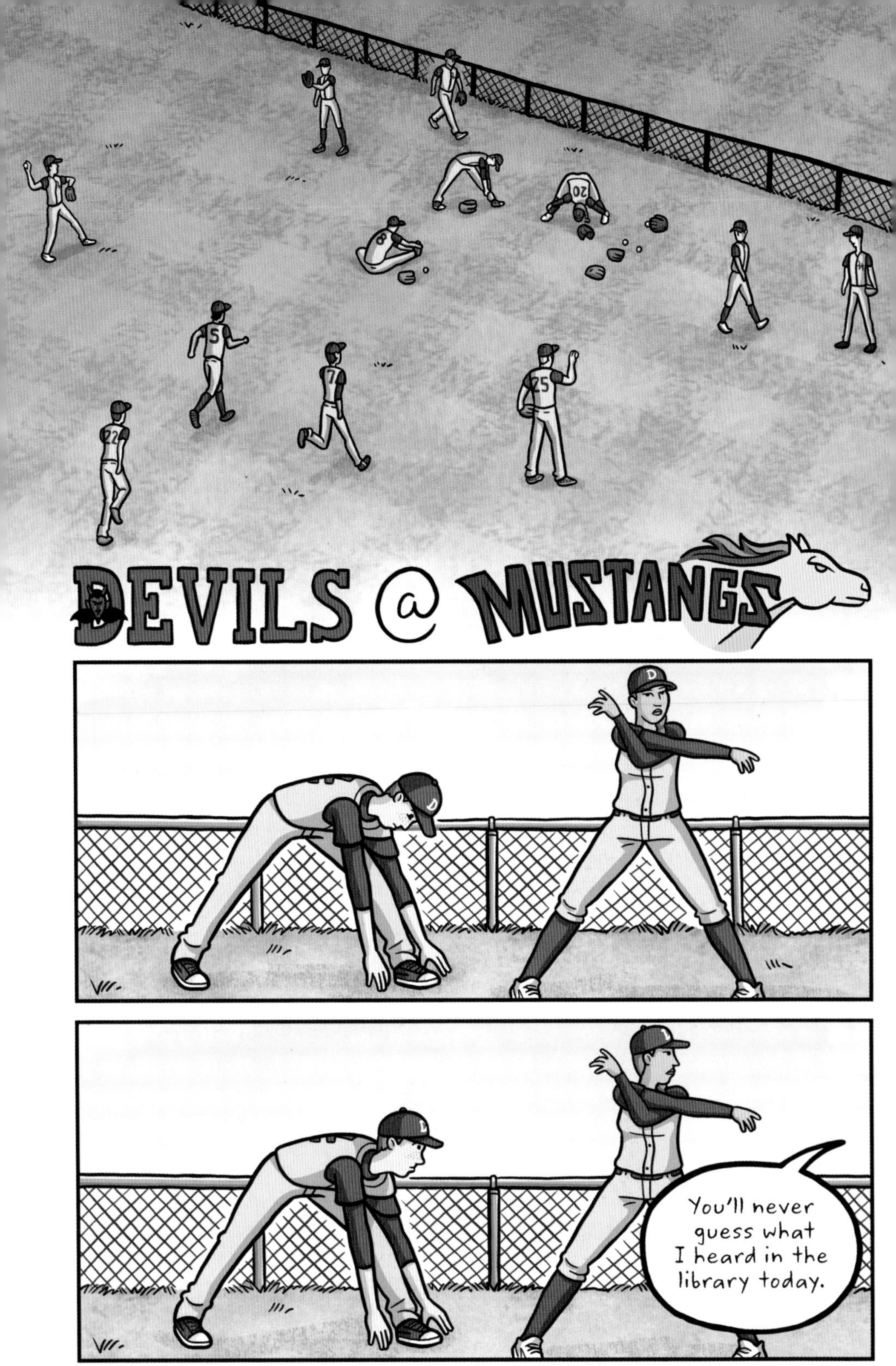
DEVILS @ MUSTANGS
You'll never guess what I heard in the library today.

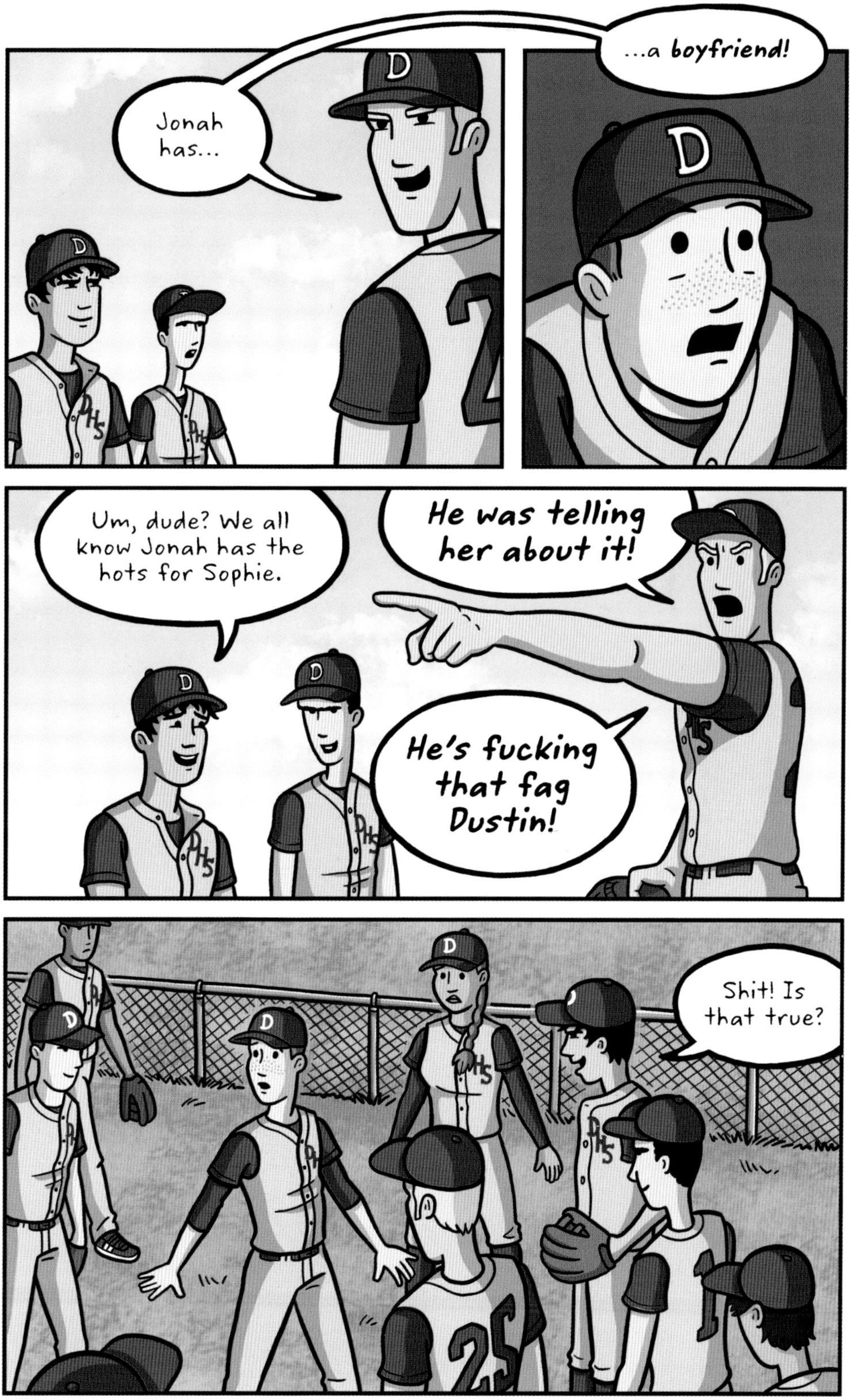
Jonah has...
...a boyfriend!
Um, dude? We all know Jonah has the hots for Sophie.
He was telling her about it!
He's fucking that fag Dustin!
Shit! Is that true?

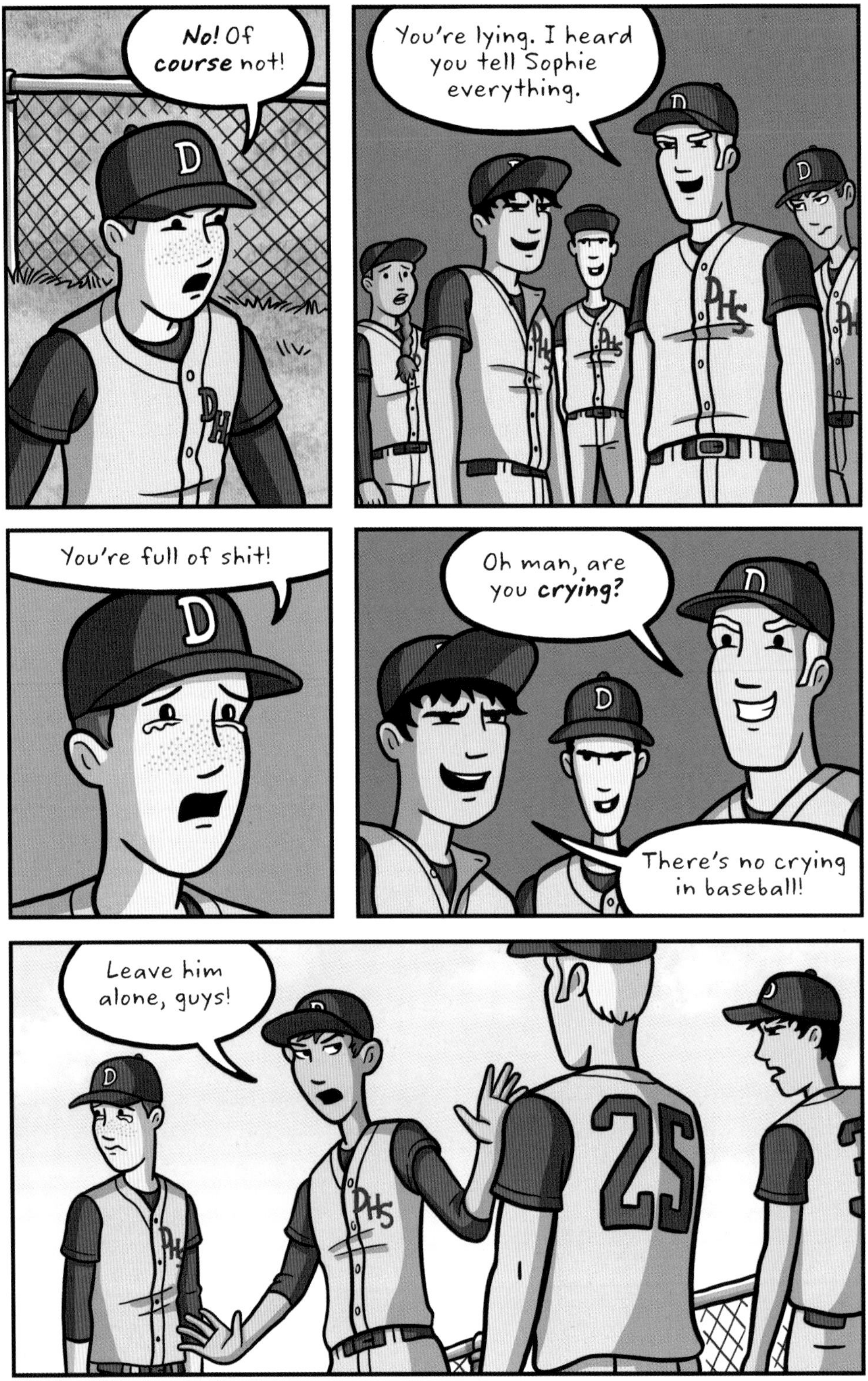
No! Of course not!
You're lying. I heard you tell Sophie everything.
You're full of shit!
Oh man, are you crying?
There's no crying in baseball!
Leave him alone, guys!

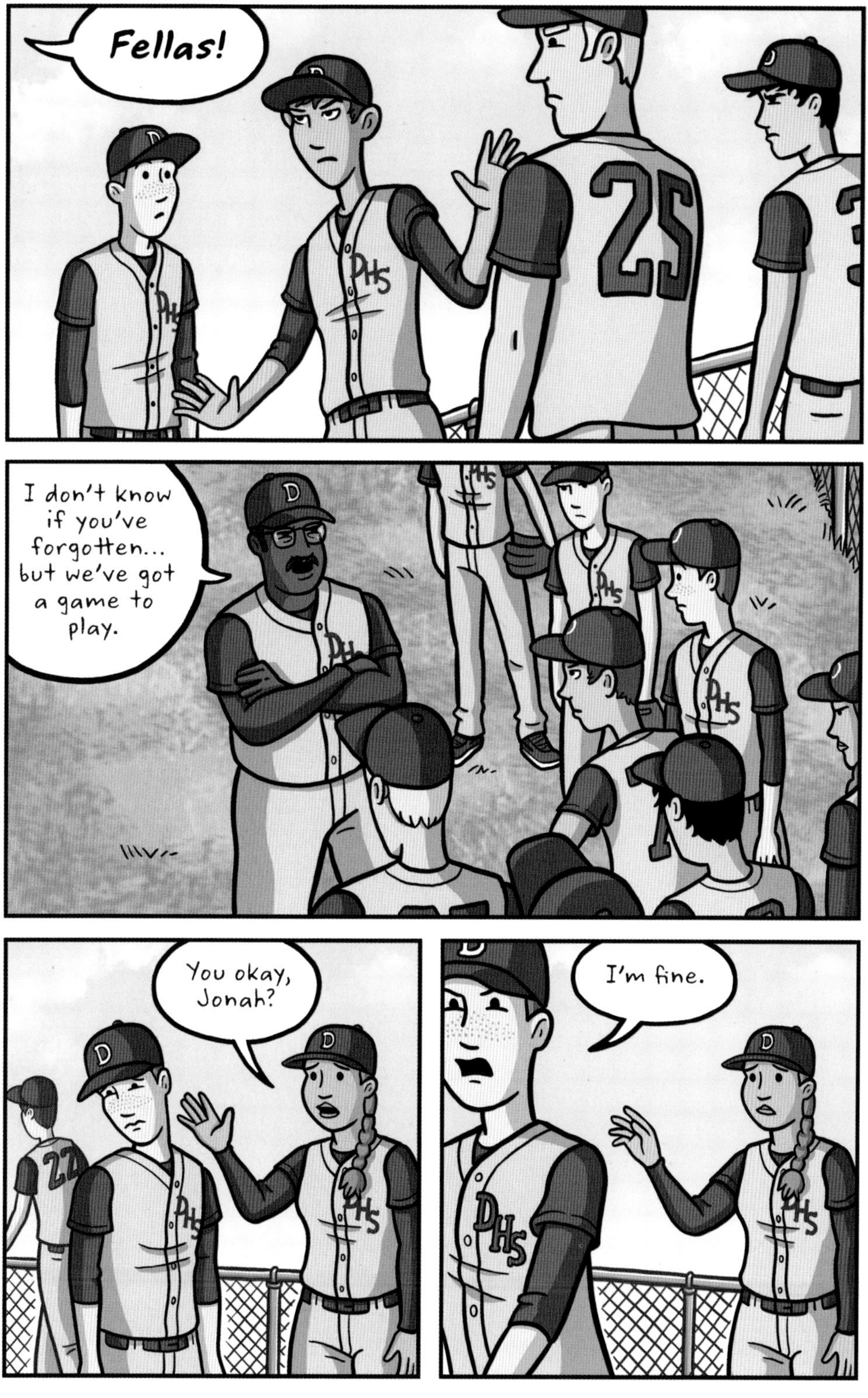
Fellas!
I don't know if you've forgotten... but we've got a game to play.
You okay, Jonah?
I'm fine.

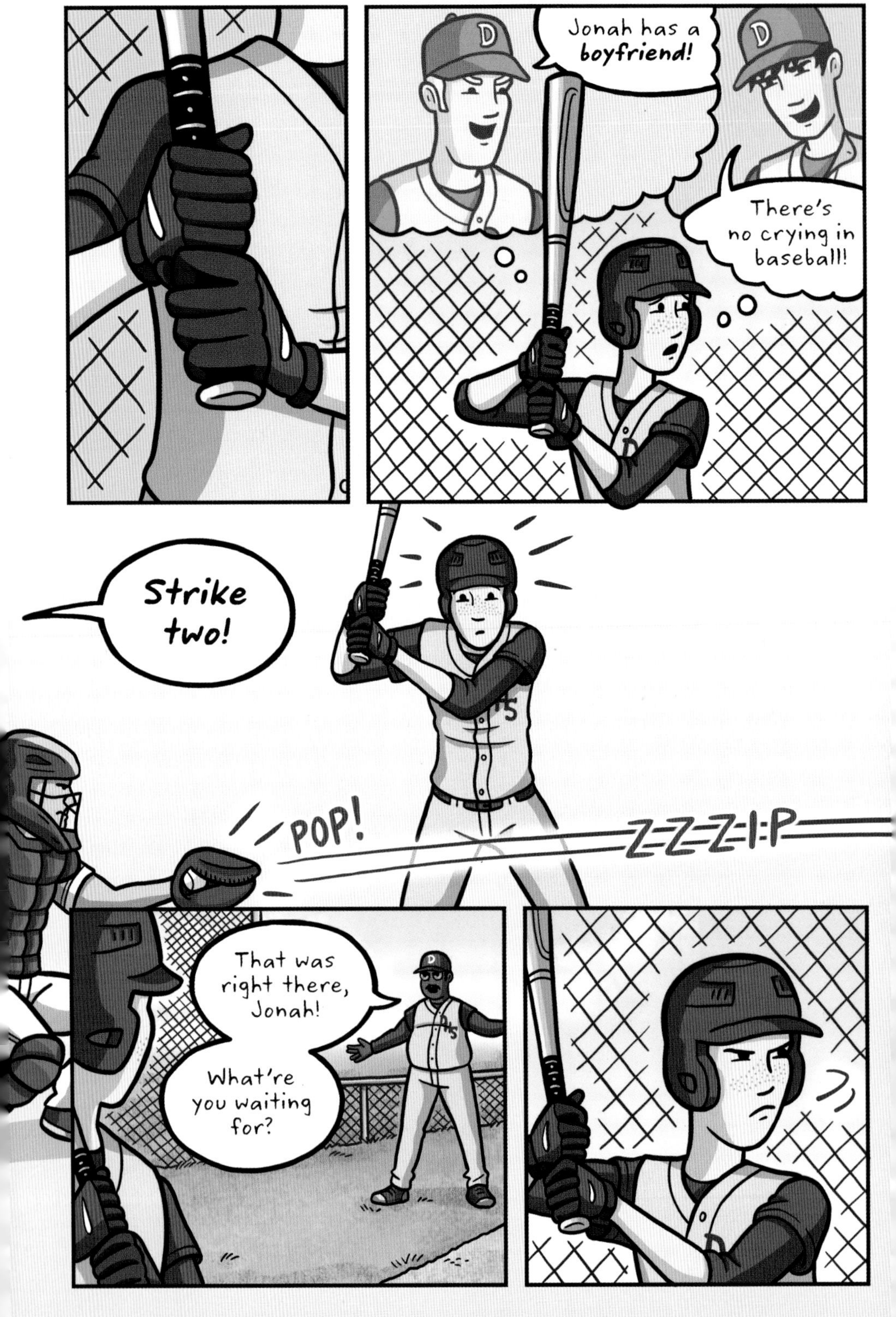
Jonah has a **boyfriend!**
There's no crying in baseball!
Strike two!
POP!
ZZZZIP
That was right there, Jonah!
What're you waiting for?

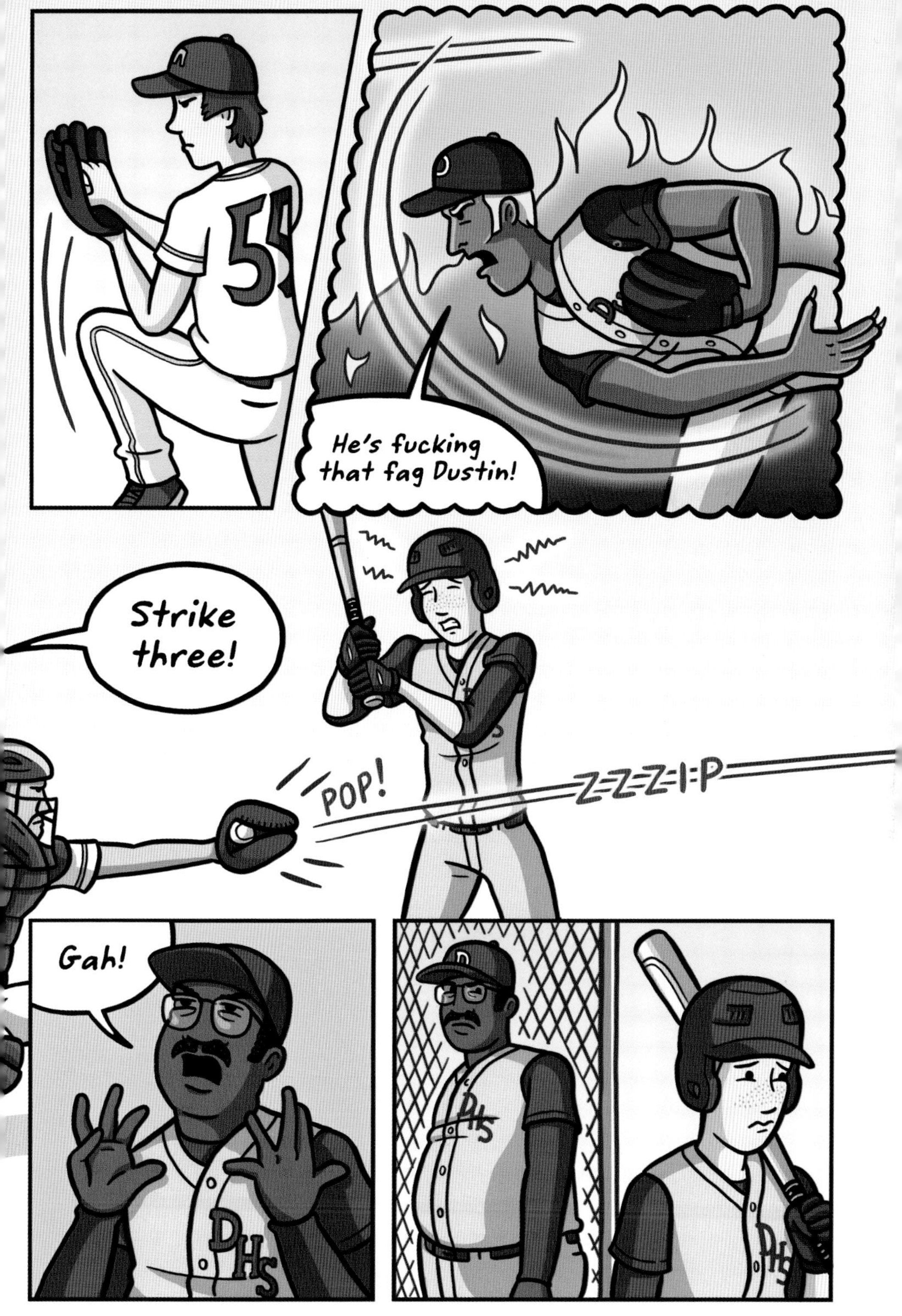
He's fucking that fag Dustin!
Strike three!
POP!
ZZZZIP
Gah!

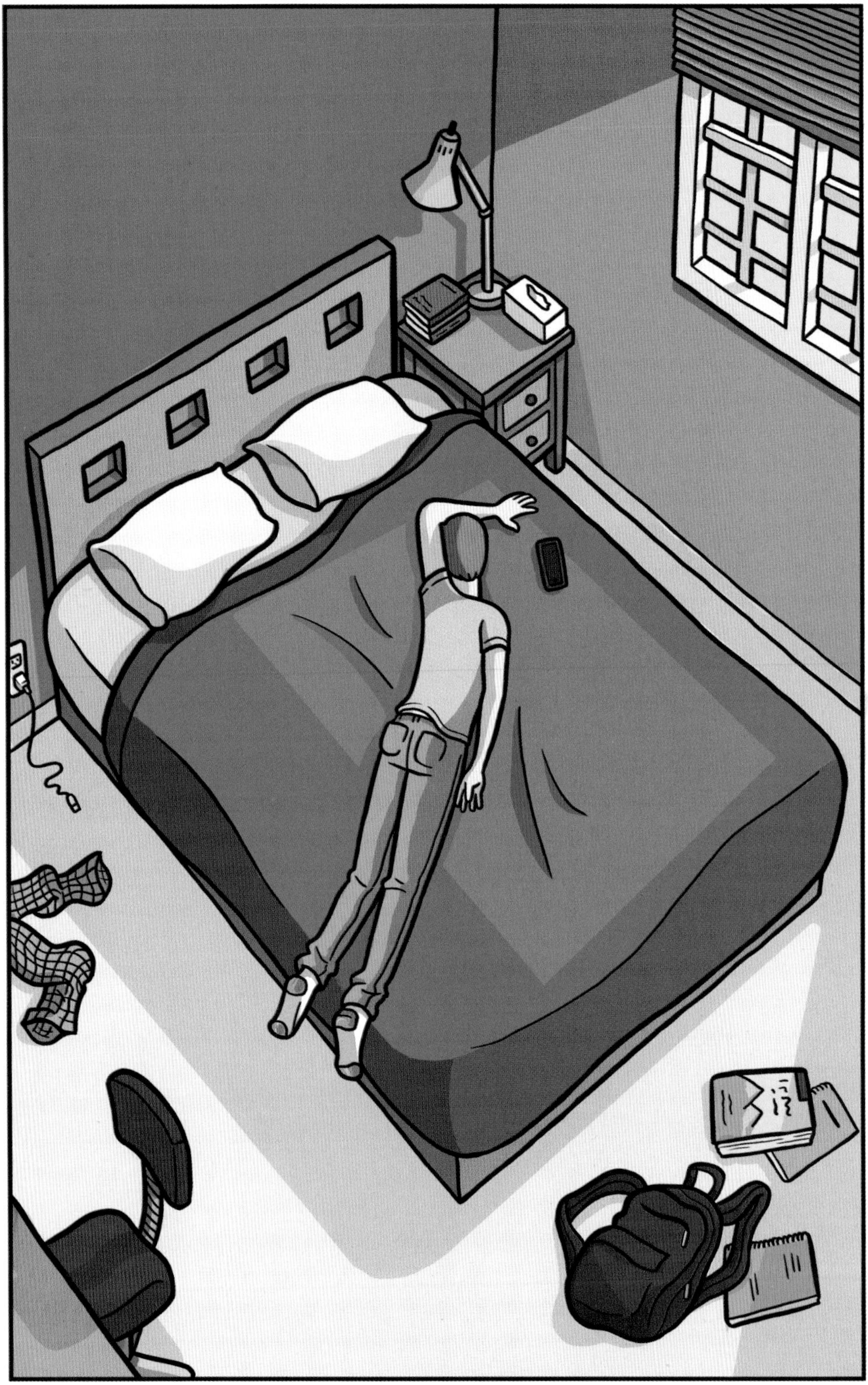

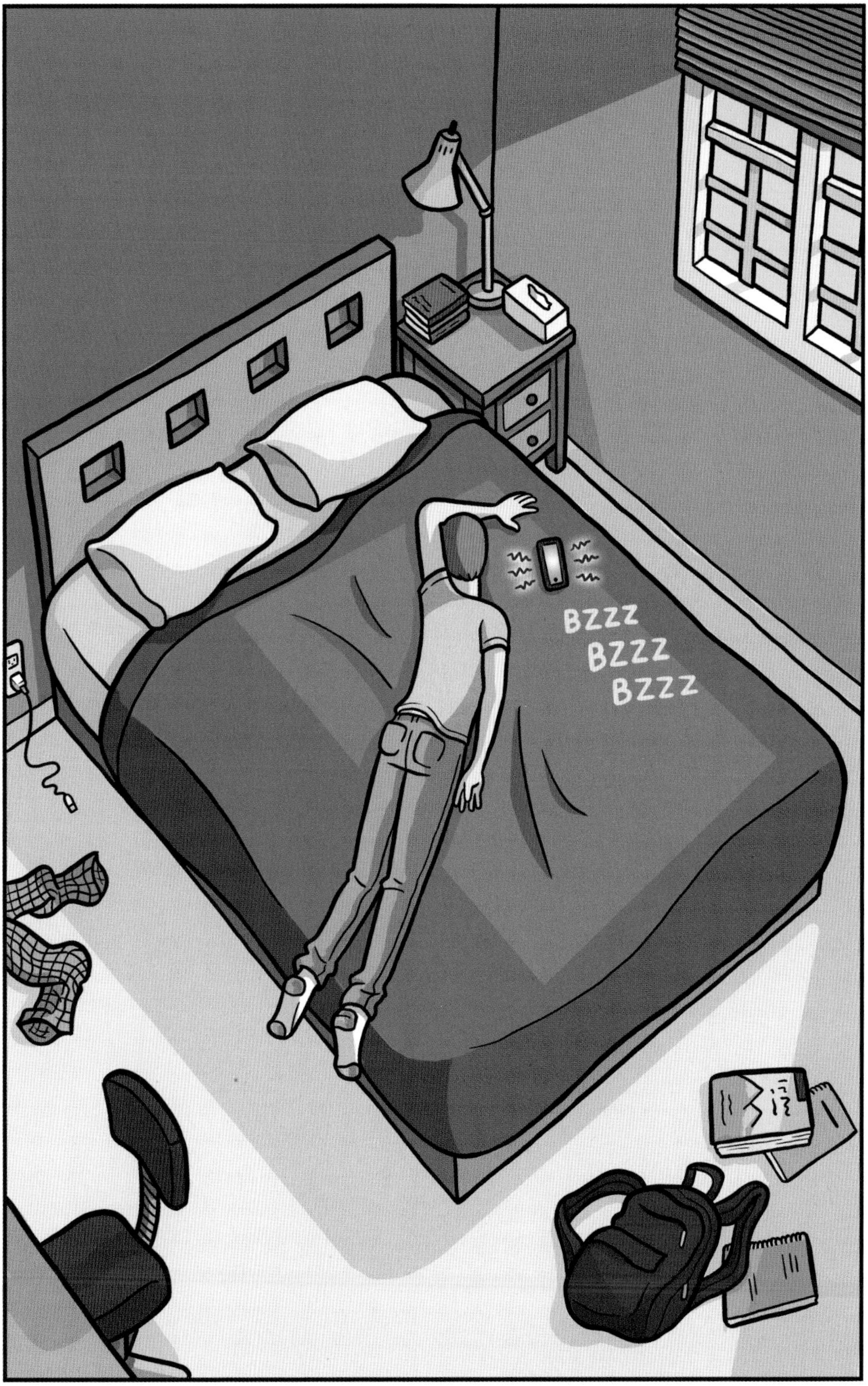
BZZZ
BZZZ
BZZZ

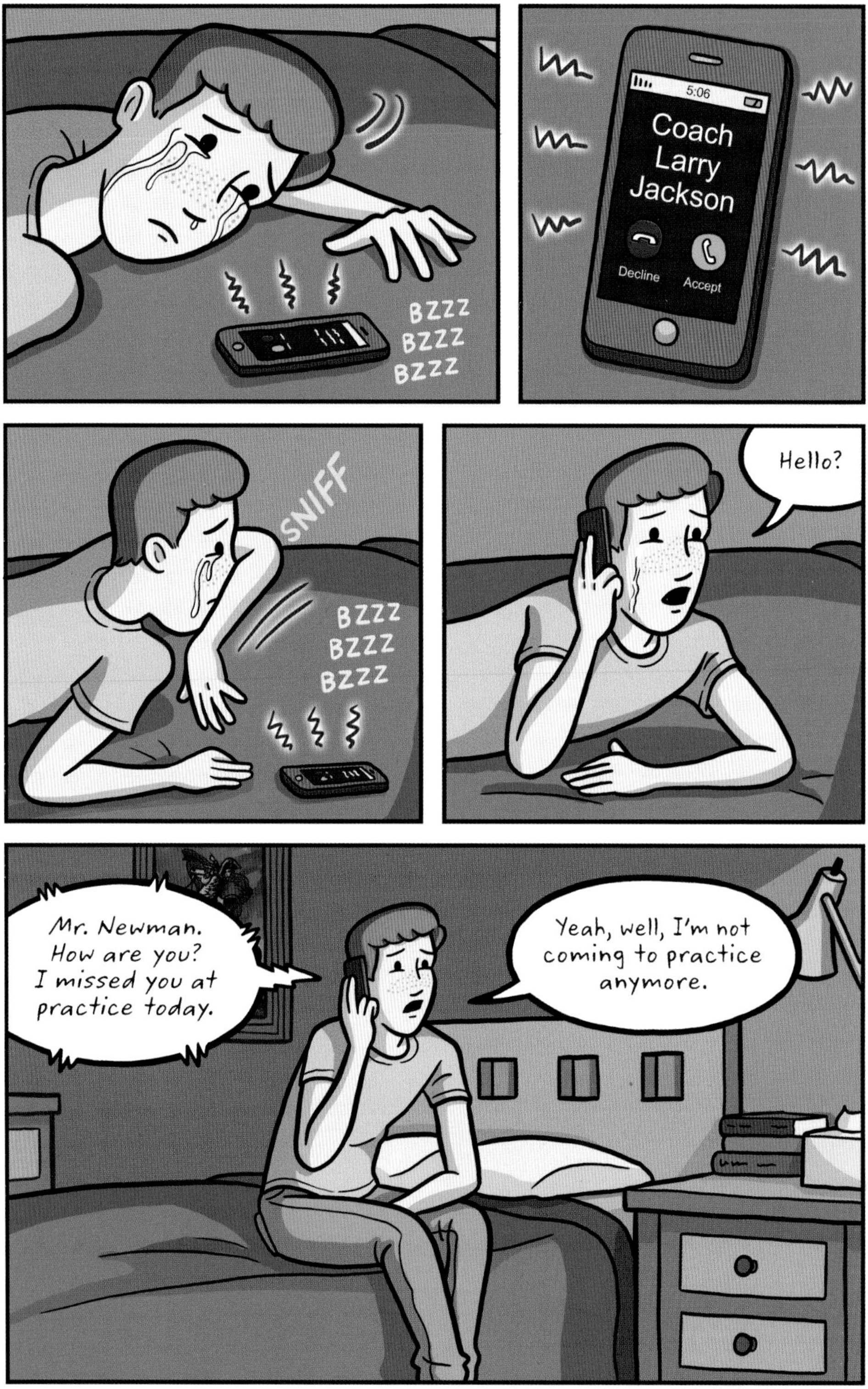
BZZZ
BZZZ
BZZZ
5:06
Coach
Larry
Jackson
Decline
Accept
SNIFF
BZZZ
BZZZ
BZZZ
Hello?
Mr. Newman. How are you? I missed you at practice today.
Yeah, well, I'm not coming to practice anymore.

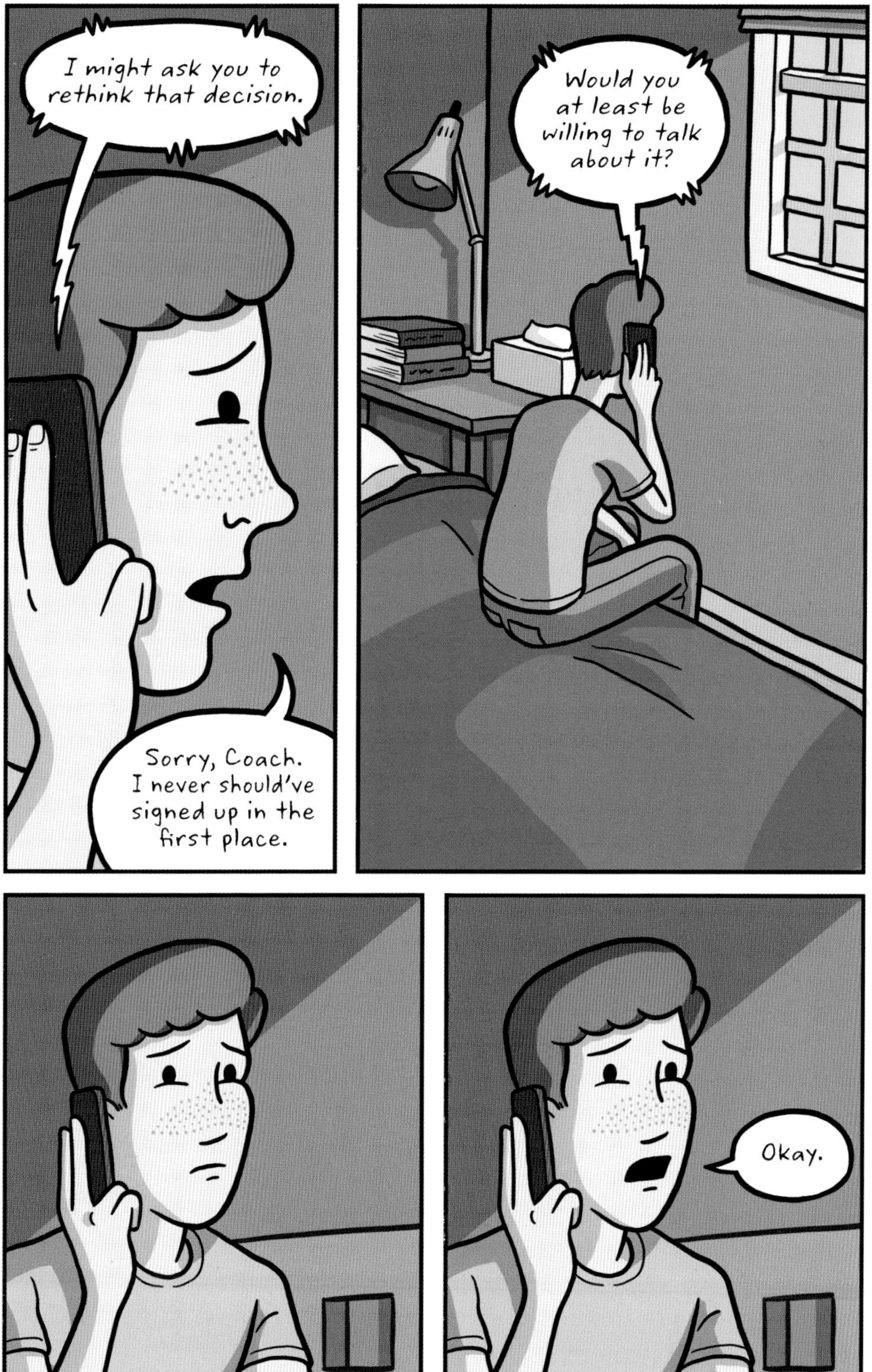
I might ask you to rethink that decision.
Sorry, Coach. I never should've signed up in the first place.
Would you at least be willing to talk about it?
Okay.

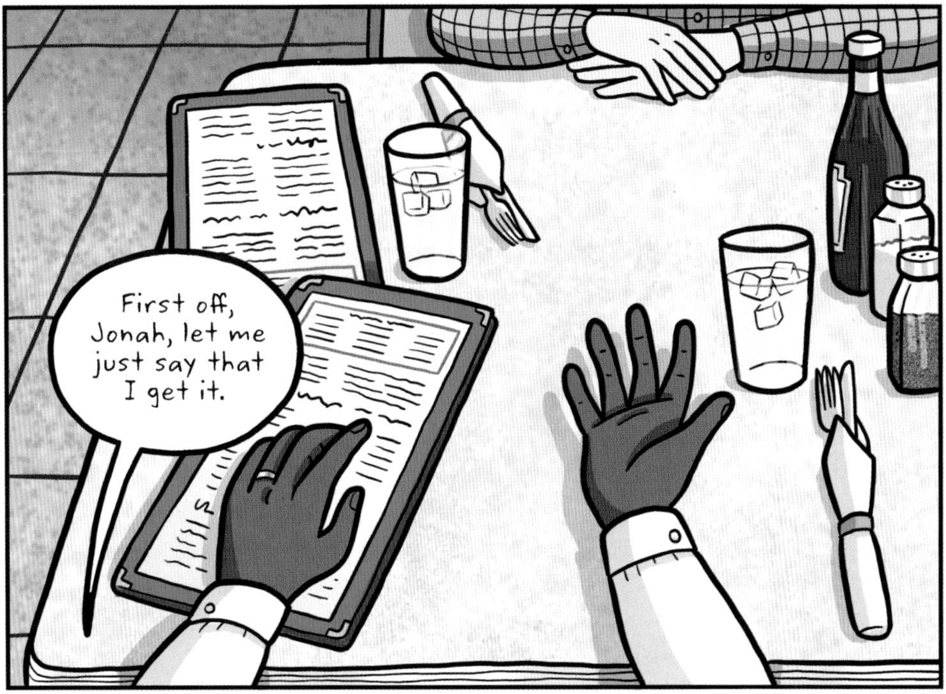
First off, Jonah, let me just say that I get it.

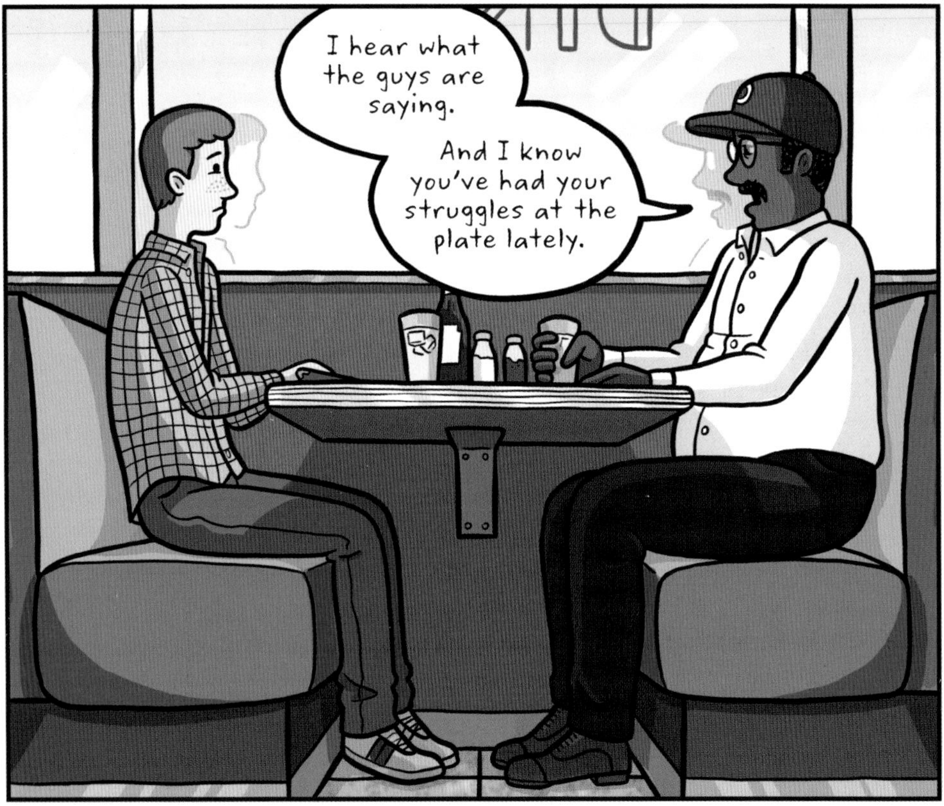
I hear what the guys are saying.
And I know you've had your struggles at the plate lately.

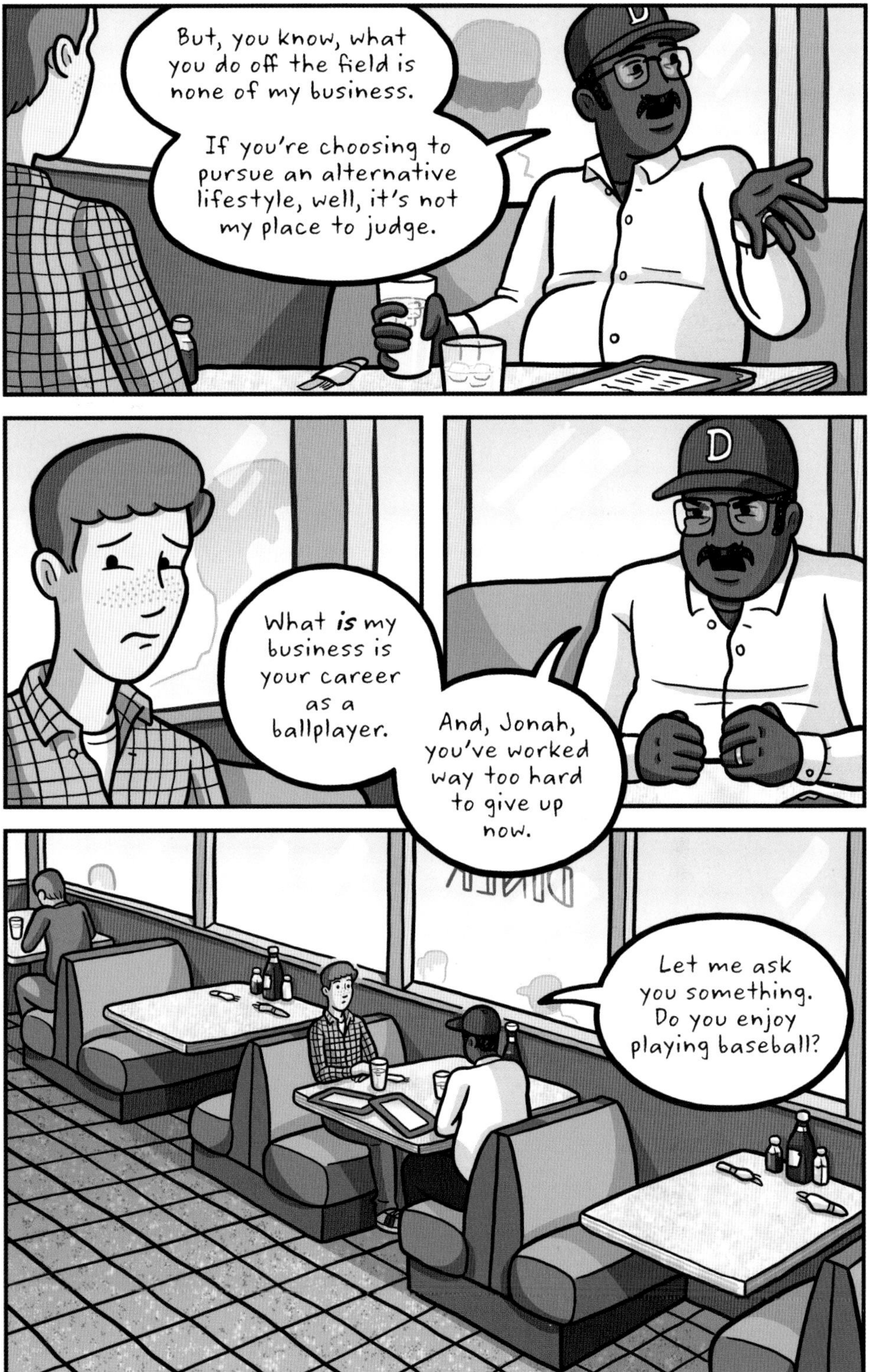
But, you know, what you do off the field is none of my business.
If you're choosing to pursue an alternative lifestyle, well, it's not my place to judge.
What *is* my business is your career as a ballplayer.
And, Jonah, you've worked way too hard to give up now.
Let me ask you something. Do you enjoy playing baseball?

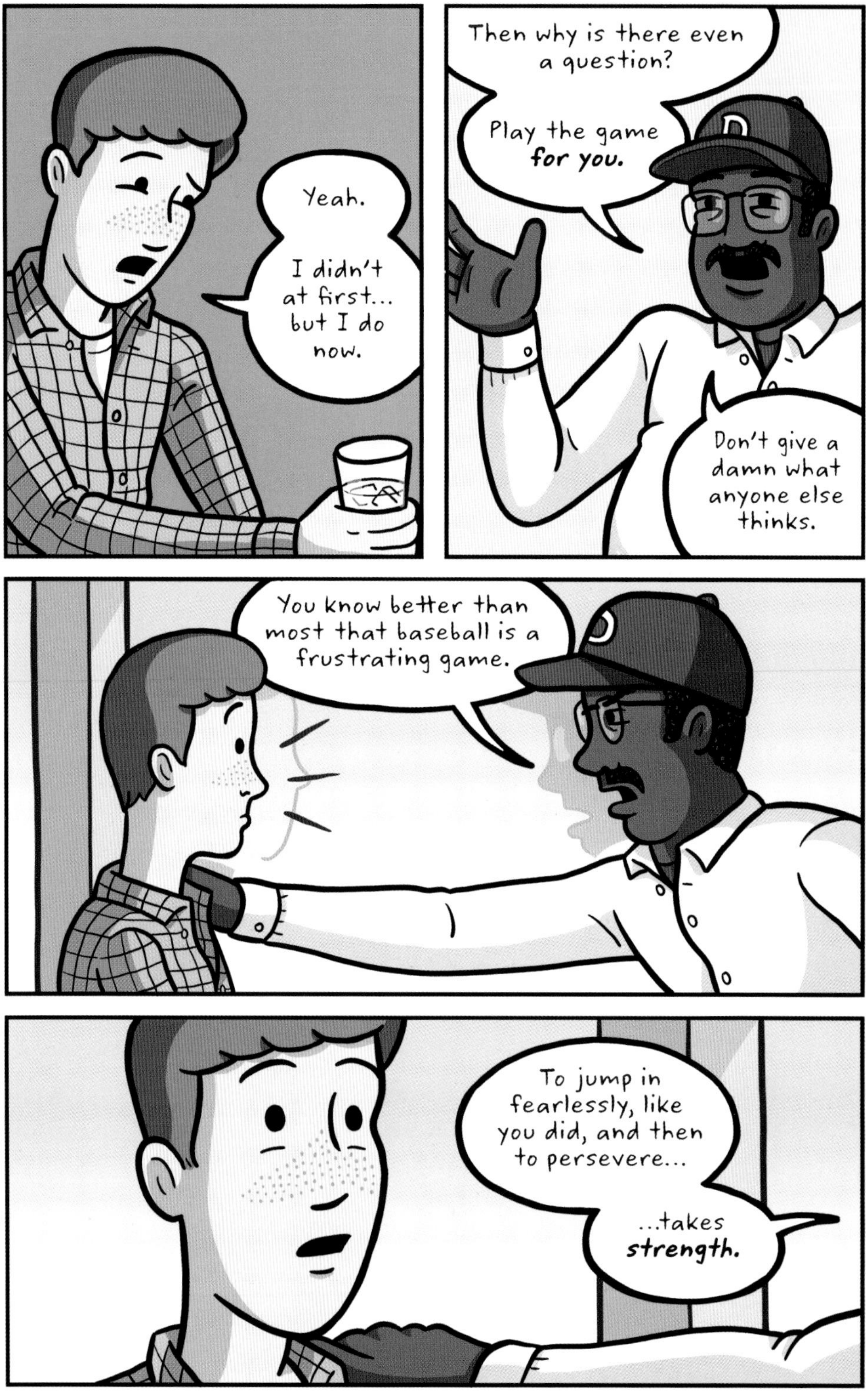
Yeah.
I didn't at first... but I do now.
Then why is there even a question?
Play the game **for you.**
Don't give a damn what anyone else thinks.
You know better than most that baseball is a frustrating game.
To jump in fearlessly, like you did, and then to persevere...
...takes **strength.**

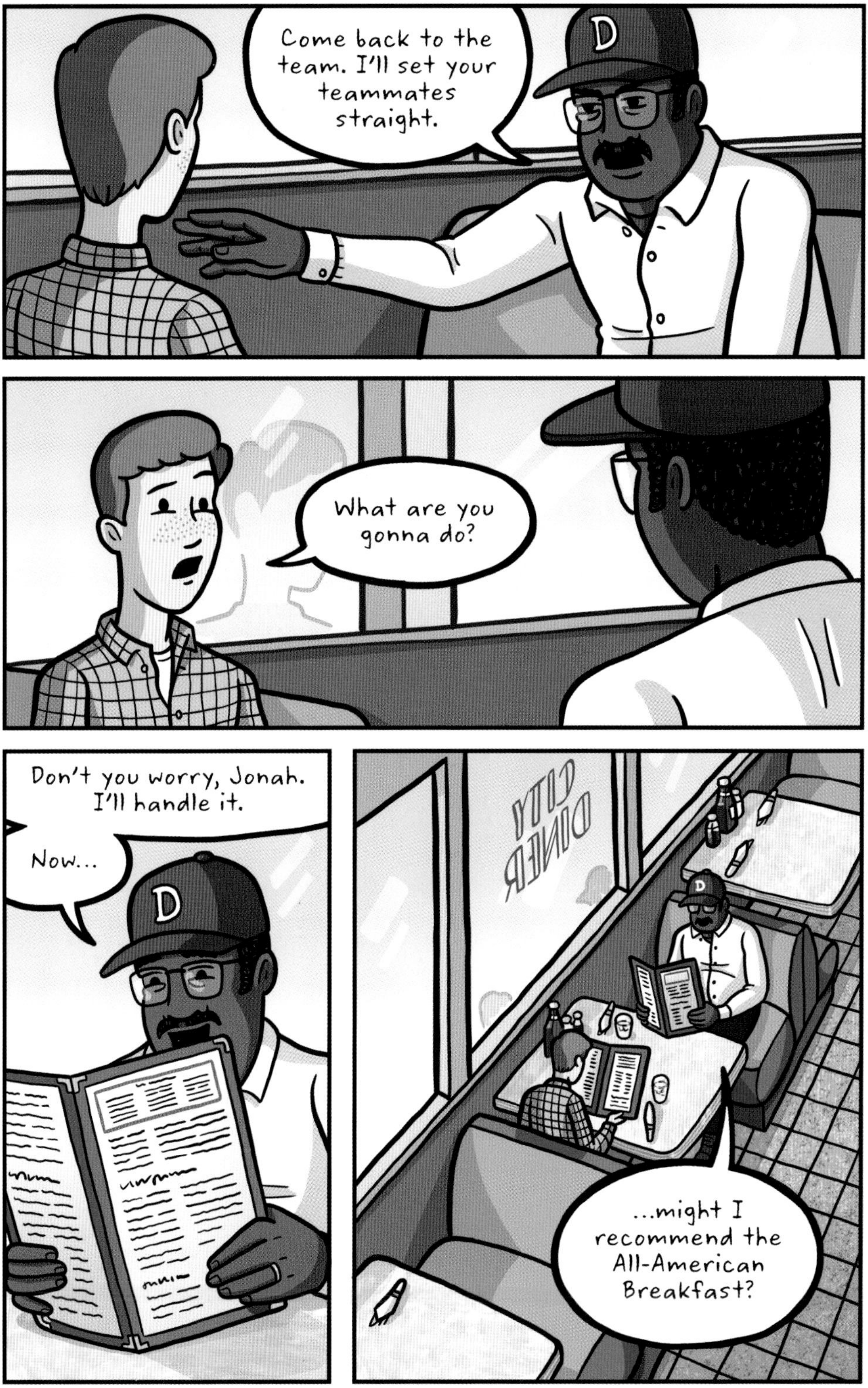
Come back to the team. I'll set your teammates straight.
What are you gonna do?
Don't you worry, Jonah. I'll handle it.
Now...
CITY DINER
...might I recommend the All-American Breakfast?

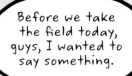

"Before we take the field today, guys, I wanted to say something."

DEVILS VS. LIONS

"It has come to my attention that certain harmful rumors have been circulating of late."

"That needs to stop. You guys are a **team**."

"Your teammates are your **brothers**. And if I hear anyone demeaning his brother again, he'll be **benched**."

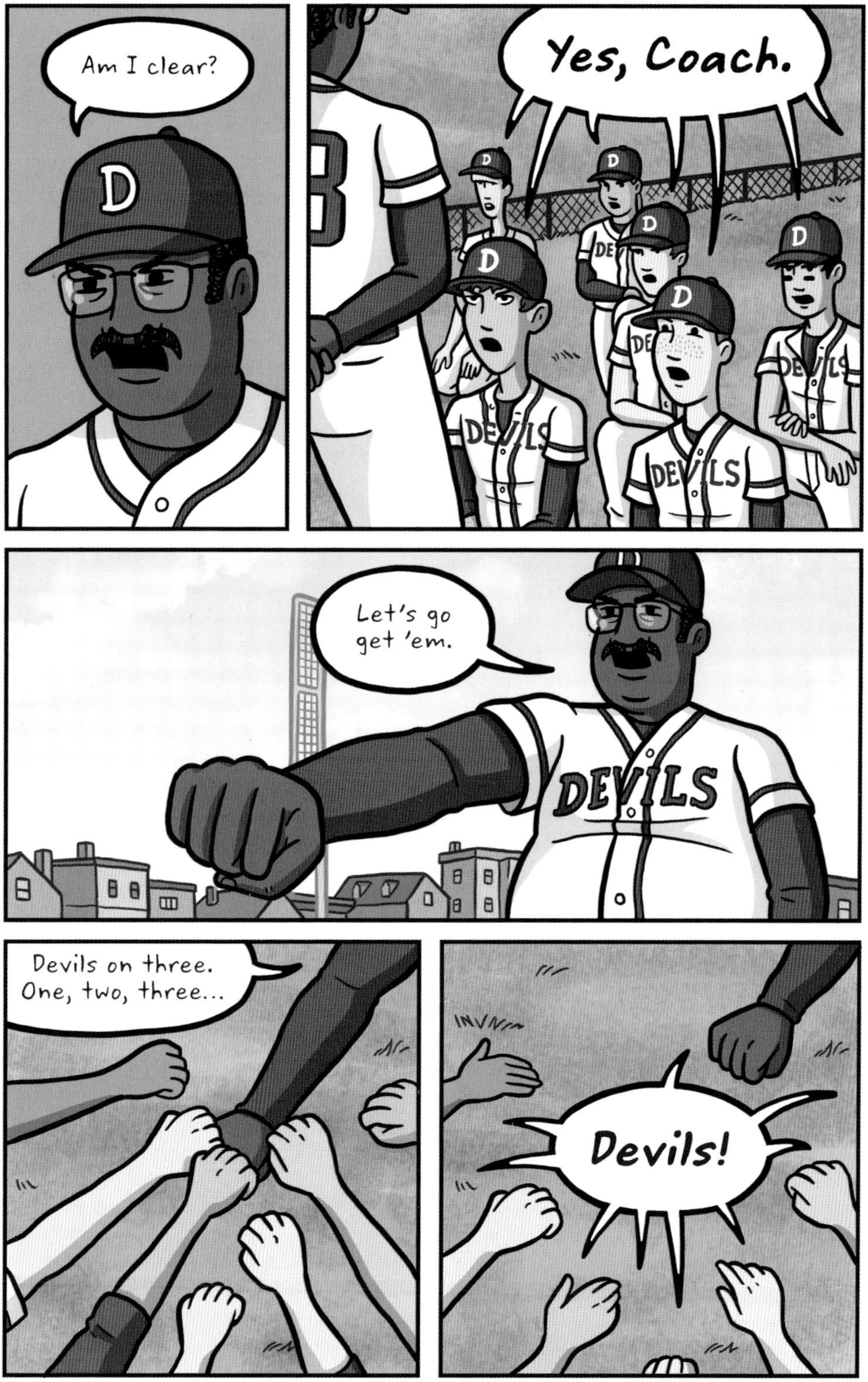
Am I clear?
Yes, Coach.
Let's go get 'em.
Devils on three. One, two, three...
Devils!

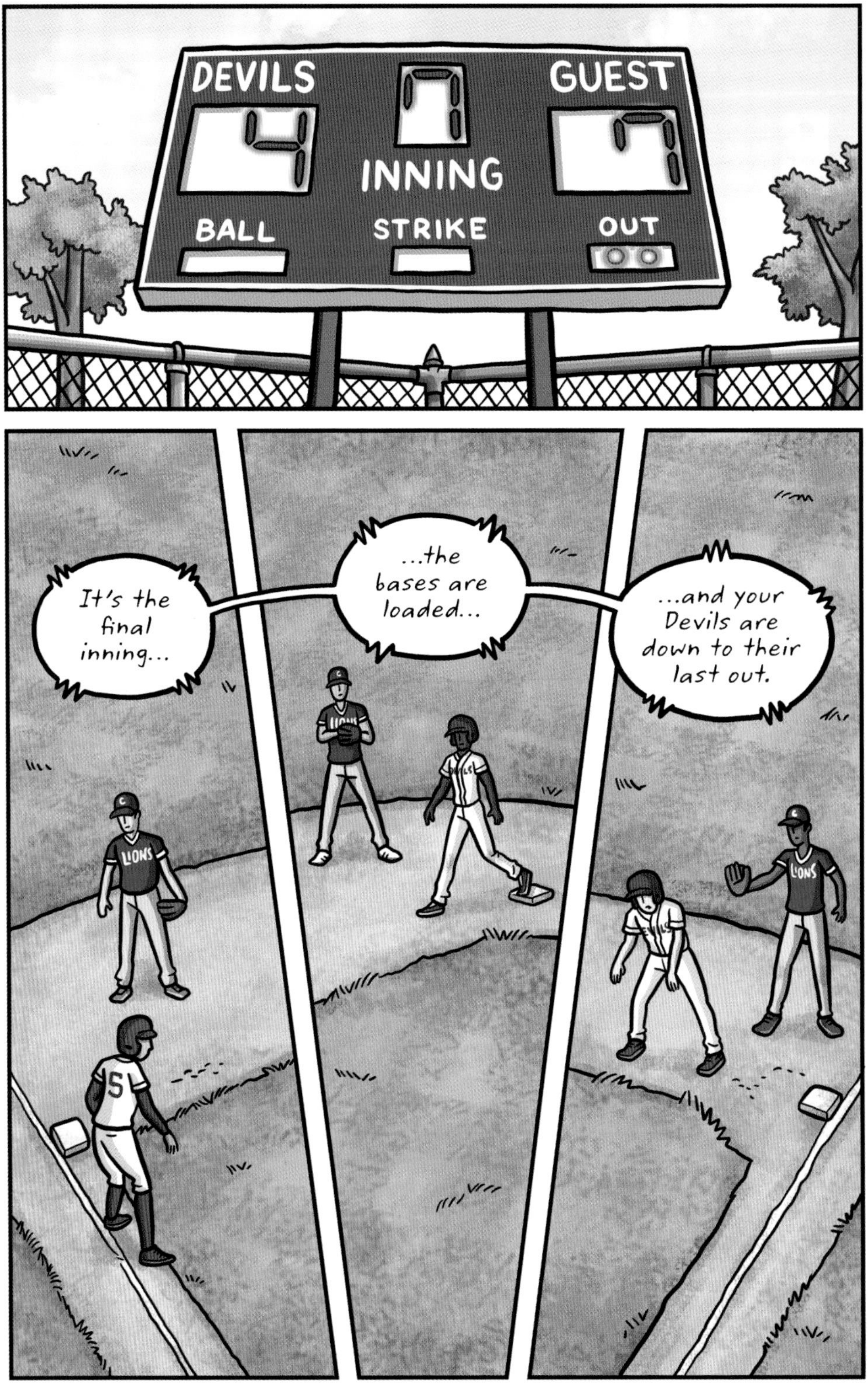
DEVILS
GUEST
INNING
BALL
STRIKE
OUT
It's the final inning...
...the bases are loaded...
...and your Devils are down to their last out.

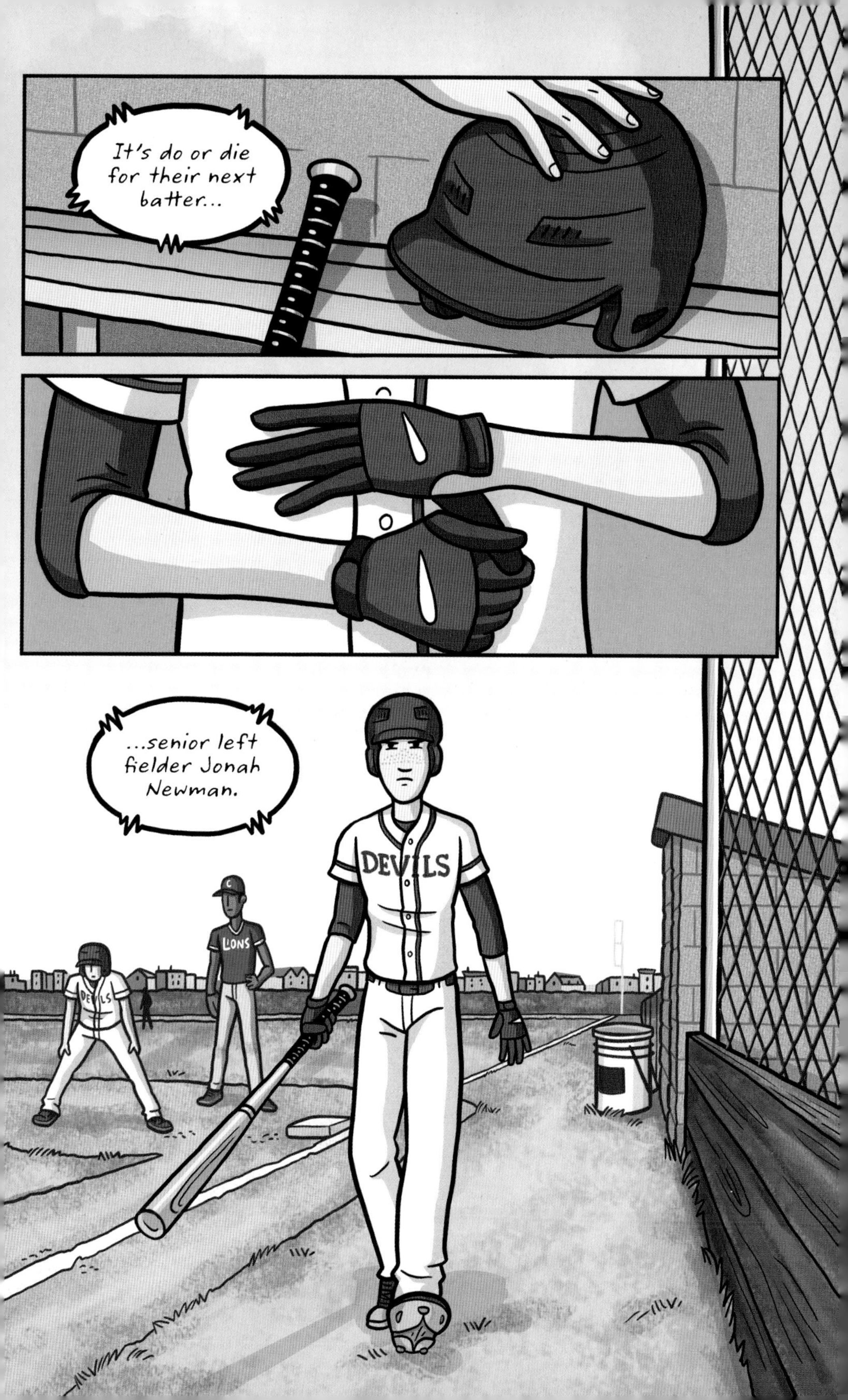
It's do or die for their next batter...
...senior left fielder Jonah Newman.
DEVILS
LIONS
DEVILS

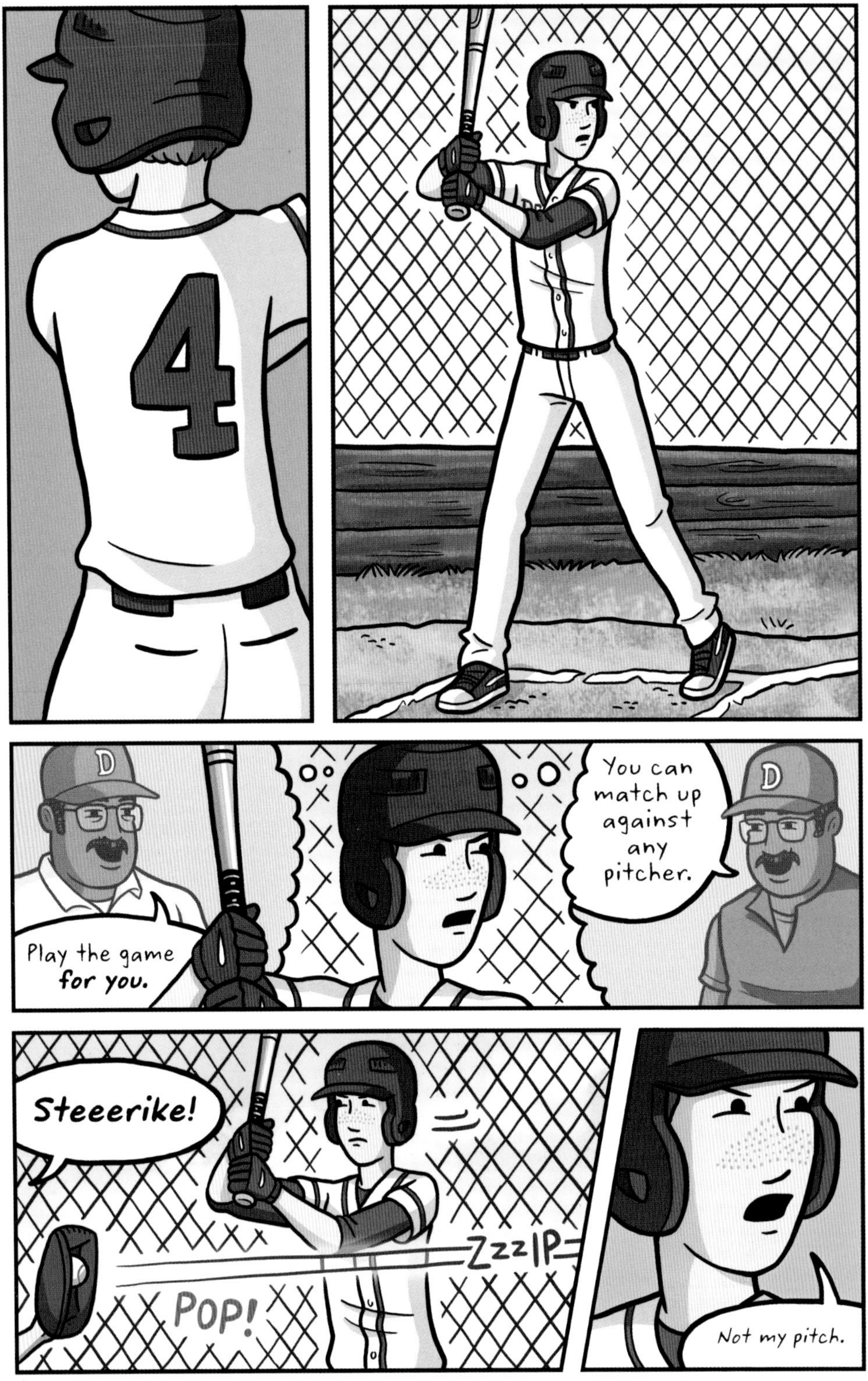
Play the game for you.
You can match up against any pitcher.
Steeerike!
ZzzIP
POP!
Not my pitch.

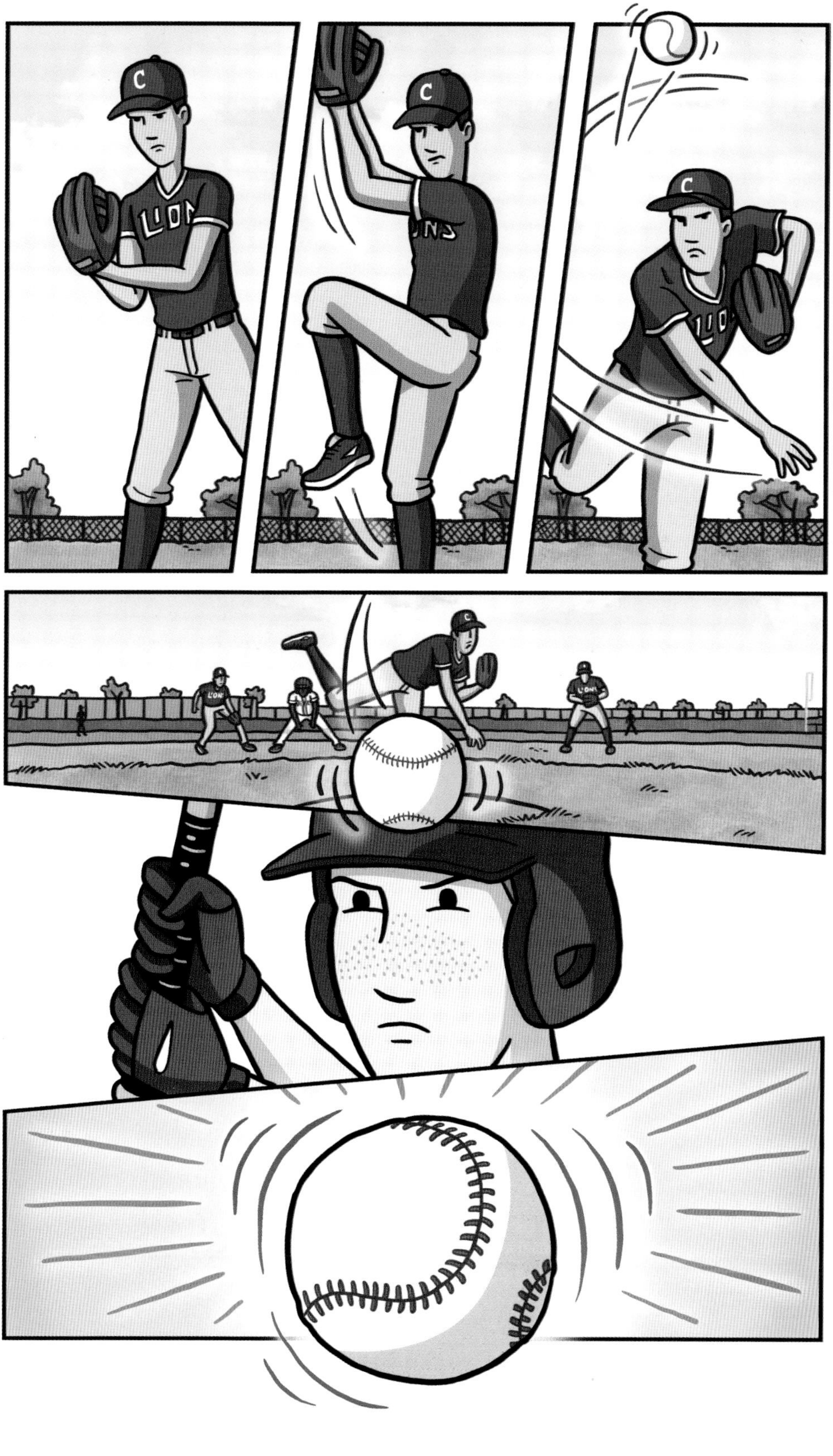

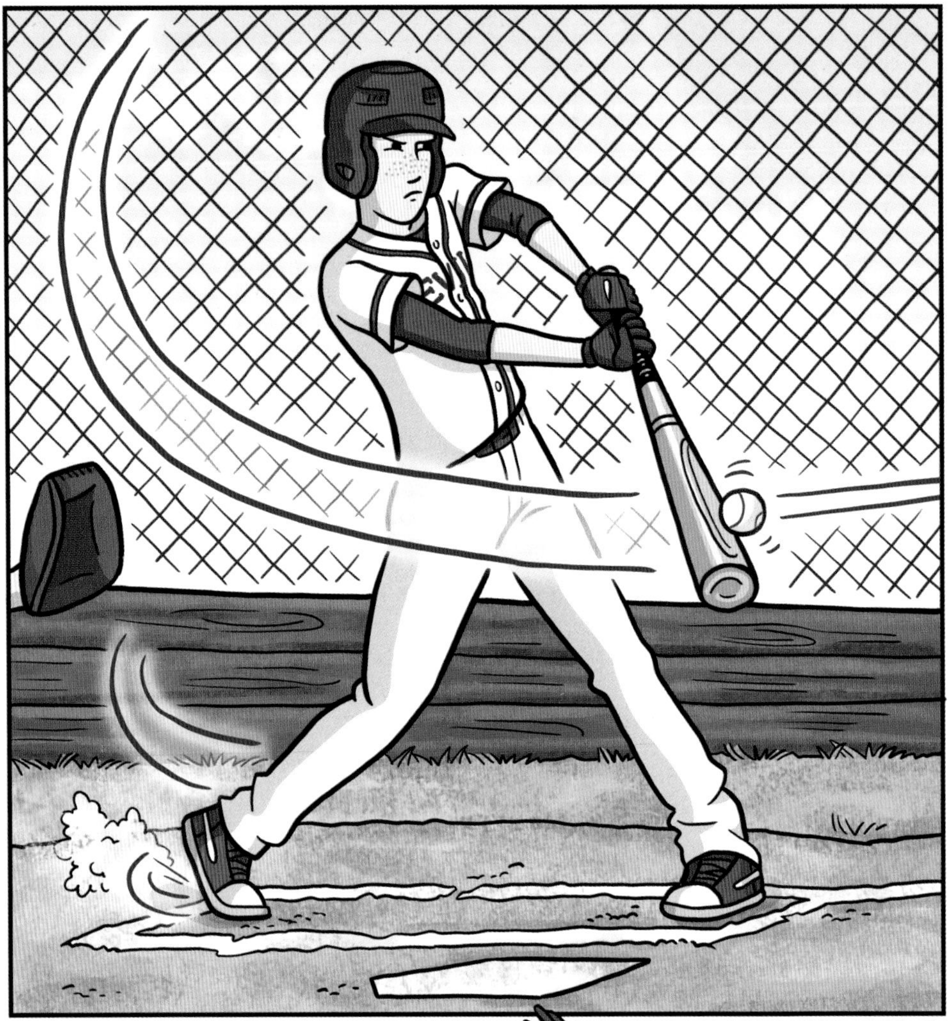

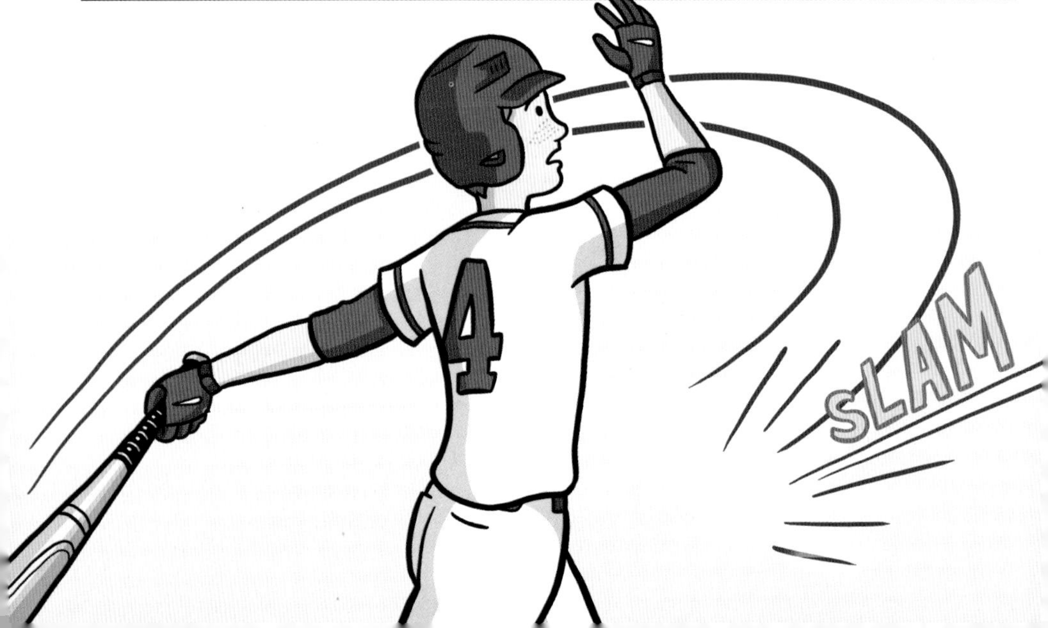
SLAM

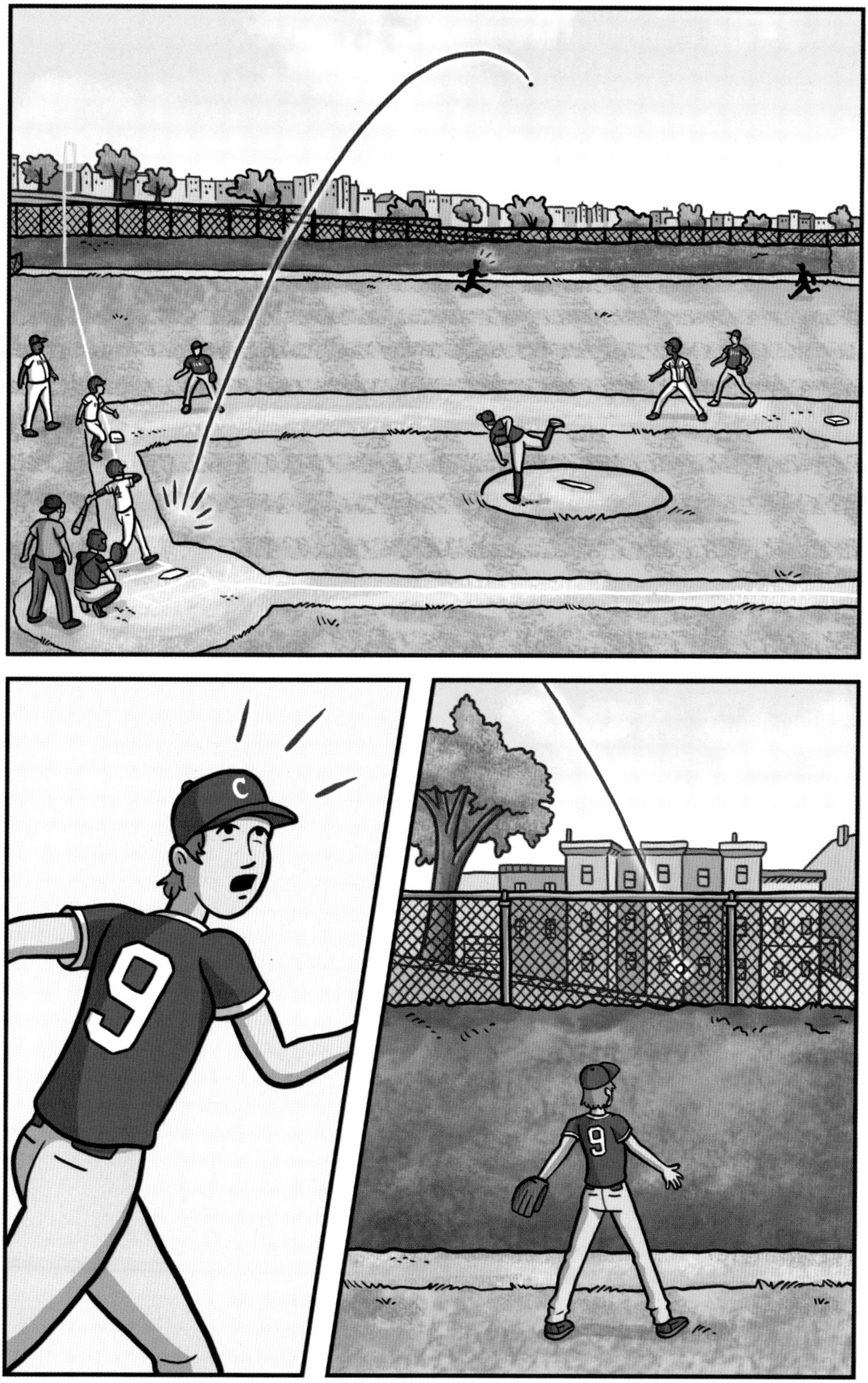

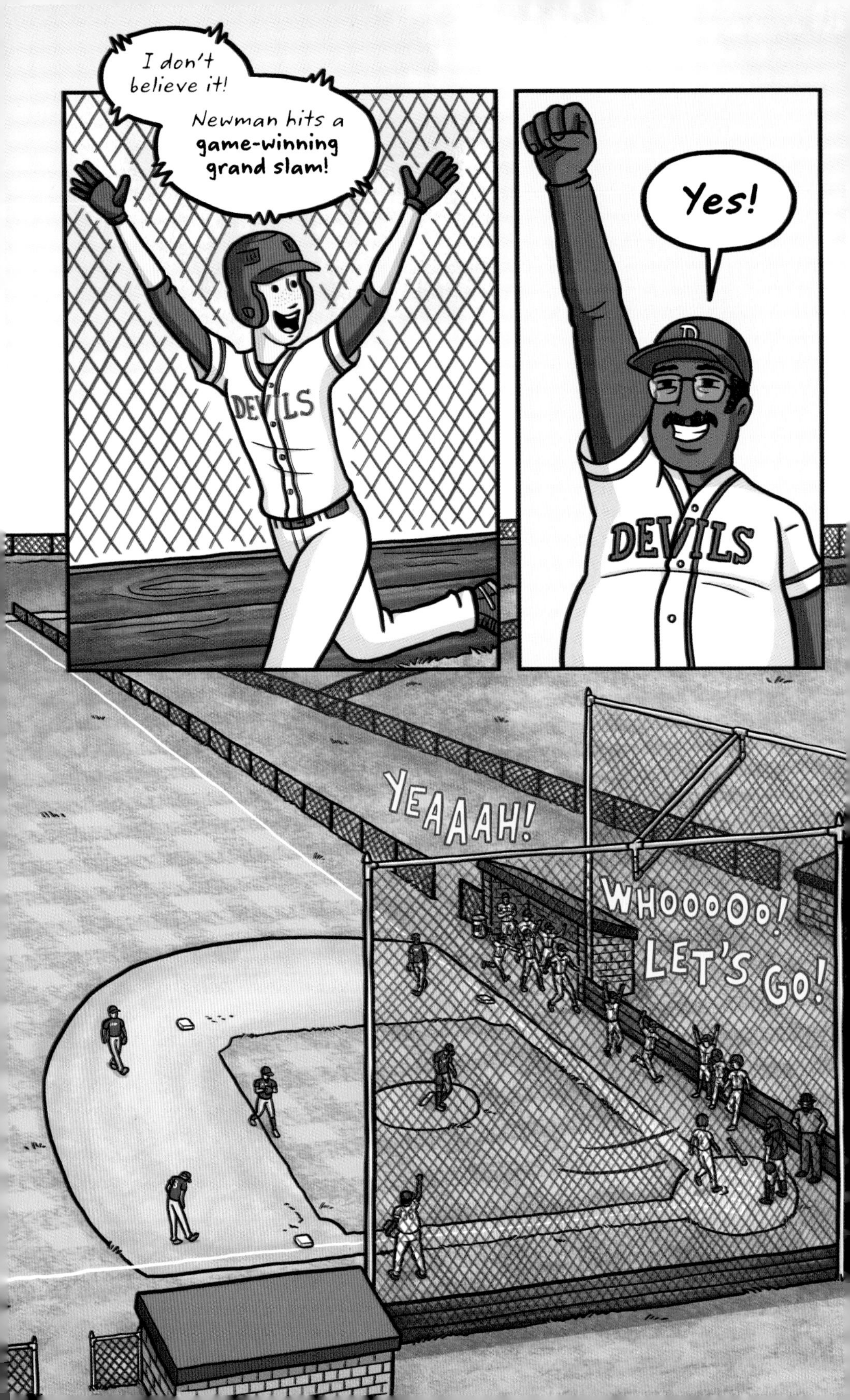
I don't believe it!
Newman hits a game-winning grand slam!
Yes!
YEAAAAH!
WHOOOOOo!
LET'S GO!

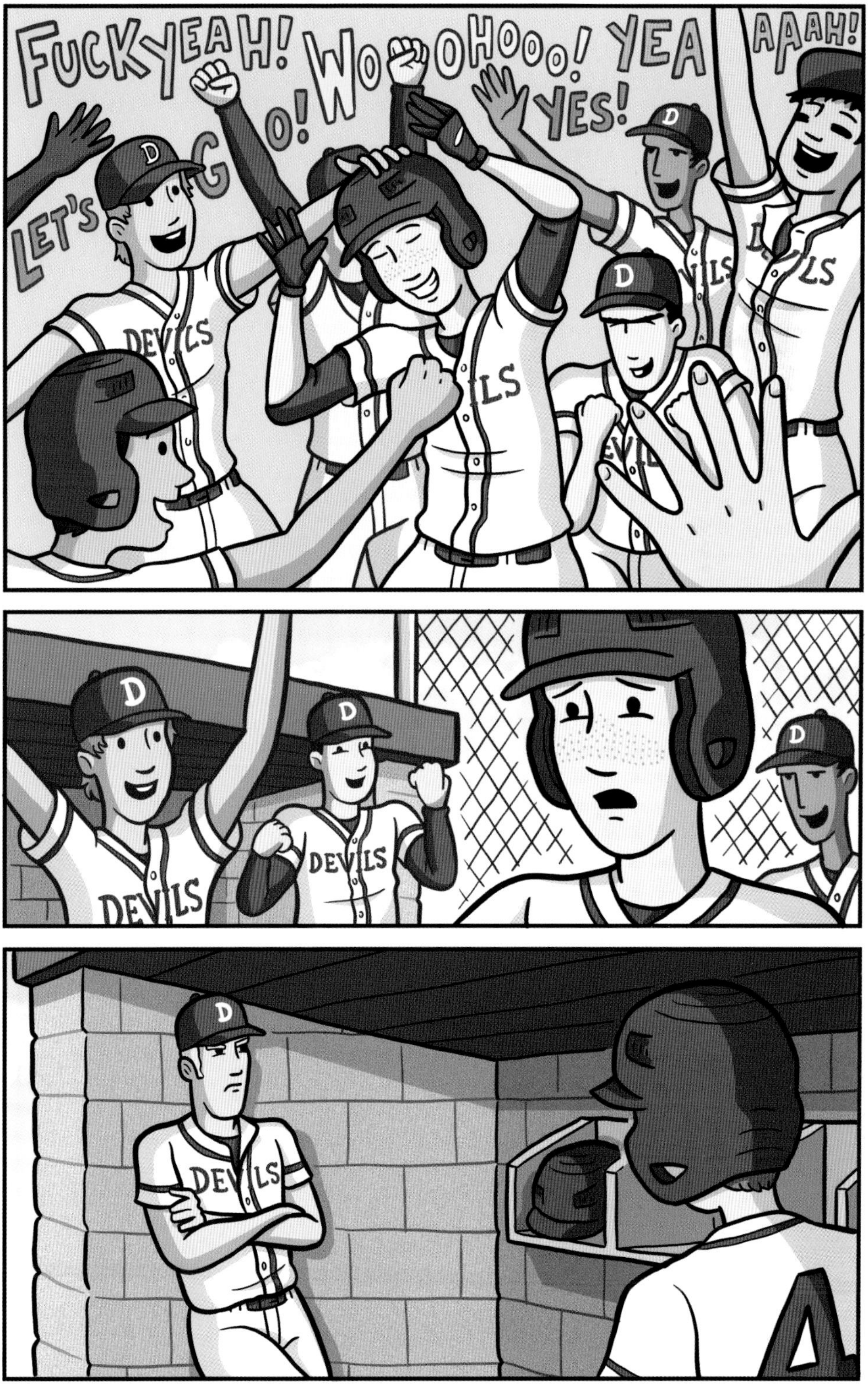
FUCK YEAH!
LET'S GO!
WOOHOOOO!
YEA
YES!
AAAH!

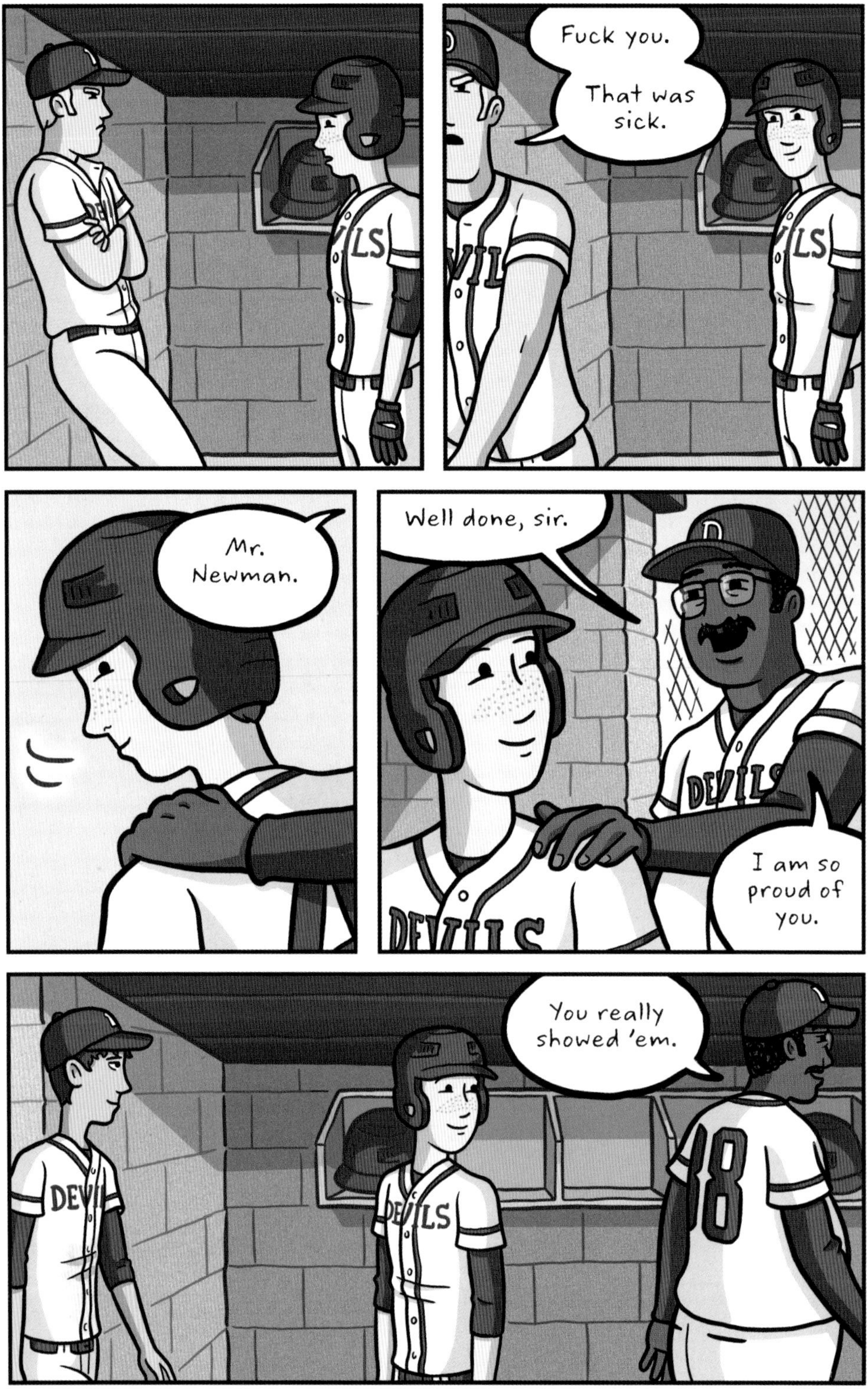
Fuck you.
That was sick.
Mr. Newman.
Well done, sir.
I am so proud of you.
You really showed 'em.

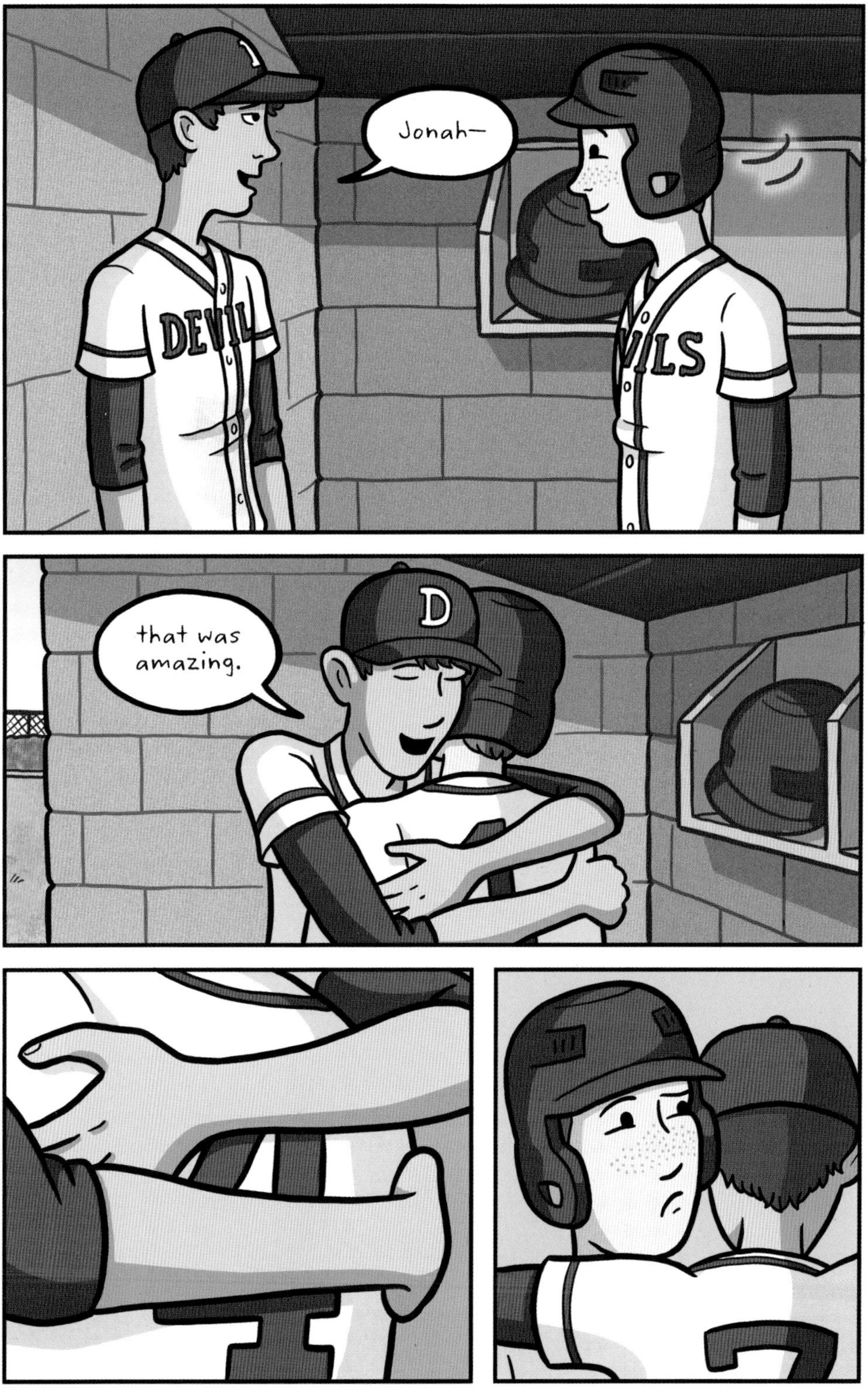
Jonah—
that was amazing.

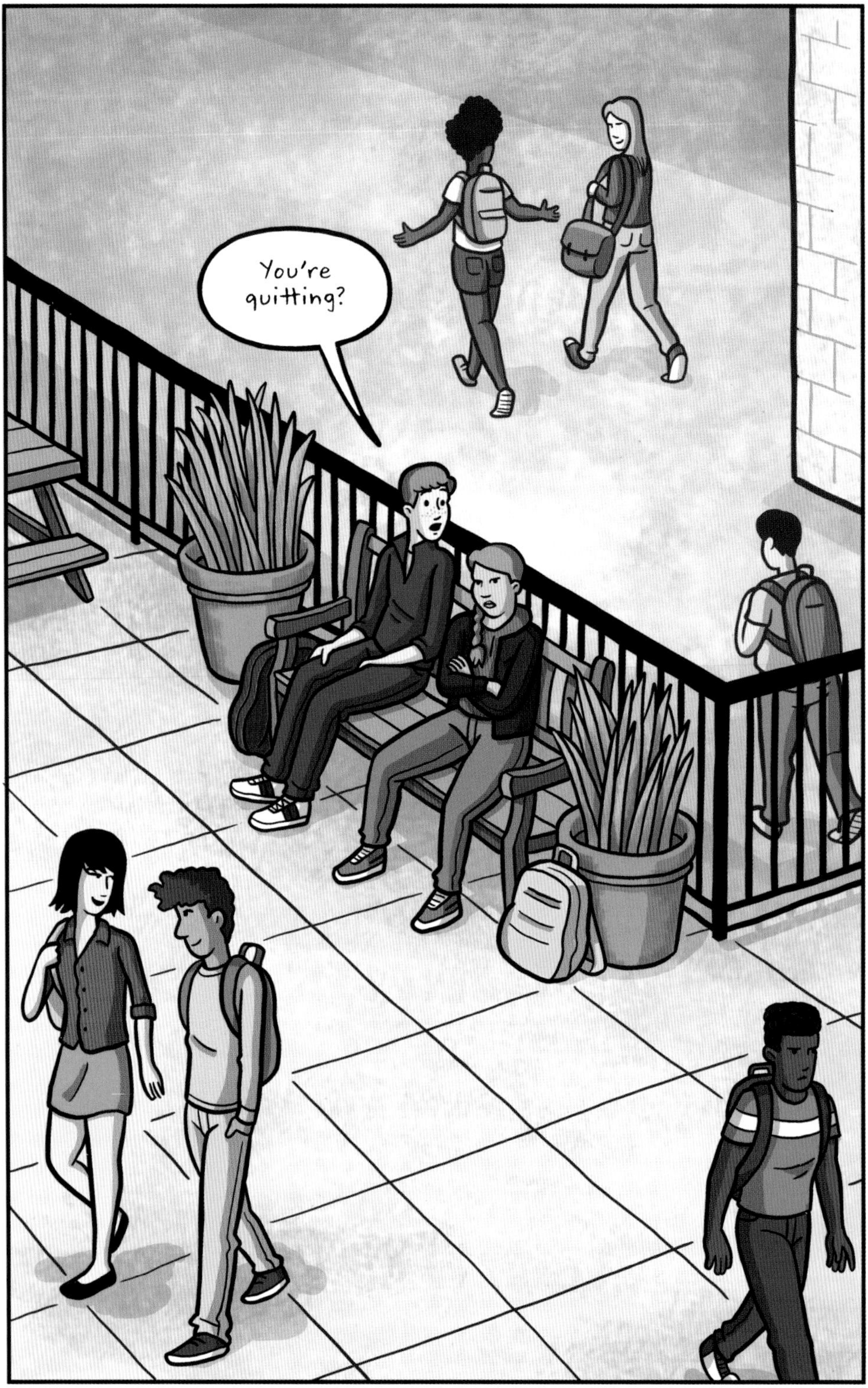
You're quitting?

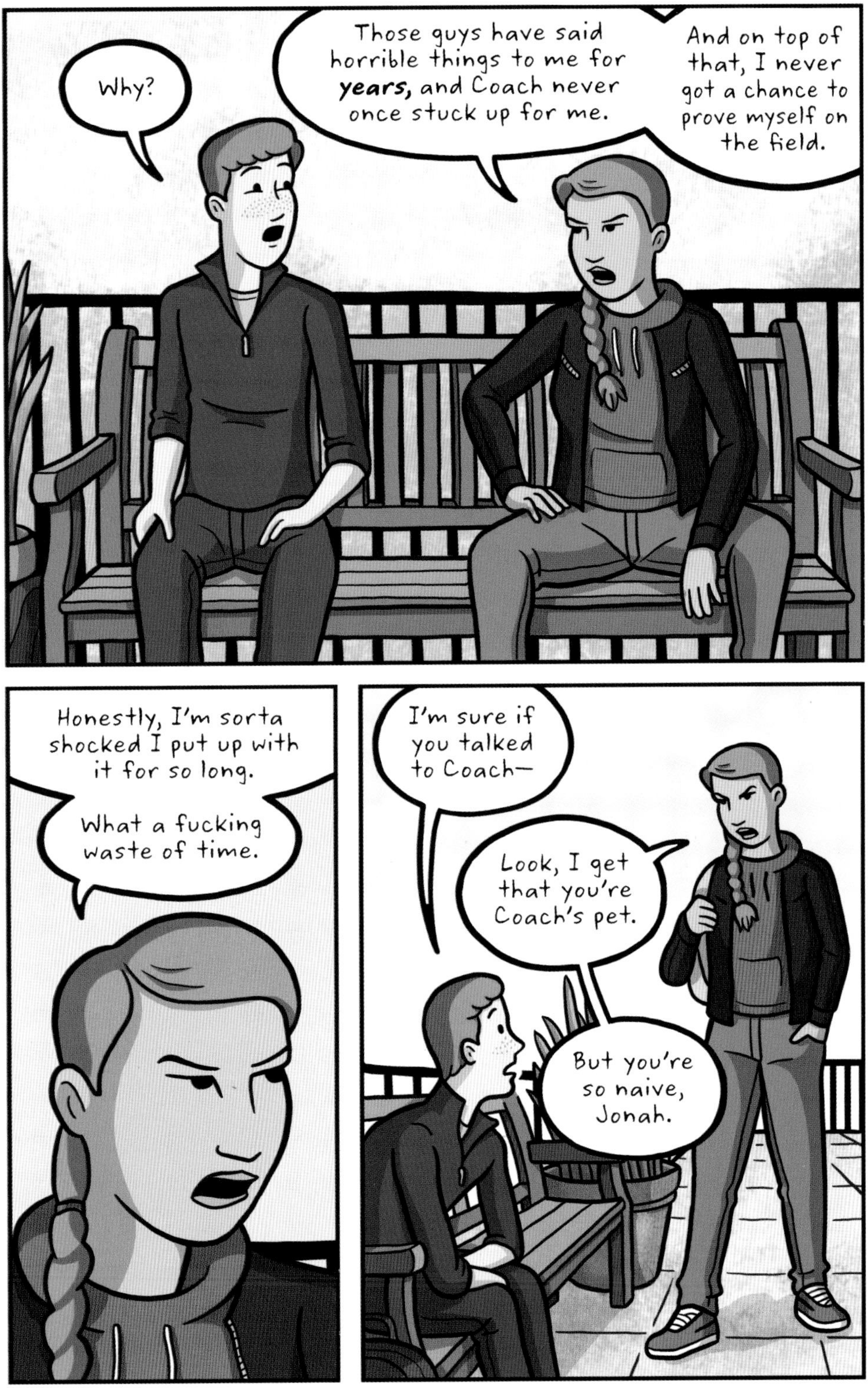
Why?
Those guys have said horrible things to me for **years,** and Coach never once stuck up for me.
And on top of that, I never got a chance to prove myself on the field.
Honestly, I'm sorta shocked I put up with it for so long.
What a fucking waste of time.
I'm sure if you talked to Coach—
Look, I get that you're Coach's pet.
But you're so naive, Jonah.

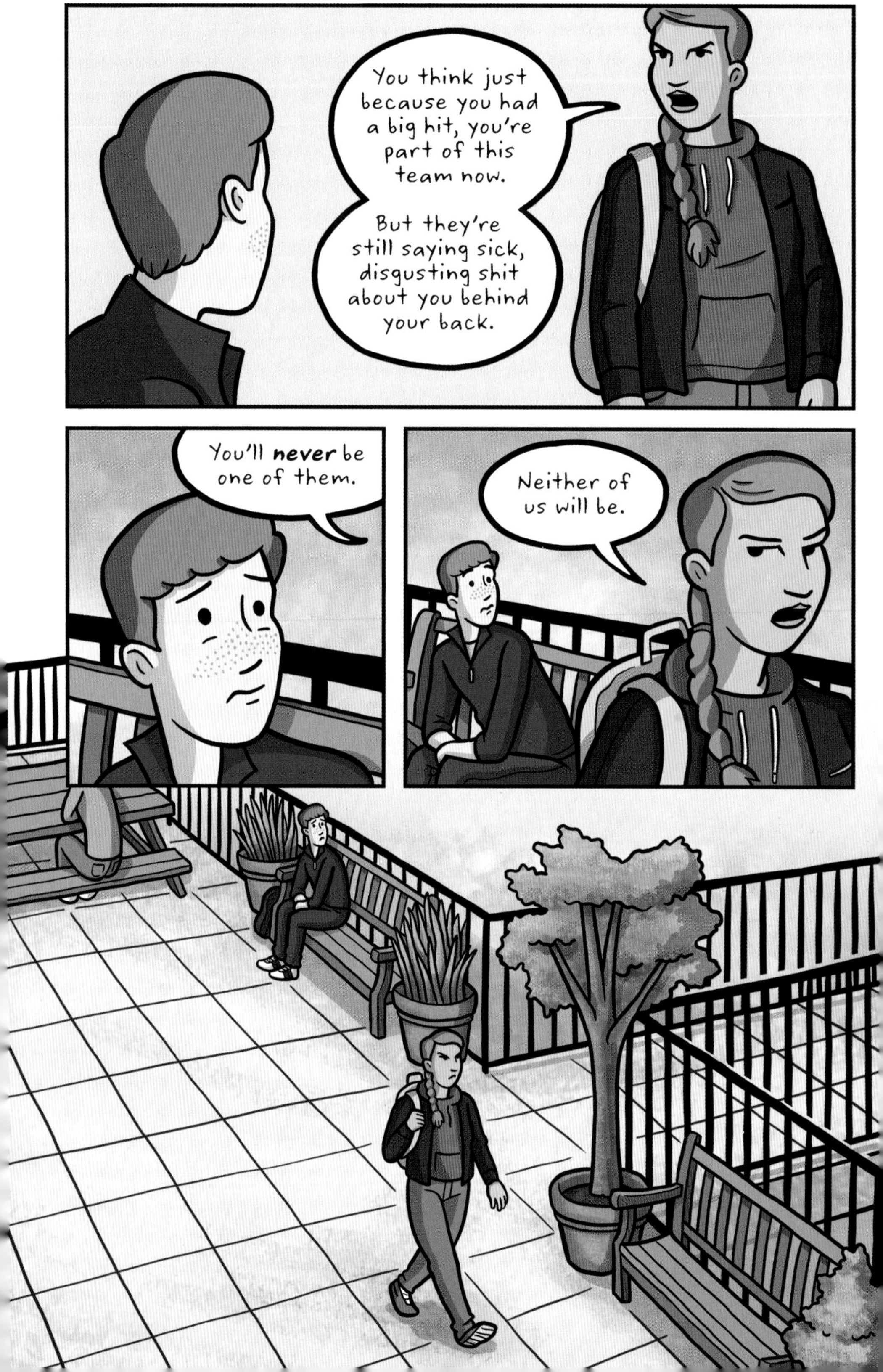
You think just because you had a big hit, you're part of this team now.
But they're still saying sick, disgusting shit about you behind your back.
You'll **never** be one of them.
Neither of us will be.

CHAPTER 6

An
Enchanted
Evening

DHS SENIOR PROM

May 5, 2012
6 P.M.
Gymnasium

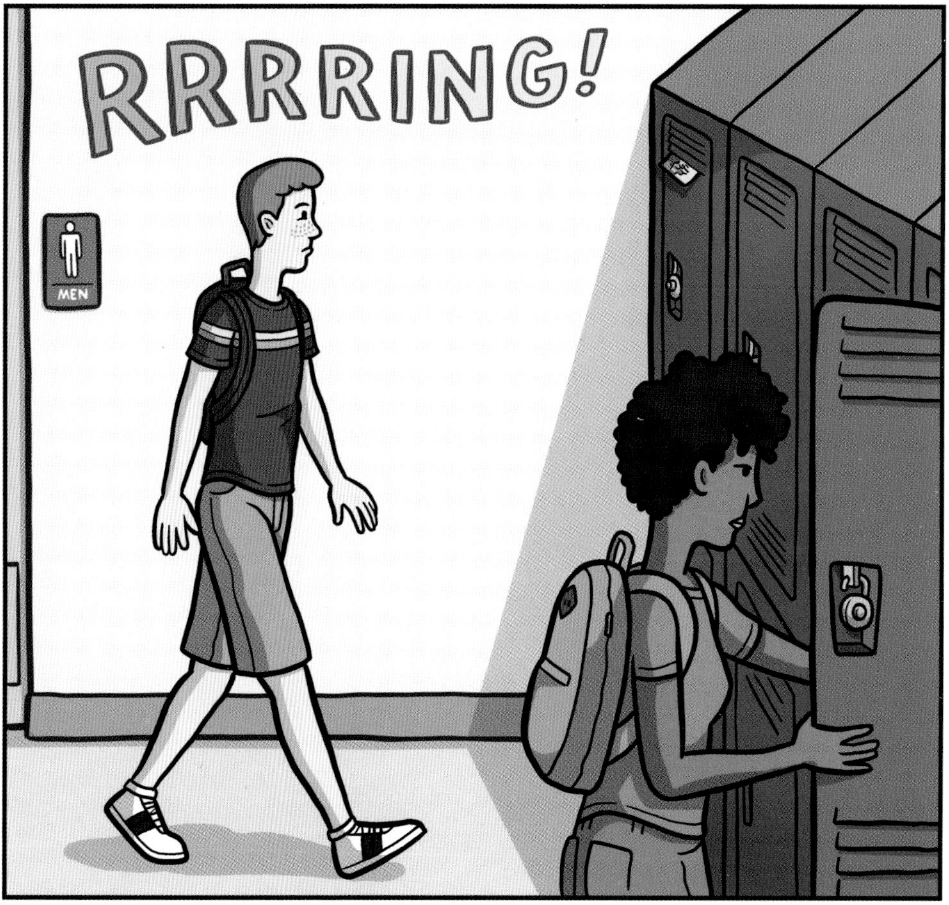
RRRRING!
MEN

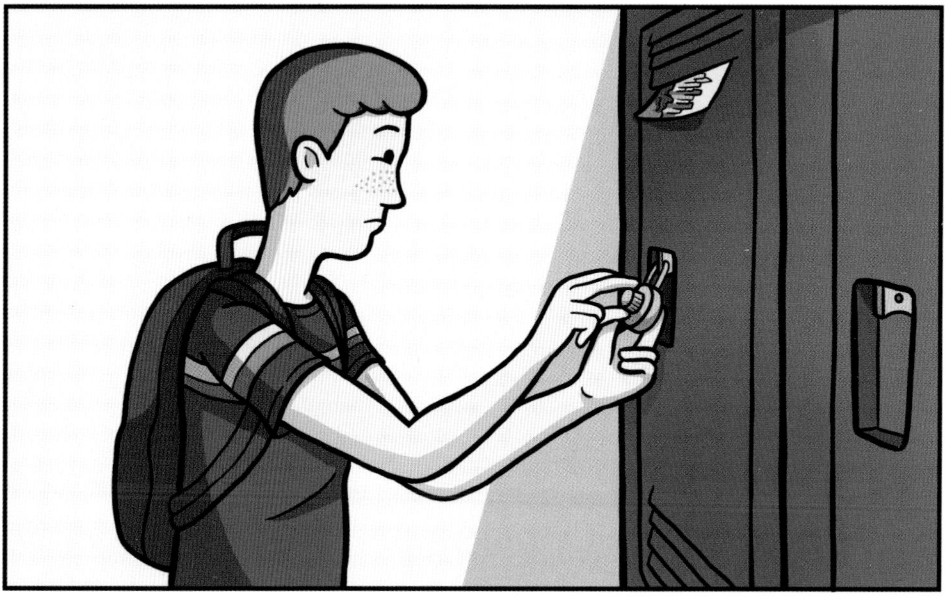

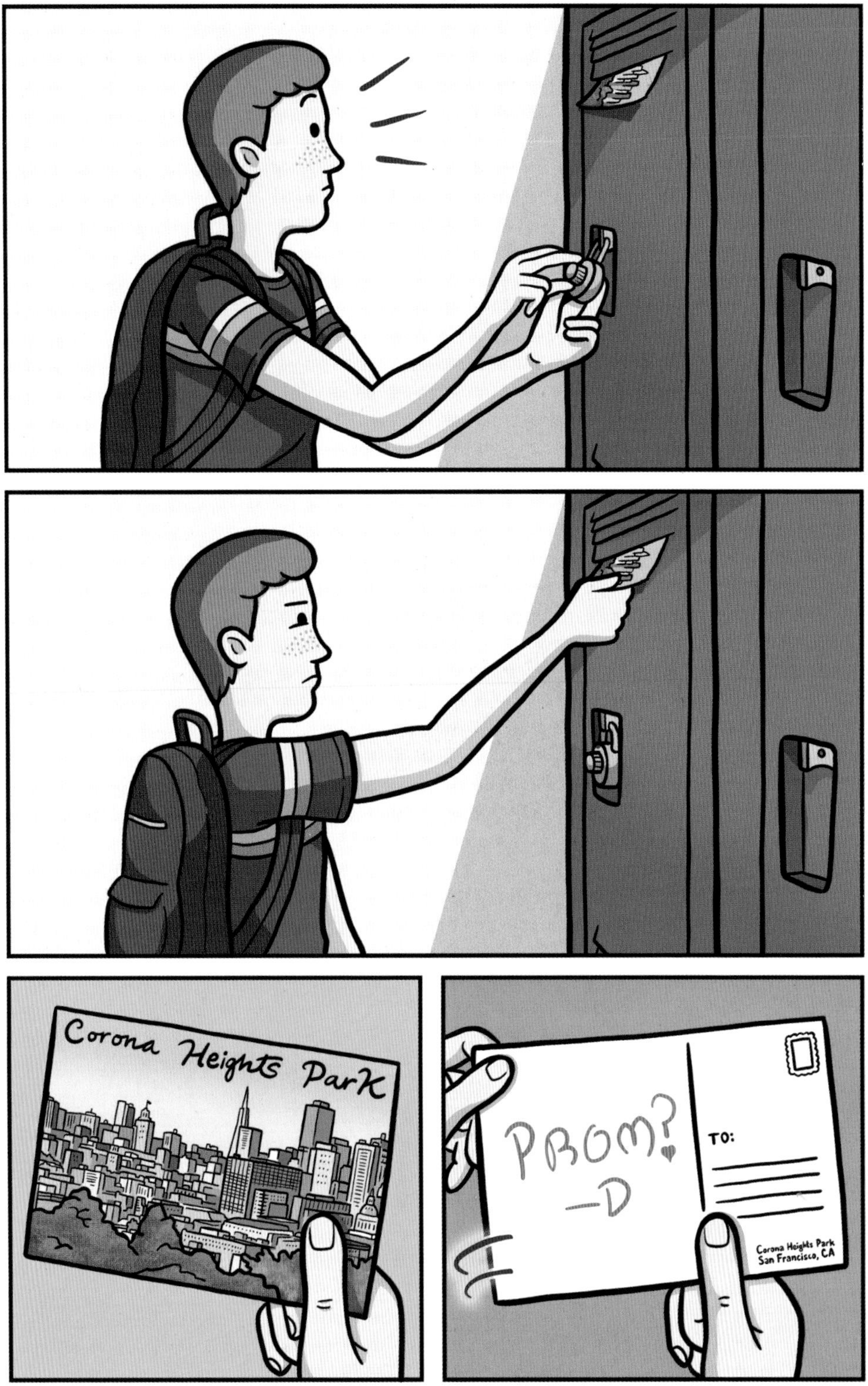

Corona Heights Park
PROM?
—D
TO:
Corona Heights Park
San Francisco, CA

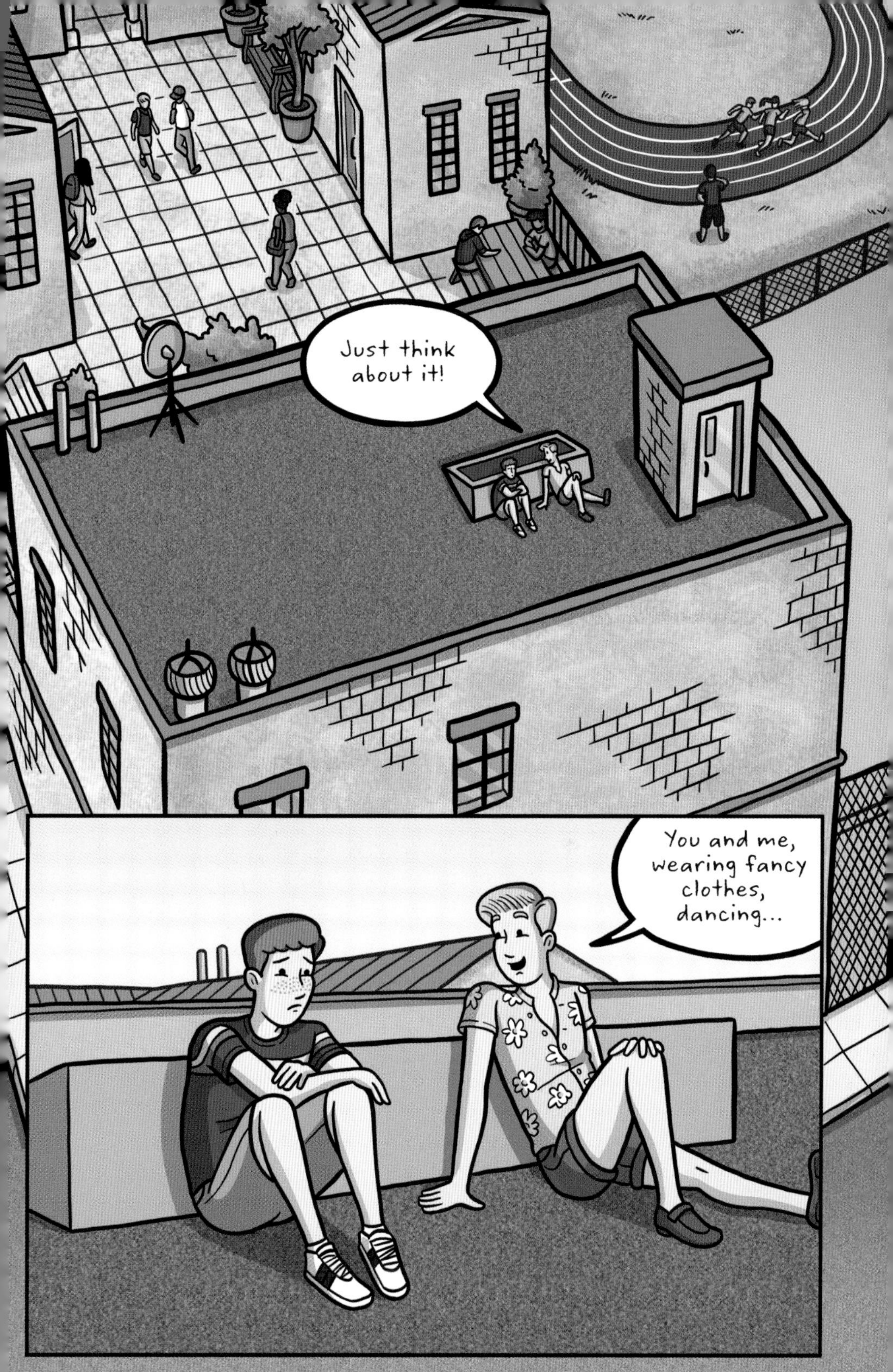
Just think about it!
You and me, wearing fancy clothes, dancing...

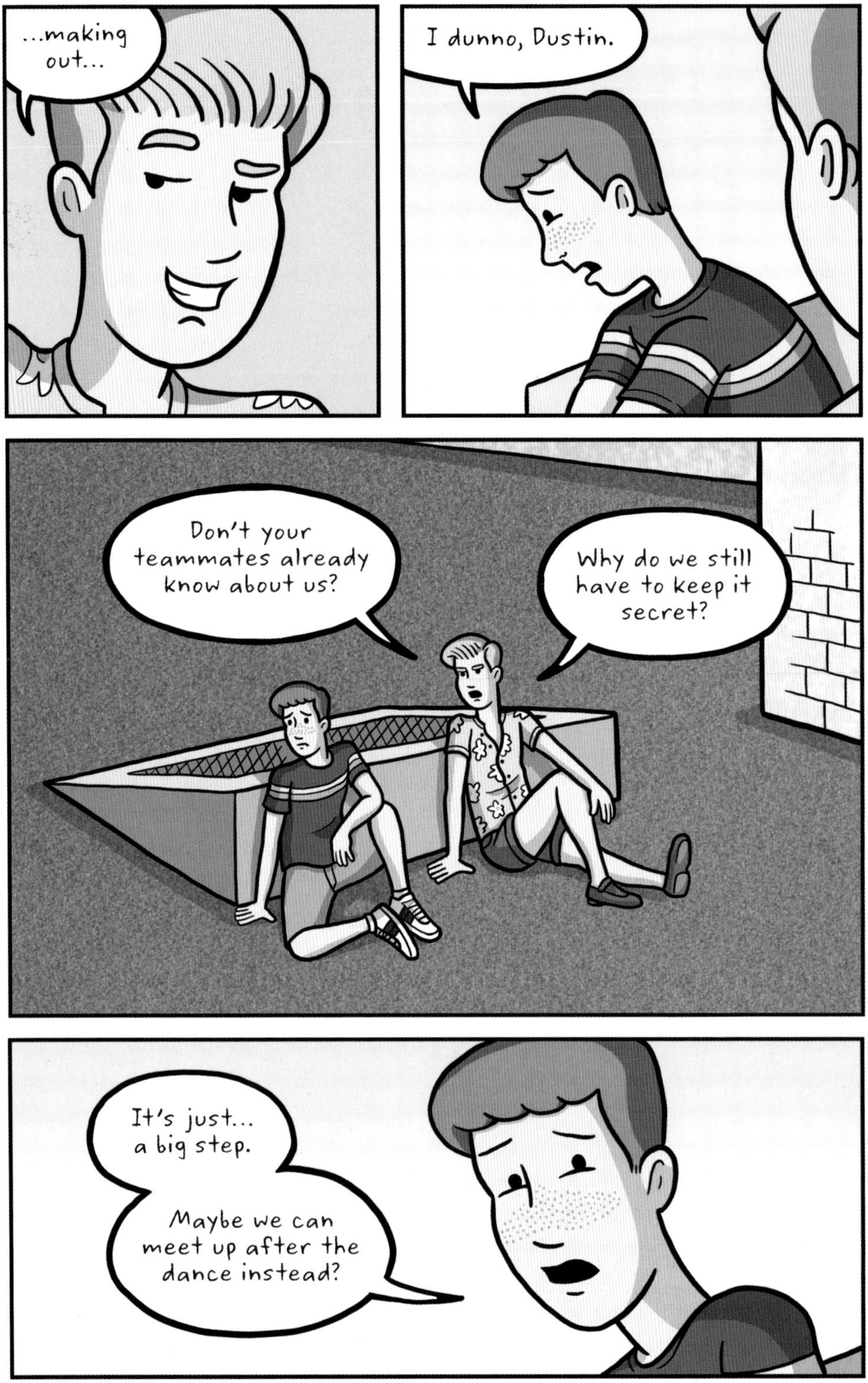
...making out...
I dunno, Dustin.
Don't your teammates already know about us?
Why do we still have to keep it secret?
It's just... a big step.
Maybe we can meet up after the dance instead?

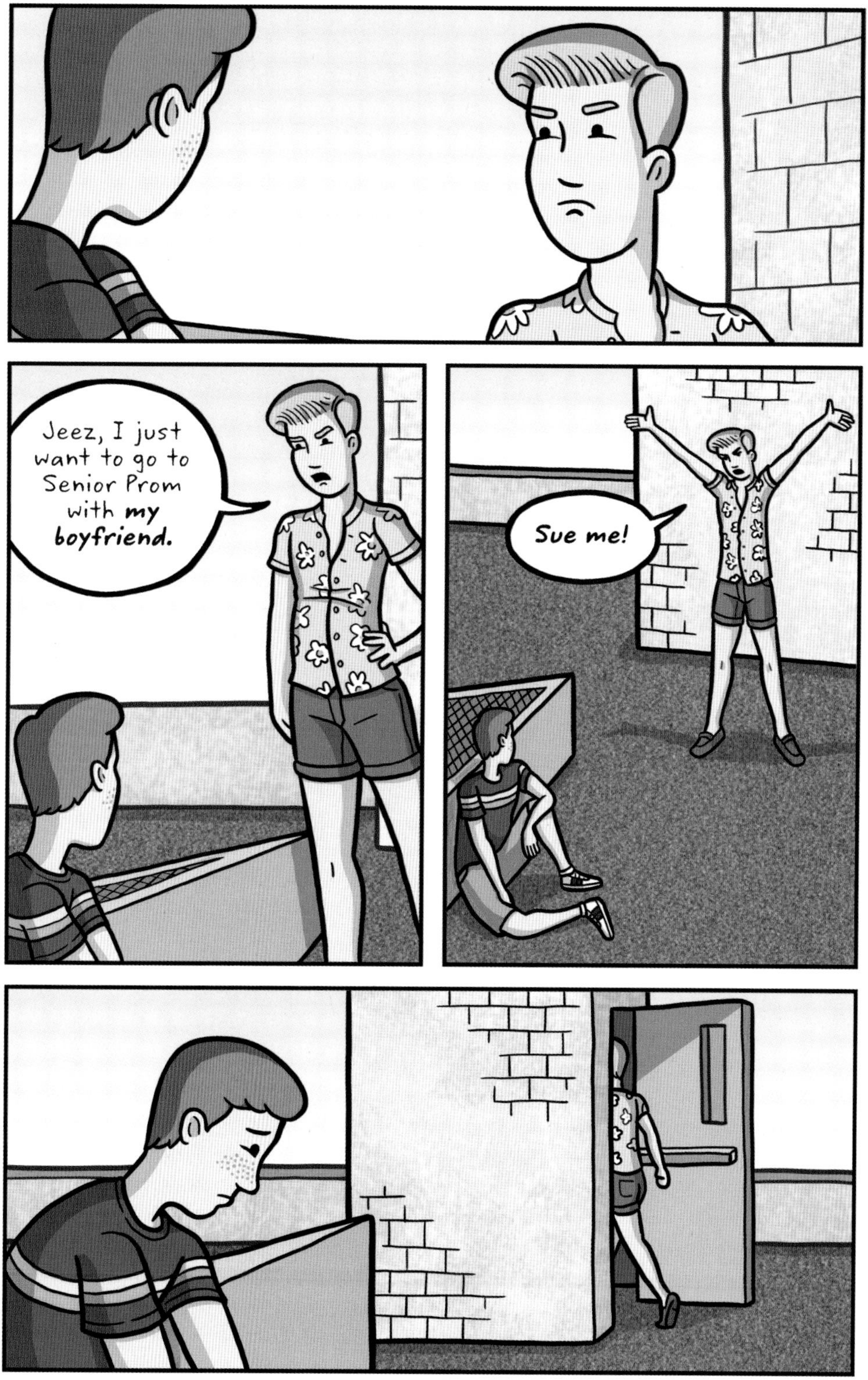

Jeez, I just want to go to Senior Prom with **my boyfriend.**
Sue me!

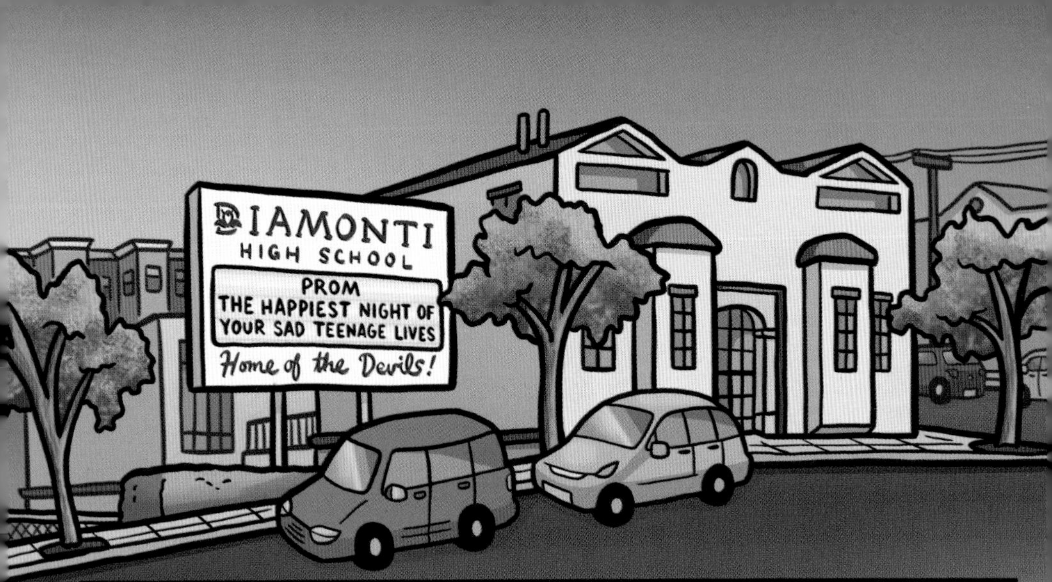
DIAMONTI
HIGH SCHOOL
PROM
THE HAPPIEST NIGHT OF
YOUR SAD TEENAGE LIVES
Home of the Devils!

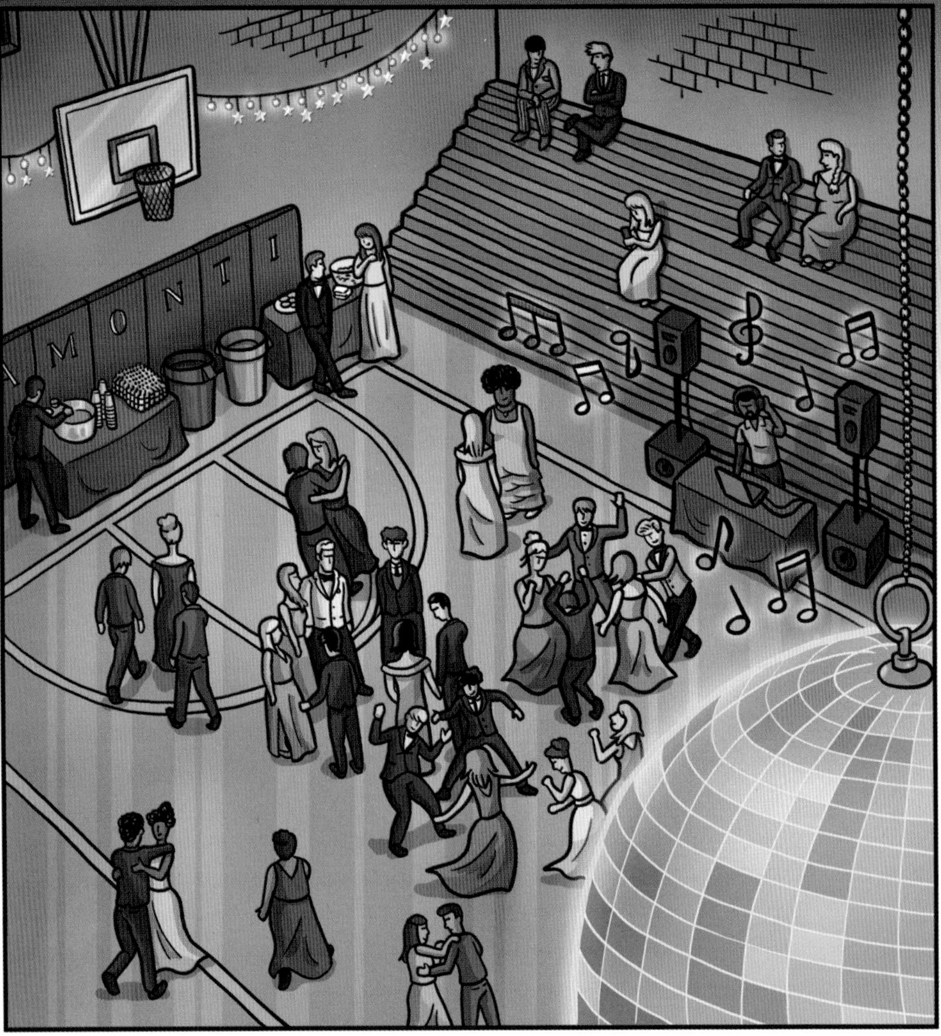

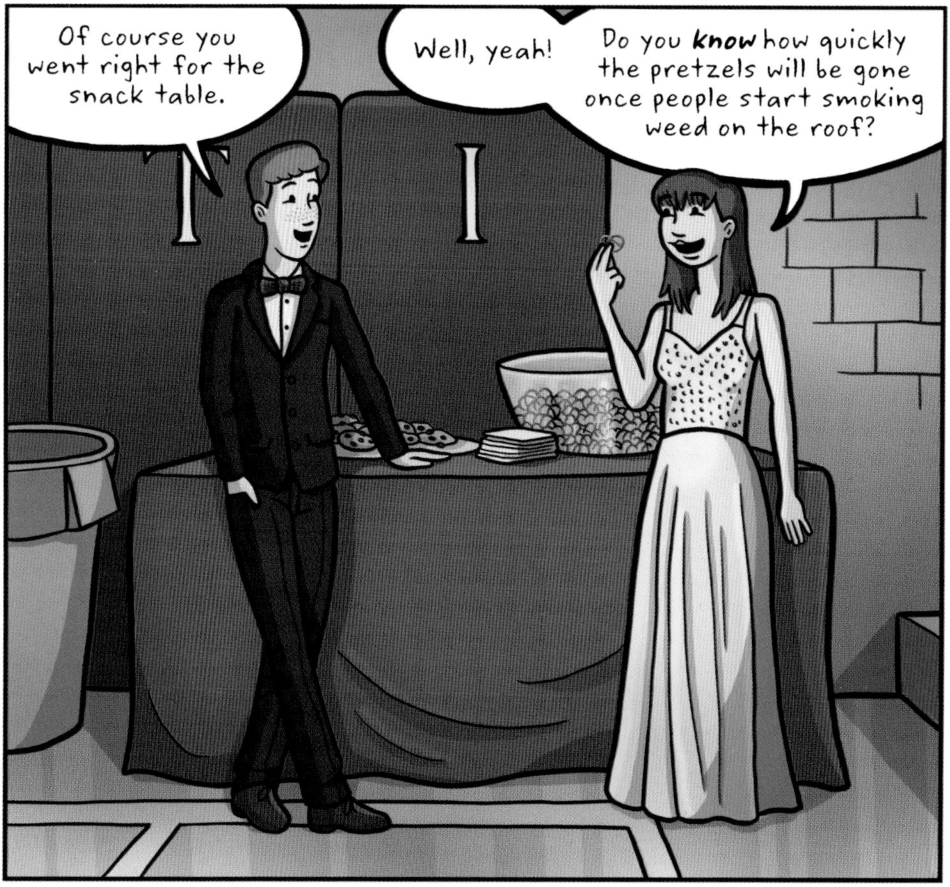
Of course you went right for the snack table.
Well, yeah!
Do you **know** how quickly the pretzels will be gone once people start smoking weed on the roof?

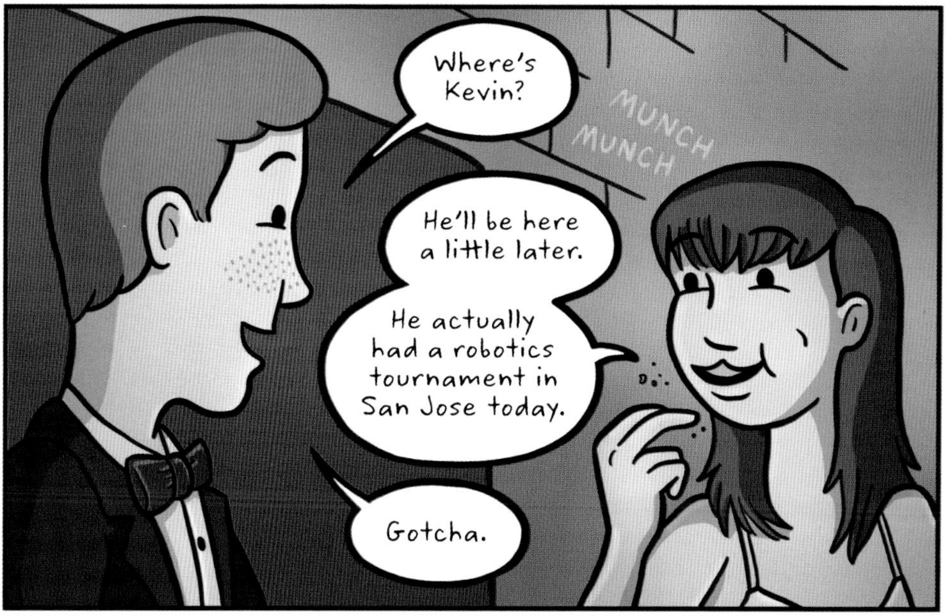
Where's Kevin?
MUNCH MUNCH
He'll be here a little later.
He actually had a robotics tournament in San Jose today.
Gotcha.

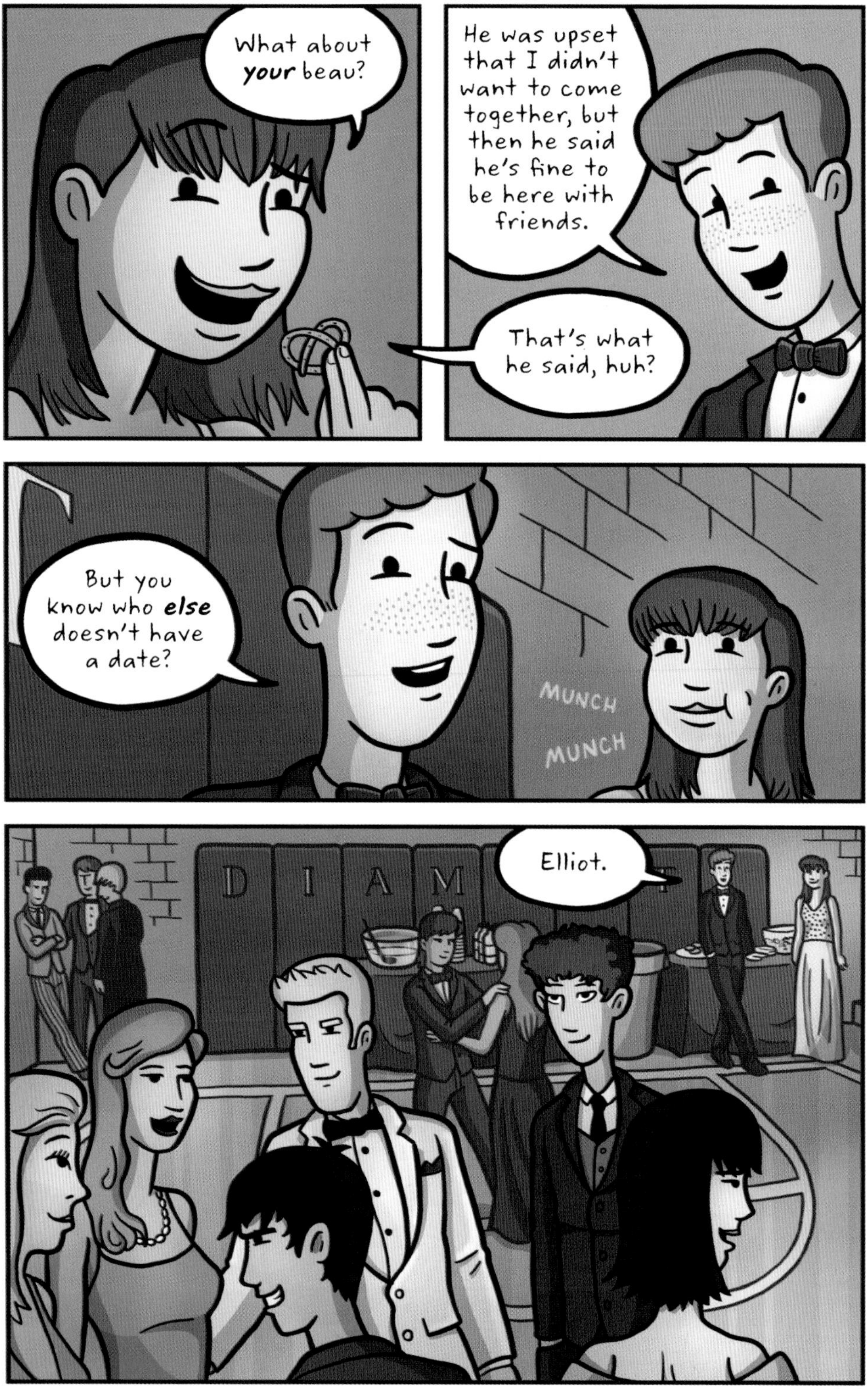
What about **your** beau?
He was upset that I didn't want to come together, but then he said he's fine to be here with friends.
That's what he said, huh?
But you know who **else** doesn't have a date?
MUNCH
MUNCH
Elliot.

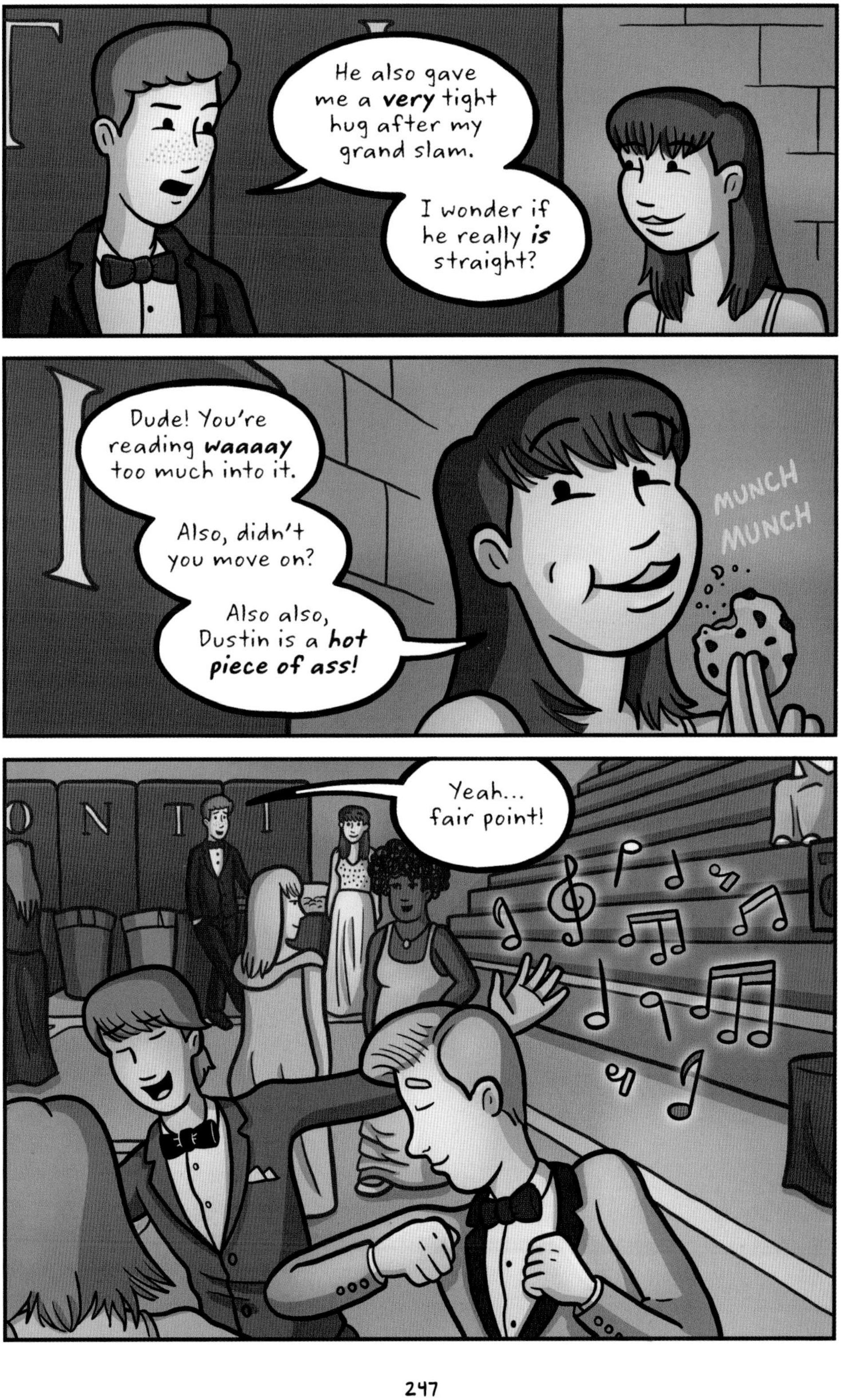

He also gave me a **very** tight hug after my grand slam.
I wonder if he really **is** straight?
Dude! You're reading **waaaay** too much into it.
Also, didn't you move on?
Also also, Dustin is a **hot piece of ass!**
MUNCH MUNCH
Yeah... fair point!

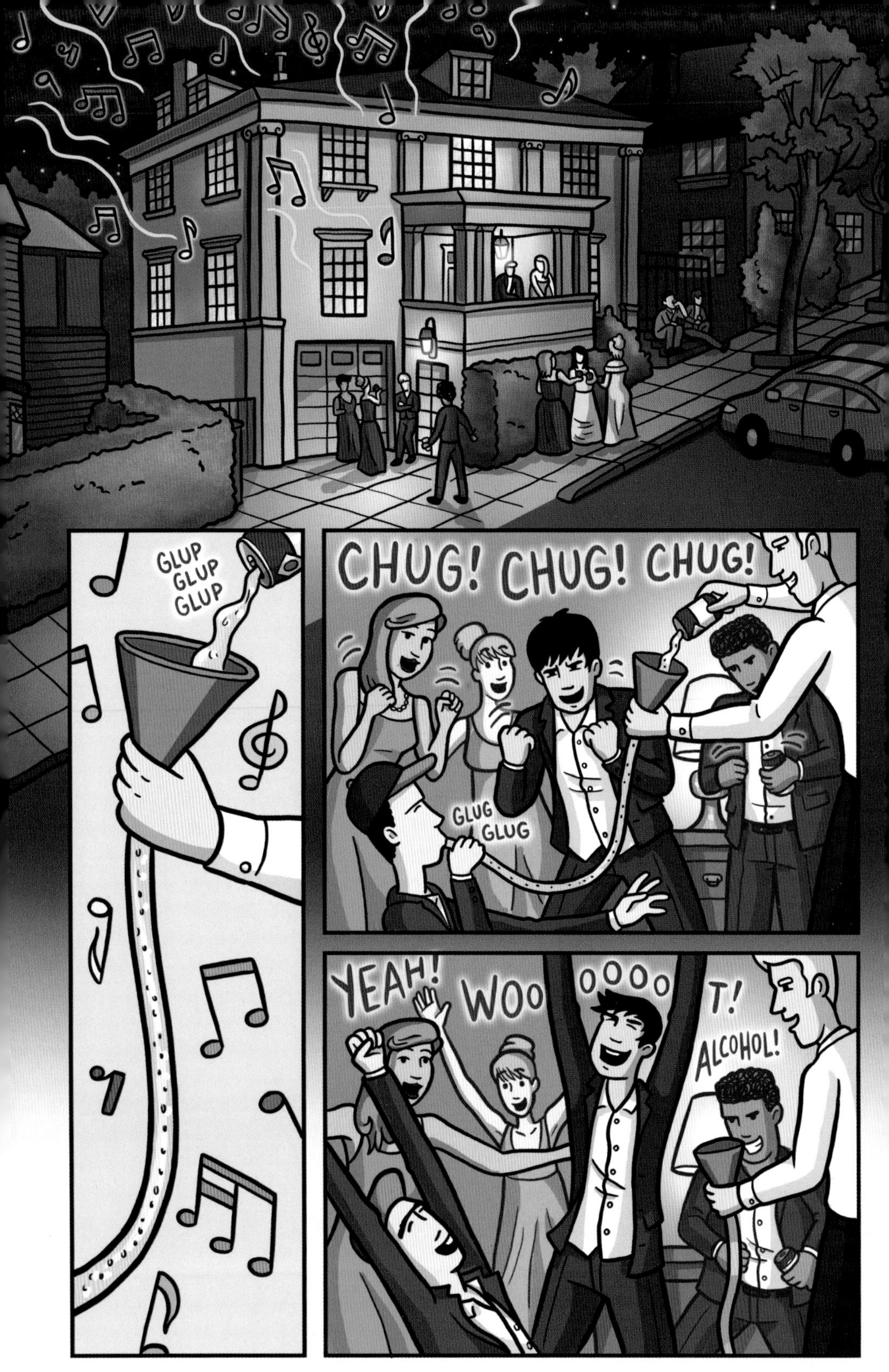
GLUP
GLUP
GLUP
CHUG! CHUG! CHUG!
GLUG
GLUG
YEAH!
WOOOOOOT!
ALCOHOL!

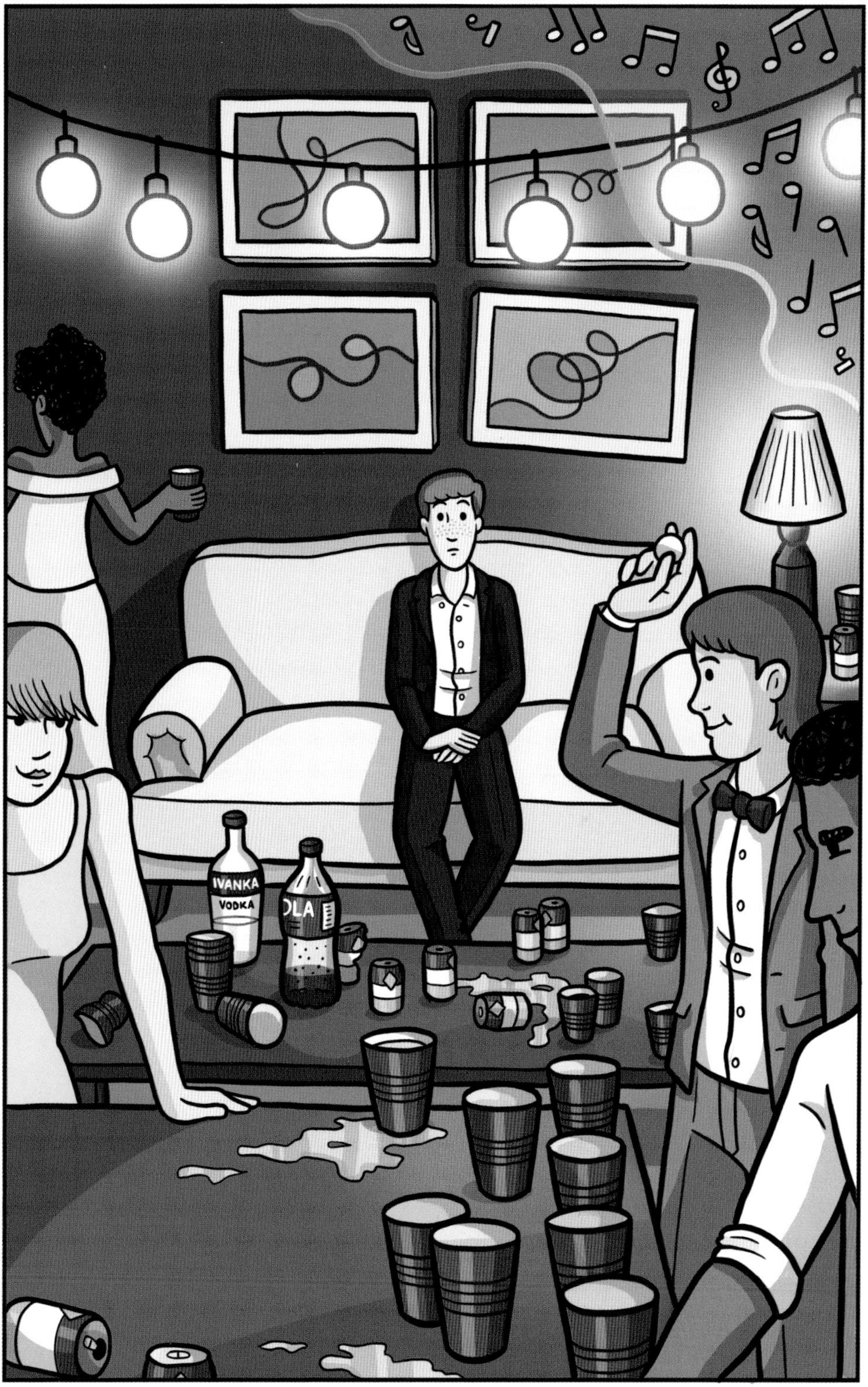
IVANKA
VODKA
OLA

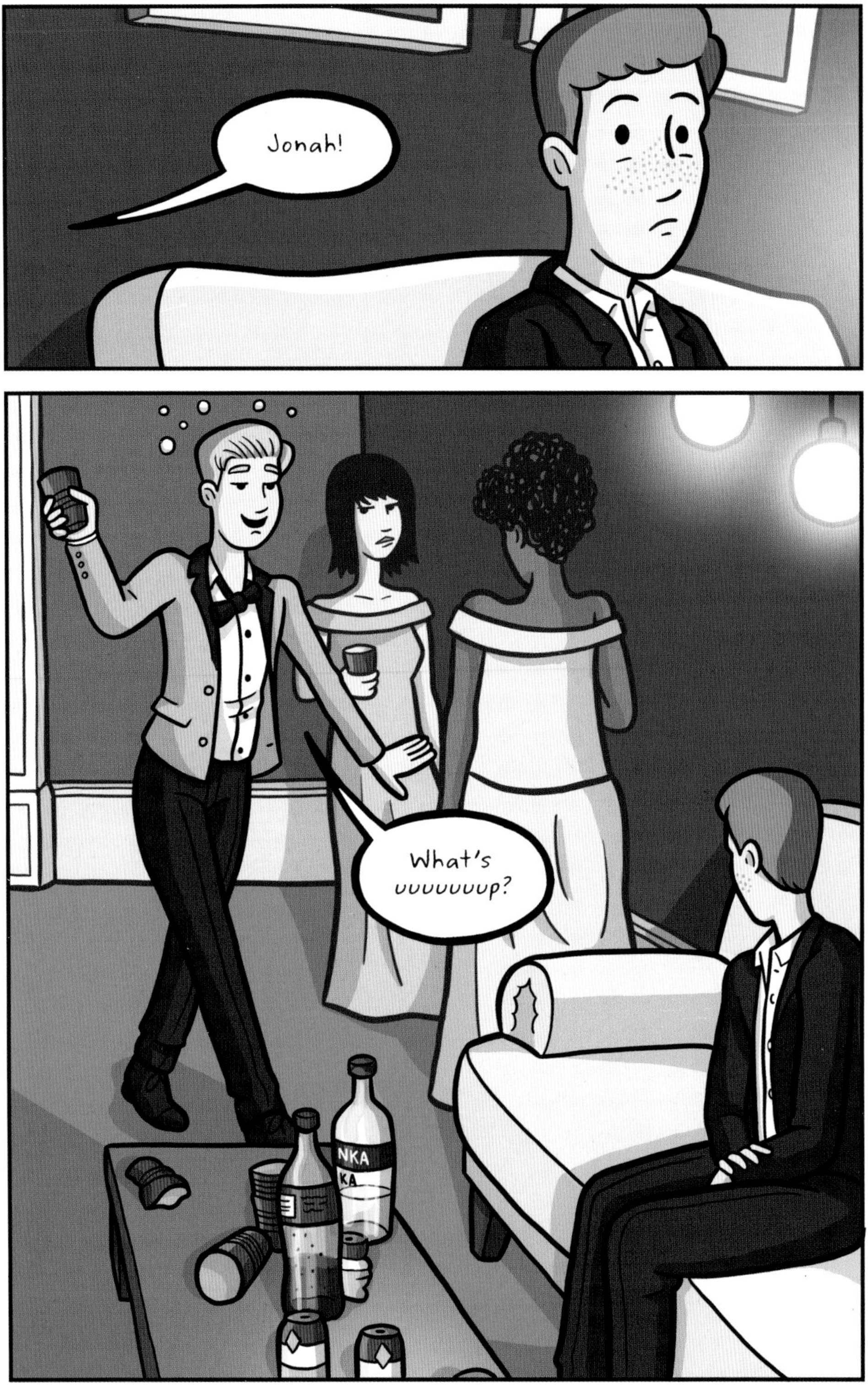
Jonah!
What's uuuuuuup?

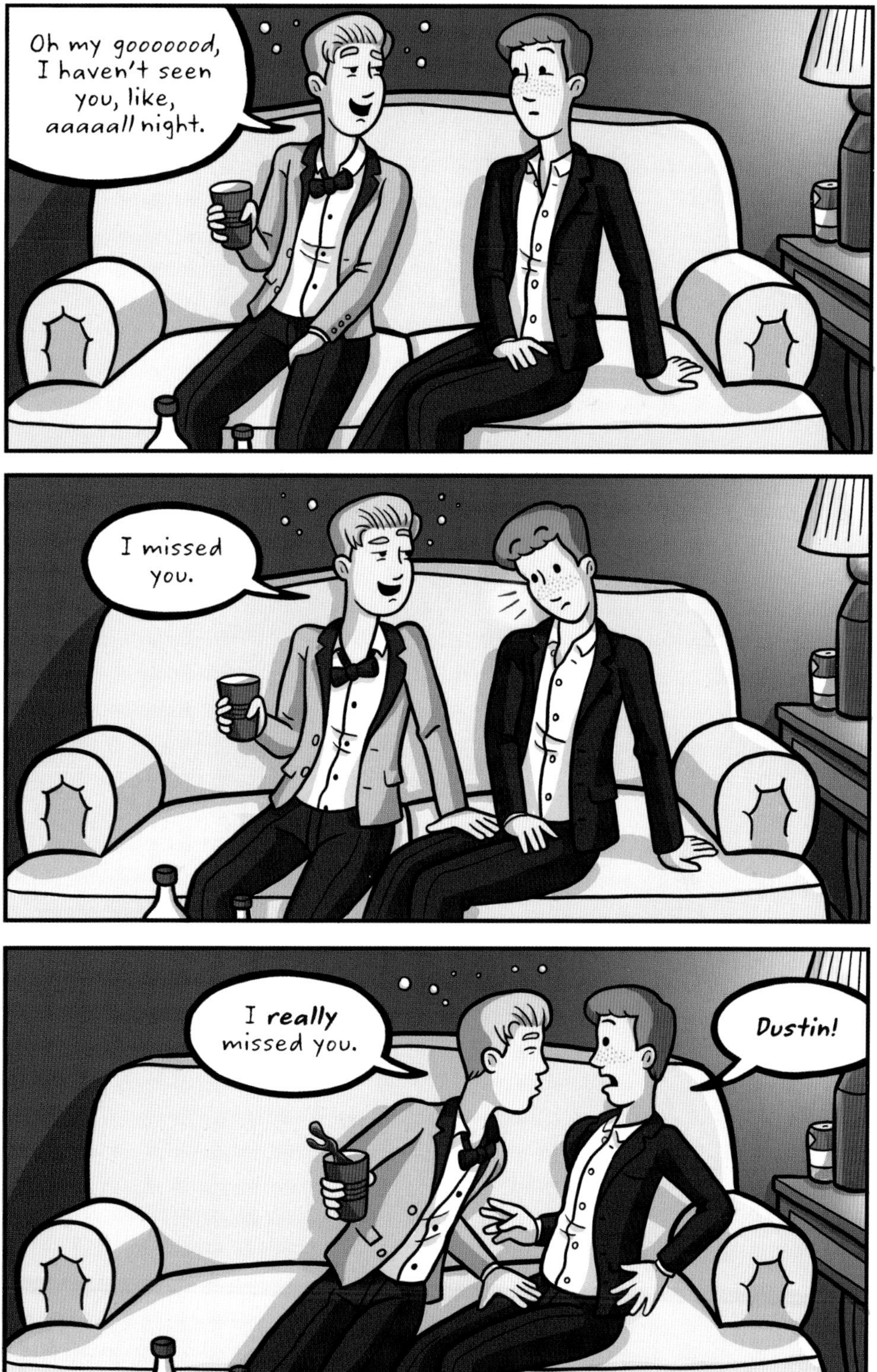
Oh my gooooood, I haven't seen you, like, aaaaall night.
I missed you.
I really missed you.
Dustin!

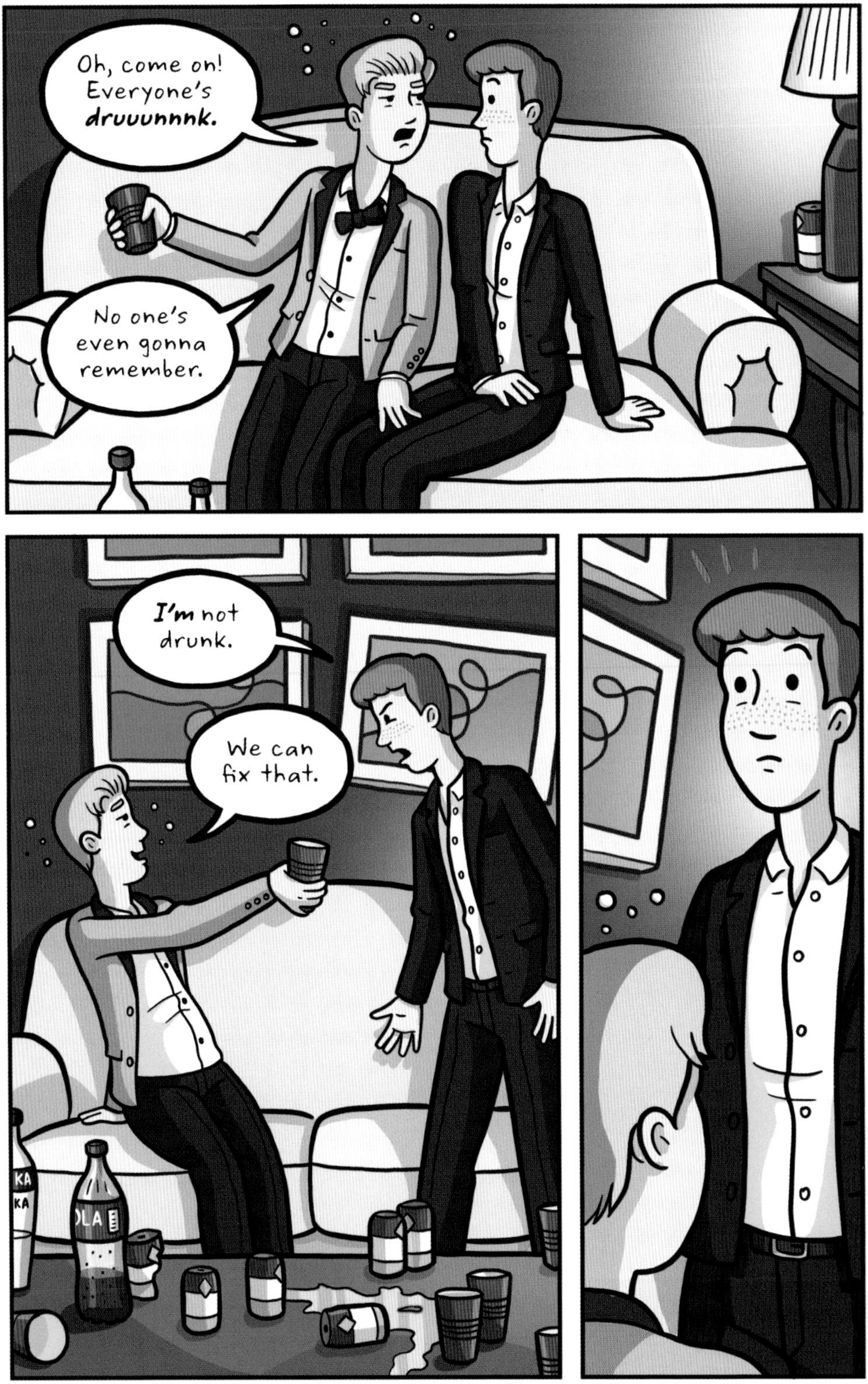
Oh, come on! Everyone's **druuunnnk.**
No one's even gonna remember.
I'm not drunk.
We can fix that.
KA
KA
OLA

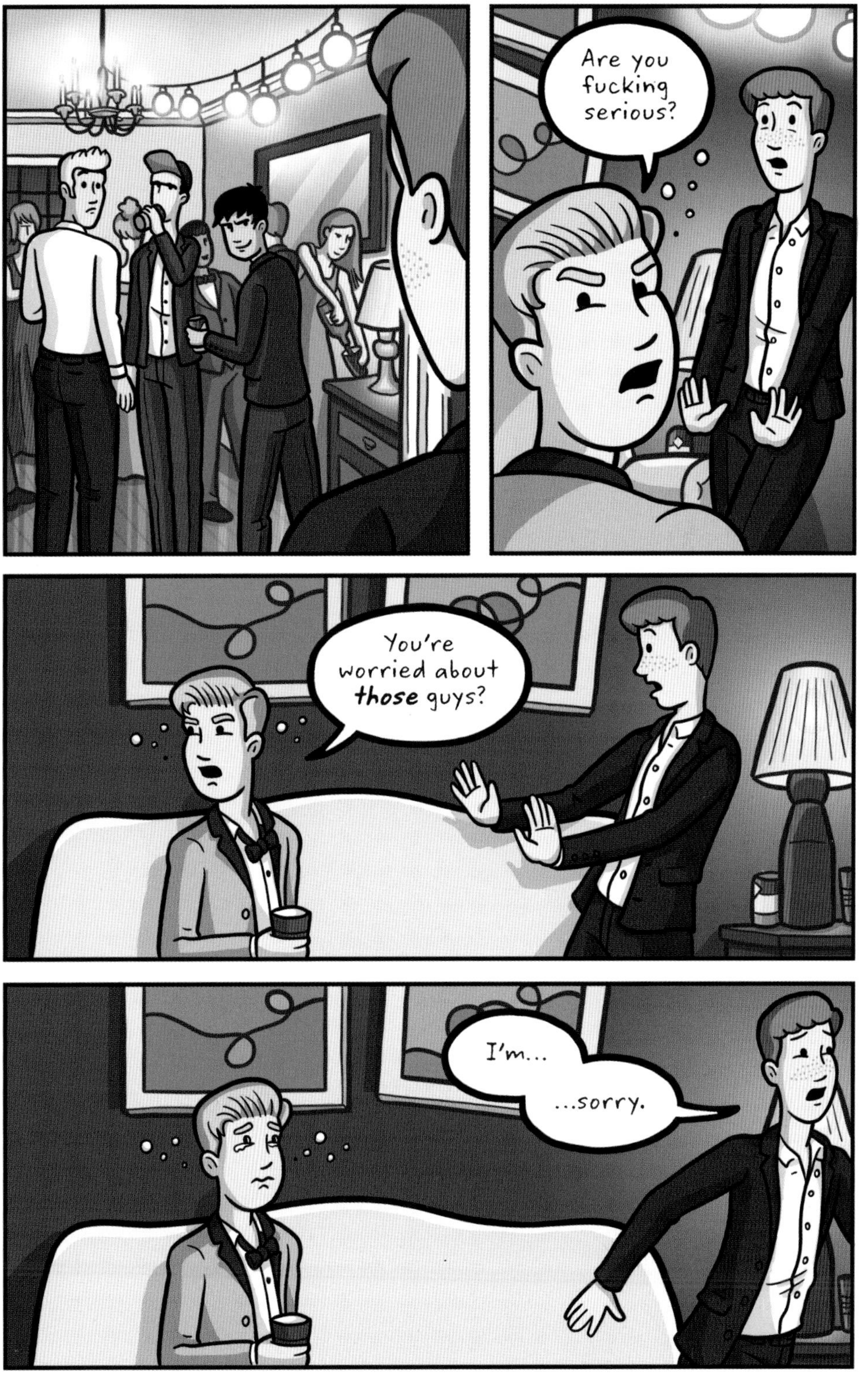
Are you fucking serious?
You're worried about **those** guys?
I'm...
...sorry.

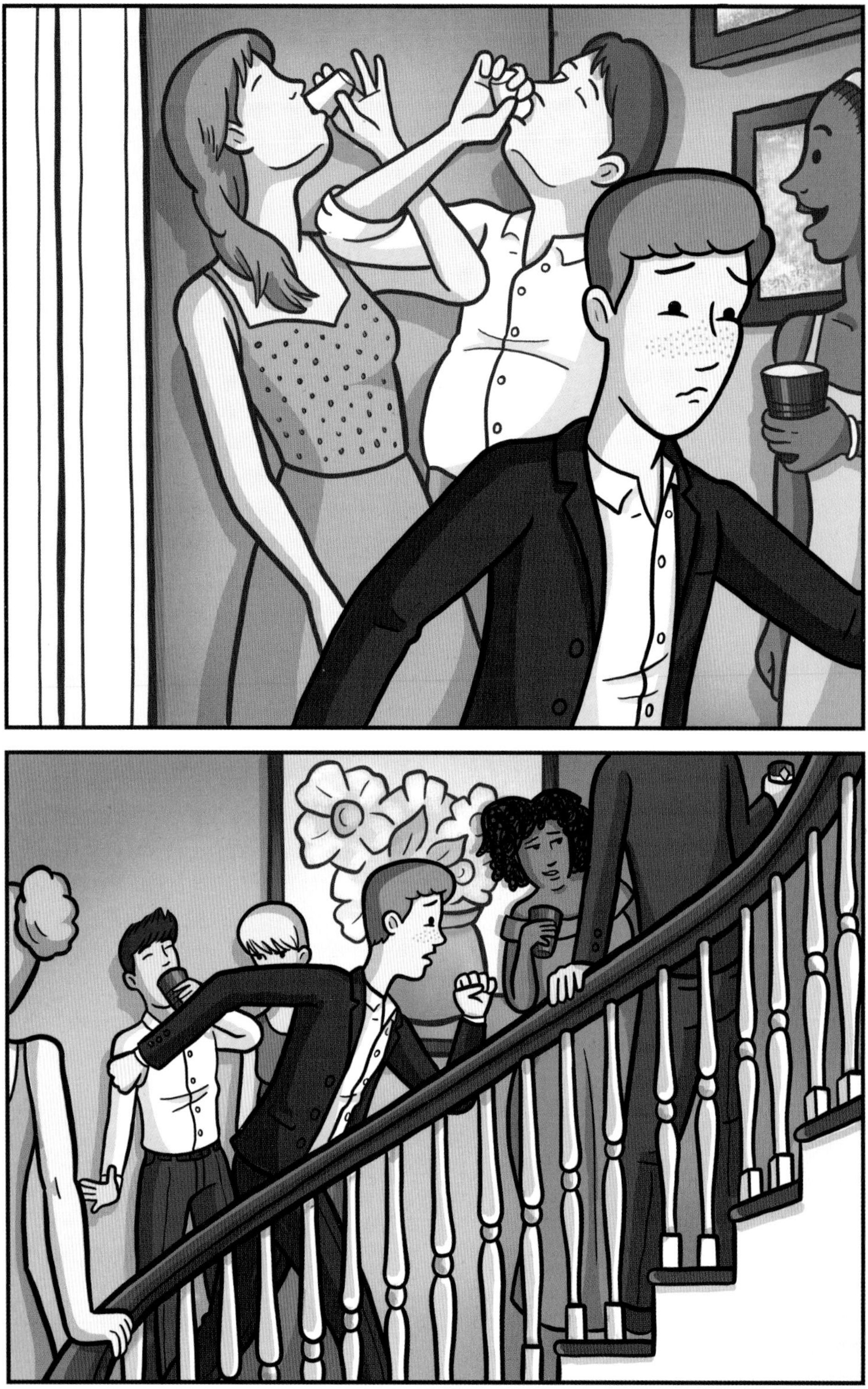

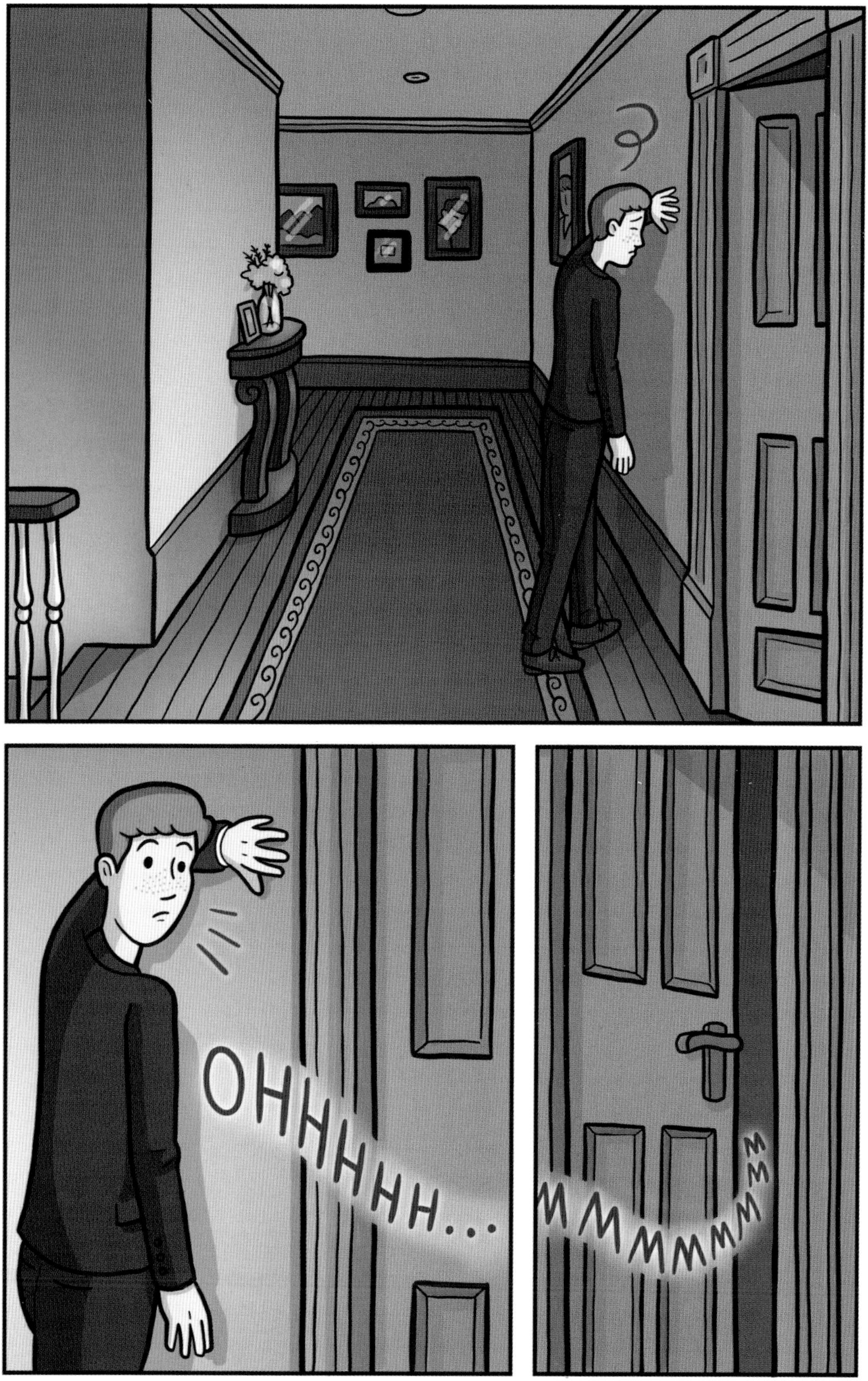
OHHHHHH...
MMMMMMMM

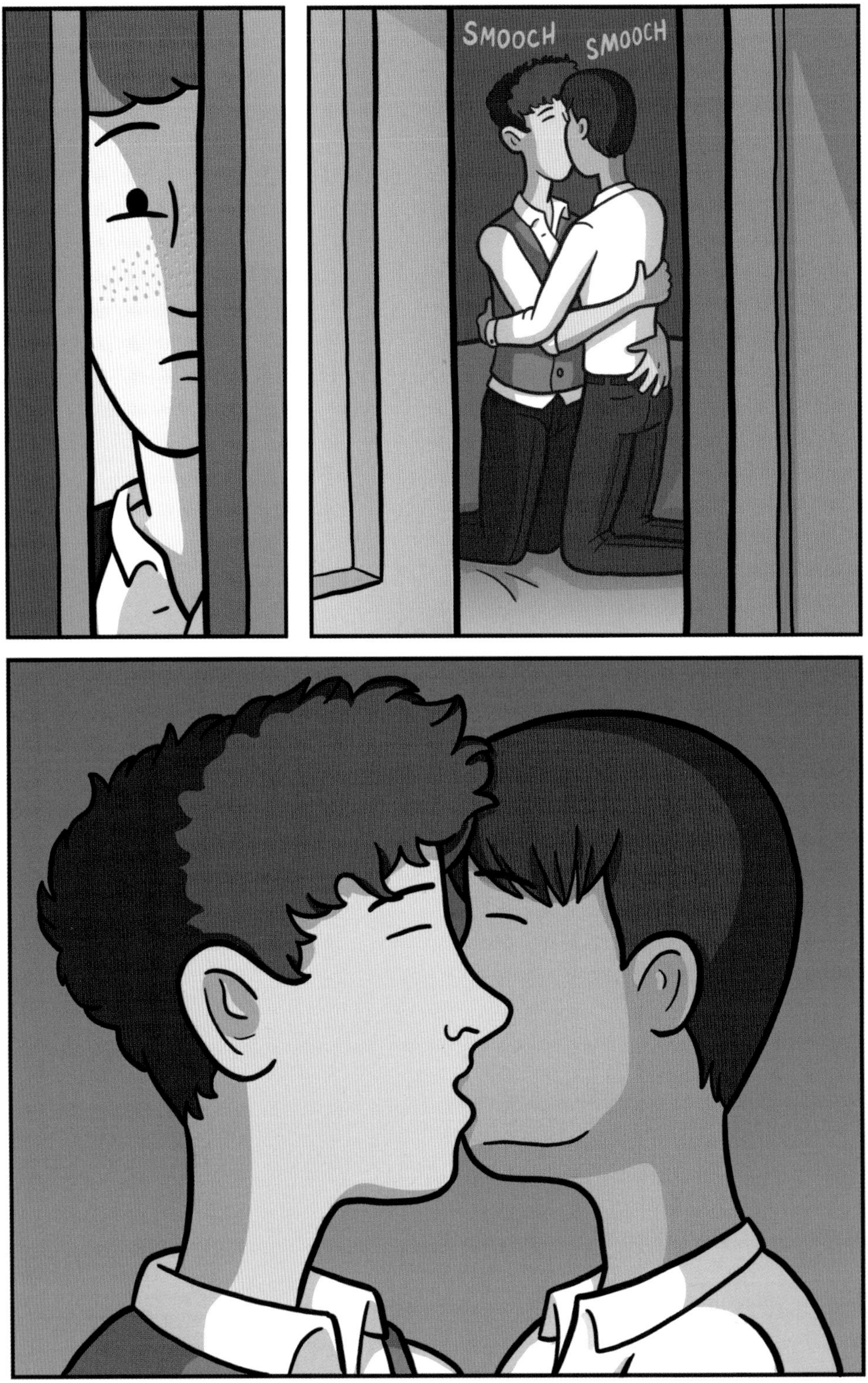
SMOOCH
SMOOCH

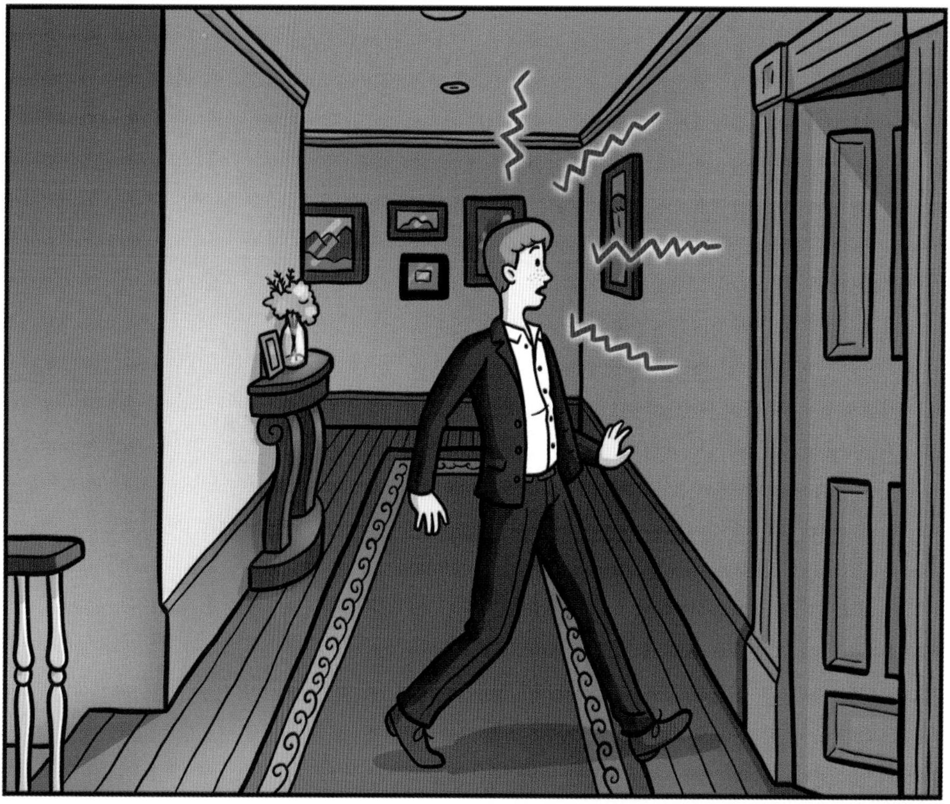

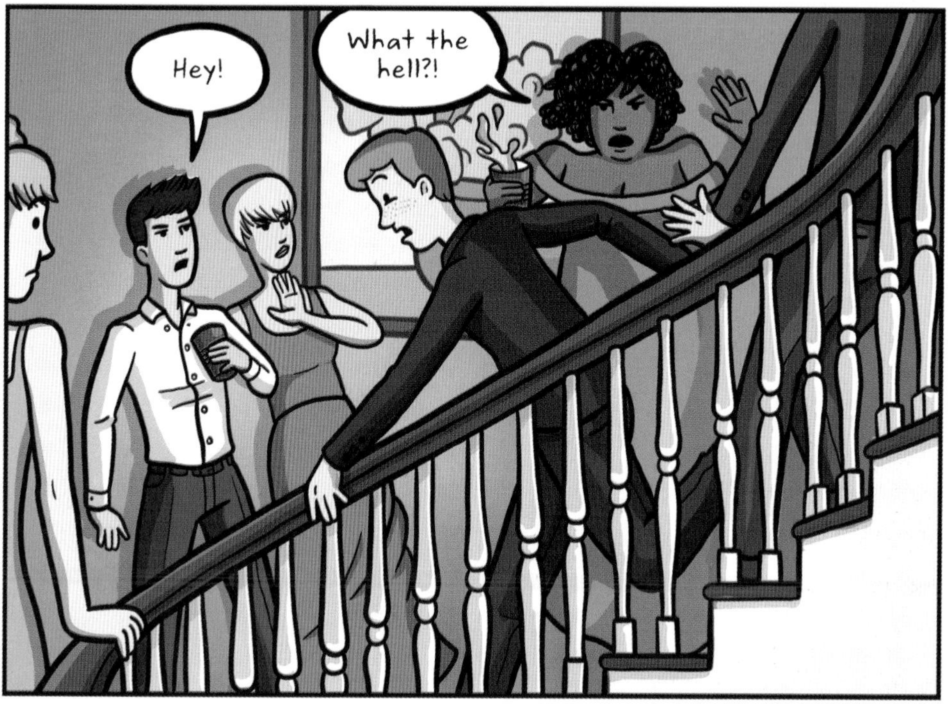
Hey!
What the hell?!

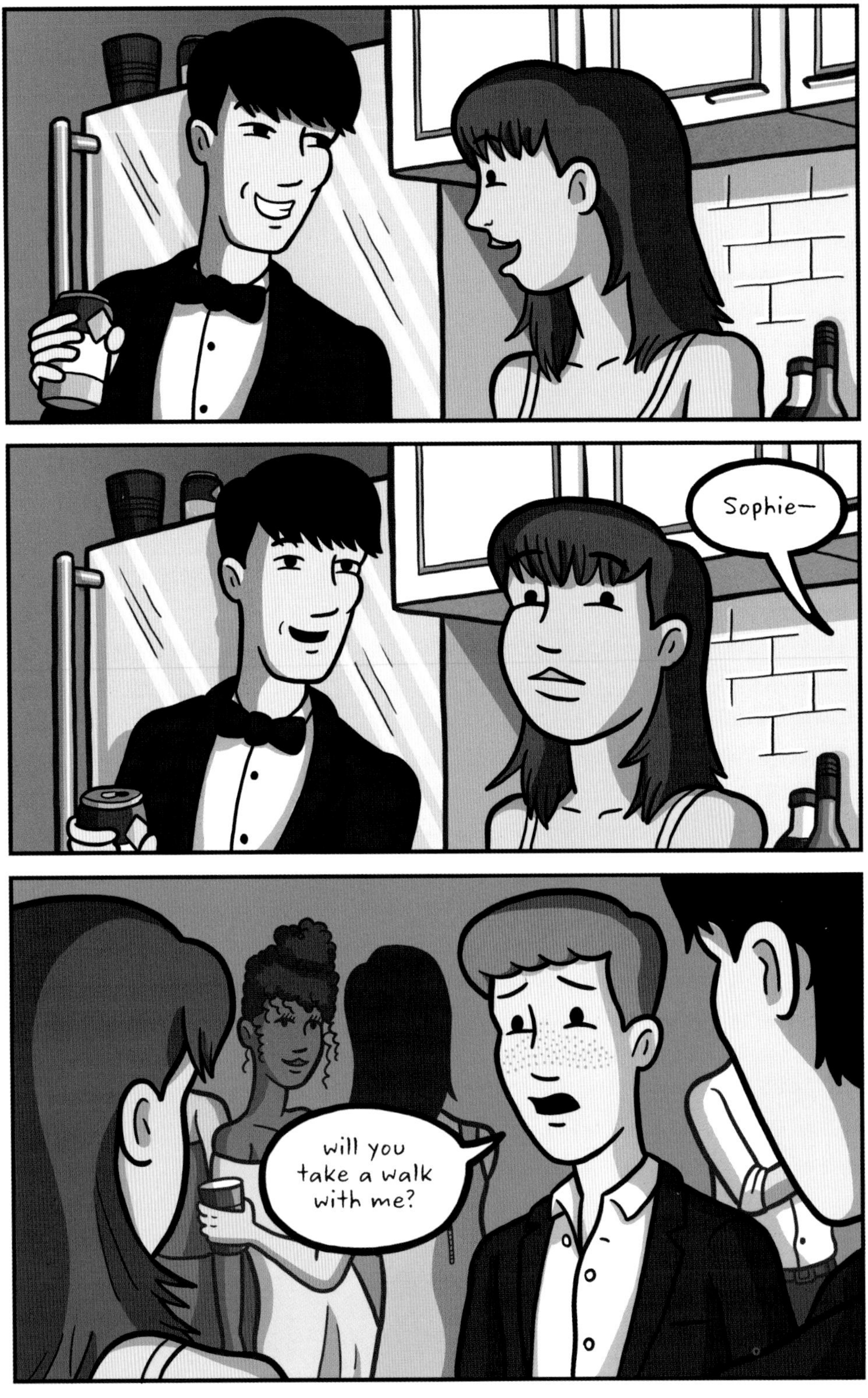
Sophie—
will you take a walk with me?

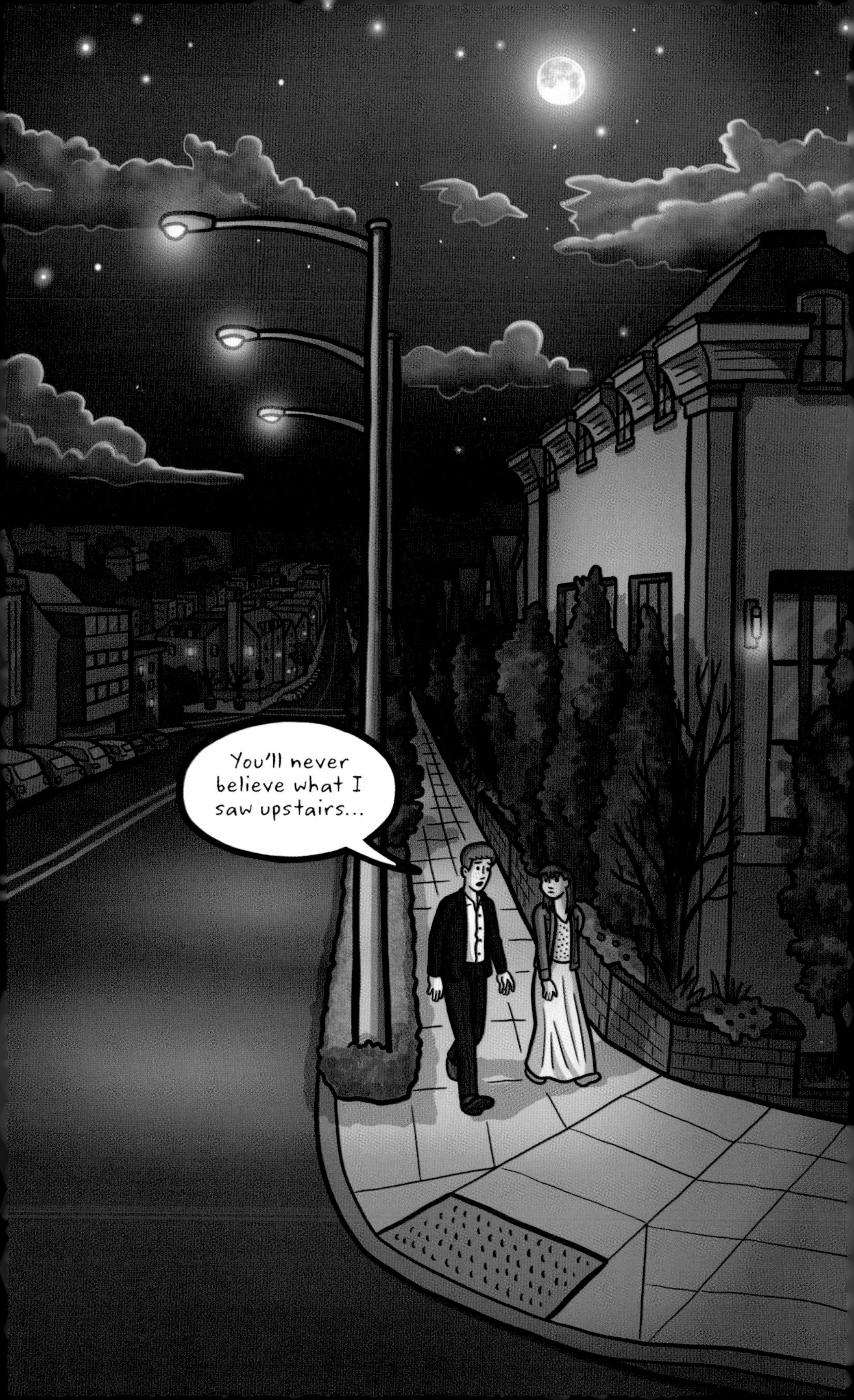
You'll never believe what I saw upstairs...

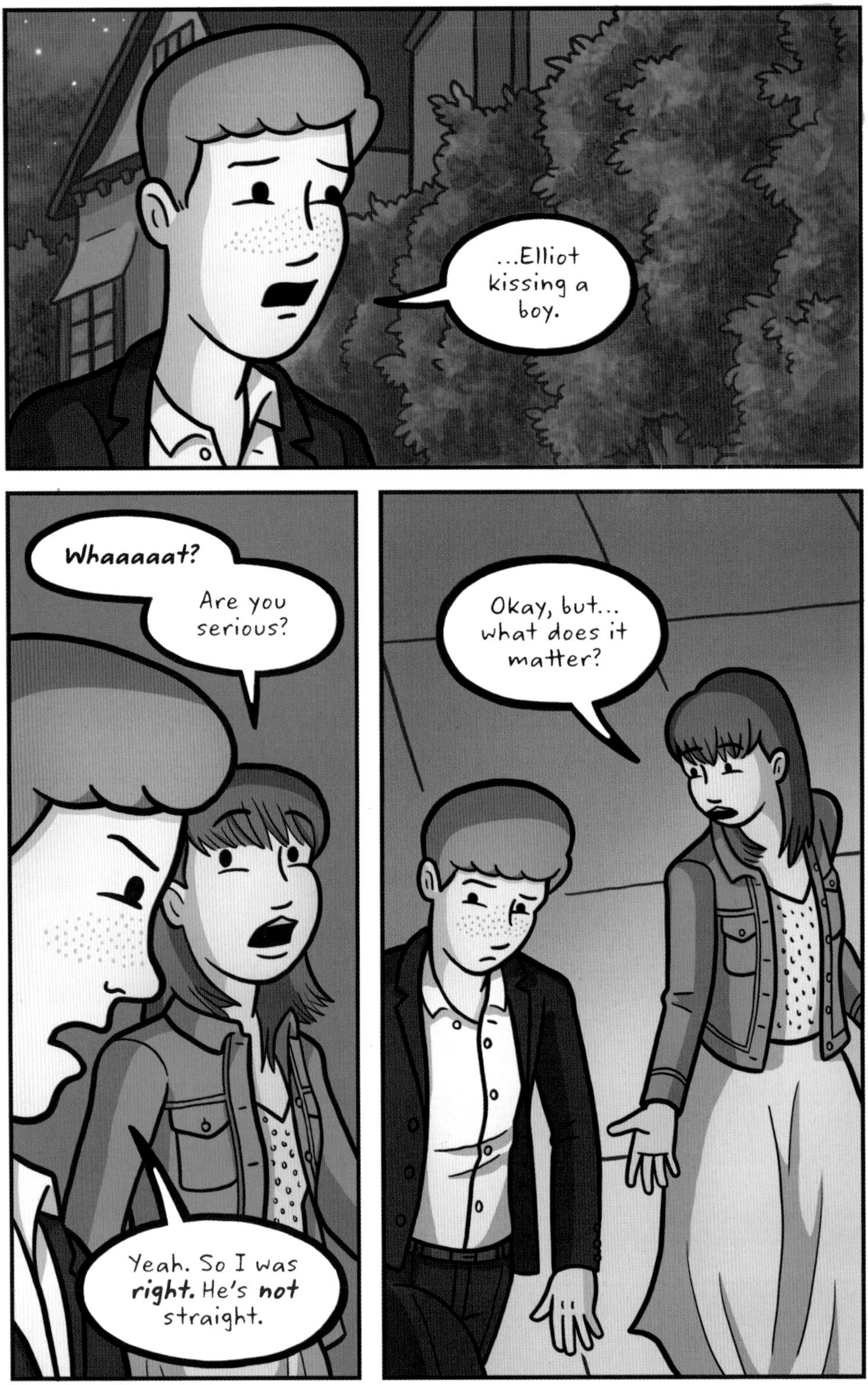
...Elliot kissing a boy.
Whaaaaat?
Are you serious?
Yeah. So I was **right.** He's **not** straight.
Okay, but... what does it matter?

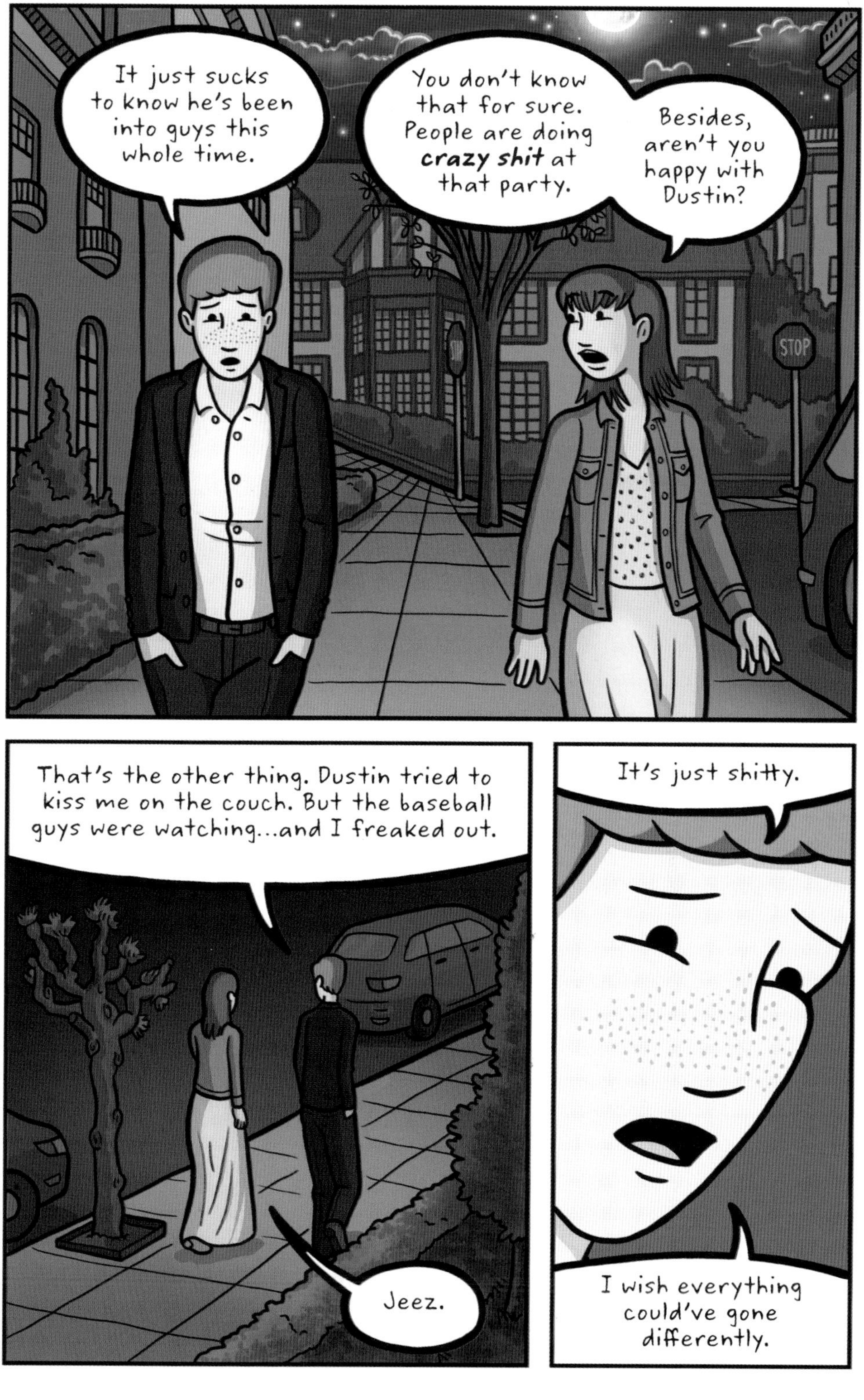
It just sucks to know he's been into guys this whole time.
You don't know that for sure. People are doing **crazy shit** at that party.
Besides, aren't you happy with Dustin?
STOP
That's the other thing. Dustin tried to kiss me on the couch. But the baseball guys were watching...and I freaked out.
Jeez.
It's just shitty.
I wish everything could've gone differently.

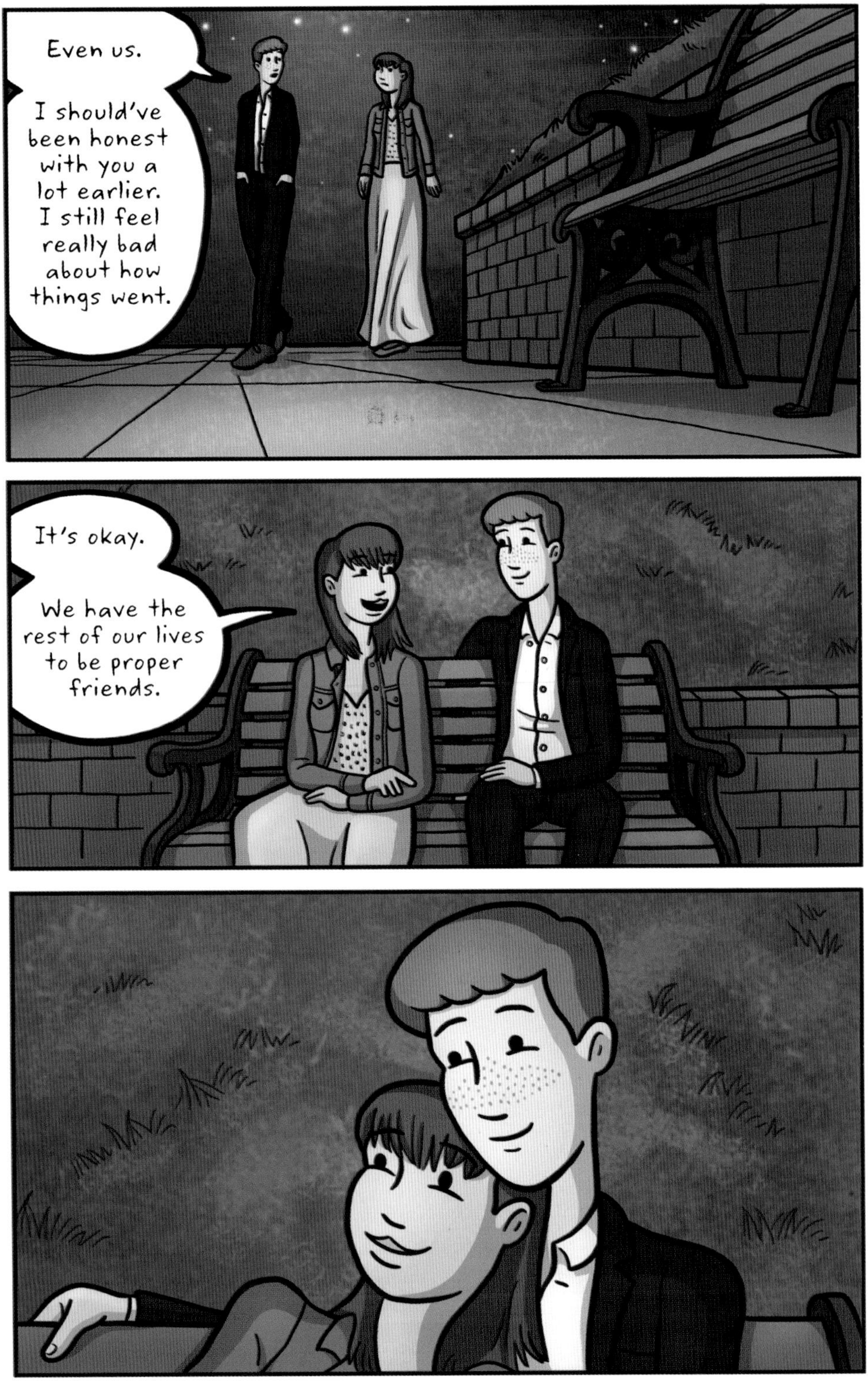
Even us.
I should've been honest with you a lot earlier. I still feel really bad about how things went.
It's okay.
We have the rest of our lives to be proper friends.

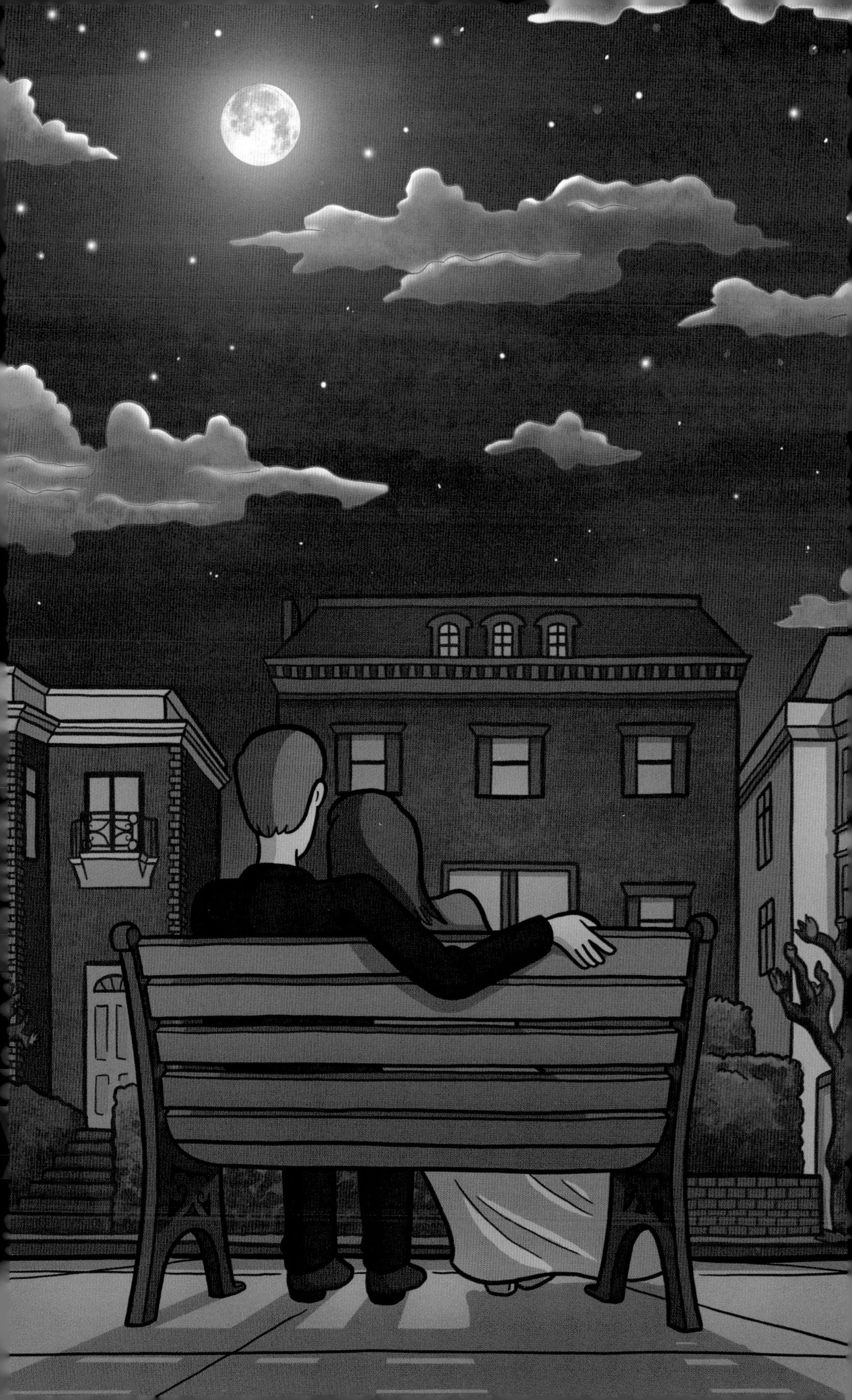

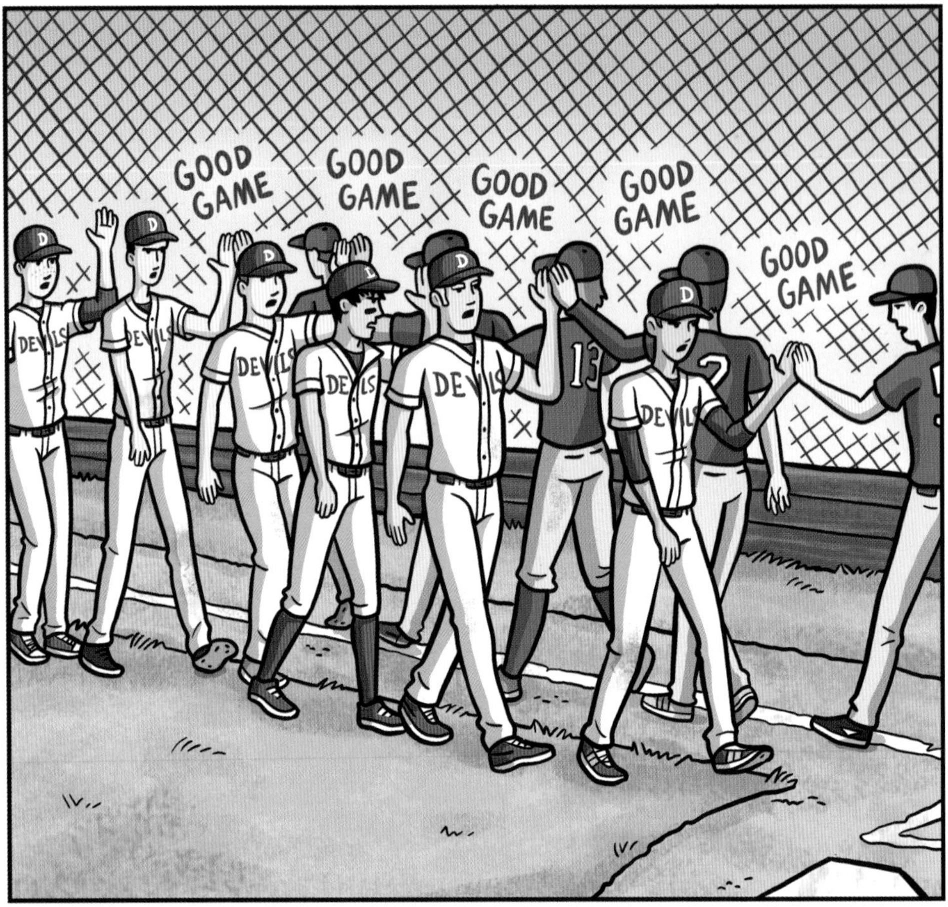
GOOD GAME
GOOD GAME
GOOD GAME
GOOD GAME
GOOD GAME

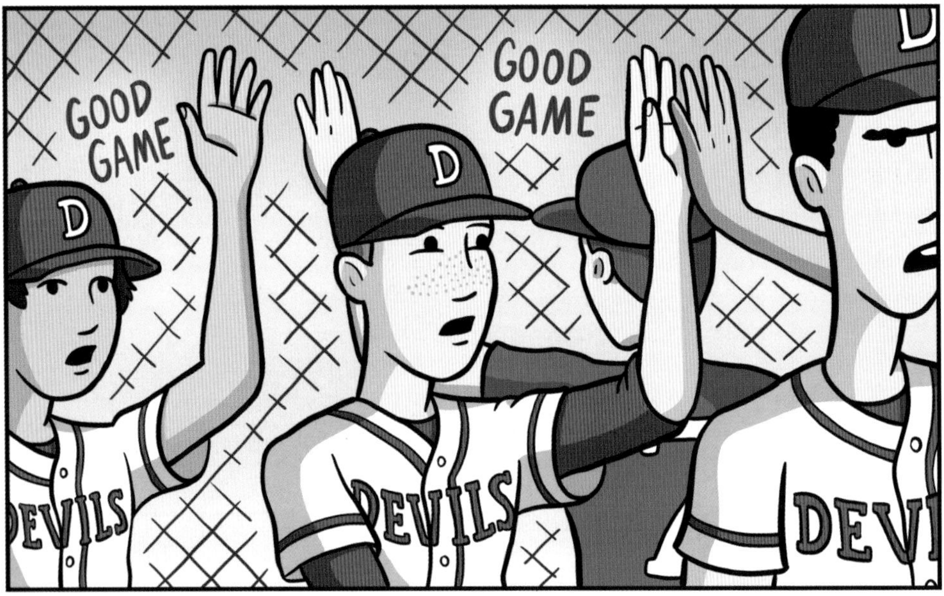
GOOD GAME
GOOD GAME

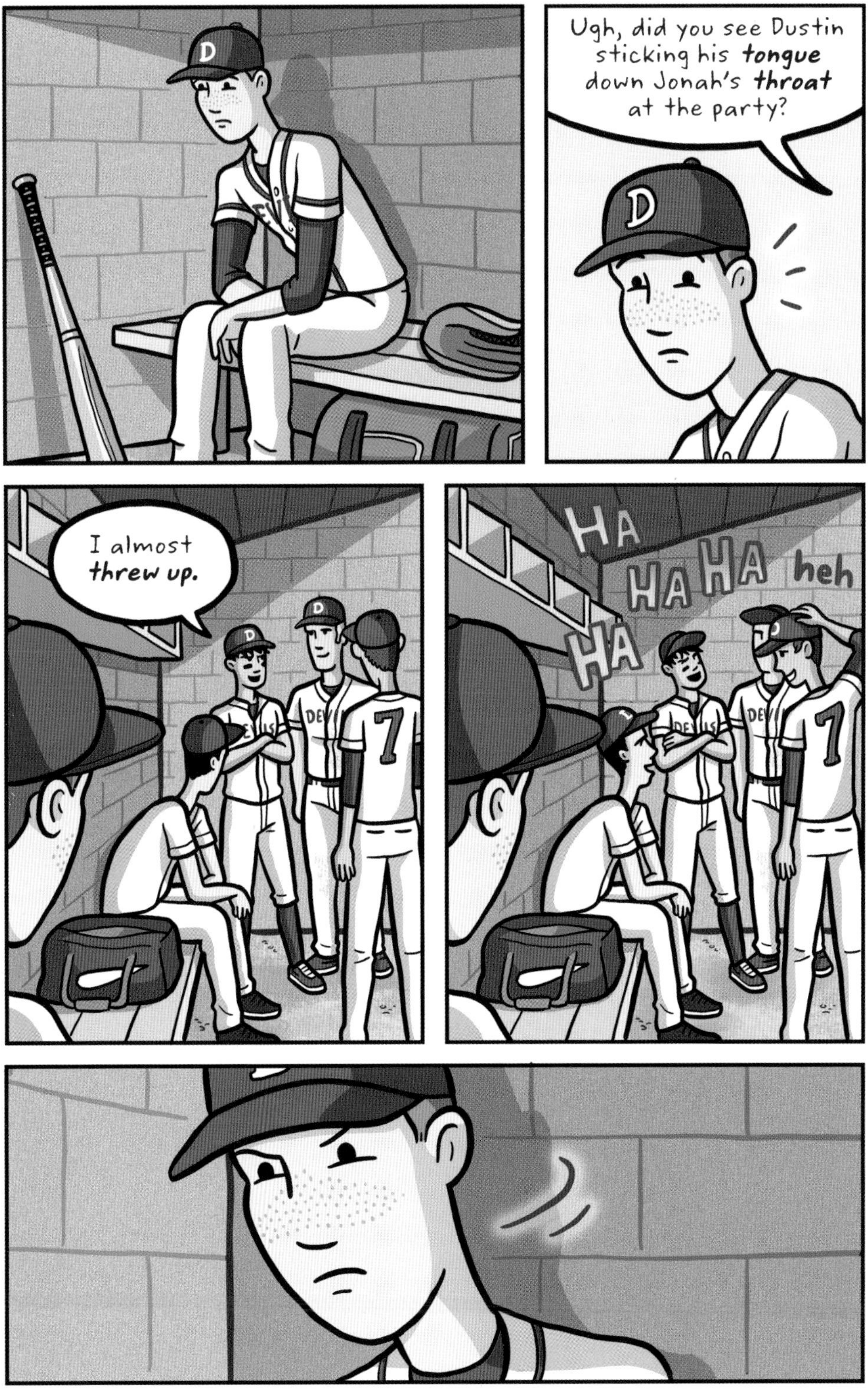
Ugh, did you see Dustin sticking his **tongue** down Jonah's **throat** at the party?
I almost **threw up.**
HA HA HA HA HA heh

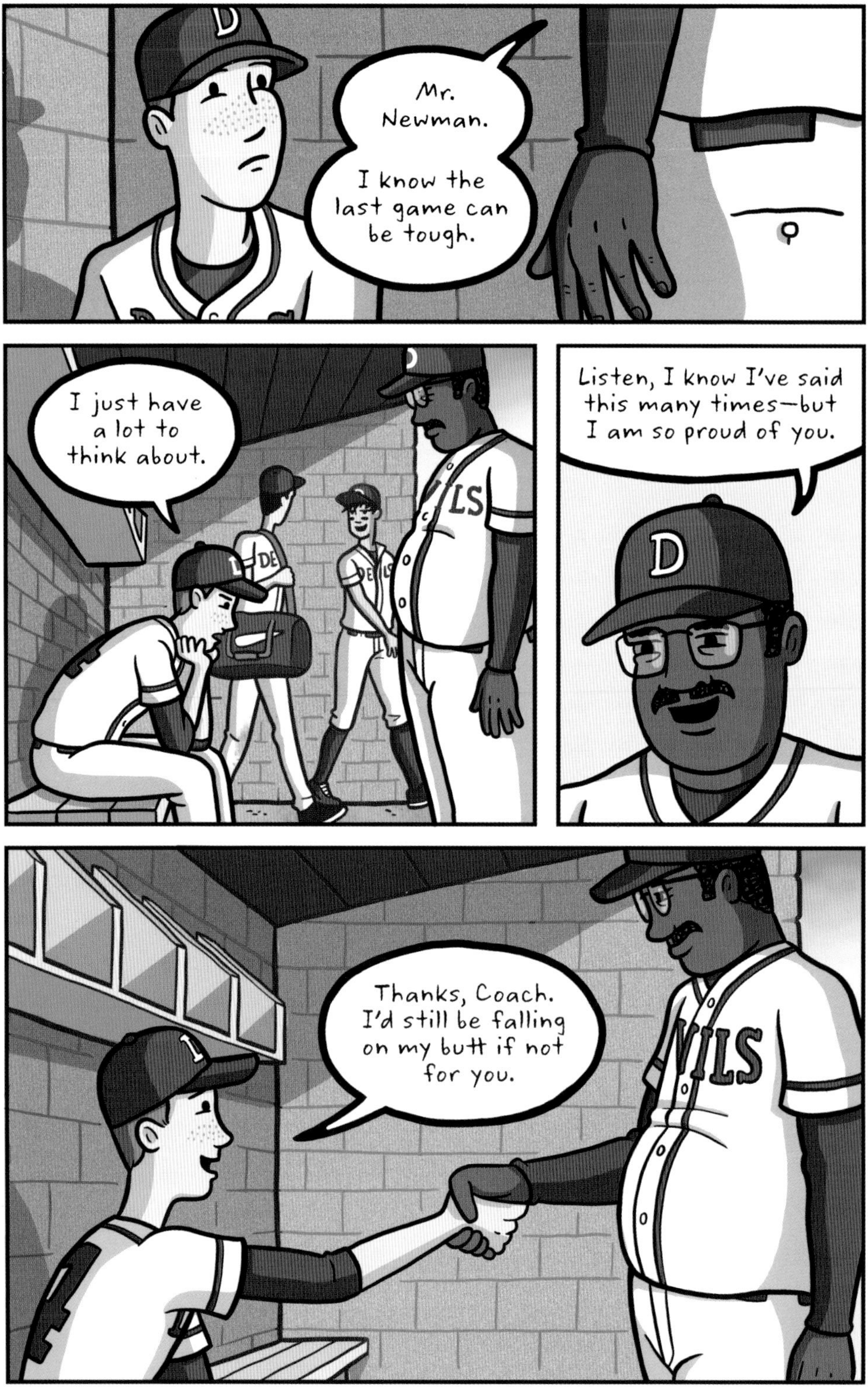
Mr. Newman.
I know the last game can be tough.
I just have a lot to think about.
Listen, I know I've said this many times—but I am so proud of you.
Thanks, Coach. I'd still be falling on my butt if not for you.

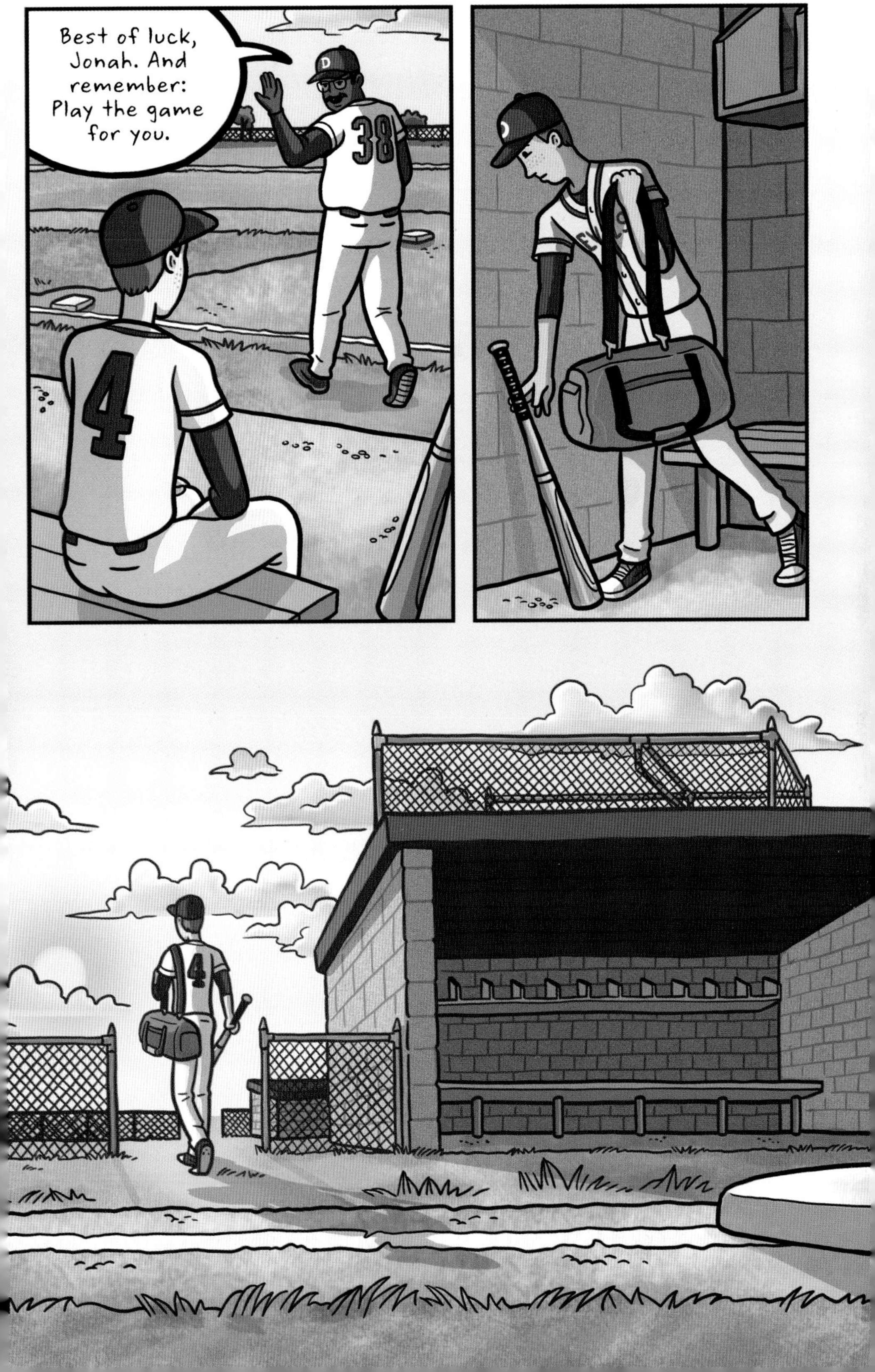
Best of luck, Jonah. And remember: Play the game for you.

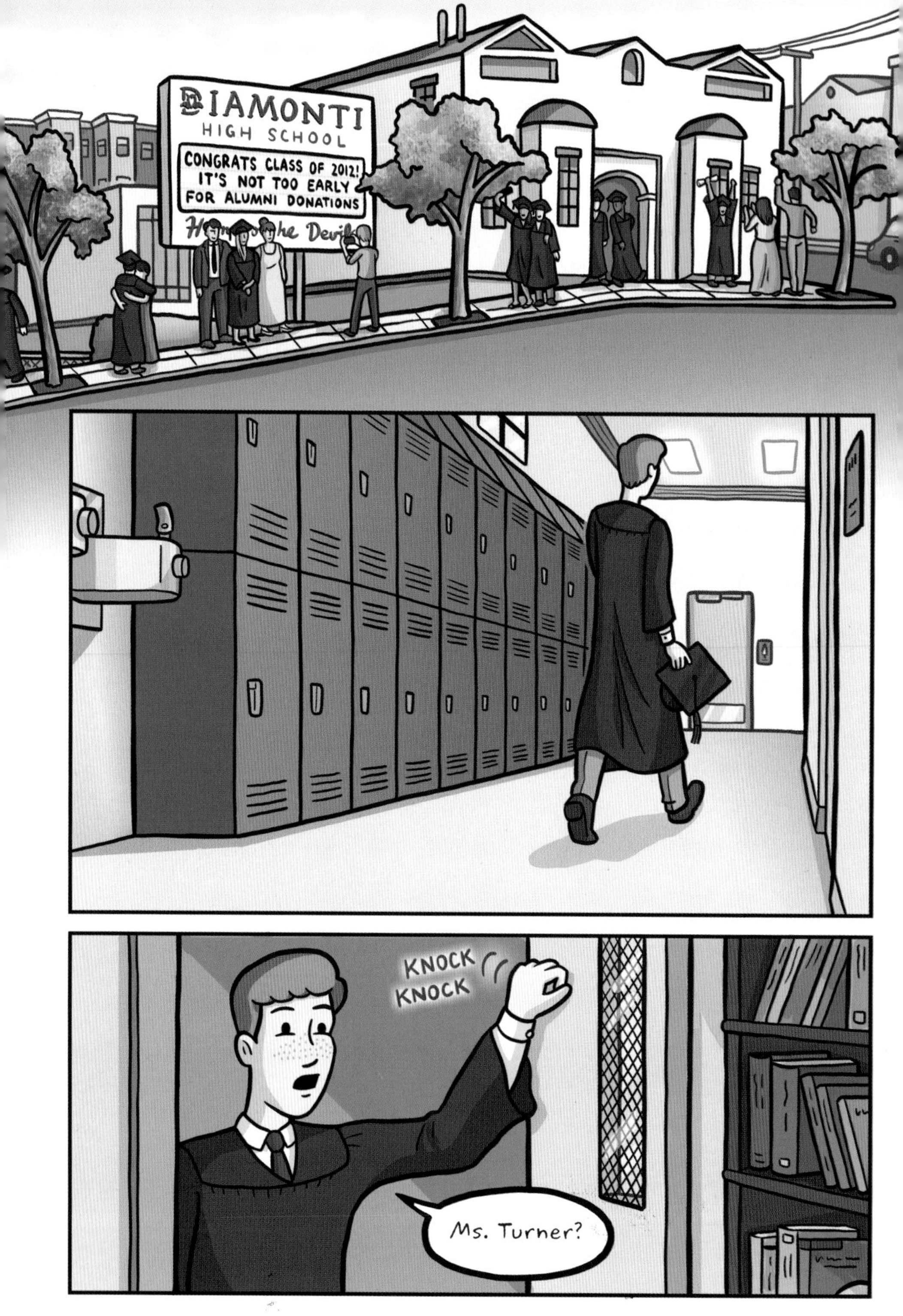
DIAMONTI
HIGH SCHOOL
CONGRATS CLASS OF 2012!
IT'S NOT TOO EARLY
FOR ALUMNI DONATIONS
KNOCK
KNOCK
Ms. Turner?

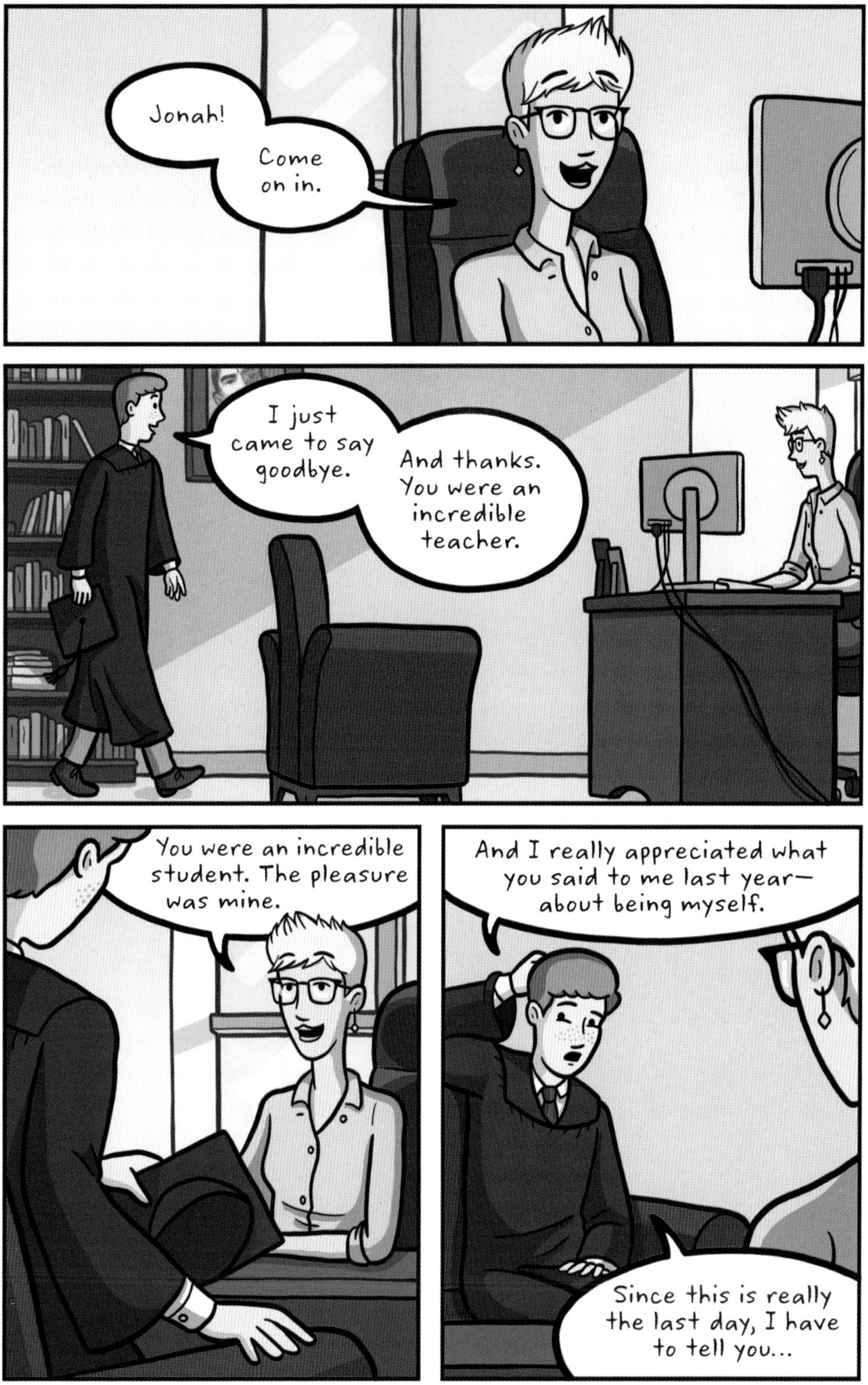
Jonah!
Come on in.
I just came to say goodbye.
And thanks. You were an incredible teacher.
You were an incredible student. The pleasure was mine.
And I really appreciated what you said to me last year—about being myself.
Since this is really the last day, I have to tell you...

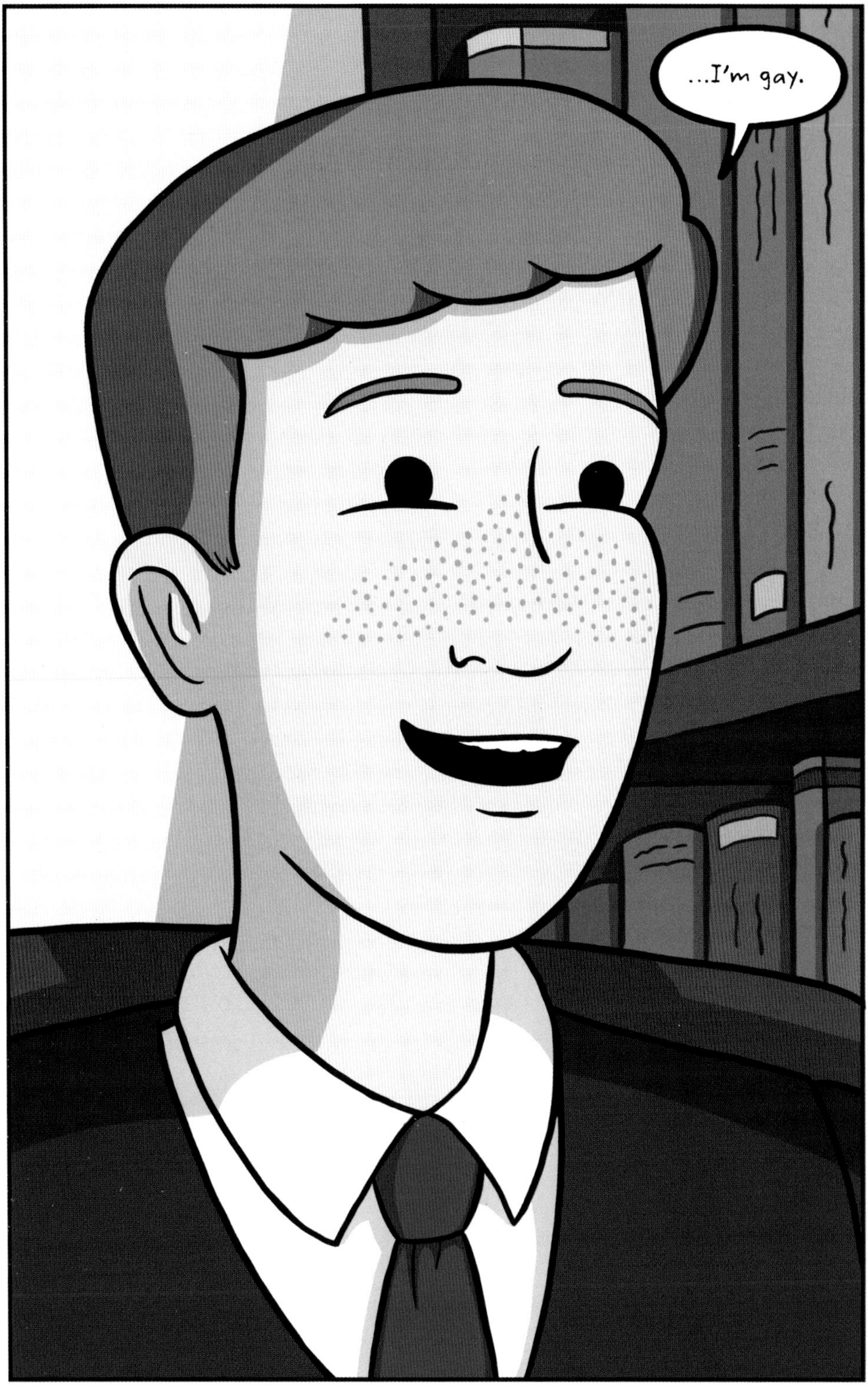
...I'm gay.

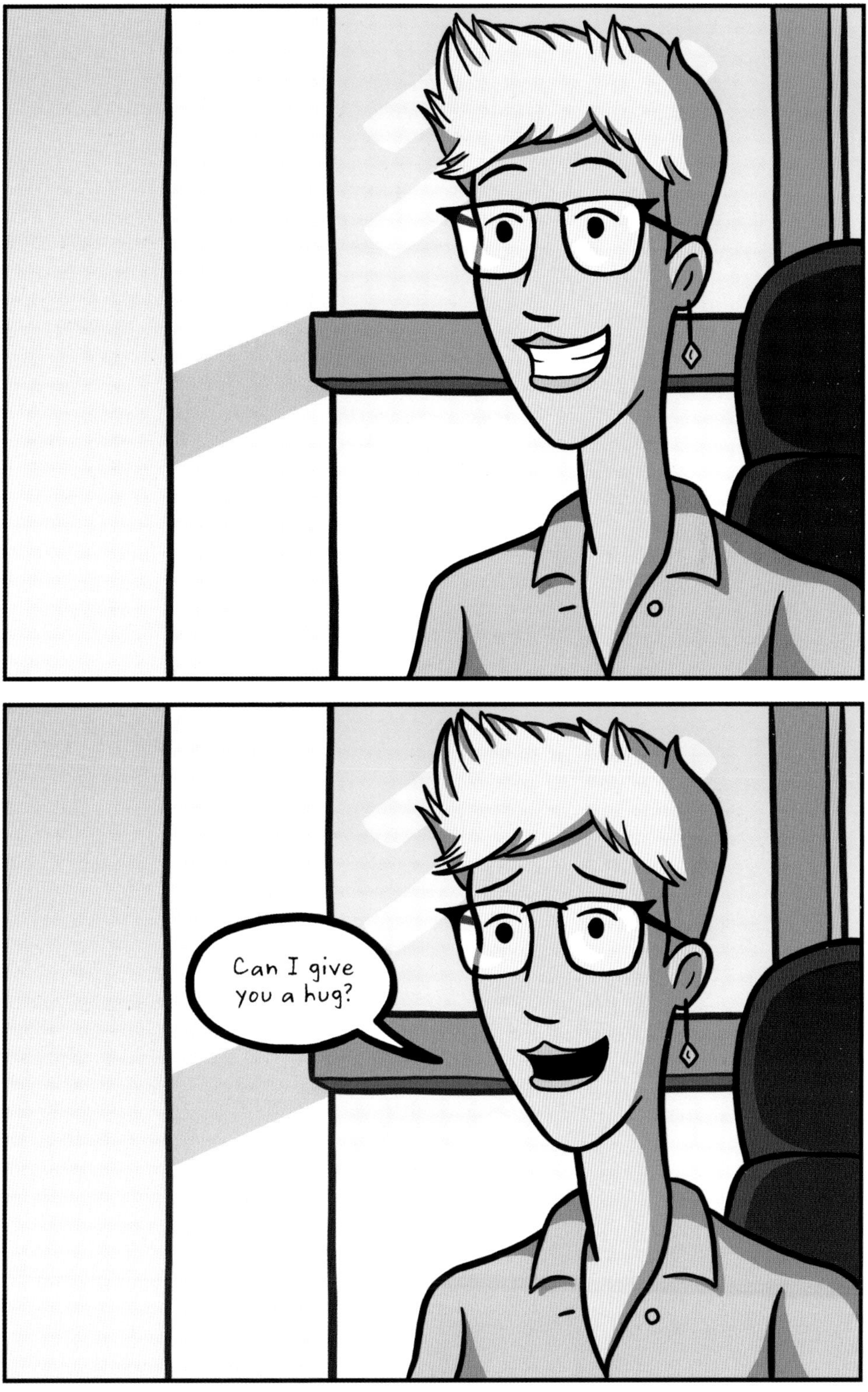
Can I give you a hug?

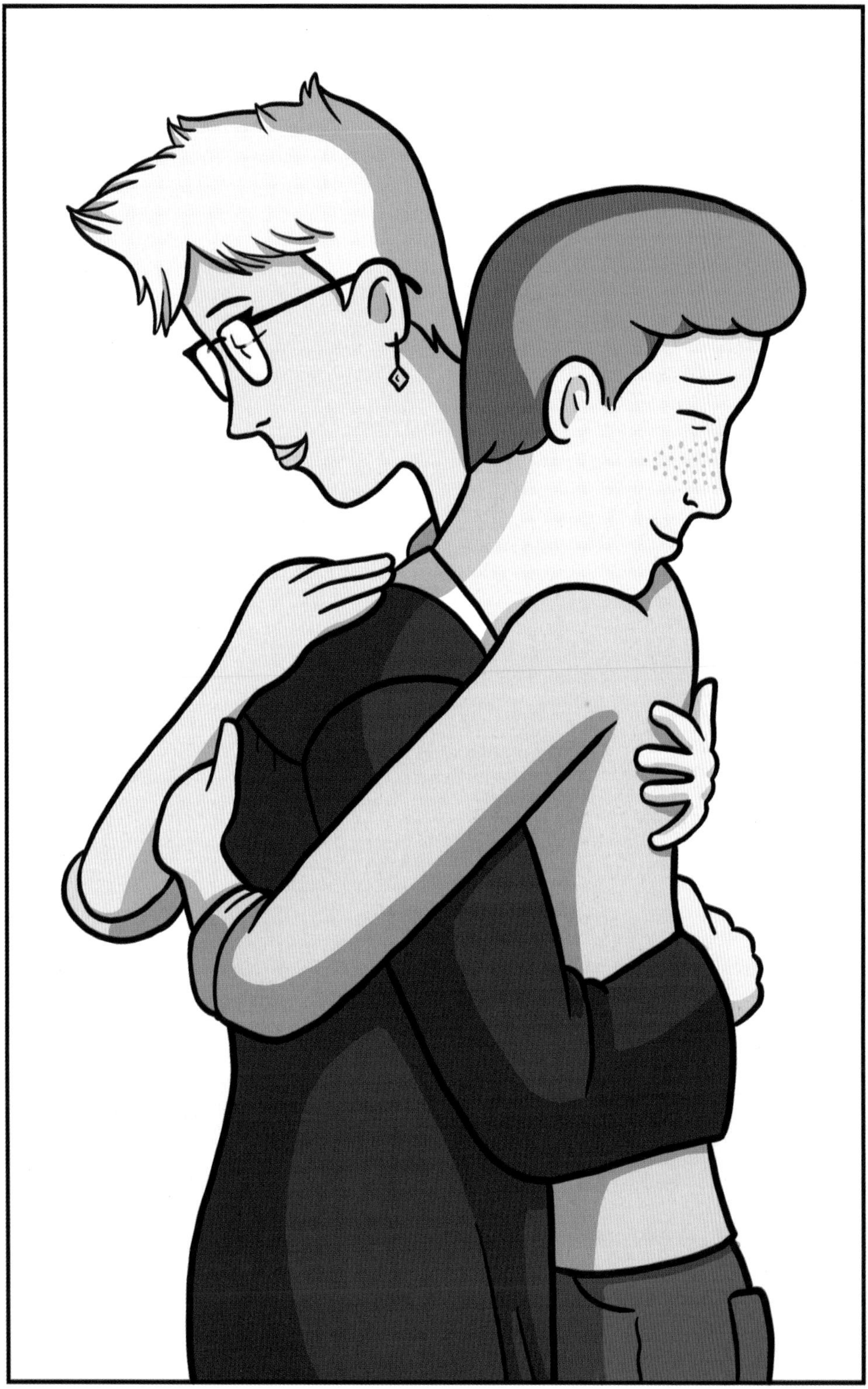

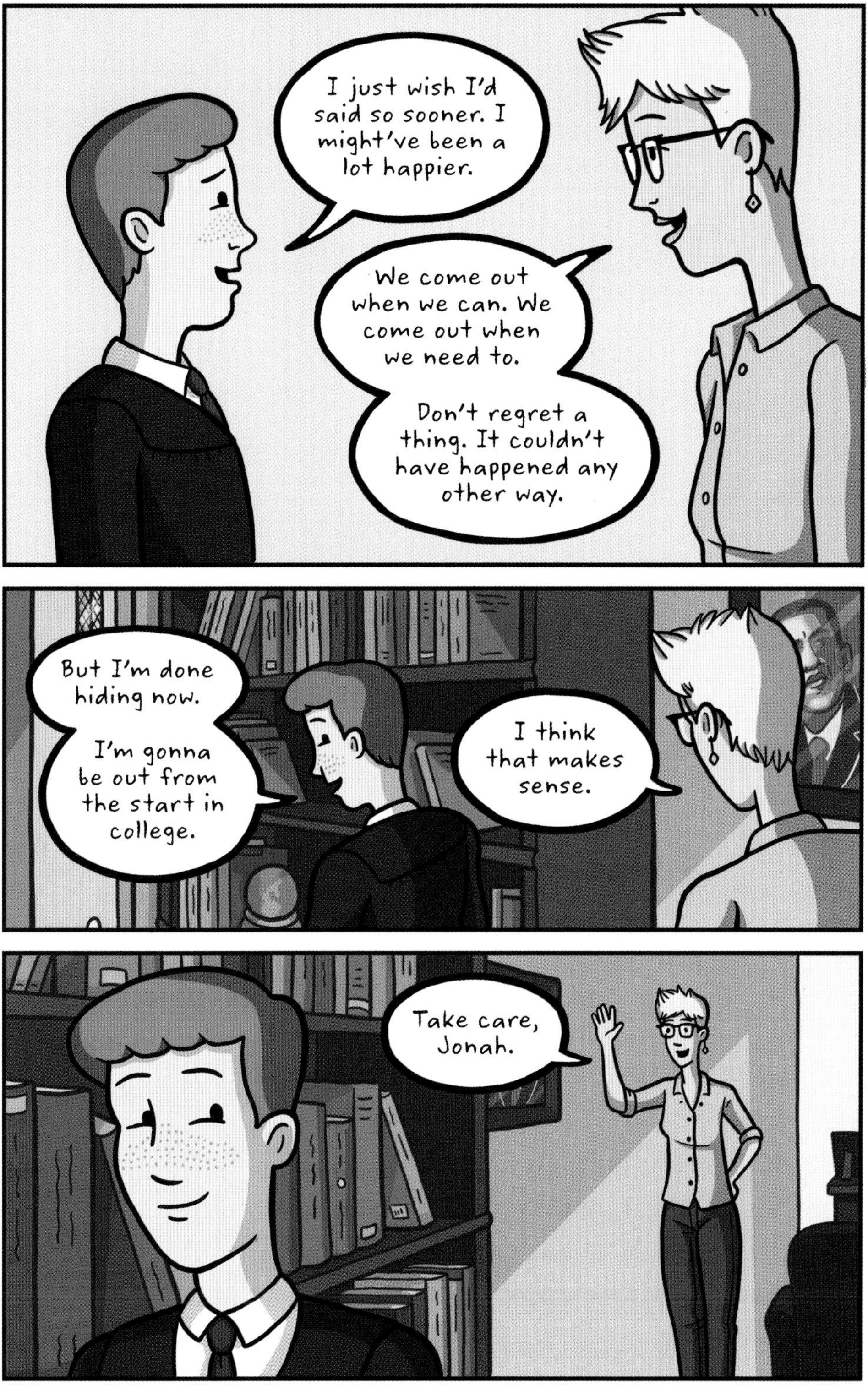
I just wish I'd said so sooner. I might've been a lot happier.
We come out when we can. We come out when we need to.
Don't regret a thing. It couldn't have happened any other way.
But I'm done hiding now.
I'm gonna be out from the start in college.
I think that makes sense.
Take care, Jonah.

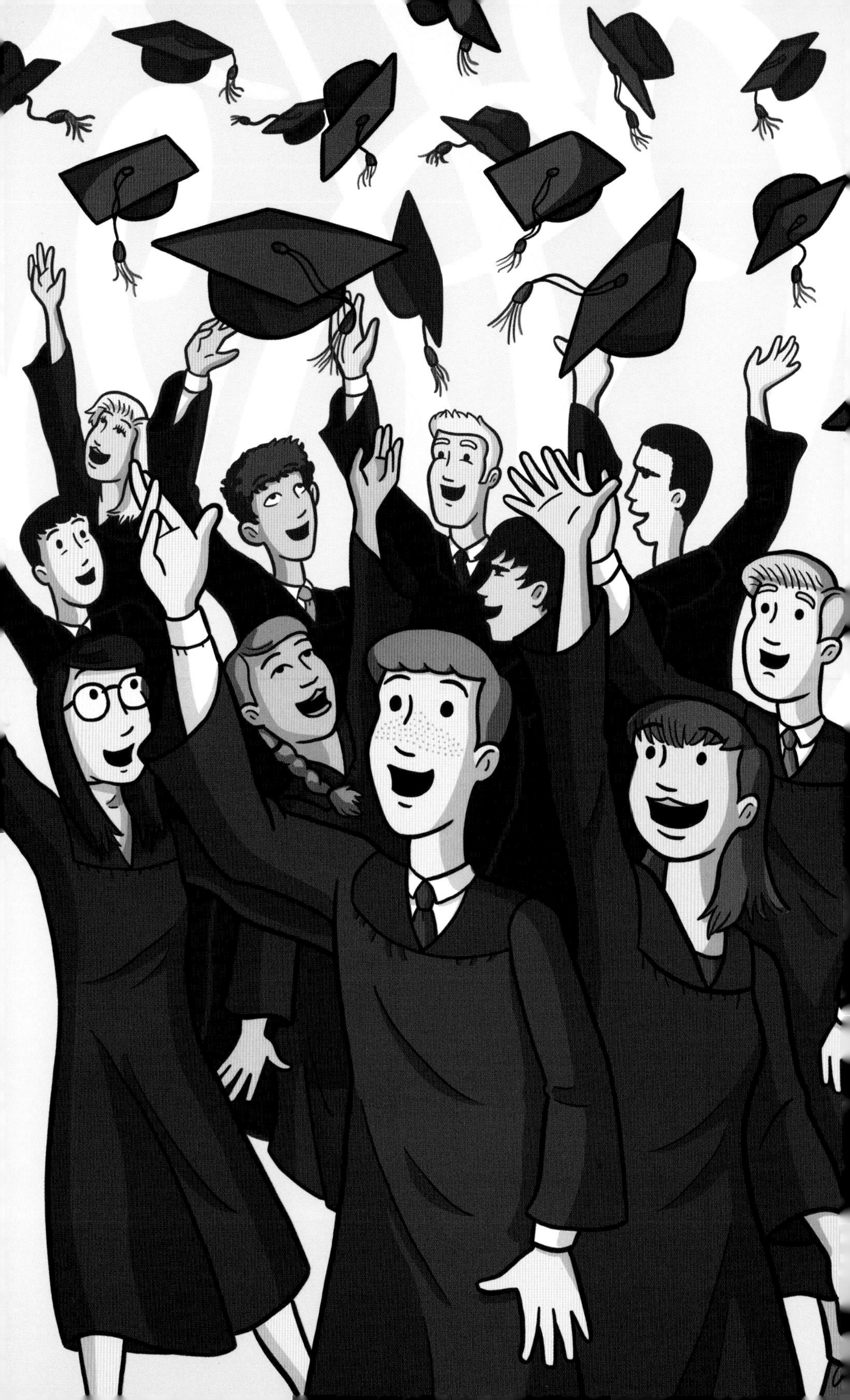

CHAPTER 7

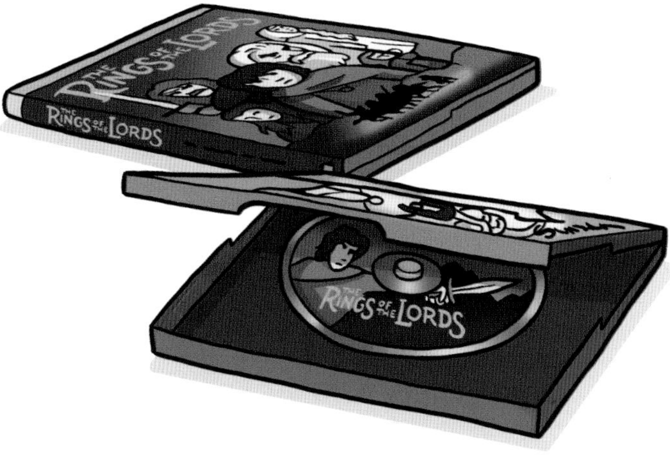

THE RINGS OF THE LORDS
RINGS OF THE LORDS
THE RINGS OF THE LORDS

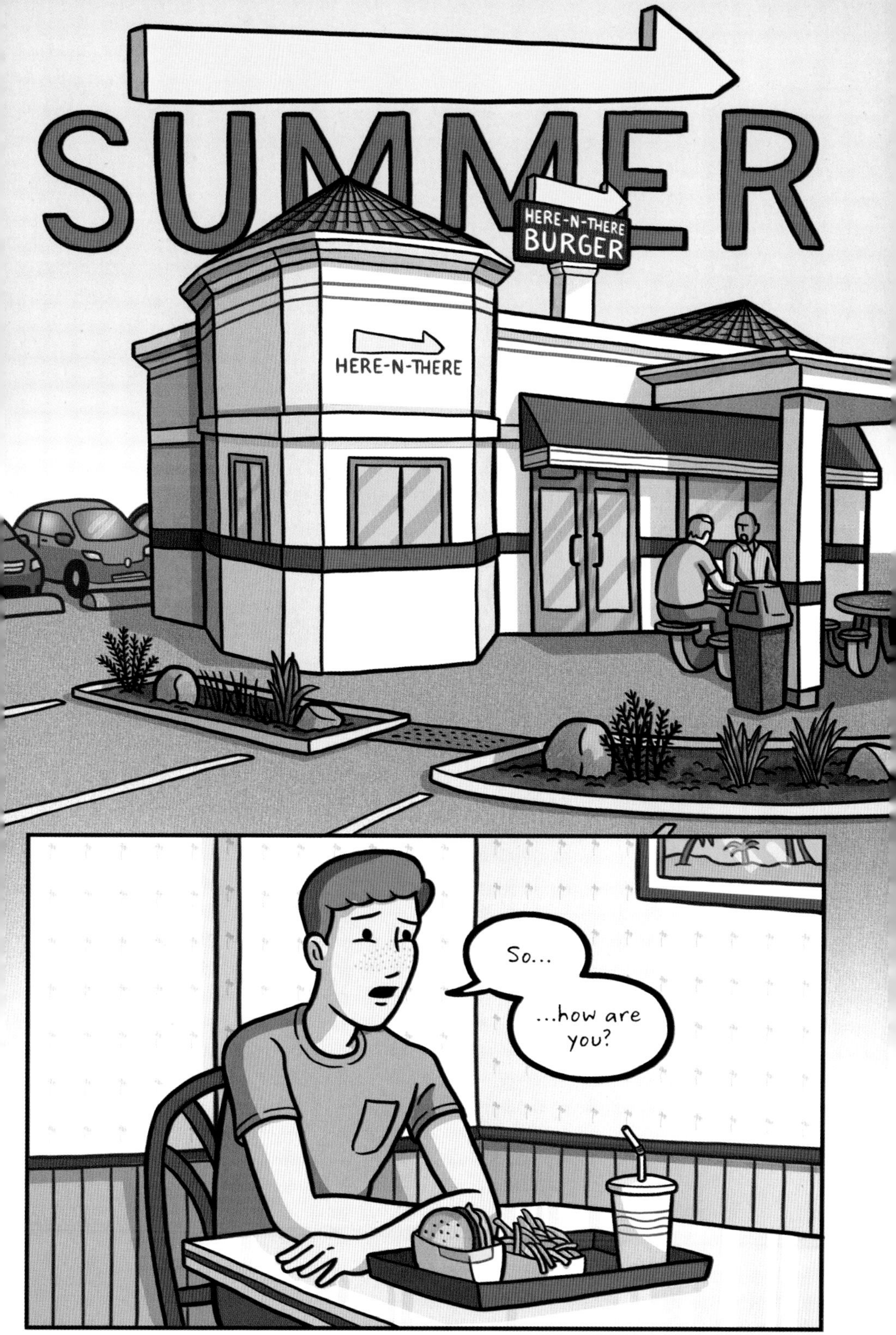
SUMMER
HERE-N-THERE BURGER
HERE-N-THERE
So...
...how are you?

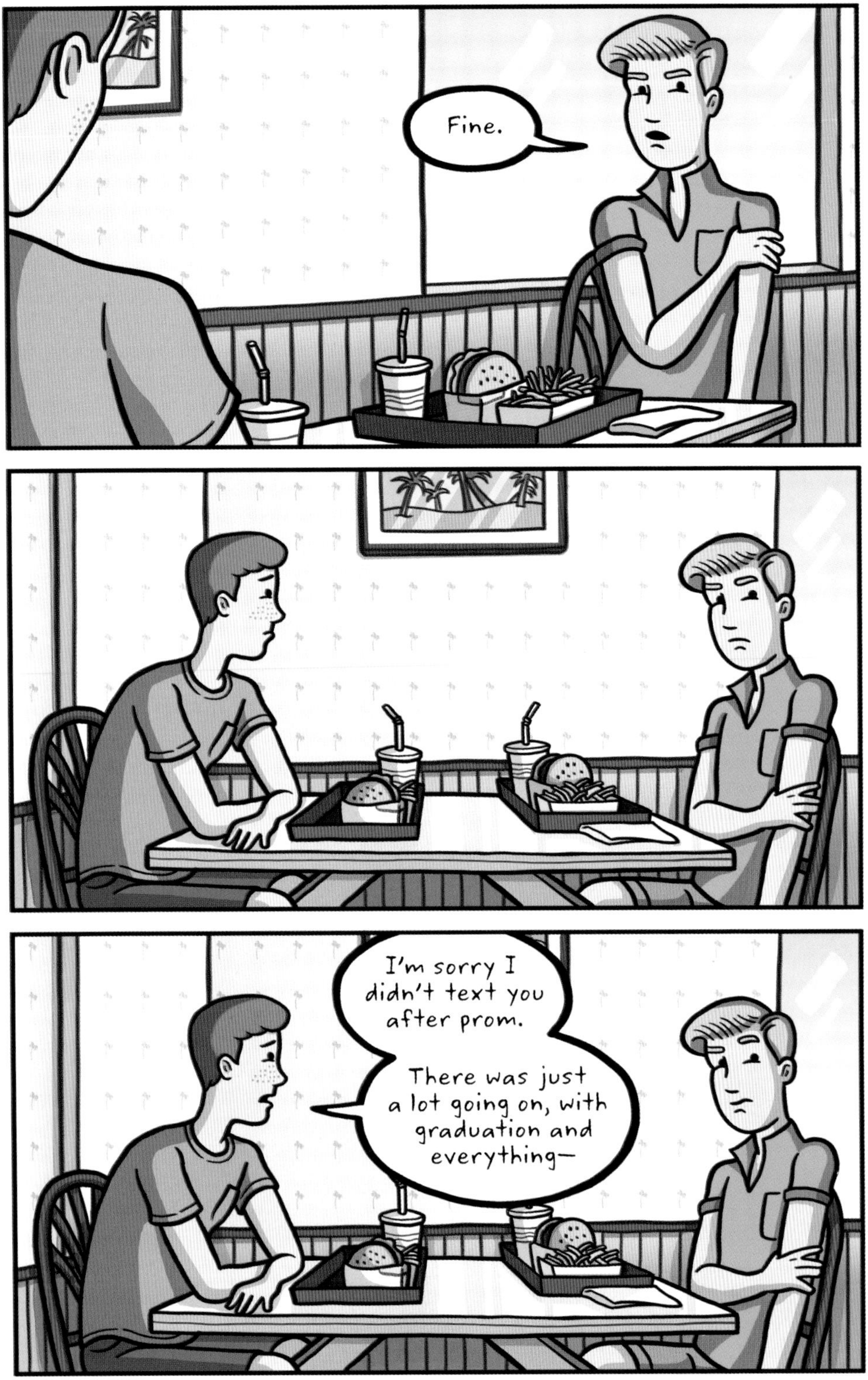
Fine.
I'm sorry I didn't text you after prom.
There was just a lot going on, with graduation and everything—

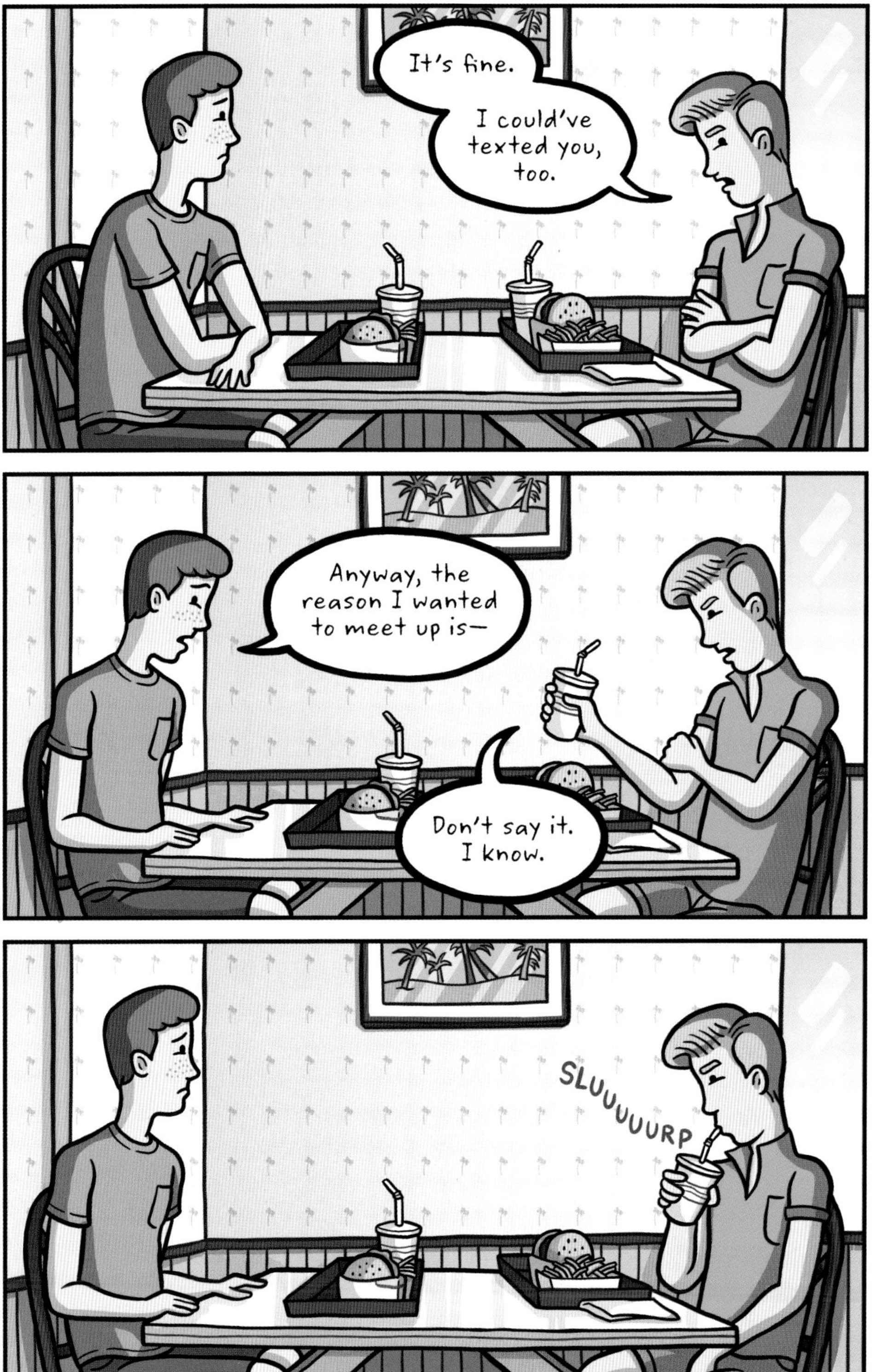
It's fine.
I could've texted you, too.
Anyway, the reason I wanted to meet up is—
Don't say it. I know.
SLUUUUURP

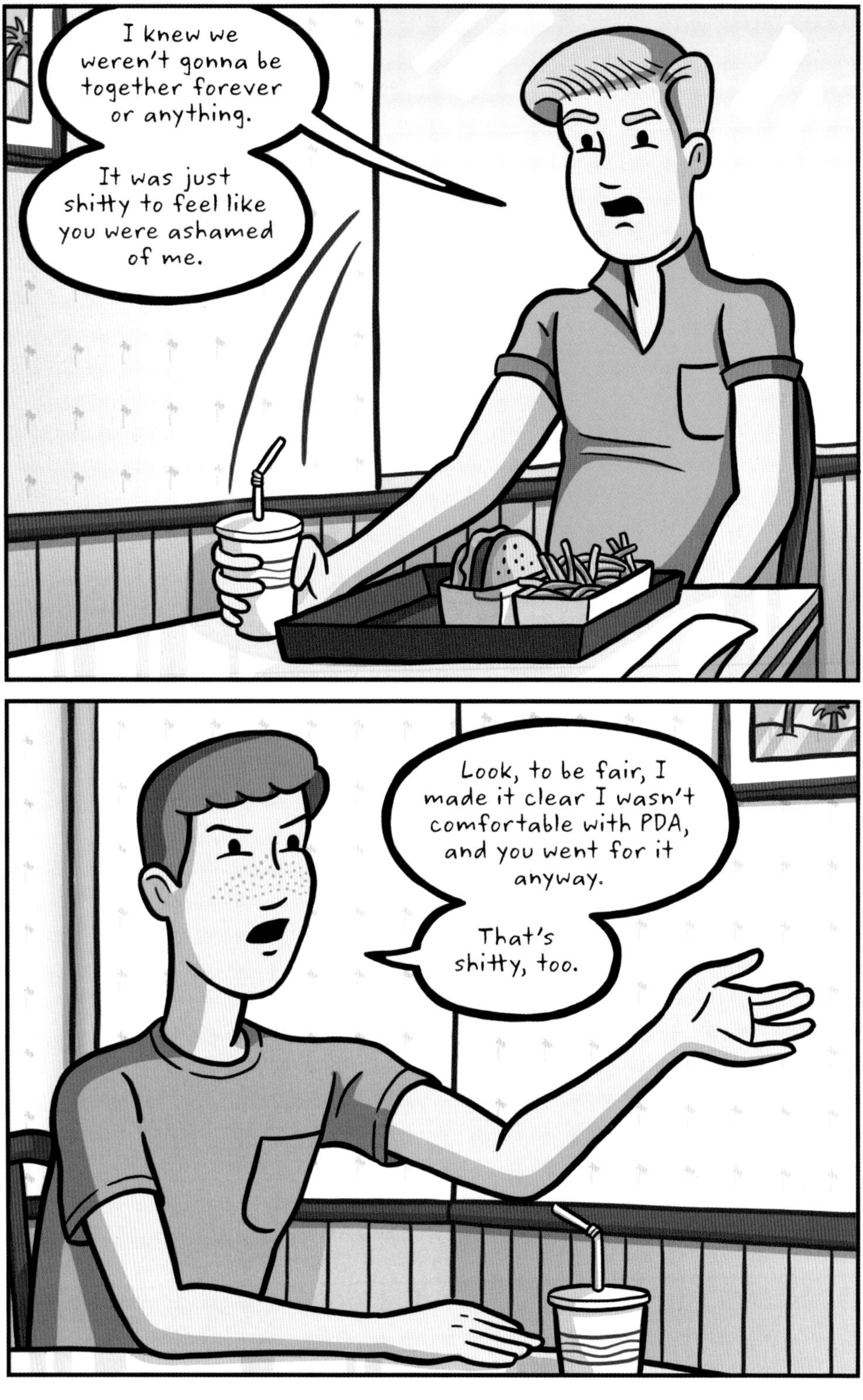
I knew we weren't gonna be together forever or anything.
It was just shitty to feel like you were ashamed of me.
Look, to be fair, I made it clear I wasn't comfortable with PDA, and you went for it anyway.
That's shitty, too.

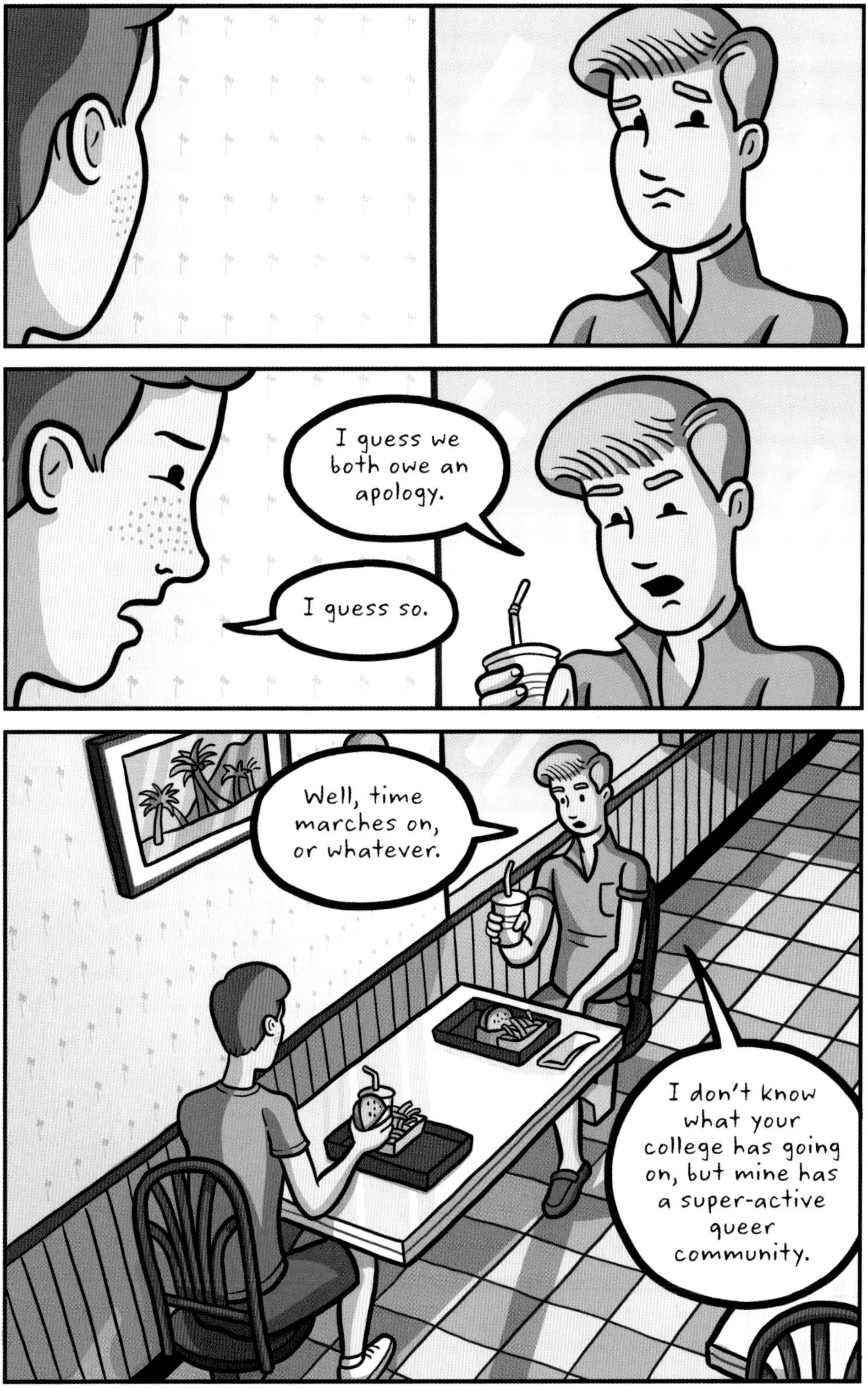
I guess we both owe an apology.
I guess so.
Well, time marches on, or whatever.
I don't know what your college has going on, but mine has a super-active queer community.

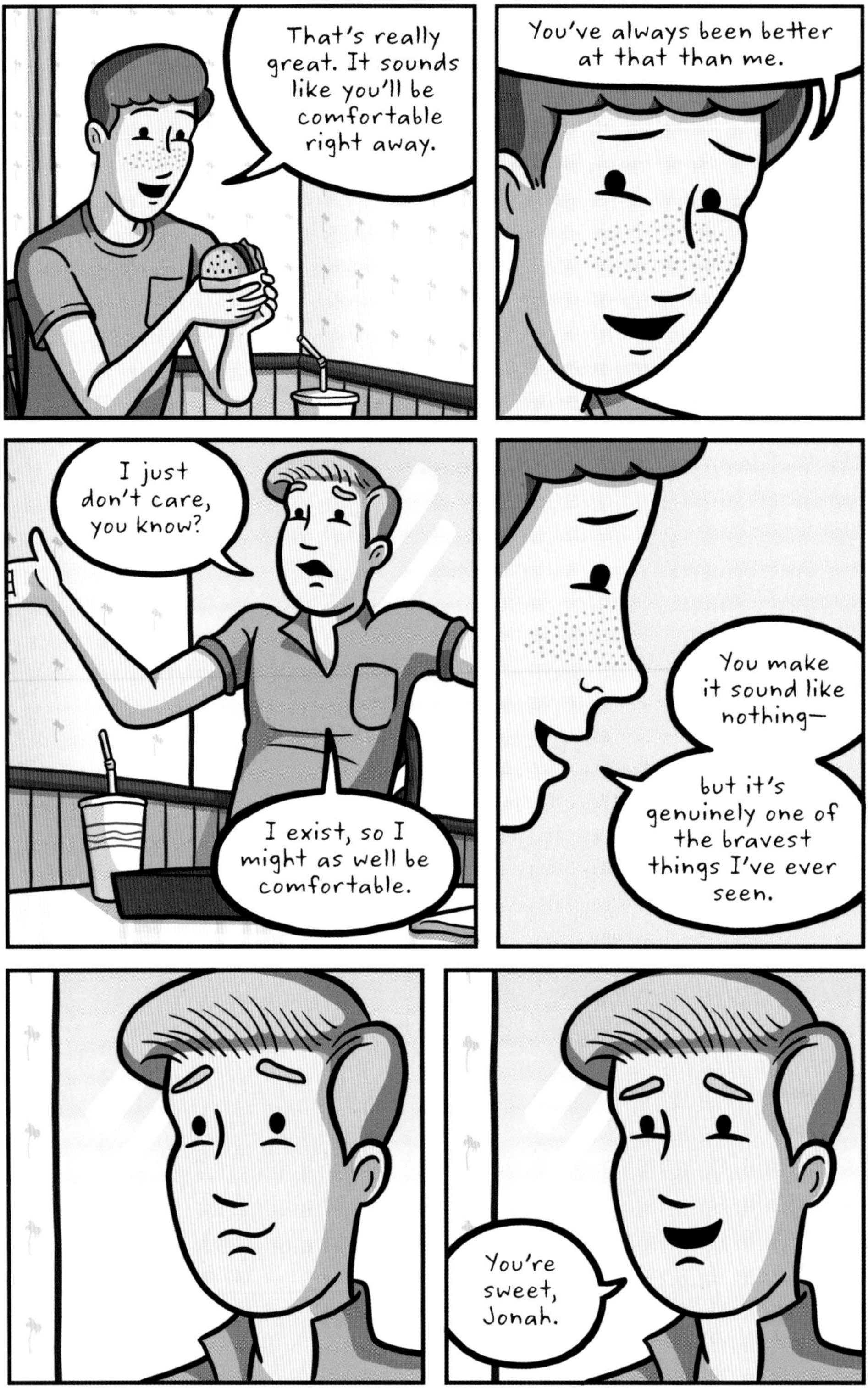
That's really great. It sounds like you'll be comfortable right away.
You've always been better at that than me.
I just don't care, you know?
I exist, so I might as well be comfortable.
You make it sound like nothing—
but it's genuinely one of the bravest things I've ever seen.
You're sweet, Jonah.

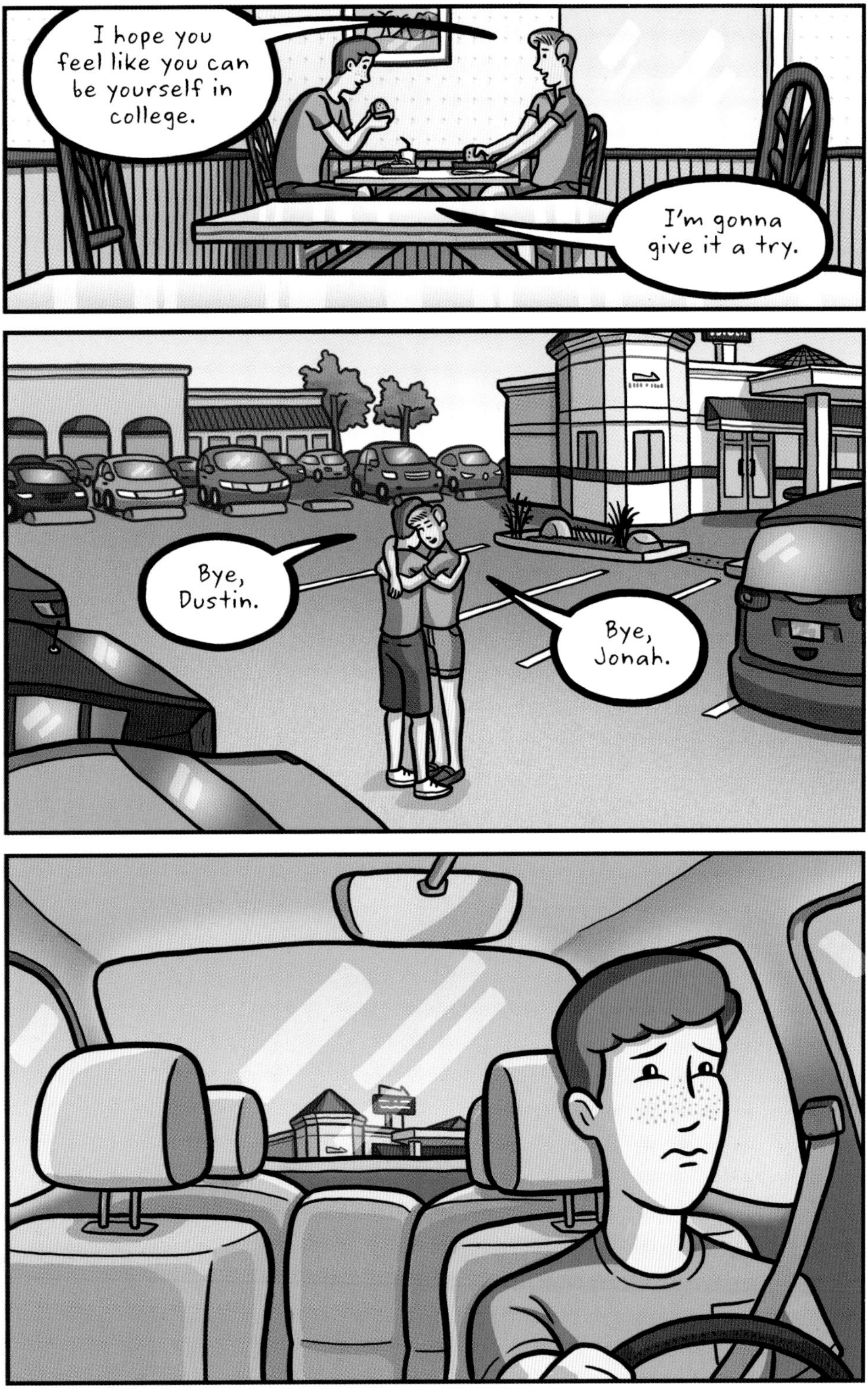
I hope you feel like you can be yourself in college.
I'm gonna give it a try.
Bye, Dustin.
Bye, Jonah.

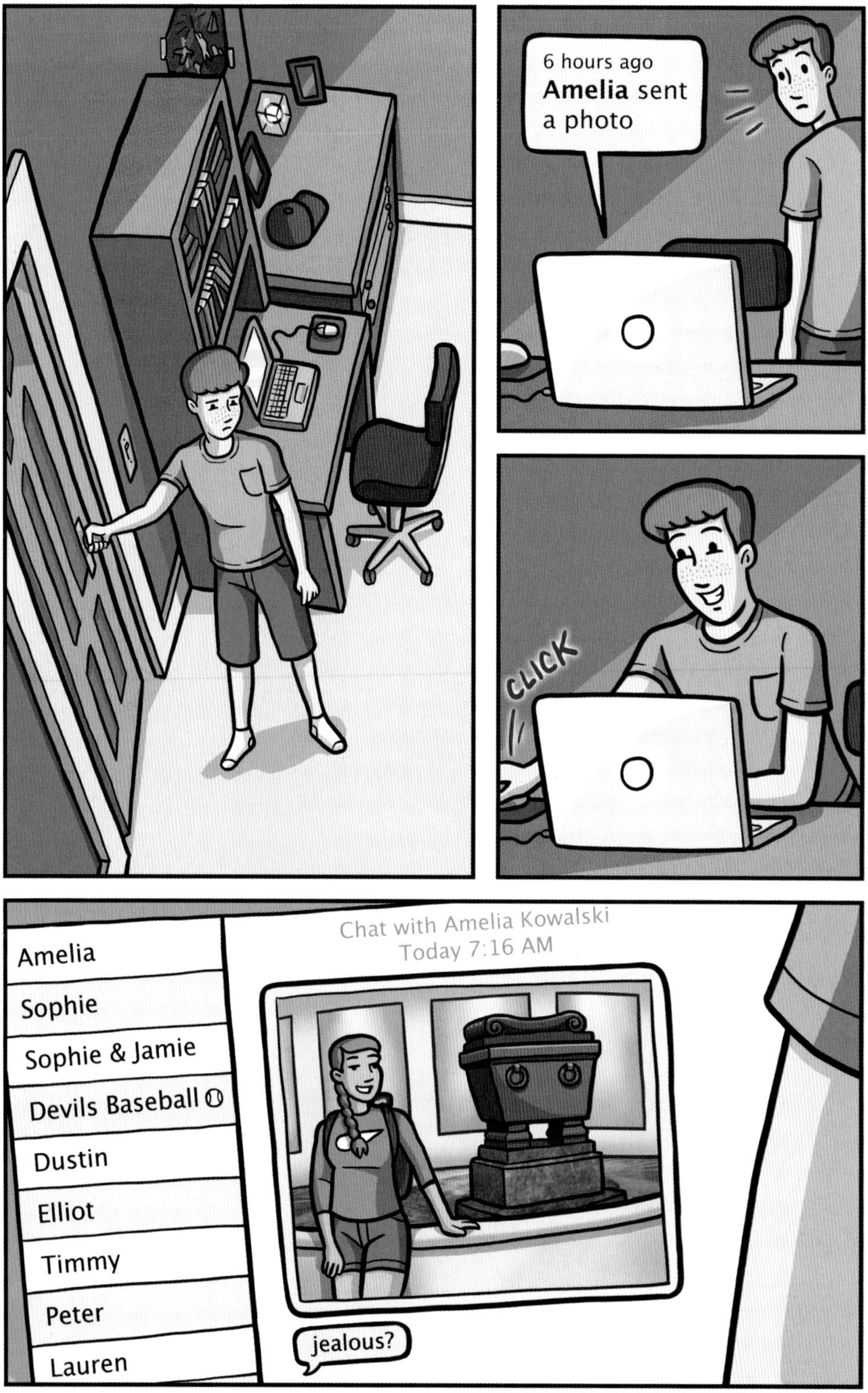
6 hours ago
Amelia sent a photo
CLICK
Chat with Amelia Kowalski
Today 7:16 AM
Amelia
Sophie
Sophie & Jamie
Devils Baseball
Dustin
Elliot
Timmy
Peter
Lauren
jealous?

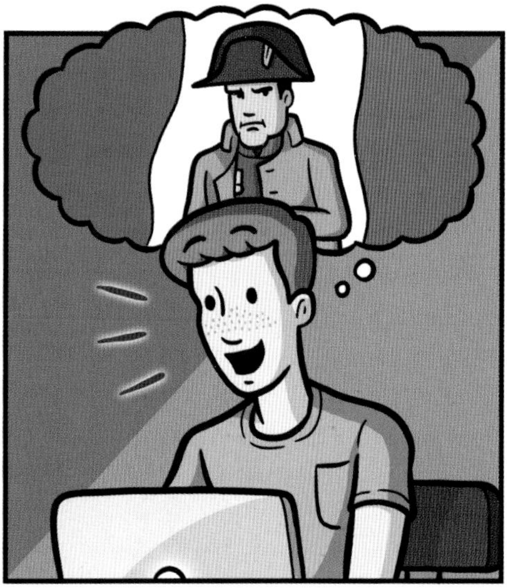

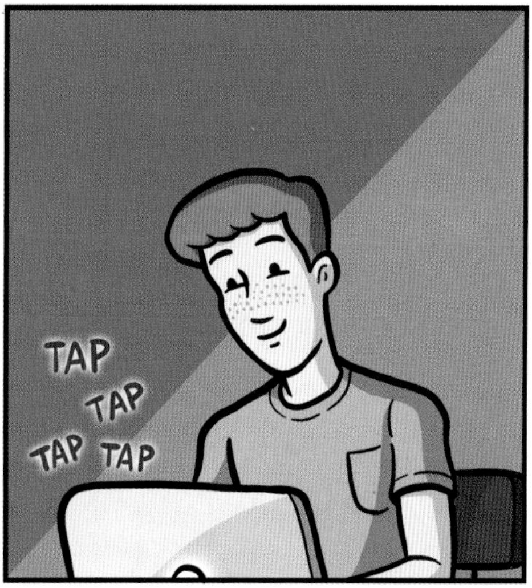
TAP
TAP
TAP TAP

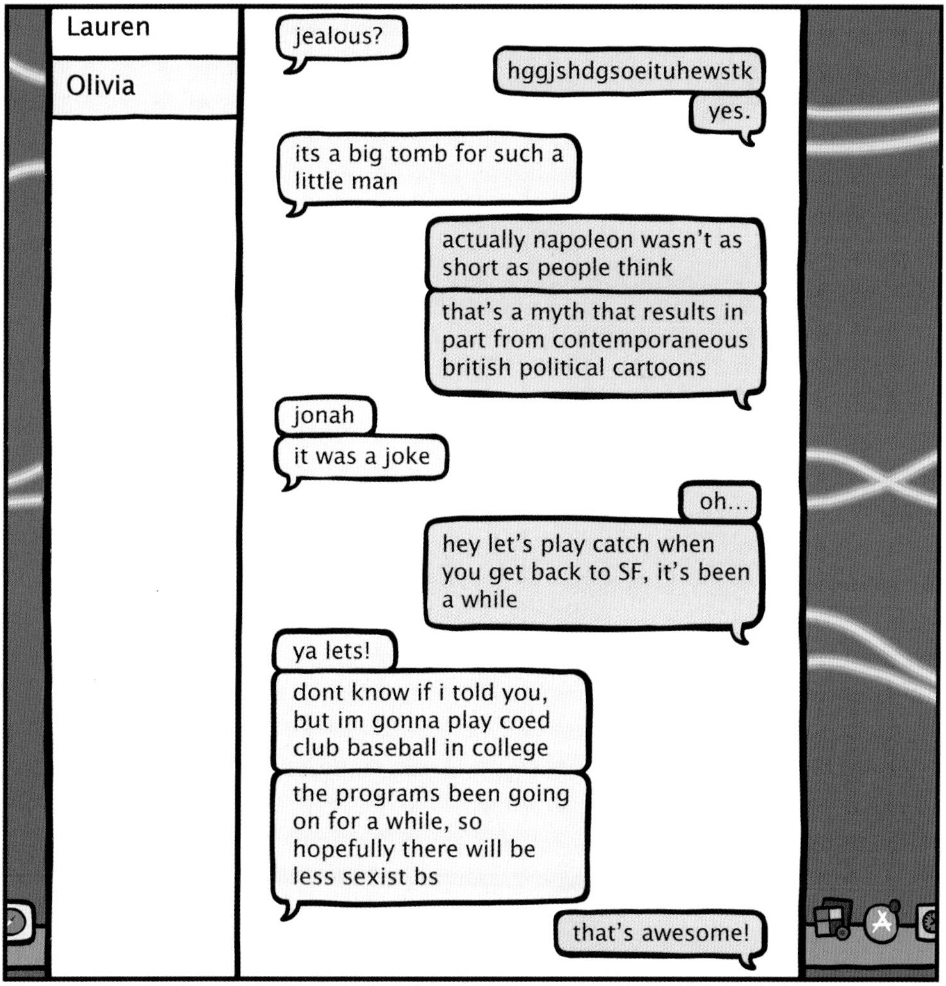
Lauren
Olivia
jealous?
hggjshdgsoeituhewstk
yes.
its a big tomb for such a little man
actually napoleon wasn't as short as people think
that's a myth that results in part from contemporaneous british political cartoons
jonah
it was a joke
oh...
hey let's play catch when you get back to SF, it's been a while
ya lets!
dont know if i told you, but im gonna play coed club baseball in college
the programs been going on for a while, so hopefully there will be less sexist bs
that's awesome!

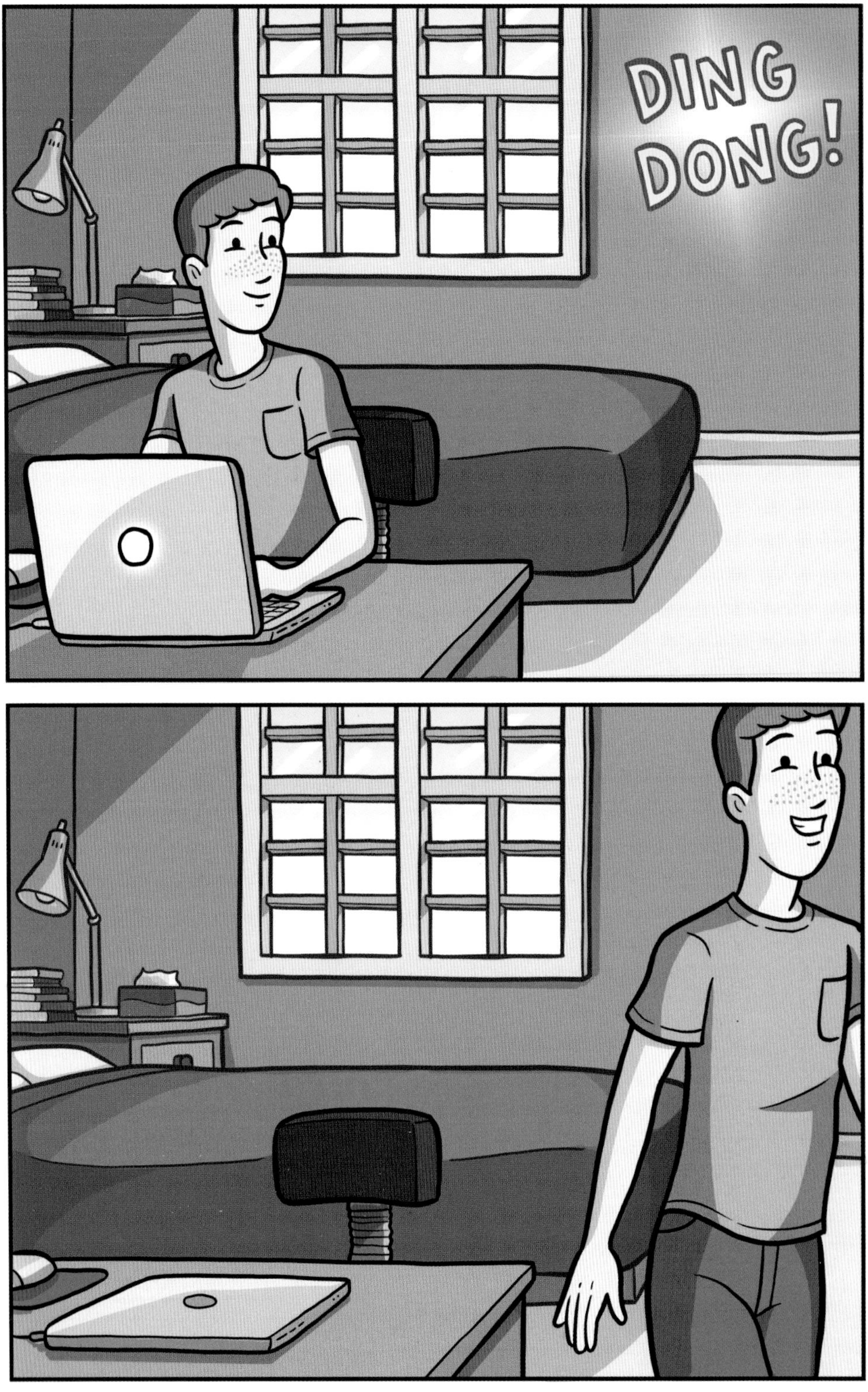
DING DONG!

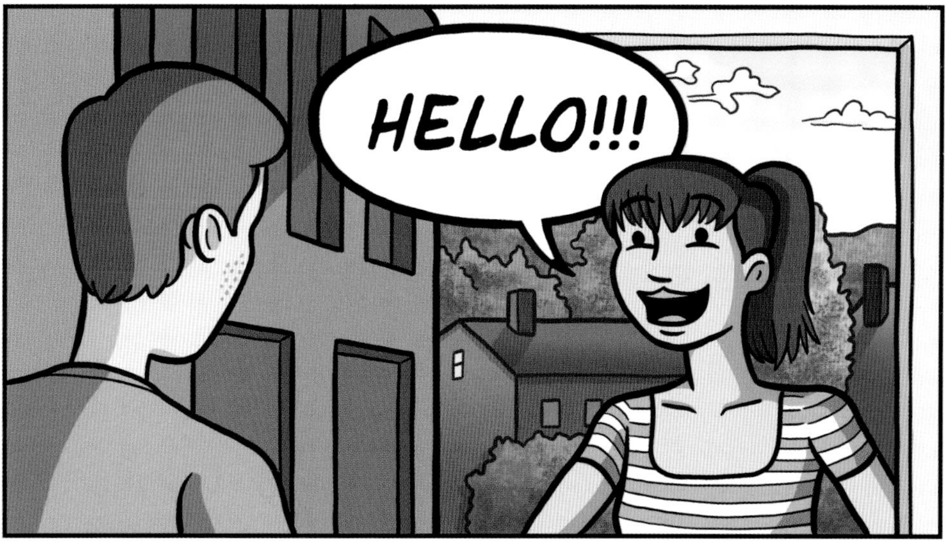
HELLO!!!

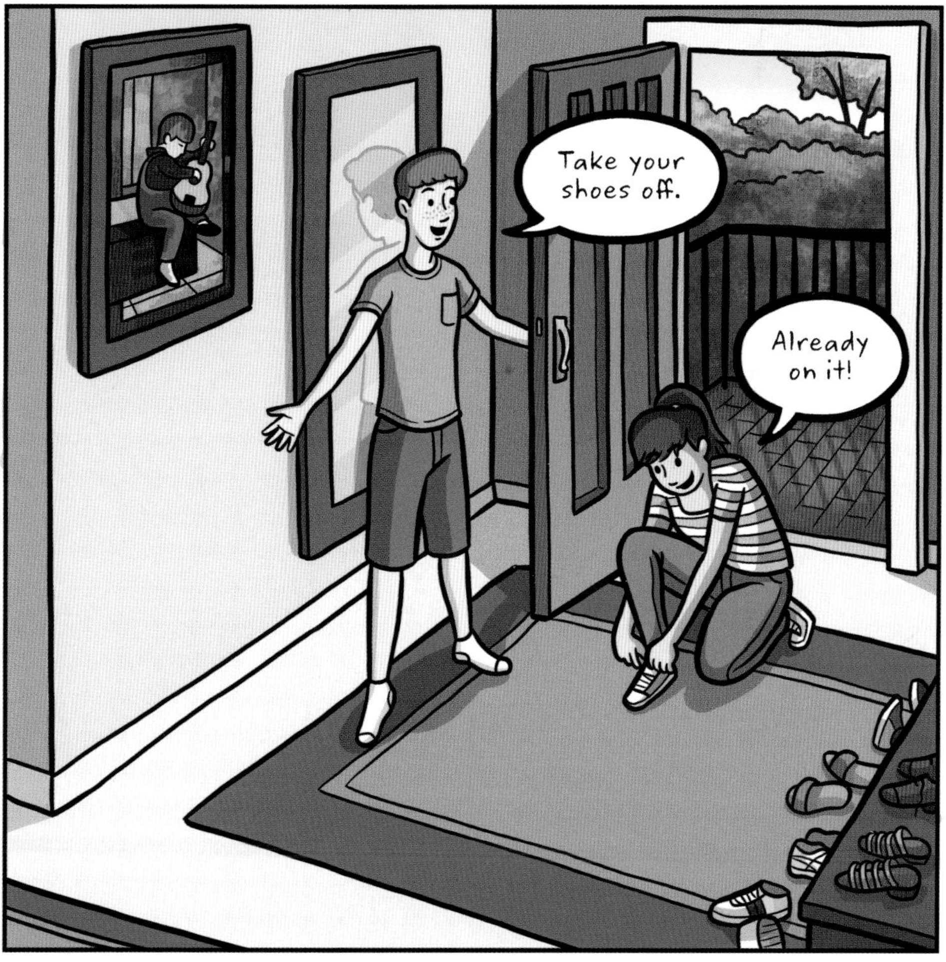
Take your shoes off.
Already on it!

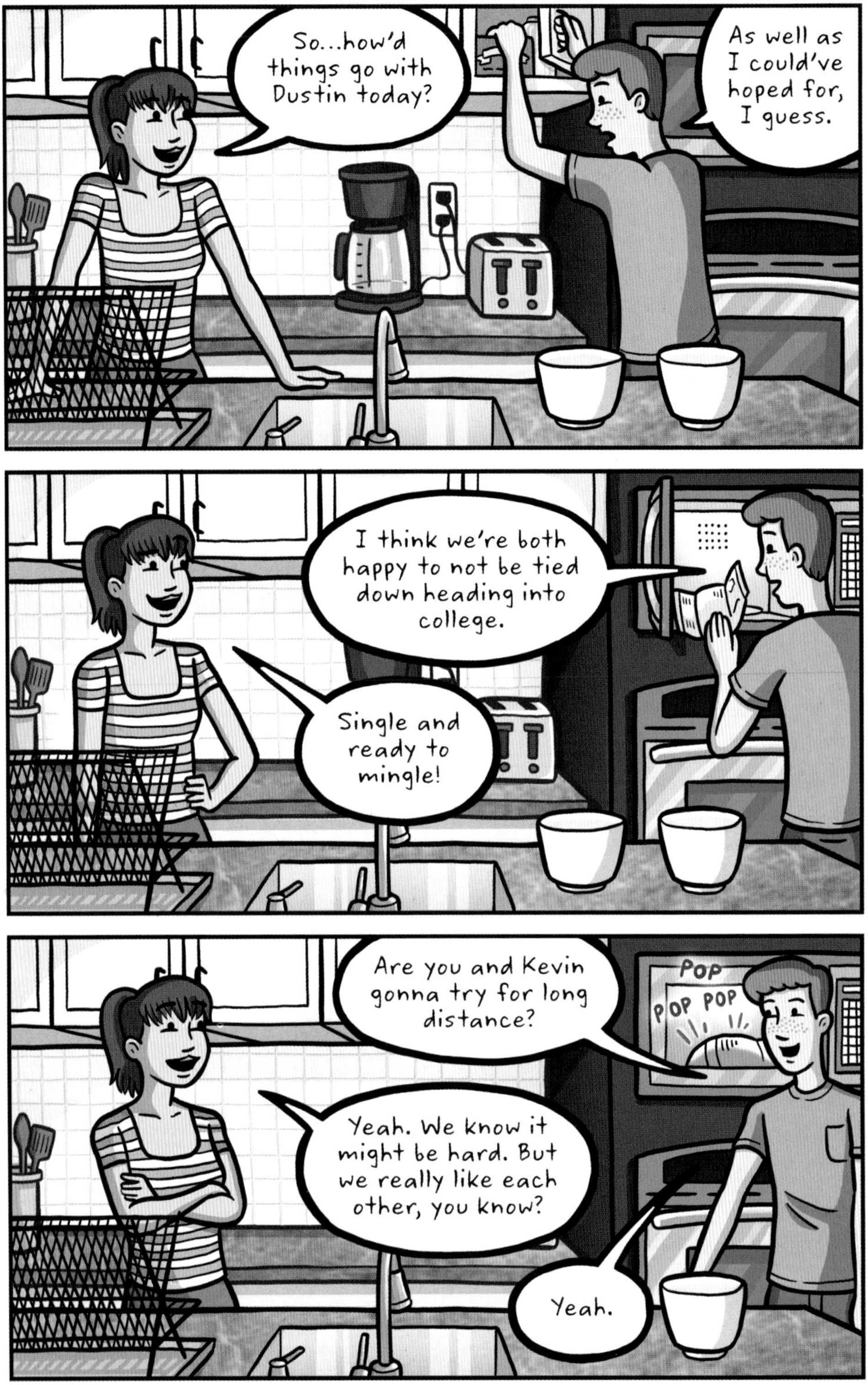
So...how'd things go with Dustin today?
As well as I could've hoped for, I guess.
I think we're both happy to not be tied down heading into college.
Single and ready to mingle!
Are you and Kevin gonna try for long distance?
POP
POP POP
Yeah. We know it might be hard. But we really like each other, you know?
Yeah.

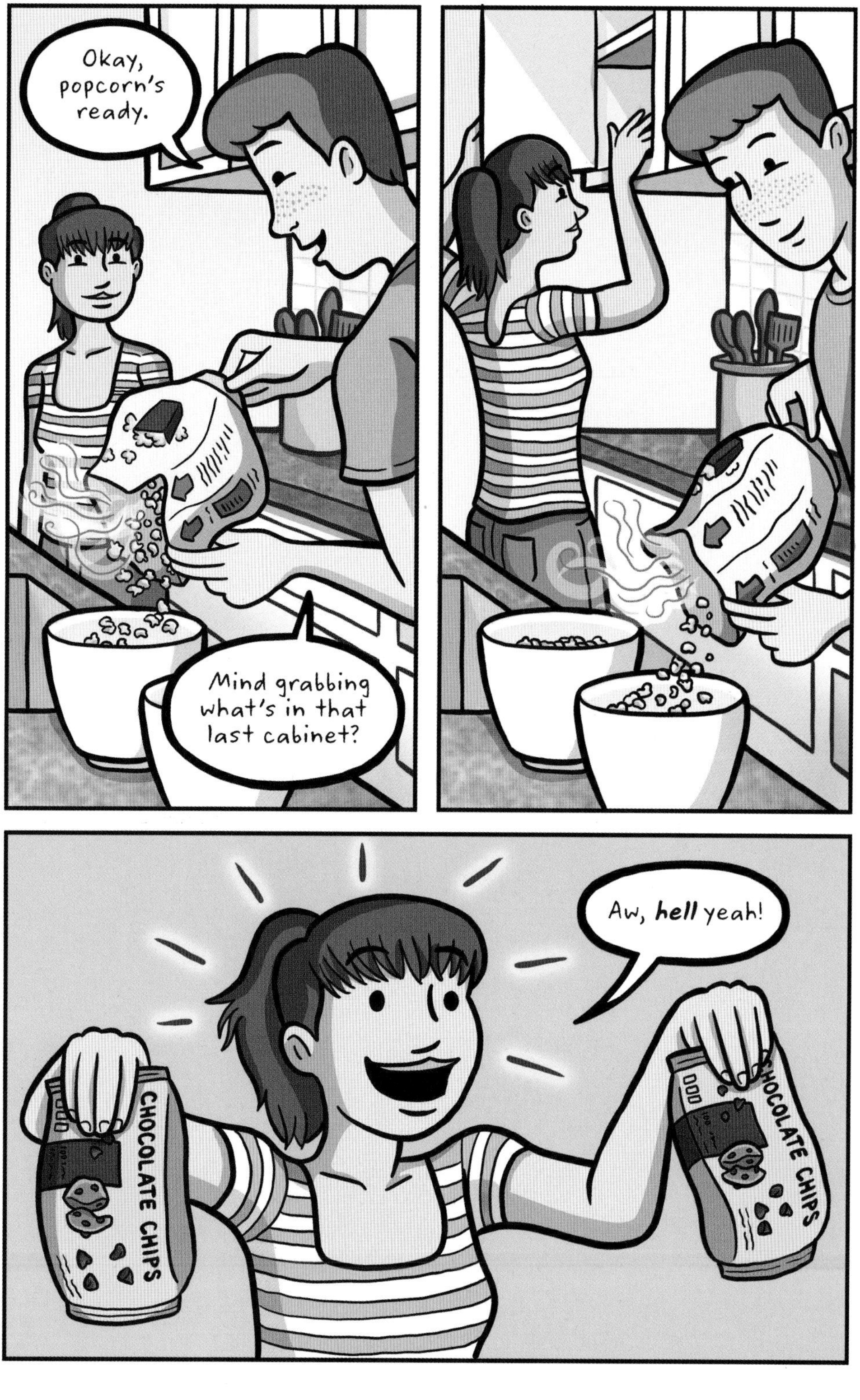
Okay, popcorn's ready.
Mind grabbing what's in that last cabinet?
Aw, **hell** yeah!
CHOCOLATE CHIPS
CHOCOLATE CHIPS

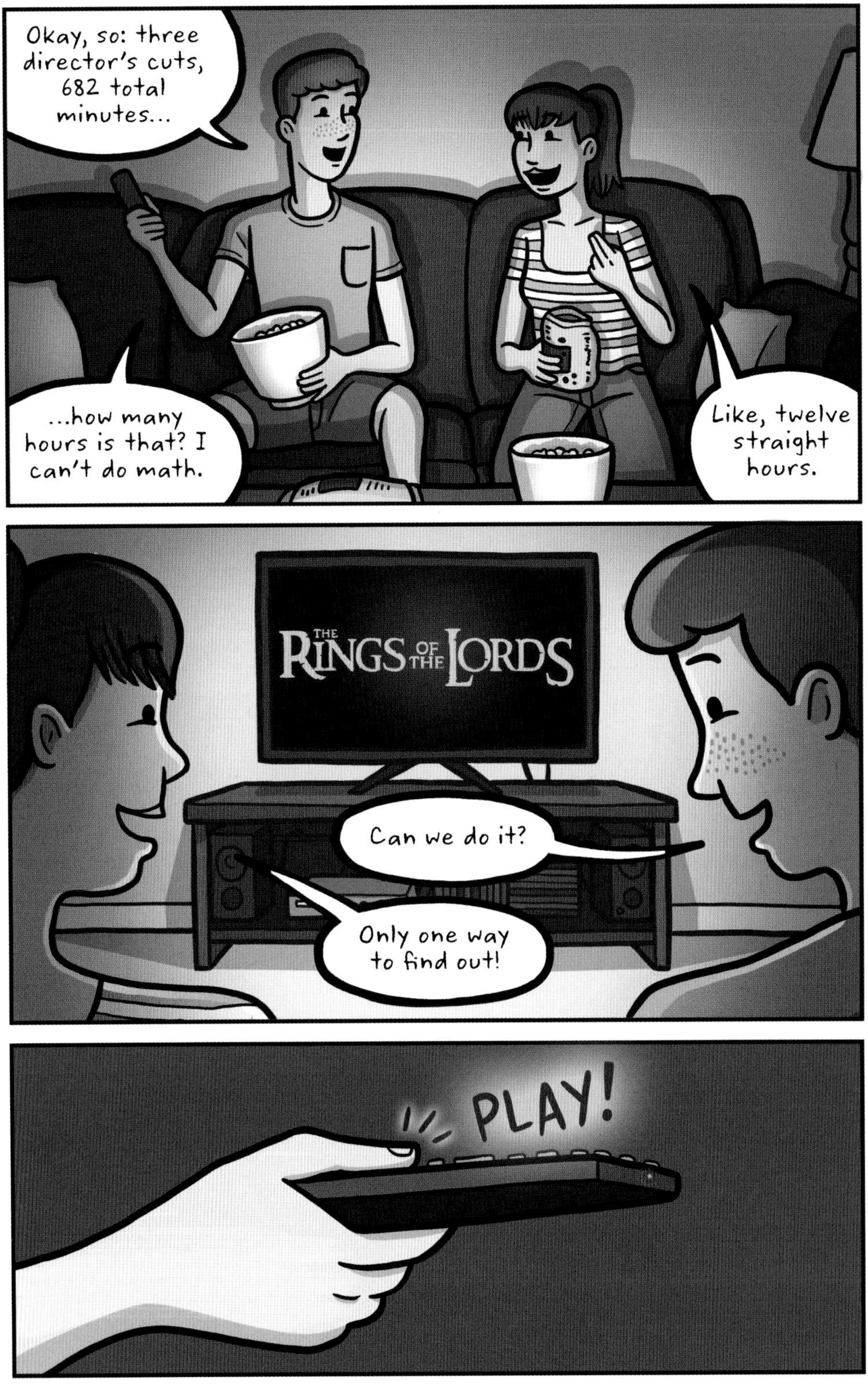

Okay, so: three director's cuts, 682 total minutes...
...how many hours is that? I can't do math.
Like, twelve straight hours.
THE RINGS OF THE LORDS
Can we do it?
Only one way to find out!
PLAY!

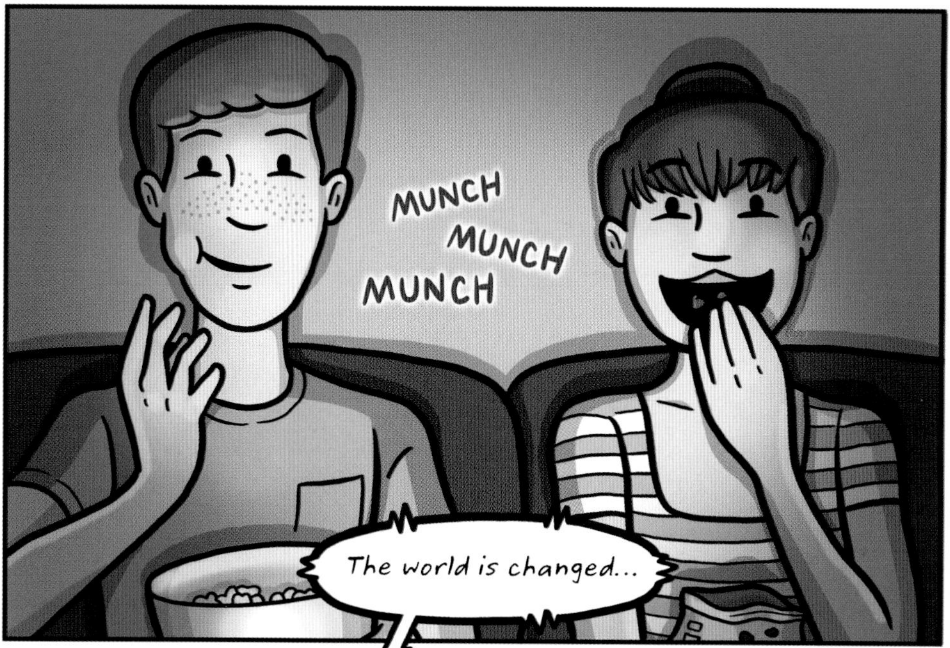
MUNCH
MUNCH
MUNCH
The world is changed...

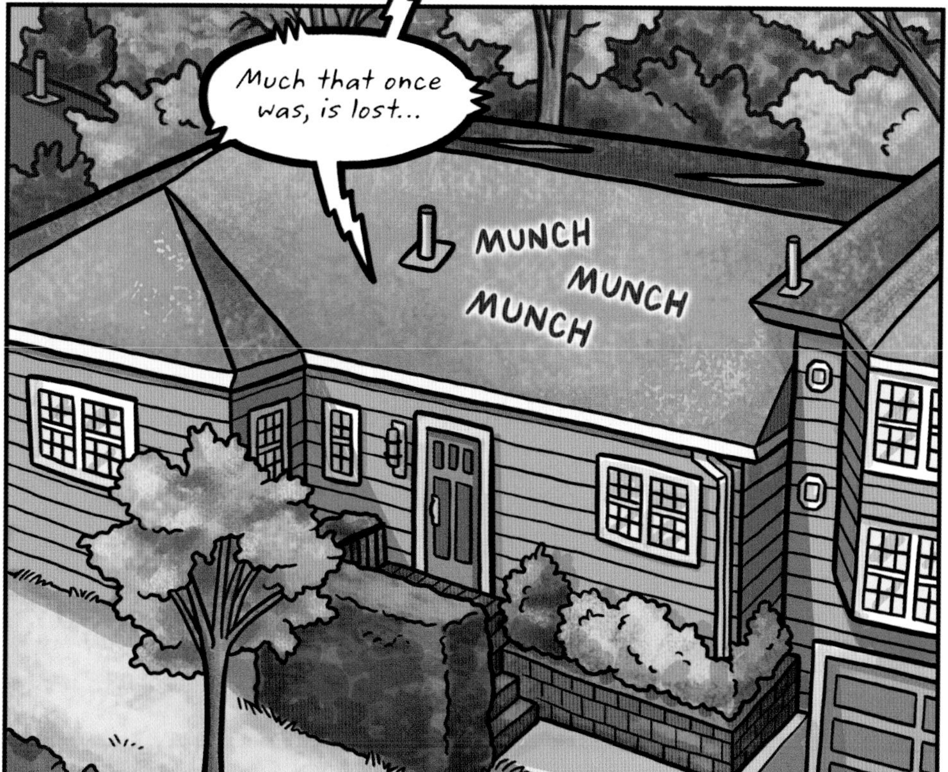
Much that once was, is lost...
MUNCH
MUNCH
MUNCH

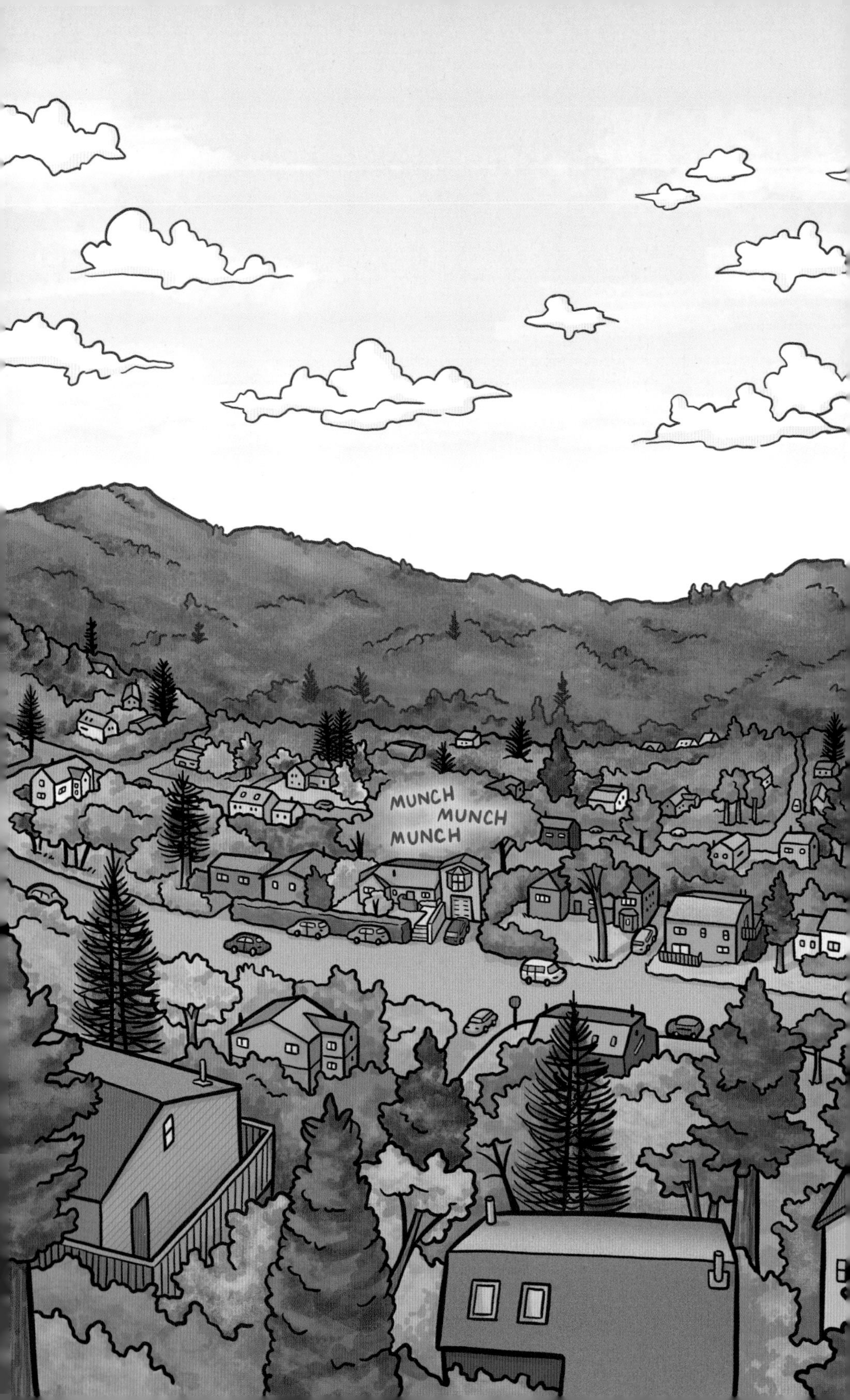
MUNCH
MUNCH
MUNCH

THE END

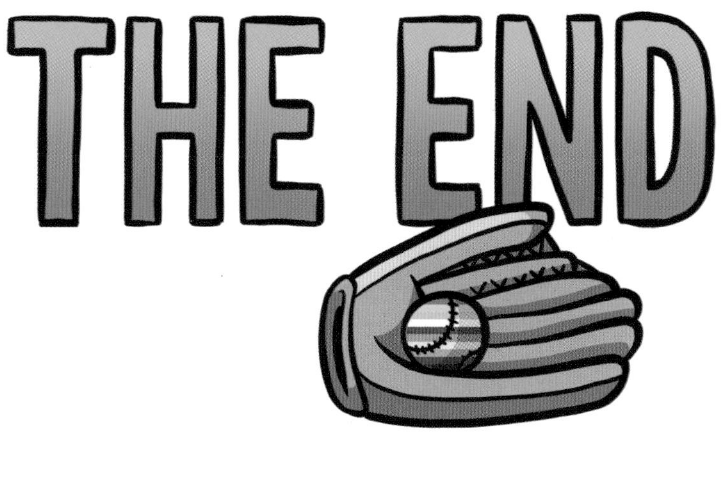

AUTHOR'S NOTE

While this book is a work of fiction, it's based on my experiences as a teenager, and a lot of it is true. I really did jump into competitive baseball as an unathletic latecomer; I really did have a secret boyfriend senior year; and I really did hit an unlikely home run. (It wasn't a game-winning grand slam, but it felt like one!)

But much more than the plot itself, the emotions in this book are true. *Out of Left Field* started as a memoir, but as I worked on it, I became less interested in depicting my life as it really happened and much more interested in transmitting those true emotions to the reader. Hopefully I've conveyed how it feels to have a secret crush, to crave the approval of some homophobic dudes, to first kiss someone of the same sex, and to finally lean into authentic selfhood. And hopefully, whether or not you play baseball or identify as LGBTQ+, you're able to relate to some of those feelings.

I think that many people struggle to become the best version of themselves, especially when they're teenagers. Doing so often involves going against social pressures, doing active and conscious work, and even screwing up once in a while. In *Out of Left Field*, Jonah the character screws up a lot, from laughing along with his teammates' offensive jokes to failing to be emotionally attentive to Sophie and Dustin. These parts of the book come from the rawest and most emotionally honest place of all. When I was a teenager, I really did make mistakes like this, some of which deeply hurt the people around me. It was important to me to depict not just mistakes, but their aftermath—consequences, apologies, and growth—because I wanted to show that selfhood is determined in part by how we respond to screwing up or being called out. Everyone makes mistakes, but it's the choices we make afterward that define us. As an adult, I'm still making mistakes, still learning, and still trying to become the best version of myself.

Thank you for reading *Out of Left Field*!

—Jonah Newman

BEHIND
THE SCENES

I began to write *Out of Left Field* in 2018. Over the next two years, I drafted and re-drafted the plot synopsis and script. I also started to sketch characters and settings.

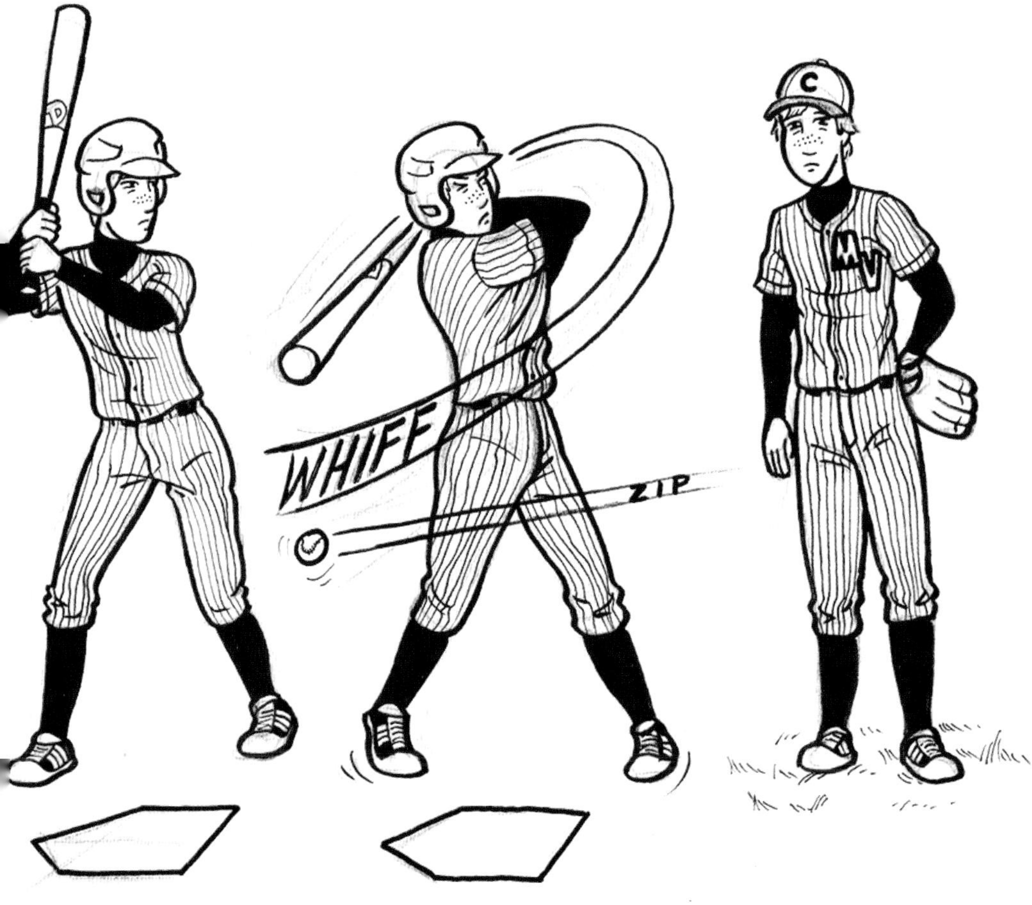
WHIFF
ZIP

Because so many scenes would take place there, I paid special attention to Diamonti High School, drawing the campus from multiple angles and sketching floorplans. I wanted to know what would be in the background no matter where the characters were and how exactly the characters would move through the environment.

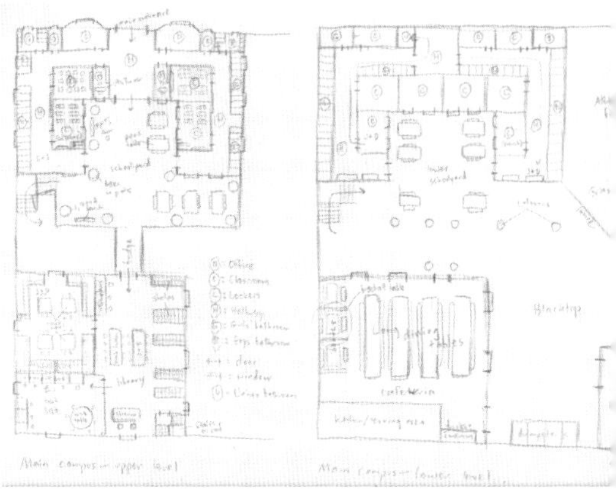

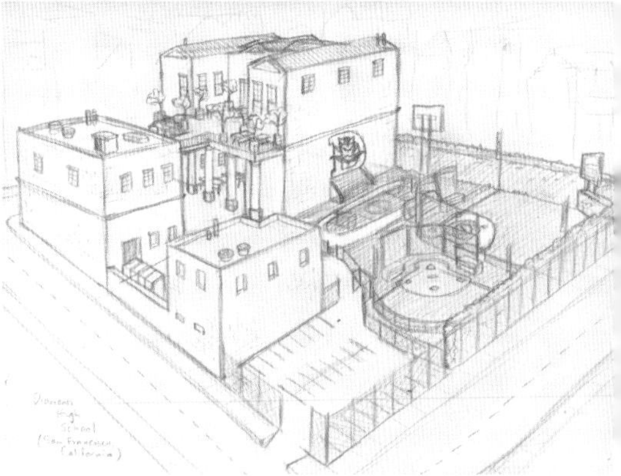

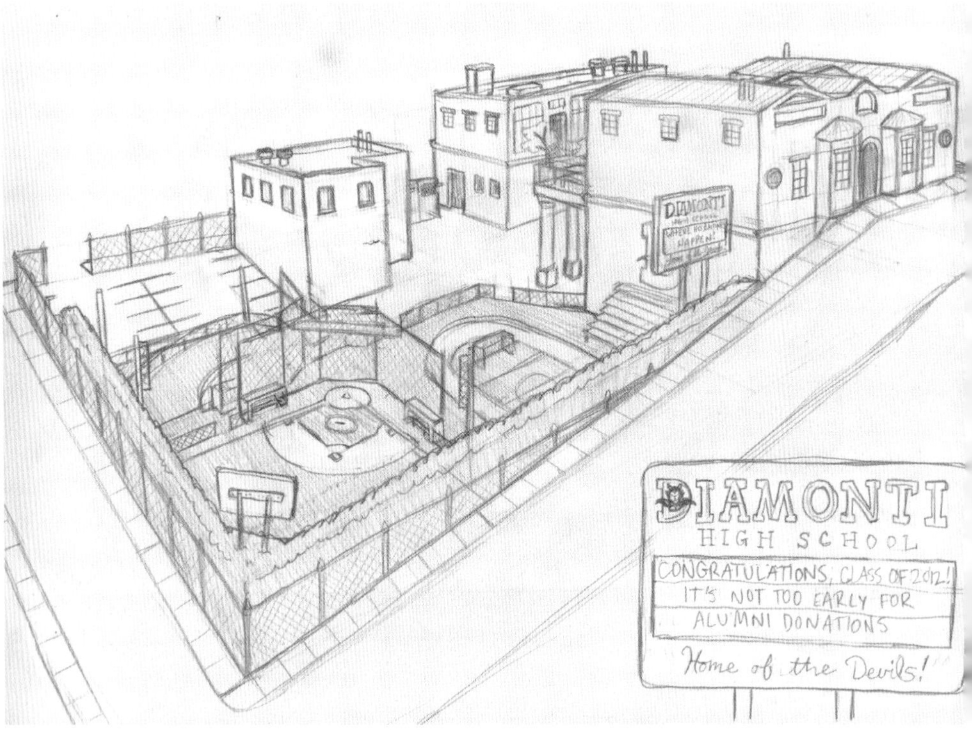
DIAMONTI
HIGH SCHOOL
CONGRATULATIONS, CLASS OF 2012!
IT'S NOT TOO EARLY FOR
ALUMNI DONATIONS
Home of the Devils!

After finishing the script, I drew the entire book on Bristol board with PaperMate SharpWriter #2 mechanical pencils. For help with unfamiliar objects or challenging poses, I pulled images from the internet or even served as my own art model!

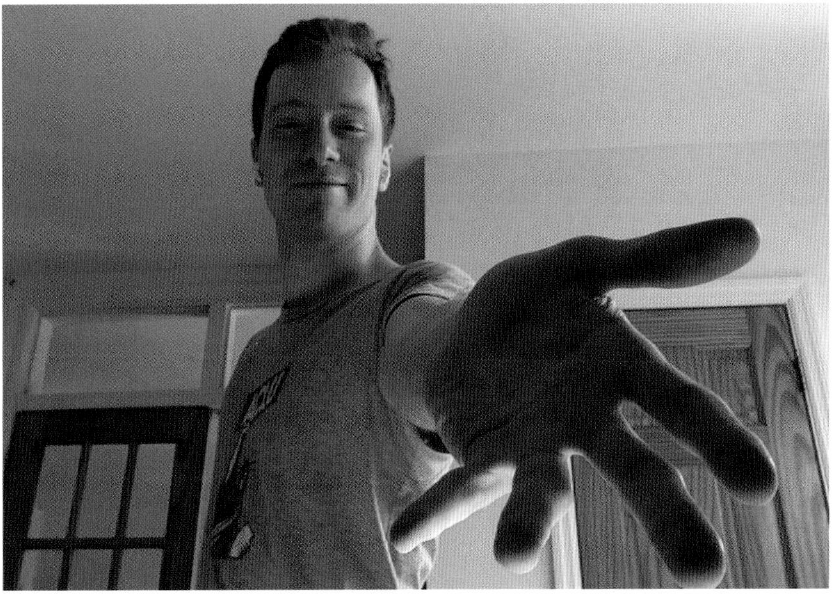

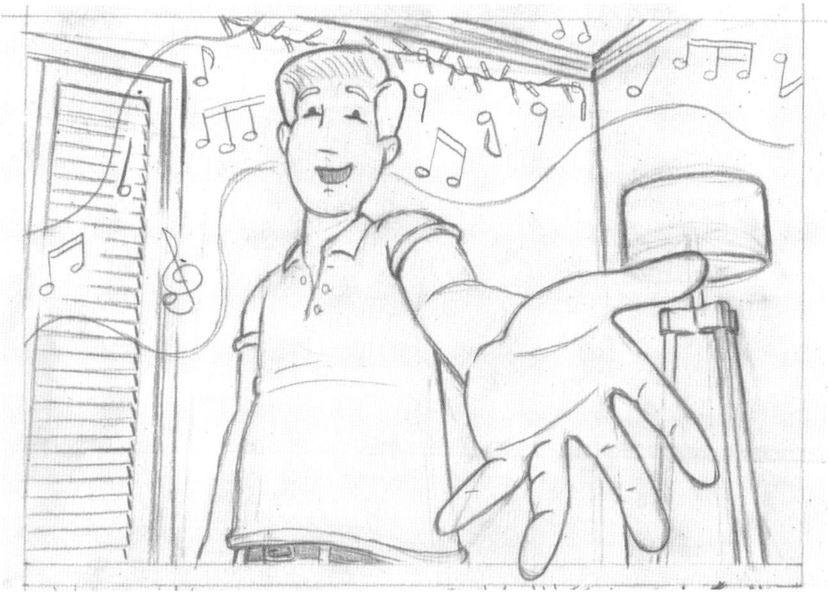

I scanned the penciled pages into Photoshop and drew the final line art on an XPPen tablet. I also laid out the text (which is in a font based on my handwriting). Then the pages were masterfully colored by Donna Oatney. I provided annotated guides and reference images to help Donna execute my vision.

RRRRING!
DIAMONTI
HIGH SCHOOL

RRRRING!
DIAMONTI
HIGH SCHOOL
WE SURVIVED ANOTHER DAY
Home of the Devils
One more, Elliot!

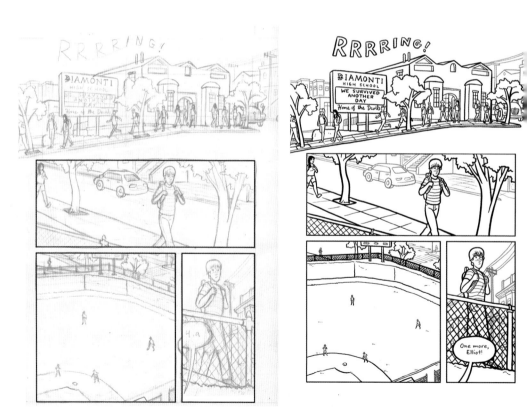

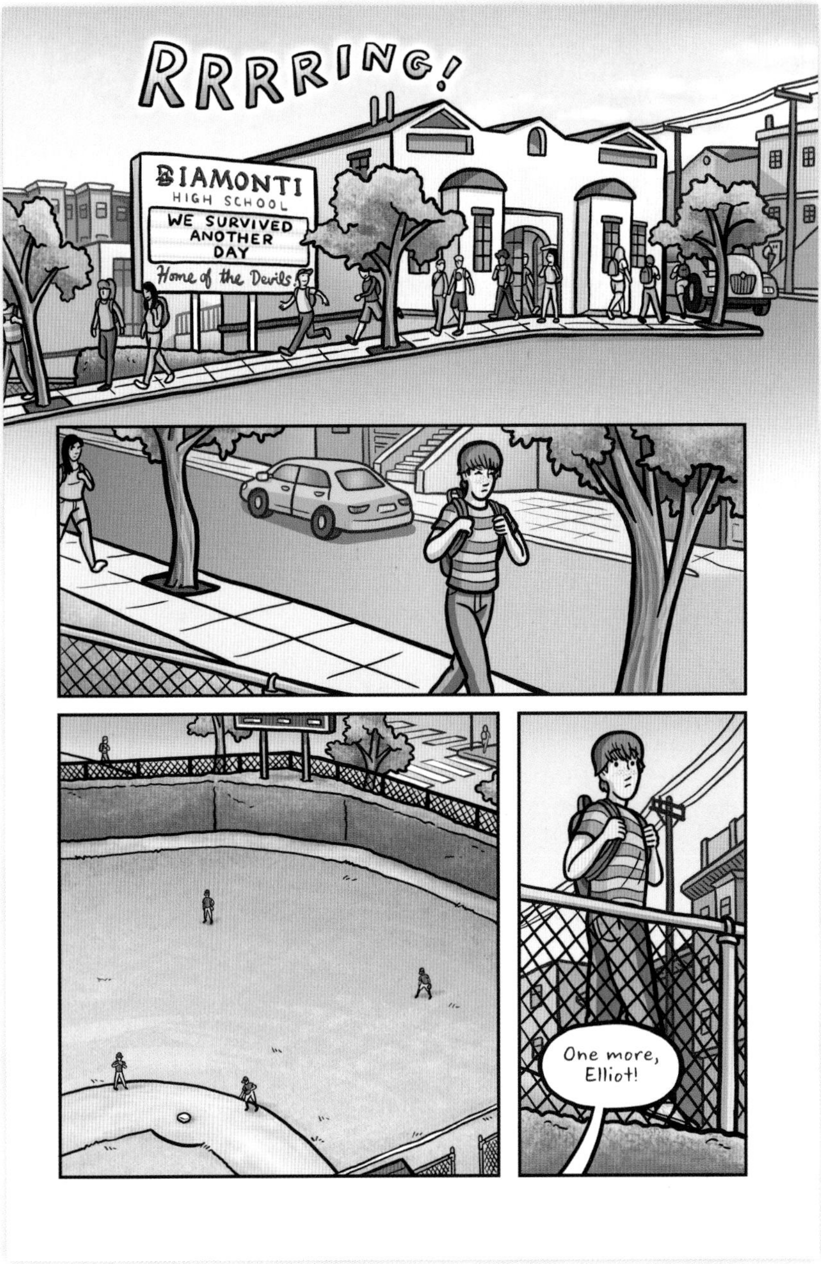
RRRRING!
BIAMONTI
HIGH SCHOOL
WE SURVIVED
ANOTHER
DAY
Home of the Devils
One more, Elliot!

The book you're holding in your hands is the product of six years' hard work and many people's creative input. Although it took hundreds, perhaps even thousands of hours to make, for me, they were intensely joyful and satisfying hours. I hope you loved reading *Out of Left Field* as much as I loved making it!

Thank you . . .

To Donna Oatney for her brilliant colors, jaw-dropping hard work, and intense attention to detail. Donna, you made my art look better than I could've ever imagined!

To Patty Rice, Kirsty Melville, Julie Phillips, Brittany Lee, Tiffany Meairs, Lynn Stoecklein, Danys Marys, Elise Thompson, Brianna Westervelt, Diane Mangan, and the rest of the team at Andrews McMeel for publishing this book so expertly and for allowing me to share my story with the world.

To Amy Berkower for her warmth, wisdom, and attentive, nimble agenting. To Celeste Montaño, Dan Lazar, and the rest of the team at Writers House for their insight, hard work, and professionalism.

To Dav and Sayuri Pilkey for their astonishing kindness, generosity, and advocacy.

To Ngozi Ukazu for taking me seriously when I was a fledgling cartoonist, for supporting my work ever since, and for being one of the loveliest people in all of comics.

To Chad and Andrea for being two of the earliest believers in and shapers of this book.

To Alex, Ama, Franny, James, Natasha, Dante, and Stefanie for timely expertise, vital lessons, and much-needed support.

To Phil for his keen eye and brilliant instincts.

To my grandparents, aunts, uncles, cousins, and friends: your excitement about this book helped me power through.

To my parents for encouraging my creativity from the beginning, and for loving and believing in me always and unconditionally.

To Adam for being the best editor, listener, supporter, and life partner anyone could ask for. I know nothing I make is good until you say it is. I can't believe how lucky I am. I love you.

If you're an LGBTQ+ teen looking for information, resources, or support, the following organizations might be able to help you:

The Trevor Project
thetrevorproject.org

GLSEN
glsen.org

It Gets Better
itgetsbetter.org

Jonah Newman is a cartoonist and editor. As an editor at Graphix, Scholastic's graphic novel imprint, he has worked with Dav Pilkey, Jamar Nicholas, Angeli Rafer, and many others. When he's not creating, editing, or reading comics, you might find Jonah binge-listening to history podcasts, playing in an LGBTQ+ softball league, or getting way too invested in his fantasy baseball team. He lives in Brooklyn with his husband (who's a human) and two kids (who are cats).